MERDEKA SQUARE

MERDEKA SQUARE

Kerry B.Collison

Sid Harta Publishers
1997

Edited, designed, and produced by
PenFolk Publishing
(03) 9807 6616

for Sid Harta Publishers
and Asian Pacific Management Co. Ltd. S.A.

First published 1997

Text:	Kerry B.Collison
Cover Concept:	Guy W. Collison
Cover Design:	Pat Craddock
Maps:	Steve Craddock
Book Design:	PenFolk Publishing
Author's photograph:	courtesy of the *Daily Advertiser*, Wagga Wagga, photo by Samantha Studdert

Printed in Australia
by Australian Print Group,
Maryborough
Victoria
Australia 3170

*Thank you for supporting our authors. The purchase of this book entitles
the buyer to membership of the Sid Harta Book Club at no cost.
Please send your name and address for future mailing purposes to:
PO Box 1102, Hartwell, Vic, Australia 3125.*

You may also wish to order further copies of *Merdeka Square* by
using the form at the rear of the book.

Dedication

I wish to dedicate this novel to the memory of

Adik Irma Surjani Nasution,

General Nasution's daughter who, at the age
of five years, was shot dead in her parents' home during
the failed assassination attempt against her father
and other members of the Council of Generals.

When she lost her life, so too did Indonesia lose its innocence.

"When in Rome..."

"Only be patient till we have appeased
The multitude, beside themselves with fear
And then we will deliver you the cause
Why I, that did love Caesar when I struck him,
Have thus proceeded."

Brutus to Mark Antony after Caesar's assassination,
Shakespeares's *Julius Caesar* Act III

* * * * * *

"Masuk kandang kambing mengembik...."

"Sabarlah dulu sampai rakjat yang bingung
serta takut sudah bisa kita tenangkan.
Setelah itu, baru akan saja djelaskan kenapa
Bung Karno, walaupun betapa djuga saja hormati
beliau sebagai Presiden, terpaksalah saja sisikan."

Perwira Tinggi, Tentara Nasional Indonesia
Djakarta 1965

Contents

Book three, 1965, coup and counter-coup

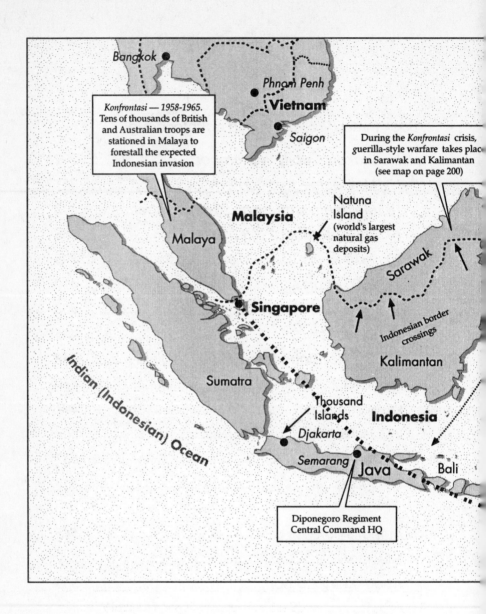

Bangkok

Phnom Penh

Vietnam

Saigon

Konfrontasi — 1958-1965.
Tens of thousands of British
and Australian troops are
stationed in Malaya to
forestall the expected
Indonesian invasion

During the *Konfrontasi* crisis,
guerilla-style warfare takes place
in Sarawak and Kalimantan
(see map on page 200)

Malaysia

Malaya

Natuna
Island
(world's largest
natural gas
deposits)

Sarawak

Singapore

Indonesian border
crossings

Kalimantan

Sumatra

Thousand
Islands

Indonesia

Djakarta

Semarang Java Bali

Indian (Indonesian) Ocean

Diponegoro Regiment
Central Command HQ

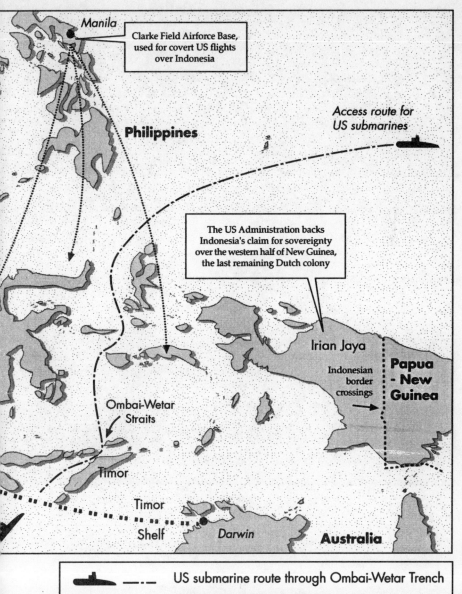

Manila

Clarke Field Airforce Base, used for covert US flights over Indonesia

Philippines

Access route for US submarines

The US Administration backs Indonesia's claim for sovereignty over the western half of New Guinea, the last remaining Dutch colony

Irian Jaya

Indonesian border crossings

Papua - New Guinea

Ombai-Wetar Straits

Timor

Timor Shelf

Darwin

Australia

US submarine route through Ombai-Wetar Trench

route taken by the British 'V' Bombers armed with nuclear bombs, 1962–65

covert flights by the US Airforce

Prologue

John McEwen, Acting Prime Minister of the Commonwealth of Australia, stood silently, pensively looking out
from the windows of his office across the well-lighted
gardens.

He remained motionless, hands clasped behind his back
in military stance.

There were no books, no decorations, nor were there any
items of personal memorabilia to identify the room's previous tenant. These had all been removed at the request of
Prime Minister Holt's widow.

It had been just one week since Holt had disappeared
while swimming in the ocean off Portsea.

Upon taking office, John McEwen had been immediately
briefed by the Attorney-General. McEwen had been shocked
and angered to discover the existence of the covert organi-
zation ASIS, and its subversive activities directed against
Australia's powerful neighbours. His Coalition partners in
government had deliberately kept him in the dark.

A file lay opened on the oversized teak desk. Above and
below the text, the page was boldly endorsed with security
classifications and warnings ...

MOST SECRET

OYSTER MO-9
AUSTRALIAN SECRET INTELLIGENCE SERVICE
EYES ONLY PRIME MINISTER

REPORT ON ASIS ACTIVITIES IN INDONESIA, 1965-66

John McEwen watched the traffic flow round the roundabout and spin off along the arterial roads to the suburbs. It was late.

He turned, almost painfully, and moved back to his desk. He stared down at the file and was suddenly overcome by waves of fatigue. He looked back through the windows as if wishing to avoid confronting the damning report which lay before him, but there was no escape. Now he could barely distinguish the shapes of the slow-moving cars, their lights dimmed by the early evening mist drifting in from Lake Burley Griffin.

The Prime Minister leaned forward, placing his hands on the high-backed leather chair for support and closed his tired eyes momentarily.

More than half a million had died throughout Indonesia. ASIS was deeply involved in the disaster.

And why should that be the only secret that Holt had kept from him?

Book one

1901-1964

Chapter 1

Netherlands East Indies — 1901
Central Java

The peasants moved lethargically as the hot, dry monsoon wind toyed with the dust causing occasional eddies of choking air to swirl about. As the villagers went about their monotonous chores they covered their heads with cloth to protect their faces from the fierce heat and dust. Their bodies were dehydrated by the dry, debilitating conditions during the day, and then further ravaged by the uncontrollable sweating in the humidity of the still, suffocating tropical nights.

Their village, Kampung Blitar, located in a desolate and isolated pocket of land, was locked behind the giant volcanoes to the north, in one of the most densely forested tropical islands known to man. This insignificant area, treated harshly by the prevailing weather patterns, was almost unknown to the outside world. But Kampung Blitar was not so isolated that it managed to escape the attention of the gods who ruled their precious Javanese realm. They watched, patiently, until the planets had achieved a suitable conjunction and, at an appropriate moment, moved to alter the destiny of their subjects below.

* * * * * *

Blitar's impoverished community was situated in the centre of Java's only rain shadow. The arid conditions and intimidating terrain had not attracted the *Vereenigde Oost-Indische Compagnie (V.O.C.)* planters. Instead, this desolate place had become a sanctuary to the thousands of *pribumi* people who had fled their colonial masters during the centuries of the Dutch East Indies Company's dominance.

17

Initially, many of the district's inhabitants consisted of escapees from police stockades. Most were merely guilty of minor offences which, at the time, attracted severe and often cruel punishments such as public flogging. These petty criminals fled to the *Blitar* region knowing that the Dutch soldiers would not follow. The terrain was dangerous and claimed many lives amongst the white foreigners who had ventured into the mountainous region. These unsuccessful incursions resulted in orders being issued by the V.O.C. Governor not to pursue prisoners who had fled into this domain. The *Compagnie* designated the area as *badlands* and the district continued to be neglected throughout the hundreds of years of Dutch occupation of the extensive archipelago.

As the Dutch East Indies entered the twentieth century and social change slowly produced a literate class amongst the indigenous people, Blitar also became home to the first political refugees. Although their number was limited, their presence was accepted by the peasants in their isolated world as these intellectuals could provide some semblance of learning to the illiterate farmers and their children.

The villagers were predominately Javanese who followed the Moslem faith and lived in simple clusters of thatched roofed dwellings scattered throughout the barren region. These *kampung* were rarely established without a mosque where the faithful could be called to prayer. As the five daily summons emanated from the makeshift minarets, the entire population would follow the established regimes, and go about their ablutions prior to commencing prayer. There were few exceptions. These rituals were essential to their lives. The people of Blitar suffered many hardships and depended heavily on their spiritual beliefs for relief and comfort.

* * * * * *

The island's inhabitants had all but forgotten the devastation cast upon them by Krakatau's explosion when they were visited by torrential rains which seemed to never end. It was the year of Nineteen Hundred and One.

Thunderstorms had lashed the countryside causing floods throughout the rich rice-bearing plains, and landslides in the mountain regions. Roads remained cut for months. Blitar had become even more isolated and hidden from the rest of Java's millions.

In one of the larger villages a small school had been constructed from the traditional mud bricks and teak trees. There were no desks. The children simply sat on small *tikar* mats which they placed on the clay floor before lowering themselves to sit cross-legged in the one-room hall. The building doubled as the *balai* or village community centre. Often the mothers would join the children and assist with the teaching. There was only one class for all the students, regardless of their age.

The school represented far more than the primary education it provided. It was a symbol which these simple people respected and desperately clung to in their surrounds of extreme poverty. The *kampung* elders had organised the building's construction as they understood the importance of providing these basic facilities for the children. The hall had taken almost five months to build and the entire village had participated, working together in the accepted manner of *gotong-rojong*.

This was one of the schools where *Raden Sukemi Sosrodiharjo* taught. He helped with the school in the neighbouring village as well, but was reluctant to spend too much time away at this time. His Balinese wife, *Ida Nyoman Rai* was heavy with their first child and he wished to be present when the birth took place.

There was no hospital here, only a midwife who also nursed the injured and sick whenever one of the villagers required her limited medical knowledge. Her cures were traditional concoctions of herbs which were often accompanied by chants and prayers. *Ibu Arifin* was respected and admired by the *kampung*, and feared by a few who claimed that the Sumatran woman was, in fact, a *dukun* who could not only cure the sick but also cast spells. Good and evil *dukun* could be found in every village throughout the islands as mysticism was an integral component of the Indonesian culture, delivered in abundant doses by means of the *Ramayana* shadow puppet shows. *Ibu Arifin* was a true believer even though she followed her traditional beliefs in parallel with her Moslem faith. She understood that the stars had cast an incredibly powerful influence over their earthly presence and that a conjunction of the sun and Neptune in the ascendant was nearing prominence. This would be, she knew, a reccurrence of the celestial conditions which had accompanied the birth of the Prophet Muhammad. As she worked, she offered a silent prayer to the *One and Only True God*, then added a supplication to her traditional ancestors and their formidable ghosts.

Demands on the woman's time and expertise had grown considerably during the year but she never complained. At that very time, there seemed to be an overwhelming number of young pregnant girls approaching term, most of whom had yet to see their fifteenth birthday. The midwife cared for them all, never admonishing these young girls for their predicament as she herself had given birth when only fourteen. Whenever those distant memories occasionally emerged, she would immediately endeavour to concentrate on some other thoughts for those earlier times had left bitter scars, which *Ibu Arifin* preferred to leave buried in her own distant village near Padang.

* * * * * *

A late afternoon electrical storm had driven most of the villagers indoors as dry winds forced a path down through their valley, ripping at trees, tearing at the poor soil and sucking all that was loose up into huge clouds of choking dust. Throughout the night, the children lay close to their mothers, clinging onto their *sarongs* as the wind screamed wildly outside, generating visions of wild demons shrieking across the evening's darkened skies. *Tjengkeh* trees, silhouetted only occasionally by the brilliance of lightning flashes, shuddered violently as the turbulence struck causing unripened cloves to be stripped from their pods prematurely. The brilliant flashes produced still portraits of eerie figures which seemed to dance momentarily as several of the women rushed bravely around outside, collecting possessions left behind in the panic, when earlier they had dashed quickly to the confines of their huts. The heavens seemed to be tearing themselves apart as lightning flashed continuously, all around, followed predictably by the deafening roar of thunder claps. It was as if the gods were at play.

The terrifying sounds ripped down through their valley, seemingly gathering momentum as the stark mountain walls on both sides channelled the fury in their direction. The villagers understood that the storm which had erupted thousands of metres above their heads and along the mountainous ridge to their north could easily bring the desperately needed rain to their dry land. But it seemed that their prayers were to go unanswered. The heavens exploded with the gods' cruel laughter, the sharp deafening cracks of thunder a testament to the power which surrounded them.

Alone, in the dark village square, the *lurah* clutched his *sarong* tightly around his body while he struggled to protect his eyes from the maelstrom of dust and leaves. He cupped one hand and held it to his right eye, vainly attempting to identify whether rain was falling further up on the slopes. More than eight months had passed since his village had been blessed with rain. Impatiently, he waited for another flash of lightning. There! For a brief moment, the village headman believed he could see what appeared to be rain falling in the distance. He felt cheated. It would seem that once again, only those who lived higher in the mountains closer to the gods would benefit from the squall. He remained outside praying silently that the storm would move closer, bringing just enough rain so as not to strip the remaining topsoil away from their land. But the squall was rainless and the old man, disappointed, turned away from the wind and limped into his sparse accommodations.

A young girl darted suddenly from one of the huts and headed directly for the *balai* in search of the midwife. It was very late, she knew, probably even morning. As she crossed the open ground between the huts, lightning flashed and she turned in terror then fled back to the safety of her home. Moments passed and the child reappeared, running directly towards the simple structure as her mother had instructed. *Ibu Rai* was not her natural mother but in villages such as these that did not matter. The orphan had been taken in by this kind Balinese woman and cared for lovingly. Every year throughout the district, many children were abandoned as their parents fell victim to disease or some other cruel condition of life. Cholera, smallpox, and typhoid were all too frequent visitors to this community. Death would always claim at least one in every fourth child, before they could even walk.

A clap of thunder exploded around the huts causing the fragile girl to fall. Screaming with fear she jumped to her feet and continued running. Her heart pumped excessively as she tried to open the heavy door, only to find that it had been jammed tightly shut from the inside. She yelled as loudly as her small lungs would permit but her screams went unheard. Terrified in the dark, she turned and retreated to her own hut only to find her mother already lying on the floor, preparing for the imminent birth. She clasped her mother's hand tightly and sat down on the *tikar* mat beside her as the moment approached. She was scared and wanted to cry. Her father had not yet returned from the other *kampung*. What was she going to do? He had not come home at all during the night. The child called frantically to her mother, "*Bu! Bu!*", but the woman's painful labour now caused confusion and the child's tearful calls did not register.

Another thunderous explosion threatened to rip the simple hut apart as the wooden door smashed inwards. The young girl jumped to her feet and attempted to lift the broken timbers back into place, but without success. As she struggled with the slats of wood her mother screamed again. Confused as to what she should do first, the child was not conscious of the figure which brushed past her, then moved quickly into the room to attend to the mother. As the girl stood in the doorway, the wind beating heavily against her tiny frame, she became aware of a strange, almost unfamiliar sensation. Holding her hands to her face for protection, the child leaned against the wind and peered outside. Immediately she knew from the sharp biting sensation that stung her arms and legs that it was raining. Lightning flashed again followed by several claps of thunder which rocked their entire surrounds. Suddenly the wind died. And the rain continued.

As she stood there with her little hands held outside cupped to catch the elusive treasure she heard one final cry, and the girl turned slowly, and witnessed the birth of her brother. She stood there for what seemed an immeasurable time watching as the baby emerged, only to be taken quickly by the adept midwife and placed in a small space alongside the *tikar*. Minutes passed as her mother was attended to and the baby cleaned. She heard her mother whisper some words which sounded to her like *ari-ari* but she was not sure, as *Ibu Arifin* removed something quickly and wrapped whatever this was in a square of cotton cloth, before placing the item in the urn on the far side of the small room. She watched, fascinated, as the midwife completed the essential tasks before placing the newborn baby in its mother's arms.

When the Balinese mother thought the moment appropriate, she would retrieve the cloth and its contents and find a suitable place to bury the *ari-ari*. It was a Balinese custom to place the placenta in a blessed place somewhere in the garden, in the belief that this represented the recently born infant's other half, and that this act would guarantee that the two halves would always be reunited. Balinese have always been known to return to their place of birth and adherence to this tradition would, in the future, be even more important as the new baby's mother was a titled Balinese woman.

The young girl was startled by a shout from outside and turned to see her father's figure scrambling across the now-soggy field. When she was certain that it really was her father, she ran quickly towards the man squealing with delight, calling to him that the baby had been born. When she reached the tired figure, he bent down to scoop the child into his arms, holding her tightly to his chest. Nearing the centre of the communal yard he observed that his neighbours had ventured outside, babbling with excitement at having been blessed with the downpour. Women ran with excitement into the small hut and examined the boy child. A loud shout brought them all back outside. It was the village *lurah*.

"*Look!*" he commanded, pointing to the sky as the rising sun's brilliance broke through the clearing storm clouds. They followed the direction of his outstretched arm and a silence fell over the village.

As the clouds dispersed the sun's rays pierced through the hot, moist morning atmosphere. The people stood transfixed by a magical sight. The golden colours merged with the most brilliant reds and greens. There was a hushed silence as the rainbow seemed to move closer and closer, its colours becoming brighter as it approached. None could ever remember having seen such a magnificent *pelangi* before, and certainly not one which appeared within reach of their outstretched hands. It was almost as if the powerful beams rose out of their *kampung*.

Ibu Arifin appeared from the hut. She was stunned by the rainbow's proximity and brilliance. Cautiously, she called to the baby's father. "*Subuh*," she said, her head raised to the sky, "*Your son was born at the prayer time of Subuh*". And the father nodded his head slowly in consent. It was an appropriate name which respected the time of birth and his faith.

His son would be called *Subuh*. As the entire village stood in awe of the mystical sign that *The One and Only True God* had given, they remained silent, almost fearful, knowing that they had witnessed an event of great significance, and that somehow the child who had been born at that moment of prayer was somehow associated with the blessing of rain their village had received.

One by one the villagers approached the proud father and gently stroked the tiny baby's feet. As the women crowded around the teacher, there was a soft cry from behind. They turned quickly in the direction of the sound and there, standing in the broken doorway, *Ida Nyoman Rai* held her hands to her face as she looked across the short distance to her newborn son. It was as if his very being was surrounded by the magnificent rainbow. An aura. It was a sign! The woman moved awkwardly towards her Javanese husband who quickly placed his arm around her waist and led her back to rest.

"We will call him Subuh", she heard him say as they entered the hut and her weary body slumped to the unmade bed. *"Muhammad Subuh Koesnasosro!"* Her husband placed their son in her outstretched arms and smiled warmly at them both as they lay together before him. In later years, many who were present in that village at that time would swear that the colourful aura was in fact witnessed by all present, and that many people came from distant villages to see the newborn child. It was as if they somehow could sense that this child was destined for greatness. He would become their country's first president.

* * * * * *

At the time the strange events surrounding the birth of the child named *Subuh* took place, storm clouds had also gathered ominously over Gunung Merapi. For days the earth had trembled as the huge volcano sent signs that an eruption was imminent. Tremors had rocked the island of Java travelling from the epicentre thousands of kilometres to even the most isolated places. Huge clouds of ash and poisonous fumes spewed out of the enormous crater. The earth continued to twist and sway as a terrifying series of tremors rumbled outwards, towards the towns and villages throughout the archipelago.

The combination of storm clouds and billowing fumes provided a spectacle which struck fear in all who witnessed it. Clouds of heavy poisonous gas flowed directly down the mountainous slopes unimpeded, sweeping through the unfortunate villages which lay amongst the rich rice-terraced foothills. None could escape the poisonous fumes. The young, the elderly, the village headman, all died within moments. Goats and chickens lay scattered where they had fallen.

Huge lava flows moved with perilous speed down the volcano's sides carrying a lake of molten stone in their path. Villages disappeared in just moments as the mass of lava swallowed the flimsy huts. As the devastating bubbling mass encroached upon village after village, the air was filled with the sounds of coconut fruit exploding on trees as the air surrounding the flow became impossibly hot, causing the ambient temperatures to rise rapidly above flash-point. Thatched roofed dwellings exploded as waves of heat engulfed the villages, instantly cremating those caught inside by the deadly gas just minutes before. The volcano roared on throughout the night. Only a few of the terrified villagers were spared as they fled.

* * * * * *

The small village of Woboro lay within sight of the incredible events which unfolded not ten kilometres away. Because it was positioned on the northern aspect of the volcano's foothills, the menacing lava flow and poisonous gases mercifully could not reach the tiny hamlet. As the eruption continued, all of the *kampung's* inhabitants waited nervously outside, gathered together as they prayed for protection. None of the villagers could remember such a violent display from the mountain, although there were tales of similar devastation which had occurred back in the ancestral days of their *nenek-mojang*.

Their prayers were led by a senior Islamic leader who had returned to this village to attend the birth of his child. His presence made the villagers feel secure, for this scholar was a true representative of their beloved *Allah* and he provided the spiritual comfort they needed so desperately at that time. They prayed continuously through the evening and, as the danger passed, fell into exhausted sleep. Occasionally, some would awaken to the sudden familiar jolt of an earth tremor, but most remained asleep until they were called for the morning prayers.

Once prayers were over, the holy man was summoned to the small room where his wife was resting. She smiled tiredly, exhausted from the ordeal of the birth, and reached out with her right hand to her husband. He squeezed it lovingly as the midwife held his newborn son out for him to examine. Waves of emotion engulfed him as he released his wife's palm and took his son into his arms. He turned and walked outside into the small village square where he stood facing the menacing volcano. The sun had risen but its brilliance was choked by the storm clouds and deadly ash. The midwife, fearing that the particles of the ash might injure the child or at least interfere with its breathing, insisted that the father return the child to its mother. The father refused. Instead, he commenced chanting while rocking the infant to and fro in his arms. He prayed. Soon he was joined by many of the villagers who had completed their prayers earlier, during the *Subuh* period, and now wished to inspect the new addition to their village.

An hour passed, and then came the fiercest of storms. The peasant farmers retreated into their huts and waited for the heavy deluge to pass. Soon they were able to venture outside once again to discover that not only had the rain ceased, but the sun's rays had managed to pierce through the filthy haze of ash and dark clouds. Suddenly there was a chorus of shouts which brought the rest of the villagers running outside.

They all stood in amazement at the spectacle. In the distance, towards the east but behind and surrounding the huge volcano, there was blue sky. As they murmured amongst themselves, the father reappeared holding his newborn son.

Immediately, there were gasps of astonishment for, at that very moment, the early morning sun's brilliance sparkled in every direction and the most magnificent rainbow appeared across the valley. The villagers turned towards the man holding the child and were surprised to see him smiling at his son, as if ignorant of the incredible spectacle surrounding them. The *pelangi* seemed to rest at the newborn child's feet. Suddenly, the new father raised his head and called for them to rejoice. He announced that this miracle had been a sign sent by the *One and Only True God, Allah!* They responded at once, falling to their knees as the man led them in prayer. Later that day, the volcano ceased to erupt and the weather returned to normal.

As in Blitar, many of this village's number were prepared to swear on the *Holy Koran* that they had witnessed the miracle of the brilliant rainbow and the volcano's abrupt silence. Many maintained that they could see quite clearly where the rainbow commenced, its proximity so close they believed they had touched the magnificent rays. Some also related, in reverent voice, that, at the moment when the brilliant colours spread across their hills, they noticed that there was also an aura surrounding the newborn child.

These were all simple people. They were not wise in the way of the *maggis* who clearly understood what was happening: that they were all in fact witnesses to the fulfilment of an old prophecy which predicted the birth of three kings at this time.

One, the prophecy stated, would be a king of his people, leading them out of the darkness of oppression. The second would also be born during the violence of nature's despair, to rise to lead his people away from their spiritual suffering. The third would be born of pale yellow skin in the islands far to the north, and would conquer the world known as the Far East.

Before the close of that mystical day when, as the sun slipped quickly away and the faithful attended the *Mahgrib* prayer period, the newborn child had been named. His father sensed a great moment had arrived but even he was not to know that his son would grow and become one of the world's greatest spiritual leaders as he introduced the philosophy of *Susila Budi Dharma*, or *SUBUD* as it would become known.

On the day of his birth, his parents selected his name and wrote it down to be remembered. He was called *Soekarno*.

* * * * * *

None of the inhabitants of either of the two villages which experienced the mystical events on that same day were aware of the strange coincidences surrounding their two communities, nor how they were inextricably tied together. That both of the chosen children born during the early hours of that morning would suffer identical illnesses within days of their birth would not have registered as being of any significance, had these simple people even known of these events.

Subuh's father carried his son in his arms for weeks as the boy's health deteriorated. *Ibu Arifin* had never seen anything like it before. She could not understand what it was that ailed the child, only that the debilitating attacks were taking their toll on the infant.

And, in their village, *Soekarno's* parents also continued to pray as they watched, in disbelief, as their son continued to suffer from the devastating illness.

The gods observed this enigma and moved to correct their dilemma. On an appropriate day, as the confused state continued threatening both children, holy men visited both *kampung* and blessed the infants. Traditional *adat*, or custom, then required that the children's parents select new names for the sickly boys, to assist with the fresh start in life each would be given.

In the small village of Blitar where rain had mystically fallen as the boy child was born, his parents ceremoniously cast away the infant's given name of *Subuh* and renamed their son. They called him *Soekarno*.

Almost one hundred kilometres to the north in the village of Wiboro, a similar ceremony took place. The parents here also prayed for their son's *kharma* to improve with his new name.

Their child's name was changed from *Soekarno* to *Muhammed Subuh*.

* * * * * *

And so the gods smiled on these two children and blessed them, and their health returned and they grew, and moved forward with their lives, each destined to fulfil the prophecies passed down from their ancestors.

Chapter 2

1928 — 1933

Soekarno leaned forward and gazed out through the window overlooking the quiet street. The provincial city's inhabitants were enjoying the mid-day break from the heat. Everywhere throughout the region, the Dutch masters and the Indonesians followed the customary habit of resting from the mid-day's heat. It was a time set aside for rest before returning to one's chores later in the afternoon. *Bandung's* residents rarely slept at this time. The Dutch had discovered that this city's moderate climate did not place the same demands on one's body as the low-lying settlements along the humid coast. Here, in the evenings, one could even experience the occasional need for warm clothing although most of the *bule* wore these heavy clothes as an affectation, or out of some sense of homesickness for their native land.

Soekarno loved it here in *Bandung* with its parks and gardens, its schools and colleges. Especially the colleges. He smiled quietly to himself and leaned back away from the view, rolling easily back onto the bed. The girl's musky fragrance still hung in the air and he closed his eyes momentarily, conjuring up images of the young student undressed again. He lay still, controlling his breathing as his mind recaptured moments he had spent with the soft, pale-skinned girl.

Since he could first remember, his close friends called him *Djago*, The Cock, or Champion in deference to his obvious schoolyard strength. And later, as his handsome features and charismatic charm developed, his prowess at winning the hearts of the ladies confirmed the appropriate title. Soekarno enjoyed the flattering nickname which had stuck since his early teens in Surabaja although, these days, he preferred to be known as *Bung Karno* as he felt that this identified him more with the people, and his political ambitions.

As his thoughts moved away from the charming and willing student who had shared his bed in the early afternoon hours, the handsome young engineer permitted his mind to wander back to other ladies he had known. Soekarno always enjoyed this feeling of post-sexual after-glow which provided the occasion for his mind to relax and his thoughts to wander carelessly. Such luxuries were becoming increasingly rare, and often eluded the ambitious graduate as his political activities and demands on his private time consumed opportunities for such interludes.

He was reminded of his early teens in the small village town of *Tulung Agung* where he was raised in the care of his grandparents. He loved them dearly and recalled the seemingly endless, almost dreamy days of uncomplicated rural life he missed so much here in the city. Living away from his own parents hadn't bothered the young teenager. In fact, he enjoyed escaping the suffocating life of the *kampung* although he missed his mother dearly, at first. It was during this period of his development, living with his grandparents, when he became enthralled by the *wajang kulit* puppet shadow plays which recounted the Hindu *Ramayana* epic.

These never-ending stories captivated his heart and soul. He recalled rapturous evenings spent at village roadside theatre depicting the ancient stories wrapped in symbolic gestures, which represented the very heartbeat of Javanese culture. Night after night, he would plead with his *nenek* to be permitted to go down to the village square where these shows were held. There he would sit with his friends and watch the shadows move behind the white screen as the drama unfolded. The puppeteer would half-talk, half-sing the story, sending his audience of children into a trance. Sometimes they would just fall asleep, as the plays could continue for many hours into the warm Javanese nights.

It was during one such occasion that the young *Djago* observed a number of girls sitting a short distance to the side of his friends. When he discovered that they were giggling and pointing in his direction, he correctly assumed that they were discussing his handsome features. Although only fifteen, he was already conscious that he attracted the opposite sex and never felt uncomfortable with this fact. As the girls continued to giggle and attract his group's attention, *Djago* remembered rising to his feet and sauntering over to the junior high school girls who immediately became quite embarrassed. None of the other boys would ever have done that! An hour later, the young Soekarno found himself fumbling with one of the girls under the copse of palm trees behind the village square. The next morning, his grandparents placed him on the bus and sent him to Surabaya. He never did understand why so much commotion had been generated from what was just a short encounter in the bushes. After their brief and clumsy sexual experiment, the schoolgirl had immediately told her mother who, in turn, related the shameful encounter to her husband when he returned home later that evening. The following morning the grandparents wisely packed his bags and sent him scurrying off to the city and out of reach of the angry father's razor-sharp *golok*.

At first, Soekarno didn't enjoy the large city. He spent some weeks with his family's distant relatives living in an overcrowded shanty on the outskirts of Surabaja Port. Some weeks passed before he received a letter of introduction from his father which requested assistance from an old acquaintance for his son. Soekarno delivered the communication and was immediately taken into the household where he maintained lodgings while completing his high school studies. This was the home of Omar Said Tjokroaminoto, the esteemed civic figure and renowned religious leader.

Tjokro treated his new lodger as if he were his own son. The two soon became close as the elderly scholar identified the enormous potential of the eager young student. As his foster son, Soekarno received a concentrated schooling in languages and religion before moving on to study politics under the older man's guidance. As time passed and the young protege eagerly absorbed whatever teachings he was exposed to, Tjokroaminoto gradually introduced Soekarno to many of his special guests who came to seek the respected leader's advice, often encouraging the young man to participate in the general discussions. It was during this time that *Bung Karno* discovered the complexity of many of the issues facing his fellow countrymen. The never-ending flow of political and religious activists who passed through his foster father's home provided a forum for him to study these emerging leaders, who spanned Indonesia's growing political spectrum.

Tjokroaminoto often observed his young protege and wished

that he was his own real son. As this was not to be, he decided on the next best course of action and, at the age of sixteen, he married his daughter Siti Utari to the confident Soekarno.

Soekarno's competitive nature and manner precipitated difficulties in his new relationship with Tjokroaminoto, whose followers had escalated in number to more than four hundred thousand. He fell out with his father-in-law, and the marriage lasted only another two years before Soekarno sent her home, childless, and established a de facto relationship with the landlady of his Bandung accommodations, Inggit Garnasih, a woman some twelve years his senior. Always the opportunist, he married this wealthy woman who supported her handsome husband while he studied at the Bandung Institute of Technology.

Inggit soon discovered that her young man had no intention of being faithful to her but she still adored her cocky, high-spirited husband and accepted his many liaisons. Eventually, as their fifth anniversary approached, Inggit realised that she had become, once again, just his landlady as Soekarno ceased sharing their bed, preferring to keep his life and activities totally divorced from her. She accepted the status quo, preferring the hurt she felt to losing him completely.

Soekarno knew that he had power over women. It never ceased to fascinate him that this was so, although he believed that he was special and was destined for great achievements in his life. Now that he had graduated he could move onto a different path. He had never really wanted to be a civil engineer but, as the Dutch controlled the colleges, he had considered himself just lucky that he had obtained any degree at all. During his years in Bandung, he consistently developed relationships with other students who shared his political views. He practised public speaking alone in his small room before venturing down to the common park areas to test his style on the other undergraduates. Soon he became a sought-after speaker as his demeanour and style attracted huge crowds. His charismatic personality and presence often mesmerised the gatherings. Soekarno's confidence grew quickly as he discovered that his popularity was not restricted to the provincial city of Bandung.

As he lay on his back contemplating his past, Soekarno knew that he had reached a major crossroads in his career. It was unlikely that he could now expect any civil service opportunity as the Dutch police had been watching his activities closely and he had already been warned several times as to the content of his speeches. He knew they were inflammatory. His captivating style depended on channelling his audience's hate and despair with their colonial masters into support for his political ambitions. And he was becoming more and more successful. The following day he was to leave for Semarang and prepare for a rally that had been organised.

Soekarno smiled with anticipation. He lived for the adoration, the mass hysteria that broke out whenever he spoke, the opportunity to consolidate his political base and, of course, the power he felt flow through his veins as the crowds shouted out in unison calling his name. *'Soekarno! Soekarno! Hiduplah Soekarno! Long live Bung Karno!'*

The following morning Soekarno joined his comrades who would support his rally and act as bodyguards in the event the Dutch secret police attempted to attack their hero. They were all dressed alike, simply, wearing their black *pitji* caps proudly. They were in high spirits. It was as if they sensed the historical import of what they were about to do.

And so they departed, taking the slow winding mountain road down the dangerous track towards the north coast of Java and the coastal towns of Tjiribon and Semarang, heading for the huge rally that would changes all of their lives forever.

* * * * * *

Semarang

Even Soekarno was astonished at the large number of students that attended his rally. The townspeople had followed the surging mass of humanity into the old soccer field more out of curiosity than anything else. Street vendors also followed and, within a relatively short period of time the entire area had taken on the appearance of some organised festival as the crowd moved around slowly creating an almost carnival atmosphere. The roadside vendors or *kaki-lima* traders sold *sate* to the clamouring high school children, while Soekarno and his team prepared an area on the side of the field from where he would address the crowd. He was extremely pleased with the turnout. His confidence grew and he strutted around smiling and talking to anyone who cared to listen. It was his way of preparing himself prior to an address, collecting his thoughts, as most of his speeches were unrehearsed.

At the back of the crowd, a young boy complained to his mother about the heat and flies. Occasionally, as small clouds of dust rose around the main pedestrian traffic, he would sneeze and wipe his nose with the back of his hand. He didn't want to be there. He had just followed his mother and she, in turn, had only followed the crowds into the field to discover what was taking place. Once his mother had determined that it was just a student gathering, she sat down alongside everyone else to wait. There was nothing else to do in the town. Their bus didn't depart for Djogyakarta for at least another three hours and so she elected to wait there and observe whatever was to take place. Her son, Soenarko, sat down disgruntled beside her.

The Javanese woman merely placed her hand behind his back and, slowly moving her fingers up towards his neck tickled him quickly to distract his attention from the conditions. She glanced at him and, satisfied that he would cope with the heat, returned her attention to the crowd. They sat in the heat for another twenty minutes or so when suddenly there was a roar as the crowd scrambled to its feet. The young mother rose with the others and then bent down to pull her son up alongside her. She realised that the boy could not see and decided to move out and away from the centre of the crowd. Slowly they made their way back towards the entrance and eventually found an area that was not as crowded. She looked down at her son and was immediately concerned. Soenarko had difficulty breathing. It was one of those attacks which had haunted him practically since birth. His mother sensed the urgency and sat down next to him encouraging her boy to lie on his side while she stroked his back. The dusty conditions only further aggravated the boy's asthma attack and he began to choke. The woman panicked and, sensing this, the boy followed suit.

Suddenly a figure moved alongside and picked the boy up. He held him upright, applying a wet cloth to the child's face, rubbing the back of his neck several times, while speaking softly to the stricken Soenarko. Moments later, the man led both mother and child outside and away from the crowded field.

'*Rest here!*' he ordered, pointing to several well-worn wooden stools normally reserved for the patrons of the roadside vendor who specialised in *bakmi goreng*. He motioned to the owner and indicated that he wanted a glass of the sweet syrup which was sold to accompany the fried noodles.

'*Drink this!*' he said, handing the pinkish-coloured mixture to Soenarko.

'*Terima kasih,*' the child politely responded but before he could sip the cold drink was struck by another attack. It lasted for several minutes, depleting the boy's reserves. He sat on the stool listlessly, held close by his anxious mother. They continued to sit quietly together for some time and the boy might have fallen asleep had it not been for the air suddenly being punctured by the crowd's deafening cries. '*Hiduplah Bung Karno!*' they shouted in unison, '*Long live Bung Karno!*' they chanted, over and over again until a hush enveloped the crowd.

Moments of quiet followed; then the woman heard a voice drifting across towards them, carried by a resonance and clarity which startled her with its strength.

'*People of Semarang,*' the voice started, pausing for a moment as the crowd became completely hushed. '*People of Semarang, you are political slaves!*' Again there was a pause for effect.

'*People of Semarang, you are prisoners in your own land!*' The voice rose slightly, developing a pitch which carried across the packed ground. '*People of Semarang, the time has come for you to unite and work together for the benefit of yourselves, your children, your futures and your independence!*' And then, with his powerful voice he called, '*People of Semarang, Merdeka!*'

The crowd screamed in unison, their voices pounding the air as they called out together, '*Merdeka! Merdeka! Independence! Freedom!*' which slowly changed into the fervent chant, '*Hiduplah Bung Karno, Long live Bung Karno!*' Knowing that his commanding presence had been felt by all those present, Soekarno then went on to speak for more than an hour. He did not rest nor did his rhetoric lose any of its brilliance. The crowd adored him. The more they called his name, the less tired he felt, until the mass of people were totally under his spell. It was as if one of the characters from the shadow plays had come to life to care for them all. They didn't want him to finish.

They listened in silence when he cajoled them for being ignorant of what was happening around them and criticised their teachers for failing to fan the fire in their hearts, the desire for freedom from the Dutch. They listened as he encouraged them to unite as one, to forget their racial and religious differences and work together to form a common front. They sighed when his voice developed a soft musical quality as he talked of love and loving, of peace and prosperity for their children. They screamed in support when he called for them to take up arms and expel the foreigners from their soil when the time was right.

Soenarko and his mother sat with the stranger who had assisted them and listened to the orator continue to speak without once resting. They knew that something special was happening around them but were content to just be a small part of whatever it was, without question. The stranger leaned closer and placed his hand on Soenarko's shoulder. He smiled and looked directly into the child's face and said, *'When I was very small I also had a sickness. My parents later told me that the village people where I was born believed that I might die. But, as you can see, I am now well again and have not suffered any such illness since my childhood.'*

Soenarko's mother looked at the man's face and believed what he said. There was a strange truthfulness about this stranger and she wanted to take his hand and hold it for comfort. Her son also sensed the man's power but was confused by its presence. He only knew that his attack had gone and that he now felt much better. He looked up at the stranger. *'Did you have my sickness?'* he asked.

'Yes,' he answered to the surprised boy. *'But as I told you, it has now gone, forever.'*

'Perhaps you gave it to me!' Soenarko accused, causing his mother to purse her lips and frown at his rudeness.

'Perhaps I did,' the stranger replied, smiling at the startled pair. *'And if I did, then I am obliged to take it away.'*

'Please don't.' The woman intoned, saddened now by this talk. She knew that this sickness would stay with her son for life. Anyone in their village who fell victim to the breathing illness suffered throughout their lives with the beast inside their chest. She looked sadly at the stranger who smiled, then placed his hand back on her son's shoulder.

The boy responded to the warmth of the man's hand and offered no resistance as the stranger closed his eyes and appeared to pray silently, to himself.

'Njonja,' he said, removing his hand from the boy while addressing the mother, *'What month was your son born?'* The woman was surprised at the question but answered as she could see no harm. She thought for a few moments, collecting her thoughts. When she gave the answer, the man's face broke into another smile and his eyes danced with satisfaction.

'It is the same month as my birth. Only you are a little younger,' he said, speaking to the boy. *'Siapa namanja?'* he suddenly asked, wanting to know the child's name. Soenarko replied politely in his clearest Javanese dialect. The woman placed her arm around her son and squeezed him softly.

'What is your name, sir?' she asked, using the polite Javanese level to address the softly spoken man. She was pleased that she had done so, for when he responded, the woman knew instantly that this stranger was not only highly educated, but was obviously from her own district in Java.

'I will write it down for the boy. I would like for him to take this paper home when you leave and keep it folded until the morning. Would you grant me this strange request?'

The woman was surprised but etiquette demanded that she agree. A small piece of paper was produced and when he had finished writing, he folded the paper and passed it to her.

'I must go now. I am sure that you will have a safe journey home. Selamat tinggal!' he said, rising slowly and lightly touching the boy for the third time on his shoulder.

'Goodbye, sir, terima kasih.' the woman responded, her hands clasped together, her fingers softly touching her lips as if in prayer.

'Selamat djalan, Bapak,' the grateful boy called as the white cotton dressed man departed. He watched the figure walk away when suddenly the man turned and waved to the boy as he called, *'Sampai ketemu lagi, Soeharto! — until we meet again, Soeharto!'*

Soenarko's mother was surprised that the helpful stranger had, in a matter of a few minutes, already forgotten her son's name and was deep in thought when there were shouts and cries close by. Frightened by the clamour, she immediately rose and led her son away from the disturbance. As they headed down the street past the *pasar* where the stench of the day's unsold produce hung heavily

37

in the air, they could hear police whistles and pistol shots shatter the air. Suddenly there were hundreds of people running down the streets nearby as they fled the savage police and their batons. They immediately took refuge in one of the stalls and waited for the disturbance to pass. Soon they were able to continue and, later into the afternoon, they boarded the bus which would take them safely home to their small house in Desa Kemusu Argamulja.

They arrived late in the evening, too tired to eat. Soenarko fell asleep immediately under the watchful eyes of his mother. As she sat there praying that his sickness would go away and leave him to live the life of a normal child, she remembered the stranger. Extracting the paper he had given her from her *tas*, Soenarko's mother leaned closer to the kerosene lantern to read the inscription. She did so then bent forward and kissed her son. Then she placed the piece of paper with *Subuh's* name on it beside her son's bed and left him alone, to dream whatever it was that little boys dream about.

* * * * * *

Another year was to pass before the sickness became so severe that a holy man was called to her son's side. She now believed he was about to die, plagued by the debilitating attacks. As she sat with Soenarko throughout those distressing days and nights, she prayed that the boy would recover, as had the stranger they had met. Soenarko's health did improve, mysteriously, and when he was well enough to rejoin his class, his friends were not overly surprised when he announced that his mother had given him a new name so that the sickness would not return. On that day, when he was called by the teacher, he politely corrected her for using his former name.

'My name is no longer Soenarko, Ibu. My name is now Soeharto!'

And, almost magically, the child known as Soeharto recovered completely from his illness. Within a short period of time even his school performance improved, attracting the attention of his teachers. He had beaten the terrible attacks and would never again suffer the disease.

As he became older and wiser, the fortunate Javanese understood that his recovery had, indeed, been miraculous. And although he came to learn that events in life were often shrouded with mystery, he firmly believed

hat the quietly-spoken religious man who had offered him comfort on
hat day played an integral part in his recovery.

And so, Soeharto never forgot the name of the stranger they had met
vhen the police had raided the political rally in Semarang, arresting the
)utspoken activist, Soekarno, and throwing him into jail. He could still
·emember the roar of the crowds as they called to their hero and these
:hants would often plague his dreams, awakening him in the dark of the
night as the multitude of voices still echoed in his ears calling, 'Hiduplah
Soekarno, Hiduplah Bung Karno! Long live Soekarno!'

Chapter 3

*1963 — Kepulauan Seribu,
The Thousand Islands*

They had agreed that *Pulau Putri* would provide the best anchorage and, now that they had settled down on the small islands' white, almost crystalline beach, Murray had to agree. There were fifteen or so in the group. The voyage from Tandjung Priok, Djakarta's harbour, had been reasonably pleasant. Murray would have preferred to sail but this had not been an option. They had approached the ALRI *Laksamana Laut* and appealed to the Navy Rear Admiral's generous nature, requesting a charter boat for the students and their Australian friend. At first, the senior naval officer was insistent that his vessels were not available for hire but when the young smiling Australian stepped forward and spoke to him in fluent Bahasa Indonesia, the situation changed. Not immediately, of course. The officer was suspicious of a foreigner possessing such uncommon skills in the local language. The Dutch had all but left Indonesia, and only a handful of Europeans who could converse fluently in the national language remained. Many of these were Soviet technicians.

When it appeared that they were not making any real headway with their negotiations, several of the female students had ushered the rest of the group out of the navy office while they remained behind to persuade the stubborn officer to reconsider. Although some rupiah did change hands, the port commander still required considerable convincing that the Australian was not from the Eastern Bloc.

'*Show me his passport,*' he demanded. Murray was summoned back into the office where the two girls were then dismissed. He requested the document politely, albeit brusquely, and examined the blue-covered passport. '*Murray Lloyd Stephenson,*' he read slowly

41

and with difficulty. *'Do you have any dollars?'*

Murray surreptitiously removed the wallet from his back-pocket and extracted two American dollar notes. An hour later, his excited group were steaming out past the breakwater walls towards *Pulau Edam* where they passed close to the lighthouse before taking a heading of 330 degrees. The ship was more than they had expected. The Russian patrol boat slipped through the calm sea at thirty knots covering the forty nautical miles in just over an hour. As the noisy twin diesels churned the water, flying fish raced before the wooden hull, entertaining the excited students. All but two of their number had never been to the magnificent string of more than one hundred coral islands which dotted the shallow sea north of the capital. Their destination was one of the more isolated islands which lay in the centre of a large lagoon, surrounded by a necklace of coral atolls. These were all densely covered with tall coconut palms and low shrubs. Kepulauan Seribu, the Thousand Islands, were virtually uninhabited as drinking water was scarce on the smaller atolls.

They had unloaded their supplies and made camp just twenty metres from where the calm lagoon's occasional ripples tickled the beach. As soon as the patrol boat had departed with instructions to return the following afternoon, everyone stripped down to their underclothes and entered the warm clear water. They laughed and splashed each other while a few of the young men ventured out into the deeper water in search of green-backed lobster. As the day wore on, the girls organised a fire and prepared a simple meal of rice and fish which they had exchanged for cigarettes from one of the passing fishing *perahu*.

The island was relatively small. Murray had ventured off to reconnoitre after the meal and discovered that he could cover the area in less than fifteen minutes. It was a paradise, he thought, wishing that he had sailed out to these magnificent islands before, when he had first arrived in Indonesia. Now he had only a few days left and the thought depressed him. The past two years living in Djakarta as an exchange student, studying at the Universitas Indonesia, had been the most significant period in his life. Murray had developed a sound appreciation of the Indonesian people and their culture. He had acquired many friends and now resented having to leave it all behind. But he knew that he really had no choice in the matter. Although his family were financially secure, it wasn't money or the lack of it which would require that he soon return to Australia. He had given a commitment and was obliged to fulfil the undertakings he had given prior to his departure from Melbourne, two years before. His thoughts were suddenly interrupted as the attractive Sundanese girl dropped beside him and rested her head on shoulder.

'Why do you sit here by yourself, Murray? Can't you decide which of the tjewek you want for tonight?' she bantered. Yanti knew that given the opportunity any one of the other girls would jump at the chance to tempt her boyfriend away.

'How did you know?' he teased, 'I thought, that as the decision's so difficult to make then perhaps I should have them all.'

'Okay, you do that and I will cut their hair off,' Yanti parried, then added, 'and maybe something of yours as well!' but Murray knew that she was only half-joking. One thing he had discovered very early in his stay and that was just how damn jealous these beautiful creatures could be, and how totally insecure they were in their relationships.

'Murray, sajang, would you take me to Australia when you go?'

'Sure,' he replied, wanting to keep the banter light. 'And a couple of Javanese girls as well.' There was always strong competition between the Javanese and Sundanese and he attempted to change the direction of their conversation. He would certainly miss Yanti when he left but there were others who were just as sweet, and he really didn't want to think about all of that on this beautiful island. He rose and pulled Yanti to her feet before her pout became permanent. 'Come on, let's go back in the water.'

'No, Murray, I have already been out in the sun too long! You will make my skin black and then everyone will say I am ugly!' she said, half-jokingly, although it was a fact that a girl's beauty was tied to the fairness of her skin. Working in the rice fields was to be avoided at all costs as the tropical sun was merciless, stamping the women as peasants with their darkened faces and bodies. Nevertheless, she followed the tall, fair-haired Australian down to the water's edge where she playfully kicked sand at his back before fleeing happily back to the safety of the shaded campsite.

Murray swam slowly out into the deeper water and lay on his back soaking up the late afternoon's warmth. Occasionally, as he drifted lazily and the mild currents carried him too far, he would turn and swim back a few strokes to avoid being washed onto the coral reef which surrounded the adjacent island. The conditions were idyllic. In years to come, tourism would spoil these islands, he knew, and then the magic would tragically disappear.

During his two years in-country, he had travelled extensively and was continually amazed at the enormous tourist potential of the archipelago, with its pristine beaches and coconut groves, its towering volcanic mountains and rice-terraced highlands, its diversity of peoples and cultures. Yes, he would certainly miss all of this, and the prospect saddened him. He reluctantly accepted that he would return to the bleak Melbourne winters and, if an old friend failed to support his return, he would remain locked behind the desk job he knew would be waiting. Murray feared that his life might then slowly deteriorate and he would, as had many of those who had preceded him, regret the decision he had made a few years before to surrender his innocence in exchange for opportunity. At the time, he had been excited with the prospect of joining the government agency. In fact, he still enjoyed several exceptional relationships which had developed as a result of his membership in the exclusive intelligence service. The opportunity had been offered and he had not hesitated.

Murray accepted that, had it not been for his association with *Central Plans*, as it was referred to by its limited membership, it would have been most unlikely that he would have ever visited Indonesia: at least, not during these politically unstable times. Brief recollections of Melbourne and his family crossed his mind as he kicked slowly causing his body to move back towards the beach. Something in his mind triggered his memory and suddenly he found himself thinking of his mother and how she often had manipulated his early life.

* * * * * *

Murray had considered himself fortunate as his mother and sister had always been loving and very supportive. His mother had made sure that he received the best of education. Attendance at Geelong Grammar School stood Murray in good stead. During the years he spent at that fine establishment, he excelled not only academically but also on the sports field. He developed relationships with other students which would remain intact for many years after he had matriculated. Later, when he had graduated from Melbourne University's Faculty of Law, Murray was really not surprised to see the occasional familiar face amongst those who had also entered government service.

He had first been approached during his final year at university. Murray's mother had accepted an invitation for them both to spend the weekend with the Bradshaws in Portsea. In later years when reminiscing, Murray would often smile when recalling his mother's telephone instructions just before that long week-end.

'You will be expected to join in the tennis. The Bradshaws are very competitive people but you should not let them intimidate you. I will meet you there.' Mrs. Stephenson never missed an opportunity to advance her son's social relationships. 'Darling, you have the directions. Oh, and Murray,' she added, 'don't forget the new sports jacket I gave you on your birthday. They dress for dinner.'

'Should I bring complimentary batteries for their hearing aids?', he asked, and immediately wished he hadn't. He appreciated his mother's aggressive approach to widening his social contacts but remembered several other invitations which had been disastrously boring.

'Murray, don't be impertinent. I am confident that you will find these people quite exhilarating and, as for the inference that we are all just a bunch of old fogies, you should be prepared for some very competitive tennis.'

His first reaction was to decline the invitation, but knowing his mother's persistence, he decided that taking a break on the coast wouldn't hurt. The undergraduate studies were more demanding than he had anticipated and, as he entered his room just off campus and identified the stack of unread reference titles, the thought of a long weekend away from the drudgery suddenly appealed.

He thought the weather was probably going to be fine, although, like most Melbournians, Murray knew that any predictions he might make about the weather were likely to prove incorrect. The following day, having packed both warm and summer clothing just to be sure, he drove south down through the old farming areas towards the Army's Officer Training School before following the directions his mother had given. Murray knew the area reasonably well but even he was impressed to see the delightful cottage in its setting so close to the sea. After parking the MG TF snugly against the footpath, Murray lifted his gear from the back seat and strolled into the rose filled front garden. Before he could knock, the door was opened by a genial Harry Bradshaw and Murray was gripped by the hand and escorted directly to the rear of the house, where a small group had gathered.

'Everybody, this is Muriel's boy,' Bradshaw called out as they stepped down onto the enclosed terrace, behind which lay the tennis court and swimming pool. 'Murray, this is my wife Susan,' he said before turning to the women playing cards. 'The lady successfully cheating your mother at gin rummy is Jean Broome, and this gentleman is to be your tennis partner. Alfred, may I introduce Murray Stephenson.'

Murray stepped forward and shook the extended hand warmly as he smiled confidently and said 'hello' to the ladies. He was surprised to find that both these women were considerably younger than their husbands. Alfred Broome maintained his grip while he took Murray by the shoulder and playfully tested the younger man's arm for strength.

'Seem's you'll do, Murray. What do you say that we give our hosts a thrashing as soon as you're settled?'

'For goodness sake, Alfred. Give the young man a chance to catch his breath.' Jean Broome called as she placed her remaining cards down on the table indicating another win. 'As you can see, Murray, I'm not the sporting type I'm afraid. Hope you will be able to carry the side as your partner's ego is far superior to his game!' With which, the Bradshaws joined in the fun laughing at the truthful statement.

'That's okay. I enjoyed the drive and, quite frankly, I've been looking forward to a game or two. Been locked away with my books for too long. Will five minutes be okay?'

'Muriel, would you do the honours please?' Susan asked, indicating the guest room alongside the pool. Murray's mother rose and took her son by the arm leading the way. She returned quickly and took her place at the card table.

'He is a fine-looking young man, Muriel. You must be very pleased.' Susan commented, not realising that the very same thought preoccupied the minds of the others present.

'Perhaps we should send the old ones home,' Jean Broome added idly, sipping her gin and tonic. This was already her third. After her eighth or ninth, she had been known to become amorous with the younger men. Her comment brought a brief scowl to her husband's face.

'We'll see who's old, my dear,' Harry Bradshaw interceded quickly. The Broomes were close friends and both couples readily accepted each other's idiosyncrasies. Bradshaw crossed the terrace and lifted Alfred's wife out of her chair and headed towards the pool. Knowing that to continue with his charade would be folly and disastrous for the weekend gathering, Harry returned his guest to her seat and kissed her gently on the forehead, just as Murray returned.

'Well, let's do it,' Susan suggested, slightly miffed at the display. 'Muriel, you don't mind do you darling? You're more than welcome to join us, you know.'

'Not today, thanks dear. I'd be happy to stay here with Jean and discover just how she always manages to win.' Amid the light on-going banter, the foursome moved onto the tennis court, and commenced with a few minutes of warming up shots before the challenge got under way. They played for an hour resting only briefly between the two sets. Murray was surprised at their level of play. He had expected a typical weekend game and was delighted that he was obliged to compete with all of his skill. His own game was normally enough to earn courtside accolades from the gallery. On this occasion he struggled to maintain his first service due to the fact that he had not anticipated such strong opponents. Underestimating his hosts' skill was indeed a major tactical error which attracted several severe and pointed glances from his partner. Alfred had expected more of Murray, from what his mother had implied on the telephone the week before, but he did not overly display his disappointment. As the set developed he was pleased that he had reserved judgement for Murray's game improved dramatically, serving well and generally covering the court, saving difficult points which might have otherwise cost them the game.

The match over they rested around the swimming pool sipping champagne and freshly-squeezed orange juice. As the sun moved behind a thick blanket of cloud, the air became chilly and they adjourned to their rooms in preparation for the evening meal. Murray was relaxed with the thought of spending the rest of the weekend with his mother's friends. He hadn't always enjoyed the company of older people. He felt comfortable here and hoped that they approved of him. As he showered, Murray's thoughts turned to his own father and he sighed, the hot stinging stream of water washing away the instant mood swing he experienced whenever he remembered the man. Quickly he put the image out of his mind and, stepping from the shower, towelled himself until his skin reddened under the onslaught. He dressed casually then added his blazer.

Upon entering the main house he cursed himself silently for not wearing a tie. The other men both wore cravats, and the moment he caught his mother's critical eye Murray wished he'd remembered her advice. They drank and talked for almost two hours before sitting down to dinner. The conversation moved from sport to politics and both the older men invited the younger man's opinions.

In fact, he was being tested for the soundness of his political views. During the Cold War years, many apparently Ivy League types had concealed their left-wing persuasions and many a government agency had been burned. The women present were oblivious to what was taking place. Murray had no idea that both of these men were senior government officials whose activities placed them in the dark and sinister world of intelligence gathering and, on occasion, espionage. This was how their covert organisation recruited the select few who now represented the most elite secret service in modern times. Had Murray been told at that moment that Harry Bradshaw was one of the most skilled field operatives in the Government's employ he would most probably have scoffed. His host was affable and gracious without the rough edges one would expect from the grubby world of spies and their intrigue. The other male guest could easily have been a senior member of the community, seen participating at fetes and church bazaars with his splendid humour and entertaining stories. Murray would also not have accepted that Alfred Broome was, in fact, the head of Australia's Secret Service and that he commanded a force of agents that was so secret that even the Parliament was not privy to its existence.

As the evening wore on, the women retired, leaving the three men to pursue more serious discussions. The older and more experienced pair led Murray into conversations which surprised him as they discussed regional politics, the Commonwealth's unhealthy position in relation to the ever-increasing American presence around the globe, and the threat of communism as it spread through Asia and down towards Australia. When he finally returned to his room, he was amazed to see that they had talked together until three in the morning. Tired from the tennis but satisfied that he had carried himself well, Murray fell asleep almost within moments of his head touching the soft kapok pillow. He was totally unaware that he was about to take his first steps along a path with a very dark and sinister destination, that his life would never again be his own, and that his mother had unwittingly delivered him into the hands of evil.

The following day, Saturday, they had a rematch but the outcome was the same. Alfred was ecstatic as some considerable time had passed since he had partnered a win over the Bradshaws. That evening, as they had on the previous night, the women retired shortly after dinner leaving the men to their discussions and, once again, the topics followed much the same pattern as the evening before. Alfred directed the conversation back to his preferred subject, communism and its spread in Asia, and the dangers of the Domino Theory while Harry checked and probed the unwitting law student as to his own loyalties and preferred political affiliations.

It was towards the early hours of Sunday morning that Murray was asked very directly whether he would be interested in government employment once he had graduated. Murray was quite taken off guard by the question, but when it was made clear that there was a sound career path opportunity for him, and that both of these men could ensure his acceptance subject to final security clearances being conducted, he was flattered that he was considered worthy of such sponsorship. They didn't dwell on the subject, suggesting that his decision would require much more than a few days to determine whether he believed he could make such a commitment. They agreed not to raise the issue again for the remainder of that weekend. On the following day, Murray was surprised that they had meant exactly what they had stated. It was almost as if he had imagined the intriguing discussions having ever occurred at all.

He remembered that it had rained throughout the Sunday and a sharp exchange had taken place between the women, Jean and Susan. He had not understood at the time as Murray was not privy to the personal secrets these two couples enjoyed. The ensuing tension made him feel uncomfortable and he went for a long jog in spite of the weather. When he returned, it was as if nothing had occurred, as they were all, including his mother, quite tipsy from the champagne Harry had broken out from his cellar. Murray joined them after he'd showered and was relaxed to discover that the earlier tension had disappeared. He quietly examined his mother's expression but there was no indication that everything had not returned to normal.

That evening passed slowly. The atmosphere became tense once again and it was obvious that the couples were suffering from overexposure to each other. It was apparent to Murray and, as the youngest present, he felt uncomfortable. Shortly after dinner he excused himself, kissed his mother on the cheek as he whispered to her, then retired to his room. He undressed slowly and then flopped into the soft double bed, wishing he had brought something to read. Murray lay in the darkness willing his mind and body to relax but he could not sleep. Hours passed before he finally submitted, drifting into a deep sleep.

The night had almost passed when he awoke suddenly, startled. He grabbed at whatever it was that moved close to him in the dark.

'What the...!'

'Shh!' the woman intoned, surrendering as her hands were gripped fiercely by Murray's. 'Shh!' she called urgently, again, indicating that there was no resistance. Confused, he released her wrists and, as he did so, felt a hand moving softly over his face until it rested on his mouth.

'Don't say anything, Murray! Please don't say anything!'

He could smell the alcohol on her breath. Murray reached for the bedside light but she anticipated the movement.

'Don't, please!' she pleaded, lifting the bedcovers and slipping in beside him. He thought the woman to be quite mad coming to his room while her own husband slept close by.

'For Chrissakes, you'll get us both hung!' he hissed as she started stroking his firm arms and thighs.

'Don't speak, Murray, just be quiet!' she implored, moving over his body and kissing him in an attempt to prevent him from talking.

It was hopeless, he knew, as already he'd been aroused. Moments passed and, as she stroked his body slowly, kissing him softly first on the neck and chest, and then slowly down his firm stomach, he realised that he wanted her to stay. A small voice warned him that what they were doing was dangerous. They would be caught! He should send her away! But the warmth moving up from his loins enveloping his whole body was a far more powerful force and, before he could offer any resistance, she had slipped into position over him and was gently rocking him into an uncontrollable feeling of ecstasy. His hands moved across her body in the dark until coming to rest as he cupped her breasts. They moved together, in harmony, their excitement building when suddenly she called out softly, stifling her cry as she shuddered.

Then she bent forward and gently kissed the surprised Murray before slipping back out of the bed, leaving quickly before he could prevent her departure. He heard her move through the darkened room and, when the door clicked closed behind her, even then he dared not turn the light on, until he was sure that sufficient time had passed for her to return to her own room. He was stunned by the sudden exit and bewildered by the woman's foolish adventure. If it had not been for the lingering scent, he may have believed that he'd been dreaming.

Hours passed before sleep returned. And even then it was not a refreshing rest, as he dreamed restlessly only to awaken without any recollection of what had transpired in his sleep. Of one thing he was certain. A woman had entered his room and made silent, eager love, leaving him concerned and disappointed with the interlude. He was irritated with himself for permitting it to happen. But more than anything else, Murray was annoyed because he was not certain which of the two wives had entertained themselves at his expense.

As he sat down to breakfast, Murray felt uncomfortable knowing that one of the women sitting across the table had cheated on her husband just a few hours before. He tried to act as if nothing at all had occurred and joined in the casual conversation, surreptitiously observing those present to see if there was some indication, some acknowledgement as to which of the ladies had been his visitor. There was just no way he could determine this as even their perfumes seemed similar and neither of the wives gave any indication of their indiscretion. It was almost as if nothing had happened. Guilt, and an uneasiness that his affair may suddenly be exposed, encouraged his early return to the city where he buried himself conscientiously in his studies. For weeks, when he lay awake at night, Murray visualised the exciting tryst and, no matter how he tried, he was unable to determine which of the women had compromised their friends and husband.

During the following months, Murray was invited back to the Bradshaws home on several occasions and he had accepted, not just because he enjoyed the strong bond which had developed with Harry but also, at first, out of a sense of curiosity. During the first return visit the programme was much the same as before. They played tennis, dined and talked late into the night, and Murray felt comfortable in their company. During his third and final visit, the tennis consisted of men's singles only, as Susan had insisted on remaining with Muriel Stephenson while the men fought it out on the courts. Murray thought it relevant that Alfred Broome's wife had also not accompanied her husband on these last visits.

Later, he had asked his mother casually about the woman's absence, but she merely shrugged, almost indifferently, and ignored the question. As the circumstances were never repeated, he believed he understood why and wondered what had happened to the flirtatious Jean Broome. He never met her again and, by the end of his final semester, the fading memory of the brief encounter no longer concerned him as he had established other priorities in his life. He completed his law degree a few months later, and immediately entered government service.

Murray Stephenson joined the sixty-three other members of the Australian Secret Intelligence Service and commenced the gruelling training demanded of agents in the exclusive agency. He attended the jungle training courses in southern Queensland and completed the basic Code of Conduct courses at the discreet Australian Army facilities in Middle Head, Sydney. Murray then went on to practise his new skills at the military installations on Swan

Island. Murray Lloyd Stephenson had entered the dark world of suspicion and intrigue and become one of its clandestine warriors.

Before Spring had revisited the Victorian capital and Melbourne once again pulsed with the promise of another Grand Final, he had completed a two-month indoctrination and assimilation course on the first floor of the old prefabricated two-storey building near the lake in Albert Park, referred to as the *Head Office*. This was the home of Australia's most secret institution, ASIS. And it was known to those select few merely as *Central Plans*.

* * * * * *

Murray's tight work schedule excluded him from enjoying any real time off during the weekends. It wasn't until he received the call from his mother that he realised just how long it had been since he had taken a break away from his duties. His mother, insisting that he attend the garden party with her, reminded him that it had been more than four months since his last visit. Murray thought that his mother had seemed a little distant, almost cool, when they spoke on the phone. Muriel Stephenson was adamant that they attend the function together. Recalling her son's preference for casual attire, she also insisted that he wear a suit. Murray was not surprised as his mother had always dictated his dress code since he could first remember.

He arrived at her house and parked his MG. Muriel Stephenson refused to go anywhere in his car, instructing Murray to drive her in her own vehicle. It was only then he discovered that the hosts were to be the Bradshaws. Murray could not remember precisely when he'd last seen Harry and Susan. Certainly, it was well before he had commenced his demanding training with ASIS. Although Harry was, in his own right, one of the most senior Intelligence Heads in the country, ASIO was not accommodated in the same buildings as its overseas counterpart. Apart from the last time he'd spent at the weekend cottage, Murray couldn't recall when he'd last spoken his mentor. He had been just too preoccupied with the demands of his new position.

Murray smiled at his mother's secretive manner. They drove up Toorak Road until Muriel Stephenson instructed her son to stop. Without waiting for him to open her door, she then stepped out and stood alongside the entrance of a church Murray remembered having passed thousands of times as he had driven into the city. She watched as he locked the car and then turned and walked through the side gate into the lawned area. Murray followed, caught up and then walked down the paved path towards the group assembled outside the church's main entrance. When he recognised the couple he smiled, and waved as he and his mother proceeded towards the Bradshaws. Bewildered by the secrecy, he continued to play his mother's childish game, stepping up and shaking Harry Bradshaw's hand, then leaning towards his wife Susan, to kiss her on the cheek. Even when the woman stepped forward and handed the crying infant for Susan to hold, it did not register that he had been invited to a christening. And then he turned and caught the expression on his mother's face. Then he turned again and looked at Susan. He was confused. Then he understood. It had been some time since he had seen the couple and now it was clear why Susan had opted out of the tennis earlier in the year. He looked at his mother and shook his head wondering why she had kept the event secret. Embarrassed that he hadn't even brought a gift, he opened his mouth to remonstrate with his mother when the minister appeared and ushered them all into the church.

Throughout the brief service, Murray glanced at his mother and he could see from her expression that something had upset her. Deeply. He knew that she could be like this, remembering the turbulent time following his father's departure. They never did see him again and he recalled the months which followed, when there was practically no conversation at all in their house. He frowned, concerned that he had missed something which so obviously worried her. The private christening took no more than ten minutes, after which the small group moved back outside for photographs. There were less than ten people present, including the proud parents. Murray took his turn and stood, holding the child between both Harry and Susan. Then he watched as his mother was given the child. Murray thought he could see tears in her eyes and then it came to him. She had become lonely. And then he felt guilty, knowing that he had been neglecting her.

They were invited to the Bradshaw's Toorak home for a brief celebration. Harry served the Moet Chandon while Susan attended to her child. Murray stayed just long enough to have a brief conversation with Harry before his mother developed a headache and had to be taken home. They drove to her house in silence. Murray parked her car, walked around to open her door but, once again, she had moved first and left the vehicle unassisted, walking directly to her front door. Murray was again confused. He walked up to the house where she waited, expecting that his mother would hand him the key to unlock the door. When he stepped up to the front step, she extended her hand for her car keys. Surprised, he handed these to her as Muriel Stephenson's hand flashed through the air and struck him fiercely on the face. He reeled back, stunned from the unexpected blow.

'What the hell......!' he began to say, as his mother calmly placed her key into the lock and opened the door. He stood there in shock. She had never struck him before, not even when he'd done the most outrageous things as a child.

'Just like your father,' she said, and stepped inside. For a long moment Murray stood on his mother's doorstep wondering what had happened. Unable to figure it out, he turned and left, angry at her behaviour. He understood that she was growing old and was suffering the pangs of loneliness. He couldn't help that, and was shocked by what had just transpired. Murray knew from past experience that, given time, his mother would respond to a telephone call and some flowers. Then he would get to the bottom of what was really troubling her. Angry that she had selected the Bradshaw's special day to demonstrate her feelings, Murray left without speaking to his mother further, believing that it was almost impossible to fathom the female mind.

Muriel Stephenson heard her son drive away and bit her lip. She refused to cry. It was not her position to tell him. Suddenly she felt so alone. And ashamed. Then, when she realised that he just might not have known, she broke into tears, devastated by the knowledge that not only had she alienated her son, but the fact that she would never be permitted to claim the child just christened as her own grandson.

* * * * * *

Murray let it go for a week before he phoned his mother. He was surprised when Susan Bradshaw answered the call.

'We have to talk, Murray,' Susan had said. Murray agreed to meet, suggesting lunch, but she had insisted that a drink would be more appropriate.

'Harry will not be joining us, Murray, so please come alone.' He did, and they met in the bar at the Intercontinental. An hour later, Murray left Susan to find her own way back as he wandered down the street, bewildered by the news she had brought. It was only when he arrived back in his sparse bachelor quarters that the enormity of what Susan had said really became apparent. He just couldn't believe it. And all that time he had thought that it had been the other woman who'd climbed into his bed and cheated on her ageing husband.

And then Murray couldn't sleep worrying about Harold Bradshaw. He lay in bed in the dark, thinking, conjuring up in his mind what the ramifications of that disclosure could bring to his life, should their secret ever be uncovered.

* * * * * *

The Thousand Islands

A girl's voice startled Murray out of his quiet reverie causing him to choke as he swallowed sea water.

'Murray! Murray! Awas! You are almost over the coral!'

He coughed and, regaining his breath immediately kicked quickly, then rolled over to discover that he was in less than two metres of water. He moved slowly, cautiously, as directly below he could identify the sharp long black needles of what the locals called *bulu babi* — pig's bristles. Murray knew that to touch these deadly sharp needles would result in the tips breaking off wherever they touched the body, causing extreme pain. The sea porcupines passed dangerously close to his stomach as he made his way carefully away from the coral and back to the beach.

As he climbed out of the lagoon, Yanti ran up and threw her arms around him. He knew that he had been fortunate she'd alerted him to the dangerous reef in time. He smiled down and kissed her gently. *'Terima kasih, manis,'* he said, wishing that he really could take her home to Australia with him. But Murray knew that this would be impossible. Even if he had not been associated with the

Service, her own political affiliations would have precluded Yanti and most of those who'd accompanied her out to the serenity of the islands from ever visiting the Commonwealth of Australia.

For Yanti was a member of the *Gerwani* — the *Gerakan Wanita Indonesia* or Indonesian Women's Movement, which was directly controlled by the *Partai Komunis Indonesia*. Yanti and her friends belonged to an advanced cell within that organisation. They were amongst the more dedicated followers on campus. Murray looked down at the smiling face and innocent eyes. It was difficult to believe but true.

This sweet playful creature, his Yanti, was not just a senior member of the Indonesian Communist Party. She was a dedicated member of an elite women's corps of communists. A very dangerous playmate, indeed. Yanti, as had many of her fellow *Gerwani* members, had undergone intensive military training. She was just one of the tens of thousands who now followed the Indonesian Communist Leaders. These tough women were considered brutal in the execution of their orders. They were feared on campus and were responsible, through their culture of intimidation, for the swift growth of their organisation throughout the Indonesian universities. There was no doubt in Murray's mind that, had Yanti been aware of his true agenda in attending the University of Indonesia, she would have been amongst the first to participate in whatever steps were necessary to protect the *Gerwani* and destroy him, without remorse.

Chapter 4

1960-63

Murray's detailed administrative training was no less strenuous than the physical aspects of becoming an ASIS agent. Much of his time had been dedicated to learning the new jargon and the complicated terminology associated with Defence and its myriad of associated spin-offs. His first field assignment was to take up temporary residence in Indonesia, posing as an exchange student. The fact that there had been no reciprocal arrangements with the Indonesian university apparently was of little concern to the government agencies involved, both in Australia and Indonesia. His brief was to establish himself using the cover of the University exchange programme and then to penetrate all the political factions which had infiltrated campus life. There were specific target groups. Murray was to befriend student members of the *Partai Komunis Indonesia* — the Indonesian Communist Party, which had grown to become, or so they claimed, the third largest in membership after the Soviet Union and China. He was to identify and associate with student leaders involved with political, cultural and religious group activities on and off campus. In short, Murray was to develop a deep cover and not alienate any of the groups targeted. This proved easier said than done, as Murray soon discovered that petty rivalries on campus could develop into deadly vendettas once away from the watchful eyes of the University *dosen*.

He had left Melbourne and flown directly to Singapore where again he was discreetly briefed by the ASIS Chief of Station in the Australian High Commission. Murray was amused at the location selected for Australia's diplomatic mission as the Consulate and other departments were located above the Hong Kong and Shanghai Banking Corporation. It was customary for all diplomatic and consulate staff enroute to Djakarta to spend a few days in Singapore, to break the long journey and provide an opportunity to obtain a tropical wardrobe from the fine Singaporean tailors. Murray, unfortunately, had no such entitlement as he was obliged to maintain the facade of being an advanced student who wished to study *Bahasa Indonesia* and the Indonesian culture. His luggage only contained an assortment of casual clothing and sporting equipment.

His briefing in Singapore consisted primarily of studying recently acquired photographs of known student activists which he committed to memory. Murray spent two days examining reports covering the latest military signals intelligence which, frustratingly, had been seriously edited by the source provider, the British equivalent service, MI-6. Information was a jealously guarded resource and even the British were cautious about who should benefit from their covert activities.

The Station Chief suggested to Murray that these concerns had created a rift between the two intelligence arms soon after it was discovered that one of the architects of the Australian Secret Service, Charles Howard Ellis, had been working for Adolf Hitler's gang during the Second World War. Just a few years later Ellis was interrogated by MI5 officers. The Australian-born spymaster not only admitted to maintaining close personal relationships with Philby and Blunt during their traitorous years as Soviet moles, but also confirmed their suspicions that he had been compromised by the Soviets some ten years before.

Murray scanned through the signals concerned with the many deletions. He was cleared to the highest level of security known in Australia and yet here, to his dismay, the names of field operatives and other essential information had been removed. At least, he thought, with some sense of quiet comfort, his own position would be less likely to be compromised as the Australians had retaliated by withholding essential intelligence as well.

*   *   *   *   *   *

He boarded the British Airways' 707 and enjoyed the short flight across the Java Sea and into the Indonesian capital. The flight stewardess had announced their arrival before remembering to pass the complicated arrival forms. Murray smiled as he completed his

Customs and Immigration forms when he read that *'pornography was a banned import without special licence.'* A heavy pungent smell permeated the air as the cabin doors swung open.

In years to come he would always remember those first moments, standing in the aisle, concerned with the air quality as the suggestion of rotting garbage and *durian* assailed his nostrils. He had moved forward with the other passengers, slowly, in single file, until reaching the exit where they were obliged to step across a wide gap onto the ancient mobile steps which, shaking precariously under the weight, threatened to spill the new arrivals onto the tarmac. He looked around quickly, surprised to see villages surrounded by coconut trees just off the runway. Children played along the airstrip, kicking a soccer ball to and fro and, as he watched, a dog entered the game, biting playfully at the children's bare feet as they chased each other. Murray looked up at the sky and immediately wished he hadn't, the sun's brilliance momentarily blinding him. It was hot.

As he stepped down onto the cracked cement tarmac, waves of heat rose through the soles of his shoes and, within seconds, his clothes were saturated with sweat. The short walk from the parked jet through the poorly maintained Kemayoran International Terminal immediately cast a cloud of depression over his excitement. The building reflected the country's economic collapse. The walls were filthy and only parts of the ceiling remained painted. There were no partitions nor doors. The entire area was one huge, unkempt hall with a number of broken ceiling fans hanging precariously in the centre of the building. There were bright red signs painted on the interior walls which Murray identified immediately as Communist slogans. He remembered that this airfield doubled also as a military facility where the Soviet Mig-15s and 17s were based to protect the city.

The unenclosed airport was practically deserted as the handful of passengers struggled inside and away from the fierce heat. There was little respite for these shocked foreigners as they slowed their movements hoping to ease their discomfort. One by one, they were checked and questioned, each passenger requiring almost fifteen minutes to pass through the immigration desk.

Customs were even more belligerent. The surly officers opened everything and, whenever they discovered a camera, the film was immediately removed. Cigarettes disappeared as these were a treasured item. The smarter visitors carried four or five cartons, knowing that the officials would leave them with at least two of these. Books were removed and examined. Clothing was checked and even letters were opened and examined for money.

Murray smiled his way though the hour it took to complete both procedures. It was not in his character to lose his cool, and anyway, doing so would not only further exacerbate whatever situation had provoked such a reaction, but would also be considered as a severe loss of face in this, and most other Asian nations. Finally he was cleared and permitted to leave the terminal. As he exited the building, a foreigner walked up and greeted him.

'Keith Wells, Head of Station,' he said quietly, extending his hand and taking Murray's case with his other.

'Murray. Murray Stephenson,' he responded, completing the formalities. Both men had seen each other's photographs and read each other's files. Wells then escorted his new arrival to a light blue Holden sedan.

'Well, thought you'd never get out of there. What happened?' the embassy officer asked as they pulled away from the large group of beggars which had encircled the car, hoping that this would guarantee that a few rupiah would be dropped from the *tuan's* rear windows. The driver placed the vehicle into first gear and revved the engine loudly, warning the filthy beggars to move. He had no patience for such displays around his car.

'Nothing out of the ordinary,' Murray replied, 'I think the two Brits ahead of me caused the delay.'

'Yep, that will do it every time. They still have quite a bee in their bonnets about the British. You'll soon discover that as you wander around the streets here. Most of the itinerants will spit at you unless you are quick to convince them that you're an Australian.' He looked at the new arrival and smiled. 'How is your *Bahasa Indonesia?*'

'*Lumajan sadja,*' he replied, knowing that he needed to concentrate of this aspect of his credentials quickly. He'd had relatively little opportunity to learn the language, what with the gruelling training courses and the incredible mountains of information his masters demanded he absorb in those few short months. 'I'll need to put in some real time, that's for sure. It won't be that difficult now that I'm here,' he added.

'True enough.' The other man looked at the back of the driver's head and motioned to Murray with his hand to be careful with what he said. Most of the drivers could understand some English and, amongst these, even after the Embassy's careful screening process, there were agents who had been placed in these driver positions by Indonesia's own secret service, *BAKIN*, the *Badan Koordinasi Intelidjen*.

They occupied the twenty minute drive with small talk. Murray was fascinated with the spectacles along the main thoroughfares. Occasional stands of coconut trees grew alongside the road. Weather-worn tarpaulins hung listlessly across broken footpaths, sheltering roadside vendors selling a vast choice of foods. As their Holden slowed from time to time, weaving through the disorderly pedestrian traffic and the three-wheeled *betjaks*, Murray caught his first glimpses of Djakarta's inhabitants. Roadside stalls were packed with customers sitting on long bench stools as they devoured their servings of hot, spicy food, while the air was filled with voices calling out to passers-by, enticing these potential clients with boasts of flavour and price. *Soto Madura, Nasi Padang, Sate, Sop Buntut*, these and many other food stalls' signs flashed by as Murray remained engrossed in the congested scene. The driver slowed, then stopped. He opened the door slightly and spat heavily onto the road. As they drove on, Murray detected something different in the car's air quality. For a moment, Murray thought that the driver had done the unforgivable; he winced and held his breath.

'God!' he said hoarsely, almost choking on the smell. The other Australian looked at Murray and snorted.

'You'll get used to that,' Wells suggested. 'It isn't what you think, Murray. That wonderful scent you have just encountered is the foul-smelling *durian* fruit which, believe it or not, the Indonesians claim is the most delightful taste ever designed by Allah.' Wells smiled before continuing. 'Our Consul tried it when he first arrived. Claims the experience would be like eating an 'off' custard cake inside an outback toilet!' with which he laughed and shook his head at the comparison. Even the air-conditioning could not prevent the powerful aromas from entering the sedan. As they drove on, Murray slowly accepted the overpowering stench as something he would have to get used to.

There were PT-76 Soviet tanks positioned on several of the main intersections and Murray wondered what amphibious tanks were doing inside the city. They looked most threatening with their 76mm barrels pointing directly towards the oncoming traffic. As they continued, he discovered that most of the vehicular traffic seemed to be of Eastern Bloc manufacture. Truckloads of armed soldiers approached recklessly from behind, blowing their horns arrogantly, causing the driver to pull over and permit the convoy to pass. Then Murray spotted what he thought was the most ridiculous thing. It was another amphibious vehicle, ploughing down the street leaving track marks along the bitumen road. He smiled at the sight of the Soviet BTR-50 Armed Personnel Carrier, complete with its nine soldiers standing aloft.

Murray was surprised to see that the soldiers standing in the back of the huge trucks were fully armed, some carrying grenades hanging from their belt webbing. Another convoy sped past, throwing thick clouds of dust high into the air as ducks and chickens squawked, screeched, and scrambled for safety, sending the pedestrian hawkers scurrying after their birds. Horns blared raucously, adding to the pervasive chaos. School children stopped and turned away from the noise, covering their ears and closing their eyes to avoid the suffocating dust. Older and more affluent students pumped along on their bicycles, handkerchiefs tied across their faces as they fought for some small share of the pot-holed roads.

Their driver elected to take the *tuans* via the large market area of *Pasar Senen*. Here the traffic ground to a halt as Wells cursed the driver for his stupidity in selecting this route. He had not been watching when the car had turned away from *Djalan Hajam Wuruk* and now would pay the price for permitting the driver to take one of his impossible shortcuts. The market area was cluttered with produce and a multitude of peasants were off-loading even more, as the ancient buses rested from their arduous journey down the mountain roads. Goats were tethered in line, as one of the many butchers prepared his section for another of the animals to be slaughtered, according to Moslem tradition.

Murray was only metres from the swift knife as it flashed once sending a bloody trail splurting across the fly-ridden table. He was shocked at the brutality of the moment, and surprised at his own reaction. As Murray knew, the meat would only be be considered *halal* and accepted by the Moslem customers if the throat had been severed in the correct manner.

Buffaloes walked lazily through the slop and mud, directed by small boys with rattan sticks. Bicycles were pushed through the mud by their owners; along the cross-bars were dozens of chickens tied upside down, ready for sale and slaughter. Men and women alike yelled and screamed at each other, abusing those who splashed mud carelessly on others, as they fought their way through the maze of baskets containing everything from vegetables to quail eggs.

Murray was astounded at the mass of humanity congested around this marketplace and wished they could move on, for the air inside the vehicle had become uncomfortably humid. But reversing out of this congestion was out of the question so the men were obliged to sit and wait for the section ahead to clear. The car's engine began to overheat and the airconditioner ceased to function.

'*Get this bloody car moving, Mas!*' the Station Chief hissed at the unhappy driver whose eyes immediately searched again for some way through. He started blowing the horn hoping that this would make the huge bus broken down up front suddenly disappear. Keith Wells shook his head in disgust and became resigned to the situation. It would not be safe to walk though the *pasar* area.

Another fifteen minutes passed when finally their sedan managed to move though the muddy section, and away from the decaying mounds of the previous day's produce, which had been just left at the edge of the market. As the driver shifted into second gear, Murray observed hordes of children, their clothes in tatters, fighting and playing in the stacks of refuse. He had read much about this country of extremes but admitted that there could be no preparation for the sights he had seen in his first hour in-country. He made a mental note to keep his injections up to date.

Within minutes of leaving the squalor behind, Murray was surprised at the contrast as they drove into the city's inner suburbs. Fine two-story residences lined many of the well-kept streets. Tall palms stood majestically beside the white wall dwellings, signalling the lush gardens hidden discreetly behind tall perimeter fences. They drove on. A further ten minutes passed and they moved from

Tjut Mutiah into Menteng, Djakarta's elite suburb where most of the generals lived. It was only minutes away from the centre of the city and, of course, the Presidential Palace. The driver turned into *Djalan Tasikmalaya* and stopped at the second house in the well shaded street. It was an old colonial-styled villa surrounded by bougainvillaea trees. The driver blew the horn impatiently. Suddenly, the iron gate opened and a smiling, toothless *babu* waddled outside to welcome her new *tuan*.

'*Selamat datang, tuan mudah,*' she said through the betel-nut-stained mouth, welcoming the young foreigner.

'*Terima kasih,*' was all Murray could find to respond at that moment as he was almost speechless at the size of the villa. 'It's fantastic!' he exclaimed, admiring the Dutch dwelling.

'Don't get too excited just yet,' Wells warned, leading the way along the footpath which wound its way through a number of frangipani trees beside the villa. Murray followed silently and, as they turned around behind the beautiful home, he discovered a small detached building similar in size to a garage. Keith Wells turned and smiled, permitting the excited housekeeper to brush past carrying the *tuan's* baggage easily under her powerful arms.

A wave of disappointment washed over Murray as he suddenly realised his error.

'This pavilion will be yours, Murray, for the next two years,' he was informed by the smiling Station Chief who was obviously enjoying the look of dismay on the younger man's face. 'Welcome to Djakarta.'

* * * * * *

Almost six months had passed before Murray felt comfortable using the language. His proficiency accelerated once he began to take the occasional female student home to his compact quarters. Although austere by Western standards, his accommodations were adequate. The entrance opened into a two-by-five metre lounge area which Murray used more as a store area than anything else. This almost verandah setting adjoined his bedroom which, in turn, backed onto a simple bathroom and general ablution area. The basic kitchen was outside, to the rear of his bedroom. An overhanging tiled roof provided protection for the kerosene stove from the rain.

More often than not, when meals were prepared in this simple place, his betel-nut-chewing houselady would ignore the *minjak tanah*, preferring to squat and fan a charcoal fire rather than risk cooking on the kerosene monster which often threatened to explode. Whenever Murray overslept and had company, she would make it quite clear that she did not approve, often ignoring to knock when entering his room, regularly catching Murray and his surprised bedmates in various states of play. He adored her almost doting ways and often would walk up behind the greying *djanda* and playfully pat her on the bottom, remembering to jump aside quickly before she whacked his legs with her *sapu lidi*. She always seemed to be carrying that broom.

Murray attended the *Universitas Indonesia* in what amounted to an 'observer' status. Although he was not enrolled as a full-time student, he probably spent more time on campus than many of the Indonesians. He registered as a part-time informal student, paying considerably more than he should have for this privilege, and attended a variety of lectures. His presence was never questioned and, as his language proficiency improved, he discovered that he actually enjoyed listening to the senior *dosen* lecture on their version of Indonesian history. He found that most of his fellow students were very naive when it came to discussing politics and concluded that their immaturity was a result of the strict government censorship imposed on all forms of communication.

Sometimes, when he participated in discussion groups he would endeavour to explain issues or historical events only to find that there was a wall of resistance to the truths he proposed. Mostly, his friends would laugh when he suggested something which they could not accept as true or accurate. But there were those who resented his presence, his colour, and his popularity. These were the student activists and he knew that, if he expected their acceptance, then it was imperative that he convince this group of his sincerity.

Murray went out of his way to encourage dialogue with the individual members of these student political organisations, but discovered that the young men were overly suspicious and the girls were extremely hard-line in their views.

Eventually, he convinced one of the young women, Yanti, to go on a date. They spent several Saturday afternoons, accompanied by at least one of her girlfriends, watching Chinese movies in the

Menteng Bioskop. Finally, Yanti agreed to go out with Murray, alone. That evening, she visited his small pavilion and stayed until morning. When he awoke on that Sunday morning, Yanti lay alongside, her eyes wide open, watching her new lover.

'I love you, Mahree!' she said, almost sadly and kissed him softly. He responded by making love to her once again and, from that day on, Yanti ensured that Murray was accepted by the other members of her group. His conquest provided the means for his successful infiltration of a major target group: the Indonesian Communist Party, which was known across the nation as the *PKI, Partai Komunis Indonesia*.

* * * * * *

Dr. Soebandrio seemed pleased with the Party's progress. Only those who knew him well understood that the powerful left-wing politician rarely displayed his emotions publicly. Today he was particularly elated with the reaction he had received during the Cabinet meeting when President Soekarno himself praised his Minister for his foresight and services to the country. Immediately after the session had noisily been terminated by Bung Karno screaming at the Military elements, they had left together to prepare for the official announcement.

They worked for hours on the speech. Mostly, the style was pure Soekarno. However, the Communist Party's line was mentioned more than once, which satisfied Soebandrio. They had agreed that he, as Foreign Minister, should make the announcement. The declaration was broadcast immediately by *Radio Republik Indonesia*, and on that day Dr. Soebandrio's name became synonymous with the war that was that day declared to crush Malaysia.

They called this action *Konfrontasi*.

* * * * * *

Murray followed the excited group down the passageway into the covered student assembly area. Already there were more than a thousand other students gathered, listening to the broadcast which had, by that time, been underway for more than ten minutes. He moved closer to the loudspeaker and immediately wished he hadn't. The distorted voice made it even more difficult for him to understand what was being said. Impatient, he reached out and pulled Yanti closer.

'What's going on?' he asked.

'War, Mahree, War! We've declared war on Malaysia!' she added excitedly, not noticing the shocked look on his face.

'What?' he asked incredulously, hoping that he had misheard her reply.

'It's true! We're going to war against those imperialist servants!' she announced gleefully. The Indonesian people knew that the new Federation of Malaysia was designed to threaten their country. The former British colonies had amalgamated to form an alliance against the only truly free and democratic state and now they would be crushed by the might of the Indonesian Military.

'Yanti,' Murray called, raising his voice to compete with the excited crowd. 'Yanti, are you sure?'

'Sure, Mahree, sudah pasti!' she responded, confirming his worst fears. 'Listen, Mahree, and you will hear for yourself!' with which Yanti suddenly left his side and disappeared in search of her other friends. He concentrated hard but with great difficulty. The distortion made it almost impossible to decipher what was being broadcast and he felt frustrated, standing there in the midst of thousands of people but unable to understand what was taking place around him.

'Are you all right, Mas?' a voice asked, somewhere close by. Murray turned and spotted the smiling face and he responded by placing his hands over his ears. She understood and laughed. 'Yes, I agree, it's too loud!' she shouted up at him. 'Do you understand what is being said?' she asked.

'Not much, I'm afraid. It is too difficult with all of the ...' with which he was lost, not knowing the Indonesian word for distortion.

'I understand, Mas. Let me help, okay?'

'Baik,' he answered, grateful for her assistance. He looked around for Yanti, annoyed that she had so suddenly deserted him.

'Dr. Soebandrio has announced that Indonesia has declared a war of confrontation with our neighbouring countries associated with the Federation of Malaysia. He has made the announcement on behalf of the Cabinet with the full backing of the President and the Military. He has stated that the neo-colonial powers will be powerless to prevent Indonesia from moving to protect itself from what the nation's leaders consider to be a *hostile assembly of puppets threatening the Tanah Air's sovereignty. He went on to say that the Military will mobilise immediately and sukarelaan forces will be formed to accommodate all of those brave volunteers who wish to fight against the aggression of the Western Imperialists' ideologies.'*

'You're very good,' Murray praised, admiring the girl's power of recall. *'Do you think he is serious?'*

'Oh, he is serious enough, Mas. We all more or less expected that one day our influential Communist friends would embroil us in a war of sorts' She turned and smiled again and asked, *'You're an Australian, no?'* and then continued with her next question before Murray could respond. *'Are you an Australian Communist?'*

'No, not at all,' he replied, stunned by her assumption. *'Why do you ask?'*

'Well, I have been here for two years now and you are here already for, how long, one year?' Murray confirmed this by nodding, his voice fading with soreness from shouting to make himself heard. She paused momentarily before continuing. *'I have seen you maybe a hundred times, and I know your name. I know a great deal about you already. What I do not know about you, Mister Mahree, is why you spend so much time with all of those Communist girls.'*

Murray was taken aback by her directness. It was so out of character for an Indonesian who was not familiar with the person being addressed. He found her attitude refreshing and smiled as he spoke.

'Perhaps they are the only tjewek who want to talk to me!'

'I don't think so, Mahree,' she answered, coyly. *'Perhaps you should widen your horizons,'* she teased.

'And how far would those horizons have to reach in order that I would know your name and where you come from, nona manis?'

'Far and high enough to see the tip of Gunung Merapi,' she replied, immediately indicating that she was of Central Javanese extraction by nominating the closest major mountain to her origins. *'And my name is Ade, Mister Mahree,'* answering while deliberately drawing out his name as if it were totally alien to her tongue.

'Well, Nona Ade, terima kasih. I will remember your kind help and comments today.'

'Are you going already?' she asked, surprised, as if he was then obliged to remain and continue the discussion. *'Don't you wish to*

know what else Dr. Soebandrio has been saying while you have been talking and I listening?' she enquired, almost with a pout.

'Saja minta maaf. I'm sorry, Ade. I have been impolite. Would you please tell me what else the famous Foreign Minister has said?'

'Of course, Mahree,' Ade replied. *'He said nothing!'* with which she turned and walked away. Knowing he had offended the young girl, Murray hurried after her and, in spite of her short stature, he had considerable difficulty following her through the crowded assembly.

'Ade! Wait' he called, *'Tunggu sebentar!'* but she feigned not hearing his call and hurried along knowing that he was following. Minutes passed and she stood out in the open ground waiting for Murray to catch up. As he approached, she pretended to turn and ignore him and then turned back and smiled.

'Do you know that it is considered impolite to chase a gadis you do not know as you have, just now, in front of thousands of curious eyes?' Murray stood alongside and laughed at her cockiness.

'Okay, Ade. I have already apologised once. For an Australian, that's already a great deal. Let's declare peace before your Dr. Soebandrio gets us both.'

'He is not my Dr. Soebandrio!' she hissed almost vehemently.

'Why do you feel so strongly about the Foreign Minister?' he asked, careful with his word selection this time. Ade hesitated before answering.

'I just don't agree with the power he and the Communist Party have been given. Our nation is one that is based on many considerations, including Belief In God. Nowhere in our Pantja Sila does it state that Communism has a place. How can we accept a belief in Tuhan on one hand yet support the destruction of that very ideal on the other?'

Murray was again surprised by the girl's response. He liked Ade immediately and decided to pursue their conversation later. Right then it was imperative that he make contact with the Station Chief in view of the Crush Malaysia announcement. Murray made arrangements to meet at another time then hurried away, hoping that he could find a decent *betjak* driver to peddle quickly, as the Australian Embassy was some considerable distance. He avoided visiting the building too frequently, not wishing to raise suspicions. His cover dictated that he maintain the semblance of a student.

There was no doubt that the declaration would have been

received with considerable alarm. These were not empty threats, it seemed. Murray understood that the Indonesian Government had, for some time, been wooing the Soviets. They had jumped at the opportunity to establish a firm foothold in South-East Asia, and military equipment and infrastructure aid had been pouring into Soekarno's Indonesia. Already, the Air Force, *AURI*, boasted squadrons of the huge Tupolov TU-16 long range bombers, the Soviets' answer to the American B-52. These had been strategically based at the Madiun airfield and represented a real threat to regional stability.

These bombers had the strike capacity to wipe out any Australian capital city and certainly all of the regional hubs such as Singapore, Hong Kong, Kuala Lumpur or even the American bases in Guam. AURI's ORBAT, or Order of Battle consisted also of IL-28s, the sophisticated bomber attack aircraft which, until then, had not been seen outside the Eastern Bloc. Missiles were installed throughout the country, many at bases strung along the north coast of Java. It was envisaged that this area might be the target of a possible first strike from the American forces stationed at Clarke Field in the Philippines.

Murray had been obliged to study this information. He had learned that the Pentagon had financed numerous missions into Indonesia, under cover of Air America, and it was during one such sortie that the Indonesians shot down an American pilot, Pope, providing Soekarno with the justification he needed to further increase the ABRI arms build-up. The CIA pilot had flown down from the Philippines, strafed a village and its church, killing seven hundred people during his attack. Murray understood the propaganda value this pilot's capture gave Soekarno, who finally agreed to surrender Pope to President Kennedy's brother when he visited. Murray understood that first it had been the British, and then the Americans who had increased their military presence in South-East Asia, and Soekarno had become deeply concerned as to their real intentions.

The President believed that the entire region was being destabilised not so much by the new republics, but more by the British and Americans in their ruthless attempts to re-consolidate their positions in his part of the globe. Soekarno watched with disbelief as the British increased their presence in Malaysia, transporting many of their soldiers from Europe to occupy bases throughout their former colonies. Even the Americans had been startled by the British build-up, countering with their own increased presence in the Philippines and Indochina. Soekarno had initiated a secret dialogue with the Burmese. Their country had been torn apart as a result of American foreign policy just ten years before. Fearful of Chinese support in Korea, Eisenhower had brazenly financed remnants of Chiang Kai Shek's former Nationalist Army to occupy northern Burma, in an attempt to open a second front with the Chinese so as to distract their main thrust through Korea. The Burmese leaders had explained to Soekarno how, as Chiang Kai Shek's men fled Mao Tse Tung's superior forces and overran Burma, these well-armed Chinese had little difficulty establishing control over the heroin trade, boosting its production tenfold. Once he had discovered the United States' involvement in the disruption of order in that country, Soekarno didn't mind accepting the Soviets' overtures and developing relationships with what he perceived to be a healthy counter to the American and British presence in his region. Besides, the USSR had re-equipped the Indonesian arsenal entirely on credit, and were apparently eager to continue to do so as long as this emerging nation maintained 'satellite' status with the Soviets.

Murray had read reports on how the Navy, *ALRI*, had also benefited from the Soviet Military Defence arrangements. Warships had suddenly appeared in Indonesian waters, their difficult-to-pronounce Russian names replaced with softer Indonesian choices such as *'The Irian'*. Murray had seen many of the new warships moored in Tandjung Priok. He had even passed close by the submarine base in Surabaja, but was unable to obtain clear photographs. He had counted five of the small but deadly ships moored together, but was not to know that three had already been taken out of commission due to personnel problems.

The Indonesian submariners generally feared going to sea, and insisted on surface steaming in preference to the claustrophobic conditions imposed once their ships dived to the oceans depths. Less than eighteen months after the small fleet had arrived in Surabaja, *ALRI* all but abandoned their plans to utilise these vessels. The crews simply refused to man the submarines.

Murray knew that the Army had secured impressive weaponry

from their new allies. In fact, the constant flow of trucks carrying men and equipment to and fro suggested the nation was preparing for war. Murray thought about the complicated Indonesian military position as he made his way down to the Australian Embassy in the Tjikini-Menteng area, off Djalan Pegangsaan Timor. They crossed the railway in front of the Tjikini Hospital and the *betjak* driver insolently clanged his bell at the Soviet PT-76 tank positioned on the corner. The Australian Embassy was just a few houses down on the right.

'Setop disini!' he ordered, with which the driver quickly squeezed the handbrake situated under his well-worn bicycle seat. Murray did not want to take the iron monster into the courtyard again as, the last time he did that, it earned him a stern lecture about protocol from the Consul. He climbed out of the *betjak*, paid the driver ten rupiah and strolled into the Embassy grounds. There was only token security at the entrance and, as he passed through, the smiling near toothless Pak Ali beamed as he mock-saluted the young Australian.

'Pagi, tuan,' he called happily, *'How are you tuan mudah?'*

'Baik sadja, terima kasih,' Murray answered, replying that he was well. He spent a few moments talking to the gentle old security guard before entering the building. Ali was regarded as somewhat of an icon amongst the small Australian community. No one really knew just how old Ali was, as he lied about this continuously to maintain his employment with the Embassy. Murray moved on, laughing at Ali's latest gossip, wishing he could spend more time with the man. He climbed the few steps and went through the foyer directly to the receptionist.

'Selamat pagi, Murray. Apa Kabar?'

'Still intact,' he joked, smiling at the middle-aged woman. *'How's your love life?'* Rukmini pulled a face and extended her tongue. *'If it's that bad, maybe you should try one of us bule for a change!'*

She laughed. *'What, and ruin my reputation forever?'* The exchange was nearly always the same. Murray always spent a moment here or there chatting idly with the local staff. They were all fond of the handsome young Australian and pleased that he usually found time to talk. Not like some of the staff members whose arrogant behaviour was often the main topic during *kopi* breaks. *'Do you wish to see Mister Keith today?'* she asked. Murray rarely asked to see anyone else except the First Secretary or the Consul.

'Thanks, *manis*,' he replied and wandered over to the rack of Australian newspapers in the corner. Murray missed them a good deal, and enjoyed his occasional visits to the Embassy where he could catch up on the sports back home. In theory, the newspapers were sent in the diplomatic bags from Canberra on a weekly basis. Unfortunately QANTAS often refused to land at the poorly-equipped Djakarta airport and it could be two or even three weeks before they arrived.

'Seems your team is still at the bottom of the ladder.' Murray turned to the man who had spoken after silently gliding up behind him. Murray extended his hand.

'Sometimes I think they believe it's where they belong,' Murray grinned ruefully. His club had not been in a final for ten years. 'How are you, Keith?'

The Station Chief shrugged and indicated that Murray was to follow as he turned and walked back through the rear of the reception and Consulate area. Murray knew just how paranoid the First Secretary was about talking in front of others, especially the Indonesian staff. He followed Wells down a corridor and waited patiently while the man knocked and identified himself. Murray always found this routine amusing as the officer on the inside could see though the spy-hole just who was on the other side of the heavy reinforced door. Moments passed before they could enter and when they did, Murray discovered that there had been changes initiated in the office layout. Where before there had been a small reception area manned by an administrative officer, there was now another wall and, to his surprise, yet another door. The officer activated the release catch from somewhere under his desk and remained seated as the two men passed through into the Embassy's political section. There were three offices located in this area. Wells finally spoke as the second door clunked closed behind.

'Just been installed. Canberra felt that this old building couldn't withstand a determined break-in and flew their own carpenters up for the week. Must say they did a bloody good job although we were all pleased to see them go. Couldn't get anything done while the bastards were here, and we both worked shifts around the clock keeping an eye on them, while they completed the installations.'

The Station Chief's office was on the right. 'Go in and sit down,

Murray while I find Davis.' Keith Wells left Murray to wait so he helped himself to the strong-brewing *Robusta* coffee. He heard them return and stood up to greet the Second Secretary, Alan Davis. He had met the Tasmanian on a number occasions during earlier briefings in these offices and once socially when he attended a quiet dinner at the man's quarters on Djalan Patimura.

'How's it going, Stephenson?' Davis asked, pouring coffee for himself. 'Shagged all of the girls on campus yet?'

'No, but I'm getting there. Why don't you come around and spend the weekend at *Djalan Tasikmalaya* and I'll set you up with a couple of freebies?' Murray responded, almost sarcastically. There was rivalry between the two and Wells pursed his lips as the two sparred with each other. Although Davis was more senior than Stephenson, they were both young and relatively new to the Service. He wished some of the more experienced agents were present, especially with the volatility of the moment.

Murray had resigned himself to the sub-standard living conditions. His role dictated that he live in the simple accommodations at Djalan Tasikmalaya, unlike the large villas the Embassy officers enjoyed at this post. Sometimes, when the electricity failed for hours as it often did due to the inadequate city supplies and antiquated reticulation system, or the water pump refused to work during the dry spells, he would drop in to one of the Embassy homes and use their facilities. These houses had stand-by generators and were equipped with air-conditioning, deep-freezers to hold their hoards of imported steaks and sausages and larders which were always filled with supermarket items not available in the local shops.

On one occasion he had suggested that, as Davis was unaccompanied on this posting, it would not be unreasonable for Murray to drop around from time to time just to use the western bathroom for a change. The Second Secretary had been adamant that too-frequent visits to his house could compromise Murray's deep cover, knowing that he would have the Station Chief's support. On the other hand, Murray was conscious of Davis' inability to strike up a successful relationship with any of the foreign women. This was not just because Davis was cursed with an unattractive body and an ugly disposition, but because, as number two in the political section, any relationship with a local girl would be considered grounds for instant recall to Melbourne. Consequently, whenever the opportunity arose Davis would dismiss his servants for the night then drive down to the *Patimura* Cemetery where literally thousands of prostitutes would congregate during the early evening hours. He would select one of these girls, take her back to his villa for a few hours then send her away by *betjak* when he had finished with the *kupu-kupu malam's* services.

It was old Pak Ali who had informed Murray of the *night butterflies'* indiscreet visits. As Davis' security, his *djaga* would refuse to leave the area entirely, remaining close by to ensure that the villa would not be broken into by the many *maling* who worked the suburbs. All the Embassy *djaga* would confide in each other, relating whatever goings on took place in the foreigners' households. Davis silently envied Murray his handsome looks and numerous conquests. He despised himself for using the *Patimura* prostitutes and, regrettably, as his tour progressed he became more and more dependant on these liaisons.

Once he contracted gonorrhoea and, fearing certain discovery by Wells should he visit the Embassy doctor, Davis was obliged to sit in a local doctor's congested surgery along with *kampung* kids and their mothers. Venereal disease was normally reported by the Australian doctor to the Head of Mission, as this was one of the conditions of his employment. Davis knew that it would be impossible for him to claim having contracted the disease from one of the foreign girls as her name would also be required by the Embassy doctor. The obvious conclusion would be that he had been carrying on an unacceptable relationship, thereby jeopardising his sensitive position.

He believed this to be most unfair, especially as Stephenson was permitted to sleep with whomever he wished, and was even encouraged to do so with the Indonesian girls. No, he was not about to make Murray Stephenson's life any easier than it already was, regardless of whatever relationships existed between the Ivy League player and the senior spymasters back in Australia.

Word had preceded Murray's arrival that he was well-connected, which only increased Davis' envy. After their first clash, Wells had suggested that the young Stephenson's star was on the ascent, and inferred that it wouldn't harm Davis if he were to make the effort and try to get along with his fellow agent. It seemed that his advice had fallen on fallow ground. The two were naturally antagonistic towards each other.

'Have you been following the broadcasts?' Wells asked. He disliked operating in this country without the benefit of the local language. Whenever an interpreter was required they would call upon one of the Military Attaché's NCOs who was cleared to assist with these tasks. He raised a sheet of paper and passed it to Murray. 'This is a translation of the Foreign Minister's bulletin. How does that fit with what you have heard?'

Murray read the page quickly. It was obviously a direct translation of the broadcast he had heard earlier. 'This is as I heard it,' he said, 'although I missed some of the bulletin due to the voice distortion.'

'What was the reaction on campus?' Wells asked. Did you have a chance to discuss the good Doctor's declaration before beating a path down here?' Murray silently acknowledged the admonition. The Station Chief was totally correct. He should have waited around to establish the student mood and reaction to the startling announcement.

'From what little time I had, I'd say that generally, the student body was supportive.' He didn't mention the girl Ade who had offered her opinion regarding the Communists. 'The PKI leaders were onto it immediately, chanting as they usually do when the opportunity arises. I didn't have much of a chance to talk to Yanti as she dashed off looking for her Gerwani comrades. How about I return tomorrow and fill you in?'

'Under the circumstances I think you should only come in if there is something really important. It would be more beneficial for you to stick close to your girlfriend and see what her little commie friends are cooking up. One thing's for sure, as we speak the British bases in Singapore and Malaya have gone on full war footing. Wouldn't be surprised to see some early action from the RAF boys in Changi Field. Seems that we have no choice but to send troops. Any threat to one of Her Majesty's Commonwealth nations embroils us all, I'm afraid. Wouldn't be surprised to see the HMAS Sydney or even the Melbourne steaming up through the Sunda Straits in response to the proclamation. The Embassy is on full alert and the Consul is busy contacting Australian citizens to recommend they prepare to depart this screwed-up country.'

'What's the Military Attaché's opinion? Will Soekarno go

through with it?' Murray asked.

'I've just finished a joint briefing with all the Attachés and the Ambassador. Seems they put the wind right up the little bastard as he immediately suggested that he return to Canberra for consultations with the Minister. The general consensus is that yes, Bung Karno must and will attack now that Dr. Soebandrio has issued the declaration publicly. It is fairly obvious that the President sanctioned the broadcast. The interesting thing will be to see just how much support the Army give him this time. It's not even a month since that last attempt on his life and the word is that the failed assassination was carried out by two field officers. We're still waiting for the new protocol lists to see who is missing. One thing you've got to say about Soekarno, he's living a charmed life. According to my count, this makes the fourth attempt to date and not once has he been seriously hurt. Why doesn't someone teach these bastards to shoot?'

Murray thought solemnly about the previous attempt to remove Soekarno, and felt saddened by the number of children who died just across the road in the grenade attack in the hospital grounds. The President had attended the official opening ceremony for the new Tjikini Hospital wing. As he stepped down from the black convertible, a number of children ran forward and placed garlands of flowers around their *Bapak's* neck. Their bodies had saved Soekarno's life as Army rebels hurled grenades from the back of the crowd of onlookers. When the dust settled, The Great Leader Of The Revolution just stood dazed, unhurt, surrounded by the broken bodies of some fifteen or twenty young children. How was it, Murray wondered, that this man continued to engender so much hate and yet, at the same time, could still be loved and admired by so many millions?

'Seems almost indestructible, if you ask me,' Davis suggested, attracting a sharp look from his superior. The thought that Soekarno was proving difficult to remove deeply concerned the Station Chief. Two of his own operatives had been involved in one of the earlier assassination attempts but neither Stephenson nor Davis were aware of the Executive Action which had been sanctioned by the man in The Lodge, back in Canberra.

'It's only a matter of time before one of his four hundred generals takes the leap himself and blows the cunning little devil away.

As far as I'm concerned, the sooner the better. The world is sick to death of tyrants like Bung Karno and I'd be willing to bet that he won't last the year once the first casualty lists are posted. I'm just amazed that the Army agreed to support this ridiculous declaration of war.' Wells, removed his hands from behind his neck and leaned forward. 'If I'm wrong, gentlemen, this will be one very unhealthy place to be should the Brits unleash some of their weaponry, just to show Soekarno that playing at war can be a very dangerous game. They could swing over here from Singapore and drop one or two low-yield atomic warheads and it would be all over. Don't underestimate the Brits. They have the capacity and would never stand by and permit an invasion of any of their Commonwealth countries, let alone three!'

Murray considered this and agreed that Singapore, Malaya, and Brunei would be protected at all costs. It seemed like madness that the Indonesians even considered such a misadventure, knowing that they would have little support for such aggression.

They discussed the situation for another half-hour before Murray departed, promising to send word as the need arose. He was escorted back through the internal security doors and left to find his own way down the passageway and out of the building. Waving cheerfully as he left, Pak Ali watched him climb back aboard another *betjak*. Murray headed down through Menteng to his quarters. The driver grunted and cursed as they moved slowly towards Djalan Tjokroaminoto while Murray remained deep in thought, ignoring the long row of tall trees as they passed by. These covered the *kali's* banks providing shelter to Djakarta's itinerants and beggars, many of whom called out for money as the *betjak* moved in their direction. Murray ignored their requests, his thoughts concerned more with the sudden turn of events. He did not believe that there would be any personal danger for himself should hostilities really begin, because there was a predetermined series of steps and actions he could take to ensure his safe departure, should this become necessary.

Murray decided that this would be unlikely. He suddenly wished he knew more about what really went on down in the Presidential Palace, with its incredible intrigue and constant power plays amongst the government leaders and ambitious military chiefs. Although question after question came to mind, he realised that his experience and knowledge of the Indonesian thought process was frustratingly limited. Nevertheless, he couldn't help but feel some admiration for the charismatic leader and his ability to remain on top of the diversified and confusing mass of one hundred and fifty million people. How could Soekarno manage to survive, he wondered, with the constant feuding, the compromise, the threats and the incredible juggling act which had become an integral part of his daily routine? Why had he so blatantly rattled the sabre at a more powerful adversary when he knew that this action would summon the strength of Britain's forces? What could have been going through the President's mind when he sanctioned the declaration of war? Murray continued to speculate, as his transport delivered him to the front of his driveway.

What in hell was the Indonesian President really up to?

Chapter 5

Djakarta

Soekarno sat quietly, eyes closed and legs crossed as he cleared his thoughts. Outside he could hear the distant traffic as it moved around both sides of the Palace, never so close that it hindered conversation. This room was not air-conditioned. He was always uncomfortable when it was too cold, preferring the slow-turning overhead fans which moved the air gently around the high-ceilinged room. This is where he relaxed, mostly alone, at the end of his long days. In here he knew that he could do whatever he wished in complete privacy and, as if this thought had just at that moment occurred, he kicked his shoes off, removing his socks with his toes. He then stretched and yawned, reviewing the day's events in his mind.

Suddenly Soekarno smiled as he recalled the morning Cabinet session. There had been no formal agenda circulated. He certainly did not solicit the opposition's opinion as to whether they agreed or not with his decision. Had they been given this opportunity, the meeting would still be under way without any resolution in sight. No, that was not the way to deal with those manipulative generals who secretly worked against him and his supporters. If only he knew for certain which of their number had been responsible for the ongoing attempts on his life.

One day they would succeed, he thought sadly, then shivered. The reality was, he knew, with so many generals around him any one of them could have been involved. After each of the first two attempts, he felt a burning rage at these acts of betrayal and vowed to have those responsible publicly executed once they had been caught. But they never were and this added to his fury. When the third attempt almost succeeded, he became philosophical about his failure to engender total loyalty from those close to him. The most recent attempt had convinced him that his *adjal* was obviously not to be for some considerable time, and consequently he almost treated these attempts to take his life with contempt, as if it were all a part of some grand game in which he was the ultimate referee.

* * * * * *

President Soekarno had anticipated the outburst from Nasution. He believed Nasution to be so predictable. On the other hand, the President considered that his powerful Ministerial ally, Soebandrio, didn't understand how to handle men like Nasution, Indonesia's most senior general. His Foreign Minister had warned that, since General Nasution had attempted a coup once before, he was likely to do so again.

'Bapak, Nasution wishes to be President. He has the support of most of the divisional commanders. He could move on the Palace at any time. Why don't you just send him off overseas as one of your ambassadors, just to be sure?'

Soekarno had dismissed Soebandrio's fears.

'How could you have already forgotten the ease with which we handled his last attempt? The man has no sense of opportunity. He had us in his sights, backed with tanks and yet, with a few soft words and promises, he folded. Ten minutes later he sat and ate together with the very people he claimed to despise. I promoted him and, in so doing, removed his power. No, Nasution is no longer a threat. We must look past this man to see who stands quietly behind in the shadows. That's where the danger lies and where we must look.'

Soekarno stared deliberately at his senior general, then explained that Soebandrio had been instructed to read the declaration of war against Malaysia. To stare at one's adversary in such a way was to invite immediate confrontation but, he believed, as President it was essential to display his authority over those present before they could establish any real form of resistance to his elaborate plan.

Soekarno could see that General Nasution was deeply unhappy. The President was aware that the anti-Communist elements had looked to the General to restrict the PKI and Soebandrio's rapid growth and, since Soekarno had removed Nasution as Army Chief

of Staff and relegated him to the advisory council of KOTI instead
of chairing this important West Irian command, the General's power
base was clearly in danger of disappearing.

*'Bapak, it would be foolish to declare war on Malaysia. We would lose
such an action,'* Nasution had pleaded. Soekarno had listened in
silence as his subordinate walked a fine line in arguing against the
declaration. The President knew he could easily find support among
the junior generals and use this against Nasution. Soekarno was
aware that the man before him had unsuccessfully appealed to
Djenderal Yani, his replacement as Army Chief of Staff, who at the
time had avoided Nasution's eyes and coughed, embarrassed that
he would appear so obvious in his lack of support for a fellow
general.

The President was aware that General Yani had his own Javanese faction to consider, and would realize that he had little choice
but to support his President or end up as impotent as his Sumatran
predecessor, Nasution. Soekarno had watched, concerned as the
Indonesian Armed Forces had undergone radical changes over the
recent years. Divisions and rivalries were still apparent and
Soekarno knew that his decisions were often considered whimsi-
cal and irrational. The President knew that it was essential to his
own survival as leader that he keep his Military opponents' alliances off balance at all times. At the President's request, and as an
act of appeasement, Yani had moved to replace the divisional commanders in Sumatra, South Kalimantan and South Sulawesi with
his own men. The previous commanders had all foolishly resisted
Soekarno on matters relating to the PKI and had subsequently paid
the price.

President Soekarno had looked up and, caught by Nasution's
troubled eyes, looked away once again.

*'Djenderal Nasution. We have reconstructed the Military in our home-
land and committed our people to enormous hardships so that your officers and men are able to enjoy the most sophisticated weaponry available.
Our Soviet allies have provided bombers, missiles, tanks and ships. Now
you must provide the men to utilise these expensive toys. Are you telling
this Cabinet that you are unable, as our country's Commander of ABRI,
to carry out the orders of your Supreme Commander?'*

Soekarno stared once more directly into Nasution's eyes,
challenging the four-star general to refuse to accept the Presidential

decision. Soekarno recalled how slowly the moments had passed
as the tension was apparent on the faces of all present. Nobody
wished to see an open split between the Army and the President. It
would be catastrophic, and the damage irreparable.

*'May I suggest Bapak that we consider appointing one of the senior
officers other than Djenderal Nasution to the specific post to take charge
of this endeavour?'*

Nasution's head had turned quickly to the speaker and he glared.
Soekarno had smiled silently, knowing that his opponent most probably had expected such a suggestion from the Minister for Air, who
carried only two stars on his shoulders. With a few exceptions,
most of those present were senior military officers.

*'That would be totally unacceptable to the Armed Forces. Or at least,
to the Army. Unless there has been a change in my circumstances that are
yet to be announced I believe that I am still the most senior officer currently serving in our ABRI and, as such, remain totally responsible for
all such military matters. I could not...'*

'That is so, Pak Nasution,' Soebandrio interrupted, *'I agree that
you should lead our forces against the Malays!'*

Soekarno knew he had ensnared Nasution in his well-laid trap.
The atmosphere had been electric as all eyes turned to the popular
military figure. Nasution had little choice but to retreat. Those
present knew it was imperative for Nasution to maintain his friendship with Yani, even though they did not always see eye-to-eye on
the important issues. It was obvious that Yani would support the
Army should a contest erupt between the Palace and the Military,
but Soekarno knew that Nasution could not be confident about the
degree of support he could expect from the Javanese Chief of Staff.

The President could see that Nasution felt frustrated by the other
generals. Having been raised in Javanese fashion himself, Soekarno
could understand Nasution's annoyance with the traditional
Javanese way of conducting business. The reluctance of the Javanese to express themselves openly, unlike the Sumatrans, never
ceased to irritate the Revolutionary hero.

President Soekarno wondered if Nasution really understood that
the Foreign Minister sitting across the long table, Soebandrio, was
behind most of the machinations which continued to weaken the
Army leadership. Soekarno had sat back and permitted this situation to develop as it was necessary to his overall strategy for political

survival. He knew that Nasution had learned much from Soekarno and his colleagues over the years. The President had out-manoeuvred the generals more than once before, but they were now becoming more and more determined to prevent any form of communist take-over.

'*The leadership of this national effort should be given to Djenderal Yani.*' Nasution had then crossed his arms in defiance and waited for Soekarno to respond. The President was surprised. Did Nasution realize that he had taken a very dangerous gamble, surrendering even more power to the capable and ambitious Yani? Soekarno thought that the general did not want to be remembered by his fellow countrymen as the man who took them to war when he mistakenly believed that peace was an available option.

'*Bapak. I would be proud to serve with this new command,*' Air Vice Marshall Omar Dhani had offered. Immediately others joined in, offering to support the war effort. Within a few minutes, almost all the officers present had committed themselves to supporting Soeharto and Soebandrio's quest to expand the country's political boundaries.

Soekarno stood at the head of the magnificently-carved teak table and observed those present. Slowly he looked from face to face as if determining what to say next while reading their thoughts. Most, in typical Javanese fashion, remained expressionless. The communist members were obviously pleased with the session's outcome and displayed this by grinning and winking at each other.

Nasution sat stone faced. He wished a thunderbolt would strike the room and exterminate the filthy communists. In his mind, the unthinkable had happened yet again. His opponents had increased their already powerful political base at his expense.

Suddenly Soekarno spoke.

'*We must show the nation and our people that we are united in this great task which lies ahead. We must educate the masses to understand that it is imperative for them to remain alert against neo-colonial and imperialistic forces which continue to endeavour to destroy our country and its people.*

We are being encircled by the British and their puppet states.

The formation of this so-called Federation of Malaysia is designed to achieve one aim and one aim only; the destruction of Republik Indonesia and Pantja Sila. The British have provoked our response. It was agreed

*during the Manila Conference that a referendum would be called in both
Sabah and Sarawak to determine whether or not the people truly wished
to join this proposed Federation of Malaysia.*

*Now, with the Malaysian Tengku's blessing, the British have decided
to proceed without the agreed referendum. The United Nations were to
conduct the polling, but these arrogant British colonialists have announced
that they would not have accepted a negative outcome, even had the choice
been put to our brothers in those two small countries.*

*We have no choice. They have refused to entertain any dialogue which
may have prevented this heavy decision I have taken this day, with your
full support. We will move forward together and destroy the British im-
perial states which, through their proposed amalgamation, will block our
country's natural development and impede the spiritual growth of our
children. We cannot permit our children to hide in the shadow of British
colonial values. We must eradicate this threat from our borders. We must
crush those who threaten our nation, chew them into small pieces then
spit their remains into the British faces. We must ganjang Malaysia!'*

Soekarno's careful choice of a slogan astonished Nasution. If he
was not as angry as he then felt, he might have also cheered and
applauded with the others. As the meeting broke up and the members departed, Soebandrio and Soekarno stayed behind, talking
together. Nasution walked out of the hall alongside Yani to show
that there were no hard feelings. The newly appointed commander
remained silent until they were alone on the steps, waiting for their
drivers.

'You've got to admit, he's very clever,' Yani said softly without looking
at the other officer. *'In one move he has managed make us responsible for
this ridiculous attempt on Malaysia and what's more, responsible when it
fails, as fail it must!'* As his vehicle had arrived first, he offered his hand
to Nasution who took it warmly and squeezed once, acknowledging
the difficult position in which Yani now found himself.

'Be careful, Yani,' Nasution warned, *'Ganjang Malaysia just may
not turn out to be the tasty meal Soekarno is led to believe!'*

Yani turned while still in earshot, smiled and whispered with a
hint of sarcasm. *'That's why he said ganjang, not makan,'* he said, and
then added as he entered the Russian four-wheel drive, *'He just
wants to chew them a little, not swallow them up!'* and then saluted
Djenderal Nasution, who was then left standing on the Palace steps,
very much alone.

* * * * * *

Brigadier-General Soeharto dressed quickly. He was annoyed at having been overlooked at the briefing session. He checked his uniform, then finished the luke-warm glass of *kopi*. He would eat later, when he returned. Although outwardly he did not display his feelings, Soeharto was furious. The announcement had taken place while he had been off-duty for the day. Tien, his wife, had arranged for the children to all be photographed with their parents, and he had broken with tradition and stayed home that day. His distinguished Javanese features came to life as he smiled quietly to himself. Their youngest son, Hutomo Mandala Putra, was barely one year old.

Soeharto was reminded of the campaign he had been given to liberate Irian Barat from the Dutch. He had given his youngest son, "Tommy", the campaign's title *Mandala* as his middle name for it was this dedicated service which had restored Soeharto to his rightful rank. For a moment he reflected. Now his children numbered five, three boys and two beautiful girls. The image of his oldest, Rukmana, passed through his thoughts as he remembered that she had already reached fourteen which, had they been but a poor peasant family living off the soil back in the villages of Central Java, would have certainly meant an arranged marriage before her next birthday.

The Brigadier frowned. There was such a fine line between what was and what could have been. He had always endeavoured to provide for his family, as his own mother had for her children. Life under the Dutch had been difficult enough. Being born into a confused state of secrecy precipitated a childhood without the support of relatives so important to the young. The truth relating to his mother and her relationship with the royal court of the Sultans of Djogyakarta had long been buried and he wished that it remain so, for her sake and his, and her grandchildren.

As a child, he had been tenderly cared for by his mother and he loved and respected her dearly for this. Soeharto remembered his childhood. He had been an only child although his family's cramped quarters were overrun with his father's offspring from a previous marriage. The family grew even more when his father married yet again, resulting in his moving continuously from home to home, never really feeling settled in any of these places. He had suffered a series of illnesses during his early years but, there again, who did not? In typical Javanese fashion, his mother had encouraged her son to complete high school knowing that the Dutch would favour those who had gained their diplomas. Soeharto sometimes reflected on the brief period when he was accepted as a trainee bank clerk. Although his mother was pleased with this achievement, Soeharto soon became impatient for excitement. He remembered also that fateful day when his clothes had been ripped by his pushbike while cycling to work. He lost his job but this did not entirely displease him. He was young and his country was bubbling with political activity. An opportunity arose and he jumped at the chance to join the Dutch colonial army where he underwent basic recruit training.

Not long thereafter, the Japanese occupied the archipelago interning the Dutch and other foreigners. Soeharto, as did many of his peers, sided with the Japanese and became a member of the Japanese-sponsored Defence Corps. He was selected for officer training and served under the new landlords until they too surrendered, granting Indonesia the opportunity to declare its independence. Soeharto disassociated himself with the emerging political groups. He avoided their rallies, preferring to listen to the speeches on radio. Often he was amused with the new President's rhetoric and would scowl whenever Soebandrio's communists held their parades.

Letnan Soeharto was deeply disappointed that the new republic was immediately embroiled in a battle for its own survival against the Dutch. He joined his fledgling country's guerrilla forces and fought alongside other heroes of the Revolution and War of Independence. They fought with what few armaments were left by the Japanese, often armed with simple bamboo spears and farmers' field scythes. He remembered the bloody encounters and the dead. In Bandung he had seen the wholesale slaughter of many innocent victims, and the memory of Surabaja being continuously shelled by the British Royal Navy still tore at his heart. Their war continued through four years until Indonesia was formally recognised, and shortly thereafter, Soeharto joined Djenderal Nasution's command and was promoted to lieutenant colonel.

Shortly thereafter, due to his dedication and capable leadership, he was promoted to command the elite Diponegoro troops in Central Java. He remembered how content he felt at that time, with his career firmly established in the new Angkatan Bersendjata Republik Indonesia, and the birth of his first child, Rukmana. His circle of friends had grown considerably and, due to his new position, he discovered that even the local Chinese business community sought his friendship.

He approached his new administrative duties in a methodical manner and soon discovered that the entire system of supply was in chaos. In fact, Soeharto identified serious problems with the divisional procedures and took immediate steps to rectify the problems. It soon became apparent that the men in his command were not receiving their correct entitlements, nor were equipment supplies and rationing handled in a professional manner. Just ten years before, when Indonesia officially took control of its own Treasury, there was less than fifty thousand guilders left to rebuild the entire country from scratch. The Military had first call on funds as these limited amounts became available. When the Soviets finally supported the Republic with its massive infrastructure and military hardware loans and aid programmes, much of the financial pressure was relieved. However, the troops still had to be fed and clothed. As Commander of the Diponegoro troops, the responsibility to provide adequate food and supplies for his men became his first priority. As Soeharto remembered those difficult times, a slight smile crossed his face as he recollected meeting the little chinaman for the first time.

The merchant could barely make himself understood. He, like so many of his race, had migrated illegally to Indonesia to escape the turmoil of Mao Tse Tung's China. As these people arrived, they quickly went about establishing themselves throughout the coastal cities, developing their links with other merchants. They worked tirelessly, building the foundations for their new futures, understanding the need to foster close relationships with the Military. But there were often many problems and the port traders of Semarang City complained bitterly as waterside costs escalated, due to overly ambitious and greedy Navy officers who squeezed many of the Chinese out of business. The Chinese traders were desperate to break loose from the Navy's grip and approached Soeharto with an offer to accommodate his needs, on the condition that he intercede on their behalf.

In typical Javanese fashion, a compromise was reached through considerable discussion with the local Chinese merchants. It was obvious to the Army that their food and other supplies were controlled by these merchants. The Military had nothing to barter with except protection and this, although greatly appreciated, did not generate sufficient funds to overcome their problems. An arrangement was suggested which provided for both the commercial and political aspects being satisfied. The Military controlled the movements of all trucks in and out of the harbour. The Navy were unable to negotiate this arrangement as their authority ended at the port's entrance. The merchants believed that the Customs and Navy were destroying their profits with their ever-increasing demands and illegal duties. The cost of moving cargo from the ships, through the warehouses and then onto Navy trucks for delivery, had reduced their margins to the point where large-scale smuggling to by-pass these harbour officials was essential to their survival. Why not formalise some commercial arrangement and eliminate the difficult sector, thereby stabilising prices and profits?

The concept was sound and the Army was desperate for supplies. A meeting was organised and Soeharto was introduced to a Chinese trader who had fled his Communist homeland and settled in Java. An interpreter was required as the merchant had not lived in the country long enough to acquire even the local *pasar* language. They sat together for hours, eating and discussing the proposed arrangements. The Army would send its own trucks into the harbour and use soldiers to unload the cargo which belonged to the trader. In return, the Chinese would provide essentials to the Army and, from time to time, credit for their supplies. It was agreed. Their relationship prospered, the men in Soeharto's command benefiting from the *kongsi* that had been born out of common needs. A short time later, documents were arranged so that the mainland Chinese trader could legitimately stay in the country.

Soeharto was never to fully understand what happened next. General Nasution had been furious that reports of smuggling though the Diponegoro Command had reached Djakarta. Accusations were hurled back and forth but, in the end, the damage was too great to contain and Nasution accused Soeharto of complicity in the scheme. He was transferred. Angry, frustrated and falsely accused, Soeharto stepped out of the limelight. He was sent to the Army Staff College to cool his heels. Many of his compatriots believed that Nasution was concerned with the sudden rise of Soeharto and moved to slow his star's meteoric rise. Nasution's faction supported his decision and the Sumatran severely damaged Soeharto's reputation. He never forgot, nor would he ever forgive, this ill-treatment delivered by the hands of his fellow officers. Dismayed with the outcome but still loyal to his country, Soeharto continued to serve diligently. He watched with growing concern as the Communists strengthened their grip on the country's leadership and infiltrated senior positions even within the Military. Disgusted with the growing number of politically-motivated promotions, Soeharto decided enough was enough and finally stepped forward, his voice among the few who were identified as fiercely anti-Communist. He was sent away from Java. At first he feared that this would damage his career forever but then, as his own group of followers and supporters began to grow, Soeharto commenced applying pressure whenever and wherever he could, in the hope that the senior officer corps would resist the PKI political machine's growing influence. His dedication and loyalty began to bear fruit and now, finally, he had established an enviable power base within the military and was able to influence others, even his superior, Djenderal Yani.

An old grandfather clock chimed in the next room and Soeharto knew that he must move quickly. The broadcast had been repeated and he knew that there would be considerable activity downtown in the Defence Department. As he left his home on Djalan Tjendana, Soeharto's aide jumped to attention and ran to open the rear door of the Soviet sedan but he waved the soldier away, indicating that he would drive himself.

He drove down to Kota and found the man sitting in his customary singlet and pyjama trousers, waiting patiently for him to arrive. The little chinaman listened in silence while the Javanese spoke. He understood the ramifications of what had happened. The entire community of Djakarta's Chinatown area of Kota had been abuzz with excitement. They were all anxious to determine just how a war with Indonesia's neighbours would affect them, their families and their businesses.

When he was satisfied that his old friend understood what was required, Soeharto left the small, narrow office and drove back up Djalan Hajam Wuruk towards the new city. Fifteen minutes later, Soeharto arrived at the Army's KOSTRAD headquarters and went immediately to his third floor office and called his aide. He was very troubled. The communists were making a move and he was agitated about being left out of the information loop. Soeharto sat behind the carved teak desk surrounded by pennants, flags and divisional plaques and brooded over his problems. He knew from experience that not only would the whole country swing into a destabilising mode due to the President's proclamation, the Chinese community would do as it always did whenever they anticipated violence. They would immediately close down all of their activities and wait, sending the commercial sector into another tailspin. He knew that this would continue until they could be assured that they would not be embroiled in the madness of Indonesia's politics or be targeted by isolated groups who could make political mileage from involving the small minority in some way.

Brigadier General Soeharto rose, then walked slowly towards the large window overlooking *Lapangan Merdeka*. Across the park, almost hidden behind the huge National Monument, he could just make out a motorcade as it entered the grounds of the United States Embassy.

Deep in thought, he squinted in an attempt to identify the embassy vehicles as they moved into the American compound but the distance was too great. Minutes passed and another motorcycle siren identified a second ambassador visiting his American colleagues. Suddenly an idea crossed his mind. Soeharto returned to his desk and collected the papers which lay there, then left the Army Strategic Command office and its view overlooking Merdeka Square.

Chapter 6

Canberra,
Djakarta,
Bangkok

The mood around the room was solemn. The group of five men sat silently digesting the information they had exchanged during the morning's marathon session in this chamber. Most were dressed as one would expect of elder statesmen and senior Public Servants. The odd man out was in uniform. The uniform was that of the Australian Army and the officer was its Chief of Staff. That the other services were not represented did not reflect on their importance in any way. The matter under discussion had not required their presence at this stage, but further meetings would, no doubt, be scheduled, once consensus had been reached with those present.

'Gentlemen,' the heavy-set leader commenced, his face clouded by the seriousness of the moment. 'Gentlemen, I believe we have no choice. It seems that President Soekarno's intentions are quite clear. He intends to take Malaysia.'

The Prime Minister looked at the others present almost as if challenging them to respond. He was furious with the Indonesian President. The impertinence of the man, declaring war on the British Commonwealth. It was, he considered, the most absurd act of aggression. The man had to be insane!

'I believe that we are all in agreement then?' the recently-knighted Sir Robert Menzies asked, though it sounded more like a statement. His political stature had grown considerably with the honour Queen Elizabeth had bestowed upon her Australian Prime Minister. He had led the country through the past fourteen years. He looked across at Holt, his Treasurer and heir-apparent. 'How will it be funded?'

'I suggest that we just increase the allocation funds currently dedicated to ASIS. This would alleviate difficulties with any audit

requirements as ASIS's operational expenditures are not account-
able to Parliament. The figure would blow out disproportionately
in relation to ASIS's own activities but, I believe, this would be the
most appropriate method of disguising the funding required.' Holt
paused before continuing to ensure they understood. 'I don't fore-
see any problems.'

'Attorney-General?'

'I agree, Sir Robert. Funding the activities is not what still wor-
ries me though. We have limited resources in ASIS and may be
obliged to go further afield for assistance.'

'What do you have in mind?' the PM asked cautiously. He had
a very sound cabinet and his most senior players were present.

'I believe that we should bring the Americans in on it.' The Attorney-General knew that this would be of concern to both the Intelligence services. He glanced at the two men, in turn, expecting
their objections.

'Why don't we try this without them for once,' Alfred Broome
suggested. He didn't want those damn Americans interfering in
what was to be his operation. ASIS may be under-funded and short-
staffed but introducing the 'cousins' into the arena would amount
to giving them control. 'Besides, this really is a Commonwealth
problem.' He knew that this would appeal to the Prime Minister's
sense of "Best if British".

'Do you agree, Deputy Director?' Harold Bradshaw was asked.
As far as his Department was concerned, it would be difficult for
his ASIO men to get even a sniff at whatever was planned. Being
Australia's domestic spy service, Harry was not permitted to operate outside the country.

'Prime Minister,' he started, having prepared for such an opportunity, 'Although the Act prevents my men from participating,
perhaps we could second our more experienced agents to ASIS for
the duration? Some of them were originally involved with ASIS.'
He looked across at Alfred who nodded thoughtfully. It would be
more palatable to have Harry's team on board than having to watch
his back with the Americans.

'That would be acceptable, Sir Robert,' Alfred advised.

'And the SAS?' the Prime Minister asked, addressing the Chief
of Staff.

'We will have them in place within two weeks, Sir Robert.'

The General could have put them into the air that day but decided that he would prefer the additional lead time. Also, he wished to negotiate with his British counterparts who would no doubt want to control the secret missions out of their bases in Singapore and Malaysia.

'Understand, gentlemen, we are not under any circumstances to imply to our allies or the Parliament that we are engaged in an act of war. As discussed earlier, I am prepared to send the SAS, conditional that their efforts are kept covert, that the men who are selected are to sign the Official Secrets Act, and that at no time is it to be suggested that I have approved even so much as a simple police action. Our soldiers will be going to Malaysia and Singapore simply as part of an exercise that had been scheduled since last year. Do I make myself entirely clear, gentlemen?'

The men all acknowledged affirmatively. They all understood that they were already co-conspirators and had been since the formation of the Australian Secret Intelligence Service. Not even Parliament was aware of this covert arm. The Opposition had no idea whatsoever what was going on and, considering the colour of their politics, it was probably safest to maintain the status quo.

Further meetings were scheduled for the Friday and the group dispersed. As Alfred walked together with Harry, they discussed availability of agents and other matters relating to the proposed overseas missions. An hour later they shared a Commonwealth car on their way to the airport. Australia's espionage and intelligence centres were in Melbourne, not Canberra, and both these spymasters wouldn't have had it any other way.

Harry agreed to visit Indonesia to determine the accuracy of Alfred's Djakarta Station reports. He had offered his services and reminded the other Intelligence Head that his previous field experience would be invaluable in ascertaining the mood and political situation should he visit the Djakarta Station. He sent an overseas cable to Murray and indicated that he was making a private visit and requested Murray's company for a short journey. Language difficulties and all that. Ten days later, Harry Bradshaw, Deputy Head of Australia's domestic spy service landed in Bangkok, enroute to Djakarta. He had elected to take the long way round.

* * * * * *

Indonesia

Murray felt certain the left-hand drive Plymouth Belvedere would leave the road at any moment and plunge into the valley on his left. He wished the other driver had agreed to the lower fare. At least his car's steering was on the appropriate side. And they were both feeling the effects of the winding road and the leaking exhaust pipe. Suddenly he couldn't take any more.

'Stop here!' he barked at the driver. Distracted, the driver almost collected an oncoming bus speeding down the mountain side towards them at an incredible rate. Immediately both he and his companion climbed out and moved away from the oversized American sedan and the effects of its nauseating smoke. *'Turn the damn engine off!'* he called but the driver refused.

'Tidak bisa, tuan. If I do that we won't be able to restart the engine'

'Well then, you stay here while we walk ahead,' he ordered. The girl looked at him as if she did not understand. He took her by the hand and started walking up the long climbing bitumen road. The air at this altitude was refreshing and slightly cool. The view to both sides of the road was covered by tea trees, their tops flattened deliberately by the picking process, creating the impression that the volcanic slopes were covered by a wide unfolding green blanket spread deliberately in this pattern by some giant hand. Alongside the winding road stood tall oak trees planted by the Dutch to prevent roadside erosion and, in some instances, to indicate dangerous corners. The oaks were painted white around their lower trunks to assist drivers who dared cross the mountain by road at night.

A soft mist started to roll towards the couple as they continued their slow stroll. The low cloud passed, leaving the sky clear once more. They had been walking for more than ten minutes when Murray became concerned.

'Where the hell do you think that driver has gone?'

'He's back there waiting for us, Murray,' Ade replied. *'You told him to wait there for us!'*

'No I didn't. I told him to let us walk ahead and that he was to follow.'

Ade knew what she heard. She also knew that the driver had not been paid and would follow when they didn't return. *'It's not far, you can see the building from here,'* she said, pointing up the slope to where the long structure dominated the mountain pass.

'*That will take at least another twenty minutes, Ade. Are you sure you're up to it?*' he challenged, knowing that she would accept. She muttered something to herself and commenced walking quickly, her short legs almost strutting as they moved on and up the hill towards the mountain coffee house. Ade had been trying to entice Murray to the Puntjak Pass since their first meeting, some weeks before. She had spoken to him on campus once or twice, and believed she'd made it quite clear that she would go out, if asked. At first, Murray appeared to be preoccupied, and it was not until they bumped into each other at a friends' house that they held a conversation of any real depth and their friendship developed. Their mutual friend was a student of religious studies and Ade was surprised the Australian had been invited. It was then that Ade learned that Murray had already developed a keen sense of observation and understanding of matters related to the Indonesian people. She was impressed with his knowledge of the Javanese culture, his ability to understand the intricate customs which, because these were so shrouded in a wealth of symbolism, most foreigners found impossible to comprehend. Ade laughed with the others present when he attempted to emulate the voice of a *wajang* puppeteer. He was relaxed in their company and extremely popular, which was obvious from the expressions of admiration he received.

As the evening had come to a close, Ade was further surprised to discover that her gregarious friend knew so little of Mohammed Subuh, the Islamic scholar. He'd sat and listened intently as their host attempted to explain the *Susila Budi Dharma* philosophy and the mystique which surrounded the SUBUD movement. Ade was particularly pleased with his interest as she was more than just another Mohammed Subuh admirer, she was also one of Bapak Subuh's most ardent followers. Along with others present, Ade urged Murray to attend one of their meetings and he had willingly agreed. They had made arrangements to meet and visit the small compound located on the city's outskirts and, to her astonishment, Murray was so taken by the experience he insisted that they return within just a few days of his first *latihan* session. Amazingly, it seemed as if he found something that had long been missing in his life. Suddenly they had something in common, something they could share. Ade built on this quickly in an attempt to discourage

99

his relationship with the young communists on campus. She had become fond of Murray but soon realised she had little influence over his choice of friends. Ade could not understand why he would want to spend so much time with Yanti and her comrades. Ade despised her fellow student; even more so, now that Murray continued to associate with the communist supporters.

They had agreed to spend the day together, after a morning *latihan* session, driving the two hours up to the pass where the famous Riung Gunung Coffee House was nestled between the shorter peaks, under the shadow of Gunung Gede. It was well-known that President Soekarno often took time away from his summer palace in Bogor, just a few kilometres from the mountain foothills. For Ade, this added to the excitement of the outing, wishing for an opportunity to see her hero again. Like many of the younger generation, Ade adored the legendary President and tales of his extramarital activities. It did not bother her, as a woman, that her hero was so promiscuous. When Murray jokingly suggested that Soekarno was no longer capable of servicing his many wives and girlfriends, he discovered that Ade was overly sensitive to comments about their leader.

'I don't wish to hear you say anything bad about Bapak. He is loved by all and is now the father of our nation. He can not help it if all of those dreadful women continue to throw themselves at him. After all, he is only a man and entitled to make some mistakes!'

As they arrived at the coffee house so did their driver. Murray told him that they would be there for at least an hour and suggested that, this time, he should turn the Plymouth around and face the ageing vehicle downhill. He watched as the driver complied but still the engine was left running.

'Why don't you turn the engine off, dong!' He called out to the obstinate *supir*, who mumbled something about the car wouldn't like him to do so. He shook his head. In a land where the culture referred to inanimate objects having life, feeling, wants and desires, Murray knew it was easier to ignore the problem than argue. As an Australian, he had found it very difficult to understand just how deeply-rooted animism was in the Indonesian culture. When he studied their official language he came to accept that the inanimate often dictated the sentence structure. For Murray, this had been extremely difficult as it contradicted his own culture. Murray

gave up and was about to enter the building when he noticed a huge eagle perched, with its left talons tied securely to the pole. He admired the magnificent creature.

'Look, Ade. It's so incredibly beautiful.' he said, standing a few metres away from the stern-faced eagle. He shook his head sadly. 'It's just a pity that it has to be tied in this way.'

Ade held his lower arm and tugged, slightly bored with all the attention the bird was receiving. 'If it wasn't tied, it would just fly away, Murray,' she said, serious in her observation. He looked at her quickly to see if she was teasing and identified another of the differences between the Asian and European cultures. The thought that someone may wish to release the bird for purely unselfish motives, permitting it to escape its prison, did not enter into the rationale of her thinking. Even after two years studying the people and their culture, Murray repeatedly found that an understanding of Indonesian logic still eluded him. He sighed, letting it go. He had been there before and knew it would have been an unsatisfactory debate. Murray checked his watch and reminded himself to return early. He had a plane to meet the following day and needed to be alert.

Harry Bradshaw was coming to town.

* * * * * *

Thailand

Harold Bradshaw handed his passport to the immigration officials and waited patiently. There was no drama and neither should there have been. His credentials described Harry as a teacher and his declaration stated that he was travelling on holidays. Unfortunately, no, he could only afford to spend the one night in Bangkok, in transit. No, he said to the official, he had nothing to declare. His baggage would remain at the terminal overnight. This was completely true, as he had entered Thailand from Hong Kong on a Cathay Pacific flight and Harry did intend departing the following day for Singapore. His flight had been delayed some hours and he was now concerned that his meeting might be aborted.

Accepting the first fare offered, he sat up front in the battered taxi and played with the knobs controlling the airconditioner, but

KERRY B.COLLISON

without success. It was steaming hot. The perspiration caused discomfort but he ignored this minor irritation. Again he checked his
watch and tried to encourage the driver to go faster but was unable to communicate. At least the man understood the name of the
hotel he had nominated, and nodded for almost ten minutes confirming that he knew where it was downtown, as he drove full
throttle along the airport highway. At least it hadn't been raining,
he thought thankfully. During his last brief visit, Harry was obliged
to leave his stranded taxi, remove his shoes and walk almost two
kilometres through knee-deep water and sewerage overflow from
the *klongs*.

They arrived at the small hotel off Soi Nana where Harry had
arranged to meet. He would not check in here. Harry had made
other arrangements. He paid the driver with the baht he'd bought
at Kai Tak Airport and walked quickly inside. The cocktail lounge
was to the left of the small lobby. He entered and sat at the bar,
ordered a bourbon and coke then casually looked around. It was
dark and his eyes had not adjusted to the lack of light. There were
a dozen or so guests sitting in the booths, being entertained by
their girlfriends. He finished his drink and was about to leave, resigned to the fact that his meeting had failed when he identified
the thick silhouette moving towards him.

'You're very late. I didn't think you were coming. This is not
good. We do not have a great deal of time,' grumbled the man in a
heavy Russian accent.

Harry didn't bother extending his hand. He disliked the man
and even under more cordial conditions might still have avoided
touching him. The heavy-set Russian smelled as if he hadn't bathed
for weeks. But they all carried that very same odour in Moscow.
Harry knew, he had spent time there, in the field.

'Flight was delayed out of Hong Kong,' was all Harry offered,
waiting for his contact to take the third seat along the bar. Harry
had deliberately placed his coat on the stool immediately next to
his. The few extra centimetres may not make that much of a difference, he thought, but at least it was worth a try.

'We will talk here?'

'Yes, it's okay,' Harry answered.

'You will leave tomorrow morning?'

'Noon flight,' he answered, already tired of the small talk.

102

'Do you have it here?' the Russian asked, leaning closer so as not to be overheard. Harry leaned back slightly, shocked with the sudden intrusion of bad breath. 'God, this man is an animal,' he thought. Harry lifted his coat and extracted a small parcel from the inside pocket. He handed this to the other man.

'Time for a vodka?' Harry asked, turning to attract the bartender's attention.

The drink was poured in silence. The Russian took the small glass and gulped its contents before placing the thick envelope in his huge trouser pocket. He then turned and walked away without even bidding the Australian goodbye.

Harry watched the Russian leave. Then he checked his watch. The drop had taken only three minutes. He was relieved. Time was running out. Harry dropped an appropriate amount on the bar, placed his coat over his arm then departed also, leaving his unfinished drink.

He left the small hotel and walked down to the eastern intersection. He hesitated, pulled a packet of cigarettes from his coat and placed one slowly in his mouth, then turned to see if he had been followed. Satisfied that he had not, Harry lighted the Rothmans and immediately wished he hadn't. His throat was dry and this was his third pack for the day. He stood on the corner for a few more minutes as if trying to make up his mind which direction to take, then turned and walked slowly back to the hotel he had just left.

This time, when he entered the bar he continued through until reaching the rear section where exit signs indicated the toilets and fire door. Harry opened the rear door and looked cautiously in both directions, then stepped out into the dark alleyway. Confident that he was alone, Harry walked up through the alley to the right and stopped just before the corner and knocked on the door marked K115B. Only moments had passed before the door opened and he stepped inside, passing his coat to the young man who stood waiting, smiling at his expected guest.

'I am so happy to see you again sir,' the boyish voice said, taking his guest by the hand. 'It has been so very long since you were here,' he continued, his voice now almost a whisper as he led the *ferang* up the few steps into his bedroom and started to undress slowly. The lights were soft and the air heavy with an almost pungent smell as Harry stood transfixed, staring at the young boy-ish figure slowly undressing before him.

'Where is Piya?' he asked. His words sounded hoarse. 'You promised me Piya,' he repeated, becoming agitated as the shape moved slowly to the soft sounds behind the cushioned bed. He stepped forward, almost lunging as he tripped on a carefully laid rug. 'Where is Piya?' he asked again, his voice rising.

'Piya is here, my darling. Piya is here,' he called softly, rotating his hips back and forth in a slow sensual movement. The ageing spymaster was momentarily confused. He looked closely at the soft young body gyrating within touch and suddenly understood. It had been almost two years since his last visit and his lover had grown. Relieved, Harold Bradshaw stepped forward and took the young boy in his arms and kissed him hungrily before falling to the bed together. Piya was ecstatic. His generous *ferang* lover had returned. And on this day of all days! He was really so fortunate to have such a wonderful surprise!

And on his twelfth birthday.

* * * * * *

Harry awoke with a start and moments passed before he re-membered where he was. He looked across at his companion and smiled. The boy reminded him of an earlier time and another place which, as he closed his eyes, brought back a flood of other memo-ries. He permitted his thoughts to drift and, as sleep evaded him, Harry recalled his early days in Europe and England, when he was still in his prime as an active field agent.

Then the image of Konstantinov flashed across his mind and he ground his teeth, willing the memory away, without success. He lay there in the partial darkness, listening to the airconditioner hum as it fought to keep the room temperature constant. He tried directing his thoughts to other things, but the memory kept re-turning to haunt him. Tired and annoyed with the invasion of his thoughts, Harry permitted his mind to wander wherever it wished, no longer resisting the distant events which flooded back into his mind.

He had been foolish, he admitted. The boy had been only thir-teen but in post-war Berlin who could tell the difference? The streets were swarming with prostitutes of both sexes as they fought to survive the aftermath of Hitler's Germany. Most were destitute and gave themselves willingly, sometimes for the price of one meal.

He had taken the boy back to the small hotel. Nobody paid any attention as he escorted the youth to his room. Or, at least at that time, he had thought that his activities had gone unobserved. Berlin at that time was inundated with agents. As the city had been carved into sectors, he had been assigned to the British Sector and had already spent some months moving across the sector lines through East Berlin, sometimes acting as a courier, other times to handle a simple intelligence drop.

Harry would never forget his shock when the bedroom door burst open and two huge men barged into his room brandishing automatics. He and the teenager were both naked. The men punched the boy unconscious and ordered Harry to remain where he was as one of the men photographed the lurid scene. The other Russian stood with one hand in his overcoat pocket while indicating with the Luger that the Australian was not to do anything foolish. The flash blinded Harry as the first man moved in closer to the bed for a clearer picture of the boy's bleeding face. Several more photographs were taken and then they turned to leave, the larger of the men maintaining his weapon in full view to discourage Harry from following or doing anything courageous. As they moved through the broken doorway the photographer turned and smiled sardonically while the other man spat on the floor. Then they were gone.

Harry was relieved when they finally made their approach. It was inevitable that he would be required to follow their demands and, at first, these were not too difficult to accommodate. Their requests were generally for information concerning British operatives and Harry provided these without hesitation. He had no choice. Disclosure of his sexual idiosyncrasies would not only have ruined his career but would also have placed his life in danger from within his own organisation. He knew how brutal the Russians could be.

Harry had seen it all before. As that year came to a close, Harry discovered that he actually didn't care too much one way or another whether the West or the Communists controlled the world. Berlin had become a cesspool of humanity and he, one of the many sucked into the filthy quagmire created by extremists from both Left and Right of the political spectrum, became a relatively insignificant player in a game which none of them seemed to understand. Even the most hardened agents became cavalier as they went about their secret lives, scoffing silently at the ideologies propounded by Moscow and the temptations offered by Washington, as the self-proclaimed leader of the West. It was when Harry was escorting a family of three through an established route, bringing a fellow conspirator's children across from East Berlin, that he became apolitical and severely critical of all who would be the world's masters.

The crossing had ended in disaster. The children had been sacrificed and it was only later that he'd discovered that even had the escape not been compromised by an unreliable cell in the Soviet Sector, they would most certainly have been killed before completing the crossing. The massacre had been intended as an explicit message to all agents who operated along the divisions separating East from West Berlin. The father had been turned, and his children had paid the ultimate price for his betrayal. Harry had survived the ordeal, but only just. The Soviets had orchestrated that he be blamed, his usefulness to them no longer in question. Later, when he discovered that he too had been marked to die during that operation, Harry went to ground for months before being discovered. The British offered him sanctuary but it was, as always, conditional. He was to leave the SIS. He was no longer considered an asset to either side and, for the first time in many years, Harry felt a tremendous burden disappear from his shoulders as he gratefully accepted the dismissal. He fled Europe and escaped to his home, in Australia, as had Ellis before him. For months he had lived as a recluse. His life had become void of all attachment and he considered taking his life. Harry became desperate, desperate for some justification to live. He had no friends. He felt drained of those emotions which demanded commitments of loyalty to King and Country, to family and friends. These were no longer part of his make-up.

After months of seclusion and self-examination, he accepted that whatever had happened, it had not been entirely his fault. Harry went to Melbourne and applied for a position with the Ministry of Defence. They were desperate for field-hardened men with

European experience. During his first month at the Defence establishment, Harry learned from hushed conversations that a new Intelligence arm was to be formed, based along the lines of the British MI-5 and MI-6. A team from London was appointed to act as adviser to the Australian Government and, amongst this number, Harry identified William Webb Ellis, a former Sydney man whom he had met on more than one occasion while on field assignments. He remembered the deep resentment many of the other agents had expressed for this man which, at the time, Harry had put down to British-Australian rivalry, as the Colonial Boy had climbed to giddy heights within the British Intelligence Service.

There had been rumours, none of which had been substantiated. Whispers seem to follow Ellis wherever he went, even to Singapore and the United States where he directed British MI-6 interests. The spy master married so many times it was almost impossible to maintain records of his marital activities. Harry was surprised to learn that one of Ellis's wives, Lilia Zelenski, was a White Russian which, considering the sensitivity of the Intelligence Chief's access, was in itself typical of the man's extraordinary behaviour. Harry decided to approach the colourful, enigmatic bureaucrat. Ellis recognised the former field agent and, shortly thereafter, Harry's future was assured. Ellis had offered his hand and Harry had eagerly accepted. Harold Bradshaw had completed the circle. He was now back in the intelligence fold, only this time, under the control of Australia's first double agent. It was through Ellis that he met Alfred Broome. After that, Harry's field experience provided a clear path for his accelerated promotion to senior roles within the embryonic Australian intelligence community.

At first, it was as if he had been given a new lease on life but, as he became more and more engrossed in the machinations of the sinister world of espionage and the confusing shadows this life cast, Harry grew to despise the creators of the world in which he had become a prisoner. Disillusioned, embittered, he found it more difficult, as time passed, to retain his sense of identity.

He made serious attempts to identify why, emotionally, he felt no real loyalty to his masters. Harry believed that the West was as culpable as their Soviet counterparts. He decided that neither side really offered any solution to the problems the masses faced as they struggled just to survive and, as the major powers improved their economic, social and political grip on the emerging countries which suffered the humiliation of being relegated to the Third World, Harry elected to remain silently apolitical and non-aligned. Reluctant to offer political opinions when asked, silent and inconspicuous even within the strange world which bred contempt for those who maintained too high a profile, Harry soon became an integral part of the upper echelons of the fledgling Intelligence community.

Harry was promoted to Assistant Deputy Director in the newly-formed Australian Security Intelligence Organisation. One of his first calls to congratulate him on his appointment was from the Cultural Attaché, Embassy of the Union of Soviet Socialists' Republic. It required only one brief meeting for Harry to consent to re-establishing their former relationship. The Cultural Attaché had shown him the photographs.

As the months passed, Harry learned to accept the compromise he had made. He established himself as a reliable officer and those around him soon developed an even greater respect for this man on whom they discovered they could always rely. Meetings with the Russians were relatively infrequent. When they did effect a rendezvous, Harry willingly accepted the envelopes which always contained a generous consideration for his services. He never did feel like a traitor, electing to consider himself more as a mercenary, a free agent. He continued to provide the Soviets with the information they required and his financial rewards increased considerably when it was announced that he would move to England to establish a new liaison centre with the British MI-6. When Harry arrived in London, he was instructed to liaise with a nominated KGB officer who was stationed at the Soviet Embassy. His name was Konstantinov and his demands on Harry drove him perilously close to insanity. The fear of discovery and the consequences of his actions chewed away until finally, when dangerously close to a complete breakdown, KGB colonel Konstantinov identified the seriousness of Harry's mental state and temporarily discontinued utilising his services. Within the year, when the Russian believed he could once again be pressured into complying with the KGB demands, Harold Bradshaw recommenced his double life.

Since that time, Harry had remained in the full employ of the KGB and, when the Australian Government established its second

Intelligence Service on the 13 May, 1952, due to his unique field experience and uncanny ability to analyse the Soviet's activities, Harold Bradshaw became Deputy Director. The position demanded that Harry attend all joint working Intelligence sessions whenever these were held, and liaise with foreign government counterparts, including the CIA and MI-6 where he soon developed close working relationships with the other spy chiefs.

In June, 1957, Harry married Susan Christina Blackmore, only daughter of Sir Ronald Blackmore, of Blackmore and Heath, London. His bride was more than twenty years his junior. He had hoped that this union would assist him to become financially independent of the secret income he had been receiving from the Soviets. Unfortunately, this was not to be. Susan's father passed away that summer leaving his estate deficient of funds due to poor investments. Although their marriage had been consummated, Susan soon discovered that her husband's sexual appetites appeared to be deteriorating at an alarming rate until, to her dismay, they ceased sleeping together even before their first anniversary had arrived.

Accepting his condition as graciously as possible, Harry watched his wife Susan throw herself into the social circuit with great energy and managed to occupy her life with social rather than physical intercourse. Susan had wandered only once. The brief affair had been discreet and intimate. She was young, attractive, and Harry knew she had become disillusioned with the physical aspects of their marriage. Harry had suspected that his wife might enter into such casual relationships and accepted this, recognising that with her looks and youth, he should prepare himself for Susan's occasional infidelities. For Harry, the marriage was, in many respects, a perfect arrangement. Susan was not a demanding woman and presented him with a perfect cover to hide his own sexual preferences.

He had never strayed into dangerous sexual liaisons while in Australia, even though such opportunities were easily arranged in Melbourne where the domestic security service was based. Even within the ASIO ranks, he knew of at least three operatives who were of a similar persuasion to himself. No, he had decided when first moving to the new organisation, he would be circumspect in selecting his sexual partners, preferring to leave these activities for when he visited Asian capitals, such as Bangkok. It was here he had discovered Piya during one such visit some four years ago. Now, he thought, remembering his surprise at the boy's change, he would need to find another reliable partner as Piya would soon be too old.

As these and other thoughts elapsed into a foggy blur, Harry finally fell asleep to the hum of the air-conditioning unit.

* * * * * *

The following morning Harry had bathed and dressed even before many of Bangkok's foreign tourists had returned to their hotels after all-night sessions in Pat Pong's infamous bars. Normally he would have slipped a change of underwear into his coat pockets for such brief stays and regretted this oversight. Even his teeth felt gritty. He would shower and change again in the First Class lounge at the airport. He checked his wallet and looked down at the sleeping boy. Harry removed two hundred baht and placed the money on the bedside table, then he left.

As the Deputy Director left Piya's rooms, he was observed. Harry walked down to the corner and up the street to find a taxi. He decided to go directly to the airport and take an earlier flight to Singapore and on to Djakarta. Harry Bradshaw smiled smugly as he approved of this slight change in his travel plans. It never hurt to be flexible in these matters, he thought, the years of field experience influencing his decision. Three hours later, as the Intelligence Director's flight taxied into Paya Lebar Airport in Singapore, details of his previous evening's activities had been encrypted, transmitted, deciphered and placed on a senior analyst's desk across the other side of the globe. Harold Bradshaw had been picked up by a surveillance team as he entered the young prostitute's rooms.

The contents of the sensitive material were then taken upstairs and surrendered to the Australian Area Operations Desk Officer who read the report slowly then smirked at the photograph pinned to the file cover. Suddenly, his face clouded

'Gotcha, you asshole!' he snarled, poking Harry's image with his finger. 'Gotcha at last, you sonofabitch!' With which, Senior Agent Richards of the Central Intelligence Agency slapped himself on the thigh and opened the top drawer of his desk, extracted his banned Havana cigars, selected one and placed it between his teeth. He lighted the expensive leaf and leaned back into his swivel chair, savouring the cigar's almost perfect flavour. It was worth waiting for, he knew. They had caught him at last and he had even provided them with a bonus.

The American closed his eyes and grunted in satisfaction. They had him cold. And Richards knew that should the need arise, this man would be obliged to co-operate. The Australian had compromised himself completely. At any time they so desired, he would become *their* man.

* * * * * *

Piya smiled as the two men arrived for their appointment. He was excited, believing that this would be a very rewarding arrangement. He peered out through the spyhole and watched the men as they approached his door. Piya was a little surprised as one of the men appeared to be Thai. He could see that the other man was obviously a *ferang*. They both held themselves like soldiers. He had seen their type before and Piya assumed that the Thai national was merely escorting his foreign friend. The young prostitute spoke to them first, establishing that they were, in fact, the clients who had telephoned earlier. He then let them enter and suggested that the protocol was to first pay him for his services. The solidly-built *ferang* whom Piya had correctly guessed was a soldier smiled as he moved closer and delivered two short but swift blows to the boy's abdomen. Piya collapsed to the floor doubled in the foetal position, sucking unsuccessfully for air as his world disintegrated around him.

The beating did not last more than a few minutes but, to the young male prostitute, it was an eternity. He lost consciousness only to be revived by his attackers. He moaned then cried, sobbing for help from the Thai man, confused as to why he had been so brutally beaten. He had little money on the premises and he knew it would not be rape; they would have done that before any attack on his small body. Perhaps they just enjoyed going around beating up people in his profession, he thought, fearful that they might still kill him.

When they finally left, Piya's battered limbs were still trembling with fear. They had threatened to return and he was certain that they would. He had told them everything they wanted to know. He had also promised to keep them informed in the future should there be any further contact from his favourite client. They had warned him not to run away and he understood their threats. Piya believed that they could find him if he deserted his premises. Besides, where could he go? He had bathed slowly after locking the doors securely. What was this all about? he wondered, still in shock.

Why were these men so interested in Harold Bradshaw?

Chapter 7

Indonesia

Murray was convinced that Harry had practised sitting in that position before. He had still not mastered the uncomfortable cross-legged lotus and was impressed with the older man's ability to sit in that way without apparent discomfort.

As soon as Murray had explained his experiences in the SUBUD community's compound, Harry had insisted that he be taken and introduced to the religious sect's head. At first, Murray was reluctant, convinced that his visitor had an ulterior motive, but changed his attitude the moment he witnessed Bradshaw's reaction to his first contact with the *SUBUD Bapak*.

They had entered the peaceful room and remained standing in their stockinged feet until the master had entered. He smiled and clasped his hands together, moving them slowly from his face towards them as if in a gesture of supplication. He spoke to them in English, welcoming Murray and his guest and bidding them to sit with him and talk. Subuh sat on the large *tikar* mat and beckoned, indicating that the others should follow. Harry immediately moved into the cross-legged position while Murray eased himself down carefully onto the woven mat.

'This is your first time in our country?' he asked politely.

'No, it isn't, Bapak.' Murray had offered directions as to how the religious guru should be addressed and was pleased that Harry had been listening. 'I have visited Djakarta and Surabaja before.'

'I am pleased that Mas Murray has brought you to SUBUD. What religion do you follow?' he enquired. Harry was momentarily taken aback. In Western cultures, it would have been considered impolite to be as abrupt in enquiring as to one's religious denomination. It had been some time since he had attended church

113

as a Christian for the sake of prayer or worship. In fact, apart from weddings, funerals and the odd christening, Harry did not recall having attended a Sunday service for many years.

'I was raised a Catholic but regretfully, I have been lacking in my duty to my faith.'

The master explained that it was irrelevant to which religion they belonged providing one believed in God. 'There are seven types of soul in the Cosmos,' he explained, 'and there are religions corresponding to these seven types. Man has long known of their existence,' he said, looking directly at the two men as he spoke. 'and these may be compared to the Seven Ages of Man, inasmuch as different forms of behaviour correspond to the various stages of growth.

'Our community here should not be confused as a new religion. Some have compared the SUBUD philosophy with the ancient Mysteries while others have suggested that SUBUD is a derivative from or a combination of Hinduism and Sufism. I will leave you to consider these thoughts to assist with your own conclusions. Our aim is to educate our members to a deeper awareness of the true nature of their souls and to purify and cleanse them. This is achievable through prayer, meditation and the *latihan*.'

He then went on to deliver a short lecture encouraging them to direct their spiritual hopes and aspirations exclusively towards God. He asked them to join him in prayer, to which they willingly agreed. They listened to the soft resonant voice fill the room as their thoughts concentrated on the great man's prayer. His words were clear and precise and, as the almost melodious tone seemingly eased whatever tension lay in their bodies, they listened as he spoke softly, willing them to relax their minds and bodies completely, urging both men to sit quite still and clear their thoughts. They closed their eyes for what seemed to be moments, only to discover, when they heard their names being called, that they had unknowingly remained in a trance for almost twenty minutes. Later, Harry admitted to feeling a sense of awareness during those missing minutes but could not remember any specific thought or words which transpired during their trance. He asked Murray if he too had felt as if his body had become a soft electric current, flowing aimlessly around his person, creating what he described as a floating sensation. Murray had agreed that he too had experienced a warmth, but compared it more to being suspended under a soft light.

When they heard the Bapak call their names, both men instantly regained full consciousness of their facilities, and opened their eyes to see the master standing before them. The ceremony was over. The Bapak left the room without any further word, leaving the men in the company of their thoughts. Both remained in the lotus position for some time, conscious of the blood flowing through their veins more freely and, for a brief time, they felt full of pure thoughts.

As they left that special place, both men knew that they had experienced something extraordinary; almost bordering on the mystic. They walked away quietly, each contemplating what had taken place.

As they moved between the small trees, Mohammed Subuh watched the men with a clarity only his eyes could see. There was a slight blur in his vision as he concentrated on the two men walking away, almost as if there was a shadow obstructing his sight. As he turned his head ever so slightly to see past it, he was alarmed that this mark remained fixed on one of the men as they walked away. He closed his eyes, attempting to will this dark blur away, then opened his eyes. He frowned. The mark remained. And it remained fixed on the departing image of Harold Bradshaw.

* * * * * *

Before Harry returned to Australia, he revisited the compound and attended the *latihan*. Harry had not objected when Murray brought one of his student friends along to the session but he was surprised that the girl was not permitted to join with the men during the latihan. The sexes were segregated for this emotional and soul-searching exercise. Before the men entered the room, which had been specifically prepared for such sessions, they were required to remove their watches and any other metal or hard objects which could cause physical harm. At first, this request made Harry apprehensive but, as the others complied, so did he. Later, he was to admit privately to Murray that this experience was one of the most incredible he had ever had.

Harry learned that the *latihan* was a means whereby followers entered into a state of self-purification. SUBUD, not unlike Sufism, offers its members the possibility of knowing Reality through inner experience, conditional on the participants' ability to purify his or herself sufficiently in order to receive such revelation. Many never achieve this pure state and for those who do, the process is a long and demanding one. This training of one's self required Harry's concentration to induce what he thought was a form of auto-hypnosis in which the direction originates from one's Higher Self. Once this process becomes operative, he was told, the *latihan* proceeds in the same manner as that in which he took breath; it would become as automatic as his heartbeat and he would be able to achieve this state with full consciousness.

At first Harry was shocked with the behaviour of those around him. Some of the members fell to the floor, crying, while others started screaming loudly. He panicked and wanted to leave the room, which suddenly erupted into pandemonium as men screamed of their lives and disappointments while others stood perfectly still as if already in a state of tranquillity. It was like a scene from some mental institution. Gradually, as he realised that there was no danger, that these men were merely exorcising their devils, he fell into the routine of things himself, and started to sing. Amazingly, he felt no shame or embarrassment and, as the minutes rolled by, discovered a sense of release from the stress under which he had lived most of his life.

When the *latihan* session had been terminated, they spent an hour alone, meditating. Soon after, all three returned to Murray's pavilion where they sat for yet another hour discussing their experiences that day. Ade had to hurry home, so Harry invited Murray back to the Intercontinental Hotel for dinner, which he gratefully accepted.

'How about we leave now and I'll take some clothes. If you don't mind, Harry, I could certainly do with a long tub in your room, that is if you don't mind?'

'Go for it, Murray. I can see why you'd enjoy some civilised facilities for a change.' Harry laughed, looking around the very basic accommodations. 'But don't worry, young man, from what I hear you will be out of here very soon.'

Murray looked at the older man with some surprise. 'What have you heard?'

'We'll talk over dinner. Come on, grab your gear and let's get the hell out of here before I become claustrophobic.'

Half an hour later, Murray lay in the luxury of a hot bath, not entirely uncomfortable with the knowledge that he would soon be returning to Australia. He towelled, changed and met Harry down in the Baris Lounge of the hotel. He strolled into the bar wearing an open-neck batik shirt. It was almost his trade mark, as the other expatriates simply refused to wear the cheap cotton cloth. Murray did so out of necessity and didn't really mind. A few familiar faces raised their hands and said 'hi' as he passed their tables. Most of those present were either journalists or embassy officials. There were only a few drinking holes around Djakarta and this, the newest, catered for those who were on government business and could afford to pay the one dollar fifty US for a cocktail.

'Murray!' a voice called and he made his way around the horse-shoe shaped bar. The bartenders recognised him and brought a large bottle of Bir Bintang as he slipped in alongside his friend.

'*Malam, tuan!*' the chief bartender said, warmly.

'*Ya, selamat malam, Mas,*' Murray responded mechanically, then remembered to smile. He was not entirely relaxed, even after the bath. Perhaps he was edgy because he knew he would be leaving soon, he guessed, or was it because he hadn't felt entirely comfortable with Harry from the moment he had arrived? Murray was concerned about having such a senior member of the Intelligence community visiting without the support of his own masters. Harry had been explicit in his cable. He was on holiday and firmly indicated that he would not appreciate having Murray's people either coddle him during his visit or feel obliged to entertain him while he was taking a much-deserved break. Harry had explained that Susan had not wanted to leave home at that time. He said she had insisted that he go alone and enjoy himself. Djakarta was no place for a three-year-old infant and so he had decided to take some private time off, just for himself for a change. When Harry had mentioned his wife, Murray had immediately felt the old uneasiness return. He had watched the older man's face carefully as they discussed family and friends and, to his relief, at no time did he see any indication that he might have known.

'Well, cheers, Murray,' he said, downing half of his bourbon and coke and immediately indicating to the barman that he wished another. Murray observed the speed with which the double shots disappeared. He raised his glass of beer and swallowed slowly.

'Can we get right into it, Harry? I can't stand the suspense.'

'It's off the record. Your own powers-that-be will advise you in their own good time. I'm not the messenger, just a friend short-circuiting the delivery process.'

'How much time do I have?' he asked.

'Give or take, I'd say, hmmm,' he paused, 'about a month.'

'Shit, Harry, that's no time at all!' he almost shouted, then dropped his voice knowing that most of the journalists in that bar could not obtain the *surat djalan* permits necessary for them to move around the countryside, and some places even within the metro-politan area, and so they survived primarily off what they heard here.

'It wasn't my call, Murray. You know that my influence is lim-ited. Besides, there is a strong possibility that you will be back be-fore you know it.' Murray grabbed at the suggestion. 'How strong a possibility?' he asked, sensing there was a great deal more that he was not being told.

'My estimate?' he asked, 'Oh, I'd say something around the high nineties.' Murray's spirits suddenly lifted with this news.

'When will I be told?'

'It seems that I am to have some influence over what will hap-pen up here,' he said, lowering his voice even more as he twirled the long plastic stirrer the barman had insisted on placing in his drink. 'Keep it to yourself. Don't want your team spitting the dummy because I pre-empted their delivery service. Okay?'

'Sure. And thanks,' he agreed, thankful for the early warning.

'As I'm leaving tomorrow, what do you say we eat upstairs then take a stroll around the traps?' Harry was not really all that inter-ested but felt that it would be out of character not to hit at least Mama Louie's before heading back to Melbourne. Murray finished his second glass and left the rest of the bottle.

'Ready when you are,' he said, edging off his bar stool not en-tirely unhappy that someone else was picking up the tab. The at-mosphere in the Baris Lounge was not exactly conducive to confi-dential discussion. There were just too many embassy ears listen-ing, their amateurish behaviour made obvious by their strained dialogue. Djakarta had become a cesspool full of foreign intelligence

118

agents, he thought, waving goodbye to the staff as he followed Harry Bradshaw.

They dined in fine style on the top floor of Djakarta's finest hotel. The Nirwana Supper Club was set in splendid surroundings, with views down both sides of the restaurant. To his right Murray could see the lights around the newly-constructed sports stadium, built with valuable dollars so that Soekarno could show the world that even the New and Emerging Nations could provide for their athletes. He smiled as the area blacked out while he was admiring the achievement. On his left Murray could see down Djalan Thamrin all the way to Merdeka Square. Suddenly he realised just how much he would miss this city and its inhabitants, even with the inherent problems of corruption and apathy which often tested his patience.

'Never get too close, Murray,' the voice interrupted his wandering thoughts. 'It's not only unprofessional, it would be dangerous.'

'Seems that the place really does grow on you after all,' he responded. 'There are worse places,' he added, almost lamely.

'Sure, but you haven't seen them all, yet,' the older man advised, remembering an earlier time and another place. He seemed to recall making a similar statement to his controller. How long ago was that, he wondered? Was it really twenty years ago? Harry pushed the memory back to where it belonged. Those times were not all that memorable. 'Come on, don't get morbid on me. Finish your steak and we'll leave.'

'Actually, Harry, I wouldn't mind staying here for a while.' Murray did not particularly wish to end up playing interpreter again for his friend. He'd had enough of that during the first few nights. It was tiring and boring task, holding a two-way conversation repeating everything twice to both parties for hours on end, while the hookers crowded around encouraging him to arrange for Harry to take them back to his room and, after all of that, Harry always refused.

Harry was happy to call it a night after dinner. 'As it so happens, young man, I am feeling a little worse for wear and would be pleased to just stay here. Will you come for breakfast tomorrow? My flight isn't until midday.'

'Wouldn't miss it!' Murray happily responded. In a way he

would be sorry to see Harry go. Apart from the interpreting demands, Harry had been good company, probably the best he had enjoyed for some time. Too long a time, he suddenly thought. Maybe it was time he went home. He didn't want to believe that he was losing some of his objectivity. They remained until the floor show was over. Harry signed the check and escorted Murray down to the lobby. He smiled as literally hundreds of *betjak* drivers crowded towards the entrance, calling out to the familiar face.

'Good night Harry,' he called, climbing into one of the three-wheeled monsters, waving as the driver turned without caution directly into the flow of traffic and cut across the roundabout towards the Soviet and British Embassies. As his driver pumped furiously to beat the oncoming traffic, Murray turned and waved once more but his companion for most of the past week had already disappeared from view.

Harry had watched Murray's transport cross the busy roundabout and then head home. He checked his watch and saw that it was still quite early. He looked down towards Djalan Blora where he knew the transvestites congregated and snorted with contempt. He stood for some moments, feeling the warm evening breeze move slowly through the night. A touch of dust mixed with the many tropical aromas hung temptingly in the evening air as Harry looked sadly at the small group of children offering themselves just outside the hotel's perimeter.

He resisted the temptation, turned and entered the hotel. Alone.

A guest dressed in a long-sleeved white shirt and charcoal trousers checked his watch as Harry entered the lobby lift. He observed the indicator lights above the doors and checked the level at which the lift stopped. The man then waited for a further fifteen minutes before wandering out of the hotel and into the car park. There, he remained sitting in a black Mercedes 190 until midnight. Convinced that his quarry would remain in his room for the rest of the evening, Dimitri Kololotov then drove away, returning to his own small premises at the rear of the Soviet Embassy.

The Russian was not the only party to show interest in the Australian's movements. Both Murray and Harry had been observed while they were at the SUBUD compound. In fact, they had been followed almost from the moment Bradshaw's flight had arrived in Djakarta. As Dimitri had concluded his duties for the night, so too did his American counterpart. By noon the following day, Harry and Murray's movements would be known from reports which had already been deciphered, scrutinized, and placed on their respective desks in both Moscow and Langley, Virginia.

The observations were practically identical. Data extracted from files was checked and updated. Harry's movements were noted along with detailed information relating to those he was seen with during the visit. When the files had been read, these were returned to the security clerks who, in turn, checked the instructions attached to the report's cover. A cross-reference note was placed in Harry's file and, as per instruction, a new file was then opened, bearing the relevant identification in bold red letters across the documents face. The new file was simply titled, STEPHENSON, M.I., and then stored in the 'possibles' section.

In both the CIA and KGB Central Registry, Murray Lloyd Stephenson had been identified as a result of his association with Harold Bradshaw during the latter's visit. In both reports he had been classified as having strong Communist Party affiliations and being a member of the SUBUD religious-cum-spiritual group. In the course of the next twenty-four hours, his name would appear on no fewer than a dozen cross-referenced intelligence situation reports. Within the week, agents from several foreign legations in Canberra, Australia, would commence the tedious task of investigating his background in order that his file be upgraded to 'confirmed' or relegated to the lesser categories in the Registry computers.

Their investigations would eventually leave their masters confused and shaking their heads.

* * * * * *

True to his word, Murray arrived for breakfast. They sat in the outer section of the coffee shop and filled in time with banal discussion until the hour arrived for Harry to depart. They drove to Kemayoran Airport together and Murray waited until Harry's plane was airborne before returning to his pavilion.

When he arrived, he was met by his servant, who informed Murray that he had guests. After Harry's demanding visit, the thought of female company for a change lifted his spirits. He had expected to find either Ade or Yanti waiting for him inside. Instead, there were two men waiting for him.

'Hello, Stephenson,' Davis said, a grin on his face. Murray looked at the other man.

'G'day, Murray.' It was Keith Wells. 'Haven't heard from you for awhile. Been busy, have we?'

'Got some great news for you, Murray,' Davis added, impatiently.

'Shut up, Davis!' Wells snarled. He had just about had enough of the Tasmanian. 'Why don't you go and wait in the car while I talk to our friend here?' It wasn't really a question. Miffed, Davis stormed out sullenly and banged the door loudly as he left.

'You're going home, Murray,' Wells advised.

Murray waited a few moments before responding. 'Guess I'm due for a break,' was all he said. There was an awkward silence before the Station Chief spoke again.

'This may be more than a break, Murray,' he said slowly.

'Meaning?' he asked, anxious now about what his superior seemed to be implying. Murray felt uncomfortable not being able to mention his discussion with Harry.

'Seems your time here is up. That's all.'

'Just like that?' he asked, incredulously. This wasn't happening the way Bradshaw had predicted. There was something wrong. He could detect the hostility.

'Just like that,' Wells replied.

'Do I need an explanation?'

'Yes, but that's between you and our masters back home.'

'When do I leave?' he asked.

'You're to be out by the end of the month. Come down to the Embassy on Monday and we'll have your tickets and funds ready.' Keith Wells then left. Murray watched the housekeeper close the gate behind them. 'By the end of the month' meant just over two weeks before he departed. He rehashed the brief and enigmatic conversation in his mind and decided that even the Station Chief may have been left out of the information loop, and that his concerns were just an over-reaction to Well's delivery style. Anyway, he thought, there was nothing he could do until he returned to Melbourne and Central Plans.

Murray commenced making mental arrangements for his

departure. There was not a great deal to do as he had little to pack. He looked around the sparsely furnished quarters. Not much for two years of one's life, he thought, ignoring the feeling of depression which hovered now with the thought of leaving. He would concoct some acceptable explanation for his sudden departure. Murray thought about his friends. He would invite them all to a farewell party! Once again he looked around the cramped accommodations and decided to arrange something special. Then he remembered the Thousand Islands. Murray believed that this would be an ideal venue for his farewell party.

He left Djalan Tasikmalaya and headed for the university to inform his friends. He knew that this would not be an easy task. Murray had developed some very special relationships on and off campus during his two years and now, suddenly, he must tell them he was leaving.

Less than two weeks later, Murray and most of his close friends chartered the Indonesian Navy vessel and spent their last week together on the idyllic tropical island. Most, that is, with the exception of Ade. Distressed as she was, knowing that Murray was about to leave, Ade was adamant. She would not spend the weekend in the company of those communists.

* * * * * *

Murray pulled a bottle of beer from the home-made, polystyrene-lined ice box. It had taken all of them to off-load the heavy cask. The drinks had not been put on ice until they made camp amongst the coconut trees a few metres from the high tide mark. Sjamsu had carried the one metre blocks of ice from the ship's freezers and broken them into more manageable lumps. These he placed in the ice box and then emptied the case of beer into the large container. Murray had tried to explain that the beer should have gone in first but, with typical Oriental logic, Sjamsu had ignored his suggestion knowing that to do so would only make it more difficult later when they needed to take the beer out. The bottles remained on top of the ice.

Murray decided that he'd had enough swimming for the day and took another stroll around the small atoll. The island was literally smothered with tall coconut palms, most of which were heavily laden with fruit. Murray looked up to ensure that he was not standing under one of the coconut bunches. He had seen the damage a falling coconut could do to a car roof and didn't need to be told not to sleep under the swaying trees. What amazed him was that the Indonesians still insisted on sitting under the palms, and would only move when one of the coconuts dislodged itself, falling perilously close. Murray thought he understood, and believed that this was not bravado, nor was it stupidity. It was simply their fatalism, their belief in *adjal*.

Yanti did not follow. She understood that Murray needed to be alone with his thoughts. His friends all understood that he was sad to be leaving. They too would miss his company and friendship and this was reflected in the group atmosphere which, on this occasion, was subdued. The girls prepared more food and, as Murray returned, several of the men had taken their small *tikar* a short distance and prepared for the Mahgrib prayer. Murray looked across to the west and counted the slow seconds as the huge dark orange ball slipped below the horizon. And then he sighed, as the sunset all but disappeared within that magical moment.

* * * * * *

In the late afternoon on the following Tuesday, Murray Stephenson left Djakarta. There was a feeling of loss as his friends waved from the open observation level. They watched as Murray walked slowly across the concrete and called out loudly when he turned and waved goodbye to them. Sjamsu called loudly as Yanti waved furiously, holding a hand written placard wishing him 'Selamat Djalan'.

As he approached the steps leading up to the Boeing 707, Murray turned for one last farewell. He could no longer distinguish their shapes, let alone their faces. Disappointed that Ade had not put her feelings aside just this once and joined with his other friends to bid him farewell, Murray looked back over his shoulder and paused for one final look before entering the aircraft. He sensed that a major chapter in his life was coming to a close.

The four-engined jet screamed along the short runway then lifted suddenly, banking to the West and passing back over the terminal building. Murray peered down below, unable to differentiate between the structures as the Boeing climbed noisily. The aircraft continued to climb as the pilot manoeuvred the jet gracefully, changing its course in accordance with the flight plan. A chime sounded somewhere within the cabin as the seat-belt and no-smoking signs were switched off. Murray unlatched his seat-belt and made his way forward from the economy class section towards the toilets.

As he passed the front section of the economy seats, Murray waited for the stewardess carrying complimentary drinks to finish serving before he continued towards the toilets. He paused, placing his left hand on the aisle seat headrest to steady himself as he stood waiting. The aircraft dropped slightly, then steadied itself as he held tightly to the seat and, as the aisle had then cleared he moved forward, turning to apologise to the passenger whose seat he had gripped during the light turbulence.

'Sorry, ...' he started to say, looking at the occupant of the seat.

'Hello, Mahree,' the young woman replied, enjoying the look of surprise on his face. Murray gripped the seat in front to steady himself as the aircraft suddenly dipped again. He stared at the passenger, lost for words.

'What are you doing here?' he demanded, confused by her presence on the aircraft.

'Why, Mahree,' Ade teased, deliberately shifting the emphasis on the syllables, 'going to Australia with you, of course!'

Kerry B.Collison

Chapter 8

Australia

After readjusting to life back in Melbourne, Murray was satisfied that he had made the correct decision. Three months before, he had been prepared to walk away from his profession and search for something less demanding on his personal relationships. Now, refreshed, away from the idiosyncrasies of Asian life with its often confusing cultures, Murray experienced a new vitality, a rejuvenation of his former self.

He played tennis, enjoying the game without the humid conditions he had become accustomed to in the tropics. Old friendships were re-established, and life moved into a familiar mode, one which provided an atmosphere of order and solidarity. He was home.

Murray's debriefing had not taken too long. During the first days, he sensed that there had been a certain amount of animosity amongst his peers. He put this down to the fact that he had been out of circulation and had lost real contact with the other agents. He set about rebuilding and consolidating these relationships.

His mother had been strangely distant when he visited her. Their first meeting was stiff and awkward. When several of her cardplaying friends arrived, providing him with the opportunity to escape, he felt relief. He had stayed with his sister during the stopover in Sydney and she had brought her brother up to date regarding family matters. He had left his travelling companion to her own plans, although he suspected that she would have preferred accompanying him into see the sights, before proceeding on to Canberra. This suited Murray. He was pleased to have the day alone with his sister.

Sitting in the quiet leafy garden, Murray reflected on the events surrounding his departure from Djakarta. He remembered being totally disorientated when he discovered Ade on the plane. He had taken the empty seat beside her as he recovered from the shock of seeing her there.

'What are you doing here?' he had asked again, his mind confused by her presence.

'You have your secrets, Mahree, I have mine,' she smiled.

'How did you manage to arrange all of this so quickly? Passport, tickets! My god, Ade, how did you even manage to organise a visa in that time?'

'I had a little help, Mahree. Professor Winton at the Australian National University made most of the arrangements. Do you remember meeting Bapak Winton at the SUBUD complex? I'm sure we talked about him. He was the one who spoke fluent Bahasa Djawa to Bapak Subuh. Don't you remember?' Ade explained, bubbling with enthusiasm as she spoke.

'When you told me you were leaving for Australia, I asked SUBUD if they would help me contact the Professor to see if he had been serious about assisting Indonesian students with courses at his university. After that, I didn't have to do anything! They were all so supportive. Bapak Subuh must have spoken directly to his old friend because they called me back to the community centre the very next day and told me the news. I didn't want to tell you in case nothing happened, Murray. It was to be a surprise. We all knew the date of your departure and it was not difficult to book a seat on this flight, as you can see for yourself,' she said, indicating the near empty plane. *'This is also why I didn't join in the island trip. By then my documents were complete and my ticket confirmed. I knew that you would be so surprised!'*

Ade giggled, and looked directly at Murray. *'You are surprised, aren't you, Mahree?'*

He sat quietly listening to her explanation and, when she had finished, he just shook his head slowly before responding. *'You should have told me, Ade. Perhaps I could have helped.'*

'But everything was well-organised and I did want to keep it a secret until we boarded. I watched you at the Kemayoran Airport with all of your friends. You were so preoccupied hugging and kissing all of those girls you didn't even notice me when I was at the check-in counter.'

Murray had cast his mind back to the departure hall. She was totally correct. The scene had been a little chaotic, he remembered. Not that he would have recognised Ade anyway, Murray thought as he observed her clothes. She was dressed in a long trouser suit and high heels. He had only ever seen her in knee-length dresses or blue jeans, normally wearing the comfortable flat-heeled casual shoes most of the younger women preferred. Ade had tucked her shoulder-length hair up under a cap making identification nearly impossible. Murray smiled at her and shook his head once again.

'What are you going to do in Australia? What about your studies at Universitas Indonesia?' he asked.

'I have already confirmed with the university lecturers that my time in Australia will be credited towards my final examinations when I return. I will not be in Canberra long. My study visa is only for three months. But you could always help me extend, couldn't you, Mahree?' she suggested coquettishly. Murray ignored the idea, talking instead about more mundane matters such as finances, clothing and where she would stay while attending the short study course at the Australian National University. He was amazed to discover that all of these had been carefully, albeit quickly, planned to the last detail by the SUBUD members. She was indeed very fortunate to be going to Australia. Especially at this time, he had thought.

When they parted at the Sydney airport, Murray had promised to call her in a few days and arrange for her to visit once she had settled. He watched her walk away to arrange her ongoing flight, completely confident and assured. As he left the airport lounge area, he turned and waved once to which she responded immediately. Murray was still considering her successful efforts to visit Australia as his taxi dropped him at his sister's apartment in Neutral Bay. He understood that the visit had been quite some achievement. He also knew that, without some intricate string-pulling, it would not have been possible for Ade to accomplish what she had, in such a short time. Obviously, he thought, SUBUD had developed some strong pulling ability and was quite capable of applying it whenever deemed necessary.

* * * * * *

'You must come down, Murray.' The invitation had been offered for the third time and he could not refuse again. Harry Bradshaw had all but insisted that he spend the weekend at the coastal retreat. 'Bring your racquet and we'll see what's happened to your game while you've been away.' Unable to provide another suitable excuse, he accepted.

He drove down to the Bradshaw's home slowly, anxiety chewing at his stomach. Murray had considered telephoning Ade in Canberra and offering her the fare if she would come down and accompany him but, considering the circumstances and the host's position, he decided against it. Ade had met Harry in Djakarta but he wasn't sure if it would be appropriate for him to invite the Indonesian girl. She had done well with her time at the university and was not looking forward to returning home, which would be soon. Murray had invited her down several times already and Ade had happily visited, staying in his apartment along St. Kilda Road. He did not take her to meet his mother, which Ade found more than a little curious. Murray believed that their relationship could not be permanent and ensured that these feelings were understood by Ade. Nevertheless, they slept together, enjoying each other as natural lovers would, ignoring the inevitable.

Ade sensed that Murray would not ask her to remain in Australia which clearly demonstrated that he did not care enough for her to do so. She also understood that, once her flight departed Australia and she returned to Indonesia, their relationship would most certainly end. With only a few weeks left before her visa expired, Ade knew that the immigration authorities would not approve yet another extension. It was clear to Murray that she wished to remain in Australia, and he knew that to encourage her to do so would be irresponsible. Perhaps it was for the best that he hadn't asked her down for this weekend, he thought, slowing down as he approached the cottage.

He parked his MG and strolled slowly towards the large cottage, kicking the iron gate closed as he passed through. The lawn had obviously just been cut. The air still carried that grassy freshness which always accompanies that chore. Rows of poppies backed by dwarf lavenders lined the footpath on both sides, their fragrance competing with the other colourful beds of flowers, most of which were in full bloom. He looked up to the front entrance and instantly caught his breath.

'Welcome back, Murray,' Susan said, smiling radiantly. 'It's been too long.' She bent down, then crouched, holding the child from behind. 'Say hello to Uncle Murray, darling. Murray, this is Michael!'

Murray stepped forward and also crouched, 'Hello tiger,' he said, admiring the boy's striking blonde hair. 'Are you my new tennis partner?' He extended his hand and touched the boy's cheeks softly. Michael screamed, turned and shrank back into his mother's arms. They laughed at the child's reaction and suddenly Murray felt the angst wash away with the moment. He followed Susan Bradshaw into the house and through to the patio. It was almost as if he had not been away from the setting. The card table and the drinks were the same, and to his astonishment, even the same people who had made up the party during his first visit some four years before were present, including his mother, Muriel Stephenson. He walked over and kissed her first before turning to the others. She responded warmly, boosting his confidence.

He then turned to Jean Broome and immediately observed that she had aged considerably, her face showing the results of over-indulgence. She clasped her gin and tonic with both hands. Obviously, her extended visits to the sanatorium had not been successful. Murray had only discovered her problem well after she had taken to disappearing for weeks at a time. Office gossip had alerted him to her alcoholism.

'Hello, stranger. You're looking in good health. The tropical climate appears to have suited you,' she said. Murray smiled, pecked her on the cheek and shook her husband's hand.

'Alfred. Looks like we'll have another tough match on our hands,' he laughed, turning then to Harry Bradshaw and shaking his hand also.

'Thought it would be fitting to have that re-match Alfred and I have been promising each other. Same partners as before, Murray, only this time you will have to run a little faster. Your partner is not as young as he was when you last won.'

Alfred Broome snorted. 'Well, let's see about that! Come on, partner, change your gear and we will give them a quick thrashing before dinner.'

They played for an hour, the Bradshaws winning easily. Harry had been accurate in his observations. Alfred had aged considerably over the past few years, which made the match even more demanding on his partner. Twice, the game was brought to a halt as the older man ran out of steam and required a short spell. When Harry offered to call it a game, Alfred insisted that they continue.

He should have heeded the warnings.

The following week, while attending an Intelligence Chiefs briefing, Alfred Broome collapsed with chest pains and died before the ambulance team could render assistance. On the Monday morning, Alfred Broome was buried in a quiet ceremony attended only by his family and a few close friends.

An urgent meeting was called by the Minister and those summoned agreed on an interim replacement for the deceased Chief. There was little discussion as to whom this should be. There was only one qualified candidate who was completely au fait with both the domestic and overseas Intelligence arms, and he was present at the meeting. The Minister was receptive when he expressed willingness to make the necessary move in the interests of expediency and continuity. The decision had been unanimous, and before lunch on that day, Harold Bradshaw was appointed the interim Director of the Australian Secret Intelligence Service. Immediately, he set about reorganising Central Plans' operational structure, increasing agent representation in all South-East Asian target countries.

* * * * * *

The following month Murray Lloyd Stephenson finally returned to Indonesia. The word 'Diplomatique' was emblazoned across the cover of his passport in gold lettering, and his other credentials declared he was a member of the Australian Embassy in Djakarta. The revised Protocol Lists circulated regularly throughout the Diplomatic and Consular missions mentioned Stephenson's arrival and status. His position in the Australian Embassy was listed as Third Secretary, Political Affairs.

* * * * * *

Langley, Virginia, USA

The Assistant Director, South-East Asia, looked across at the other officer and nodded, in concurrence. It would appear that the other man's evaluations supported his own conclusions.

The Australians had weakened their overseas intelligence capability while perhaps strengthening their domestic service with the appointment of Bradshaw as Intelligence Chief, ASIS. The vacuum created within ASIO would be of little consequence, providing 'Finger Jar', the designated code name allocated to Bradshaw within the CIA, had no influence over whoever was appointed to fill his former position as Deputy Director.

'Getting to be like those goddamn Brits,' the ADSEA grumbled. He had come in from field operations almost ten years before and still cursed the MI6 for the SIS operations which had cost the CIA one network and a number of valuable agents. After the Philby and Burgess fiascos, there wasn't one American operative left still prepared to risk exposing themselves to the British agencies. The Agency had decided that the Australians had been too close to the British, resulting in their secret intelligence operations often being compromised.

'What do you expect, Sam,' the other man responded, feeling the frustration of not being permitted to just move in and resolve the mess as they would have before Johnson became President. 'Our inexperienced friends Down Under were not even aware that the very man who virtually co-founded their Secret Service was not just a former nazi collaborator but also served the goddamn Russkies for years before he was isolated.'

'Well, what are we going to do with this lot then?' the ADSEA Head asked in an almost perfunctory manner. He knew what he would do had the decision been his alone to take.

'What we always do, Sam. What we always do, goddamnit!' As Assistant Director, Australia and New Zealand, his work load had suddenly doubled since the Brits had enticed their Commonwealth brothers into joint operations against the Indonesian 'Crush Malaysia' campaign. Until President Soekarno started playing with the Soviets, his sphere of operations had been relatively uneventful. He, too, was tired. Tired of the bullshit and tired of having his hands tied when there was so much he could have done to rectify many of the 'situations' which had suddenly pushed his distant Pacific area into a 'hot' status.

'We will have to take them out of the loop until they rectify the problem.'

'Why for godsakes don't we just goddamn tell them?'

'The Director feels that with the Vietnam involvement building up we will need their international support. Besides, we can

continue to contain any damage 'Finger Jar' may be responsible
for by moving into a direct relationship with him. It would be more
beneficial to keep him as one of our 'friendlies' by alerting him
discreetly to the information we hold. Should the Aussies move to
replace him, God knows who they would select as his successor.
Besides, we're getting used to the Brits screwing up. It's just bad
luck that the Australians are so dependant on their relationships. I
wouldn't touch another British agent for the next generation after
what that asshole Maclean and his playmates did to their Intelligence Service, not to mention ours.'

'So we just sit back and not inform their Prime Minister that his
most senior Intelligence Chief has not only compromised himself
and his Department, but possibly the domestic agency as well?'

'No. Not even that. As far as we are able to determine, he's been
very careful. Apart from the Bangkok fairy he visits, we have no
other evidence that he has similar liaisons outside Australia. As
for what he does on home territory, we have only assumptions to
go on as there has been no evidence of 'Finger Jar' breaking the
law in his own country. Not even the hint of any homosexual activity. Let's hope that he keeps it that way. I, for one, would not
wish to be involved in the decision-making process which would
necessitate any extreme action. Our jobs are difficult enough and,
if I'm right about Lyndon B. Johnson and his Texas oil friends, we
can expect more and more escalation in the Indochina conflict.' He
paused for a moment as the memory of Kennedy's assassination
flashed through his mind. At the time of his death, American losses
in Vietnam were almost negligible, the sudden escalation pumping American losses through the roof. The ADSEA believed that
the new Administration would continue to increase American presence in Asia in what could be a futile attempt to encircle Ho Chi
Minh. The United States would need domestic and international
public opinion to support their war effort.' The bottom line is, we
will need to maintain the very best relationships possible with our
inexperienced friends from Down Under, as they say.'

'What about Indonesia, Sam?' he coughed, cursing the habit
which needed almost three packs per day. Sometimes he wished
he could have a quiet moment with that 'Marlboro Man.'

He coughed again and his opposite number waited patiently.
He looked at his old friend. The word was that he probably

wouldn't make it to year's end. 'Do we beef up our presence?'

Samuel John Forrester looked at his friend and sighed. No one really understood what the hell was going on there. They had penetrated almost every known apparatus of government, placed their agents in sensitive positions, financed the hell out of the place and still all they got was a load of crap intelligence as to who was doing what and why! They had more than fifty operatives active in the arena and he could guarantee, based on the intelligence he had seen flowing through over the past eighteen months, that not one of the so-called experts knew what the hell they were talking about! He just felt so frustrated with the lack of professional reporting. It tore at his gut. When he remembered the amount of 'green' that had been dropped to grease the information flow, he wanted to throw up. The so-called 'intelligence' which he had personally evaluated was just a bunch of crap. In his opinion, they had no real representation in situ and, because the White House had refused to acknowledge Soekarno as a real threat to global peace, much of his resources had been redirected to Laos and Cambodia.

'Sure,' he said, 'let's send in another dozen agents so they can sit on their green asses and justify their presence with the crap this Agency is in dire threat of drowning under!' He rubbed his tired and pulsating temples. God, he wished he could have one of those damn cigarettes. 'There's so much shit on file right now it would take more goddamn desk officers to evaluate than you could fit into Yankee Stadium. Whatever happened to quality, for Chrissakes?' His heavy chest sucked in a large amount of air as he placed his head between his huge hands and rubbed his jowls briefly. 'The short answer is, no. There is no budget. Soekarno has moved down in priority because now the Pentagon has persuaded our Executive Branch that 'Nam needs all of our attention right now.' He rubbed his face briskly again, then leaned back into the uncomfortable chair. 'It seems that we must do with what we have.' His tired and bloodshot eyes peered across the table at the other sector officer.

'Okay. I've got it,' the other man responded wearily. 'We'll hold any action in abeyance until this asshole craps in his own nest. Is that it?' he asked, referring to Bradshaw.

'Sorry, Pete. That's about it.' He looked down and suddenly rolled his head to exercise the tight neck muscles which threatened to lock his head in one permanent position.

'Fine, Sam. Hope he doesn't become an expensive asset, that's all!'

'Me too, Pete. Me too,' the weary Assistant Director sighed.

Chapter 9

1965, Indonesia

Subuh had just departed, leaving the President in a foul temper. The Palace staff could hear his tirade from the next level and they knew it would be an unpleasant day for all. Whispered voices carried news of the unusual outburst through the Palace corridors and, within a very short time, the story was circulating throughout the halls of most Government departments.

The President had summoned the respected figure to his office. He had wanted to know why the man had been in the habit of receiving foreign nationals who, according to the Indonesian Intelligence Co-ordinating Agency, BAKIN, were obviously foreign agents. Soekarno had exploded when he had first read the list which, unbeknown to the President, had been provided by the Soviet KGB Station Chief in the USSR Embassy, through one of their contacts in BAKIN. There were at least a dozen American names contained in the damaging report. According to Soebandrio, one of his confidants in the intelligence community, having examined the report, informed him that many of the foreign names listed were known representatives of foreign intelligence services, the majority being from the CIA. The President warned Subuh to be more discriminating in the selection of his *bule* followers.

Minutes after this uncontrolled burst of anger, Soekarno had immediately regretted what happened. Such behaviour was atypical for a Javanese and this had caused him to lose face. Indonesians favoured discussion and consensus. The President was chastened by his own behaviour and, to mollify the situation, he had then taken Mohammed Subuh and hugged him warmly.

Soebandrio had remained in the adjacent room until Subuh had left. Having heard the President's harsh attack just minutes before,

137

he was reluctant to show his face just in case Soekarno was having one of his temper tantrum days. The Palace staff had observed recently that such incidents were occurring more and more frequently, and they realised that the Crush Malaysia war effort was mainly responsible for their leader's volatile outbursts. Soekarno felt that he had been betrayed by the Military. He had been embarrassed by their failures and refused to accept that the Indonesian soldiers could not defeat the Malays in the jungles of Borneo. All he had heard for the past months had been lame excuses as to why the elite of his forces had been unsuccessful in their campaign to take Sabah or Sarawak, on the northern side of Indonesian Kalimantan. Troop losses had been astonishingly high. Morale had deteriorated severely amongst his forces, and rumblings of dissatisfaction could be heard along the corridors of the Department of Defence.

Soekarno realised that his position would be seriously weakened should his Crush Malaysia effort fail. He blamed the British for he knew that they were supporting the Malaysian resistance throughout the newly formed Federation.

'*Sialan*,' he muttered, believing the Tengku had betrayed him. Soekarno was convinced that the Malaysian Federation was an attempt by the British to encircle Indonesia, and he had no choice but to destroy their efforts. He would sit alone and listen to many of the foreign broadcasts. He despised the Voice of America and British BBC for their attacks. They accused him of being erratic, confused, and a threat to world peace. As these broadcasts increased, so too did his own radio sessions with Radio Republik Indonesia. Whenever they called him a tyrant he would respond by accusing the West of neo-colonial and imperialist motives. Soekarno understood that he must assert his own and Indonesia's claim to regional leadership. The Asian political sphere had changed dramatically over the past fifteen years.

Soekarno understood that British Empire influence over its former colonial states had waned considerably . The concept of the Malaysian Federation was, he believed, an attempt to re-establish the European presence and prevent Indonesia from expanding its own sphere of influence regionally. He desperately needed to succeed with his policy of Confrontation, as domestic issues were overwhelmingly in need of such a distraction. The President was convinced that *Konfrontasi* provided the solution to all of his major problems.

Soebandrio entered the large room where Soekarno had just finished his meeting with Subuh. He tried to determine whether the time was appropriate for him to raise the issue of replacing some of the anti-Communist Military commanders. He had planned to use their recent losses as an excuse to have these senior officers posted to less influential positions. The *Partai Komunis Indonesia* had increased its power base considerably and now needed to develop a Fifth Power to sit alongside the Four Armed Forces.

The concept had been proposed initially by Aidit, the Party Chairman whose audacious plan to arm five million workers and ten million peasants would place the PKI in a position of strength which even the military could not oppose. The communists must have control of their own militia if they were to control the country. Soebandrio was concerned, as were his comrades in the Party, that their President may not survive long enough for them to achieve their goals. Already Soekarno's health had deteriorated. The long years he had served in prison had not helped and recently he had complained of a recurring kidney ailment. As much as they adored their leader, the Party leaders had agreed that preparations to establish a communist military force must be completed, before the country was faced with the possibility of losing its President. Soebandrio realised that, should the Great Leader of the Revolution pass away suddenly, there would be a scramble for power. A communist he might be, he thought, but before that, he was an Indonesian and understood clearly what would follow any sudden vacuum occurring in the country's leadership.

There had never been a change of government without bloodshed in his country, even as far back as the mighty kingdoms created a thousand years before. Soebandrio knew that whoever held the gun when the stage became empty would control the next leadership challenge.

For now, it was the Armed Forces under the control of many anti-Communist officers. Slowly, he and his party faithful had eroded their opposition's strengths and even orchestrated the successful placement of their own officers in command. But this had not been enough. The anti-Communist factions were strong amongst the Military.

Soebandrio had recently become aware that a group of senior ABRI officers had established their own secret alliance, a Council of Generals. He had been unsuccessful, however, in establishing the purpose of their covert activities.

He approached the President and waited. Soekarno turned, his arms crossed.

'The country is overrun with foreign agents. How did we let this happen?' The question, Soebandrio knew, was rhetorical. He waited. *'The Americans want to play on both sides of the fence. First, they offer training for our young officers and, once they have them over there and away from the influence of their motherland, they set about indoctrinating our men with their own form of imperialism.'* He unfolded his arms and bent down, resting on a carved settee. *'Do you realise that the American Embassy has almost five times the staff of any other foreign legation in our country? And what do these representatives do with their time? They subvert our leadership and plot our overthrow!'* he said angrily, punching the coffee table with his fist as his voice became raised.

He would never forgive the Americans for their past attempts to destroy Indonesian unity. The Eisenhower Administration had been incapable of understanding his neutralist position and non-aligned policies. He and the people of Indonesia had suffered at the hands of the Americans. Soekarno would always remember their attempts to support open rebellion in both Sumatra and Sulawesi, and the threat of direct invasion by their Seventh Fleet back in 1958. It was a time when dissident parties moved to create their own countries within the Republic. The Sumatrans demanded their own independence, confident that they had the support of the United States, while in Sulawesi, fighting had flared up again between government troops and local elements which were backed by the Americans out of the Philippines.

Before it was all over, his generals had committed most of the sixty-nine battalions enrolled in their three Javanese divisions to fighting on both fronts, Indonesians killing Indonesians, encouraged by the United States. Soekarno knew, at that time, as long as the Dulles brothers maintained their powerful positions as Secretary of State and Director of the CIA, his government would remain under threat. As he considered those earlier events, he shook his head sadly. Why couldn't the Americans have understood that non-alignment did not translate into anti-American activities? He had expected more from the West. Instead, they joined forces to destroy him and his country. The final straw came when the might of the American Navy was used to intimidate his people. It was an obvious ploy to provoke a reaction from his poorly-equipped country. The American Seventh Fleet had established Task Force 75 which was then ordered to Singapore. The Task Force was comprised of the heavy cruiser USS *Bremerton*, the destroyers USS *Eversole* and *Shelton*, and the attack aircraft carrier, USS *Ticonderoga* which carried two battalions of marines.

As the American Fleet assembled in Singapore, he remembered the tactics they used in their attempts to further provoke an Indonesian reaction. President Soekarno knew that rumours had been concocted by the United States Ambassador who even had the audacity to request confirmation that he intended sending AURI's planes in to bomb the Caltex oil fields in Sumatra! He was enraged when foreign radio reported US Navy officers in Singapore publicly stating that they would move into Indonesian waters and evacuate Americans from the trouble spots in Sumatra. It was an obvious attempt to justify an American invasion.

It was then he saw Nasution at his best. In a lightning pre-emptive strike, General Nasution caught the Americans off-guard. The Army Chief moved five battalions of marines and RPKAD paratroopers by air to eastern Central Sumatra. He had dropped two companies of the paratroopers directly into Pekanbaru Airfield where they discovered that the Americans had overflown just hours before, dropping weapons and supplies in anticipation of their own invasion. Nasution's men laughed with excitement when they identified the modern machine and anti-aircraft guns complete with ammunition lying there, waiting for them. Immediately the tide had turned, and Nasution had thwarted the United States' attempt to divide Indonesia into separate states.

Soekarno remembered with bitterness just how many thousands of Indonesian lives were lost due to the American tactics of covert support for the rebels, and open intimidation against his legitimate government. He turned towards Soebandrio and suddenly smiled.

'Perhaps the Americans are going to inundate us with their own people until there are more of them than us,' he joked, but his mind was troubled.

Soebandrio saw an opportunity immediately. *'Why don't we consider improving our reporting? Perhaps Bapak should consider replacing the djenderal with someone more sympathetic to the Palace. It is impossible to believe that our own Intelligence Agency has not placed these foreign elements under surveillance. And, even if that is their position, it is unacceptable. It is well known that the BAKIN leadership is anti almost everything Bapak has proposed over the past three years. Perhaps they are a part of this Council that is rumoured to have been formed by senior echelon army officers.'*

'I already know all about that!' the President snapped. *'It's Nasution again. He won't be satisfied until he becomes President. What else must I do to that damn Sumatran? Sialan,'* he growled, rising again to his feet. *'I should have locked the bangsat up when I had the opportunity. Now it is impossible.'*

Soebandrio changed tack. Soekarno had not responded to his earlier suggestion and, given the President's volatile mood, the Foreign Minister resisted promoting his own solutions. He knew that the President's wild mood swings could permanently ruin one's career. He was confident that the Intelligence Agency would be run, eventually, by a PKI loyalist.

'Why doesn't Bapak consider sending Nasution away, perhaps as Ambassador to one of the South American states?' The President re-crossed his arms and snorted at the suggestion.

'If only that were possible. Nasution has no wish whatsoever to leave. I have already had these suggestions made and he refused.'

'Do you suspect that he is really considering an Army take-over, a coup?'

'No, not again. He could not muster the support to effect such a move. Also, the Tjakrabirawa guard would not let him within sight of me without first alerting the Garrison Commander.' Soekarno suddenly looked tired. He returned to the ornately carved teak settee and lowered himself carefully. Soebandrio observed the stiffness with which the President moved. Soekarno's face was blotchy and puffed. Soebandrio noticed how thin his leader's hair had become in recent weeks. The Foreign Minister wondered if this is why the Bapak was never seen in public without his *pitji*, the black cap he wore everywhere. The President was tired. Soebandrio agreed with his own Party's Internal Committee conclusions. Soekarno could die at any time.

'Bapak,' he said softly, *'you look tired. Why don't you rest for a few days?'*

Soekarno stretched himself upright then leaned forward, placing both hands on his knees for support. *'I am leaving for Bogor tonight. I have decided to spend some days there.'*

'Bapak, may I bring Low Jooi Keng?' he asked. The Chinese doctor had already treated the President when earlier illnesses had occurred. She was considered to be one of the finest Chinese doctors in Kota. Soekarno merely nodded. He still suffered from the occasional lower back pain.

Soebandrio decided not to pursue their discussions about Nasution. He excused himself and went immediately to arrange for the doctor to be present when the Bapak arrived at the Bogor Summer Palace. He would have to hurry, he knew, as the President would most likely already be there within the hour.

* * * * * *

Major-Djenderal Soeharto stood smiling at his sixth child. He had agreed that she be called *Siti Endang*. The doctor had quietly told the general that this would be the last child. He was not unhappy with this. His wife was not a young woman any more and *Tuhan* had already given them so much blessing. Now they had three boys and an equal number of girls. He believed that this was more than mere coincidence. The religious leader Subuh also enjoyed an identical number of children! The Javanese father slowly shook his head in acknowledgement of what the older man had said. He would always be very grateful to this spiritual leader, for his prayers and, now, for his advice. In a sense he felt there was some unexplainable mystical bond between them. It was if they were brothers living in each other's shadows.

He touched his newborn softly with his right hand then left. He had matters to attend to, serious matters. He would confront Yani immediately to discover why he had not been invited to join the so-called *Council of Generals*.

* * * * * *

Lembah Njiur

The meeting was held in secret. As the evening prayers of Mahgrib had been attended to and the sky darkened in the absence of a moon, the vehicles arrived, one by one. Guards, inconspicuously dressed, manned the perimeter. Although their corps identification had been removed, the surrounding villages knew that these soldiers were members of the army's finest. They had seen them here before.

Yani was the first to arrive at Djenderal Nasution's mountain villa. The lieutenant general sat low in the back seat as his unmarked sedan passed through the hillside *kampung*. Several children were dragged unceremoniously back by a concerned mother as they had moved to see who could possibly be passing through their village at that time of the night. Thick clumps of bamboo and native grasses lined the dirt road, scratching at whatever vehicles struggled past as they bumped their way through the three kilometres of heavy rain forest. Large sections of the dangerous track had collapsed into the steep ravine causing further delays, as the military vehicles moved cautiously around the winding route.

Another hour passed before the others had all arrived. Nasution nodded to the group as he entered the villa's main lounge and waited for his *djongos* to finish serving coffee and leave the room before addressing his officers. Nasution had spent almost the entire year formulating his plan which would require the absolute support of the men who were present. As he looked around the group of Indonesia's most senior Army officers, whom he believed were his trusted supporters, Nasution experienced a sense of sadness that there were not more who could have been invited to join his Council. He smiled at Yani and then at the others before welcoming them to the meeting. He was not overly concerned with the security arrangements surrounding his villa. The men who stood guard outside would kill any intruder. Even the drivers had all been selected from this elite group of loyal soldiers.

As he looked at the men present, he wondered if any had compromised their relationship by telling others the true nature of these meetings. Nasution knew just how difficult it could be to maintain secrecy. He was conscious that several of these officers had more than their share of domestic problems and it would not be inconceivable that one of their members could unwittingly disclose his whereabouts to a wife or girlfriend. Nasution was aware that at least two of their number had difficulties maintaining their quota of wives, as well as small town-houses in Tebet, where they frequently rendezvoused with their young *tjewek*. Sometimes he wished his officers had been more monogamous in their relationships, setting a higher standard for the others but he knew that, as long as their laws and culture provided that men could take up to four wives, then it would be an impossible task to change their attitudes.

The evening air was considerably cooler than the men were accustomed to in the capital. They had all lighted their clove cigarettes, the pungent smell heavy in the sealed room. Nasution signalled with another gesture that they should come to order.

'Gentlemen', he commenced, crossing his legs and leaning back into the leather chair. *'We have much to discuss tonight. I trust you have all made arrangements?'* The generals understood. None had informed their families or others as to where they would be that evening, or when they would return. As military men such situations were rarely a problem. Those around them were accustomed to the sudden disappearance of the senior officers and accepted their absence without question. These men were all painfully aware of the consequences should there be a breach in their security. There was no doubt in their minds that they would be arrested for treason and, most probably, not even be given the benefit of a *Mahmilub*, or Court Martial. They knew that should their activities be discovered, most likely they would just disappear or suffer a tragic accident. It was an occupational hazard, serving in a Military infested with communist cadres and informants. They all murmured in response to their Commander's question.

'We should not underestimate Bung Karno and his communist friends. They are far from being stupid. As we progress with our plans, it will become even more important to our survival that you continue to be diligent, and never discuss our association with others unless we are all in agreement. We must be extremely selective in our recruitment of fellow officers and their men. The PKI has penetrated every division in our Army and even, I am sad to say, my own offices. AURI, our Airforce, can no longer be counted on for any support. This is another reason why we must agree to restrict our Council only to Army officers. The Navy is borderline and, as for the Police, ...' he raised his hands in a gesture of hopelessness.

'It would seem that we could expect support from the majority of our men. How will we contain the Airforce when the time comes?'

The question was raised by Major General Harjono, Third Deputy to the Minister and Chief of Army Staff. He was considered to be one of the brightest in the upper echelons of the Army.

'It would be imperative that we secure Halim Perdanakusumah Air Force Base and Bogor simultaneously. We wouldn't want them airborne with those damn helicopters.' The voice belonged to Major General Parman who was well known for his outspoken views regarding the President's confusing leadership. The others nodded in agreement. The Russian Hound helicopters were based just outside Bogor and could easily move into the Capital within minutes, when needed. They were well-armed and could carry more than a dozen crack troops.

'I would be more concerned with what would happen to the AURI units in Madiun and Djuanda,' Major General Soeprapto said. 'It would be impossible to maintain control over both of those fields without the support of the Diponegoro Divisional Heads. Madiun has at least five of their TU-16s fully serviceable and we could not afford to have any of their communist pilots tearing off with the bombers. Should they have support from the Surabaja Fleet Air Arm in Djuanda Field then, gentlemen, we would most likely lose East Djawa to the communist forces.'

'Our Brawidjaja units should be positioned in close proximity to both fields to ensure that we don't lose control of those AURI squadrons. I have seen what the IL-28s can do and would not want to have those aircraft in the hands of Aidit and his crowd. It would be difficult, I agree, but I don't see any alternative but to arrange to have enough of our own men close to those bases when we are ready to move.'

The officers discussed their problems and strategy well into the night. From time to time, Nasution permitted his *djongos* the opportunity to enter and refill the empty glasses of coffee and remove the overflowing ashtrays. As the men became weary and it was obvious to all that, although they had come a long way in their discussions during the course of that evening, there was still much to consider and plan.

One thing was certain. Without exception, all present had agreed that the Communist Party had to be eradicated before they gained further control of the country. They would effect a military coup d'etat. They would save the Republik Indonesia from the overwhelming tide of communism which had swept through their country, poisoning their culture. Yes, they had agreed, they would act to remove the communists and the *dalangs* behind the scene. Each man had given his solemn oath to the others that they would work towards this aim and the elimination of Dr. Soebandrio, Chairman Aidit and their chief sponsor, President for Life, Great Leader of the Revolution, Bung Karno.

* * * * * *

Canberra, Australia

When he had first been invited to the Soviet Embassy in Canberra, Harry had thought at the time just how ridiculous it would have appeared to anyone who knew of his sensitive post as Head of Australia's Secret Service, had they observed his entering the obscure building. As a matter of protocol, Harry always complied with the reporting requirements of his own Department and logged his visits with the ASIS Deputy. In so doing, he skilfully established these occasional visits as a necessary activity within the framework of his maintaining conduits with all foreign intelligence representatives in the country. The courtesy calls were never considered sinister by station watchers and other intelligence observers. To the contrary, whenever Harry made arrangements to visit the Russians, he was always driven in one of Her Majesty's Commonwealth cars. The Security Chief would merely instruct his secretary in Melbourne to make whatever arrangements were necessary, and an official car and driver would meet him at the Canberra Airport and remain at his disposal until he departed.

Amongst Canberra diplomatic circles, Harold Bradshaw was relatively unknown. His counterpart, and successor to his position, was quite a different story. The domestic agency, ASIO, was well-known and its Director often invited to formal functions throughout the foreign community which maintained a presence in the Australian capital. As Harry had previously been Deputy Director of this agency, a substantial number of Canberra observers also maintained a watching brief on the man as his former position continued to attract considerable interest.

After some months had passed, and Harry's name had all but disappeared from the Public Service Lists, most accepted that he had been shunted sideways into some obscure position of little significance within the Department of Defence. Even Susan resigned herself to her husband's move out of the social limelight, electing to maintain her own circle of friends.

Mostly, Susan Bradshaw mingled with the Broomes, through whom she met Muriel Stephenson, an old acquaintance of Alfred's. Harry seemed pleased with this particular relationship although Susan never did examine his reasons. She assumed that this was because both her husband and Alfred worked together in the Defence Department in something she had overheard them refer to as Central Plans.

Intrigue never really held the same fascination for Harry as it so obviously did for the current generation of operatives he had witnessed passing through the Head Office. He believed that many of the men and women who had graduated from the demanding courses to be selected as field agents suffered from what he'd once described as the flick syndrome. The experienced Director had seen looks of disbelief on many of the new graduates' faces when they discovered that only a small minority of their number would actually venture out into the field as agents. It was obvious from extensive psychological testing over the years that many of the applicants were initially attracted into the Service in search of excitement. Some resigned, disheartened when they discovered that the often tedious tasks they would be obliged to endure would often be the limit to whatever excitement they might experience during their careers. Very few eventually qualified to be selected as field agents. Due to the extreme secrecy which surrounded the very existence of the covert organisation, recruitment had become increasingly selective and demanding. A growing number of personnel had been exposed to the existence of ASIS. The Director knew that, in time, this would be their weakness. It was therefore imperative that security clearances were staged in conjunction with staff recruitment, training, and indoctrination, so as to avoid full exposure to candidates who were unlikely to proceed past a specific point within the administration or operational aspects of the Service. Harry felt uneasy even with the limited number who had achieved the highest level of clearance. There were less than seventy, he knew, as he could recall every name on the list buried in the Attorney-General's Department.

As the black Government limousine pulled into the driveway,

Harry instructed the driver to wait in the vehicle. It was good practice not to permit drivers to talk, especially to members of foreign legations such as this. The Director alighted and walked briskly up the dozen or so steps before being escorted directly through the foyer and up the staircase to the second floor. Harry observed that nothing had changed as he climbed the carpeted steps. It was always the same, he thought, right down to the silent escort leading the way while another followed behind. Both men looked like they could strangle gorillas with their bare hands. What was it, he thought, that made all of these people smell the same? It was probably some sort of Russian genetic deficiency. He shook his head and squeezed his nostrils together as he continued to climb the stairs. At the top of the stairway they turned down the right corridor where Harry was directed into a small room and left alone for some minutes. The escorts had closed the door behind him after he entered, but Harry could still smell their presence. He was certain that they would be waiting just outside the room if needed.

Harry looked around the familiar surroundings. He had attended meetings here before. The decor's lack of colour and the portrait of Khruschev's unpleasant features contributed to the cloud of depression which threatened to envelop him as he sat uncomfortably in the austere surroundings. He bit on a fingernail, a habit he had not suffered since early childhood.

'Welcome Comrade,' the voice boomed, startling the Director who had not expected the KGB officer to enter as silently as he had. The man's frame filled the doorway as he entered, his movements slow and almost stiff. Harry rose quickly.

'Thank you, colonel,' Harry replied, preparing himself for the vice-like grip which somehow, always left him feeling inadequate.

The Russians were in the habit of playing a little joke on their Western counterparts. The most senior KGB officer in their overseas missions always filled the post designated as Cultural Attaché. Often, it seemed, these men would play role reversals with the other staff, just to keep the host intelligence services on their toes. Harry had read a recent report in which Konstantinov had been observed driving around the city with his allocated driver enjoying the ride from the rear seat. Harry did not enjoy these childish pretences. He believed this displayed a serious character flaw and wondered what other games the KGB colonel might enjoy when others were not looking.

'We will start, then,' Konstantinov said, almost impatiently. 'We have something of interest to you, Comrade.' Harry wished the colonel would desist from referring to him as if they were ideological partners.

'I'm all ears,' Harry responded dryly. He hoped that the Russian did not want to play word games as he had in the past.

'You will remember our recent discussions with respect to Indonesia?'

'Yes, colonel. You went to great lengths, if my memory serves me correctly, to explain how disappointed Mr. Khruschev has been in relation to the Indonesian's refusal to permit the Soviet Fleet anchorage in their ports.' He hesitated. 'Has there been some change to this?' Harry was surprised. There had been nothing from his own agents to this effect.

'There may be,' the colonel replied, 'but only if we are able to push them a little.' The ASIS Director looked quizzically at the KGB officer and waited. 'We are in possession of a most interesting document, Comrade Director,' Konstantinov continued. 'Moscow has permitted me to divulge some of its contents as you will need to know this information before conducting some business for us in Indonesia.' Harry's heart rate increased slightly. He did not like the direction this conversation was heading in, not at all.

'Let me remind you of our position, Comrade Director.' Harry wondered why Konstantinov insisted on calling him 'Director'. The Soviets had no knowledge of the existence of ASIS and, as he had informed them of his move from the senior position, hoping to discourage too much further interest in his affairs, he was curious as to why the Russian continued to address him in this way. Harry tried to recall what their reaction had been when he first advised them of his apparent demotion, and he remembered that there had been relatively little curiosity. He assumed that they believed he was still involved in senior intelligence matters and accepted the apparent ruse in the normal course of intelligence business. Harry listened intently as the colonel continued.

'The Russian people have been betrayed by the Indonesians. When they pleaded for our support, we unhesitatingly gave it. When they begged for our aid, we provided whatever they needed. When their own President requested that the USSR provide military equipment, we delivered our most sophisticated weapons. And what do the Indonesians give us in return?' he asked, his voice rising angrily, 'I will tell you Comrade Director, they give us nothing. Nothing!' he added, banging the desk with his huge fist for emphasis. 'But now we have the opportunity to change all of that! Their President smiles behind his hand at us but now we will show him that we Russians still exert considerable influence in his country. What do you know about the Indonesian Army's Diponegoro Division?' he asked, unexpectedly.

Harry was momentarily caught off guard, and hesitated. 'It doesn't matter,' the colonel interrupted before Harry could respond. 'All you will need to know is here, in this file.' The Russian tapped the thick document slowly with his stubby index finger. 'I want that you should read this file,' he said, picking the bundle up with both hands and passing it to Harry.

'What! Now?' he asked incredulously, staring at the bulky package. 'It would take me all week!' he exclaimed, shaking his head.

'No, Comrade, you may read this later. We give you our permission to take this very valuable document away to read, then return to us.' The KGB colonel stared stonily, Harry shifted uneasily in his seat. He was surprised that they would even consider permitting such information out of their sight, let alone out of the building.

'When am I to return this file?'

'Three days, Comrade, three days only. After that,' he smiled and snorted at his own joke, 'as the Americans say, we will send in the cavalry,' with which, he leaned forward and slapped Harry's leg painfully. 'Now I stop joking and you will listen.' Konstantinov immediately became serious once again. 'In these documents you will see that we have edited much of what was originally contained. This was done, obviously, to protect our source.' The colonel looked over at Harry as he spoke to ensure that he had the man's undivided attention.

'What is the country of origin?' Harry asked, not expecting that the Russian would reveal such information.

'The United States,' he said clearly, his face showing the slightest indication of a smile. The KGB had obviously scored big, Harry thought. He straightened his back and waited for more. 'We have successfully penetrated their Pentagon at the highest level,' he announced, waiting for Harry's reaction. There was none.

The Australian Intelligence Chief resisted smiling. If anyone had been penetrated, it would have been the Soviets, he scoffed silently. Even if they had successfully compromised some cipher clerk of a junior administrator, they would always be vulnerable to the possibility that they had been played by the clever men at Langley. Junior officials were often deliberately placed within reach of Soviet agents with the intent to confuse or lay bait for bigger fish.

Harry was disappointed with what he had just heard. He was surprised that such a senior player had been sucked into what would inevitably be a typical CIA operation. Konstantinov sensed the reaction and moved his head forward slightly, his upper lip curled as he spoke.

'No, Comrade, do not assume that we Russians are all stupid!' he almost hissed. 'We have a copy of one of their field agent's reports. The information we have was not sourced in the usual manner. We now have a most reliable source ensconced within the American Department of Defence — specifically, at the Pentagon itself.'

Harry showed surprise. It was not like Konstantinov to disclose so much unless their source had already been repatriated — or killed! His interest rose as he opened the file and identified markings and other verification with which he was most familiar. CIA Intelligence exchange continued between the Western Alliance and, on more than one occasion, Harry had sighted identical markings and references on documents provided by his counterpart in the United States. He read on, turning the page as he scrutinised the information and, as his excitement grew, he flipped through the remaining pages to see if there was some way he could authenticate the data. He knew that this would be practically impossible. He looked up at the colonel almost in disbelief. The Attaché had watched Harry searching through the bundle impatiently and now sat with a thin smile on his lips.

'This is incredible!' Harry said, knowing that what he held in his hands was most probably an excellent example of the finest intelligence gathering he had seen for some time.

'We will talk more. First, we will take a vodka.' Harry was about to refuse. He rarely drank before evening but remained silent as he realised that the colonel wished to celebrate. He didn't hear the buzzer but knew that there must have been one somewhere within the Attaché's reach for suddenly, taking Harry by surprise, the door snapped open and the colonel barked an order in Russian to one of his minders. The man returned immediately with a full bottle and two glasses. The colonel dismissed the huge shape, opened the vodka and filled both glasses almost to the brim.

He handed one to Harry. 'Russia,' was all he said before downing the entire contents. Harry followed, wishing he was elsewhere. The colonel refilled the glasses. The Australian knew it would be impossible to refuse. 'To the Party,' the Russian offered, once again emptying his glass. Again, Harry complied. Konstantinov looked pleased with himself as he filled the two glasses, this time, only to half. Harry sighed and accepted the measure one more time. He waited for the Russian to offer the toast. Konstantinov smiled and held the half measure up and clinked glasses with his co-conspirator. 'To the Diponegoro Regiment,' he said, drinking the vodka quickly before banging the glass on the desk. Harry followed, hoping as his brain commenced its downhill slide that this would be the final toast.

'Comrade Director,' the colonel started, 'there is going to be a coup d'etat in Indonesia!' Harry looked incredulously at the Soviet colonel.

'A coup?' he asked, sure that he had misheard. 'In Indonesia?'

'Yes, a coup!' the colonel continued, seemingly enjoying himself with the revelation. 'And we are to ensure that it is successful, Comrade Harry!' he added, the vodka taking effect. A cold chill passed down the ASIS Chief's spine. He heard the statement and knew that he wouldn't enjoy what was to follow. 'You, my Aussie friend, are going to help Mother Russia recover some of the ground we have lost. Okay?'

'What do you have on your mind, colonel?' he asked cautiously. The effects of the vodka slurring his words. He silently admonished himself for permitting the Russian to manipulate him as he had. 'How can I help the USSR with its problem?'

'You, Comrade Harry,' he replied, leaning forward as he moved his weight around to a more comfortable position, 'will assist the KGB by supporting the elements in the Indonesian Army who plan to take control of their Government!'

'The Diponegoro Command?' he asked sceptically, 'you really

believe that the Diponegoro Command has the capacity to effect such an incredible task? It sounds like foolishness!' Harry snapped, immediately wishing he had been more selective in his word choice.

'You will read this report,' the colonel insisted, once again prodding the thick document with his finger. 'You will understand more when you have completely examined the information there. The Americans have already placed one man inside. Do you think that they would bother if there was not substance behind the initial reports. Look for yourself. Their own agent's reports are included.'

Harry was stunned. He flicked through the file but was unable to locate the specific document to which the colonel referred. Impatient, the Russian snapped the file out of his hands and rummaged through the pile of data until locating what he needed. He turned the bundle around for Harry to read. 'There!' he barked, cheeks reddened from the alcohol.

It was all there. Harry shook his head in amazement. It just seemed incredible that the information even contained the agent's name. The report described a number of meetings that had taken place, where they were held and who contributed to the secret assembly of officers intent on revolution. He started to read on when the file was snatched back out of his hands.

'Later,' the colonel snapped. 'Now it is time for your to listen.'

The delayed effects of the vodka had thrown a blanket across Harry's mind. He no longer felt threatened by the Russian; after all, he remembered, they were in his country, not some back street off Lenin Square. Then he remembered that it was imperative he maintain his composure. After all, he was still on foreign soil, so to speak.

'Mother Russia has exposed its soul to these backward people. Our investment cannot just be counted in terms of currency, even though the USSR has given the Indonesians more than two billion American dollars in aid, military hardware and credits. There is a great deal more at stake here. Comrade, listen!' he commanded, moving to the edge of his seat, dangerously close to tipping the balance with his huge frame. It was as if the effects of the three oversized vodkas had already dissipated. 'The Indonesians are no different to the other satellites which embarked on a path of Communism as a means of satisfying the masses. The Chinese, Koreans, Laotions, Vietnamese and even the Malays have played with our great ideology, corrupting its very essence to favour their own interpretation and domestic needs. Already we have seen Chairman Mao Tse Tung lead six hundred million peasants away from Moscow's influence. Ho Chi Minh has sided with his great enemy and now, having sucked our country dry and unable to repay our great gifts, the Indonesians follow some poorly-conceived axis which they believe will deliver the whole of Asia into their revisionist hands.'

Harry struggled to concentrate but did so, knowing that what the colonel said was essential to the document he now held tightly in both hands.

'This Soekarno believes that he can now distance his country from Russia while maintaining some ridiculous concept of what he calls ...' he hesitated, searching for the correct word. 'NASAKOM. Yes. That's what the fool calls it, NASAKOM! This man has taken Communism and twisted its very heart, preaching his revisionist version to accommodate all that contradicts the true meaning of Communism. The people are obviously confused. How could they accept this man's corrupt teachings? That he endeavours to create a new ideology by throwing Nationalism, Religion and Communism into one melting pot only proves that the man is not a true thinker!' Konstantinov paused for a moment. Harry grimaced as the colonel looked at the half-empty bottle. Moments passed before the KGB officer continued, as if he had rehearsed this dialogue well before.

'This man, Soekarno, he is not good for Russia.' Again the colonel paused. 'He has permitted the Indonesian Communist Party to grow, and it is now the third largest in this world. You might ask, Comrade Harry, is this not a good result for World Communism? We would answer you, no! The Indonesian communist is not like a true communist. He thinks he can pray to his gods when in need and play with communism only when it suits. Their President has taught them this. Now, it seems, he may just be successful in developing this very dangerous axis between the Asian communist leaders. Soekarno is close to developing a very powerful alliance which, if he is successful, would run from Indonesia, through Malaysia, into Ho Chi Minh's North Vietnam, Laos and even Cambodia, leading up to the welcome arms of Chairman Mao.'

'Why would this be detrimental to Russia?' Harry felt obliged to ask. He was confused by Konstantinov's presentation.

'The Asian communist deals in revisionist Marxist theory. That is what is dangerous to world communism. Look at Castro, he is a real communist, not like these pretenders who merely play with the words in order to create even more power for themselves. No! Soekarno and his friends are not real communists. They have created a pseudo-communist ideology to accommodate the uneducated peasants who follow their leadership blindly. How can they be communist and still embrace their gods? How does this Soekarno believe it possible to follow pure communist doctrine when immersed in religious dogma, nationalism and whatever else he feels necessary to feed to his followers?' Konstantinov paused. 'They destroyed their only true communists during the Madiun Rebellion.'

'Then why do the Soviets continue to support the Asian communist leaders?' Harry managed to ask.

'Because we must keep our foot firmly inside the door.' The colonel reached out and held the vodka bottle, tipping it slightly to examine its contents. 'And,' he continued, 'because the Americans are moving to establish themselves firmly in Vietnam and Indonesia, we are prepared to overlook the idiosyncrasies of the Indonesian leadership for the time being. Also, we have not been paid and must protect our substantial investments. We have given those people our technology, our money, and our friendship. They have repaid us by refusing to acknowledge their debt and have placed even greater demands on the Soviet Union. Now they want steel mills to be completed in Tjilegon, dams to be constructed throughout the island of Java and many, many more infrastructure investments which run into billions of valuable foreign exchange.

'It is quite apparent to Moscow that, unless there is a clear change in leadership within the Indonesian Military, the Americans will be encouraged to displace our country's interests and Russia will no longer lead the world's communist effort. In the event that Soekarno's Military leadership continues to make overtures to the United States and such efforts remain unchecked, the Americans will develop a defensive strategy involving Vietnam and Indonesia which will result in an American presence in Soekarno's country even before he realises what has happened.'

'Most of the country's generals have already been recruited by the enemy. There is a very strong possibility that they could tear the leadership away from Soekarno. We would prefer that he remain in power, preferably only as a figurehead, even though our best interests are not being served. At least, the Americans would not be able to swoop in and take our rightful place in the country.'

'These officers from the Diponegoro Regiments. Why would you want to support them?' Harry asked, still confused.

'These soldiers have turned against their superiors who have grown fat from the funds sent by the Americans. They have sold their country to the CIA. There are many of these senior officers who sit in Djakarta, enjoying their large houses and cars, sniffing around after the Americans who inundate the capital as we speak. We must support these soldiers. They are our only choice. Without them Russia will have no future not just in Indonesia, but all of Asia. Should the Americans gain a foothold there, it will be impossible to maintain our relationship with these people. Already we have seen the British remove the Communist Party from Malaysia and even Singapore. Next, the Americans will endeavour to support the South Vietnamese until even Ho Chi Minh is forced back into the mountains of North Vietnam. No! Mother Russia has decreed that this will not happen.'

'What makes you believe that the Diponegoro Command, assuming what is in this report is reliable, will agree to any relationship with the Russians?'

'We have no idea whatsoever what their reaction would be.' He hesitated, and immediately Harry felt that Konstantinov was lying. He was hiding something. 'We have decided that there is no real risk. It would be just as favourable for us should they be successful in eliminating the pro-American lobby. That will give us the opportunity to reassess our approach and commitments in order to consolidate our presence in the country. The pro-American generals must go! We are fortunate that the opportunity has arisen,' he said, once again pointing at the file, 'and we may be able to accelerate their removal. You must go to Indonesia and talk to these men.'

Harry looked at the colonel. The alcohol's effects had caused a slight dull ache at the base of his neck and shoulders. He straightened his back and rolled his head gently, collecting his thoughts.

'And just what am I to say to these men when I meet them for the first time? Hello, there, I have a message from Boris, we want to support your impossible efforts to overthrow the government? For Chrissakes, colonel, who's responsible for this idiocy?' he snapped, not caring that he may have overstepped the mark. The Russian's suggestion that he go to Indonesia and even attempt such a poorly-conceived attempt to win over the isolated group was beyond comprehension. Konstantinov's eyes narrowed as he glared at the ASIS Chief.

'You are no fool, yet you talk like one,' he admonished. 'Take the file, read it then return when you have formulated your approach. You are not merely being asked to carry out this task, Comrade Director, it is not as if you have a choice.'

Harry resisted responding. His temples thumped adrenaline. He felt the rage but managed to contain his feelings. What he had been instructed to do was impossible! Konstantinov had placed him in a no-win situation. If he refused, he would be exposed. If he accepted, his relationship with the Indonesians could be at risk. What if they refused to deal with him again after he revealed the information he had obtained concerning their subversive activities? What if they exposed him to any one of the 'friendly' operatives already established within the target area? His life would be hanging by a thread. Harry rose to his feet, his heart filled with hate. He lifted the file and placed it almost casually, under his arm.

'Good!' The colonel exclaimed, as he also dragged himself upright. He reached into his coat pocket and extracted an envelope. 'Expenses,' he merely said, extending his arm.

Harry glared at the Russian. How he despised this man. He hated Konstantinov for what he was and for the power he exerted over him. But he despised himself even more. He took the envelope and buried it inside his coat. An hour later Harry Bradshaw returned to Melbourne.

* * * * * *

Melbourne

'We are acting alone on this one,' Harry advised the surprised Director of Military Intelligence. 'The Prime Minister has agreed.'

The statement required no response; the DMI understood that the PM's concurrence was sufficient.

'May I ask why, Harry?' General Thorpe asked, knowing that whatever the response from the cloak and dagger Chief, the answer would most likely to be a deliberately distorted truth. He sometimes wondered why he even bothered.

'John,' Harry started, clasping his hands together while preparing his response. He needed the DMI's support which, he knew, would not be forthcoming unless he could convince the Army Director that what he was being asked to do would not compromise his own Department. Harry had not endeavoured to establish any real personal relationship with any of the three Military Intelligence Directors. He considered these men as necessary conduits for the dissemination of intelligence material but, as they were not directly involved in the direct collection of intelligence as were his field operatives, Harry encountered considerable difficulty when seeking their support for his clandestine operations. Australia's signals intelligence was virtually under the direct control of the man sitting across the highly polished mahogany table but it was not this area of support the ASIS Chief needed.

'The PM agrees that our activities should be more in support of our Commonwealth interests than, say, our American cousins. The US sees global interests only in terms of themselves against the Soviets. They really don't give a damn in respect to Australia's own position. Their world revolves around the US of A. The PM is quite adamant. We will do this one alone because, if we don't, our national interests will be damaged beyond repair. You know yourself, John, how bloody casual the Americans can be about Australia's interests. They have been beating their own drum ever since they pushed the Japs back from our shores.' Harry rubbed his face with one hand; he was tired. It was not obligatory that he explain to the DMI. He knew that it was just good politics to do so.

'The Americans want control over all of our Intelligence in the target area,' he lied, knowing that this would be sufficient for full DMI support. None of the agencies would stand for such a development. S.E. Asia was Australia's backyard and the Military would insist that they maintain some semblance of independence in the region.

'And you have convinced the PM that we could end up out in

the cold again?' The DMI's reference was to Vietnam. The Australian Forces had only been involved after the Americans required international support for their continuing presence in Indochina. The Australian Military had wanted to send their own advisers years before but the Americans had politely refused. Now, it appeared, the Yanks wanted control over Australia's intelligence gathering services in Indonesia. No, the DMI concluded, not while he had any influence in the matter.

'Exactly,' Harry lied again, while nodding his head.

'Well that's it then, as far as I'm concerned. You'll have your request, Harry.'

'Thanks, John. Knew we could count on your co-operation. I will inform the PM,' he added, both men rising to their feet and shaking hands. The DMI departed leaving Harry to sit and contemplate on his next course of action. He returned to his desk and commenced preparations for the next step in his complicated scheme. Now that he had secured the services of the Army's Military Attaché in Djakarta as an acceptable cover, he believed that what he planned was achievable.

Harry rose and went to his own safe and played with the double tumbler action until both combinations permitted the heavy handle to open, revealing the most secret papers he hoarded there. Selecting a thin brown file without any security markings to designate its sensitivity, Harry informed his secretary that he was not to be disturbed until lunch. Then he sat down and read the file once again, brooding over the damaging contents. It seemed as if only minutes had passed when his secretary, Madge, buzzed to advise him it was time for his luncheon appointment with his deputy, Anderson.

Harry returned the file and re-locked the safe. As he tested the handle to ensure that the contents were indeed securely hidden, Harry knew he would not have much time to implement his plan. He thought about those around him who would be essential to its successful realisation and sighed deeply. He hoped he could still rely on young Murray.

* * * * * *

Merdeka Square

Djakarta

The first riots occurred along Djalan Nusantara, across the canal from Pasar Baru where the majority of Djakarta's foreigners shopped. Several thousand students pushed and shoved their way along the street towards the Palace grounds, chanting as they held placards high above their heads.

'PKI, PKI,' the students sang, waving to their fellow citizens who merely moved away from the oncoming crowd of communist students from the University of Indonesia. There had been rallies all over the city, supported strongly by their Party. Chairman Aidit had encouraged the students to go to the streets and show the people just how large their numbers had grown. It was an attempt to intimidate, the populace knew, and reacted accordingly. As the large crowd dressed in white cotton uniforms and red bandannas moved toward the fringe of Pasar Baru, the Chinese shopkeepers immediately closed their premises and boarded the shop fronts to prevent pillaging. They had seen this all before and most were concerned with the growing frequency of such demonstrations.

As the young communists moved en masse along the main road chanting 'PKI, PKI' their voices could be heard across the other side of the city block, and as far as the radio station. They approached the high white-washed walls outside of which the Presidential Guards stood and watched, prepared to move should the students provoke a response. The crowd continued to move towards the main gate and the Guard Commander issued the order for the soldiers to cock their weapons. They knew that standing orders required that the first volley be fired over the demonstrators' heads but the contingent were all just as prepared to fire directly into the crowd should they attempt to enter the Palace grounds.

The communist students came slowly to a halt outside the President's offices and continued to chant, drowning out all other sounds as they called their Party's name. The soldiers stood tense, waiting for the inevitable rocks to be thrown. Minutes passed and the students moved closer to the gates, annoyed with the lack of response from within. As the students became bored with the inaction and their chanting lost rhythm, another sound could be heard faintly above the noisy mob. It was another large crowd of students, apparently moving towards the Palace gates as well, chanting loudly. The first group turned to greet their fellow students and immediately there were angry shouts as they discovered that these were not from their student union.

'Abolish the Communist Party,' the newcomers cried loudly, 'Down with Aidit!' they challenged, moving towards the PKI supporters. As the large numbers of students approached, it became evident to those who watched from across the street that there would be serious trouble as the two rival factions clashed. The anti-Communist students moved forward into direct confrontation with the PKI demonstrators. Immediately, all hell broke loose as the opposing groups ran towards each other, brandishing their placards as weapons. The Palace Guards braced themselves for the inevitable. And then the rock throwing commenced.

Students reached down and picked up lumps of tar and rock which lay alongside the broken edges of the road, then hurled these with all their force at the opposing students. Within an incredibly brief period of time, the street was transformed by the savage riot. Students punched and kicked at each other brutally, boys and girls fell unseen, their agonising screams smothered by the tumultuous roar. Rocks and other missiles thrown without aim cracked heads indiscriminately, and as the injured fell they were in danger of being trampled to death.

It became impossible to distinguish between adversary and friend. The main body of rioters crushed and trampled students in the centre as it gathered momentum towards the Palace gates.

The officer of the guard shouted a command and instantly shots were fired into the air. For a brief moment there was a stunned silence, followed immediately by a roar as the students turned on the soldiers, pushing forward without fear. Incredibly, they seemed to amalgamate as one body and turned on the green-uniformed guards. As they surged towards the small contingent of guards, a hail of rocks sailed through the air, injuring several of the soldiers. Instantly, they retaliated. The second volley of shots ripped through the front line of students tearing through clothes and young bodies. Bullets penetrated deep into the astonished crowd and the air was choked with screams and gunfire. Panic-driven students fell over each other in a futile attempt to escape. But the soldiers did not stop firing, and scores of students fell with each volley. Suddenly the ear-piercing rapid fire ceased. The soldiers had run out of ammunition.

The more fortunate students stumbled in terror, away from the bloody killing ground, anxious to flee before the soldiers changed magazines and recommenced firing. Those who could ran without looking back, knowing that they were leaving friends behind, friends who still screamed in fear for their lives. Friends who would surely die when the soldiers opened fire once again. A loud shout shook those who remained and they tensed, waiting for the next barrage of bullets. Another shout, this time louder, and the soldiers obeyed the command. The officer stepped forward and positioned himself directly in front of his men and barked another order, removing the automatic from its holster to ensure compliance to his command.

The disgruntled guards paused, considering their positions; then turned and moved back inside the Palace grounds. Their Captain moved swiftly, re-locking the large iron gates as he issued more orders to the men. He then turned and viewed the scene before him. He attempted to count the bodies which lay spread across the wide road. There were several mounds he could see, where students had fallen to the ground together, dead as they hit the road. When the young officer counted thirty, he swallowed, with great difficulty, then continued the bloody task. It was difficult to know how many had died from being crushed in the panic to escape, but the Guard officer understood that protocol dictated his report should only apportion the most conservative number of dead to gun fire.

Later he would indicate in his report that two students had been accidentally shot as they had grabbed the guards' weapons while the rest had died as a direct result of the bloody clash between the opposing factions. The bodies had been quickly collected by an Army detail and disposed of without ceremony behind the city's notorious Senen Prison. Grieving families and friends would be told that many of the bodies had been so badly mutilated that identification had been impossible. They would never see their children again.

* * * * * *

Murray had moved quickly to investigate the demonstrations once word had arrived at the Embassy. This was one of his functions. Being fluent in *Bahasa Indonesia*, he was considered the only appropriate officer to send out whenever these disturbances occurred. Murray would take one of the Embassy Holdens and drive directly to wherever the students held their rallies. Often he would walk alongside their flank, talking to them and getting a feel of what the rank and file really thought they were achieving with their demonstrations. This provided Murray with the opportunity to photograph student leaders in action.

Although many of the faces he identified were those of friends he had made over the years, he soon discovered there were now many more he could not recognise, who had become prominent with the accelerated spread of communism throughout the Republic. Murray was disciplined and understood that his role was that of an observer. It was essential that he not become embroiled in any of the student activities. He was now a diplomatic officer and could not demonstrate allegiance to any of the participating factions. He was there only to collect information and then provide an assessment of the situation. The intelligence reports detailing his observations would be his sole responsibility.

Murray had instructed the driver to pull over near Djalan Veteran, from where he walked the remaining few hundred metres towards Djalan Nusantara. The driver was relieved that the *tuan* had not insisted on taking the vehicle any further.

'*Aduh,*' he had thought when ordered to take *Tuan* Murray down past Merdeka Square. The entire driver pool had heard the news about the latest demonstration and none wished to venture outside. Often their cars were stopped by the demonstrators then wrecked. It was a terrifying experience, Achmad knew. He had already been caught twice and was extremely nervous, knowing that he was to take the young *tuan* down to take a look at the excitement. Achmad just couldn't understand why this *tuan* always went out in search of trouble.

'*Achmad. You wait here for me, understand?*' he had instructed the agitated driver.' *Tentu sadja, tuan!*' he had responded. '*Of course I'll wait here,*' he thought to himself silently, '*only a fool would proceed any further.*'

Murray carried the small Minolta in his left hand and walked quickly along the small side street until reaching the corner of Djalan Nusantara. He stood for a few moments observing the military vehicles pouring past, heading west in the direction of the Palace gates. He assumed that the road would be closed off within minutes and so elected to cross the small bridge which led directly down through Pasar Baru. Once on the other side Murray turned to the left and followed the narrow lane bordering the *kali*, and running parallel with Djalan Nusantara which was then on the other side of the canal. He walked quickly, concerned that he had missed the demonstration. Minutes later, he was pleased that he had. As Murray neared the roadway opposite the Palace Guards, he could clearly see the aftermath of what had obviously been a serious clash. Even at that distance he could make out the bodies lying like large broken dolls, scattered across the road and, in some places, already stacked in piles awaiting collection.

He counted the dead as accurately as he could, his task made more difficult by the soldiers as they moved the bodies around, dragging some in one direction while dumping others together. Soon it was almost impossible to differentiate between bodies he had, and had not yet counted. Murray estimated there were approximately fifty to sixty dead. There did not appear to be any wounded. He assumed that they had either escaped or had been taken to hospital by the Military Police who appeared to be actively conducting the clean-up. Murray lifted his camera again and took several more shots before being startled by a soldier who came clearly into his lens view, holding his rifle to his shoulder and peering down the sights directly at Murray.

He froze instantly, perspiration suddenly covering his body as he waited for the crack of the rifle shot. Slowly he lowered the camera and turned away. He knew that the soldier would continue to watch until he moved far enough away to satisfy the man that his presence was not threatening. Although he knew that he needed to get the hell out of there as quickly as possible, Murray also knew that to run would be a major mistake, and would most likely provoke the soldier into taking a shot. He walked slowly, the trickle of sweat flowing down his spine, his body tense with the knowledge that he could be shot in the back at any moment. As he approached the rusty steel pedestrian bridge Murray permitted his head to turn slightly, just enough to provide a quick glance from the corner of his right eye. The soldier was still watching, his rifle resting in a less aggressive stance. Murray decided to leave the scene; his presence was obviously considered provocative to these soldiers who probably wouldn't understand his right to Diplomatic Immunity in the event that they should challenge him again. Most of these men were poorly educated and easily excited.

He elected to return to the car and report back to the Station Chief. A thought crossed his mind and he frowned. He had identified the PKI banners lying around and suddenly wondered if Yanti or any of her group had been involved. Murray sighed. He would drive over to the quarters where she boarded, once he had filed his report. He felt tired and leaned back to rest as they drove back through Tjut Mutiah into Menteng.

It was only when the vehicle entered the Embassy grounds ten minutes later that his hands began to shake. As he climbed out of the back seat, Achmad held the door open, permitting the *tuan* to lurch forward and away from the Holden just in time as he commenced heaving, the shock suddenly taking effect.

'Tuan Murray,' the driver called in surprise. It was quite uncommon for the foreigners to become ill in such a short journey, even from his driving. *'Can I help you, tuan?'* he asked sincerely.

Murray remained bent over for some minutes before recovering his composure. As he walked up the steps and into the lobby he realised just how lucky he had been to return unharmed. He went immediately into the inner sanctum and delivered his report directly to the new Station Chief. He did not mention his near fatal encounter and, as he lay awake that night reliving those few terrifying seconds, Murray questioned his own judgement as to why he had omitted this information, but decided that as they had never really established any real rapport, the other man might have just scoffed at his retreat.

Murray could not understand how Alan Davis had managed the promotion. Wells had been a capable and very experienced Station Chief. He was not confident that Davis, now that he had returned to Djakarta to fill the Chief's position, would be able to handle the pressures associated with the job. Unable to sleep, he read until the early hours of the morning when he decided to take his *mandi*, change and go back into the Embassy to catch up on outstanding reports.

As Murray's current position was described as Second Secretary Political, having moved up one level since his arrival, it was essential to his cover that he perform some of the more mundane tasks associated with the position he held. At the moment, he felt inundated with the tedious tasks related to the United Nations Family Planning Programme for which, much to his dismay, he had been delegated the responsibility of maintaining a watching brief for the Australian Government counterpart agencies. This, and similar functions, consumed a considerable portion of his time and he discovered that once backlogged, it was almost impossible to recover from the mountains of reading material which poured incessantly into his receiving tray.

Murray decided to take a *betjak* from his residence on Djalan Serang to the Embassy where he found all the security guards asleep. He just smiled and crept past them quietly, as the duty-driver swung into the driveway and dimmed his lights. He jumped out of the station-wagon, left the engine running and hurried towards Murray.

'*Pagi, tuan,*' he said, his face reflecting the long night shift he had worked. '*Tuan Murray, would you accept this cable please? It would save me having to drive out to Kebajoran to wake Tuan Evans and then bring him back to the Embassy.*'

Murray willingly accepted, just to help out. He knew what it was like to be the duty officer as the chore came around every two months and created havoc with one's social life. Communications were very poor. Apart from the covert radio installed in the rear of the Naval Attaché's office, there were no direct links to the international community, resulting in an inadequate system of cables and telexes sent on a scheduled basis from governments to their embassies in Indonesia. Even highly classified material was moved in this manner.

The Duty Driver would check the central post office on an hourly basis. Whenever such a communication was received, it was his responsibility to awaken the rostered officer and have him taken to the Embassy immediately to carry out the decoding. The officer would commence deciphering the message in the usual manner in the Central Registry where a number of machines had been installed for this complicated process. The first line of every message identified a name followed by a security classification which would indicate whether the officer may or may not proceed. The double encoding system ensured that the integrity of the signal's contents remain intact.

Murray strolled up the steps, unlocked the front doors, checked his mail box, then went through to his own section, unlocking then relocking doors as he proceeded. Most Embassy staff could enter their own sections at any time, as a series of combination locks provided accessibility only to those who were given the numerical sequences to the tumbler security system. A number of alarms had been installed throughout the old building — not that this would prevent a well-organised band of thieves from breaking through the front doors into the main lobby. Anyway, they would not find anything there. The sensitive sections were buried in the building's bowels, with the walls, floors and ceilings all recently constructed from reinforced concrete. All classified material was locked away in huge, room-size Chubb safes providing a formidable challenge to any who believed they could steal Australia's secrets.

Murray turned lights on as he ventured into his own section, leaving them to burn brightly as he settled down beside the boring unclassified material left to the side of his desk some weeks before. He opened the small envelope and spread the five-digit coded message in front, betting to himself that this was probably another of those 'urgent' messages for the Air Attaché's office merely advising that one of the RAAF aircraft overflying to Vietnam had changed pilots and felt the necessity to advise the Embassy in case, he assumed, the plane fell out of the sky and embarrassed everyone. He muttered to himself, observing the cable, knowing that he would have to go through to the Registry and hook up the machines.

He did this and, fifteen minutes later as the heading was deciphered, he discovered that the first line indicated the message was, coincidentally, addressed to him personally. This required that he return to his own section and insert the relevant tapes into another set of decipher equipment. He patiently threaded the two tapes and punched the start button. As the machines clacked away in unison, interpreting the five-digit code imprinted on the narrow tape in the form of puncture marks, Murray was surprised to see that the message bore the highest clearance and was addressed personally to him. He read the two-part message:

TOP SECRET

First code batch for Registry.
Pass to addressee only for final code.
This communication is for the addressee only:
Sec/Sec/Political. Pls pass urgently.

TOP SECRET
OYSTER - MO9
ADDRESSEE EYES ONLY.
ADDRESSEE: M.I. STEPHENSON
SENDER:DIRECTOR. ASIS
Date:7th February, 1965

TEXT: YOU ARE TO PROCEED TO SINGAPORE FOR ONE-ON-ONE
DISCUSSIONS STOP MEET NEXT WEEK MAYFAIR HOTEL NOON
12TH STOP NATURE OF MEET MOST SENSITIVE STOP IN CONSE-
QUENCE YOU ARE NOT TO ENTER INTO ANY DIALOGUE WITH
OTHERS IN THE DEPARTMENT STOP WILL ADVISE YOUR SUPERI-
ORS YOU ARE ON PERSONAL LEAVE FOR TWO DAYS THOSE
DATES STOP RGDS STOP HB ENDS
TOP SECRET

Murray re-read the signal and then put the message through
the shredder. He was surprised at the contents but pleased that he
would be able to get out for a few days. He checked his watch and
when he discovered that it was already after six o'clock, he locked
up and went in search of the duty-driver. Murray decided to take
Yanti to breakfast and see what her involvement had been in relation to the ongoing PKI demonstrations that were tearing the city
apart. When he arrived at her lodgings Yanti was not there. The
old *babu* who cleaned and cooked for the students under her care
had just shaken her head when he asked to speak to her.

*'Yanti is not here. Neither are her friends. They have all gone away. I
don't know where they are. You come back tomorrow. Maybe Yanti will
return by then.'* The toothless grey-haired woman closed the door.
Murray heard the lock snap shut as he walked away.

* * * * * *

'Mahree, you haven't been out to the Community Centre for such a long time!' Ade admonished. Murray kept his arm around her shoulder as they sat together on his sofa. The residence in Djalan Serang was as grand as any of the other Embassy houses with the exception, of course, of the Ambassador's magnificent mansion on Djalan Teuku Umar. The home contained three bedrooms, all air-conditioned, as were the oversized lounge and dining rooms. Embassy houses were allotted according to rank and position. As a Second Secretary, he was expected to entertain regularly and was provided with a suitable expense account for this purpose. Mainly, whenever Murray did entertain, the majority of his guests were Indonesian, unlike many of his fellow officers in the Embassy who mostly only invited other Europeans to their homes. He could understand their problem filling a guest list which included Indonesian guests as, at that time, very few could comprehend English.

He tickled Ade with his other hand and she responded playfully. *'I don't have as much time as before, manis!'* he said, in response to her complaint about the infrequency of his visits to the SUBUD compound. And this was true, he thought. His days were becoming longer in terms of the number of hours he was putting into building his network while maintain old relationships as well.

'But it seems you still have time for your Gerwani friends.' Ade argued.

'Look,' he started, not wishing to get into another of these discussions. *'Yanti is my friend also, you know that. I thought we'd agreed not to do this any more? Let's leave it alone, okay?'* Murray knew without looking that by now Ade would be pouting. She always did. *'Okay?'* he asked again, tickling her once again. Ade's small but strong fingers found their way to the fleshy spot under his ribs and pinched his skin fiercely, just to let him know that she was not happy with the ongoing arrangement Murray maintained with Yanti and her friends.

Ade knew that Murray was sleeping with his communist friend but blocked that out of her mind. It was his right, she thought, reluctantly, even though she also spent the night in his bed at least once every week. Ade looked at Murray and decided that, rather than risk losing him altogether by insisting on his disassociation with Yanti and his other communist friends, she would just persevere until he realised that the *Gerwani* were not only dangerous, but also untrustworthy.

'*When will you return from your trip?*' she asked.

'*I'm only going for a few days, manis. I will return from Singapore before the weekend.*' Murray knew it was pointless in hiding his destination. These were secrets that were impossible to keep in such a closely-knit community as the Australian Embassy. Once he had booked his ticket, it seemed that everyone in the Chancery knew he was going to Singapore for a few days. Immediately, he was inundated with requests to purchase this and that for wives, as the shopping in Djakarta provided few of the luxury items so readily available in 'Singers' as they affectionately called the shoppers' paradise. Murray accepted the small orders, ranging from lipstick to nail polish, knowing that all Embassy officers given the same opportunity to spend a few days 'out of station' would do likewise.

'*Don't forget my oleh-oleh!*' Ade reminded him. It was customary to purchase a myriad of small gifts when one was away as these indicated to the recipients, upon return, that they had not been out of mind during the absence, however short this may have been.

'*I'll buy you some perfume,*' he teased.

'*Okay,*' Ade replied, surprising him. She left the couch and returned with fifty sen, half of one rupiah. Murray looked at the domino-sized note, worth no more than one cent Australian.

'*That won't buy you much!*' he laughed, accepting the crumpled note.

'*No, Murray, that's not to buy the perfume. It's a token gesture only. It is our custom to always pay a little something for perfume, for we believe that such a gift will cause a break in friendship unless the one you give the perfume to pays something towards its cost.*'

Murray smiled again. It seemed that he would never stop learning this country's customs. He squeezed her again, then rose and led her back into his bedroom where they remained through the rest of the afternoon. That evening Murray took the Garuda flight to Singapore and, upon arrival, went directly to the Mayfair Hotel. And Harry Bradshaw.

Chapter 10

Singapore

Murray sat comfortably in the floral-covered chair listening attentively to the Intelligence Director. His mood was solemn. Harry's revelations were, to say the least, startling.

'We have a mole, Murray. I'd never thought it possible but there it is. One of our own.'

'What makes you believe it's Davis?' he asked, still not convinced of the accusations.

'We can never be absolutely sure unless, of course, he stepped forward or confessed when confronted with the charge. It is most unlikely that any of these opportunities will arise. Rest assured, young Murray,' he said, almost paternally, 'we will cover your back at all times. If, in the event that it comes to light that Davis is not our man then, with the arrangements we have made, there would be negligible damage to the Service and, of course, Davis' career.'

'Why don't we just confront him then?' Murray asked, confused as hell. He still refused to accept that his current Station Chief was responsible for the leaks mentioned by the Director. Davis had returned to Head Office for a few short months before being selected to replace Keith Wells as Djakarta Station Chief. Although Murray disliked the man and believed him to be bigoted, these were not sufficient grounds to distrust him. He looked at Harold Bradshaw. The Director looked exhausted, the crows' feet lines now more obvious, spread like deep scars around the corner of his puffy eyes. His hair had thinned considerably since they had last met, just a few months before. Murray noticed the heavy stained fingers, evidence of the three packets of cigarettes the ASIS Chief consumed daily. He watched Harry light the smoke and draw heavily.

'What would you do in his place?' the Director asked. 'Would you just step forward and calmly place yourself in the care of Her Majesty's prisons for at least thirty years? Or would you deny any charges of impropriety, placing the onus on your accusers to produce evidence? Come on, Murray, don't you see just how bloody impossible the situation is?'

'So you intend leaving him in situ, knowing that he may be responsible for compromising the Service?' he asked disbelievingly. 'It sure as hell doesn't build confidence, Harry. That's my arse sitting over there in a sling with Davis!'

'Now you appreciate the importance of keeping him out of the information loop with what we have discussed. It is imperative that he not have access to this intelligence. Do I make myself very clear, Murray?'

'Sure,' he answered, not entirely happy with his predicament. The Intelligence Director had explained that he had already arranged through DMI in Melbourne for the Military Attaché to request Murray's services as interpreter to accompany the colonel on a brief tour through Java, visiting Indonesia's Military Commands. The request to visit had already received official HANKAM approval. The Australian colonel was not briefed on the reasons for Stephenson's accompanying him on the tour, merely that it would be so. The Embassy interpreter would be called away for the duration to create the necessary request for Murray's assistance. This would be sufficient to convince the Station Chief, Davis, that all was above board and not arouse his suspicions as to the real purpose of his Second Secretary's being seconded to the Military Attaché's office.

'Let's go over it again, Murray. I know I don't need to tell you just how damn important this is to us in Central Plans. Our necks are stretched way the hell out on this one. If we pull it off without complications, you could easily find yourself sitting in Davis' chair before the end of the year.' Murray's eyes widened. Now that was something he'd not expected to hear.

'Let's see,' he started, recalling the early morning brief. They had breakfast in Harry's room and commenced immediately after room service had responded to their request to clear the trays. 'Colonel Sulistio was trained in the States. It appears that he was recruited

174

by the boys from Langley during his tour Stateside. He returned to his Division in Semarang and moved quickly into Diponegoro Command HQ. Since then, he has maintained a steady stream of intelligence flowing back to Langley. He claims,' Murray recited from memory, emphasising claims as information that had yet to be substantiated, 'that the middle ranking officers of Diponegoro have established their own unit within their Command to effect a military coup d'etat against the most senior generals in Djakarta. Sorry, Harry, I'm still having trouble with this. It just doesn't jell for me.' He paused, leaned down and rubbed his left foot which had fallen asleep. 'Why? The Diponegoro Command is one of the most highly respected of all the Indonesian Commands. Why would they insist on removing their own generals?'

'Murray, listen. I have already explained that their mood is indicative of what is happening through the Armed Forces. The field officers look to their generals in Djakarta and all they see is men whom they once admired, sitting back, permitting the Communist Party to make incredible inroads while they get fat on their backsides, enjoying life in the Capital, lining their pockets while their rank and file continue to experience incredible hardships. You know only too well what has happened to their 'Crush Malaysia' programme. I can confirm that they have lost literally thousands to our SAS boys operating in Malaysian Borneo. This so-called unofficial war has cost them more than just men and equipment. Their President's standing has deteriorated. There are strong rumblings throughout their defence corridors that Soekarno should go and, even though we strongly support such sentiment, only the Diponegoro officers have actually developed a workable plan to rid us all of their pro-communist President.' He stretched his legs across the bed moved his toes to improve circulation. 'This group that call themselves the Council of Generals. Who do you think is behind it?' he asked.

'Seems little doubt that it's Nasution. My guess is that Yani would be involved, along with most of his supporters. Surprisingly, there's not much leaking out. Could be just another of Nasution's moves to protect the Army from further encroachment by Aidit and Soebandrio. Those two have hurt the Military's power base drastically over the past year. Wouldn't surprise me if the Council is just a club of senior officers looking for a forum to air their many grievances against Soekarno's NASAKOM. Not that the Army seem to be in a hurry to withdraw support for the Crush Malaysia effort. Most of these guys are getting fat off the proceeds generated by the conflict.'

'Exactly!' Harry interrupted. 'This is one of the prime factors behind the resentment expressed by the officers in Semarang. They want a change in their Military leadership and we intend supporting them. We must convince them that it would be in their interests to discontinue this ridiculous war effort of theirs. Surely they must realise just how futile their efforts have been against the Brits and our own boys? Christ, we've taken no prisoners during the Sarawak action and Soekarno is being told that these dead soldiers, reported as having disappeared, were purely deserters who have run into the jungle to hide! Surely the man couldn't be that naive?'

'Okay, Harry, so we approach the Diponegoro boys and offer our support. Why would they want anything to do with us?' he asked, rubbing his foot again as an ache developed from the uncomfortable position.

'The PM has agreed that we may offer some attractive incentives. Firstly, providing they take Soekarno out and put the reins back on the PKI, we would be receptive to guaranteeing our full support in the United Nations for their legitimate acquisition of West New Guinea.' Harry saw the look of surprise on the younger man's face. 'It is a foregone conclusion, Murray,' he said, displaying the open palms of both hands. 'The Indonesians will take it anyway. Any United Nations efforts to implement a referendum there would, in our opinion, be compromised by the Indonesians building a substantial non-indigenous population during the lead-up, moving tens of thousands of Javanese across to settle before any vote could be called. So we can't do much to prevent it and might as well take advantage of the situation.'

Harry reached for another cigarette, ignoring the half-finished stick still smouldering in the bedside ashtray. As he inhaled, the effort caused him to cough harshly. 'Secondly,' he continued, rubbing an itchy right eye with the back of his free hand, 'we'll guarantee them asylum if they screw it all up. This would be an unconditional offer.' Harry's voice reflected his fatigue. He had not had much rest during the past two nights. Particularly the evening before, in Bangkok. He aborted his customary appointment when he discovered he was being followed. It had shaken him badly.

'Seems reasonable. They may just take it.' Murray mused. An escape to Australia should the officers fail. He wondered how many would actually make it and decided that the offer had no real downside for the Australians as it would be unlikely that any of the conspirators would survive. They rarely did.

'You are to target the officers whose names are listed here,' Harry indicated, pointing to the file left on the round glass covered coffee table. It bore no markings to identify the volatile contents. 'Go with the Military Attaché, have a good time in Bandung and Surabaja. But when you hit Semarang, Murray, do what must be done. Identify those officers, spend time with them alone, if possible. You understand their language; they'll warm to you. Don't under any circumstances even consider broaching the subject we have discussed. You're to establish direct contact with these men and, upon your return to Djakarta once the tour is finished, contact them again and foster whatever communication there is between yourself and the men we have targeted here,' he instructed, pointing again at the manila folder.

'And then?' Murray asked, already guessing what the other man's response would be.

'Then, Murray, my man, you will arrange another meeting for yourself to visit Semarang independently, only this time I will accompany you.'

'Could take some time,' Murray suggested.

'Time,' Harry sighed, 'time, unfortunately, we don't have. I need to be able to return and meet with these officers in less than three weeks. Events could easily overtake us all, Murray, and that could be disastrous.' The Director sighed again. He had to have everything in place before the Americans became aware of what was happening.

'Three weeks!' he protested. The time-frame was impossibly short.

'Sorry, chum. That's all you get.'

'And you'll take care of Davis and the other arrangements?' he asked.

'All of it. I just want you to remember how crucial your developing contact with these officers is to the play we are about to make. We can't afford to screw this one up, Murray. It would be disastrous.'

Murray sat silently considering that possibility. It would be dangerous, he knew. 'Okay, Harry,' he said, understanding the extent of the commitment he had just made.

'Thanks, Murray,' the Director beamed. 'I knew I could count on you.'

* * * * * *

Indonesia — Java

They were both tired. The evening before, their Bandung hosts had insisted on entertaining the Australians. Following an early dinner courtesy of the local Chinese restaurant, the visitors were escorted down to a grotty place well-hidden behind the officers' mess. The moment they entered the dismally lighted room the Military Attaché turned to Murray and shook his head. He was not having any of this! A selection of poorly-dressed village girls sat quietly, their features barely visible in the low-wattage light. One of the girls said something and the others laughed nervously. Another rose and walked towards the foreigners, then said something in their local dialect. Murray could not understand the girl, but when she stood alongside Colonel Wharton, the Military Attaché and made a motion with her hands attracting even more nervous laughs, it became clear that the colonel's large frame was the object of their fascination. The Attaché towered over the others present, and the young prostitutes were obviously concerned as to who would have to partner the *bule* visitors.

'Murray, I don't care how you do it, but get us, or at least me, out of here.'

'Give it a few minutes, George.' he had replied. 'We'll sit and keep them company for a while then drift back to the guest house. I'll talk to them. You can just sit there and continue to frighten the hell out of them.' The colonel agreed. He understood the importance of face. It was just so damn annoying that he could not communicate. Not having control of the situation was absolutely alien to his nature and military training.

He squatted down on one of the short stools so as not to intimidate the girls further and listened as Stephenson entertained them. The village girls were obviously surprised that he could speak their language. After a reasonable time had elapsed, impatient to retire

178

in preparation for the long gruelling next day's drive, the colonel checked his watch and indicated to Murray he thought they should leave. As soon as both men emerged from the unofficial brothel, their hosts reappeared smiling, and then insisted on accompanying their guests back into Bandung to the Savoy Hoyman Hotel. They tried to protest but the Area Commander refused to listen. He had organised for the beer garden to remain open and, he said, the band were also waiting. The Australians had no choice but to agree, returning to their rooms in the Army Guest House well after midnight.

They had little sleep, rising early to tackle the long drive down through the mountains and across to Semarang. Both men sat silently in the rear of the Embassy Holden as it wound its way through the narrow, dangerous road which, in places, was barely wide enough for one vehicle, let alone the buses and trucks which forged recklessly down the mountain pass. The men both felt uncomfortable with the conditions but neither complained. Instead, they kept their eyes glued to the road and the steep embankments where, from time to time, they observed evidence of where some earlier driver had missed a corner, plunging his passengers to their death some hundreds of metres below. The road wound through a dense teak forest, the sun's rays hidden by the trees' thick leafy crowns. Monkeys wrestled together along the roadside oblivious to their dangerous choice of playground, scampering to safety only at the very last moment as cars and trucks approached perilously close. Birds of impossible beauty swooped on injured prey left to die by the passing traffic, their shrieks of warning to the approaching intruders echoing through the canopied jungle. Twice the men spotted brilliant green snakes twisting their way with incredible speed as they fled the oncoming car wheels.

Several hours passed before the driver asked if he could stop for a cigarette. The *tuans* were pleased to do so, stretching their legs as they stood outside in the cool morning setting, enjoying the fresh mountain air. Before the driver could finish his *kretek* with its clove aroma, dozens of villagers appeared out of nowhere and squatted around the two foreigners. The men laughed as they climbed back into the car. There was no village visible and yet, as they had experienced in almost every place they had visited in the country, wherever they stopped there would be a crowd of inquisitive children present, within minutes.

The remainder of the drive to the northern port city was un-eventful, just tiring. As protocol dictated that they report upon ar-rival, the men agreed to go directly to the Diponegoro Command HQ before cleaning up, to advise their hosts of their presence in Semarang. They were warmly welcomed, advised of the pro-gramme schedule arranged in honour of the Australian Military Attaché's visit, then escorted by Military Police, sirens whining loudly as they cleared the traffic for the diplomatic car.

That evening, the Diponegoro Commander held a reception at the Hotel Istana, one of the few remaining venues suitable for such purposes. Apart from his senior officers, the general invited a small number of government officials, all military appointees. There were also several local traders present. Murray smiled knowingly when introduced briefly to these men. He knew that the businessmen would be expected to pay for the extravagant function. Murray dressed in formal attire, his white jacket requiring some hasty last-minute attention. Colonel Wharton dressed in formal military evening dress, the gold accoutrements adding to his distinguished bearing. The two rows of decorations for service and courage had already been carefully pinned in place on the white penguin-cut jacket by his wife as she packed the evening uniform prior to her husband's departure.

The colonel was not alone in expressing his pleasure that they were staying in the Hotel. Murray had been through this region many times during his first tour, and had suffered endless sleep-less nights whenever obliged to sleep in local bug-infested *losmen*. The reception was to commence at six o'clock. Murray accompa-nied the colonel downstairs to join their hosts, where they stood alongside the Diponegoro Commander as they were introduced to the other officers and guests. It was then that Murray finally met Lieutenant Colonel Sulistio. The colonel surprised both the Aus-tralians with his command of English. Immediately, Murray solic-ited the soldier's help, suggesting that it would be greatly appreci-ated should the officer take some of the pressure off him, feigning ignorance to military terminology and therefore difficulty with the interpreting.

'I would be pleased to do so,' the Javanese officer willingly agreed. It was an opportunity for him to flaunt his recently-acquired skills in front of the general. He knew that this couldn't hurt his future prospects. Very few of his peers had acquired this language proficiency, even amongst the several thousands of Indonesians who had been trained by the Americans. Murray was instantly relieved. He would now have an opportunity to speak directly to all of the officers whose names he had memorised. He would return to the CIA mole later, Murray decided, encouraging Colonel Wharton to accept the Javanese officer as his temporary replacement. The Attaché agreed, not displeased with the arrangement. He was not aware of the Indonesian's treasonous relationship with the Americans.

As the reception wore on, Murray was successful in making contact with most of the senior officers listed by his Director. He encouraged their questions and established a strong rapport with the men and their wives. Murray flattered the women, and they responded. Before dinner was served, most of those present knew his name while that of the other Australian was totally lost on them. He spoke at length with the ladies, knowing that they were attracted. This never bothered Murray, who enjoyed the extra attention and used it to his advantage.

As the exotic buffet was replenished with even more seafood and rice dishes, Murray roamed the room, talking to their hosts and other guests, stopping occasionally to chat with the senior officers' wives before moving on to speak briefly with some of the government officials. As the occasion was nearing its close, Murray decided it was time for him to reposition himself beside his Military Attaché.

'Thank you for assisting Colonel Wharton,' he said, shaking Sulistio's hand warmly but not with the customary firm Western grip. 'I would never have had the opportunity to enjoy myself so much had you not come along.'

'But have you not been here before, tuan Murray?' the kolonel asked.

'Yes, several times in fact.' Murray went on to explain his student days prior to his joining the Embassy. 'But I never really had the opportunity to move around this freely.'

'Ah, yes. Of course. You would not have had the benefit of your current status. Tell me,' he asked, looking directly into Murray's eyes, 'did you have the benefit of a surat djalan at that time?'

'Not really,' Murray responded. The document to which the kolonel had referred was the mandatory travel paper issued to all foreigners when they moved outside the Capital.

'I had friends in high places,' he joked, half-expecting the officer to enquire further.

'Ah, I see. Tuan Murray really does understand how my country works!' Sulistio smiled. *'And are those friends in high places in the Army?'* he asked, pleasantly, but Murray sensed that he was moving into dangerous ground.

'Tidak, Pak Kolonel,' he answered in the officer's own tongue. *'No friends in the Military, I regret to say.'* Having provided the opening, he waited.

Sulistio turned his head from left to right then smiled at Murray. *'Seems that is about to change. You have made many friends here tonight,'* he said, then added in English, 'Especially amongst our ladies!'

They laughed together as the others guests moved to depart. The Australians stood alongside their hosts once again, shaking hands cordially as the evening came to a close. The following morning they were taken to the Army Command Headquarters where they spent the entire day, discussing each other's weaponry and training procedures. The visit went well and by the time they were ready to depart for Djogyakarta and Surabaja the next day, Murray knew that he had achieved what he'd set out to do. One by one, he had approached each of the officers on the ASIS list and they had responded warmly to his attempts to cultivate their friendship. He believed that the next objective would not be difficult and immediately commenced planning how he would approach these men to arrange the following visit. With Harry Bradshaw.

* * * * * *

Canberra — Australia

Konstantinov looked hard at the man he would normally have despised. The Russian usually had little time for such men who, having compromised their own integrity, did not have the intestinal fortitude required to extricate themselves from their predicaments. Still, he above all others in his profession acknowledged that, without such players in his world of intrigue, little would be achieved. Blackmail had become an essential tool in the application of his dangerous trade. Harry was different and, Konstantinov, for reasons unknown even to him, respected the ageing spy.

'Why do you wish to continue with the original assignment. Surely this changes everything?' Harry asked. He had just finished rubbing his brow but, for some reason, the tension remained. He rubbed the area briskly, again. 'How reliable is this information? It seems just a little fortuitous to me!'

'Totally reliable, Comrade, totally reliable, I can assure you.'

'Well?' Harry waited. The situation was verging on the chaotic. It had suddenly become very dangerous for those involved in the rapidly-changing scenario.

'You should still proceed with the original plan. Only now, you will have more to offer. Once you have disclosed this information to the Diponegoro officers they will have no choice but to trust you in the future.'

'Colonel,' he started, still confused by the dramatic changes in events, 'please explain why it is that Moscow wishes to reveal this information? Surely it would mean the end of your only foothold in the country?'

'We expect that once you reveal what the Indonesian Communist Party has planned, the Semarang officers will move to pre-empt such foolishness. This would not only diffuse a volatile situation but most probably result in the Communist Party surviving for the future. The PKI leadership would most certainly be removed, paving the way for more moderate thinking. We believe this would precipitate a return to the Moscow Line and sever the proposed alliance between the Indonesian, Vietnamese and Mao communists.'

'But what if it goes too far? What if they completely eliminate the PKI or simply just ban its activities?'

'Moscow will not permit that to happen.'

'How?' he asked, almost angrily. The scheme bordered on the insane.

'That is not for us to argue, Comrade. Besides, do you really believe that any group is strong enough to completely wipe out Indonesia's millions already dedicated to the principles of communism? Comrade, the suggestion is ridiculous.'

'My God, colonel,' he whispered hoarsely at the ramifications of what was planned. 'This could so easily back-fire. It's too risky!'

The ache in his forehead had moved. His temples throbbed fiercely as he attempted to convince the Russian that what they proposed bordered on lunacy. Konstantinov glared at the Intelligence Chief.

'You know what you must do, Comrade. Just do it!' The discussion had ended. There was nothing left for the ASIS Director to say.

Harry Bradshaw left the Russian Embassy and returned to Melbourne immediately. He filed one report of his visit to the Soviet Embassy with Anderson, his Deputy, and then went about making final arrangements for his imminent visit to Indonesia. He sent out the relevant communications advising of his movements, then left the Head Office and went directly to the Intercontinental Hotel. There he used the concierge to send an international cable. It was addressed to Bangkok. The next morning, an hour after the message was delivered, the recipient made a brief and enigmatic call within the Thai capital then hung up.

'It's Piya,' the boy's voice had said, 'he's coming!'

* * * * * *

Semarang — Central Java

Due to time constraints, Harry had insisted they fly to Semarang. Murray attempted to convince his Director that it would probably be as fast driving the four hundred kilometres, in spite of the road conditions, as it would using the domestic airways. Then there was the safety factor. These short domestic runs by ageing Dakota were extremely bumpy at this time of the year. Murray, for one, hated the idea of flying through the cunimbulus clouds almost at eye level with the smouldering volcanoes that lay in the flight path.

Murray calculated that, considering the taxi rides at both ends, the three-hour delay when Garuda couldn't find the mandatory missing aircraft, the actual flight time virtually amounted to the driving time. But the obstinate Director refused to listen to him.

They arrived during the tail-end of a local thunderstorm. The aircraft was easily buffeted at the restricted altitudes they flew, sending people lurching into the cluttered aisle, gripping their seats each time the plane dropped suddenly. The cabin was choked to capacity as four more passengers than seats stood bravely in the aisle. At the rear of the converted freighter, the ground crew had placed crates containing two of the largest white pigs Murray had ever seen. Another passenger had brought his fighting cocks along. These stood restlessly in cages, blocking the side exit. As the aircraft commenced its final approach, one of the children sitting up forward retched, setting off a chain reaction. When the Dakota taxied to a halt, both Murray and Harry helped open the doors then jumped before being totally overcome by the foul air inside.

They checked into the Hotel Istana. The reception clerk remembered Murray who requested a double room for them both. This avoided the problems with Harry's travel documents. He did not carry a diplomatic passport. Neither did he possess a *surat-djalan* travel pass. Prior to Harry's arrival, Murray had confirmed arrangements with the officers he had contacted. They had expressed surprise that he was returning this soon, but quickly extended an invitation to meet and *makan* together. Murray dressed casually, wearing an open-neck short-sleeve shirt while Harry changed into his safari suit.

It had been difficult for Murray to orchestrate a meeting with the specific officers whose involvement in the planned coup d'etat had come to his Director's attention. During their meeting in Singapore, Harry had concocted an acceptable story, explaining to Murray that the information had been released by their counterparts in Langley on a Director-to-Director basis. Due to Murray's immediate superior being under a cloud himself, it had been decided that he would be left out of the information loop until such times as his position could be clarified beyond doubt. Murray accepted the plausible explanation. Upon his return to Djakarta with Colonel Wharton, he had contacted the Diponegoro officers and expressed his gratitude for their hospitality and suggested that he might return the following week on a private visit, en route to Bali. He had asked for the opportunity to reciprocate their kindness, suggesting another meal at the Hotel Istana, knowing that it would be unlikely for the soldiers to refuse such an invitation. The problem he had was resolving how to cull out the officers they did not wish to meet. In the end, Harry suggested that they arrange a later meeting with the officers concerned, and that this could be organised during the dinner. It was messy, and neither felt relaxed about the tedious but dangerous task which faced them.

Murray was disappointed that almost a dozen of the officers attended the dinner, including Colonel Sulistio. Harry appeared apprehensive when first introduced to the American-trained soldier but Murray decided that the Director, with his extensive field experience, could handle anything which might arise during the evening. And he did.

Once Murray was convinced that Harry had remembered which of the men present were those he wished to meet discreetly, he went about directing the conversations to those officers. It went smoothly and, as coffee was served, Harry excused himself, went to his room and returned with a box of cigars which were quickly opened and handed around the table. Murray was impressed with his style. He watched Harry smiling and laughing with the Indonesian soldiers, never once indicating that the language barrier posed any problem. From time to time, Colonel Sulistio joined in interpreting for the group, permitting Murray the opportunity to initiate separate conversations.

Only a few of the officers drank alcohol, which suited the agents. They knew that these men were unaccustomed to spirits and even one or two beers would normally make them ill. As ten o'clock approached, the soldiers indicated that they thought it time to return to their respective quarters. It appeared that there would be no opportunity to speak to even one of the targeted officers privately. The group started to break up when suddenly one of their number decided to use the toilets before departing. Murray took the initiative and followed the brigadier general through the lobby and out into the toilet area. He waited for the officer to step back out into the rear courtyard.

'Pak Djenderal,' he commenced, knowing that he might have only this one opportunity to make his pitch. 'Pak Djenderal, there is something very important that we wish to discuss with you in private.' The brigadier general stopped, surprised at the statement.

'What is it?' he asked, curious as to the foreigner's behaviour. Normally when these people wanted a favour, they would have one of the junior officers make the approach.

'Pak Djenderal, we wish to meet with you in private. It is most urgent.'

'What is there to discuss? I have no business with you or your friend.'

'Pak Djenderal,' Murray again tried, feeling the opportunity slipping away from him. *'What we wish to discuss cannot be said here, nor do I think would you want it to be said in front of the others.'* The Indonesian bristled and began to move away, angry with the arrogance of such an intrusion. These *bangsat* are all the same, he thought angrily.

'Make an appointment with the Kolonel. Then I will see if it is a matter for our further discussion.' He turned and had walked no more than three paces when Murray caught up and whispered urgently, bringing the general to an abrupt halt.

'Diponegoro mau kudeta,' he whispered just loudly enough for the startled officer to hear. Immediately the general turned and snarled at the accusation that his Command was involved in planning a coup d'etat.

'That is a very dangerous statement,' he said, glaring at the *bule*. Murray took a chance. He knew he had to go in all the way. There was no turning back.

'It is only dangerous to those who plot such an action, Pak Djenderal.' he said, knowing that the Javanese was looking for more before he could respond. *'We have information relating to the plan,'* he added quickly, taking the offensive. *'It is this which we must discuss with you in private, Pak Djenderal.'*

'Who are you?' the shocked general asked, his voice almost choking with rage. *'Who are you who dares to insult me in this way?'* he stammered, while clenching his fists.

'Pak Djenderal,' Murray spoke softly, *'we are here to support you.'* For several moments he waited, expecting the other man to scream for his junior officers to join him. Christ! Murray suddenly thought, what if someone had made a colossal mistake? What if he had just approached the wrong man? He tensed.

What seemed like an eternity passed as the two men faced each other. The general continued to stare fiercely at the foreigner who had made the wild innuendo, while the other stood firmly, his hands deliberately loose at his sides. Suddenly the Indonesian spoke.

'We will talk now. Follow me,' he ordered as the relieved agent did as he was instructed. They returned to the lobby where the other officers waited. The general barked at his aide and nodded to the other officers who immediately came to attention, bade farewell to their hosts and departed quickly. Only one other remained behind.

'Pak Djenderal, may I stay and offer my assistance?' Kolonel Sulistio

said. Murray watched Harry stiffen as the exchange took place. He guessed as what might have been said. The Commander looked at his officer and attempted a smile.

'I will be all right by myself,' he said, obviously pleased with this officer's response.

'But Pak Djenderal,' Sulistio insisted, incurring a look of dismissal which he clearly understood. *'Kalau begitu, selamat malam, Pak,'* he said, acquiescing then bidding his superior goodnight. He turned to the Australians. *'Good evening, gentlemen,'* he said, a little too officiously, *'please take good care of our Commander.'* with which he stepped back and saluted instead of shaking their hands, then marched away stiffly.

'Seems we have upset that one,' Harry said to the general, which Murray considered inappropriate and neglected to translate.

'Yes, you have,' the Commander said sternly to the two shocked Australians. Then he looked at their expressions and smiled resignedly. 'Yes, gentlemen, I do speak some English. Come, we will talk. But not here,' with which he turned, and the others followed the general outside, where his aide waited patiently beside the Commander's Jeep. He motioned for the Australians to climb into his vehicle. Murray was not sure that this was such a good idea, considering they had just alerted the officer in charge to the fact that they were aware of his complicity in an anti-government plot. Harry nodded and Murray climbed aboard with the others.

They remained in silence as the Jeep bumped its way back towards the Divisional Headquarter. Just before the main entrance, the aide turned left and drove down several streets before turning once more and coming to a stop outside a large two-storey building. He flashed the Jeep's lights. Two armed soldiers appeared, rifles held in the ready position while they checked the Army vehicle. Satisfied that it was their Commander, they then opened the heavy iron gates and ushered them inside.

'My home,' was all the general said, climbing out of the uncomfortable Jeep and walking directly into his house. Minutes later, Harry sat opposite the general in his study, with Murray on his left. The room was not large, nor was it air-conditioned. The general waited until his staff had placed coffee in front of his guests and left the room, closing the tall green doors behind. Murray detected a mustiness in these quarters, as if the room was rarely used.

He noticed the photographs hanging on two of the cream walls. Neither were of faces he could recognise. An outdated calendar displayed a painting of the Borobudur temple.

He glanced at the ceiling and spotted the tell-tale water marks where rain had poured through from the broken roof tiles above. Several flags hung listlessly in the corners as if waiting for some breath of fresh air to bring them to life. A wash-basin rested against the far wall, confirming the original designer to be Dutch. Water dripped from the single tap, following a permanent brown stain that no-one had bothered to remove. The room's appearance reflected an absence of wealth, of power. Considering the tenant's position, Murray had not expected such obvious neglect. It was certainly out of character for what he considered to be the norm with other high ranking officials. The general indicated that they should commence.

'We speak English. Later, if too difficult, he can speak for both of us,' the officer suggested, pointing at Murray.

'Fine. Then perhaps I should begin,' Harry remarked, anxious to control the direction of the conversation from the outset. 'Firstly, general, I should clarify just who I am but, before doing this, I must have your assurance that what I am about to tell you must, for the moment, remain with you only. Is that agreed?' The Javanese listened, then indicated that he understood.

'General, I work with the Australian Government. Murray here is my official interpreter and is privy to the information I am about to disclose to you.' The brigadier general held his hand up and looked at Murray who immediately translated what had been said. 'I wish to assure you that the purpose of my visit is to help, not to create problems for you or those in your Command.' Harry waited to see if his host had understood before continuing. 'What I am about to show you will prove that we are genuine friends and look to you for your trust.' Harry extracted a sealed envelope from his pocket and ripped the seal off before removing the contents. He then placed two pages in front of the general. Minutes passed before the officer had completed reading the information. He looked up at the ASIS Director.

'Who wrote this report?' he asked. Harry did not hesitate. Looking sideways at Murray he stated clearly, 'One of your own officers, general!' Murray's cheek muscles tensed. Surely they weren't going to expose the American agent?

'Which man wrote this?' he asked again, slowly, obviously determined to discover the identity of his own enemy within, his *musuh dalam selimut*. He was shocked, given the knowledge that one of his close officers had betrayed him. Immediately the brigadier general showed signs of losing control. 'You must tell me!' he demanded, his voice rising almost to a shout. Murray looked helplessly at his superior. What the hell was going on? he thought.

'The man's name is the officer we met tonight named Sulistio. His name is Kolonel Sulistio.' For a moment there was complete silence. Murray was speechless. God! he thought, the bastard's compromised a friendly agent! What in the hell is Bradshaw up to? he struggled to understand.

'You lie!' the general shouted, then looked at the other man. '*Bohong!*' he repeated in Indonesian.

'No, general. I'm sorry, but it's true. Your man was already in the pay of the Americans well before your plans were even discussed. He willingly became one of their agents while undergoing training in the States. It is always difficult when these disclosures are made, general. Believe me, I know. The fact is, the officer has been reporting regularly exactly what you and your officers have planned to remove the senior Military Establishment in Djakarta.'

'I do not believe you. Why do you not help him if he is working for the Americans? Why come to me with this story? The Australians and Americans are allies! No, you lie!'

'There is more that I must tell you, general. Of course, we are friendly with the Americans and it is true that they are our ally.' Harry paused to ensure that the officer had understood. 'General, although to you it is already a very serious charge that one of your men has been providing secret information to the Americans, there is something far more serious. That matter is the real reason for my meeting with you.' Murray listened intently. He had no idea what the hell was going on.

'What can be more serious than your accusations?' the general snapped.

'General, listen. Please listen to what I am about to say, General, the Australian and British have confirmed reports that the Indonesian Communist Party, your PKI, plans to overthrow your government!' Harry said, dropping the bombshell in a clear and precise manner. There was a moment of silence before the general slapped the table loudly, then scoffed.

'The PKI ?' he repeated, snorting as he spat the words scornfully. '*The PKI could not put out their children's washing without falling all over themselves. Why do you come to me with this nonsense?*' he demanded, reverting to his own language. Murray quickly translated for Bradshaw.

'General. Your superiors in Djakarta have already been approached by their American associates. We don't need to discuss that issue here but you are fully aware that your Military leadership has already moved into the American camp. As Australians, I must admit that we are not unhappy about this. The problem is that neither the Americans nor your senior generals believe that the PKI are planning such a move against your people, Now that does concern Australia. It would seem to us that we have a common interest. Since your own leadership prefers to ignore this danger, then we would be pleased to support any intent you have in moving first to establish control.'

'You can understand my own government's predicament. Yes, we are allies with the Americans, but please consider the risk my Government has taken in jeopardising that relationship, here today. Should the Americans become aware of our support for the Diponegoro Command to assume leadership control in lieu of their own preferred faction, it would be disastrous for all concerned. In short, the Americans would never support your efforts, preferring to maintain a strong relationship with your existing leadership who refuse to accept, as you just have, the possibility that Mr. Aidit and his gang are planning their own party. General, this is why it was imperative that I met with you and explained about Sulistio first. Whatever you have discussed, whatever you have been planning, even whoever is involved with you, all this information is now in the hands of the Americans.'

The brigadier general appeared to understand.

'If this is true, why haven't the Americans already informed Djakarta?' he challenged.

'They most probably have. If your superiors refuse to accept that the PKI is plotting to overthrow the government, then why would they believe that their own highly esteemed Diponegoro Command could even consider such an outrageous suggestion?

Have there been any recent transfers of those involved?' Murray, stunned also by these revelations, watched to see if the general had understood the damning information revealed by the ASIS Director.

The general thought for a moment then frowned. Three of his more senior officers had been moved to other Commands during the past month and all were supporters of his covert actions. Slowly, the skin around his mouth tightened with anger as he realized that his entire operation may have already been compromised by one of his own.

'Give me proof,' the Commander challenged. Harry had anticipated this request and had already removed another document from the pocket of his safari jacket. He placed the page next to the other documents.

'There, general, is your proof,' he said, pointing to a line in the centre of the page. 'You can see, sir, this is an extract of a CIA report. It clearly mentions that Lieutenant Colonel Sulistio of the Diponegoro Command is the source of the information contained in the other documents. You will also recognise, general, that this report is stamped 'Top Secret' and, by showing this to you, my country has placed itself in a most difficult position, not to mention that I and my interpreter here would forfeit our careers should the Americans discover that we have passed this very sensitive material to you.' Harry looked to Murray and nodded. Murray repeated all that had just been said in the general's own language. As he did so, the officer looked from one page to the next and then back again, as if cross-referencing the contents. He shook his head in disbelief. Murray looked at the soldier sympathetically while wondering if it had also crossed the general's mind that Sulistio may have more than one master. The very thought that the Diponegoro plans may already be known in Djakarta seemed an obvious possibility to him. The general rose to his feet.

'You go back to the Hotel Istana now. We will check with Sulistio. If what you say and have shown me is true, then I will meet you again tomorrow. If it is not true ...' he left the sentence unfinished but the threat was clear.

'General. I don't want to tell you your business but it is essential that you move to contain this officer by removing him from sensitive positions. We don't want this man to be hurt in any way. That should not be necessary. We ask that you consider this.' Harry looked at Murray as he spoke then quickly glanced away again.

'We will meet tomorrow. Please go now.' He walked out of the room and stood silently beside the large side doors through which they had entered earlier. He did not offer his hand as they departed, and only grunted when both thanked him for the meeting. They returned to their hotel in the Jeep and Harry cautioned Murray with his hand, indicating that they should not go to their room immediately. They found one of the staff and ordered a bottle of *Bir Bintang* which was served warm over brown-speckled ice. They walked out to the small beer garden and sat, quietly discussing what had just transpired.

'Harry, you just burned a friendly! What's going on? Is this something to do with Dirty Tricks?' he asked, referring to the Secret Service's department which specialised in operations of this nature. 'If so, don't you think I should have been told before letting me walk into the crap I just witnessed back there?'

'It's not crap, Murray. We have confirmation that the Indonesian Communist Party is definitely planning a move. We just don't know when. As for their man Sulistio, well,' he lied, 'the Yanks were going to dump him anyway. Seems he has strayed a little from their camp as well.'

'What then is our game plan Harry?' Murray asked again. 'And how does Central Plans suddenly develop resources that the Yanks don't have? How did we manage to confirm the PKI's intentions?' he asked, looking directly at the Intelligence Chief. Harry Bradshaw just stared back at the younger man. He could see the fire in Murray's eyes and suddenly he remembered a time when he, too, experienced those very same emotions.

'Let's just say that we have a man who is very friendly with the Russkies,' he said tiredly and rose, indicating that he wished to go inside. Murray walked with him as far as the lobby, permitting the older man to enter their room and use the bathroom first. As Harry climbed the wide wooden staircase, Murray observed the slowness of his gait, watching the man until he disappeared from view.

He stood there for a moment, staring up at the empty space, wondering who it was the Director had referred to as being so close to the Soviets he was able to produce such incredible intelligence. Murray shivered in the warm tropical night. In a way, he didn't really want to know.

* * * * * *

It was still dark when the Jeep left with the small group and drove thirty kilometres away from the city, heading into the hinterland once they'd crossed the first line of hills overlooking Semarang. There were five of them including the driver. The driver turned off the sealed macadam and followed a dirt road for a further twenty minutes before the track disappeared altogether. They left the Jeep and moved down to the edge of the swift flowing stream where they squatted, smoking *kretek* cigarettes together. The general turned to Sulistio and stared into the man's eyes. The *kolonel* raised the cigarette to his mouth and drew deeply, then sighed, resting his head between his knees. He heard the men move to stand and knew that this was the end. He closed his eyes and refused to whimper or beg forgiveness. He was a Diponegoro *kolonel* and would die like one! Sulistio knew that the man standing behind him would be the djenderal. His Commander always insisted that a good officer should never shirk his responsibilities he remembered, and ...

The single shot to the side of his skull exploded through the stillness of the night, tearing away his face. As the brigadier general stepped away from the body, the other officers moved in quickly, stripping clothes and other identification from the dead officer's remains. Satisfied that they had missed nothing, they then pushed their former comrade's body into the stream.

The following morning the Commander sent for the two Australians.

* * * * * *

The meeting took place in the general's villa. Once again, only Murray and his Director were present. Neither had slept, apprehensive as to the outcome of their earlier discussions. The Commander commenced the conversation by indicating that he accepted the information passed to him the previous evening. The Australians looked quickly at each other.

'And Sulistio?' Harry asked. The general frowned and flipped his right hand casually.

'He has been dealt with.' Both men understood the ominous

gesture and response. Murray chewed the inside of his lower lip. There had never been any doubt in his mind that Harry had anticipated such a reaction. The general had no choice, given that his own officer had betrayed them all. Harry Bradshaw immediately used the opportunity to raise some of the issues he believed should be resolved when the leadership changed. They discussed the support Australia would provide with respect to Irian Barat and future joint defence co-operation. The general was pleased. Harry moved on to more current problems.

'General, my government would appreciate your assurance that, when the situation changes, you and your associates will support a full cessation of hostilities against Malaysia.'

'We would agree to this. The Crush Malaysia strategy was designed by the communists. We are not interested in carrying on with this fruitless action. Many of us have worked towards convincing our superiors in Djakarta that the war is senseless and should be stopped. They have ignored our Armed Forces losses and continue to send our men into the jungles of Kalimantan where already we have lost thousands. You may tell your Government that we will stop the *Ganjang Malaysia* action as soon as we remove those who support it.'

'General, just who are the members of this Council of Generals?' Harry asked. The general was very surprised by the question. He smiled thinly at the Australian.

'It would seem that you are very well-informed!' he said. 'Most believe that there is no such group, that it is just rumour, nonsense, so to speak.'

'Would it not be reasonable for us to assume that these officers are the same men you referred to earlier?' Harry pressed.

'It would be reasonable for me to suggest to you who is and who is not a member of the exclusive group,' the Commander replied, uncomfortable with the knowledge that the foreigners appeared to know a great deal more about the inner machinations of the Indonesian Armed Forces than they should. Harry Bradshaw understood. He withdraw a notebook from his safari jacket and commenced writing. The general sat silently, and would have normally been amused with this behaviour had the situation been different. Murray knew what his associate was writing. He acknowledged Harry's quick thinking although he did not believe that it would be successful.

'General, I have made a list of the senior officers in Djakarta whom we believe are members of the Council. You understand that this information is indeed relevant to our own position. The Australian Government would not wish to continue developing relationships with those who may, in the future, have little say in Indonesia's leadership.' Harry removed the small page from his notebook and passed it to the general. The Commander read down the list quickly. He looked up at the Intelligence Chief.

'I can't be entirely sure about these,' he said, pointing to the names, one by one. 'This one, however, I am certain would not be involved with the Dewan Djenderal. This, is a good man,' the general said sombrely. 'He once worked here.' The Commander removed his own pen and ran a line through the name before passing the list back to Harry.

'Thank you, general,' he said, smiling confidently. They talked for another hour before the meeting broke up, both sides apparently pleased with what had been achieved. The visitors were driven back to the Hotel Istana where they prepared for their return to the capital. Shortly after noon, the Garuda DC-3 departed, surprisingly, almost on schedule, beating the afternoon storms which approached the coastal city at alarming speed.

As they flew along the muddy coastline, Murray remained silent, pleased that the weather was reasonably calm. He looked at his co-passenger and smiled knowingly. Although there were still many questions he felt were left unanswered, Murray believed that what had transpired during the past twenty-four hours had tremendous significance in terms of future Indonesian-Australian relations. He admitted that many aspects of the discussions he had attended were still unclear in his mind, but of one thing he was certain; Harry Bradshaw was one hell of a negotiator. Murray suddenly felt a sense of pride and gratitude at having been accepted into the Director's confidence. He turned and smiled at the older man.

'Is that the list?' he asked. Harry had the page in his right hand and was staring at the names he had written.

'What?' he responded, startled. His mind had wandered, his thoughts preoccupied with other issues. 'The list?' he asked, remembering where he was, 'Yes. This is the list.' He passed it to

Murray and watched the younger man's expression as he examined the names. Murray thought about the senior officers mentioned and made no comment. He passed the page back to his Director, who seemed distracted.

The aircraft commenced losing altitude as it approached Kemayoran Airport. As the small twin-engined plane circled over Tandjung Priok Harbour before lining up against the sea breeze to land, Murray's thoughts remained on the list he had read, and that also of the recently-appointed major general whose name had been scratched off by the brigadier. He was deep in thought as the aircraft's tyres bit savagely at the runway and screamed, jolting his memory. Then he remembered. The officer whose name had been removed was also a former Diponegoro Commander. Now he held one of the most powerful positions in Djakarta, as the Commander of KOSTRAD, the Army's Strategic Reserve Command. And his headquarters were located on Merdeka Square.

Book two

1965, January to August

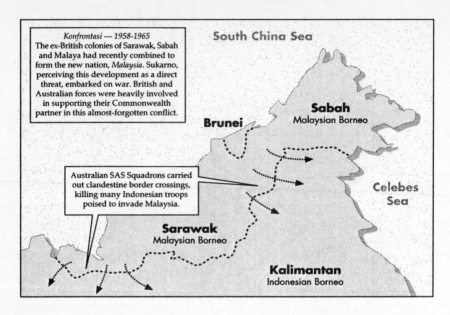

Konfrontasi — 1958-1965
The ex-British colonies of Sarawak, Sabah and Malaya had recently combined to form the new nation, *Malaysia*. Sukarno, perceiving this development as a direct threat, embarked on war. British and Australian forces were heavily involved in supporting their Commonwealth partner in this almost-forgotten conflict.

Australian SAS Squadrons carried out clandestine border crossings, killing many Indonesian troops poised to invade Malaysia.

South China Sea

Brunei

Sabah
Malaysian Borneo

Celebes Sea

Sarawak
Malaysian Borneo

Kalimantan
Indonesian Borneo

Chapter 11

Sarawak — Malaysia — Borneo

Major Zach wanted to slap the mosquito as it sucked blood through the side of his neck but dared not move. He watched through his open sights as the soldier on point headed directly towards him. He held the SLR Armalite rifle firmly as rain fell incessantly, drenching the weapon's stock, covering the open aperture, making it almost impossible to maintain a clear shot. It was his imagination, Zach knew. Mosquitoes would disappear in such torrential downpour. Slowly he bit into his left cheek, forcing his concentration to return. The sudden salty taste of his own blood cleared his thoughts.

Again, he peered down the blurred corridor, the thin dark metal points confused by droplets of rain which clung to the sights. The soldier raised his head not more than a few centimetres, silently cursing the conditions. The rain never ceased, the mud clung at his boots sucking his feet down into the jungle's quagmire, while vines and other thick foliage pulled at his camouflaged clothes and weapon. Still, Zach dared not move. There were others. He knew, without doubt, that the sergeant would be ready over on his right flank, even though he couldn't be seen. The area off to his left had been left clear. This is where they would pause, uncertain, listening as the rain thundered down, making it impossible to distinguish between the jungle's natural sounds and those which could warn them of impending death.

Lightning flashed, followed immediately by a thunderous clap which shook their surrounds. The enemy paused as their platoon commander moved his hand ever so slightly indicating that they were to remain still. He watched; and waited. His breathing slowed, as the forward soldier stood less than fifteen metres directly in his

201

sights, and turned his head, as if suddenly aware of a foreign presence. The major's finger flexed, squeezing softly as he peered over the rifle, his target so close the blurred vision no longer mattered. His could see the Indonesian corporal's eyes, as the soldier peered cautiously into the heavy foliage ahead. The major exhaled slowly as he continued to squeeze the Armalite's fine trigger.

Suddenly, the world erupted around them as the other SAS soldiers followed his signal, releasing hundreds of rounds of ammunition before the Indonesian point man's shattered body had hit the soggy ground. Camouflaged soldiers leaped forward, shooting at the Indonesian patrol as they swooped down the slight incline, struggling to maintain balance on the slippery jungle floor, heedless of the thorny undergrowth which ripped flesh from hands and stung faces fiercely.

The Indonesians, caught by surprise, barely had time to return their enemy's fire before it was all over. The eight-man patrol had been annihilated in less than three minutes.

The savage noise of gunfire was followed by a moment of deafening stillness. Then, suddenly, the forest's creatures shattered the tropical air with screams of terror as monkeys, birds, and other creatures fled to safety.

The major crawled towards his first kill, and crouched over the dead soldier. It was almost impossible to distinguish the officer's form shrouded in camouflage, his tools of war deliberately darkened so as not to betray him, his face blackened to blend with the surrounding forest. He paused, signalled to his NCO, then continued forward. Together they counted the dead. There were seven. Quickly, almost silently, the men moved from body to body removing whatever they found. Letters, identification, paper money. It was all collected. The rain eased momentarily.

The surviving soldier had been hit in the stomach and lay in shock. Corporal Lewis moved towards the wounded Indonesian to complete the kill. He grabbed the soldier's head expertly with his left hand, pulling the man's chin in an upwards motion as his knife commenced its path across the terrified Sumatran's throat.

'Wait!' a voice hissed urgently. Corporal Lewis remained in position, fighting the adrenaline charge. His blade remained at the soldiers neck. 'Lewis!' the voice called again and he stopped, tilting his head sideways to check. It was the major. Lewis kept the knife at his prisoners throat. 'Lewis, how bad is he?' the officer asked.

'One through the side of the stomach. He'll bleed to death,' the corporal whispered.

'Wait!' the major ordered, then turned and signalled to his sergeant. The NCO scrambled across quickly. 'Give him a shot,' the officer instructed, 'then drag him over there,' he said, indicating a huge decaying tree trunk covered in moss and vines. The sergeant positioned himself alongside the wounded soldier and glared at Lewis. The corporal glared back then withdrew the blade. They dragged the bleeding man over to the dead tree and lifted him slightly so that he leaned against the rotting trunk. Another soldier joined them and ripped the Indonesian's bloodied uniform away to expose the gaping wound. He looked at the major and shook his head. Under normal circumstances the man could be saved. Here, in the jungle, the soldier would die within hours. The morphine was injected unceremoniously as the officer crouched down beside their prisoner and spoke.

'What is your name, mas?' he demanded. 'Siapa namamu?' The wounded soldier stared at the white man before him in disbelief.

'Sekali lagi, siapa namamu?' the major asked for his name again. The NCO raised a water can to the man's parched mouth and tipped the aluminium container slightly. The soldier attempted to move but couldn't.

'Tolong, tolong,' he cried, pleading for help.

'What is your name, you bastard!' the officer hissed. 'Tell me your name or I will cut you with this,' he threatened, holding his blade in front of the man's face. The solider sobbed.

'Hartono, tuan,' he answered, eyes wide in fear. 'My name is Hartono.'

'What unit do you belong to?' the major demanded, moving the knife slowly before the soldier's face.

'Regu Harimau, tuan,' he responded, informing the white soldier that he was part of the Tiger Team. A soldier behind swore. These were communist bandits, not even regular soldiers. The major glared over his shoulder at the Corporal. Three of his men understood the bastardised form of Malay. They had picked up their experience killing communists during the Malay Emergency.

'Why aren't you wearing uniforms?' the officer asked, impatiently.

'We changed before leaving Kampung Saleh.' the Sumatran replied, before breaking into a coughing fit which almost choked him. He was given another sip of water.

'What were your orders?' he was asked.

'We were moving towards Kampung Tanah Tinggi. Our orders were to kidnap some of the villagers. I don't know which ones.'

The major stared down at the soldier. His clothes were obviously Army issue, but neither he nor his dead friends wore any distinguishing flashes. Not even name tags. The sergeant leaned over and tapped his wrist watch. They were running out of time. The major nodded.

'Which one of these is your officer?' he asked, moving his hand in an arc covering the bodies which had been dragged into one area as he questioned the prisoner. Major Zach glared at the Indonesian. The young soldier was probably about twenty, he thought. He asked the question again.

'I don't know, which one, tuan, I can't see from here!'

'What was his name?' he growled, conscious of the dangers in remaining where they were after the ambush.

'Bhakti, tuan. His name is Comrade Bhakti.' His answer was followed by another grunt from the corporal. The sergeant waved his wrist at the officer and shook his head. The major sighed, and rose to his feet. He nodded and moved away. The SNCO stood beside the wounded man and gestured for his men to move out.

'It's okay, Sarge,' Lewis said, his hand ready with the razor sharp weapon. The sergeant stared at the corporal. They had worked together in Malaya when the communists were pushing the British soldiers around the plantations north along the Thai border. He stepped away and made room for the other soldier. Immediately, the Indonesian realised what was about to happen and sobbed. He started to scream as Corporal Lewis bent down and grinned as he displayed the knife. He held the man's head as before, turning his body slightly away. Weakened by the loss of blood, the Sumatran offered little resistance.

'Tuhan, tolong! God help me ...!' he screamed, his cry for help cut short as the SAS Corporal's knife severed his throat.

'Filthy bloody commo,' Lewis spat as he pushed himself away from the pumping blood, wiping the blade on the dying soldier's torn clothing. He joined the others. Major Zach motioned with his hand and the SAS team moved out, covering as much ground as possible. They knew it would be folly to remain. Knowledge of the encounter would already be spreading through the surrounding villages. The sergeant checked his bearings and indicated the direction to those behind. Rain started to fall again, but the soldiers maintained their gruelling pace through the thick jungle. It would have been faster following the tracks, but they didn't dare. If they were observed, their standing orders were to kill those who might identify them for what they were.

Three hours passed, the soldiers refusing to rest as they continued their forced march through the extreme conditions, pushing on towards their destination. By late afternoon they reached the edge of the jungle, and their camp, ten kilometres from Simanggang. Exhausted, they went about cleaning their weapons before bathing in the jungle stream and taking their rations.

Across the river from their camp, villagers went about their lives, as if it were normal for these foreigners to be present on their primitive doorstep. From time to time the soldiers would return a wave, acknowledging the fiercely proud people who tolerated the Australians within their close proximity. These were people of the Dayak tribes, whose ancestors, and theirs before them, had hunted, fished and borne families along these rivers long before migratory tribes had encroached upon their territory. They were allies of the Australians primarily because of the common enemy, Indonesia.

This ancient ethnic group understood what was happening to their people, their communities isolated by political lines drawn by others without knowledge of ancestral ties or responsibilities. The Dayaks were the rightful inhabitants of Borneo. Their families had grown throughout the centuries, spreading along the river shores throughout the incredibly large island. They knew what would be lost if the tribes from the southern islands established control over their land. The Australian soldiers were careful when dealing with the smiling river people. They were known to eat their enemies.

The men ate, talked quietly and listened to their officer outlining the following day's activities. There were smiles all around when the major announced that they were not crossing the Indonesian border again the following day. Instead, the SAS soldiers had been ordered to return to Company Headquarters. Zach grinned at the SNCO and the sergeant returned his smile. The special unit had been out in the jungle for twenty-one days straight, crossed into Indonesia more than a dozen times and killed more than one hundred Indonesian soldiers before these intruders could enter Malaysian Sarawak. It did not bother the Australian soldiers that they had violated another country's sovereignty and killed its people. Theirs was an undeclared war. There were no rules, only enemies. The SAS had been ordered to cross the imaginary lines which officially separated British Commonwealth Malaysia from its aggressive neighbour, Indonesia, and prevent Soekarno's terrorists from infiltrating into the newly-created federation where they murdered villagers and kidnapped children, before escaping to the sanctuary of Indonesian Kalimantan.

The Australian soldiers wore no identification which would have compromised their country in the event of their capture. These men understood the enormous responsibility they carried into Borneo's jungle. They reluctantly removed their insignia and the highly-regarded shoulder flashes, knowing that these would be worn again, soon, once they returned to their regiment.

Major Zach rested well that evening. They had not lost a man. At least, not during this expedition. As he closed his eyes, he thought about the others who had not been so lucky, and immediately blocked these memories from his mind. His tour was almost over. He would be happy to return to Australia for a little R& R, go and visit family, get away from the Regiment for a few weeks and find somewhere with a decent bath. Maybe he would drive up to the snow for a week, he thought, enjoy the cold and the beauty of the mountains, get his mind off the jungle. As these thoughts occupied his mind, Major Steven Zach, SAS, slipped into a restless sleep.

When morning arrived, the Australian soldiers broke camp and moved across the river. There they negotiated with the Dayak elders, sitting cross-legged in the long house as terms were negotiated and arrangements put in place. As the morning sun beat down on the soldiers, their impatience was obvious and tempers grew thin. The villagers pushed their boats into the river and primed their powerful outboard motors in preparation to take them on the six-hour journey downstream.

* * * * * *

'You're going home, Steve.' Colonel Peter Jones smiled, handing the can of Victorian Bitter to his friend, and junior officer. He was pleased that Zach was there. That he was safe. They had been close friends for some time. And, of course, he was particularly pleased with the major's promotion. Zach was the only SAS officer of his rank still permitted to actively participate in the patrols. This was normally left to more junior officers but, due to his uncanny skills in the jungle, his request to remain directly involved in the border crossings was reluctantly approved. 'Well, colonel,' Jones laughed, lifting his own can in recognition of what he believed to be a fine decision by the Army Board back in Canberra.

The Hungarian-born Australian SAS officer laughed and lifted his own can in salute. Lieutenant Colonel Zach, Steve thought. It had a good sound to it.

'Do the lads know?' Jones asked, referring to Zach's men.

'The sergeant major is probably down in the Mess telling your SNCO as we speak.' The Commanding Officer wandered across the raised timber floor and looked over the damp ground towards the other barracks. 'Your men will miss you, Steve,' he said, knowing that he would also. Steven Zach was one of the finest men he had known: not just as a friend, but as a professional soldier. The man had commitment and integrity. His men followed him almost without question.

'I'll drop down for farewells before heading off. They're good men, Peter,' he stated, although he knew he didn't have to tell his colonel this. Their successful patrols spoke for his men's professionalism in the field. Zach had been lucky. During a patrol earlier in his tour, he had lost five of his men in a crossfire ambush to RPKAD troops. These were the Indonesian Army Paracommando forces. There had been no court-martial. The British intelligence had been totally screwed up, placing Zach and his men in extreme jeopardy. They had virtually been ordered to cross into a 'hot zone' which had been cleared by Intelligence as safe. When Zach's men were knee-deep and half-way across the swift flowing stream, the Indonesians had opened fire, killing three of his patrol in the first seconds. The survivors fought their way out of the devastating ambush, refusing to withdraw until they had managed to recover their fallen comrades' bodies. These they dragged back across the river, fighting as they withdrew. Two more men died before they reached the river's embankment. Zach's remaining men carried their dead into the heavy jungle where they remained until a SAS support team arrived and transported the bodies back to their base.

Zach had then returned to the river with his remaining men and, armed with the knowledge that the other embankment was in enemy hands, encircled their encampment and mounted his own cross-fire, placing the Indonesians between his handful of men and the river. They killed more than thirty RPKAD regular Indonesian troops in the brief but savage encounter before slipping quietly away, recrossing the river and returning to base camp. From that moment on, Major Steve Zach's star was on the ascent. His men trusted him, and his peers respected the man who had shown them all the qualities an officer should have. He had come a long way from the horrors of Occupation, first by the Germans and then in 1956 the Russians, when they stormed into his country in one final attempt to destroy the very soul of the Hungarian people. Although his great-grandfather had been German, Zach had considered himself only as Hungarian. Now he was an Australian.

As Steven Zach threw the empty can expertly across the quarters into the designated bin, he experienced a sense of achievement, of success. He was pleased with himself. And why not? he thought. He had just been promoted and ordered back to Australia. There would be no more patrols, and this particularly pleased him. No more ploughing through thick jungle, living in the same clothes for weeks on end. At last he would be leaving the filth and insects which had nearly driven him crazy during those first months, and the monotonous humidity which permanently saturated one's clothes. Yes, he thought, it would be just great to be back in Australia for a change.

The following morning the newly promoted Zach boarded the helicopter and headed for Kuching. From there he was transported by British RAF Andover to the military field in Changi, Singapore. The same day, he caught the QANTAS Boeing 707 directly to Sydney where Movements Control had arranged an interconnecting flight to Melbourne for debriefing. Zach was required to dedicate considerable time being prepared for his next posting. Due to the nature of the position and the sensitivity of access, Steven Zach was obliged to submit to a further security clearance before he could proceed any further. It was towards the end of his stay that he was briefed regarding the existence of ASIS, and met with Harry Bradshaw.

Two months later, Lieutenant Colonel Steven Zach boarded yet another QANTAS flight and headed north, to Asia, once again. Only this time he would not be returning to fight in the jungles of Malaysia. Instead, he would be living amongst the very people he had fought, whose brothers and sons he had taken in battle, extinguishing their lives without remorse. Now, he would offer these people his hand, and develop relationships within their community. It was not what he personally wanted, but what was expected of him. He had been posted to Djakarta. When he passed his diplomatic passport to the Immigration desk at Kemayoran Airport, the official made a note for BAKIN, Indonesia's equivalent to the CIA, that Australia's new Military Attaché to the Republic of Indonesia had finally arrived. Steven Zach was now in the land of the enemy.

* * * * * *

Djakarta

Murray scratched his crotch and made a mental note to stop his new *babu tjutji* from starching his underclothes. His previous washwoman had not returned from the *Hari Raja* holidays. Many of the servants changed jobs at this time in the year, he knew. Once they had received the customary additional month's rice and salary for the *Idulfitri* period, some would go home to their *kampungs* and would not return, while others merely changed households without telling their former employers.

He was looking forward to the weekend away from the city, his first in more than two months. Now his section had additional staff, Murray decided to take advantage of an invitation and fly to Djogyakarta. Tickets and hotel confirmation slips lay on the glass-topped desk. He had little difficulty in arranging accommodation at the Ambarukmo Hotel, occupancy rates being what they were. Foreign tourists avoided Indonesia, what with the ongoing street violence and poor infrastructure. Not to mention the confusing two-tier currency exchange system which made staying at one of the four Intercontinental Hotels expensive, by Australian standards.

Murray checked his room-rate and made a clicking sound of dis-approval. Even with the Embassy discount, he would be charged 32 American dollars for each night. On top of this, there would be food and bar bills to cover. Murray wondered just how many tour-ists fell off their bar stools when they discovered that a beer in the Government hotels could cost as much as a dollar Australian. Hell, he thought, gasoline was only fifteen cents a gallon, his cook only cost him a dollar per month for salary on top of the thirty kilos of *beras* she received from the Embassy, and yet the Government in-sisted on charging these exorbitant prices in their four-star hotels.

He reminded himself to take plenty of rupiah. The exchange rate was always lower in the provinces. Murray knew that he could have stayed at the Ramayana Hotel or even one of the other cheaper hotels but he had decided not to on this trip. This time he would stay at the recently-constructed Ambarukmo, built with Japanese War Reparation funds.

Ade had asked him to join her to visit some of her SUBUD friends in Djogyakarta. He had jumped at the opportunity to escape Dja-karta's monotonous routine, agreeing on the condition that they fly down together on the Friday afternoon. Murray knew that this would appeal to her. They had spent very little time together re-cently and he was intrigued with the suggestion that her friends would take them both on a journey neither, she promised, would ever forget. He had informed Davis, his Station Chief, and relegated some of the minor tasks to the new Third Secretary.

'Who are you going with?' Davis had wanted to know. Their relationship had not improved much beyond that when Murray still attended Universitas Indonesia. Murray still wondered how this man could have been selected to become Station Chief. His character flaws were obvious not just to those who worked with the First Secretary, but to the others within the Chancery. When Davis had completed his first tour, there had been no traditional farewell function. Almost everyone had been relieved that he was leaving. To their dismay, Davis returned within months to fill the void created by Keith Wells' departure as First Secretary.

'Haven't decided yet,' he lied. Ade was private time.

Yanti, however, was a different matter altogether. Murray religiously submitted reports regarding their relationship, their dis-cussions and any meetings that occurred. Yanti was business, and he understood the necessity of maintaining their close bond in the interests of their ever-demanding intelligence gathering requirements.

'Taking one of the round eyes?' Davis enquired in his typically derogatory fashion.

'Maybe,' Murray replied, not really wanting to get into another of these discussions with Davis. The First Secretary was still unpopular with both the Australian and Indonesian women on staff. Rumours persisted relating to his extra-curricula sexual activities but Murray no longer cared. There were far greater concerns regarding his Intelligence associate. Ever since Harry Bradshaw's startling revelations, suggesting that Davis could possibly be involved in leaking information, Murray had established a direct operational link with the ASIS Director, by-passing his Station Chief whenever necessary. He could not understand why Davis continued in his post if there was, in fact, substance to the allegations that he had compromised the Service. It made it bloody difficult to function effectively, he thought. He was angry with Bradshaw for not rectifying the problem by removing the agent.

It was apparent that Central Plans had no hard evidence on Davis. Murray sensed that there had to be another agenda. He refused to accept that Head Office would leave Davis in place unless they were uncertain of their suspicions or, as he was more inclined to believe, there was another game afoot and Davis was to play some part without his knowledge. And this would be just the way Bradshaw would operate. Bradshaw's reputation as an experienced field agent was legendary. His uncanny ability to anticipate and resolve complicated problems was equally matched by a deviousness which often startled even the most hardened agents. Murray understood the enormous respect the other officers felt for their Director. There were few who did not admire this man whose valuable empirical knowledge was so envied by others in the Service. At times, his own relationship with the Bradshaws had been a burden. Murray's initial encounter with Susan Bradshaw had later left him feeling confused and disloyal. His earlier concerns that Harry would discover his wife's infidelity and the outcome of that liaison had gradually disappeared as it became apparent that Susan's indiscretion would remain their secret. Murray was grateful that the status quo would remain unchanged. He had the greatest admiration for Harry Bradshaw who, in many ways, had become more than his mentor.

Murray Stephenson's rapid progress within the Service was a direct result of his dedication and talent. That he had been appointed to his current position merely underscored the ASIS Chief's confidence in his ability to execute his duties in a professional manner. Although there were those who whispered that Stephenson's relationship with their Director ensured his ascendancy within Central Plans, the majority acknowledged their fellow agent's abilities and ignored the innuendo. Murray knew that Davis could be included in the minority of people who saw his friendship with the Bradshaws as being the main contributing factor supporting his career. It didn't bother him, especially coming from Davis.

'When will you be back?' Davis asked, annoyed that Murray could be confident of having female company whenever he wished.

'Late Sunday night, Alan,' Murray answered, irritated by the man's persistence.

'Good!' Davis said, as if this fitted into his own plans. 'We have a two-hour briefing session first thing Monday morning.'

Murray raised one eyebrow slightly. 'What's on?' he asked.

'We're having a one-on-one with the incoming Military Attaché,' Davis responded, peering at the single-sheet classified memo in his hand. 'Seems he has quite an impressive record,' he added, squinting to read as he spoke.

'Great,' Murray replied, wishing the other man would return to his own office. 'Could do with some style around here.' Davis looked quickly to determine whether or not the comment was directed at him. Unsure if he had detected sarcasm in Stephenson's voice, he turned and walked slowly back to the adjacent office.

Davis set about re-reading the new Military Attaché's ASIS profile. As he studied the supporting documentation, he discovered that the career officer's records indicated that the half colonel was fluent in four languages, including Bahasa Indonesia. A smile crossed the First Secretary's face as he examined the officer's file photograph. Steven Zach presented well, he observed, surprised that the handsome Attaché was unmarried.

Another thought crossed his mind as the aristocratic features stared back at him. Davis decided he would enjoy having the new Military Attaché around, pleased that Stephenson might finally have some competition around the Embassy. He returned Steven Zach's dossier to his own registry safe, reminding himself to invite the newcomer to dinner as soon as was appropriate.

* * * * * *

Djogyakarta

'Can't you feel the mystique all around?' she asked, holding his hand tightly as they stood on the final level surrounded by huge stone bell formations. It was as if they were suspended by the clouds resting gently on the temple's roof. The climb had not been difficult although many of the original stones had broken away, leaving sections exposed to the weather. As they reached the top, Ade moaned as she peered down the multitude of steep steps, almost wishing she had remained below. Minutes later, as they walked carefully around the magnificent temple's crown, the view unfolding before them, Ade knew that the climb had been worth the effort. They rested there, leaning against one of the intricately carved *stupas*, the cool morning breeze on their faces, the soft sounds of children's voices drifting up as they played far below. Murray opened the tin he had purchased as they entered the temple grounds and extracted a flat piece of what appeared to be tobacco leaf. Ade seized the *dendeng* playfully, and snapped the dried beef into manageable sections before stuffing several of these into her mouth. Murray nodded silently as he chewed the chilli-flavoured meat, smiling at her.

Although they would soon return to Djakarta, Ade was extremely happy. The weekend together had been a wonderful experience for them both, and she felt that their relationship had reached a new level of understanding, of compatability. She was delighted that Murray enjoyed her friends' company. Ade was surprised that he even participated in the rituals, not making light of their beliefs as their group camped for part of the previous night around the ancient Buddhist temple.

Ade explained that this area was considered a holy place, not just by those involved in the SUBUD following, but also by many of the Central Javanese. *Tjandi Borobudur* was visited by many who believed that they could be purified by the mystical atmosphere which surrounded the thousand year old structure.

'This is where we believe our culture was born, Mahree,' Ade had explained. 'We believe that there is a triangle which stretches from here to the ancient feudal courts of Djogyakarta and Surakarta within which there is a powerful vortex of psychic forces. We believe in the sanctity of these forces and often some of the younger Moslem boys sleep here, in search for answers through their dreams.'

Murray had listened intently, admiring Ade for the strength of her convictions. He envied the Javanese girl her cultural heritage. She explained the significance of mysticism and spoke of Subuh in terms of reverence. As she spoke, the soft musical tones of her voice captured Murray's thoughts. He experienced a sensation of tranquillity he had hitherto not believed possible as Ade explained why they worshipped this special place. His thoughts drifted as the others joined in the gentle discussion, and eventually he fell asleep under the watchful eyes of Borobudur's guardians. The moon silhouetted the temple, casting a spell over them all.

Later, as they returned to their hotel, Ade teased Murray. Earlier, her friends had all laughed when Murray had suddenly sat up straight and smiled, not conscious that he had been asleep for several hours. The sensation he recalled before losing consciousness remained with him throughout the following day. It was later, when he stood together with Ade atop the Borobudur Temple, enjoying the mood which lifted his spirits to new heights, that Murray remembered the floating state which engulfed his being the evening before. He was surprised that he had not recognised the sensation earlier. Concerned with the consequences of what could transpire during these sessions, Murray decided to be more circumspect when exposed to the influence of these group meetings.

His mood suddenly changed as he tried to recall what had transpired during his first experience with the religious sect, and when he couldn't, Murray silently admonished himself for permitting circumstances to evolve outside of his control. Considering the nature of his profession, he realised just how stupid he had been. He would definitely not, he decided, attend any more latihan with the others. It was just too risky. He would find a suitable excuse next time Ade asked him to the meditation exercises.

* * * * * *

MERDEKA SQUARE

Djakarta

As the cocktails flowed, the level of conversation increased. Alan Davis leaned forward on tip-toe in search of the guest of honour. There were at least a hundred guests present. It was traditional for the outgoing Attaché to host at least one function to introduce the incoming officer and, on this occasion, even the Indonesian soldiers were accompanied by their ladies.

Davis looked around with hidden contempt. One would never really know, he thought, whether the women present were wives or current girlfriends, as many of the Army officers present had an adequate supply of both. As several of the guests shuffled away from him, Davis spotted Steven Zach talking to the Indian Military Attaché. The new arrival had not attended his briefing as arranged. Davis was concerned. As Station Chief it was imperative that the Military understood where they sat in terms of intelligence gathering.

He moved towards the officers. He winced as he overheard yet another Embassy wife complaining about her own domestic incidents and other menial problems. These women seemed to thrive on useless chatter, he thought, pushing between two of the more buxom Indian ladies who stood directly in his path.

'Davis,' he said, finally making it to the corner where the men stood. The Indian Colonel smiled and shook the shorter man's hand.

'Subramanium,' the Military Attaché replied, smiling broadly, displaying his startlingly white teeth under a thick walrus moustache. Davis viewed the four rows of campaign ribbons and was impressed. He hoped he would not be required to repeat the man's name.

'Hello, Alan,' the other officer said. 'Quite a bash.'

'You'll get used to it,' Davis replied in patronising manner while wishing the Indian with the unpronounceable name would move on.

'No doubt I will,' Zach replied, immediately identifying the man as obnoxious. He had obviously signalled his dislike because Davis looked slightly perplexed by his response. Steven understood that, as the new boy in town, he didn't need to start life in this closely-knit community by putting this man down. 'Perhaps you would be kind enough to give me a few pointers when the opportunity arises,' he suggested, hoping this would be enough to mollify, remembering his earlier coolness.

Davis was immediately placated. 'Steven,' he said, 'I would be delighted to show you the ropes.' He then moved in closer and half-whispered. 'Sorry you couldn't make it to last Monday's briefing. You should sit down with us within the next few days.'

Zach looked at the man with hidden contempt. Up until five weeks before, he had known nothing of the existence of the Australian Secret Service. He had almost choked laughing when the DMI had explained that the original name was only changed by adding the word 'intelligence' to avoid being referred to as ASS. Steven Zach felt it was fitting that this 'ass' was their senior representative in Djakarta.

'Other priorities, I'm afraid, ...' he answered, groping for the First Secretary's first name.

'Alan,' he said, not at all offended. 'It's Alan.' In fact, he was quite pleased that the colonel had made the attempt. So few others did. 'You really must arrange some time so that we can brief you on our side of things.'

'Okay, Alan. I understand. I'm sure that you'll also appreciate the pressure I'm under to participate in all of these handover-takeover functions. What about you and I having lunch as soon as Colonel Wharton leaves?'

Davis smiled. 'Great,' he responded warmly, believing he had established rapport with the new colonel. 'I'll look forward to that.' Zach then smiled and apologised, excusing himself as he responded with a wave to an imaginary person across the room. He squeezed Davis on the side of the shoulder as he moved away. The Station Chief was happy. The natural order of things had been put right and the colonel clearly understood his position. The First Secretary wandered back through the room, selecting a whisky soda as one of the houseboys passed carrying a mixture of cocktails. He sipped the double and winced.

'Have to watch old Ali there, Alan,' Stephenson said, smiling at his superior. The senior *djongos* had a reputation for spiking the *tuans'* drinks. He knew that Ali acted under the misconception that an intoxicated *tuan* would be grateful for the additional strength pourings and remember always to put a good word in for the ageing houseboy.

'Murray,' was all Davis could muster. He had quickly fallen from his momentary high.

'Have you arranged a revised meet?' Murray asked, referring to the failed first briefing attempt with Zach.

'All arranged. I'll let you know,' he added. Murray smiled. 'Supercilious little prick', he thought, struggling to let the remark go by in the interests of harmony.

'Okay, Alan, you do that,' he said, moving swiftly away and was immediately welcomed by the couple standing nearby. Murray was a popular figure. Davis despised him for that.

The outgoing Military Attaché was obviously enjoying himself. His tour was over. Three years 'in-country' had taken its toll, and both he and his wife were not unhappy with the prospect of one more posting until his retirement. As Murray approached, Colonel Wharton's wife turned and took him by the arm.

'Well, didn't think you were going to make it!' she exclaimed, pleased that he had.

'What, miss saying goodbye to the best-looking woman in Djakarta?' he teased.

'Murray, my dear, I am going to miss you very, very much!' she laughed, flattered, wishing that she had been twenty years younger. Dorothy Wharton continued to hold his arm, waiting for the opportunity to break into her husband's diatribe. He was lecturing his replacement on how to do things in this country. She waited patiently, accustomed to playing her role. Mrs. Wharton continued to smile, squeezing Murray's arm as they both stood, attentively, listening alongside the two colonels. She had heard it all before. For a moment, Dorothy Wharton felt relieved that it was finally over, although she had reached this moment with mixed emotions. Life had been good to them here. Her husband had held a position of respect, while she had survived with servants and a reasonable social life. Apart from the occasional altercation caused when the colonel became over enamoured with the *babu dalam*, or one of the other female servants, their lives had, for the most part, survived in almost perfect harmony. She was not entirely unhappy with the prospect of returning home. At least, people used toilet paper there, she thought, not really knowing what the local ablutionary habits might have been. The colonel's wife had never visited an Indonesian household in the three years she had lived 'in-country'.

'Thank God you two have run out of breath,' she exclaimed, launching herself into the conversation as one of the men paused to respond to the other's question. 'Steven, have you met Murray?' she asked, moving to one side, pleased with herself to be standing with the three men while some of the other ladies looked on enviously. She knew that the gin-and-tonic had tasted a little too strong and could feel its warming effects flowing through her body. She turned while maintaining her hold on Murray, looking for the culprit. Her husband's handsome replacement spoke before she could spot old Pak Ali.

'Yes, we have met briefly,' Zach replied, holding out his hand. 'How are you, Murray?' he asked politely.

'Hello, Steve. See the colonel has your ear. We'll have time to catch up later, enjoy!' he said, shaking the new colonel's hand warmly before turning to leave them to continue their discussion. Dorothy Wharton continued to cling to his arm.

'Take me over there, Murray,' she instructed, her syllables now noticeably slurred. He permitted the woman to guide them towards the terrace. It didn't bother him that she was tipsy. Most of the wives spent their time drinking themselves into oblivion while their husbands were preoccupied either with the business of the day or some sweet and discreet interlude which offered a refreshing change to what was waiting for them in their palatial residences.

They stepped outside and immediately Murray identified the tantalising smell of barbecued chicken. The aroma of *sate* drifted across the small garden area as the vendor's sing-song voice cried out, *te, te,* tempting those who could hear, to buy his charcoal-cooked chicken sticks. He breathed deeply. Dorothy laughed and squeezed his arm tightly.

'You're something else, Murray' she complained, not unhappily. 'Inside we have smoked salmon, caviar and quail eggs and yet you still pine for the local food. Little wonder none of the foreign girls have managed to get their hooks into you.' She turned and was about to move back into the main room when two others joined them on the terrace.

Murray immediately went on the defensive. One of the men was the Military Attaché from the Soviet Embassy who had enjoyed the position for some years. The position designated the colonel as an active member of the KGB. Murray looked at the other man. He was tall, thin and very distinguished in appearance. There was something familiar about the man but Murray could not immediately recall what it was. He started to move inside, nodding as a matter of courtesy, as he went past.

'Good evening,' the thin man offered, partly extending his hand towards Murray. 'I'm Eric Whitehead. This is Colonel Kololotov.' He smiled at Dorothy. 'Mrs. Wharton,' he acknowledged his hostess before turning to the other men present. 'And you are ..?'

Murray had no choice. He took Whitehead's hand and pumped it quickly, before briefly shaking the KGB colonel's hand. Why did Whitehead look familiar? Murray tried to recall if he'd seen this man around the Embassy recently.

'Murray Stephenson,' was all he offered. He was very familiar with the Russian. Kololotov was listed in the protocol sheets as the longest-serving foreign Attaché in Indonesia. This remarkable achievement placed him at the head of the Attaché Corps which held monthly functions for all Military Attachés, regardless of their political affiliations. What the public did not know was that this man was one of the most senior KGB members in the Soviet Service, and the first to achieve the rank of general while serving overseas.

'I'm an Australian here on business,' Whitehead offered. 'The colonel is with the Soviet Embassy.' Murray looked at Dorothy who, in spite of her alcoholic intake, recognised the sudden change in Stephenson's demeanour.

'I'll be back in a moment,' she promised, moving away and into the crowded room.

'Don't forget my *sate*,' he called after her, wishing Dorothy had remained.

'You're with the Australian Embassy, aren't you?' Whitehead asked. Instantly Murray wished he had followed Dorothy Wharton inside. 'Haven't we met before?' he persisted.

'I don't think so. And who do you work with?' Murray decided to change to the offensive. It normally worked.

'Oh, I work for myself, Murray. Haven't you heard of Eric Whitehead and Associates? We are very prominent in the public relations arena.'

Murray cursed himself. Of course! He should have known. Eric Whitehead was virtually the commercial front for Central Plans'

South-East Asian operations. He had not met the man personally until now. Murray then remembered where he had seen the prominent well-groomed Australian before. He had seen the senior consultant sitting tete-a-tete around the pool a few days earlier. With Alan Davis.

'No, I'm sorry,' he replied a little too hastily. 'But please don't be offended by that. I've spent most of my adult career overseas. How does public relations work?' Murray asked clumsily as he groped for a reasonable response. Whitehead was about to explain when Dorothy Wharton reappeared.

'Gentlemen,' she interrupted, 'have you met our new Military Attaché?' Murray was instantly relieved. He wanted to grab the woman and hug her. Dorothy smiled coyly in his direction and left the men to carry on alone.

'I'm sorry, colonel,' Whitehead said. 'You were preoccupied when we arrived. I'm Eric Whitehead, this is Colonel Kololotov and our fellow Australian here is Murray ...' he trailed off, having forgotten Murray's surname.

'Good evening, Mr. Whitehead,' Zach responded formally. 'Murray,' he said, smiling, and then turned to the third man present. 'Good evening Colonel,' he said, addressing the Soviet Attaché in perfect Russian. There was a hushed silence. Even the KGB officer was stunned. 'Forgive me if I do not address you as Comrade!' Moments passed before the Russian could regain his composure.

'Good evening, Colonel. Your Russian is excellent! Where did you learn to speak our language so well?' he enquired, while both Whitehead and Stephenson stood silent, not understanding the exchange.

'A peasant language is not difficult to learn,' he answered, forcing a smile for the others present.

'Ah, I see,' Kololotov responded, nodding his head in an almost condescending manner. 'You are not an Australian at all. Let me guess where you were born.' For several moments there was an uncomfortable silence as the other Australians waited, not knowing what was transpiring between the other two. 'My guess is, let's see ... German? No,' he answered his own question, 'more likely you are from Lithuania? Perhaps Czechoslovakia?'

'Let me save you the effort, Colonel. I am a Hungarian Australian.' Zach said coldly.

'Very good, Colonel. Very good. And how did you manage to crawl *out of that dung heap all the way to Australia?'*

Zach's hands immediately turned into fists. Stephenson real- ised what was happening and stepped between the two men.

'Gentlemen,' was all he said. Murray stared challengingly into the Russian's eyes. He remained in this position until the Russian suddenly broke out into laughter and slapped Eric Whitehead on the back.

'You are new here, Colonel. You should learn some manners,' he said, smiling for the benefit of the others.

'And how would the Colonel be able to identify this change?' Zach replied, also smiling as if their interchange was hospitable. *'Since when does a Russian understand the meaning of manners?'* he added, hoping the barb would score.

'I will leave you here with your friends, Comrade,' Kololotov knew that this would earn a response.

'Go screw yourself, pig,' Steven Zach replied, smiling benevolently as he stood his ground and waited for the infuriated Soviet Attaché to storm back into the main body of guests. The public relations consultant frowned at the other Australians then turned to follow the Russian inside.

'Shit,' Murray said. 'I'm impressed!'

Steven Zach laughed, almost sincerely. 'Sorry,' was all he said. Stephenson knew that the exchange had been volatile. He wished he had understood what had precipitated the hostility. Zach had an impressive service record, he knew, having read the officer's profile on the morning their briefing had been postponed. Steven Zach had telephoned on Wednesday and asked Murray across to the Army Attaché's office. They met informally, and held a general discussion regarding Djakarta and Embassy life. They had agreed to meet again, privately, once the formalities of the colonel's first week had been attended to and his schedule permitted. Murray had made himself available to assist Zach with his settling-in pe- riod. The offer had been warmly acknowledged, both men obvi- ously taking an instant liking to the other. As Military Attaché in this post, Steven Zach was privy to the knowledge of not only the existence of the Australian Secret Intelligence Service but who the station operatives were.

Murray looked at the other man. They were about the same height and build, but the colonel was more than five years his senior.

The good-looking officer was not married and there was nothing in his dossier to suggest that there had once been a Mrs. Zach, Murray had noted, as he perused the newcomer's documents. It was not unusual for an ambitious career officer to remain single, in fact maintaining single status was particularly relevant to active field officers in his line of employment. Murray waved to a passing *djongos* carrying an assortment of canapes and removed two before the houseboy offered the tray to Zach.

'*Tidak, terima kasih,*' the colonel refused the finger-food. '*It looks good, perhaps I will have some later. Can you find me another drink?*' he asked the surprised *djongos*.

'I heard you were bilingual,' Murray said as the servant went in search of the drink-waiter. 'In fact, the staff tell me you are fluent in the local lingo,' he lied. It was less embarrassing than revealing that he had found this information in a highly classified report attached to the colonel's ASIS profile.

'They tell me the same thing about you,' he smiled, pleased the incident with the Russian had gone no further. Zach was angry with himself for permitting the Soviet to bait him as he had. In the past, when confronted with similar situations, mostly Zach had been able to resist such displays of animosity. Sometimes he just could not control the hatred which had consumed most of his conscious hours for almost twenty years. The Hungarian-born officer had once sworn to kill all Russians for what they had done to his country. And his family.

'What other skills do you have that we should know about?' Murray asked, politely.

'Thought you would probably already know that, Murray,' he responded, inferring that his personal papers would most certainly be known to the clandestine service, operating under cover in the Embassy. He didn't mind. Considering he was born in a foreign country, one which was now a Communist satellite state, Zach found it difficult to believe that he had successfully crossed that bridge of suspicion which almost always precluded foreign nationals from obtaining security clearance to sensitive posts.

'Ouch,' Murray grinned, remembering not to underestimate this fine soldier.

'It's okay, Murray,' Steven said, smiling genuinely. He approved of the other man. Zach had been well briefed by the Director of

Military Intelligence in Melbourne before leaving for Indonesia. 'Stephenson's all right', the general had advised, 'but watch the Station Chief, Davis. The man is out of his depth. Best you deal with Stephenson anyway, he is well-wired to the top and is going places. He has established himself as a sound and competent officer, and has an intelligent understanding of what is really going on in Soekarno-land.'

'Want to tell me what just happened back there?' Murray asked, curious as to what had transpired. It was obvious that the Russian had lost his cool. Not bad, he thought, Zach had managed to alienate the Dean of the Attaché Corps in his first week.

Zach looked at Murray and the younger man immediately wished he hadn't pried. Murray identified the cold, steel, penetrating look in the colonel's eyes. He had seen it once before. In Semarang. When the Diponegoro Commander learned of his junior officer's betrayal.

'Why not,' Zach said suddenly, to Stephenson's relief. 'The Russian insulted my heritage and I responded accordingly. You might as well get used to it, Murray, I just can't stand the bastards!'

'Shit, Steve, who can?' he agreed, just as the drinks arrived. Murray waited for Zach to select his cocktail first before deciding on the Bacardi and Coke. He checked the ice before the *djongos* was permitted to pour the mix. 'Anyway,' he continued, as the waiter disappeared, 'Kololotov shouldn't be around too much longer, from what I hear. Rumour has it he's about to be promoted and that, my friend, would mean Moscow for Boris.' Murray smiled, hoping to take some of the remaining tension out of the air.

'I really don't care one way or the other. He can stay or go.' Zach then stepped closer to Murray and lowered his voice. 'Maybe you can expand my briefing when we finally sit down together. I would appreciate an update of their activities.' Murray was surprised and Zach noticed the raised eyebrow.

'Spare-parts, Murray, spare-parts. Looks like Boris is about to negotiate a new deal with the Government to recommence supply. Seems there is a thawing in their relationship and, if this is to happen, we'll want to know bloody quick which of their armoured divisions would have the capacity to back up their Malaysian campaign.' Zach noticed Whitehead approaching. 'We'll talk later,' he suggested, with a conspirator's wink.

'Gentlemen,' the distinguished figure said. Minutes before, when the slight altercation had broken out between the Russian and Steven Zach, Whitehead had felt it diplomatic to accompany what he considered to be the offended party inside. His company, Eric Whitehead and Associates, had grown into one of the largest public relations groups in Australasia. Now he was in the process of establishing offices throughout South-East Asia, supported strongly by the Australian Government. The quid pro quo being that many of his country managers sent from Australia were, in fact, ASIS operatives who gained a direct entree into the target countries by utilising his company's established infrastructure and resources. He enjoyed considerable access to Government contracts back in Australia in consideration of his support. The public relations executive was not, fortunately, privy to more than the knowledge that Australia wished to collect intelligence in those countries where he had established his promotional activities. Harry Bradshaw had refused to give the civilian information which would reveal the existence of Central Plans.

Soon after the arrangements had commenced, the company developed the reputation for having an exceptionally high staff turnover, particularly with its overseas representatives, as many of these either refused to return at the end of their assignments, or merely resigned while they were 'in-country'. Now, it appeared he had plans to expand his activities in Djakarta.

'Gentlemen,' he said again, as the three stood alone. 'I must express my surprise at your treatment of Colonel Kololotov, especially you, Colonel,' he continued, pointing with the hand which held his drink, one finger extended. Murray waited. He could not believe that the public relations entrepreneur was venturing down this path.

'What?' Zach asked, frowning at the older man.

'Mr. Whitehead,' Murray interceded, 'perhaps we could let it drop for some other time?' he suggested. 'After all, neither you nor I have any idea as to what really occurred between the two officers. Let's just let it go. Okay?' He didn't like these amateurs and was as concerned as the other agents that people such as Whitehead were a little too close to their activities. Murray believed that these 'fringe dwellers' were totally unreliable as they were motivated by financial gain and often destroyed entire networks with their amateurish antics. Whitehead looked at Stephenson, trying to establish who he was and what his position may have been in the Embassy. Before he could respond, Murray took Steven Zach by the elbow and started to move away from the inebriated guest.

'Mr. Whitehead, the colonel must attend to his duties. He is the guest of honour here tonight, or perhaps you have forgotten?' said Murray. Zach permitted Murray to lead him back into the crowd of tipsy expatriates. The few Indonesian officers who had attended had left immediately after the buffet had finished.

'Ah, there you are,' their hostess cried, 'thought you'd been kidnapped! Come along, now, Steven, these are people you must talk to,' she said, taking her husband's replacement by the arm, and ushering him towards the noisy group standing beside the temporary bar.

'Oh, Murray,' a voice called, and he turned to see Davis moving in his direction. He could see that the Station Chief had also had a few too many. Seemed as if most of the guests had decided to lay one on for the evening. 'Want you to meet a very interesting guy I spoke to earlier,' his voice slurred. Murray looked for an excuse to escape but it was too late. Davis looked around and suddenly identified the object of his earlier attention. 'There he is now. Let's have a few words together,' the Station Chief insisted, walking back towards Whitehead from whom Murray had just, with difficulty, extricated himself.

'Not a good idea, Alan,' Murray resisted. He was annoyed that Davis had not identified the man for who he was. It was not considered to be in their best interests to develop any public relationship with this man.

'Hello there again,' Davis called, 'have you met Murray Stephenson?'

'Yes, I have. Do you two work together?' he asked, causing Murray concern.

Davis answered. 'Yes, First and Second Secretary, Political Section.' These positions would have meant little to Whitehead. He was unaware of their covert activities. 'Murray, Eric here was explaining to me earlier that he is in the process of making application to expand his operations into Moscow. Can you believe that?' Murray looked at the entrepreneur and understood why he had been so put out earlier, when they had first met. Whitehead needed

Kololotov to provide an entree into Moscow. Murray suddenly wanted to smile. Instead, he encouraged the man to discuss his activities and plans for their Djakarta office, leading the conversation away from their own functions in the event Davis screwed it up. Finally, identifying an opportunity to move on, he excused himself and asked to speak to his Station Chief in private. They walked outside and stood alone on the terrace.

'Alan, don't you remember who that guy really is?' he asked, still concerned that Davis had consumed too many whiskies. 'Doesn't the name Eric Whitehead and Associates mean anything to you?' he asked incredulously.

'Sure, Murray,' he answered, looking smugly up at his subordinate's face. 'I remember exactly who he is. Eric Whitehead is the man who might just become my new employer,' he grinned, enjoying the expression on Stephenson's face. 'We have already had discussions, Murray. The position offers double what I'm making now, and the opportunity down the track to earn share options in their company structure. What do you thing about that!' he said, poking his finger into Murray's chest, almost aggressively.

'I think you're a little pissed, that's what I think,' he answered, angry with the absurd proposition. He was convinced that Davis had lost it, and obviously had no recollection whatsoever as to the relationship the Service enjoyed with the public relations firm. 'Tell you what, Alan,' he said, his tone more friendly than before, 'why don't you and I go down to Mamas' place now, just slip out and look for some real company?' Davis stared back at the suggestion. They had never been out together before. Never. The idea of accompanying Murray appealed to him and he agreed.

'Okay, let's go,' he suggested. Relieved, Murray steered Davis quickly outside, placed him in the care of his driver, then returned to thank his hosts. Twenty minutes later he held his Station Chief with one hand while Davis yelled and screamed obscenities as the cold shower continued to pound his head. Murray cursed the man when he had stumbled, and thrown up in the shower cubicle. He left him there in his own mess, the shower still running, while he sat in Davis' lounge listening to his record collection and sipping the expensive cognac he had found buried behind the bar.

Some time passed, the fourth LP fell noisily onto the turntable and started playing a Cliff Richard album when Murray decided that Davis had probably recovered enough to understand what he needed to say. He went back into the bathroom and was surprised to hear the shower still running. He peered in though the shower curtains but there was no one inside. Murray took the three steps required to bring him to the en suite toilette and knocked. There was no answer there either. He pulled the door open and found Davis lying prostrate on the floor. He was dead. The Station Chief had choked on his own vomit and died.

* * * * * *

Melbourne

The Secretary to the Minister for External Affairs reviewed the reports for the umpteenth time and was convinced that what had happened, although tragic, required no further action from his Department. After all, he considered, the man did not really belong to their Foreign Affairs Department and there were strict guidelines as to how his Department should act under these special circumstances. He signed the report off, indicating that no further action was required, with the annotation that the file was to be returned to him personally, once the Attorney-General's office had accepted his findings.

The file was then delivered by security courier directly to the Attorney-General. His office gave the contents a cursory perusal, before onforwarding the findings to Melbourne. Once the documents had been received there, they were personally carried through the maze of offices along St. Kilda Road and delivered under signature to the Director. Central Plans had grown considerably during these two years. Harry Bradshaw relished playing the role of its Head, the Chief of the Australian Secret Service, ASIS.

He gave the report a perfunctory read before signing the document off for return to Central Registry. There was nothing contained in the highly classified document which he had not already known. Davis' death had been treated as an accident, his body returned to Australia within days of his demise, and buried quietly in his home town in Tasmania.

The Director sat looking at the brown file stamped in oversized red letters designating Central Plans' identification codes. Harry had no feelings for the loss of Alan Davis. There was now no risk of complications developing, despite the Director's suggestion that the incompetent Station Chief may have been involved in questionable relationships or that he may even have been compromised. Opportunity had provided Harry Bradshaw with a choice; he could place a temporary senior in Djakarta, or risk rank and file criticism by following his first instincts.

He wrote the message and buzzed his assistant. The signal was encoded and despatched. Within the hour, the message was taken by a supervisor and matched with the coded reference numbers. She checked the unreadable five letter word groupings in the original telex and aligned this yet again for further encryption. As the telex machines clacked away together in unison, she held the thin paper tapes punched full of identification holes, feeling the gaps pass over her experienced fingers. Satisfied that the commencement points had been aligned correctly and that the message had been prepared in accordance with Cipher Centre instructions, the supervisor removed the new tape and placed this on her international machine. She then dialled, by-passing the Australian operator, identifying the correct recognition answer back code of her first addressee, then squeezed the activate button, sending her machine through the thousands of randomly punched holes in her tape. Ten minutes later, the garbled five letter message was received in full by the Indonesian *Pos Telegrap dan Telepon*. Once the P.T.T. supervisor had ensured that the duplicate had been retained, the original was then placed in the appropriate box for collection.

Almost an hour passed before the Embassy driver picked up his hourly collection for delivery to his employers. Another hour passed before Murray, to whom the priority message was addressed, could be located and driven to the Embassy. There, once he had discovered the secret nature of the initial text, he moved to more secure premises. There, he removed the tapes and returned to his own section where a duplicate, but far more classified arrangement, was in place. He placed the tapes on the matching decoder machines and listened as they clattered away, almost in harmony. The noise stopped and the officer tore the text from the top of the Navy grey deciphers. He read the message slowly, then smiled. It was from Harry Bradshaw. He read the signal again. Murray laughed loudly in the huge lead-lined cavern as he spun the swivel chair around in excitement. They wanted him back in Melbourne immediately.

He had just been appointed Chief of Station, Djakarta.

KERRY B.COLLISON

Chapter 12

Melbourne

Susan enjoyed having her friends visit once again. She sat, dabbing her face lightly with the damp cloth, removing the small line of perspiration which had appeared on her forehead. The weather had been excellent, providing their guests with an opportunity to play several sets before the wind suddenly came in from the west, making conditions difficult on the court. Disappointed, they had ceased play and showered, only to discover that the inclement weather had moved on in that brief time, leaving a warm but gentle breeze to tempt them outside once more.

Murray had brought a New Zealand girl along as his partner. Susan would not have expected the young woman except Harry had informed his wife just hours before they were expected. She was not upset. Although Susan had regretted her indiscretion with Muriel's son, she was more than pleased that her moment of passion had not deprived either her or Murray of their friendship, and that the delayed fruits of their brief coupling had not resulted in some contentious dispute between those involved.

Susan had not been overly concerned that her husband was obviously aware that he was not the child's father. She was pleased that the issue never arose and was delighted that Harry eventually came to enjoy his role as father. Or at least, he appeared to, when others were around. Harry continued to be preoccupied with his work which, to her relief, required considerable travel. Her husband had become more and more secretive over the past year, making communication almost impossible between them. Susan maintained her circle of friends and, of course, there was her son to consider. He had already commenced kindergarten, creating yet another void in a life which already had far too many empty hours.

She knew that she could not go on like this forever, just marking time.

These occasional weekends filled with visiting friends helped Susan maintain her balance with reality and forget, briefly, that her life had become dull, even monotonous, to the point of despair. 'Thank God for Muriel Stephenson,' she thought. Often, whenever she felt really depressed, a simple telephone conversation would be enough to raise her spirits. She smiled, knowing that her boy was in good hands. Murray's mother had volunteered to watch the child and they were, at that moment, watching the Mickey Mouse Show together in his room.

Susan Bradshaw smiled as Murray returned from the room he always occupied whenever visiting their cottage. She admired his tall, athletic body, sun-tanned from his years in the tropics. Betty, the young woman who had accompanied Murray, was attractive. As they walked out together, she slipped her arm around his waist. Susan looked on, with a twinge of jealousy.

'Ready for another set?' she called, surprised by this brief sensation. There had never been any further sexual contact with Murray after that one brief encounter. Susan had strived to maintain a relationship between them both which not only preserved their friendship, but also protected their secret.

'Not for me,' Murray replied. 'Have to keep my strength,' he joked, winking at Susan. 'Why don't you two girls have a game?' he suggested, flopping down into one of the deck chairs beside the pool.

'Actually, I would prefer a swim now if you don't mind, Susan,' Betty said.

'Good idea,' she responded, pleased at not having to play alone with the younger woman. They rearranged the heavy poolside chairs to face the afternoon sun. Susan then disappeared inside, in search of the others. She found her husband proudly displaying his most recent acquisition, an opium pipe from China. The other guests stood around feigning interest in the item. Susan identified the bored looks and went immediately to their rescue.

'Come on, people, drinks,' she called, taking the younger couple and leading them back to the terrace which overlooked the kidney-shaped pool. Harry turned and followed, passing by the bar where he stopped briefly and collected the bottle of Moet Chandon, which had been resting in ice. The group settled around the pool, sipping the champagne as the rays of the afternoon sun warmed their bodies. They talked, laughed and enjoyed each other's company. Harry related an anecdote he had heard during his most recent trip into Asia, causing the men to roar heartily while the women almost choked in their attempts to resist laughing along with the others, as the raucous story ended.

'Why don't you go along on one of Harry's trips?' Anne Lawson asked. This was her first weekend invitation to visit the seaside home. Her husband had recently commenced working for the Government. Something or other to do with Planning, she thought, knowing that Government jobs were all a little vague, and boring. The men exchanged quick glances.

'Now there's a good question,' Susan agreed, clapping her hands together in appreciation of the suggestion being raised. She looked across at her husband to watch his reaction.

'It most certainly is, young lady,' Harry laughed, surprising all present. 'Why don't you join me on one of my excursions, darling?' he asked, seriously, reaching for the flute of wine. The glass was Bohemian crystal. It was all he had kept from those earlier times.

'I can't imagine myself gallivanting around with you in Asia, Harry,' Susan responded, smiling at the guests. 'You're always complaining that you don't have sufficient time in any of the places you visit. What would be the point?'

'Right again, my dear.' Harry laughed. 'Perhaps we should just send you off to one of the more exotic places by yourself.'

'Now that is a very good idea,' Susan agreed. 'How about leaving your wallet out Harry, and I'll go shopping in Hong Kong?' she teased, although the idea was appealing.

'Best to do your shopping in Singapore, Susan,' Murray advised. 'You would be guaranteed better quality and the prices are much more competitive. We all use Peter Chew's on High Street. He has never let any of the Embassy people down and will even arrange to have you met and escorted to his shop.' The group laughed, enjoying the thought that one could find such service anywhere these days.

'And you could just drop down and have a look around Djakarta and Bali while you're in the area,' Lawson offered, joining in with his unsolicited advice. 'It's only an hour's flight, and you have friends on the ground there,' he added, pleased that he had been able to contribute. Murray frowned and looked across at his host.

'Normally I would probably agree,' he tried to make light of the conversation. 'But Djakarta is no place for a woman and child, I'm afraid.'

'Oh, nonsense, Murray,' Susan interjected, 'all I have heard from the two of you has been nothing but talk of islands and beaches. I think it's a fabulous suggestion. Don't you Harry?'

'Murray's right, my dear. Djakarta is not exactly an appropriate tourist destination at this time, student demonstrations and all that,' Harry answered, certain that foreign women were rarely in danger in Indonesia. Apart from the street urchins and thieves who preyed on unsuspecting visitors for the most part, it was reasonably safe to wander around the country. The ongoing student demonstrations would be of concern though, he thought.

'But surely these are confined to the city, right, Murray?' She looked to him for help, suddenly determined to at least have the option to visit, even if only for a few days. 'Harry, this is a wonderful idea,' she said, leaning over and running her hand down his forearm. Susan then looked across at Murray. 'Well, am I invited or not?' she challenged. Bradshaw thought quickly. It wasn't such a bad idea. He nodded his head slightly, as he considered the request. As he looked around the circle of guests, Harry suddenly laughed, recognising that they were patiently waiting for his response.

'Harry, I don't think ...' Murray started to say before Susan interrupted again.

'Wait,' she asked, rising to her feet. 'No decisions yet. I will be back shortly,' with which Susan Bradshaw left her guests and entered the cottage.

'Harry,' Murray started again, 'it's no place for Susan right now. Especially with a young child,' he added.

'What if we just send her off to Bali and Djogyakarta for a week?' Harry suggested. 'Susan would be in raptures, I'm sure.' Murray was surprised with the response although he had to admit that travelling through the outlying areas and provincial capitals could be a pleasurable experience. Political unrest was mainly concentrated in Djakarta although he believed that it could spread at any time. Violence lay perilously close to the surface in Asia. Murray knew. He had been exposed to the sudden and violent eruptions which predicated massive unrest and destruction.

'Perhaps, if Susan were to just visit Bali?' Murray suggested as Bradshaw's wife rejoined the group.

'I thought we'd agreed to hold the discussion until I returned?' she asked. 'Harry,' she continued, smiling with enthusiasm, 'Muriel has agreed to look after Michael if I decide to go. So, now it's just a matter of where, and when. What do you really think?' Again she placed her hand softly on her husband's arm. Harry felt the warmth of her touch and rested his own hand on hers. He looked across at Murray for support.

'Susan, if you really want to go, then by all means go. I'm sure Murray would be only too happy to provide you with whatever assistance you'd need.'

'Of course. That goes without saying. Susan, we'd be delighted to have you visit. If you wish, I could probably arrange for you to visit the Thousand Islands while you're in Djakarta.' Harry Bradshaw was not displeased with the outcome. He knew that he could depend on their friendship to ensure that Susan would be adequately cared for during her visit. He smiled in appreciation as Murray glanced in his direction. The ASIS Director was confident that his new Djakarta Station Chief would have little difficulty in being able to make the necessary arrangements.

The following Monday, Susan Bradshaw filed an application for her passport. Three weeks later, bogged down since his return to Djakarta with the additional responsibilities of First Secretary, Murray Stephenson sighed heavily as he read the coded personal message from his Director. Susan Bradshaw had obtained her visa and was scheduled to arrive within days. He looked at the unfinished mound of files and shook his head, remembering his other mounting commitments. Murray was disappointed that she was arriving at this time. Everything seemed to be happening at once.

He thought through his problem and an idea came to mind. He then raised the receiver and punched the internal dialling codes through to the Defence section. An assistant answered and he asked to be connected to the Attaché. Moments passed before the familiar voice answered the phone.

'Zach.' The colonel had not meant to be abrupt. Murray smiled tiredly at the familiar voice.

'Steve, it's Murray. I need a special favour.'

* * * * * *

Djakarta

The crowd roared when the roof finally burst into flames. As the chanting continued, black smoke poured from the building and rose quickly into the breezeless sky. Across the city, other fires were developing quickly. The students had commenced their campaign of terror against the American offices, before focusing their attention on the various United States Aid agencies. The police stood by and watched, almost disinterested, as the devastation took place, often laughing as foreign representatives fled their buildings under a barrage of verbal abuse.

Heat emanating from the building finally forced the crowd back. Dried timbers exploded noisily as the fire raged unchecked. Fire engines had arrived but were blocked by militant students. The men stood and watched, as the building finally collapsed on itself, testimony to their helplessness. The brigade officer knew that any attempt to force his way through the onlookers would have resulted in his tender being destroyed. A thousand hands could lift even the heaviest of his fire-fighting trucks and smash it to the ground, rendering the equipment useless. A loud explosion was greeted with yet another cheer as the remaining wall collapsed upon itself sending a wave of hot ash and cinders into the crowd of onlookers. Startled, they moved back and waited, expecting some exciting finale, but there was none. The fire died down quickly, having exhausted the dry timber and other fuel within minutes.

The mob became impatient, disappointed that the excitement had finished. Someone threw a rock through the air, smashing one of the American cars parked down the street. A loud murmur of approval rose from the students and, within seconds, they turned their attention to the vehicles parked along that street. Shouts of encouragement filled the air as the crowd lost direction, swelling in ranks at great speed as people spilled into the streets and joined in the mass demonstration. Gradually, the crowd grew into an uncontrollable mob, spilling down into the side alleys, chanting and screaming slogans as they went.

A roar of approval thundered through the morning air as several houses fell victim to indiscriminate fire-bombs thrown randomly into the air.

'*Lagi dong!*' a young girl screamed in excitement as Yanti's throw burst through a window, exploding as it entered the second-storey window. Yanti turned and accepted another Molotov cocktail, waiting for the dirty rag hanging from the top of the beer bottle to be ignited. She held the bomb at arm's length as a comrade lighted the cloth wick then suddenly, satisfied that the simple but deadly incendiary was ready, Yanti hurled the bottle over the heads of the screaming mob directly into the building's entrance, where it exploded fiercely in flames. '*Another,*' her friend urged, thrusting a third bottle into Yanti's eager hands. This too was lit and thrown, landing directly where flames from her previous attempt had now engulfed the structure's entire front. The crowd cheered as an upstairs window shattered. Then suddenly they stopped and there was a hush as they stared in horror at two children who screamed at them for assistance, their small bodies framed by the gaping hole, as flames licked precariously around the second level.

'*Ada anak!*' a woman screamed loudly, pointing to the terrified pair. '*There are children up there!*'

'*Bantu'in, dong!*' another cried, insisting they be saved, but the onlookers stood petrified at the spectacle. By now the fire had broken through to the roof and black smoke billowed from the entire building. The firemen stood helpless. Their equipment was inadequate and none dared brave the blazing home, then totally engulfed by flame. One of the children disappeared from sight, having fallen to the floor of her room overcome by heat and smoke. The other child continued to scream and attempted to crawl from the window but could not, her escape blocked by remnants of shattered, razor-sharp glass still embedded in the wooden window sash. A woman in the street screamed as the young girl finally collapsed also, lost to the fire. Immediately the crowd's mood turned even more ugly but now it was directed at the elements responsible for the children's demise.

'*They did it!*' a voice screamed, pointing at the group of *Gerwani* women.

'*Grab them, somebody!*' another voice demanded as others yelled curses at the group of PKI rioters.

'Yanti, quick! Let's get out of here, now!' a friend hissed, sensing their danger. Yanti yelled a command to her group and they obeyed immediately, running down the street away from the angry crowd. Unable to keep up with the others, several of her slower comrades fell as rocks took their toll. They were left to fend for themselves. That was the rule.

'Run!' she screamed as her girls began to slow, and another fell. Yanti heard the shot and knew that somewhere behind, the rifle would be taking aim for a further kill. *'Run faster! They're shooting!'* she yelled, almost out of breath as they neared the small intersection. *'Keep going, around to the right!'* she ordered as her communist gang reached the corner. Terrified, they ran on, then turned as instructed, hoping to flee the deadly rifle fire. Yanti pushed them on, screaming at them not to stop as several of her troops slowed, already exhausted.

'Stop here and you will die!' she warned, grabbing one of the young women by the arm and forcing her to continue down the narrow street towards safety. Minutes passed before the weary women were able to change direction once again and slow to an exhausted walk. Yanti led them away, not stopping to rest until she was absolutely certain that they had not been followed.

* * * * * *

To the south, guests and staff of the Hotel Indonesia stood watching the billowing smoke fill the uptown sky. Although the Nirwana Supper Club was closed for lunch, guests had little difficulty accessing the well-appointed restaurant, permitting a clearer view of the riots below. Sirens wailed as military vehicles sped dangerously through the streets, one having already flipped over as it failed to negotiate the *Selamat Datang* roundabout directly below. A number of BTR-40 Soviet APC's poured into Djalan Thamrin from both Imam Bondjol and Djenderal Sudirman, slowing as they converged on the major intersection. Shots were fired into the air to disperse the demonstrators whose numbers had grown into tens of thousands around the city's new centre.

The angry mob was out of control and surged towards the army vehicles, ignoring the dangerous weapons mounted on the APCs. Another round of shots was fired. The crowd roared its disapproval. Suddenly the scene turned even more ugly, the air filled with screams and shouts as rocks were hurled. The soldiers did not hesitate. They fired directly into the mob, killing indiscriminately.

Alarmed, the crowd panicked and fled in all directions, trampling those before them. The violence continued as both soldiers and demonstrators became confused in the melee. More shots were fired, then again, until most of the crowd cleared the area.

Susan watched in horror, transfixed by the brutality of the moment. She hadn't meant to stay, watching the bloody scene. Something had held her there as the violence unfolded in the streets below.

'Wished you stayed home?' Zach asked. He could see just how distressed she was.

'Not exactly what I'd expected,' she said, standing with her arms crossed, still confused by the violence. 'Now I wish I'd listened to Murray,' she added, distressed by the sight of the bodies lying where the panic-driven crowd had trampled them.

'Why did you continue to watch this then?' he asked. Susan didn't respond. Steven was pleased he had decided to arrive earlier than agreed. He was to take her to lunch in the Tjahaja Kota, promising the finest froglegs in town. They had talked to fill in time and were preparing to depart when the streets outside suddenly became congested and an enormous crowd had gathered. Sensing the danger, Steven had suggested they remain in the hotel. When the rioting commenced, he'd escorted Susan to the observation point in the west wing, where they witnessed the partial siege of the city. Zach knew that Susan had never been exposed to such violence before and understood how distressing the scene below must be for her.

'We should move back inside, Susan,' Steven suggested, concerned. Susan turned and shook her head.

'No, I'll stay,' she replied, forcing a smile. Nothing like the mountains, is it?'

* * * * * *

At first, when Murray had requested his assistance, the colonel had been less than enthusiastic. Agreeing to escort an unseen partner

239

had its pitfalls, Zach explained. When it seemed that Susan might be left unescorted, Zach changed his mind and volunteered to assist. Murray had hosted a small dinner party, introducing his guest to a few close friends. Steven had smiled in approval as Susan was introduced. As he observed Murray's attractive house guest during the course of dinner, Steven Zach wondered how she came to marry Harry Bradshaw. He put the thought out of his mind, deciding it was not really any of his concern but, as the evening progressed, the question remained in his thoughts.

Murray was obviously relieved that Zach would shoulder some of the responsibility in ensuring Susan Bradshaw remained occupied during her visit. Murray forewent his rostered turn for an Embassy bungalow in Tugu, offering his weekend allocation to the Military Attaché. Zach jumped at the opportunity, and arranged for a small group to accompany Susan to the hill station. Once she had seen the small cluster of cottages nestled amongst the tea plantations, Susan began to unwind, pleased that she had not balked and refused the invitation. At first, she had felt uncomfortable that Murray would not be joining them but, when the others arrived, Susan quickly settled down and enjoyed the mountain air.

The evening was special. Gone was the sticky, humid weather of the capital. Here, at more than one thousand metres, the temperatures dropped just enough for the guests to enjoy an open fire. The *djongos* burned small tea tree logs and, as the aromatic smoke lingered in the air, Susan detected faint evening sounds emanating from the distant village, further adding to the tropical ambience. The evening passed too quickly for Susan. She experienced a genuine warmth in those around her, and realised just how long it had been since she had relaxed in the company of those her own age.

Late the next morning, Steven convinced Susan to join him for a long walk through the adjacent tea plantation. They strolled slowly through the green maze, Steven explaining how the planting cycle was maintained, and how the fields were first planted hundreds of years before. Susan listened attentively, occasionally asking an appropriate question, pleased with his company. The hours slipped by without their noticing the time. They rested in a small clearing and watched the plantation workers move in line across the difficult slopes, picking the finely-coloured leaves to shape the bushes. Susan could just see their bungalow's roof-line in the distance, partly obscured by a tall, thick stand of bamboo. Towards the west, the sun had moved behind Gunung Salak, indicating that the day was almost spent.

'It's so beautiful,' Susan said, admiring the orderly rows stretched out as far as she could see. 'This is how I pictured Indonesia would be.' She turned to Steven and placed her hand on his arm. 'Thank you for bringing me here, Steven. It will be a memory I will cherish.' Steven accepted the gesture for what it really was, a friendly touch which required no response. He smiled at her.

'Gets better as you go further away from the cities.' Steven rose and pulled Susan to her feet. 'Better be heading back,' he said, pointing to the low cloud rolling down the mountain side. Although the distance was not overly far, Zach knew that it would take almost an hour for them to make it back. As they walked through the well manicured rows, the wind grew in strength, signalling a mountain squall. Steve steered them both towards a simple structure which had been erected as a rest post for the plantation workers, to shield them from the heat of the tropical midday sun. No sooner had they crept under the simple cover when the light squall struck, thrashing the air with heavy rain.

The timber construction was barely three metres long and, having no walls, provided little protection from the horizontal rain as it cut across the mountain slope, stinging their faces and arms. They remained there until the wind abated, imprisoned by the heavy deluge. The sky remained black and threatening, lightning flashing all around as thunderclaps shook the mountain sides. Steven had stood with his back to the initial gusts of wind, protecting Susan from most of the heavy rain. He looked at her and Susan tensed, holding her closed fists to her mouth as a sudden flash signalled another close strike. She attempted to cover her ears, petrified by the ear-splitting thunderclap she knew would follow.

Steven moved closer to her side and placed his arms around the trembling woman. He didn't speak, but merely held her to provide comfort in her moment of fear. Zach could see that she was terrified by the sharp crashing sounds accompanying the tropical storm. He felt her tremble, then turn and bury her face in his chest, and cry out as another brilliant flash heralded the dangerous lightning which seemed to strike the village across the nearby field. Susan trembled and he held her tightly, telling her that she would be all right, as she clung to him in fear.

The tropical mountain storm was typically brief and, as the thunder and lightning dissipated, leaving the reluctant rain behind, Steven continued to hold Susan firmly. They were both saturated but neither felt the slight chill which followed the squall. As the rain eased, the sun broke through distant clouds to the west, casting beams of sunlight over the valley far below. Rain dripped through the weather-worn roof, finding a path down Susan's back, causing her to shiver slightly. She leaned back looked directly up into Steven's eyes.

His masculine smell touched her senses gently, causing an awareness inside that warmed her body, as he continued to hold her reassuringly. Susan tilted her head back slowly, her eyes closing softly as she parted her lips, and lifted her face to his. Steven looked down into her beautiful face and hesitated, kissed her gently, pulling her closer to his body. Susan moaned, her mouth becoming more passionate as they held each other tightly. Moments passed and they separated, staring at each other in surprise. Neither spoke as they stood there, holding each other.

It was Steven who broke the silence. As he spoke, quietly, his fingers drifted softly across her cheeks. She listened as he talked, and held her close. He started to apologise and she placed a finger on his lips to silence his words.

'Don't say anymore, Steven,' she whispered. He looked at her and slowly moved his head from side to side. They had been foolish, and caught by the moment, he felt. Steven smiled sadly and took her arms in his hands, slowly pushing her away.

'This can't happen, Susan,' he said, holding her at arms' length. 'I'm sorry.'

'Sorry? Why be sorry, Steven. I'm not,' with which she crossed her arms quickly and lowered her eyes, embarrassed.

'Susan?' The colonel placed his hand under her chin so that she would look at him.

'It's all right,' she murmured, searching for words to hide her disappointment. 'I suppose you think ....' she hesitated, her lips trembling as she fought back the tears.

'Shh!' he said, moving to draw her back to him, to comfort her as the tears rolled down her cheeks. 'It's okay, Susan. It's okay,' he said soothingly. Susan let him hold her for a few moments before she broke loose and turned away.

'I'm sorry also, Steven,' her voice choking as she fought against the tears. Susan turned and walked quickly away, in the direction of the bungalow.

'Susan,' he called, 'wait!' but she ignored the call. She stumbled, then regained her footing, then proceeded to walk quickly away, wiping her eyes with the back of her hands. He watched her go. Steven knew that he should follow, but felt that she would be best left alone. He stared after her, cursing himself for what had just happened. Steven watched Susan moving quickly along the plantation tracks, until the outline of her figure became smaller, then finally disappeared along the narrow path, through the hibiscus hedge leading to the bungalows. Satisfied that she was safe, he strolled slowly back in the same direction.

That evening, the atmosphere was more subdued. Fortunately the other guests were still present, agreeing to remain until early Monday morning when the traffic would not be as heavy. During a lull in the dinner conversation, Steven smiled as he caught Susan's eye which she rewarded with a playful kick under the table in response. Steven was instantly relieved, pleased that their relationship could continue on an amicable basis. They had returned to Djakarta early the next morning, Steven promising to take Susan for an experience he boasted she would never forget.

'Frog's legs, Susan,' he had said, indicating the size with both hands. 'Best I have ever eaten.' She laughed as his car drove away, already looking forward to their luncheon appointment. Susan was pleased she had moved into the hotel. She sensed that Murray was uncomfortable having her stay alone in his villa, and knew he was relieved when she opted to move to where, she suggested, there was a splendid pool and other women to talk to.

Now, as she stood high above the city centre, Susan wished they had remained in the mountains. The contrast between the tranquil hill station bungalow setting and the chaotic scene below was almost incomprehensible to the young woman. As she stood overlooking the carnage below, a number of two-man Scout cars suddenly poured onto the roundabout and opened fire on the few remaining onlookers with their deadly 7.62mm guns. Susan caught her breath sharply as she witnessed a group of stragglers collapse to the ground like oversized rag dolls. Shocked, she turned away sharply.

'Okay, that's enough! Please take me back to my room, Steven.' He did so, insisting that she remain there until he returned. 'Where are you going?' she asked, concerned.

'I must go the Embassy, Susan. They will be looking for me there. I'm sorry, it's bad luck. I will try to get back in a few hours. Providing the phones are still working, I'll ring you in, say,' he said, checking his watch, 'two hours.' He looked at her worried expression and smiled. 'It's okay. I'll be back before you know it.' Steven Zach left. Minutes later, he found himself standing behind other hotel guests blocking the lobby as they watched the end to the violence not fifty metres from the hotel driveway.

Steven exited via the northern wing rear entrance and crossed the car park. He walked through the Karya Wisata Hotel, out through the service area and across the small pedestrian bridge which brought him to Djalan Teluk Bitung. He walked quickly back towards Djalan Djenderal Sudirman and turned right, hurrying away from the hotel roundabout until reaching the Djalan Blora underpass, some three hundred metres from where he had started. There he found a *betjak* driver who, having been offered twice the normal fare, agreed to take Zach to the Embassy on Pegangsaan, by following the railway track. Twice they were forced off the small road by speeding Ferret Scouts as they, too, were obliged to seek alternative routes down to the riot centre. Fifteen minutes passed before the *betjak* delivered the shaken colonel to his Embassy. Zach went directly inside, where his assistant, an Army Warrant Officer, was obviously relieved that his colonel had returned.

'They're holding a prayer meeting extraordinary, now, sir,' he advised the Military Attaché. Zach merely nodded and left. He had expected as much. 'Prayers' were normally held Tuesday mornings, and were attended by the three Military Attachés, the Ambassador, his Counsellor and ASIS Station Chief. The riots had obviously demanded an urgent session be called to determine what course of action the Embassy might take, if deemed necessary. The Ambassador's secretary escorted Zach into the room.

'Gentlemen,' he said, nodding first to the Ambassador as the ranking officer present, and then to the others.

'Pleased you could make it, Steven,' the Head of Mission announced in a patronising tone. His deep resonant voice always surprised first-timers. The Ambassador stood not much taller than the exquisite mahogany desk behind which he ruled his miniature kingdom. The Military Attachés only gave the posturing Ambassador such respect as his position demanded, while normally ignoring whatever suggestions the undersized tyrant proffered during these sessions. Zach thought it quite appropriate, that, in his absence, the Ambassador was regualrly referred to as the King from *The Wizard of Id*. 'Our political section was in the process of briefing us,' he said. 'Please continue, Mr. Stephenson,' he ordered, waving a small podgy hand through the air.

'Thank you, Mr. Lovenight,' Murray responded. He disliked the little man immensely and refused to refer to him directly as Ambassador, electing instead to use the man's surname. 'I'd only just commenced, colonel,' he stated, formally. 'The position report is basically this. There are at least three major demonstration points. The worst appears to be centred around Djalan Thamrin leading up to the Hotel Indonesia. The city's Garrison Commander has placed a ring of troops around the embassies located off Iman Bondjol and behind Djalan Madura. They don't want the demonstrators to hit any more embassies although the Brits are not convinced that they won't be targeted yet again.' Those present were painfully aware of how the British Embassy had recently been gutted by fire, a result of past demonstrations. There were at least ten foreign legations situated within the danger area, including the Soviet, the New Zealand and what was left of the British Embassy.

'American offices are taking a pounding,' he continued. 'None of their citizens have been injured, although a number of local employees have been reported killed or are suffering serious injuries. It would seem that they are taking the brunt of the demonstrations. There are other and less serious reports of riots, but the majority of these appear to be strictly incidences of looting. We have estimates of around three hundred dead with no less than fifteen foreign offices and homes destroyed.'

'What's happening outside Djakarta?' asked the Air Attaché, explaining that he planned a visit to Sulawesi as part of his annual tour around the archipelago.

'So far, it seems, nothing,' Murray replied. 'But don't count on that situation continuing, Group Captain. Our information is a little loose out there in the provinces but it would seem that there definitely is a groundswell building. My advice would be to post-pone, or even cancel, your journey for a few weeks, at least. There is pressure mounting on the Military to prevent these communist demonstrations and we should not be surprised if they do take some action. Soebandrio's power play must have them concerned. After his recent appointment as Deputy Prime Minister, we have confirmed reports that the PKI have been told that their represen-tation in Cabinet will shortly be increased, to the detriment of the Army and Police. It seems that their Airforce, AURI, has made con-siderable inroads into the Army's traditional power base. Seems there's to be a major visit to China within weeks.'

The Attachés discussed the situation at length, agreeing to con-tribute to a final situation report which would be radioed within the hour to Canberra. As the meeting concluded, Murray took Zach aside as the others returned to their offices.

'How's Susan?' he asked anxiously.

'Still in the hotel. Agitated, distressed, but we shouldn't expect less. She watched the Ferrets open fire on the crowd. I told her to stay put until I returned. How are the phones?' Murray grimaced.

'Useless,' he answered.

'Okay, then. I'll prepare my contribution for the situation report and send it over to the Counsellor. Then I'll shoot back to the ho-tel.' Zach looked at his watch and swore.

'Tell Susan I'll call by later. And Steve,' he said, placing his hand on the other man's shoulder, 'thanks!'

Zach smiled and nodded, then returned to his office. A further two hours passed before he could leave the building. He took one of the Embassy vehicles down along the circuitous route he'd taken by *betjak*, instructing the relieved driver to drop him near Djalan Blora. From there he walked towards the Hotel Indonesia, surprised to see the area cleared of demonstrators, although two menacing BRDM Soviet Scout cars remained on both sides of the rounda-bout, maintaining an ominous presence. Further down the proto-col avenue smoke was still evident, and black clouds reached high into the air behind Sarinah, Djakarta's only department store.

He telephoned from the lobby then went directly to Susan's room. She refused to leave the hotel but did agree to join him down-stairs for cocktails. Steven escorted her down to the Baris Lounge Bar which, by then, was packed with guests and foreign journalists.

'I'm ready to return home,' Susan announced. Steven was not surprised. He had half expected this reaction. 'Would it be possible for me to leave tomorrow?' she asked.

'We could try, Susan. It won't be easy, the few flights to Singapore will undoubtedly be full. Wait for Murray to arrive. He should be here around five. Maybe he'll be able to call in a few favours if you're really determined to leave.'

'I couldn't stand another day like today,' she admitted, moving the small candlelight away from the centre of the low table. She looked at the *katjang goreng* and, deciding that the peanuts had been cooked in too much salt, pushed these to the side. Steven watched her. She was suffering from shock. She talked without listening, preoccupied with her own thoughts, the day's violence obviously heavy in her mind. He had seen this reaction before, but on a more exaggerated scale. Often, soldiers returning from their first confrontation with the enemy would either remain silent for days, or babble on incessantly like some excited child.

The bar lounge lighting was deliberately soft as this was where most foreign couples congregated during the early evening. It really didn't seem to matter whether it was early afternoon or late evening as the lighting never changed. Small smokeless candles set snugly in *bangka* tin holders provided flickers of light, further diminished by delicately-made red light shades. Even in this subdued light, Steven could see the anguish in her eyes.

Steven felt bad about Susan. In less than a week she had travelled from what was a relatively parochial society into a world where violence lay just below the surface at all times. He was annoyed that her husband had not, with his obvious understanding of the region, prevented her from travelling to Indonesia at this time. And, of course, there was Murray, he thought. Surely he could have dissuaded Susan from venturing into the country knowing just how volatile the political atmosphere had become. He leaned across and placed his hand over hers. Susan looked up into his eyes and smiled, just as Murray entered the bar and made his way over to where they sat. One of the waiters carried a low stool over for the familiar figure. Murray joked with the man, then ordered a Bacardi and Coke. He looked at his friends and immediately sensed the woman's tense mood.

'Looks like the worst is over.' He looked at Susan Bradshaw.

'Hear you had a bad time. Are you okay?' he asked, gently stroking her arm.

'Susan wants to go home, Murray. Tomorrow, if possible,' Zach informed him. Murray peered across at his friend in the dimly-lit lounge.

'Well, that's a pity, Susan,' he said, almost nonchalantly. 'I have managed to arrange a few days out on the islands for you, as promised. Do you remember what I told you about the Pulau Putri group of coral atolls?' he asked, sure that he had recounted stories about the Thousand Islands to Susan over the past few years. Murray sensed the mood and tried to lift her spirits. 'Hey, Susan,' he said, 'we are talking about crayfish, white sand, blue water and coconut palms!'

'And what else?' she asked, guardedly.

'It's a different world, Susan. And totally safe, I can assure you. Besides, today's violence is already history. Trust me, Susan, you wouldn't forgive yourself if you passed up this opportunity.' Murray looked to Zach for help but found none there. Steven Zach was disturbed by the fact that Stephenson seemed so cavalier about what was happening around the city.

'Murray, I think Susan has made up her mind,' he said, looking at them both. 'There has been a suggestion that even tomorrow wouldn't be too early.' Murray had expected this response. He looked across at Steven Zach but the lighting did not provide the opportunity for Murray to signal his friend. He tried another tack so as not to appear obvious. Hell, he thought, Zach was not to know that all international flights had been grounded for at least another forty-eight hours and there was no point in further panicking Susan with this detail. When he had discovered the airport's temporary closure, Murray considered the options. Susan could remain penned up in the hotel until flights returned to normal, or he could arrange for her to visit the idyllic islands just a few hours by power boat from Djakarta's harbour. A cruise out to the islands where he knew it would be completely safe would not only remove Susan from the dangerous city, but also from his immediate concern. There was no guarantee that, should she refuse, Susan would not become bored and venture out into the unsettled surroundings. He knew her well enough to be concerned about this.

'Susan, you really should consider this trip. Okay?' Murray

asked, wishing that Zach would support him. 'Tell you what,' he added, before she could refuse, 'if you agree to go, I will personally guarantee you the largest green crayfish you have ever seen. Okay?' he tried again. Steven looked across at Susan and was surprised that she appeared to be considering the offer. He frowned, then stared at Murray in the difficult light, trying to attract his attention without alerting Susan.

'Back in a moment,' Zach said, finally catching Murray's eye, as he excused himself and walked in the direction of the toilets. Several minutes passed before Stephenson entered the men's area and discovered Steven waiting patiently beside the wash basins.

'Took your bloody time! I was getting dish-hands wiping the damn things every time someone walked in or out of the place,' he complained. 'What's going on, Murray? Why the push for the islands?' Murray brought Zach up to date on what had happened at Kemayoran Airport. He shook his head and cursed the airlines, as he listened to the Station Chief justify his suggestion for Susan to spend the next few days out on Pulau Putri. They discussed the alternatives briefly, then Zach returned to the bar lounge. Susan gave him an enquiring look.

'I had to check in with the Embassy, sorry,' he lied. Then he leaned over the low table and asked, 'Are you seriously considering the island trip, Susan?'

'Could I still leave for Sydney tomorrow if I decided against the boat trip?' she asked. Steven looked directly at Susan. She was obviously not to be fooled and he decided to be frank with her.

'It may be some days before we could get you out via Kemayoran Airport anyway, as flight restrictions have been imposed. I agree with Murray. You could either stay here in the hotel bored to death, or go swimming out on the beautiful islands.'

'Alone?' she asked, now tempted to go, but not by herself.

'Of course not,' Zach replied. 'We'll make a few calls and see who amongst the wives would like to join you. Our Naval Attaché has his own thirty-footer complete with boat-boys. His wife is a water freak and would jump at the opportunity to take you out with some of her friends. Actually, the more I think of it the better this excursion sounds. You would be in safe hands and out of this confusion. Okay?' Susan thought for a moment and sighed. It would be better than sitting around the hotel pool there, she agreed.

'Could you both join us?' she asked, hopefully.

Zach frowned again. It would be impossible with the current situation and the monitoring requirements. 'We'll try to make it out on Friday. That way we could all come back together on the Sunday afternoon. I'll speak to Murray. If we can't make it, we'll let you know. The captain's boat is fitted with SSB which will keep everyone in touch.'

'SSB?' she asked as Murray returned to their table.

'Single-Side-Band radio,' he answered simply. Zach looked at Murray. 'Well, looks like we have a starter,' he said, now feeling more comfortable with the arrangements. Murray checked his watch and pulled a face. He finished his drink and rose, leaned over and kissed Susan on the cheek.

'Sorry, must be off. Besides, have to catch up with our friendly Navy Attaché and get things organised for this trip. Will you be all right?' he asked Susan as he stood, preparing to leave.

'Not if you're both deserting me,' she smiled, and looked questioningly at Zach.

'Of course not,' he laughed, waving to the waiter for drinks. Murray nodded, and left his friends while he returned to the Embassy and made the necessary arrangements for the island excursion. It was already late but he knew that the captain would probably still be in his office. While Zach entertained Susan Bradshaw, Murray went about organising the trip, driving out to the captain's house to speak with the Attaché's wife, and then despatching his driver down to the harbour area to alert the two-man crew that they would be departing the following afternoon. By ten o'clock that night, everything was in place, right down to the captain's wife having arranged for another of the wives to join in the boat trip. Provisions were not a problem; she merely drew on the substantial stocks in their store.

The three ladies were driven to Tandjung Priok by the colonel's driver the following day, where they boarded the captain's private launch and immediately went about covering their bodies with suntan oil. As they passed through the harbour's entrance just after midday, sipping gin tonics, and laughing at each other as they stumbled around the boat, the powerful twin Evinrude outboard engines pushed the launch through the calm seas at more than twenty knots, and took a heading for the farthest point in

The Thousand Islands.

The women settled down to enjoy the voyage and, within minutes, as they approached the first of the small coral atolls in the chain, Susan felt as if they had entered another world. She looked back towards the city, almost hidden beneath the heavy smog fed by diesel-driven buses and trucks, and immediately experienced a sense of release from the devastating events of the previous day. As the senior boat-boy steered the vessel around Pulau Edam with its historic lighthouse, Susan caught one last glimpse of Djakarta's distorted skyline through the distant haze and sighed, raising her glass in salute to the men she had left behind.

* * * * * *

Semarang

General Prajogo, the Diponegoro Commander, stared at the intelligence report in disbelief. It had taken months to acquire and, even then, the damning document left numerous questions unanswered. He rose from behind the heavy teak desk and moved to the window. His thoughts were clouded with the information contained in the BAKIN foreigners' desk file, a copy of which now lay open on his desk. His own Intelligence Officer had taken the initiative in the end, visiting the Indonesian Intelligence Co-ordinating Agency in Djakarta where, subjected to considerable persuasion, his brother-in-law had permitted him access to the sensitive files.

The general felt betrayed. But this was not a new sensation for the veteran army officer, as he considered the very existence of the Council of Generals a clear indictment of the senior Military leadership's intention to move his country away from the preferred policy of non-alignment, and deliver his people into the hands of the Americans. Not that he had any time for the Soviets, either! And then, of course, there was the other imminent threat of the communists moving to take control. The general cursed the PKI under his breath as he considered the unexpected complication disclosed in the folder lying on his desk.

He knew that the success or failure of their plan would be in the timing and now, with the evidence he had received, the general was convinced that their plans would most certainly fail should they continue as originally scheduled. No, he thought, he would not lead his men into the well-prepared trap. He and his officers were certain that the PKI must be close to finalising their plans as their presence in the capital had grown considerably, fuelling speculation that their move to take control was imminent.

Having considered all of these matters, the Commander decided to take the Javanese approach to the problem, preferring to see how the situation developed first, before launching his own plan to wrestle control from the Council of Generals. A window of opportunity had opened and he now knew what it was that he must do. No, he decided, the Diponegoro Command would not move first to snatch the reins of government from those in power! Instead, he would wait for the communists to first make their move and then thrust his soldiers into the arena to challenge the PKI leadership. It would all come together perfectly, he believed, just as long as they were patient. His men would defeat the communists' attempt to snatch control and, while this was happening, his officers would ensure the removal of the members of this so-called Dewan Djenderal, who sat around idly ignoring the obvious as they grew fatter with the help of their American friends.

The Commander was convinced also that the people of Indonesia would applaud his actions in restoring the Government and dealing with those responsible. The *rakjat* would support the Diponegoro Commander when he explained why it had been necessary to remove the current military leadership. The people, his *rakjat*, would understand. Of that he was certain.

The general turned back to the folder which had, once he had discovered its secrets, resulted in his drastic decision to place his own plans in abeyance until the communists made the first move. He looked down at the report and shook his head once again at the annotations made by the senior Intelligence officer responsible for the contents. He just couldn't understand how this man had so obviously fooled even his own Government and still managed to maintain such a senior position. There was little doubt in the Commander's mind that his Command had been compromised by the foreigner mentioned in the file. It was obvious, he concluded, having read of the man's constant association with the communists. Most likely, the PKI were just waiting for the generals to move first and had prior knowledge of his intentions. The communists were clever. They could then use this in their favour to gain even greater control over the President and the country. No, the Diponegoro Divisions would wait. He would play their game and see, just who would win the final play!

General Prajogo looked disapprovingly at the passport sized photograph taken from their Immigration files and attached to the report. His fingers scratched at an irritation on the crown of his head. Then, almost absent-mindedly, the Commander cleaned the dead tissue from under his fingernails with the *Djogya* silver letter-opener, a gift he had received from his fellow officers. Still deeply disturbed by the revelations disclosed in the open folder lying across the large sheet of blotting paper, he frowned once more then drove the sharp point directly through the photograph of the man he considered responsible for the major shift in his strategy.

'Bangsat!' he growled, looking down at the folder, but Murray Stephenson's face just smiled back at him, mockingly.

* * * * * *

The Assistant to the Naval Attaché, Chief Petty Officer Ron Brindles, himself a Milne Bay veteran, stared through bloodshot eyes as he assured Colonel Zach that the crew had understood the captain's instructions clearly. His condition was more a result of his alcoholism than time put in behind the unofficial Embassy radio. The vessel would be standing by in Tandjung Priok Harbour at 0800 hours on Saturday morning, to transport the Military Attaché and other guests to Pulau Putri, the Chief had said. The ladies would remain on the island while the launch returned to fetch those passengers intending to spend the weekend on the coral atoll. Chief Brindles relayed the information as if he were reading the departure details to the passengers of some ocean-going liner. As it turned out, there were only two. The captain had decided that as the Indonesian Navy did not appear to be involved in the political disturbances, there would be little point in his forgoing an opportunity to spend time out on the islands. Armed with additional supplies, the two officers boarded the vessel, which covered the forty nautical miles in two hours and arrived at their destination as the women were preparing an early lunch.

ALRI, the Indonesian Navy, controlled these islands, most of which were uninhabited and covered with thick stands of coconut trees. Fisherman landed from time to time, mainly out of curiosity or to sell their catch to the few foreigners who occasionally visited the small paradise. A makeshift jetty had been constructed although the captain still preferred mooring away from the shore. Two timber shacks had been erected and the women had established possession of these with just a few rupiah. At the rear of the dwelling a western toilet had been installed adjacent to the *mandi*, where one could bathe with fresh water, providing the overhead tanks had recently benefited from rain. A cooking pit prepared with coral lay between the beach bungalows and the lagoon. It was an idyllic place.

Zach could not believe the magnificent setting as their vessel turned carefully into the wide lagoon. At first, he thought their destination was the centre of the beautiful, elongated crescent-shaped island directly in their path. The water was clear to incredible depths, reminiscent, he thought, of Australia's north-eastern coastline. A pod of dolphins lept out of the water, leading the way through the narrow channels and brilliantly-coloured coral reef. As their launch moved farther into the setting, Steven discovered that, what he had believed to be one long island suddenly fractured into a chain of tiny coral atolls, numbering more than fifty. Each of these minute islands was smothered with coconut trees, which swayed gently in the tropical sea-breeze. Zach saw as the launch glided past that the palms were thick with bunches of yellow and green coconuts. It was as if they had entered an untouched world, Zach thought, almost at a loss for words as they became encircled by the beautiful group of islands.

The women waved as they wandered down to the water's edge, watching the vessel moor alongside the shaky jetty. The men stepped ashore, leaving the crew to manage the supplies and start up the small diesel generator to prevent the perishables from spoiling, and prevent the ice from melting further in the ship's oversized freezer.

'Well, we made it!' Steven smiled, removing his sneakers. The fine white sand felt great beneath his feet. He removed his shirt and sat on the narrow beach. 'Think I'll move the office out here!' he joked. He looked up at Susan who seemed totally relaxed. Zach was pleased. 'Have you learned how to scamper up one of those yet?' he asked, pointing to the coconuts high above their heads.

'Sure,' she replied, also laughing. 'We did that first thing this morning when we discovered the men were coming.' She was obviously in good spirits, he thought, relieved that sending her out with the others had not been an error in judgement.

'Murray said to say 'hello'. Obviously, he couldn't make it.'

'What's happening back in Djakarta?' she asked, some hint of weariness in her voice.

'It has quietened down, thank God.' Steven watched her face. 'Airlines have space available if you wish to return on Monday.' Susan looked down at the sand and moved her toe around, doodling.

'And if I say yes?' she asked, digging into the sand with the heel of her foot.

'It would be easy enough. We could just radio the Embassy and the Duty Officer would make the arrangements over the weekend for you.' He watched her move sand around unconsciously. 'That is, if you really want to go on Monday,' he added.

Susan seemed to be deep in thought. She looked up and smiled. 'We don't have to make that decision immediately, do we?' she asked.

'No, of course not.' Steven replied, rising to his feet. 'Now, Jane, how about some food for Tarzan,' he joked, making light of the moment. It worked, Susan entered into the spirit of his mood as she led him to the bungalow and made them both a vodka mixed with canned orange juice. They sat outside on the narrow stretch of sand leading down to the lagoon where occasional ripples broke the glass like appearance of the water's surface. The sun warmed their bodies as they sat, quietly enjoying the tropical ambience. Steven could see the tips of coral exposed as the tide receded. Before he had finished the vodka, reef was evident all around. He watched, fascinated, as an area almost the size of a football field slowly appeared, exposing sea life of considerable variety. Coral fish continued their dangerous adventure, swimming through the now shallow waters in search of food, oblivious to the sharp-eyed prey waiting high above for an opportunity to pounce. Crabs scurried around, playing hide-and-seek between the outcrops while sea-slugs, those succulent, cucumber-shaped tropical delicacies, lay indolently just below the surface. Soon, Steven could see that it would be possible to walk most of the one hundred metres across to the adjacent island, in the ankle-deep lagoon. Just a few steps to either side of the natural causeway, Steven observed how quickly the shelf fell away to much greater depths where larger fish fed lazily off the rich coral reef.

They remained there, together, enjoying the atmosphere and each other's company as the others, drinks in hand, wandered down to join them. As the sun reached its zenith, the men entered the deeper waters and snorkelled, while the women stood, waist deep, holding their drinks and chatting contentedly.

As the day wore on, they continued to enjoy the setting, eating crayfish and crab bought from passing fishermen for lunch, while consuming what appeared to be a never-ending flow of cocktails. By evening, the men were hungry again, insisting that they break out the steaks. The meal was cooked and consumed, along with several bottles of Italian wine obtained from some dubious supplier back in the capital.

Steven rose to his feet and stretched. They had finished eating and he'd had more than enough to drink. He strolled slowly down to the water's edge and remained there, admiring the evening sky. The lagoon remained dead calm, untouched by the soft breeze which moved, unnoticed, as it gently touched the tall palms standing like self-appointed guardians over the island and its tenants. He yawned, but he was not tired. Zach breathed deeply, savouring the tropical salt air. There were few clouds and, as the moon suddenly broke loose casting its golden spell across the waters, he became mesmerised by the magical setting.

He sensed someone moving close but did not turn to look. Nor did he flinch when she placed her arm around his.

'It's so incredibly beautiful,' she whispered. Zach remained silent, as he knew words were not necessary. They stood, together, captivated by the balmy tropical evening. 'Let's walk,' she suggested, encouraging Zach to follow as she moved away, holding onto his arm. They stepped into the tepid water and strolled slowly, away from the bungalow's lanterns and the others. They followed the sandy shoreline where phospherescence sparkled as their feet stirred the shallows. As they moved together, their arms locked around each other's waists, Susan rested her head on Zach's shoulder. Out of view, they stopped momentarily, under a tall stand of coconut palms. They didn't speak. It wasn't necessary and, as Susan lifted her mouth to his, Steven responded with a tenderness she had forgotten was possible. The warmth of his kiss engulfed her, and she pressed for more. Steven reached down and lifted Susan into his strong arms, moving towards the palms. He placed her gently on the sand, continuing to kiss her softly as his hands found their way over her body. He removed her clothes, then his, kissing the soft white areas as she encouraged him with her hands. She kissed him again, urgently, and Steven responded, almost impatiently, causing her pain which went unheeded as they joined passionately. Suddenly, Steven moaned and Susan cried out, her body arched and trembling in ecstasy. Then it was over.

They lay in each other's arms, resting, Susan stroking her lover's back as he kissed her mouth, then neck, softly.

'Steven,' she started, but he kissed her again, silencing her voice. As the warm air washed over their bodies, and the soft moonlight occasionally broke through the tall palms, casting shadows across them, they fell asleep. Clouds moved lazily across the evening sky blotting out the light, as Susan and her lover lay together. A gecko lizard scurried across a fallen coconut trunk, seeking refuge from birds it sensed watching in the darkness. Soon, the morning stars brought a colder breeze.

Steven woke, and shook his companion gently. Susan lay quietly listening to the ocean's sounds as the tide encroached. She placed her hands on Steven's face and whispered his name. They embraced, then kissed, and as Susan moved her hands across his body Steven became aroused, touching her body softly, caringly. As they made love again, this time with greater tenderness than before, Susan closed her eyes and wished that the moment would never cease; that the indescribable warmth which flowed though her body would never end and, as their bodies slowed, she sighed, deeply, in contentment.

As the morning sun threatened to spill over the early horizon and the evening hunters returned to the sanctuary of their nests, Steven and Susan walked slowly back to their bungalow, and their friends. Neither spoke, for there was little left to say.

They both understood what had happened and the consequences of their actions. But, at that moment, neither seemed to care.

Chapter 13

Presidential Palace
Djakarta

Bung Karno stood facing the northerly aspect of the Palace grounds. He had a great deal on his mind. Below, he observed a Toyota jeep enter through the main gate. From it emerged the figure of a man he had grown to despise. Soekarno snorted. His military now boasted almost four hundred officers of general rank amongst whom, he felt, to his dismay, less than a handful could be trusted. The President stepped back from the tall window and withdrew to the small ante-chamber where he normally rested. He would make the general wait. Soekarno looked at the Dutch grandfather clock and noted the time, before disappearing into the adjacent room. There, he removed his shoes and lay on the couch, closing his eyes permitting his thoughts to flow freely as he waited, anticipating his personal assistant's announcement that Nasution had arrived. Soekarno closed his eyes willing the pressure at his temples, to go away.

His dream of a non-aligned nation was quickly dissipating, forced into oblivion by the British, who were using regional conflict to reassert their colonial presence. He wondered if Nasution was part of this latest conspiracy. He sighed. If only the British would leave well enough alone, he thought. It seemed that they were determined to force the issue over the Federation of Malaysia up to the very end. The British had mobilised forces far beyond what he and his advisers had envisaged. None could have anticipated their transporting so many of their soldiers from Europe into Malaysia to support the newly-created Federation of Malaysia with its eastern alliances. At least Brunei remained outside the British-conceived amalgamation. Singapore too had been obliged to reconsider its position.

He was pleased, at least, with this development. The Singaporeans were, in his opinion, astute and their neutrality essential to the ultimate realisation of a Pan Indonesia.

He knew that his authority and stature had grown as a result of his non-aligned policy. Soekarno believed that the new emerging nations needed to position themselves on the international dais using their collective voice to demonstrate to the neo-colonial powers that the world had changed. He urged the other newly independent nations to emulate Indonesia, unified under a common philosophical front, to shun British and American overtures to surrender their political independence in exchange for economic bondage. He had a greater dream for his people, one which would provide not only an independence to achieve those freedoms denied under Colonial Rule, but one which would also guarantee their right to exist without the fear of reprisal from the British and Americans for Indonesia's stance on non-alignment.

He felt tired. It had been only six years since the Americans had positioned their Seventh Fleet in Singapore, in preparation of their Sumatran invasion, a move he had recognised at the time as being intended to split the fledgling nation into chaotic and more easily influenced states. The Americans had, of course, failed. Now he was faced with another attempt by an old rival to challenge his power. The British had embarked on a course which, having been discovered, proved beyond doubt that they would never accept an Indonesia under his leadership. A telegram addressed to the British Foreign Office and signed by the British Ambassador, Andrew Gilchrist, lay on his desk. It was the most damning indication yet that the British would stop at nothing to subvert his Government. His Deputy Prime Minister, Dr. Soebandrio, had produced the letter which contained documentary evidence of a plot against both himself and his Foreign Minister. The communication was proof that the British had established close connections with local army elements who would support the overthrow of Soekarno and his Government.

The President knew that Chou En-Lai's visit had ruffled feathers in the West. When the Chinese visited in April to participate in his tenth anniversary celebrations of the Bandung Conference, Soekarno realised also that anti-communist factions within his Military had deliberately boycotted the ceremonies to demonstrate their displeasure at having Mao Tse Tung's right hand man present. He knew that his generals suspected Soebandrio of arranging arms for the purpose of creating a Fifth Force in Indonesia, to be called upon in the event the communists gained control of the Government. When he had urged his Commanders to give this 'Fifth Force' serious consideration their reactions were, as he had anticipated. Nasution had excused himself from the meeting and had not returned. Several of the others present were obviously agitated by his suggestion but not prepared to display their displeasure openly. These, he believed, were the nucleus of what was deemed to be the secret Council of Generals. Soekarno smiled as he considered his provocative proposal to develop a fully armed party to counterbalance his own Military. It was, in fact, just a ploy. But he knew that his generals had not understood the tactic. Instead, they viewed his proposal as one which would undermine their own powerful positions. His thoughts returned to the man who would now be waiting outside, angry with being deliberately kept cooling his heels. Soekarno knew what Nasution wished to discuss. No, not discuss, he thought, it would be more like a confrontation, again. Someone inside the Palace had apparently informed General Nasution that he had sent Omar Dhani to Peking to negotiate a secret small-arms deal. An aide had reported that the senior general had been livid when he discovered that the communists were arranging for weapons to be delivered covertly into the Republic. Soekarno realised that Aidit, as Chairman of the Communist Party, had overstepped the mark recently, publicly announcing that they would arm five million communist workers and up to ten million peasants to carry on the war against Malaysia, should the TNI continue to fail in this mission. Aidit had created even more enemies amongst the Indonesian Armed Forces with that outlandish statement, Soekarno knew.

In order to appear impartial, he decided to maintain an ambiguous position, openly favouring the creation of such a Fifth Force while never really moving to introduce such an ambitious plan. He had to be seen to be still in charge of the powerful factions. It was, he felt, the most difficult balancing act he had yet attempted in his political career. On one hand he was faced with the monster of his own creation, a mass of more than twenty million workers who could clearly overwhelm the military should they become

KERRY B.COLLISON

armed. Their union movement, SOBSI, had volunteered to fight alongside Indonesia's regular forces if the country were ever subjected to aggression. On the other side of the coin, he was faced with the Military and its many factions. Soekarno thought solemnly for a moment. This Dewan Djenderal was a real threat, and he had little doubt that those involved in the secret Council of generals were receiving support not only from the Americans, but also from the British. That damn letter sent by Ambassador Gilchrist was proof! There was a knock at the door as his aide peeked into the chamber. Soekarno waved impatiently for him to enter.

'Bapak, Djenderal Nasution still waits,' he said, almost timidly. The Palace staff were all aware of the differences which existed between their President and the Sumatran general. Soekarno lowered his feet to the floor and rubbed his feet on the Persian carpet.

'Tell him I will be there shortly,' he instructed, sending the young officer away. He dressed slowly, then checked himself in the long mirror, ensuring that his many rows of military campaign ribbons were straight. Satisfied, he smiled at his reflection and marched out into the formal office area to greet his most senior military officer. Nasution rose to attention as Soekarno entered.

'Bapak,' he said, the obvious lack of deference evident in his eyes. The President indicated that Nasution should sit again, as he selected a large, ornately carved chair for himself. Soekarno then crossed his legs, permitting the toe of his highly polished shoes to point in the officer's direction. Nasution observed the offensive movement, leaned back into his own seat and emulated the President's behaviour. There was then a moment of silence as they viewed each other, before the general finally spoke.

'No doubt you know why I am here, Bapak,' he commenced.

Soekarno remained perfectly still, without responding. Nasution sighed silently. It was going to be as difficult as every other time they had met, he felt immediately. He looked directly at his President. What is really going on in the man's mind? he wondered. How can he continue this madness against Malaysia, with the incredible losses their men had suffered at the hands of the British and Australian SAS in Sarawak? Why is he permitting the communists to arm? Surely he must expect the Armed Forces to react to such a provocative step? As these questions ran through his mind for the umpteenth time, still there were no answers.

'*Bung Karno,*' he started again, selecting the form of address he knew Soekarno would appreciate. He had to try to convince the President to cease supporting the communists openly against the Military. It was flirting with disaster, he knew for certain. Many of his officers had already expressed a desire to ban the Communist Party. Like him, they also could not understand why their President had permitted the communists so much power within the Government. Their representation was directly disproportionate to the *rakjat's* wishes. This had been clearly demonstrated and still the Great Leader of the Revolution failed to recognise just how much power he had already given Soebandrio and Aidit.

'*Bung Karno, I have come to seek your assurance that you will not support the arming of the PKI,*' he said. '*There is considerable unrest amongst the Military at the suggestion that this so-called Fifth Force has your blessing. We have been informed that you have sent senior AURI officers to China to arrange for the purchase of weapons.*' He paused, looking to see if Soekarno had registered the fact that knowledge of the Air Force contingent's mission had leaked from the Palace. '*I have come here today to seek clarification of this matter.*'

Soekarno uncrossed his legs and leaned forward as one of Palace household staff entered and made his way towards the country's two most senior men. In Javanese style, the old man bent forward, so that his head would be lower than that of the President and his guest. Incredibly, the ageing *djongos* managed to balance the silver tray with its load of drinks and *makanan ketjil* without spilling either the cold coffee or the sweet sickly cakes, as he knelt on the floor and served.

'*Dhani's trip to China was simply within the framework of responding to an invitation extended by Chou En-lai during his visit. It is nonsense that the purpose of his visit is to secure weapons for the communists.*'

'*Bapak President,*' Nasution responded, careful not to permit his anger from becoming evident. '*It would be inappropriate for Dhani to enter into any agreements with the Chinese without first obtaining approval from the Armed Forces' Chiefs of Staff.*' He avoided accusing Soekarno of lying, even though the President's lack of candour was obvious to Nasution.

He waited for a response but Soekarno remained still, as if considering his reply. Then the President looked at his highly polished shoes, almost as if disinterested in continuing the discussion. The powerful men sat facing each other for several more moments while a Dutch grandfather clock standing in the near corner ticked away the seconds. Suddenly Soekarno rose to his feet and walked slowly towards the steel-framed window overlooking the palace's southerly aspect. He stood still, hands clasped behind his back as he stared at the activity in the courtyard below.

'Dhani will provide a full report concerning his activities upon his return. He is not on a mission to purchase weapons from our Chinese friends.' The President then turned and smiled at Nasution. *'You have my word,'* he added.

Nasution then rose to his feet also and looked directly at his Commander-in-Chief. He knew that Soekarno was lying and wished it were otherwise. In spite of their differences, the Sumatran acknowledged that his President had made considerable contribution to their country. If only the man had not permitted the communists to grow into the force they had become, threatening the very existence of the *Republik*. He knew it would be unwise to challenge the President's integrity as such a move could only result in a further deterioration of his position as the Military's most influential general.

He sighed silently, disappointed once again with Soekarno's obvious attempts to disguise whatever scheme the Airforce Chief of Staff had initiated during his current visit to China. Nasution was certain that the information he had obtained was reliable. Realising that the President was determined not to reveal anything relating to the covert arms purchase, he decided to leave. Even before he had sought this audience, Nasution had somehow known that any attempt to dissuade Soekarno might fail, and would not deter the President from the dangerous course the country had now taken. He stared at the man he'd once admired and suddenly knew what had to be done.

'Then I will inform the other Chiefs of Staff that Dhani's journey to Beijing is merely one of Muhibah,' Nasution stated, indicating he had accepted the explanation that the Airforce general's visit was one of a goodwill nature. Soekarno looked directly at his senior general and their eyes locked momentarily. Both men knew that the other had lied. There was nothing left to be said. Nasution nodded slightly in the President's direction.

'*Bapak,*' he said politely, then came to attention, retrieved his cap and marched from the regal setting. Soekarno turned back to the window as if disinterested and observed the scene below. Moments later, he watched Nasution emerge from the building and walk determinedly across the court-yard to his jeep. As the Army vehicle sped away almost injuring one of the palace guards who had foolishly failed to identify the four-star general, the President frowned. He was annoyed with the information leaks from within his own close circle. It was almost impossible to maintain any secrecy these days, he thought angrily, turning away from the window as he wondered whom amongst his trusted confidants had betrayed the real purpose of Dhani's mission to China.

His mind clouded with these worrying thoughts, the President instructed his aide to inform his Japanese wife, Dewi, that he would not be visiting that evening. Already he had become bored with his Japanese acquisition. Instead, he would visit his most recent conquest and spend the hours with her instead. He needed to experience the luxury of the girl's innocence and youth. Suddenly the pressures of the moment disappeared as an image of the young Javanese girl entered his thoughts and he smiled, delighted with his decision. The heavy matters of state could wait, he decided, anticipating an evening of pleasure with yet another of the willing students only too eager to discover for themselves the truth of the President's legendary sexual prowess.

The Indonesian President stretched as he made his way back to the private chamber, removing his clothes as he went. Having removed all of these, he then stepped into his favourite sarong, pulling this up loosely around his waist and climbed onto the hard four-poster bed. Then he closed his eyes to rest in preparation for the evening's activities and, moments later, he felt the tensions of the day fade away. Soekarno fell into a deep and comfortable sleep, unaware of the dangerous elements which were moving to engulf his Presidency.

And the people of Indonesia.

* * * * * *

Lembah Njiur (Bogor)

It was apparent from the mood that not all of those present were happy with having been summoned to the secret hillside rendezvous on such short notice. Major Djenderal Harjono moved to console the other senior officers as they waited impatiently for Nasution to arrive. He observed Parman and Soeprapto, and was concerned. The generals' faces reflected the constant stress under which they were obliged to operate. Both men had been working to maintain some semblance of authority within their own Commands whilst the communists continually destabilised their power base. It was apparent that they were all deeply worried by the intensity of the communist elements encroachment throughout the Military. It seemed as if overnight, many of the middle-ranking officers had shifted their loyalty to the communists, challenging the once firmly ensconced TNI leadership. The PKI had indeed become a major force within the Military and, as their numbers grew, the communist officers became even more apparent, often showing open disdain for their senior officers who had refused to identify with the powerful political party.

Worn brakes indicated the arrival of another vehicle as the jeep came to a noisy and abrupt halt outside the bungalow. They all knew it would be Nasution. They listened as a door opened, then closed. There was a brief but muffled exchange then he entered, and they all rose to greet their leader. Without exception, those present admired and respected the Sumatran general. He was an honest man. A hero. He had assumed leadership when General Sudirman had passed away, leaving the fledgling Republic's Military in Nasution's capable hands.

As he entered they could see that he too displayed signs of exhaustion. Tired as he was, Djenderal Nasution smiled at each one in turn, shaking their hands as he moved amongst their number. They were all quietly relieved. None had dared say it, but there was not one present who had not feared that Nasution's delay may have been at the hands of their enemies, for these men understood the ruthlessness of those dedicated to destroying the anti-Communist officers within the military.

The men waited for Nasution to sit before they too returned to their chairs. Yani knew from his friend's weary features that their position had become critical. Nasution had aged dramatically over the past months. Yani admitted silently that none of them would survive Soebandrio's machinations if they delayed longer. Of this he was certain. General Nasution spoke.

'Well, my friends,' he commenced in sombre voice, 'I can confirm that Dhani is on a mission to purchase arms for the communists.' The four-star general looked directly at Yani, his closest ally amongst those present. 'Your intelligence has now been confirmed. Soekarno all but admitted that our Airforce colleague is, as we speak, licking Chou En-Lai's feet and arranging for the Red Chinese to ship weapons to the Indonesian Communist Party.' Nasution observed the faces of his Council. Major General Harjono merely shook his head in disgust. He had developed a deep distrust for the Airforce general ever since the President appointed Dhani to KOGA, the Komando Siaga, an inter-service body formed to wrest control of the Malaysian campaign away from the Army. He had been instrumental in foiling Dhani's attempts. Nasution went on. 'We must now assume the worst, gentlemen. The PKI is moving to arm its cadres and that, we must believe, will result in armed insurrection and a communist take-over.' He paused, sipped the cold thick coffee, then placed the heavy glass back on the aluminium coaster. 'We must now agree to pre-empt such action. We must move before they are armed.'

'When will these shipments arrive?' General Parman asked, concerned that the weapons may already be in the Tandjung Priok Harbour.

'Within the month,' Nasution replied.

'But that leaves us little time to prepare!' Soeprapto exploded. He, more so than the others, understood the logistical problems which faced the Armed Forces at that time.

'This is why I summoned you here tonight. We cannot wait any longer. I have appealed to Bung Karno but he remains deaf to our suggestions. I have no doubt that our President supports the arming of this so-called Fifth Force as a counter-balance to the Military. He is a fool. Soekarno has developed other appetites which distract his attention from the guardianship of our country.'

'We are not ready. We need more time to prepare,' Soeprapto complained again, still concerned with the complex arrangements he would be responsible for when they made their move against the communists.

'We must determine a date, now!' Nasution demanded. 'We can't delay any further.'

Yani rubbed his face to assist with the circulation. Like the others, he too was tired. He wished the problems they faced would disappear without the inevitable confrontation which he knew would throw the country into further turmoil.

'We need an appropriate opportunity to disguise any sudden troop build-up within the capital,' he suggested. 'Why not take advantage of the Fifth of October?'

Soeprapto raised his eyebrows at Yani's idea. Then he slowly nodded in agreement. There would be adequate time for him and the others to prepare their Commands. The date suggested was appropriate. The Fifth of October was Armed Forces Day, which required substantial increased military presence to accommodate the demands for the many parades which traditionally took place around the city on that day. Soeprapto almost smiled at the thought of moving additional men and equipment into Djakarta without raising suspicion. He nodded in consent, again, in the direction of the astute Army Commander. The others also warmed to Yani's suggestion, pleased that they would not have to fight their way into the city through a mass of communist supporters.

The meeting continued for several hours before the men returned to Djakarta. As each sat silently contemplating the evening's events, not one amongst their number was in the least concerned that their actions did, in fact, amount to treason. Without exception, they were convinced that their proposed actions were in the national interests, and that as guardians of the *Republik*, it was their duty to take whatever steps were necessary to ensure the stability of their nation. The communists had to go. And along with them, the Great Leader of the Revolution, President Soekarno.

* * * * * *

Djakarta

Major General Soeharto looked at the report and frowned. He understood that past personal differences might justify his not being included in whatever Nasution and Yani were up to but, as a matter of principle, he believed his exclusion from the Council of

Generals represented a deliberate attempt to isolate him from any chance of achieving the Army's top post. Being Javanese, the thought of a direct approach to those he believed to be members of this Dewan Djenderal just did not enter his mind. To do so would be too confrontationalist and out of character. He considered the conundrum and decided to attack the problem from another angle. The KOSTRAD Commander removed the intelligence report from the other sensitive documents and placed this in his jacket pocket. He would wait to see just what Nasution and his crowd were up to before making his move. The situation was becoming even more confused, he felt, the capital tense with rumours spreading quickly suggesting the President was very ill, even dying, and that Dr. Soebandrio and his fellow communists were preparing to arm themselves in the event of Soekarno's death.

The general rose from his desk and moved to the window to think, as he had so often done before when confronted with a difficult decision. As he peered across towards the United States Embassy, a thought suddenly entered his mind which caused him to smile. He had been invited to join the American Ambassador for dinner that evening and had accepted, knowing that this would provide an opportunity for him to consolidate his position even further with the United States defence establishment. He had elected to develop these lines of communication realising that the Soviets would soon cease most of their military support for his country and, when that time arrived, his keen political sense told him that only the Americans would be able to fill the void created when the Soviets reneged on their commitments.

He returned to his desk and locked the confidential file in the top drawer. The general them summoned his aide and issued instructions before leaving his office and driving down to old Kota. He had to visit his old friend. There was much to discuss and these conversations were best held discreetly. Soeharto understood that it would not be wise to have the Chinaman visit his office on Merdeka Square.

Chapter 14

Djakarta

Murray was concerned when Susan expressed reluctance in leaving Djakarta. Later, during the course of the dinner at Steven Zach's residence, he was horrified to discover that they were obviously having an affair. He sat in disbelief, observing their glances and listening to their light-hearted banter on the weekend on Pulau Putri.

'Then he almost drowned me!' Susan said in mock reproach. Murray pretended to be attentive while she laughed and described how Steven, while showing off to the others, had tipped the rubber Zenith dinghy over, almost drowning them both. Murray could not imagine the Military Attaché behaving in this manner.

'Guess you'll be returning to Melbourne soon?' he asked. They sat sipping coffee and liqueurs in the corner bar in the main guest area. Immediately, he sensed the mood change as both Zach and Susan became silent. 'Just let me know, if you wish, and I'll organise the flight for you.'

'I'll do that, thanks Murray,' Zach replied. He looked directly at the Station Chief. 'Susan thought she may spend a few more days here before returning home,' he added, turning to her and smiling lightly. She responded, leaning across and placing her hand briefly on his.

'It's okay, Murray,' she said, unconvincingly. 'I will ask for your assistance though, if you wouldn't mind.'

'Sure,' Murray answered, his stomach sinking at the evident warmth his friends displayed for each other. 'What did you have in mind?'

Susan sat thoughtfully before responding. 'I have known you for some time, Murray. I believe that we have been more than just close friends.' She leaned over and took Steven's hand in hers. 'Don't be alarmed,' Susan said, observing the sudden frown which had appeared on Murray's brow. 'Without going into any detail, I just wanted you to know that I will not be returning to Harry.' The words hung momentarily in the air and the room seemed to become quiet. Murray could hear the soft humming airconditioner as the compressor cut in sending cool air in their direction. A gecko's throaty call broke the silence.

'Have you told him yet?' he asked, a little too loudly.

'No,' she answered, 'I haven't had the opportunity. Besides, these things are best discussed in person.' Susan continued to hold Steven's hand as she spoke. 'Murray, I know that this is difficult for you. Please understand,' she asked, touching his arm with her free hand. Murray didn't know what to say. He just smiled at his two close friends then raised his glass.

'Well, whatever the outcome ...' he said, draining the glass quickly. He suddenly felt the need to leave.

'Murray,' Susan started, seeing that he was uncomfortable. She slid off the bar stool and stood alongside Stephenson, taking his hand and squeezing it firmly. 'Murray, please,' Susan pleaded, hoping he would understand. He smiled without warmth and rose to his feet.

'Best be going,' was all he could manage. He shook hands with Zach and kissed Susan lightly on the cheek.

'Will you join us tomorrow?' she asked, now agitated by the strength of his reaction.

'Probably not,' Murray replied, abruptly, as he strolled towards the door. 'I'll no doubt see you in the morning, Steve. Goodnight,' he said, forcing a smile for the houseboy who had suddenly appeared from nowhere to open the door. He walked quickly to his car and barked at the driver. Murray was unusually silent as they drove towards his house in Djalan Serang in the elite suburb of Menteng. He could not believe that Susan had been so rash, and Zach! Murray felt overwhelmed with disappointment. For some reason he could not explain, he felt betrayed by his two friends. And then there was Harry. How was he going to react to the news that his wife had decided to leave him?

'God,' Murray thought, 'what a bloody mess!'

As they pulled away from the Military Attaché's residence,

Murray had been too preoccupied with Susan's disturbing revelations to notice the Chevrolet which had pulled in behind the Australian Embassy Holden and remained there as they wound their way through the streets of Kebajoran. It was only after he had noticed his driver altering his rear-vision mirror several times to deflect the other car's lights that Murray recognised the surveillance vehicle for what it was. He instructed the driver to return to the Military Attaché's home and, as the other vehicle continued to follow, Murray was then certain that he was, in fact, being tailed.

'I've changed my mind,' he advised the driver, 'I've found my wallet, it was in my pocket all the time,' he lied. 'Let's just go home.' The *supir* remained silent. He really did not mind driving the *tuan* around, even if he did wish to travel around in circles. The driver did as ordered and entered the Prapantja Roundabout once again before joining Djalan Djenderal Sudirman. Again he adjusted his mirror, cursing silently as the other vehicle's lights blinded his vision. Murray did not attempt to identify the other vehicle. It was not so unusual to be followed, he knew from experience. Mostly it was just inconvenient and bloody annoying. When they approached the Embassy villa, the driver was obliged to slow down considerably as armed soldiers partially blocked the small road. The driver knew that one of the more important generals lived close by in this street. He stopped, moved the stick into first gear then proceeded carefully so as not to alarm the trigger-happy guards.

It was then that Murray turned quickly to see if he could recognise the other vehicle which had stopped just far enough back to prevent identification. He squinted though the glare as the Chevrolet reversed a few metres then turned and sped away as his own driver slowed to avoid the military barricades strung along this street. He rubbed his eyes briefly then touched his driver on his left shoulder, instructing him to stop. Murray had identified several of the soldiers and, as his villa was only a few doors down the quiet street, he decided to walk, hoping to shake the cloud of depression he felt descending.

'I'll get out here. Terima kasih, Mas,' he said, as he opened the door and left the driver to return to the Embassy compound. Murray walked the remaining distance to his villa, past the familiar barb-wire blockade surrounding his neighbour's house. He stopped, opened a packet of *Gudang Garam* cigarettes, lit one, then offered the remaining packet to the soldiers. They didn't hesitate, smiling as they accepted the near-full packet.

'*Terima kasih,*' they called, as Murray continued on his way, waving one hand in acknowledgement to those he had left behind. His *djaga* opened the heavy sliding gate, permitting him to enter.

'*Selamat malam, tuan,*' the security guard welcomed, smiling as Murray touched him gently on the shoulder.

'*Ya,*' he responded, '*Selamat malam.*' He really did not feel like entering into his usual discourse with the servant, continuing on his way into the magnificent residence. The other servants all scurried into the lounge as he entered. It was always the same. The cook would lead, followed by his *djongos* and then the other servants. Murray's depression lifted immediately. 'How could one remain unhappy surrounded by people such as these?' he thought.

The *koki* insisted that he have something to eat. Murray knew that she would have been aware that he would have already eaten elsewhere. There were no secrets from the servants. He accepted a small dish of *bakso* and consumed just enough to satisfy the cook. It was a game they all played. But it was an important gesture, Murray understood.

He then showered, standing under the hot stinging water, mulling over the bombshell Susan and Steve had dropped on him. He breathed deeply, running his hands slowly through his thick hair, enjoying the warmth of the shower as the water stung his skin. He opened his mouth, permitting the spray to touch his tongue and, enjoying the sensation, he moved his face slowly from side to side as the water pellets massaged imaginary pressures from his head. A noise suddenly made him stiffen then, identifying the familiar sound and scent, Murray relaxed. He held his hand over the shower head as the girl closed the screen door behind and placed her arms around his waist.

'Allo, Mahree,' Ade said, smiling as she stood on her toes and kissed Murray sweetly. The water cascaded down over her thick, shining black hair as he knelt, placing his arms under hers, lifting her off the shower floor.

'Allo yourself,' was all he said, savouring the moment. He kissed her gently as he relaxed his hold, permitting Ade to slide back onto her feet. She laughed, then slapped him playfully on the thigh.

They showered together, taking turns to rub the other's back as they bathed, laughing as their hands ventured into sensitive areas. They did not make love. Instead, once they had changed into sarongs, Ade sat on his bed and commenced brushing her hair. Murray sat next to her and gently rubbed her shoulders and neck.

'*Awaslu!*' she warned, happily, enjoying the sensation. A soft knock on the bedroom door interrupted the moment.

'*Maaf, tuan,*' the *djongos* apologised, '*there is a driver here for you from the Embassy,*' he whispered hoarsely. Murray checked his watch and swore. He changed quickly and left, first kissing Ade softly on her forehead.

'*Won't be long,*' he promised, escaping before she succeeded in pinching his stomach playfully. As he appeared, the driver handed the message directly to him. He sighed, resenting the tedious task ahead. Murray left the villa, waved to the soldiers outside and was immediately driven to the Embassy. He checked to see if he had been followed again but the streets were already devoid of traffic. Once at the Embassy, he went through the monotonous routines which consumed most of an hour before he was able to decipher the incoming communication. It was from Harold Bradshaw, his Director. He read though the text quickly and decided that a response could wait until the following morning, remembering that it was already early evening back in Melbourne anyway. He placed the decoded message carefully inside his wallet, then secured the communications centre and locked the building behind as he left, anxious to return to his villa.

As they drove the short distance back to his villa, Murray frowned when he observed the duty-driver adjust his rear-vision mirror. He turned quickly and identified the Chevrolet which had followed him home earlier in the evening. As his vehicle approached Djalan Serang once again Murray elected to walk through the barricaded street rather than have the soldiers move the obstacles aside for the diplomatic sedan. After his driver sped away, he remained standing on the side of the road, staring back around the corner at the long dark sedan with oversized tail wings. The driver had killed his lights and parked not a hundred metres down the road. Murray turned and walked towards the Chevrolet. Annoyed, he wanted to know who they were.

As he approached, he heard the engine roar into life as the driver flattened his gas-pedal to the floor, powering the eight-cylinder machine forward with incredible speed. Immediately he realised that he had been foolish and turned to escape. As his legs carried him back towards the junction, he looked desperately for a means to evade the oncoming car but the surrounding houses all lay behind high walls covered with barbed-wire and broken glass to prevent such intrusion. Only seconds had passed when he accepted that he would not make it, the vehicle's brilliant headlights silhouetting his frame as his feet pounded the footpath. Murray had only a few metres to cover before reaching the corner when the Chevrolet's off-side wheels mounted the footpath directly behind and swerved towards him. As the engine's roar filled his ears, Murray panicked, and lept desperately for the top of the adjacent wall. The machine seemed to leap after him and smashed into the concrete perimeter fence, before continuing along the footpath amidst the screams of tearing metal.

He screamed in pain then fell hard to the ground and rolled, unable to avoid the broken curb-side rubble. His head struck the ground savagely, stunning him. Dazed, he struggled to his feet before his attackers could return and complete their mission. Pain stabbed at his ankle as he staggered back towards his street, his bleeding right hand raised to the wall for support. He heard the squealing tires as the heavy sedan turned violently, and he cried out in pain as he forced his twisted ankle to carry him back to safety.

He heard the car approach and Murray knew that he would not be able to reach the corner in time. The engine screamed, locked in second gear as its driver bore down on him again. Murray half-turned. Immediately blinded by the light's high-beam, he lifted his uninjured hand to lessen the glare. He held his breath, waiting, as the car roared towards where he leaned against the wall. He cursed out loud; the corner was only metres away. The glare blinded his vision but he identified the clunking noise as once again his attackers steered their vehicle up onto the footpath. He braced for the impact. Suddenly his world exploded into sounds of screaming metal and rapid fire as the machine-pistol's bullets punched through the air sending shock waves, slapping his eardrums fiercely. In the moment Murray fell to the ground, he caught a glimpse of the soldier standing almost alongside, and he heard the staccato sounds continue as the machine-gun punctured the night, shattering glass and piercing metal as the oncoming sedan suddenly swerved violently away.

The general's guard continued to fire from the hip as the Chevrolet suddenly swerved, the driver fighting for control as he turned sharply and gunned his engine even harder than before. Murray lifted his head and peered in the direction of the escaping vehicle. He breathed deeply and pushed himself upright. A hand gripped him roughly under his shoulder, and he succeeded in making it to his feet. Barely seconds had passed before he was surrounded by more than a dozen soldiers who half-carried, half-dragged the Australian back to his villa where he was taken inside and deposited safely on his lounge. Convinced that the foreigner's injuries were superficial, they then left him alone with his servants and returned to their duties outside, as if nothing had happened. They were accustomed to such incidents and were not overly concerned. The attack had not been directed at their general and he was not even there at that time. They would not even file a report unless asked to do so. The soldiers knew that even if they did, the incident would most probably be ignored at higher levels.

Murray sat on the lounge and removed his shoes and socks, exposing the damaged ankle. His hand was bleeding profusely. His servants fussed over him, believing that he had fallen on the broken footpath. They had not witnessed the attack and he did not wish to alarm these easily frightened people. Although they had heard the gunfire, none had associated the two incidents as the sound of weapon fire was commonplace throughout the capital. Often the soldiers would just fire into the sky out of boredom. The houseboy tended to his cuts and bruises. Murray's hand continued to bleed. He knew that the wound should have been stitched but decided against alerting the Embassy doctor. He would keep a close watch on the wound himself. The old cook could see that he was badly shaken. She had the *djongos* pour Murray a large whiskey which he thankfully drank. Soon he stopped shaking.

Murray then remembered his house guest and limped painfully into the bedroom. He entered quietly, and found Ade curled in the foetal position, eyes closed and hands clasped almost as if in prayer. She had slept through the noise and gunfire. He looked down at her and shook his head in wonder at this realisation. He limped into the bathroom and undressed, checking bruises and torn skin.

The area surrounding his temples ached and, as his hands explored the skin under his thick crown of hair, he discovered a tender lump where his head had hit the pavement earlier. Murray ran the bath and soaked himself, holding his injured hand and leg outside the tub as he scrubbed the other parts of his body. The warm water almost put him to sleep as he lay there quietly, reviewing the attack on his life. He wondered if he was responsible for provoking the men who had followed him earlier. Would they have gone about their business had he not approached their vehicle, or would they have waited for a similar opportunity to do him harm? Who were they?

He levered himself out of the *mandi* carefully, then dried himself slowly. He was just too tired to think. As he re-entered his bedroom, Murray looked at the beautiful woman in his bed and was pleased that she was still there. He lowered himself onto the bed carefully so as not to wake her. He lay on the sheets, his head nestled against the soft pillows, and closed his eyes. Ade sensed his presence and moved closer, still half-asleep, nestling gently alongside so as not to disturb her lover. Murray lay quietly watching as her chest moved slowly, the soft sounds of her breathing blended with the muffled tropical calls of deep-throated bull frogs and geckos. The airconditioner hummed through the night, wafting the artificial breeze around the room. As he slid gratefully into the sheets, Ade moved her arm across his chest, almost possessively. Finally, he fell into a restless sleep.

The night passed without further event and, as the early morning brought familiar sounds of the new day, Murray remained in a deep sleep. Later, when most of Djakarta's citizens had already risen and completed their ablutions, Murray was finally awakened by his throbbing injuries. He sat upright slowly and then reached for the beautiful young woman beside him. But Ade was no longer there. Instantly, the recollections of his near encounter with death flooded his mind and he lept out of bed only to curse himself as the pain shot though his lower leg. Murray sat back down on the bed and rubbed his face and, as if by signal, immediately his head began to ache. He groaned, then made his way into the bathroom and, as he stood in front of the mirror examining his face and bruised torso, a thought flashed though his mind.

In pain, he hobbled back into his bedroom and searched for his trousers. For a moment he could not remember where he had placed them. Then he remembered. They were still on the floor lying half-hidden under the bed. Murray bent down and retrieved the cotton slacks and immediately his hand went anxiously to the back pocket. He checked again. Nothing. He then checked the other pockets and discovered that these too were empty. Murray lowered himself painfully to the floor where he looked under the bed. Still nothing. He searched around the room with a similar result and, struggling into his sarong, he went out and called his servants. He instructed his houseboy to search the lounge where he had rested while bathing his injured foot and then outside along the street, but still there was nothing.

He cursed himself for his stupidity. He had lost his wallet. And the sensitive contents which should never have left the Embassy restricted area. Murray returned to his bedroom and sat alone on the bed, his hands gripping his pounding head as he struggled to collect his thoughts. The seriousness of his security breach and the possible ramifications of his stupidity grew in his mind as he recalled sections of the decoded communication from the Head of Australia's Secret Service.

Somewhere in the city someone now possessed a most incriminating document. And then, as he sat there on the cold linen sheets, another thought crossed his mind which he immediately tried to dismiss. Why had Ade left so early without saying goodbye?

* * * * * *

Their numbers had grown dramatically over the past months. The holy man was most pleased. Each day he would dedicate as much time as possible to speaking directly to the new converts who came from many parts of the globe. Bapak Subuh was most pleased that his teachings had spread so far. And so quickly. Followers of his philosophy visited from countries even he had not envisaged and, without design, SUBUD had grown into a formidable sect with an enviable financial base. Many of his foreign followers were middle-class men and women whose careers covered the professional spectrum.

Even he had been amazed at the number of lawyers, doctors, accountants and engineers who had flocked to hear him preach his philosophy, which embraced all cultures, all religions, and all political leanings. He knew that there were many sceptics amongst those who visited. But he also knew that none of these departed a lesser person for, once they had met with the man who provided them with the opportunity to reach though the window into their souls, their noble natures invariably capitulated to their new capacity for love and understanding. And then they accepted his teachings.

On this day, he felt troubled. A recurring dream had dominated his thoughts throughout recent weeks, and now he believed that his interpretation of the events which presented themselves clearly as he slept, predicted dark days ahead. He decided to seek a further meeting with the man whose spirit occupied so many of his sleeping hours. Even he sometimes did not understand how the universe moved and controlled their lives, although it was clear that there was a sequence to everything that mattered, and that he played but a minor role in the Greater Order.

As he sat deep in thought, contemplating his troubled interpretations, Subuh suddenly smiled as he recalled the first time he had encountered the young sickly child in Semarang. He knew that their meeting had been prearranged. It was just a matter of destiny. Then his smile faded as quickly as it had appeared as he remembered the ominous visions which had continuously invaded his dreams. The holy man willed his anxiety to retreat, providing a purer path for his mind to deal with the demons which threatened to take control of his consciousness. He closed his eyes and moved his being onto another level, another plane, as his physical presence began to separate from his spiritual core.

An hour had passed before Subuh suddenly opened his eyes, totally refreshed from the *latihan*. His first thoughts were to make arrangements to meet with the younger man. The spiritual leader smiled in anticipation as he rose to send a short personal note requesting yet another meeting with his friend: a friend who had grown not only in stature amongst his peers, but whose character reflected the very substance of Javanese tradition. He was delighted with what this man had become. The words of request flowed from his pen with humility and respect. When he was finished, he sealed his letter. Subuh then wrote carefully across the envelope, and placed the letter carefully inside a small folder, calling for one of his attendants.

That evening, as he sat alone in his home along Djalan Tjendana, the recipient read the letter over and over again. He was not displeased with the contents, only concerned that they had not met in person to discuss the holy man's interpretations in greater depth. The general took the letter and placed it inside his desk drawer, knowing that it would not be disturbed there. He decided to make time and meet discreetly with the respected spiritualist. The general acknowledged that it would be in his best interests to heed the warning contained in the letter. But he needed to know more. He sensed that the communication left a great deal unsaid, and this was of immediate concern to him. The city was rife with rumours and he understood clearly that there were undercurrents flowing which could, if he was not careful, drag him and many others away into a dangerous sea of conflict. He reached across his teak desk and smiled at his mother's photograph. And then, as always, the memories of early childhood came flooding back as Soeharto remembered those difficult early childhood days when he had first encountered Subuh in Semarang.

* * * * * *

United States Embassy, Djakarta

The flag moved listlessly as the Marine Guard ceremoniously raised the colours. The day was already suffocatingly hot, and the American could feel sweat rolling down his back as he slowly pulled the cord through white-gloved hands. Black residual lines appeared on his gloves: proof, he thought, that living in Indonesia's polluted capital was dangerous for one's health.

Inside the United States Embassy, there was already a flurry of activity, even at this early hour. In all, the total complement of American citizens officially accredited to this mission numbered sixty-two: in reality, more than three hundred operated out of these facilities, making it the largest foreign representation in the country. Apart from the diplomatic officers and their families, the complex housed a myriad of small offices which accommodated United States Navy, Army, Air Force, Marine and other Defence personnel. The congested building was like a rabbit warren. Its occupants moved around their tight quarters, squeezing past each other through the narrow corridors which connected the complicated maze of offices.

Marine Guards working in shifts around the clock manned positions throughout the complex, and it was not possible to pass through the different levels or sections without every movement being monitored. The steps to the immediate right of the foyer entrance led to the first level. There, yet more tireless watchers maintained close scrutiny of the pedestrian traffic which passed through the Defence Attaché's offices.

The corporal smiled as he recognised the approaching civilian and rose to his feet as the CIA Station Chief, Samuel Preston, passed his security post. The tall fair-haired Chief merely nodded at the guard as he strolled past, continuing along the passageway until arriving at the colonel's office. He knocked then entered without waiting for a response. He was expected.

'Frank, Pete,' he said, nodding to the two men who remained seated as he lowered himself into one of the under-sized chairs. It seemed that everything in this wing had been miniaturised to accommodate their swelling numbers. He was unable to cross his legs comfortably in the restricted space. 'What's up?' Preston asked, as he moved around in the rattan chair trying to find a comfortable position for his large frame.

'Thought you should see this,' the colonel remarked, handing a folder across to the CIA Djakarta Chief. The file cover was crossed with a thick red band marked 'Top Secret'. He opened the file and read the document while the others remained silent. As he came to the end of the first page the experienced agent let out a soft whistle then looked up at the colonel.

'Source?' he asked, handing the sensitive material back. The colonel accepted the file then threw it casually over onto his desk. He looked at the officer his men referred to as the Chief Spook and immediately wondered just how much mileage he could get out of the situation. The fine line which separated Military Intelligence from their country's more clandestine service often provided for territorial jealousies, and the colonel believed that he had scored heavily by securing the document.

'Not able to say, Sam. At least, not right now,' the colonel answered, his smile not evident as he sat there enjoying this rare opportunity to play advantage over the CIA. The Station Chief stared at the colonel through thick heavy-framed bifocals and tilted his head.

'How can we verify its authenticity, Frank?' he asked, not quite testily, but close. 'You don't have the in-country resources to substantiate that,' he said, pointing directly at the file. 'My Director in Langley would insist that I verify the document. That means disclosing the source, Frank,' he insisted. The colonel leaned over and recovered the folder and opened the file. He looked at the document as if deciding whether or not to reveal how the information came into his possession. Then he threw the file back onto his desk. He had scored enough points and knew that, ultimately, he would be obliged to surrender the detail the senior agent demanded.

'To tell you the truth, Sam, we're not absolutely sure,' he admitted.

'Come on, Frank,' he coaxed. 'We're on the same team here.' The Station Chief could have said almost anything else and not rattle the officer. The colonel's face reddened but he managed to keep himself in check. He hated being patronised.

'Pete here believes it came from someone in BAKIN,' he responded, indicating the Major with a nod of his head.

'BAKIN?' the Chief said in surprise. He was tempted to scoff at the suggestion that the Indonesian counter-part agency to the CIA was responsible for providing the sensitive material.

'Pete, you'd best fill Sam in,' he ordered. Major Peter O'Brien cleared his throat and commenced.

'I attended a briefing with our Defence Co-operation team over at BAKIN late yesterday. We were there for a couple of hours discussing matters of mutual interest.' He hesitated, embarrassed. 'During the course of our visit, there must have been at least twenty or more of their people in and out of the conference room throughout the afternoon. Most of us left the session for a leak at least once during the discussions, although I'm certain that our team never left our files unattended at any time. Not that these contained anything of a sensitive nature. We always follow the guidelines.'

'And?' the CIA Chief prompted, impatiently.

'Well,' the major answered, obviously bewildered by what had transpired, 'when we returned, I passed my papers to Meyers for filing and it was he who discovered the document at the bottom of my folder. Somehow I must have picked it up by mistake while we were there, or one of the Indonesians slipped it into my papers, although I can't see how.' He looked down at the floor briefly and coughed again, nervously. 'As soon as Sergeant Meyers gave the document to me, I immediately called the colonel here.'

'And so we are unable to confirm its source,' Sam stated, almost accusingly. 'That doesn't give the information much credibility, gentlemen.' The three men sat quietly, thinking.

'Why would the Indonesians pass such information to us?' the Defence Attaché colonel asked. Preston paused, considering just how much information to reveal regarding CIA covert operations within the country.

'It's quite possible that one of our people inside BAKIN took advantage of your visit to make the drop. It is also possible that one of their Intelligence officers decided to initiate a play of his own. Without knowing who is responsible, then I'm afraid, gentlemen, the contents must remain suspect. Having said that, I would appreciate the original for onforwarding to Langley. I'd suggest that you warn the sergeant not to discuss the document with anyone else and shred any copies that have been made. If the information proves not to be false then we wouldn't want half the world to be in on it. Okay?' The two Army officers knew that this was not a request. The Station Chief had the authority and they knew that his instructions were appropriate.

'There are no copies, Sam,' the colonel stated, reaching for the file once again and passing the folder to the CIA Chief who struggled out of his chair, preparing to leave. He smiled briefly and nodded at them both.

'Thanks for your co-operation, gentlemen,' he said, then left. The Station Chief then returned to his own office and worded a brief communication to Langley. He took this personally up to communications where the message was encrypted by one of his own men and then despatched immediately. Within minutes, the information had been passed to the senior desk officer, who read the signal and, in turn, telephoned upstairs to request a meeting with Richards, the Australian Area Operations Desk Officer.

Less than an hour had passed when Senior Agent Richards made the necessary amendments to the profile, then buzzed the registry clerk to retrieve the thick folder and re-file the report under its revised classification. The Top Secret documents titled STEPHENSON, M.L. had been updated and reclassified. His file had been removed from the 'possibles' section into his new category. The CIA had now confirmed Murray as an active agent working together with Harold Bradshaw. The only question which remained in the American Intelligence Agency's mind was his role and relationship with the Indonesian communists. Senior Agent Richards had underlined the grading classification in red and annotated, 'possible double' due to Murray's association with the Partai Komunis Indonesia.

* * * * * *

Melbourne

Harry Bradshaw was miffed with the news that Susan had elected to remain in Djakarta yet another week. and the fact that this information had been received via an impersonal telex sent from the Embassy. It was not so much that he needed her around, or that he missed her company. Harry was just annoyed that he had not been consulted before she had arbitrarily made the decision to remain.

Harry had phoned Muriel to see how young Michael was faring. He knew that the woman was extremely fond of the boy. Harry thought about the child who carried his name, and wondered if he had been correct in assuming who his real father had been. Harry knew that the child could not have been his own son but having Michael in his family contributed conveniently to the image he wished to project. Although earlier concerns had diminished with time, he still wished he could be certain about who had really fathered his son.

He considered Susan's extended stay, then carefully penned an acknowledgement, thanking Susan for the message and wishing her an enjoyable stay. Harry then wrote a brief message to Murray and marked the despatch for encryption. He then checked his watch and made a mental note of the time, planning his day to accommodate an early morning departure the following day to Canberra.

The Secret Service Director chewed at his upper lip as his thoughts turned to the Russian. He wondered why Konstantinov had advanced their scheduled meeting by almost two weeks. It was obviously important enough for the Russian to ignore established contact regimes. Harry had been deeply disturbed when the enigmatic message had been relayed to him at the Toorak Club. Harold Bradshaw was completely conscious of the dangerous possibility that he could, at any moment, be compromised by such amateur behaviour. He also knew that, should his betrayal be discovered, it would be most unlikely that he would ever face the courts. As for Konstantinov, the Australian Government would merely make him persona non grata, upon which the KGB officer would most probably retire to some lakeside *dacha* and be rewarded with an overly adequate pension for his years of service to the Kremlin.

Harry had decided that the Soviet ploy involving the Diponegoro Command went much farther than the Russian revealed. He was certain that, as Moscow supported the Central Javanese Command, it would be logical that they had identified 'friendly' senior officers within that Command. They knew who was prepared to maintain an ongoing relationship with the Soviet Union once the senior echelon of officers currently ensconced in the nation's capital had been successfully removed. This made sense to the Director. What concerned him most about this precarious scheme was the inherent danger always evident when there were two or more players in the game. Bradshaw wished there were some means whereby he could identify which of the Diponegoro officers were pro-West, and which were plotting to betray their own men by delivering their country into the hands of the Soviets. Harry also realised that these conclusions could not be raised with Konstantinov. He had no choice but to go with the flow, so to speak, and wait for developments to direct his course of action. There was little doubt in his mind that the stakes were enormous. His own position could easily be sacrificed should Moscow consider this to be to their advantage. He shuddered involuntarily at this unpleasant thought.

The information flow originating from Djakarta Station and roving agents all indicated that the situation in Indonesia was becoming more and more tense. It was obvious that the communists were getting closer to making a move. Reports concerning the Indonesian Airforce Chief, Omar Dhani, and his so-called goodwill visit to Mainland China convinced his fellow Intelligence associates that arms shipments for the Indonesian communists were imminent, and once these had been completed, Dr. Soebandrio and Aidit would most surely make their move. The conundrum was: who amongst the established members of the Indonesian Armed Forces, the TNI, would support a communist take-over?

As Director of the Australian Secret Intelligence Service, Harold Bradshaw was privy to considerable American intelligence which flowed regularly from Langley to Central Plans. He had become concerned about the deterioration in the quality of this information exchange during the past six months. At first, Harry had put this down to the fact that the Americans had become bogged down in establishing further networks throughout Indochina as a result of the escalation of their involvement in Vietnam. But after challenging the veracity of several CIA-sourced reports relating to the Council of Generals, Harry began to sense that there was a deliberate effort afoot to reduce the information flow through the Australian Intelligence agencies. He believed that the Americans were increasing pressure on some of the generals to arrest Soekarno and seize power, presumably because they were concerned with the Indonesian President's proposed alliance with their new enemy, Ho Chi Minh.

It was apparent to the Australians that the Americans believed there was an imminent danger that Soekarno would open a second front. They feared he would further escalate the regional conflict by moving against the Philippines, even though his *Crush Malaysia* campaign was rapidly losing steam. The Australian Prime Minister had become alarmed when Harry learned that the American President, Lyndon B. Johnson, was considering an option to drop 'the big one' on Hanoi or even Djakarta. Bradshaw's office also alerted MI6 in London, and the British responded by warning the Americans that they could not support such extreme action. Their view was that such a drastic response would be likely to drive many millions more into the arms of the region's communist leaders.

It seemed to Harry that the West was rapidly losing whatever influence it may have had over the Asian states. This would, he expected, delight his Russian masters as they too manoeuvred to expand their sphere throughout the region. Harry sighed. His life had become dangerously complicated, and he wondered how much longer he could continue as events gathered momentum around him, threatening his very existence. He wished he could get away for a few days. Perhaps even visit Thailand. And Piya. It had been too many months since his last visit. Harry reluctantly dismissed these pleasant thoughts and returned to the matters at hand. He busied himself with arrangements for his following day's flight to Canberra. And his appointment with Konstantinov.

* * * * * *

Semarang

General Prajogo listened attentively as the two men delivered their report. His firm Javanese features in no way betrayed his feelings. He was not angry with his men. They were excellent soldiers and had proved their loyalty to him time and time again. He accepted what they had said as unblemished truth. When they had finished, both men stood silently, their berets tucked neatly under their left shoulder epaulette, waiting for the general's admonishment over their failure. Instead, their Commander simply nodded and thanked them for their report, then moved outside to inspect the damage.

He walked around inside the high-walled enclosure several times then grunted. He had seen worse. The general barked an order and his small team of men immediately went to work repairing the vehicle. It would take weeks, he knew, and possibly longer if they were unable to source parts for the damaged bodywork. The left-hand drive sedan was badly damaged along its entire off side. The right-side double headlights had disappeared and most of the side panels had been ripped viciously away. Only two of the side windows remained intact, while shattered pieces of the windscreens were spread throughout the car's interior.

The general was amazed that neither of the men had been injured. It was a sign, he believed, as he moved closer to the Chevrolet and counted the rows of holes which ran up the bonnet and across the solid roof. Relieved that they had not been caught, he turned and smiled at his two soldiers and nodded in quiet admiration at their lucky escape. Then his mood changed as he remembered the object of their failed mission and swore silently to himself that their enemy would not be as fortunate in the next encounter. Of that he was certain. Even if he was obliged to kill the Australian himself.

* * * * * *

Canberra

The KGB had never been known for its subtlety. Harry knew that. As his driver took him back to the Fairbairn Airport terminal, he decided that the visit had been a total waste of time. His meeting with Konstantinov had lasted less than fifteen minutes and, for the first time since he could remember, there was no vodka.

He had been ushered upstairs in typical style and unceremoniously left alone to wait until Konstantinov suddenly appeared, flushed from some tete-a-tete in the Soviet Embassy. Harry wasn't at all annoyed, just bored.

Konstantinov had been full of his customary bonhomie, perhaps even more so as he cracked jokes about Lyndon Johnson and offered the ASIS Director a cigar, forgetting that Harry had long given the habit away. The Intelligence Chief had observed the heavy-set Russian's flushed, jowly cheeks, and decided that this accounted for the lack of vodka. Harry did not object. Sometimes the effects of these sessions with the great bear sized Russian would remain with him for days once he had returned to Melbourne.

They had spoken briefly of events generally before the KGB Attaché moved the conversation to Indonesia, and the Diponegoro 7th Division. Harry had reiterated most of what he had disclosed before, and was surprised that Konstantinov had insisted that Harry identify, again, the list of officers the Diponegoro Commander had written down as possible members of the so-called Council of Generals.

'I have given this to you already, once before,' Harry suggested, thinking that in typical Soviet style he was being tested as to the accuracy of earlier reporting. Sometimes, he thought, they acted like children. He then wrote the names down again, knowing that Russian sources within the Indonesian Military would already have provided such information. Nasution's membership had grown and, with that, the rumours of just who were members of his clique.

As he was about to leave, Harry was surprised by Konstantinov's unfamiliar display of friendship. The man had grabbed him in a suffocating embrace and promised him that soon things would be different. As the ASIS Chief climbed aboard the Australian Airlines Fokker and took his seat in first class, he remembered the Russian's foul-smelling breath and deep, thick body odour. Suddenly Harry shivered, and he looked up to see if the plane's air-vent was blowing directly at him. It wasn't.

Chapter 15

PKI-Gerwani Training Camp
Sukabumi, Java

Yanti looked with admiration as her trainees came to attention. The hour was late and they were all tired. She could see that this had been one of the better intakes as most of the young women had been able to complete the physical training without any serious incidents. The Gerwani had indeed become a force to be reckoned with. Many more thousands of young women had joined the Communist Women's Movement and participated in combat training camps. At first, Yanti ignored the soldiers as they laughed at their female comrades struggling to complete their physical training exercises but, as her own skills developed, she often challenged the men, displaying a deadly accuracy with handguns.

The women were not issued with standard weapons. Only senior members such as Yanti were permitted sidearms and even then, these were handed back into the store before leaving the camp training area. The others were trained to use the simple farmers' *golok*, the deadly sharp-bladed tool which, when wielded as instructed, could separate an enemy's head from his shoulders with one swipe. For uniforms, they dressed in dark pyjama clothing and wore white bandannas around their foreheads. These made them appear most threatening as they leaped forward, then back, then forward again, brandishing their deadly blades in practised movements.

Yanti had been away from Djakarta for more than a month. She missed seeing Murray and was eager to finish training this last group and return to the capital. There was an air of excitement as their *Komandan* had alerted them to the possibility that they would soon be called upon to demonstrate what they had learned at basic training. Yanti believed that she would be given a prominent

291

role to play in whatever was planned, as she had excelled as one of the more senior members of the Gerwani. Although she wished to put the incident behind her now, she had even proven her loyalty by submitting to the requests made of her just the week before when their camp had been privileged by a visit from Comrade Aidit himself.

The unexpected surprise had come as they had finished their evening meal of rice and salted fish. Their *Komandan* had called the young women to assembly and advised them to remain silent as they were addressed by their country's most senior communist, their Chairman. The girls were ecstatic. Few had ever seen their leader and, when he arrived accompanied by a dozen or so soldiers, they had all cheered and clapped as Aidit had stood before them and told them just how proud he was of their contribution to the cause. Yanti had enjoyed meeting the man and was even impressed with the officers who accompanied their Chairman, although she was surprised to see several officers wearing the regimental colours for the President's own guard, the elite *Tjakrabirawa*. Later, when her trainees had moved into their quarters, Yanti had been summoned by her *Komandan*. Without any subtlety whatsoever, she was told that the Chairman and his soldiers expected to have company during their brief visit. Yanti was not only surprised, but offended. At first, she refused. How could she possibly ask her girls to do such a thing, she argued, but the *Komandan* was adamant.

He explained that it was expected of them and that to refuse would not only be a direct insult to the Chairman, but to their cause. Yanti had argued against their demands, unsuccessfully. The *Komandan* had insisted that she was over reacting to what was considered quite acceptable behaviour. Then she was warned that her failure to co-operate would most certainly end in her being overlooked in the future, when the Party would need women of her calibre. Yanti had finally agreed. She had returned and discussed the demands with her group and was astonished to discover that most of the girls were not unhappy with the proposition. Yanti escorted ten of her volunteers back to where their guests were temporarily billeted and left them to entertain these visitors. No sooner had Yanti returned to her own quarters when she heard her door opened and two of the *Tjakra* soldiers brazenly marched in and started undressing. She did not resist. Yanti knew to do so would only be folly. Instead, she lay there until the men were finished and had left. When she was certain they had gone, Yanti ran to the end of the line of simple huts and remained there, washing herself in the *mandi* until she felt clean once again. Then she returned to her bed where she sat, cross-legged, angry and belittled.

A week had since passed and Yanti had managed to come to terms with what had happened. She decided to erase the incident from her mind and, to a greater extent, her strong Sundanese will succeeded. As a result of the encounter, Yanti's dedication to the cause grew. She felt that she had now given all that she had to her country, and that one day she would be rewarded for her unselfishness and loyalty. Yanti pushed ahead with the last few days of the demanding course, pleased that she would soon be in back in Djakarta, and in Murray's comforting arms.

* * * * * *

Melbourne

Harry seemed confused by the discussion. It was almost as if he had not understood the import of what she had said. Susan stopped talking and looked at her husband.

'Harry, do you understand what this all means?' she asked. Harry crossed his legs and remained silent. Damn her to hell! he thought, deciding that Susan could not have selected a more inappropriate time to announce a separation. His whole world had started to crumble. He stared out through the colonial glass window towards their deserted tennis court. Susan had selected the venue. She had telephoned upon her return from Indonesia and advised his secretary that she would not be available for a few days, and would contact Harry when she had recovered from her trip. When he had received the ominous message, Harry already feared that he had lost her.

Somehow he had always known that this day would arrive. He had been a fool to expect Susan to continue their relationship with the constraints they both endured. She was still young, and needed more in her life than he could provide for her. Harry turned back to listen.

293

'... and we should do this, Harry. Please, listen to me!' she pleaded, determined not to cry. Susan felt drained. She still adored Harry dearly but he could not give her the physical attention she so desperately needed. Why couldn't he understand this?

'Susan,' he started, leaning forward and taking her hands in his. 'I would be lying if I said that it's all right. I admit that I have taken so much for granted over the past years but, is there no way I can persuade you to just take some time to consider your decision first? Aren't you being just a little too hasty?'

'Harry, there is someone else,' Susan said, knowing that this would hurt him deeply, and wishing there was some other way to bring their discussions to a head. 'I'm in love with someone else, Harry. I'm sorry.' She lowered her head, not from shame but because she suddenly felt drained of all energy. She had known it would be difficult, but not like this.

'Is it Murray?' he asked, his voice almost a whisper.

'Good grief no!' Susan replied, a little too quickly and then added, 'how could you even suggest ...?'

'Well, who, then?' he demanded, but not angrily. Already he felt very tired and wished the discussion finished so that they could talk about other things.

'Harry,' Susan started, not wanting to get any further into this. She was concerned that her husband may become irrational. There was something obviously wrong. He was not responding as Susan had expected. She tried again. 'It doesn't matter who. What is important is that we must settle how best to end our marriage and, if possible, Harry, in the most amicable way.' She looked at her husband closely, concerned with the almost vacant response. 'Harry?' she asked, frustrated by his unexpected loss of concentration.

'I'm still here, Susan,' he said, 'I'm still here.'

'Well?' she demanded.

'What about Michael? What will happen to him?' he asked, hoping this might change her decision.

'Michael is my problem. I will take care of him. You know that.'

'But it wouldn't be fair to him,' he argued.

'Harry, you know he's not your child. Let's not make this messier than it already is. Please!'

Harry sat holding her hands, knowing that their relationship had ended.

'Harry?' Susan asked again.

Harry then shook his head sadly and released her hands. 'Do whatever you must, my dear, but please keep it as discreet as possible.' He then smiled thinly. 'You know I don't want this. Isn't there anything I can do to resolve the differences? If I agreed that you could continue your relationship with whoever you've found, without a divorce, could you live with this, say, for another year or so?' he felt, desperate that Susan should not cut him off without the opportunity to prepare himself for such a dramatic change.

Susan shook her head. 'No, Harry. I'm sorry.' She then rose and moved across to the cocktail cabinet and poured herself a stiff shot of vodka. She turned and raised her eyebrows but Harry merely shook his head. He had never seen her take a drink by herself before. He felt desperately tired but steeled himself to complete the grisly details.

'Okay, Susan. How do we do this?' he asked, his voice but a whisper.

Susan placed her drink down and moved quickly across the room and knelt beside her husband. She gripped his hands and kissed him lightly on the cheek, then rose and returned to where she had placed her vodka.

'I believe that we both deserve for this to be kept as civilised as possible. What would you accept as a fair arrangement, Harry?' she asked. Harold Bradshaw wanted to laugh but couldn't. He had lost his wife to another man and traded his soul to another government. He had no children, no future, and soon, if he was not extremely cautious, possibly no life. He looked up at Susan and didn't know what to say.

'I would like to keep the bungalow,' she said, awkwardly. 'After all, I have spent far more time here than you.' She looked carefully across the room for his response.

'Whatever, Susan. If you want it, take it,' he answered in a tired voice. 'Why don't you just tell me what you want and how you wish to settle the whole mess?'

'Fine, Harry,' Susan replied, strangely angry that he had not even attempted to fight for the home they had made together. 'How about we have something drawn up by your solicitor?'

'Fine by me,' he answered wearily, rising unsteadily to his feet. 'Well, guess that's about it then?' with which he picked up his keys and moved towards the door. 'Be a darling and pack my things for me, Susan?' he asked, his face now pale as he forced a brave smile. 'Best send them over to the Toorak apartment. I'll stay there until things are settled.'

'Of course, Harry. I'll attend to that. You don't have to go now, you know,' she said, unconvincingly. He walked slowly to her side and took her hand softly, then kissed her gently on the forehead as he had so many times before.

'Goodbye, Susan,' he whispered, and squeezed her hand softly. He smiled and moved towards the door, then hesitated. 'If it doesn't work out ...' he started, pausing as he opened the door. He stared at his wife and forced one last smile, offered a slight wave, then turned and closed the door quietly behind. Minutes passed, and then in the sudden emptiness, she cried.

Book three

1965, coup and counter-coup

Kerry B.Collison

Chapter 16

*Djakarta,
early September*

The general mood in the capital was solemn. Another bloody day of rioting had ended with hundreds lying dead. Once again the people had flooded into the streets to protest escalating prices and rice shortages. When the crowds gathered around the Palace, elements of communist units had infiltrated the demonstrators' numbers and started their familiar chanting, demanding food for the people. Within minutes, the crowd had been turned into an unruly mob and, as the soldiers and police moved to disperse the angry gathering, they were met with a hail of rocks. At first, batons were used to force the demonstrators back from the main gates, but these were not enough to deter the crowd. As their numbers grew, they surged forward, crushing the Palace guards.

The first volley of shots was fired directly into those immediately in front of the main gates but, to the astonishment of the Guard Commander, the crowd merely surged forward again. He yelled for a second volley and pointed his own revolver at the sea of screaming faces pushed hard up against the gates. As the shots reverberated through the Palace buildings, those inside prepared to barricade the doors and windows. The Tjakrabirawa Guards were likely to have great difficulty in preventing the demonstrators from entering the grounds.

The President was not present. He had presented yet another radio broadcast from the nation's central broadcast station, Radio Republik Indonesia. He appealed for patience while the Government endeavoured to correct the immediate problems of food shortages. As he spoke, elements of the communist PKI moved to a number of other locations around the city, and commenced throwing stones through Chinese shop windows, exacerbating the capital's security problems on all fronts.

The Council of Generals continued to meet covertly to discuss preparations for the Armed Forces Day on the Fifth of October, and their secret agenda. They had quietly permitted the rioting crowds to have their way, letting off steam as the Military prepared to mobilise its forces to move into the city, ostensibly as a prelude to the massive parades planned for the year's celebrations. The generals had laughed together when Yani related details of his conversation with Soekarno, and how pleased the President had appeared when he was advised that this year, the Tentara Nasional Indonesia would present the people of Indonesia with a parade they would never forget. The President had eagerly agreed to the massive demonstration of military power to be held along the capital's protocol roads, believing that this would distract the hungry masses from their more immediate problems, and even intimidate those who continuously moved to destabilise his Government.

Soekarno had made a number of public appearances to eliminate ongoing speculation regarding his health. It was true that he had been seriously ill, and still suffered fatigue from the debilitating kidney complaint, however Chinese doctors flown from Beijing had managed to remove some of the painful stones with their time-proven herbs and elixirs. During his brief recuperation, the President continued to depend heavily on his trusted confident, Foreign Minister and Deputy Prime Minister, Dr. Soebandrio, who continued to act as the catalyst for the growing bond between the Government and the Indonesian Communist Party.

Chairman Aidit now believed that he had the numbers to force the Indonesian Military to bend to his Party's wishes, and sufficient influence over Soekarno to ensure his support. Arms shipments from Mainland China had commenced and he expected that sufficient numbers within the PKI would be fully armed and ready within three months.

The Commander of the Dioponegoro 7th Division in Central Java waited patiently as the country slowly moved to the boil, maintaining his Command's preparedness for the moment he knew would surely arrive. The general was resolute in his plan to save his country, as Indonesia moved closer to the brink of chaos.

* * * * * *

Murray Stephenson walked slowly from the car towards the Embassy steps. The airconditioner had failed and his mood reflected the discomfort he felt as the hot, sticky weather caused streams of perspiration to run down his back, causing damp patches on his clothing. It was mercifully cooler inside the building, and he checked his watch with the large clock which hung behind the Consulate reception, noticing that one of the two was incorrect. Murray made a mental note to check again later, when he listened to the Radio Australia Broadcasts from Melbourne.

He moved through the maze of corridors until he reached his own section, buried well behind the main entrance. He nodded at other officers as he loosened his tie and unbuttoned his collar. His Number Two opened the final access door after he had punched the buzzer impatiently. Murray had looked at the Second Secretary and thrown his jacket across the room aiming for the corner chair. He then stood directly in front of the Carrier window-unit airconditioner and unbuttoned the rest of his shirt, permitting the refrigerated air to cool his body. He looked back at the other man and noticed his look of concern.

'Don't ask,' he said, kicking his shoes off. He removed his trousers and placed these on a hook close to the cool artificial breeze. During the previous Station Chief's tenure, there had been a painting of Sir Robert Menzies' stern face hanging there. Murray had removed the Prime Minister's picture as he had discovered a more practical use for the wall hook.

'Aircon gone again?' the agent asked. Murray nodded as he continued to undress, removing his socks.

'You'd think they'd fill the bloody things with freon from time to time,' he complained. Embassy maintenance had gone to hell once the new man had arrived. Murray had seen it all before. Some of the expatriates just could not handle being stationed overseas, let alone in a difficult post like Djakarta. The new maintenance officer just could not assimilate, running around screaming at his local staff and, in frustration, attempting to carry out the work by himself rather than entrust the task to his quite capable Indonesian technicians. The end result was a substantial back-load of job orders which had become unmanageable. Murray had suggested to the Consul that the car-pool maintenance be given to Sjaiful, a particularly competent supervisor who probably knew more about mechanical repairs than anyone else, including the Australian, but he was politely reminded that this was not his domain. As a result, more than half the Embassy fleet ran without adequate air-conditioning. The high ambient temperatures and extreme humidity took their toll. Tempers were often frayed and the atmosphere amongst the small community suffered as the country prepared itself for the imminent monsoons.

'There's a 'priority' signal for you, Murray,' the agent advised, handing the message to Murray who now stood almost naked, scratching at a spot on his behind. He read the heading, checked the references and dropped it on his desk. He would decipher it when his clothes were dry. He felt his backside stinging from where he had scratched the skin.

'Shit,' he muttered through clenched teeth, 'it never fails. Every time I visit those bloody offices my backside ends up feeling like I've sat in stinging nettle. You'd think the Indonesians would spray those stinking rattan chairs. Christ!' he exclaimed, stretching to see the large welt as he pulled at the skin around his buttocks. He had been bitten by the tropical lice which thrived in the rattan chairs commonly used in government offices. Dust accumulated between the layers providing a suitable breeding ground for the savage bugs. He cursed, knowing that the severe itch would remain for hours, leaving welts the size of a two-shilling coin. He resisted scratching the bites further.

'What's your schedule for today?' he asked.

'Wanted to check with you first,' the agent replied. 'Colonel Zach has asked if we want to sit in on his discussions with the Indonesian Army. If the answer is yes, I'd best make a move as their meeting has been set up for twelve.'

'What's in it for us?' he asked. Many of the discussions were merely an excuse for the Indonesian officers to put their hands out, often providing nothing in return.

'Zach thought you might be interested. Says he is meeting with one of the team leaders who recently returned from Kalimantan.'

Murray smiled. 'Should be an interesting meet. This time last year the colonel was over there knocking those bastards off!' Doesn't seem to be of particular concern to us. Got anything else pressing?'

'No.'

'Might as well accompany the good colonel then. I'll be here when you return.' The other man nodded then left. Murray then removed his underpants and inspected the welts. He removed his trousers and replaced these with the cotton underclothes. He was confident that he would not be disturbed, as this was the most secure office in the entire building, access only being given to his Number Two and visiting agents. Murray towelled himself and checked his drawer for something to ease the itch. He found an opened tube of cream left from previous attacks and rubbed this into the area affected. He then stood, thinking about his current activities and the deteriorating political scene.

Murray also thought about his friend Zach, and Susan Bradshaw. He shook his head in disbelief. Even after almost two months he still had difficulty coming to term with the fact that his Director's wife had entered into a relationship with Steven Zach. Having examined his own feelings, Murray admitted that he had been disappointed only because there had existed a bond directly between himself and the others, and that the nature of this relationship had automatically changed the instant Steven and Susan had entered into their affair. He was still fond of Susan and continued to be Zach's friend even though this did, from time to time, prove to be awkward. They had set aside some private time and talked it through and Murray was pleased that Zach understood his predicament. But he never mentioned the child.

Susan had not returned to Djakarta although Murray was certain that she maintained close contact with Steven. She had written to him explaining what steps were being taken regarding her marriage to Harry. Murray had been saddened when he read the letter. He decided against communicating a personal message to Bradshaw. He thought it best to wait until they met and Harry had the opportunity to tell him in person when he next visited Djakarta.

Murray's eyes dropped to his right hand and he clenched his fist, then opened his hand to check the red scar tissue. The wounds had taken weeks to heal, requiring stitches across his right palm and most of his fingers. He winced as he remembered grabbing for the top of the wall, his left hand grasping the edge as his right struck the row of broken glass embedded along the top of the cement to prevent intruders. He knew he had been extremely lucky.

Not only could he have lost his hand but his life as well. Murray was most indebted to the soldier who had been guarding his general's house just down the street when his attackers moved in for their kill. There had been no incident recorded. Murray had decided against this as he could see no benefit in alarming others. Instead, he later communicated the incident directly to Central Plans in Melbourne, on an 'eyes only' basis for Harold Bradshaw, his Director. Murray did not disclose the fact that he had broken with procedure and removed sensitive material from the security of the Embassy as he assumed that his wallet, and its contents, would have been thrown away once the money inside had been removed. He believed that it had fallen out of his trousers during the attack, and had most probably been recovered by one of the numerous itinerants who could have passed by any time before he had discovered his loss.

As for his attackers, Murray had no idea whatsoever who they might have been. Nevertheless, he increased security at his residence by employing an additional *djaga* and, whenever he moved around the city Murray did so with extreme caution. He had made a serious enemy out there somewhere, and he was determined not to make their tasks any easier. Murray couldn't be sure that he had not provoked the attack by confronting them in their car.

Although he believed that was possible, why did they return for a second attempt? Was it just a rush of blood on the driver's part or had there been others in the vehicle directing the operation? These, and many other unanswered questions, continued to occupy his thoughts as he went about his activities. He understood that the very nature of his position could have resulted in the attempt on his life. The attack could have been related to any of his clandestine activities as Station Chief. After all, that's what he had been trained to do. He just wished there weren't so many damn restrictions relating to his carrying a weapon. The Agency directive was quite explicit. Unless extreme prejudice was evident, agents were to store their weapons by the most secure means available. In Murray's case, this clearly meant leaving his automatic locked in the small office safe along with his other tools of trade. Unconsciously, he massaged his right hand as the image of his P9S crossed his mind. To hell with the standing orders. They should all be armed when moving around this city, he thought.

Murray checked his watch again and decided to listen to the half-hour news broadcasts. When these were finished, he adjusted his watch, dressed and went over to central registry, clearing the inner decoding safe of other officers as he set about deciphering the message he had received an hour earlier. Murray stood in front of the telex machines as they rattled away noisily, spewing tape down onto the floor as the message took readable form. When the clatter had finished, he reached up and tore the paper from the machine. Murray had already read the detail as each word had formed during the decoding process. He then extracted the two tapes and locked these away, ensuring that he had not left the carbon copy on the machine. He then re-read the signal, memorising its content before he ran both copies through the shredder. As an additional precaution, he removed parts of the finely-cut paper and placed these in an adjacent shredder's bin, knowing that one could never be too careful. Murray then returned to his own section and considered the information contained in the document he'd just destroyed. He frowned. Harold Bradshaw was on his way to visit the Djakarta Station. Murray thought about this and wondered if the visit was personal or professional. Then he shrugged his shoulders and decided it was probably both.

* * * * * *

Changi Airforce Base, Royal Air Force, Singapore

The second pilot indicated with a thumbs up and immediately commenced rolling the deadly bomber in tandem with his team member. Both aircraft moved swiftly across the concrete tarmac as they taxied from the hard-standing area reserved for their squadron, across from the row of hangers and then waited for clearance before moving out onto the runway. There was considerable traffic overhead and both crews listened as other aircraft communicated with their respective towers. The three main operational fields on the small island led to considerable congestion. Changi housed the largest contingent of British aircraft and personnel. The RAF had more than doubled their presence two years before, when the Indonesian President embarked on his crusade to destroy the fledgling Federation of Malaysia.

Other aircraft, including several squadrons of SAR helicopters which could double as gun-ships, were located in both Seleta Airforce Base on the other side of the island and Changi Field. The commercial airstrip at Paya Lebar continued to accommodate the world's airlines, bringing thousands of tourists to the friendly Singaporeans.

As the pilots of both aircraft waited patiently for their final clearance, they observed the distorted perspective created along the runway as the tropical sun baked the airfield's surface, covering the long stretch of concrete with layers of imaginary water. As the minutes ticked by, the pilots offered their silent gratitude to the British engineers who had designed their aircraft and support systems. The temperatures inside the cockpit would have been unbearable had it not been for the airconditioned suits. As the flight commander looked over his left shoulder, his radio crackled and they received clearance for take-off on the main runway. Winds were light and weather over Singapore was still fine, although late afternoon thunderstorms would roll in and dump their rain before the aircraft had completed the first leg of their mission.

Both pilots responded to the tower with a 'roger' and immediately commenced rolling onto the main runway. They lined up their aircraft and released the thousands of horsepower required to thrust the sophisticated aircraft into the sky. Within two minutes, both aircraft had left the military field behind and climbed at an incredible rate as they followed a heading away from the Indonesian islands just a few nautical miles to the south. They eased their noses around to the north, then west, then south again as they gained sufficient altitude to make their run. Fifteen minutes later, as the aircraft reached fifty-thousand feet some one hundred and fifty nautical miles north-east of Singapore and over the Malaysian islands of Anambas in the South China Sea, they turned, and marked their new direction as the crews went into full battle alert.

Minutes later, the aircraft entered Indonesian air as they crossed the Equator and the pilot snapped an order to both crews. There was a moment of turbulence as the cockpit indicator flashed, acknowledging that the mechanisms had functioned. He glanced over at his wing man and confirmed that the other aircraft had followed suit and was in the correct mode. Both aircraft then flew with their bomb-bay doors open. Their bomb load was armed with atomic warheads as instructed, to deter the Indonesian Government from launching any attack with their recently-acquired Bear Bombers which, at that moment, sat quietly along the runway at the AURI Airforce Base in Madiun in East Java. The RAF Vulcan bombers then commenced the first leg of their run through enemy territory, conscious of the SAM missiles which no doubt lay on their revetments waiting for the command to launch. There was little comfort, these pilots knew, that the Soviet SAM's strike capability lay between six and forty-five thousand feet. They had been known to reach greater altitudes, although the airmen knew that the SAM's accuracy went to hell once it pushed past its recommended threshold.

Fifteen minutes passed and the bombers crossed the island of Bangka, maintaining their heading for the Indonesian capital. Another twenty minutes had ticked by when the Royal Air Force pilots banked to port and corrected their heading to fly almost due east. They were now on their second leg, which would take them directly over the squadrons of Soviet TU-16 bombers, the Russian answer to the American B-52's currently bombing the hell out of North Vietnam. The pilots could not see the Java coastline but they knew the cities below by rote, as their squadron had flown almost identical missions twice weekly, over the past two years. In every instance, the Vulcans had been armed with atomic warheads and the aircraft flew with their bomb-bay doors in the operational ready mode.

As they checked their instruments, the aircraft passed over Tjirebon, Pekalongan and Semarang where a further course correction was made to the south-east to enable the deadly loads to fly directly over the huge Soviet aircraft based below near Surakarta. Turbulence rocked the aircraft as they crossed the string of active volcanoes, their craters up to seventeen thousand feet above the sea. The flight commander checked his instruments and alerted the crews. They then changed course for their final leg and closed the bomb-bay doors. Two hours later, the aircraft had landed in Darwin and were already being refuelled for their return run.

The crews remained in the immediate area as this process took place. Then, as they carried out their final checks, the RAF crews waved to their Australian counterparts and flew out of the Darwin base under cover of darkness. They retraced their steps over Indonesia, covering the same targets again, before returning to Changi Field.

President Soekarno went to great lengths to ensure that only a limited number of his Military and Cabinet were advised of these flights. It was humiliating. He was painfully aware of the commitment the British had given the Malaysian and Singaporean Governments and, in fact, he had been personally advised by the British Ambassador that these flights would continue as long as the Indonesian President persisted in his attempts to invade either of those two British Commonwealth countries. A direct warning was given to the President that his Airforce was being continuously monitored and, in the event any of the Indonesian Airforce Tupolov long-range bombers so much as strayed outside the immediate surrounds of Madiun, he could expect that either Djakarta or Surabaja would be subjected to a pre-emptive strike by aircraft armed with atomic warheads.

At first Soekarno thought it was all bluff until he was shown the radar tracking reports. He was livid and delivered a stinging attack on British Imperialism to his followers during that year's Independence Day celebrations. He then ordered that the flights be kept from the Indonesian people. Soekarno believed that his *rakjat* would never believe that, even with the sophisticated weaponry introduced by the Soviets, they were still unable to prevent the West from violating their airspace at will. The flights continued and Soekarno issued direct instructions to Omar Dhani that the TU-16's were to remain grounded.

* * * * * *

Clarke Airforce Base,
United States Airforce, Philippines

The American Airforce general removed his shields and rubbed both eyes slowly. He was tired and ready for some shut-eye. He glanced over the data recorded on the 'flights in progress' board and shook his head in disgust. There was one still out somewhere, and there had been no radio contact for well over an hour. He knew his arse would be in a sling if they had a repeat of the Pope flight although he did not believe that they were faced with a similar problem.

The general appreciated that things had changed considerably since then, what with the continuous bombing runs on 'Nam which originated from his field here in the Philippines. The one-star general straightened and drew in several deep breaths before rubbing his face again. Suddenly, the radio, set on the specific frequency allocated to the southbound incursion, came to life. Immediately all signs of fatigue disappeared as the pilot identified his position and advised that they had suffered some light ground fire. This had interfered with their earlier transmissions as they were completing their final drop near Makassar. Now they had completed their mission and were over the Sulu Sea off the west coast of the central Philippine islands. They reported that their run had been successful and that only minor damage had been sustained.

The general was pleased. He disliked lending his boys to the Air America flights but he accepted that they were all on the same side. He knew that his pilots enjoyed these missions, even though no record of their flights and hours in the air was recorded in their log books. Neither did they wear uniforms or dog-tags whilst on these flights. The up-side was that the CIA Station Chief paid each of his men a cool grand for each mission, and that was big money in anyone's book. He had to be selective when choosing pilots for these clandestine runs over Indonesia. Married men were never selected. He preferred the boys who had already scored time over 'Nam as they wouldn't be gun shy if things came unstuck. As for the aircraft they flew, that was another consideration. The general disliked using vintage aircraft. They had been good in their day but, as he had discovered himself when having to ditch one of the old ladies just the year before, those C-47's were definitely ageing, and really should not be used for covert flights.

The men were never briefed as to who were the beneficiaries of the night cargo drops. He could only speculate as to the purpose of the tonnes of weapons tied to darkened parachutes that his men alone had thrown out of the ancient cargo planes. Suddenly he chuckled as he envisaged these dangerous loads swinging through the evening sky and landing, as they often did, on village roofs or even on people in the streets. It didn't concern him. They were dropping shitloads of high explosives to the north all over 'Nam.

Why shouldn't this asshole Soekarno, get some too? They were surrounded by commies everywhere, he decided, wishing he could return to active flying duties. He really missed those missions. The movements officer approached and then waited at an appropriate distance until his general waved him over.

'Whattaya got?' he demanded, taking the clipboard from the major before he could refer to the data annotated there. The general shook his head and swore. 'Goddamn it, Major, we have one of those old birds limping its way back in as we speak. Now what do they want?' he snapped. The junior officer took a deep breath.

'The spooks have asked for fifteen more flights before the end of the month, General. That will mean utilising the other two birds in hangar two-two. I need your authorisation to ask the colonel over there to give us some urgent support crews to bring them on line again.'

'How deep are the targets?' the general asked, angry with the additional demands being made by the Station CIA Chief. They must have something really hot on their plates, he thought.

'All the way, General. All the way.'

'For Chrissakes,' he spat, knowing that he would be especially tight for crews. 'Get onto the rosters and tell the boys the bad news. Give me a list of those who've already had more than two runs this month. Don't want them to get too greedy,' he ordered. The major turned and disappeared quickly while his CO continued to monitor the days' flights over Hai Phong in North Vietnam. The officers all knew that their Commanding Officer had their best interests in mind and always took their position whenever it came to it. Just the week before, his men had been dragged over the carpet for dropping their load too close to the British freighters in the North Vietnamese harbour. The general had cursed and shouted, furious that his men were obliged to avoid hitting the limey ships delivering much-needed supplies to Ho Chi Minh. He just could not understand what the Brits were doing there. Weren't they supposed to be America's allies?

As he glared out through the thick plate-glass windows overlooking Clarke Field Airforce Base, the general snorted in contempt and muttered something unintelligible to himself. Then he remembered the additional flights requested into Indonesia and his face became even more serious.

All the way, the major had said. And he knew only too well what that meant.

* * * * * *

DJjakarta

Aidit listen intently as the other members of his *Dewan Revolusi* spoke. Soebandrio was present and was a senior member of this Revolutionary Council. Aidit looked around the room and felt confident that their plans would be realised. And soon.

For he now believed that he had the support necessary to effect a successful coup d'etat against the Council of Generals before they acted first. He had been informed that news of Air Marshall Omar Dhani's real purpose in visiting Red China had reached Nasution. Aidit was most concerned that the arms shipments would be interrupted by the anti-Communist TNI generals. As he listened to Untung outline specific responsibilities for the Military officers present, the Chairman of Indonesia's Communist Party watched the effect the lieutenant colonel was having on the others as he assumed control over the meeting.

The gathering consisted of members of almost every facet of Indonesia's multi-layered society. Apart from Colonel Untung, Brigadier General Soepardjo was present, as well as Colonel Latief and Majors Soejono and Agus Sigit who would all play significant roles when the time arrived. Aidit considered their ongoing need for President Soekarno's support although, at times, even he seemed to waver. Aidit accepted that there had been compromise and the necessity to identify his own interpretation of Communism as the accepted ideology within his Party. In securing Soekarno's protection, Aidit realised that the PKI had lost much of its doctrinal purity, not to mention its revolutionary will. Still, he believed, in typically pragmatic fashion, that it was imperative that he adjust the basic philosophy to accommodate the Indonesian mentality. The Party Chairman looked across at their host.

The house where they congregated belonged to Wahjudi, one of Aidit's most devout supporters. They all wore civilian clothes to avoid detection as the members were obliged to pass through a narrow gang in order to access this meeting place, which was located directly behind another building with no vehicular access. The members of the Revolutionary Council were aware that their plans had moved into a critical phase and, even more so than before, they had to be careful. Aidit sensed that they were near to achieving their goals and cautioned his inner circle of conspirators to maintain diligence at all times, fearing that the slightest slip would tear their dream of a communist state asunder.

Latief had proposed that they establish a Central Command within the Revolutionary Council, to be headed jointly by Untung and Soepardjo. They had all agreed. Next, they finalised the list of all those units which could most definitely be counted on to support their actions. Aidit listened excitedly as even he was surprised at the number of companies and units which had already committed themselves to the movement. Ever since their President's health had deteriorated, their rank and file had become seriously concerned that, should he die, there would be no-one left to protect the communists from the Council of Generals, the members of which were either known or assumed to be known to Soebandrio and Aidit. These senior Party officials warned that, in the event Soekarno passed away, these senior Military officers had made it quite clear that they would not only abolish the Indonesian Communist Party, but had promised to incarcerate its prominent membership. Aidit continued to listen as Untung spoke.

'That leaves us with a target date to determine. We should agree on that now,' he suggested. Those present immediately looked towards Aidit who nodded in affirmation.

'I agree. We must select the most opportune date for our move. What are your suggestions?' he asked. The members discussed this important issue for almost an hour until they reached agreement. They decided on the tenth day in November. It was the national holiday which celebrated the Heroes of the Revolution. Not long thereafter, the meeting broke up and they returned to their homes. Aidit had remained behind to speak with the Tjakrabirawa colonel.

'Comrade Untung,' he addressed the Palace Guard officer, 'we should speak more about Nasution and his Council. I believe that you and I have a clearer understanding of what their fate must be if we are to be successful in our efforts to take full control of the Military?'

Colonel Untung smiled at Aidit. He had been promised an appointment as the new Armed Forces Chief once the communists had taken full control of the Government. Under the new regime, there would be no rank higher than that of colonel. There would be an immediate rationalisation of officers and their ranks. He, in turn, would be promoted to this most senior Military position over his superiors, in consideration for his loyalty. He relished the thought of eliminating the current *TNI* leadership. The colonel then extracted the list of officers who had been targeted for immediate arrest. There had been considerable debate concerning which of the generals belonged on the list. They had agreed that all of Nasution's so-called Council had to be included. There were others, but these had been discussed at length and removed from the final list.

Aidit addressed the Deputy Prime Minister, Dr. Soebandrio. *'I'm not entirely comfortable leaving him out,'* he argued, referring to Soeharto, the Strategic Reserve Forces Commander. *'Although your arguments are strong, we must remember that he would be one of the most senior ranking officers once Yani and Nasution are removed.'*

'Not under our proposed reorganisation of the Military. Besides, it is a known fact that he and Nasution have been feuding for years. Also, he is not a member of the Council of Generals. We would do well to remember that, once we've taken power, we will need to maintain strong relationships with the Chinese, both politically and commercially. This man has developed considerable strengths within the local Chinese community. I recommend that his name is removed.'

After further debate, they all agreed. In the end it was decided that providing the most senior officers were arrested, the others would fall into line. After all, they had their President's blessing, he argued.

'It would be detrimental to our maintaining leadership should these officers remain alive. There would always be the danger that they may gather enough support to move against us in the future. Besides, should they be swept away in the excitement, their supporters would be like a dragon with no head. We should eliminate these men immediately upon our units moving into the capital. You would need to think through this very carefully. We need to have at least one team dedicated to this important task. A team which we could totally depend upon to carry out the necessary executions,' Aidit insisted.

'I will make the arrangements, Comrade Aidit. In fact, we already have such a unit which would be well-suited for this mission. They are

completely trustworthy and have already proven themselves to the Party,'
Untung advised.

'Then I will leave this in your capable hands, Comrade,' the Chairman smiled, satisfied that the powerful members of the Military leadership would be dealt with as he seized control of the Government. They talked a while longer; then, so as not to attract attention, left separately to attend to their other duties.

Several days passed before Lieutenant Colonel Untung made his final decision. He selected several units from the Gerwani to assist in accommodating the Party Chairman's request. He had seen these young women as they trained and was convinced that they would carry out the executions when the time arrived. He searched his mind for the team leaders he had encountered in Sukabumi when he and the others visited the field training camp. Then he remembered and made a note to make direct contact during the next few days. He wrote in his diary, *Gerwani — Sukabumi — Check names of the team leaders.*

The following Monday, Yanti was summoned to PKI Headquarters.

* * * * * *

Bangkok

Harry sat uncomfortably in the back of the airport taxi as the traffic ground to a halt. He leaned forward and peered ahead through the heavy downpour. The intersection was blocked by stranded vehicles, unable to move further when their saturated distributors had ceased to function under the waves of water which inundated the capital's roads whenever it rained. He looked out through the side window and estimated the filthy water to be at least knee-deep.

Harry knew the city well and, considering the remaining distance to his hotel, decided that he would wait until the driver managed to extricate them from the congestion rather than wade through what was probably a combination of rain water and raw sewerage. There was a *klong* not two hundred metres off to their right and he had little doubt that this canal would already have spilled its filthy effluent into the lower areas. It seemed that

Bangkok was sinking. Almost every visit he had made had resulted in his being bogged down in the rain somewhere on the city's over-crowded roads.

An hour passed. The driver had killed the engine as he was running short of gas. The man turned and smiled through irregular yellow teeth, and offered Harry a cigarette. Harry declined, wishing his command of the language was good enough to tell the man not to light-up in the confined taxi's interior. As the smoke drifted across to the rear seat, Harry quickly opened both windows but this made little difference. The driver waved the cigarette around as he fidgeted impatiently, tapping his fingers on the steering wheel to the beat of some imaginary song. Another hour had passed before the police had cleared the congested intersection and they were able to proceed. By then, the Director's clothes were saturated by the suffocating humidity and heat. The driver lit another cigarette just after Harry had closed the rear windows to benefit from the airconditioner. Then the taxi moved slowly forward into the stream of down-town traffic, the driver touching his brake, then accelerating, then braking again, riding his clutch and making Harry feel distinctly nauseous.

When they finally arrived at the Intercontinental Hotel, Harry checked his watch and was dismayed that the entire trip from the airport had taken most of four hours. He completed the registration formalities, went immediately to his room and showered. Then he dialled the local number and waited. As he listened to the dial tone ringing, unanswered, Harry became concerned. He acknowledged that he was late, but that had never been a problem in the past as Bangkok residents were quite relaxed about appointment times, due to the city's notorious traffic problems. The tone changed indicating that there was no one there. Harry dialled again, with a similar result. He frowned. As was his custom, he had sent a cable advising details of his arrival although he couldn't be sure that this had not gone astray.

Suddenly, Harry felt the skin on his neck prickle. Immediately, he became even more alert. His years in the field and inner senses told him that something had gone wrong. He knew from experience that it was most out of character for Piya not to wait. He decided to go down and check the premises for himself. Clearing the round coffee table, he placed his briefcase down flat, then extracted a small nail-file from his personal vanity set. He removed four brass screws which held the lower section of his well-worn leather case, then separated the two sections. Harry pulled one of the chairs closer and made himself comfortable while he examined the contents exposed in the hidden compartment. He removed the short cylinder and inspected this first, before placing it back in the indentation designed to hold it secure. He then coaxed the 7.62 mm pistol from its own slot and checked the Soviet Tula Tokarev's eight-round magazine.

Memories came flooding back as he held the pistol confidently. He had opted for this weapon specifically when he first arrived in Berlin as it was standard issue in the Soviet Army and, as he spent most of his time in their territory, Harry felt more comfortable carrying one of their handguns. He knew that the TT pistol was common throughout the Russian satellite states. It suited his hands, weighing less than two pounds. He was not concerned with its range, believing that no one in their right mind should attempt to take out a handgun target in excess of fifty metres.

Harry extracted another clip containing gilded steel-jacketed bullets and placed this in his back pocket. He removed the small cylinder once again and connected this to the pistol. Satisfied, he unlocked the silencer and placed this in his side pocket. He then changed shirts, selecting one which he could wear, hanging outside his trousers. The automatic under his belt was well hidden behind the curve in the small of his back, and covered by his loose fitting shirt. He checked himself in the full length mirror. He was ready.

Harry left his poolside suite and returned to the lobby to check personally for messages. There were none. Ignoring the concierge's attempts to steer him towards the hotel taxi service, Harry elected instead to walk the short distance to the main entrance where he hailed a private taxi and issued directions for the driver to follow.

Unknown to Harold Bradshaw, his movements had been closely monitored. As the unmarked pirate taxi pulled out into the traffic, an inconspicuous figure hurried across the hotel car-park and hissed at his companion to hurry. Moments later, the relatively new Fiat leaped into life as the driver accelerated quickly and followed the Intelligence Chief on his journey across the city, to meet his lover. It soon became obvious that the Australian was heading for the destination about which they had been briefed, and that their quarry was taking evasive surveillance measures. They decided to drive directly to Piya's small flat, convinced that Harry Bradshaw would soon appear for a rendevous with his young friend. They arrived not moments after the Russians had left, having baited their trap. The CIA agents remained outside, well hidden in the shadows, waiting.

* * * * * *

Piya had watched in fear as the telephone continued to ring. He glanced up at the two men who stood, menacingly, their huge frames filling the room. He shivered and looked at the window airconditioner unit to see if he had remembered to turn it down, then realised that it was fear that was responsible for the chill in his spine. He needed to use the bathroom, desperately. Piya inadvertently made eye contact with one of the men and immediately wished he hadn't. His stomach churned as he remembered their earlier visit. And the beating.

He closed his eyes and prayed to his gods. Piya could not understand why he deserved so much unwarranted attention. First, he had been beaten by the American. But that had been months ago. He had thought they had forgotten about him. Now there were others, with accents he did not understand at all. He was consumed with fear. He could hear the television in the adjoining apartment as his neighbours' children played with the volume controls. Piya wished he could call out but realised to do so would only hasten his demise. He sniffed, fighting back the tears, which earlier had earned him a stinging slap to the side of the head. He glanced at the bedside clock. It had been a gift from the man Piya knew had just telephoned. He bit his lip, fighting to control his tears and, as an uncontrollable sob escaped from deep in his chest, his head exploded with a flash, and he fell to the floor stunned by the blow. He lay there, terrified, waiting for the vicious kick, covering his head with both hands.

'Get up, you little whore,' a voice snarled at him. He struggled to his feet and sat back on the side of the bed. 'And stop your snivelling!' The one who spoke then checked his wrist-watch and cursed. 'He's not coming.'

'Give it another thirty minutes. He'll come,' the other man said confidently, 'he'll come to see his little friend here. I guarantee it.'

'No more than thirty minutes, okay? And then I get to carve this little piece of shit into dog meat!' he grinned cruelly as Piya's eyes opened wide. The other man smiled knowingly at the suggestion and winked at his accomplice.

'Sure, why not?' he agreed, enjoying the fear on the young Thai's face. They then both remained silent as they waited, tensing from time to time as occasional pedestrian traffic passed close to the apartment's entrance, before moving away. Piya stared at the clock unable to control his fear. There was little time left. Would Harry come, he wondered? Again, he closed his eyes and prayed, pleading that someone would make these men go away.

* * * * * *

Harry waited in the taxi for some time, until certain that he had not been followed. Then he paid the taxi and walked the remaining distance towards Piya's flat. He stopped half a dozen times and checked over his shoulder but could still not detect anyone following. Strange, he thought, he just had that feeling. He knew he should slow down, double check, anticipate. Harry deliberately dallied on the last corner, feigning confusion as to his whereabouts. He could not identify anything out of the ordinary but, there again, he realised anything could go unnoticed in Bangkok's sleazy backstreets. He noticed the Fiat down the street but decided that its presence was not threatening. The car's occupants had slid, unobserved, low into their seats as Harry had arrived.

He stood across from the apartment and observed the building and its neighbouring structure. Harry could not see any movement amongst the street's shadows. Again, nothing appeared out of the ordinary except the absence of the welcome light which Piya would normally leave on when expecting his visit. Harry discounted this, now almost convinced that his cable had not been received, accounting for Piya's obvious absence. He moved closer to the building, then stiffened. The airconditioning unit hung out over the footpath where it had been ever since he had first visited this location. He looked up and listened to its hum and observed a few drops of condensation fall close to where he stood.

Immediately he sensed that there was something wrong. Piya would never have left his apartment, not even for five minutes, without first turning the airconditioner off. It was just one of young Piya's many idiosyncrasies. Harry knew that someone waited inside.

He paused outside and considered his options. Whoever occupied the apartment would not expect him to be armed. He decided to force the confrontation. A couple approached and he waited for them to pass and turn the corner before he climbed the narrow steps and knocked loudly on the solid timber door. There was no answer. He knocked again as he gripped the door handle and turned the knob, pushing quickly with his left hand while holding the Tula Tokarev with his right.

The door flew open into darkness. Harry threw himself to the left and extended his right arm preparing to shoot. Dim light fell through the open doorway as he stood still, his senses alive, his finger tensed on the pistol's trigger. He realised that he had stopped breathing. Slowly he released the breath he had been holding and sucked fresh air in through his dry mouth. He cursed silently as his fingers groped along the wall for the light switch near the door.

'Piya?' he whispered hoarsely, suddenly identifying the fierce stench in the room. 'Piya?' he called again, his fingers locating the switch as he flicked the lights on and dropped to the floor, his weapon still extended towards the centre of the room. He sat crouched in this position looking directly across to the large double bed as his eyes adjusted to the sudden infusion of light. Suddenly, he groaned and cried out loudly, as he sprang to his feet then turned pointing the automatic around the room in search of others present. But there were none. Only Piya. He lay spread across the length of the oversized bed, his legs dangling across the side as if he had been doing exercises then gone to sleep. But Harry knew that this was not so. The twisted expression on the young man's face told him otherwise.

Harry felt the blood drain from his face as he stared at the once handsome boy. He bent over the body and closed Piya's eyes, unable to avoid looking at the blood-stained torso as he did so. For several minutes Harry stared at the corpse, anger building as it had once before, many years ago. Too late, he remembered the open door and, as he turned to remedy the oversight he just caught a glimpse of the huge fist before it crashed heavily down on the base of his neck, smashing him to the floor. His body buckled with the impact, causing his pistol to fly out across the room where it fell noisily on the polished tiles. That was the last sound he heard.

Below, in the street, the Fiat's driver looked at his passenger and raised his eyebrows when the Russians slipped into the apartment. They had not expected to see them there.

'Wait,' the other man ordered, gripping his associate's arm to prevent him from leaving the vehicle.

'You didn't recognise those gorillas?' the driver asked incredulously.

'Sure,' his partner answered, 'that's why we should wait. Let's see what Boris is up to first before we make out like the cavalry.' The driver killed the engine and they sat quietly waiting for the Russians to leave.

'What do you think he's doing meeting with KGB?' The taller man looked across at his partner sitting behind the wheel. Sometimes he wondered how the man qualified as a field agent. Langley must really have screwed up with this one, he thought.

'Maybe they've organised a gang-bang together, Jerry. Shit, man, how the hell would I know what those mothers are doing there with the target.'

'We should take some shots. The boss will ask us why we didn't take any shots.'

The other agent thought about Jerry's suggestion and admitted that he was right. He rummaged around on the rear seat, then dragged the entire assembly across and onto his lap. There he rearranged the lens, replaced the film to compensate for the light and adjusted the focus. The agent activated the shutter release several times to ensure that the film had been picked up by the sprockets. Then they waited.

When the door finally opened only one of the oversized bear-shaped Russians re-appeared. The Americans watched as he walked away and disappeared around the corner, but not before they had shot several frames of the huge man as he was caught in the brief shaft of light from the doorway.

Jerry looked across at his partner and raised his eyebrows, then turned his attention back to the apartment's entrance, waiting for the second man to leave also. He didn't. Jerry was becoming restless when the dark-coloured Mercedes 180 slowed then stopped directly outside the target's apartment. The driver left the engine running and moved to the rear of the sedan, opening the trunk. The two CIA agents were almost caught off-guard when the door opened quickly and the Russian ran down the steps carrying a large bundle over his shoulder, which he unceremoniously heaved into the Mercedes' open trunk. The agents continued filming as both men lept into the sedan and drove quickly away.

The Americans looked at each other and, without speaking, sprang from their Fiat and ran up the steps and into the apartment. Moments later the one called Jerry was doubled over the bathroom basin heaving from the sight of the bloody and mutilated corpse they discovered lying on the bed.

'Come on Jerry, let's go, man!' his partner called, cursing as he attempted to drag his associate up off the floor. 'If we get caught in this shit, man, we'll end up wishing that was us,' he hissed, pointing to the body as he dragged Jerry out of the apartment. Suddenly he paused, saw Harry's weapon and bent down to retrieve the automatic, shoving it quickly inside his belt as he continued to push the other agent out of the building. They ran back to their car and left the scene quickly, before someone called the police. Above all else, it was their duty not to be compromised by these situations. Both men reported directly to the CIA Station Chief at home, who instructed his agents to go directly to the U.S. Embassy, develop their film and complete their reports. He told them to wait there until he arrived.

Later, he listened to their observations, read through their reports and checked the photographs. The image was not as clear as he would have liked but, he acknowledged, the photographs were good enough to identify the Russians at work. The CIA Chief scratched his head as he examined the picture showing the one Soviet agent carrying a bundle in what appeared to be a carpet or something similar. There had been no evidence that Harold Bradshaw, or 'Finger Jar', was dead, he thought; otherwise, why would the Russkies bother to remove the Australian's body?

He completed his own analysis and sent the entire report up to communications for encryption and despatch. Let Langley work this one out, he decided, knowing that the lights would burn throughout the night when news of Harry Bradshaw's abduction reached the Director's desk back in Virginia.

* * * * * *

He couldn't breathe. His tried to free himself from inside the carpet but discovered that his hands had been tied. Harry could smell the exhaust fumes as the deadly smoke leaked into the trunk compartment. His throat was hoarse from coughing. They had tied something around his mouth to prevent his calling out. He knew that if they did not stop and attend to him soon, he would die from asphyxiation, or at least carbon monoxide poisoning.

Harry had regained consciousness only to pass out again. He had no idea whatsoever where he was until he identified the poisonous fumes and then cold realisation returned. He had been kidnapped. But, by whom? Rational thought dictated that there had to have been a mistake. Why would he be kidnapped? It most certainly would not be the Soviets, his mind argued, nor the Americans or Brits! What would be their benefit? Obviously, someone wanted something from him. And in earnest, he admitted, remembering the body left behind which had been used as bait. He had been professionally set-up, this he knew. Someone had gone to extreme lengths to arrange for his abduction. Someone, again obviously, who was familiar with his secret liaison with Piya. Harry winced with pain as the car hit a pot-hole somewhere, driving his head hard against something solid. The fumes seemed to increase as the car reduced speed, turning left, then right, then left again, then slowing to a stop. He could hear voices, then the vehicles moved forward again, but not too far before it came to a halt and the engine noise died.

He heard men's voices, then a rattling sound as the trunk was opened and he was lifted bodily from the suffocating hole. The carpet was removed and he squinted as bright lights attacked his eyes. His hands and feet were untied leaving him to stand groggily in the basement garage. One of the huge men dragged him by the shoulder, forcing Harry to follow quietly. Immediately he recognised these men for what they were, and was confused. He could see from their features that they were Russians. They even smelled like Russians, he thought bitterly, as he stumbled, cracking his knee on the first of the steps which led to the building's ground floor.

They passed through several fire exits before he was ushered into a lift which took the three men to the third floor.

Harry identified the building as the Soviet Embassy. Now he was even more confused, although feeling slightly more confident. Surely if they wanted him dead, he would have been killed already and left beside Piya? They entered a small room devoid of anything on the walls. It was an interrogation room. He had used them himself, in the past. His two guards then left, leaving him alone with his thoughts and the two chairs which had been positioned facing each other. The door opened and he turned.

'Hello Comrade Director,' Konstantinov bellowed, enjoying what he perceived to be an amusing moment for all. 'Sit down, Comrade, sit,' he ordered, placing his huge frame on one of the chairs. Harry sighed and did as instructed. The door opened and an unfamiliar face entered, carrying a tray with two glasses and a bottle of vodka. He looked at the KGB officer and accepted one of the glasses as it was poured. Both men swallowed the contents without hesitation. The glasses were then refilled and the attendant retired, leaving the men alone. Konstantinov swallowed the second shot and kept his empty glass raised until the Australian followed suit. Harry coughed as the spirits burned all the way down, sending a pleasurable flush through his tired and battered body.

He looked at the Russian and waited. He knew that Konstantinov would get to the point soon enough. Harry felt that he had experienced enough surprises to fill a life-time already. What was the KGB man doing here in Bangkok? And why had he orchestrated his kidnapping?

'Well, Comrade, seems that you have been overcome by events,' the Soviet spy-master commenced. His mood was convivial as he refilled both glasses. Harry waited. There seemed little point in interrupting. He wanted Konstantinov to get to the point quickly, and tell his story. Especially the part which finished ... and that's why we killed Piya. He lifted the glass and swallowed its contents in one swig. Konstantinov was impressed.

'Harry,' the Russian started again, this time sending a cold chill through the ASIS Chief's body. He had never called him that before. 'Harry, I believe I have some good news for you. Or at least, I would hope you will consider it good news.' Konstantinov smiled, almost benevolently, as he held his fourth glass of vodka steady, then raised it in salute before finishing it quickly. Harry waited.

'The good news is you are going home, Comrade,' the Russian said, pleased with the announcement. Harry looked at the KGB officer suspiciously. Why kidnap him to tell him that?

'You will leave tomorrow morning with some of the Soviet staff and families who are returning to Moscow by Aeroflot,' he announced. Harry was stunned by the statement. Home? To the Kremlin? Konstantinov must have flipped! His mind raced as the implications of what had just been said dawned on him. My God, he thought, they want me to do a Philby!

'I see you are pleased, Comrade. This is good. You see, there are those in Moscow who wished to terminate our relationship with you in a less friendly fashion. I argued on your behalf. They now all agree. You have been a faithful warrior to the Kremlin and now you are to be rewarded. You will be given an apartment in Moscow, treated with respect, permitted to travel freely within the Soviet Union and even an adequate pension.' Konstantinov paused to examine Bradshaw's reaction.

'Why?' he asked, still stunned by the news. He felt as if someone had gripped his guts with ice-cold hands and would not let go. His mind raced, searching for answers but there were none there. 'Why Moscow?' he asked in disbelief.

'Why?' Konstantinov responded. 'I would have thought that quite clear, Comrade Harry,' he smiled, pleased with their new relationship. 'You are being retired. And in a pleasant way.' There was a hint of menace in his voice. Harry was almost lost for words. What in the hell was going on here?

'Why can't I just retire in Australia?' he asked, fearing that he already knew the answer. Konstantinov looked at Harry's drink and observed that it was empty. He refilled both glasses.

'Because if you return to Australia, my friend, you will most surely die,' he said solemnly. Somehow Harry had anticipated the answer although he was still confused. 'Our masters in Dzerdzhinsky Square have decided to put you out to pasture, Harry. The reasons are many and complicated. I can tell you, though, it is because of what is taking place in Indonesia that you are to withdraw from your own country's involvement there as our interests will most certainly be compromised should you remain in the game. Remember, Harry, it could have been worse. There are still those who would feel more comfortable knowing that your retirement was more, ... let's say, permanent.'

Konstantinov explained how he had argued on Bradshaw's behalf, stating that the Australian Intelligence Chief would be a considerable asset in terms of propaganda alone. The West would be stunned to discover that one of their most respected officers had defected. Konstantinov relished the idea of such a disclosure, coming not so many years after the British scandals involving McLean, Burgess and, of course, Kim Philby.

And then, of course, there was the immediate risk. The Kremlin would be vulnerable if the man they had turned remained within reach of the discretionary powers of his own Government. Moscow had been emphatic. Repatriate or remove Bradshaw, and quickly. It had taken years for the KGB to successfully infiltrate the American Central Intelligence Agency and now, with one of their deep-cover agents positioned close to the decision-makers in Langley, they had discovered that Harold Bradshaw's activities had already been known, and he was currently suspected by his Western ally of having been compromised in some manner. Their mole had even verified the Australian's allocated code-name within the CIA: Finger Jar. Moscow insisted that he be removed from the arena immediately, convinced that he could be turned again at any time, by the Americans. There was too much at stake to consider the interests of just one man. Now Konstantinov was not certain that he had taken the appropriate position by supporting Bradshaw's repatriation to the Soviet Union.

'Why didn't you discuss this with me during our last meeting in Canberra? Harry asked. 'Why was it necessary to go to these elaborate steps here in Bangkok?' He paused. 'Your men were excessive,' he added, almost sullenly. The Russian looked at the Australian and smiled.

'Come, Comrade. Would you have entertained leaving Australia if we'd asked? Also, you must admit, these things are more easily arranged from Bangkok than say, Canberra, no?' The Russian continued to observe the other man's reactions. 'We decided that, as you were already here, the most difficult step had already been overcome by your leaving your own country voluntarily. After all, Harry, we wouldn't want the embarrassment of repeating the Petrov fiasco.'

Harry was stunned. His mind raced but he knew that this

decision was already a fait accompli. The Russian had obviously taken steps to ensure he would not return to Australia. What had they done? He understood that retirement to the Kremlin may be his only choice. The alternative was patently clear. Harry looked hard at the Russian facing him. The jovial expression betrayed only by the cold, piercing eyes. Harry could not believe this was happening to him. Desperately he decided on one last course of action. He paused then raised his glass.

'When did you say I'd be leaving?'

'Tomorrow, Harry,' Konstantinov answered, 'tomorrow,' raising his glass in a toast. 'I will now tell you how pleased I am that you have made the correct decision, my friend. Had you refused ...' he left the words hanging. Harry thought for a moment.

'Am I permitted one last night on the town?' he asked, forcing a mischievous grin. For a moment he thought he had gone too far, as he observed the flicker in Konstantinov's eyes as they momentarily clouded over. The KGB officer didn't answer immediately, pouring the remnants from the bottle into his own glass, then spilling half of this into Harry's.

He had suggested to Moscow that, should Bradshaw clearly be receptive to his being repatriated to Moscow, then this would be the preferred course of action. Konstantinov had been instructed that, should there be the slightest hesitation evident in Harry's response, then the Australian was to be eliminated. There had been considerable resistance to the idea of having the Australian living in Russia. Several had argued that, at some point in the future, Harry would become a major liability if he was not totally receptive to the idea of spending the rest of his days behind the Iron Curtain. Konstantinov had agreed to test Harry Bradshaw's response, and accepted responsibility for the final decision. It now appeared that he had little choice. In his own way, Konstantinov felt a little saddened by the decision he knew he must make. He had given the Australian his chance and the KGB general now decided to correct an earlier error in judgement. It just never paid to be sentimental, he knew. Especially when one's own position may be at risk.

'I don't see why you shouldn't have one last fling in the decadent West,' he smiled, then added, 'or in this case, the decadent East.' They both laughed. Harry looked at the other man and rose to his feet.

'I would appreciate just a few hours to pick up my things from the hotel, have a few quiet drinks at the bar. You know, sort of say goodbye by myself.' Konstantinov looked at the Australian, then nodded.

'I can't let you go alone, Harry. You know that.' He then rose to his feet also and extended his hand. 'I will send one of my men to escort you. Sort of keep you out of further trouble, yes?' He smiled as they shook hands. 'You must now remember that you are a member of the greater communist community, Harry,' he said, pumping his hand. Harry considered this and smiled through the alcoholic haze and assured the Russian he would do so. As they laughed together, the attendant appeared and cleared the empty bottle and glasses. Konstantinov then told him to wait. Minutes passed and Harry struggled to clear his head. The door opened and one of the guards motioned for him to follow. Pleased to be given the opportunity to leave, Harry followed. Konstantinov was waiting outside. They shook hands once more, and Harry turned to follow the enormous mountain of a man who was to accompany him.

As they walked away, Konstantinov's cold eyes followed. He had waited for the man to become indignant at the murder of his friend, and he hadn't. He had waited also for Harry to try to negotiate a deal which would have been more in character. Instead, he lied. Konstantinov had then known that Harold Bradshaw had no intention of living in the Soviet Union. Anyway, Harry would have been a tiresome problem for the rest of his days and it would have been on his head for recommending that the Kremlin accept him in consideration of his years of service. Konstantinov heard the heavy steel exit doors close behind the departing Intelligence Chief, and knew that he would never see the man again.

* * * * * *

The thick set guard sat in the back of the sedan as the Mercedes left the Soviet Embassy compound and headed back towards the King's Palace grounds. The Intercontinental Hotel occupied a large section of the Royal property and provided its guests with magnificent gardens and walkways across small streams which meandered through well-manicured lawns. When the driver reached the intersection, he continued on through instead of turning towards the hotel.

Harry lay unconscious in the vehicle's trunk. He hadn't expected the expertly-delivered blow he received as he bent to enter the car. They had not even bothered to tie his hands or feet. He had been tossed, once again, into the rear of the sedan as it was parked in the garage basement. Although Harry was well past his prime, the Russians took no chances. They wanted him alive when he hit the *klong*. A post-mortem would reveal the excessive amounts of alcohol in his blood, and this would be considered a contributing factor in his drowning.

The car continued through the city, leaving the outskirts of the capital until the bright lights all but disappeared. Traffic thinned as they moved into the rural area and still they drove on, stopping only when they arrived at the river junction which was fed by deep flowing streams. The driver remained in the vehicle as the KGB guard removed Harry's limp body from the trunk and carried him down to the *klong*. There he placed the unconscious man beside the muddy river and lowered his head into the water, gripping his victim's wrists from behind. At that moment, the water partly revived him and Harry opened his eyes under the murky waters. He panicked, and coughed as water flowed into his lungs. He struggled vainly, kicking with no effect, as his killer held him down. Slowly, he lost consciousness. The Russian continued to hold Harry's head underwater, even after his victim's efforts to resist had ceased. Within minutes it was all over.

The killer checked Harry's pulse then, having ascertained that the Intelligence Chief was dead, he pushed the corpse further out into the dark *klong's* current. He watched until he was satisfied that the body would drift downstream towards the city, where, hopefully, it would be discovered. The authorities would report the death as a tragic accident.

Satisfied that he could contribute nothing more, the KGB killer moved quietly back into the darkness. Rain began to fall as the Mercedes sped towards the Soviet Embassy and, within the hour, Bangkok's canal system was once more subject to a tropical downpour which filled every available catchment area, then spilled over, flooding the capital yet again.

The body rolled, and turned, before finally disappearing under the swift and muddy torrent. In the morning, it swept past unsuspecting villagers as they squatted alongside the embankments washing clothes. The corpse travelled on, past the floating markets, and finally drifted out into the sea.

Chapter 16

*Melbourne
mid-September*

The Deputy Director, John Anderson, sat quietly observing his Regional and Station Chiefs as the meeting was called to order. Conversation died as he stood, tall and gaunt, at the end of the long conference table and placed his hands in his pockets. He did this out of habit, and all present were familiar with his mannerisms. Anderson was popular within the Service, although he had bruised enough politicians in Canberra to warrant more than his share of criticism for the invariably tough position he took in relation to Australia's security.

Anderson was generally admired by the Intelligence community for his unique ability to cut directly to the core of a problem. He was known for the contempt he held for politicians, which often brought him as second most powerful Intelligence officer in Australia, into direct confrontation with members of Cabinet. When his name was mooted as a temporary successor to the missing ASIS Chief, there was considerable resistance in Canberra. Fortunately, he had the support of not only the Military Intelligence Directors, but also the Head of ASIO and the Attorney-General's permanent Secretary. Within two weeks of Harold Bradshaw's disappearance, Anderson had assumed the mantle of the missing Director.

There had been an immediate inquiry. Ultimately, the Prime Minister's office had decided that, because of the sensitivity of the position Bradshaw held, his disappearance should be investigated internally with all findings to be delivered directly to his office. Two teams were established for this purpose, one of which spent just two days in Thailand, where they held confidential discussions with the local police before returning home to Melbourne.

Most of the investigation was perfunctory. Anderson had

personally briefed the Prime Minister in relation to the personal discussions he had with Langley's Chief of Station in Australia. The Deputy Director had been shown copies of the reports filed from their Embassy in Thailand. Anderson immediately moved to have the investigation severely curtailed to avoid further embarrassment to the Australian Secret Intelligence Service. Bradshaw's sexual preferences had not been a well-kept secret. The Americans had returned Harry's unfired weapon, which ASIS confirmed through forensics as being his automatic. The Director's fingerprints were all over the Soviet pistol. The Thai police had co-operated fully, discreetly shredding all official evidence which implicated the Australian in the murder of one of their nationals. Anderson had personally approved the substantial payment made to the Thai investigators, although he had scoffed at the suggestion that these funds would be passed on to the dead boy's family in Chiang Mai.

There was no commemoration of his passing, not even a memorial service, as Harold Bradshaw was merely missing, not dead. Anderson had informed Susan Bradshaw of her husband's demise and was impressed with her stoic acceptance that Harry may have disappeared from her life forever. The Deputy Director had confirmed that, although Harry was officially considered only missing, the Government would ensure that Susan and her son would continue to receive whatever benefits they were entitled to under the Act. The room became quiet as Anderson withdrew one hand from his pocket and coughed, signalling that the meeting had commenced. He looked at the members of his inner sanctum and cleared his voice.

'Before we start, we'll have a moment of silence so that we may pay our respects to Director Bradshaw. I'm confident that there is not an officer here who has not, in some way, been touched by Harold Bradshaw. He served our country to the full.' Anderson hesitated, permitting Wells the opportunity to recover from his sudden coughing fit. The senior Intelligence officer almost choked, suppressing an attack of laughter as Anderson mentioned the word 'touched'.

Anderson shot a severe glance at him and Wells regained control. The Director lowered his head and uttered a silent prayer. He then tilted his head and swept the room with an authoritative look.

'Gentlemen, let's not allow our former Chief's demise to affect our judgement and good sense. Suffice to say, we have all suffered a great loss and I wish to remind you that he did leave a family behind. I will be speaking to you on an individual basis concerning Director Bradshaw's disappearance. In the interests of Central Plans and the security of our country, I wish to reiterate that rumour-mongering in any form will not be tolerated. Our jobs are difficult enough without creating internal conflicts.' Anderson then lowered his voice as if others may be listening. The officers leaned forward as he continued. 'We must assume that Harry is dead, and get on with business. Most of you are already aware that I have been appointed Chief pro tem. The Prime Minister has suggested that we maintain this position for at least six months considering the circumstances surrounding Harold Bradshaw's disappearance.' The acting Chief then looked around those present, pleased to see from their expressions that they appeared to support his appointment.

'I want you all to feel confident that there will be very few immediate changes within Central Plans. This meeting was not designed to be a briefing session, but merely an informal discussion with you all as the new Head of our Service. However, if any of you wish to take this opportunity for general discussion, then I invite you to do so.' Anderson looked around those present, his eyes coming to rest on Murray Stephenson sitting opposite Wells.

'Will we have access to the Bradshaw files?' Stephenson asked. This drew a surprised glance from others present. Anderson frowned slightly. The directness of the question had caught him off-guard.

'Limited access only,' he replied, moving on to another officer in an attempt to cut short further discussion of the missing Director.

'Will the current policy on overseas travel be maintained in view of what happened?' the second officer asked. Anderson indicated that this would be so.

'Considering that Station Chiefs must continue with whatever they had in play when Harry disappeared, wouldn't it be more appropriate that we have complete and immediate access to his files?' Stephenson asked, refusing to let Anderson stone-wall him again. 'My sector has ongoing operations which could be seriously jeopardised, even terminated, unless we move quickly to restore direction and continuity. We are operating under the most difficult circumstances in an extremely hostile environment. May I ask again, if the Director's files will be made available to me, as Station Chief?'

Anderson moved to block the challenge. It was no secret that this officer had developed an advantage over his peers due to his close personal relationship with Bradshaw. Anderson felt that Stephenson's demands were an attempt to challenge his authority while revealing what many of those present had long suspected. The Acting Chief had not always been fully briefed by Harry Bradshaw who, much to the chagrin of his Deputy, had conducted many of the covert operations without revealing any detail whatsoever of his clandestine activities. Murray observed his new Chief's reactions, convinced that Anderson really had no knowledge at all of the sensitive operation he and the missing ASIS Director had initiated.

'My position remains unchanged. Limited access will apply. Even to the most senior operatives who may believe that there are special circumstances which may dictate otherwise.'

The room became quiet as the other officers identified the poorly-disguised reprimand. Although there were some who disliked Murray because of his relationship with the Bradshaws, most considered him to be one of their finest officers and were surprised at the evident personality clash which had just occurred before them. Anderson then asked if there were any other questions and, when there were none, closed the meeting and left without muttering another word. He was furious with the Djakarta Station Chief and, once he had regained his composure, he had his secretary, Madge, send for Stephenson immediately. Anderson knew that he had to place his stamp on the whole Service quickly. He could not afford to have his authority challenged in any way. Even if this resulted in his losing some of his senior operatives. And this included Murray Stephenson.

* * * * * *

Djakarta

Colonel Steven Zach completed reading the file, adding his comments in a hand-written memorandum for the other Attaché's and then called his assistant. The thick folder contained information relating to Indonesia's ORBAT, or Order of Battle, an information schedule which listed the Military's armaments. His eyes were tired from checking through the fine detail which covered the Republic's military hardware purchases over the past seven years. Zach never ceased to be surprised at the incredible sums this country had expended on arms purchases.

He read the Pentagon report which detailed Indonesia's acquisitions from the Eastern Bloc. Had the man on the street back home in Australia been aware of the substantial military build-up just off their shores, he felt sure there would have been fewer anti-conscription demonstrations in his adopted country. The figures were boggling. He wondered how Soekarno had intended paying for the 275 tanks and armoured cars, the four destroyers and 24 torpedo boats and submarine chasers, not to mention the submarines and sophisticated fighters and bombers which now graced the country's military airfields. Zach compared Australia's paltry Airforce with Indonesia's AURI. How could Australia defend itself against squadrons which boasted fifty jet interceptors, forty jet and piston trainers, twenty long-range bombers and as many transport aircraft which gave support to Indonesia's massive number of ground troops? Zach shook his head at the American allies. The United States had run dangerously hot and cold in their relationship with Soekarno. He hoped the Americans would not regret their military aid package which provided weapons for 20 of Soekarno's infantry battalions, along with trucks, radio equipment and small ships for the Navy. They had also given them enough equipment for a company of Indonesian Marines, complete with a 60 mm mortar section. On top of all of this , the Americans had recommenced pilot training for the AURI pilots.

Steven Zach was, in a way, pleased that he was in the Military and not one of the civilians responsible for the present convoluted political situation in Indonesia. Even with his background, he found it most difficult to understand Soekarno's non-alignment policy. How had he managed to successfully seduce both the Soviets and the Americans as he reconstructed his country's Military strength! The clever dictator had developed alliances which clearly associated the Indonesians with all that was considered unholy by the West.

The Warrant Officer entered, listened to his instructions, then left with the classified file. Zach leaned back in his swivel chair and stretched. His thoughts moved to Susan's letter, which had arrived just days before Murray had told him of Bradshaw's sudden disappearance. He wished he could be with her in Melbourne. Apart from Murray, they had not discussed their relationship with others, although naturally the Attaché wives had gossiped after their return from the Pulau Putri weekend. Zach had sent her a cable, offering his condolences. Not sure who else might see the communication, he remained discreet, electing not to mention anything which could compromise her at this difficult time. At least Murray would have the opportunity to look in on her during his rush visit to Melbourne. Zach knew why Stephenson had needed to go to Australia. It seemed appalling that Bradshaw could disappear without trace, and he had suggested to Murray at the time how improbable it was that an official of Harry's experience could vanish without leaving some trail. The Station Chief had wanted to leave then and there for Thailand but, Zach knew, something on the boil in Djakarta had prevented Stephenson from visiting Bangkok before leaving for Australia.

* * * * * *

Bangkok
United States Embassy

The officers had been ushered into the Ambassador's private quarters and treated to lavish servings of American ice-cream and apple pie. The United States officials went out of their way to make the small delegation comfortable. The three Indonesian officers were suitably impressed, reacting warmly to the Ambassador's friendly manner and sincere interest in the proposal they carried.

Each of these officers had been hand selected by Major General Soeharto. They had served with him in Java and Sulawesi, and their loyalty to him was beyond question. This was their second visit.

The first had occurred only weeks before, during which they laid the groundwork for these current discussions. They had not been presented to the Ambassador during their previous meetings. Instead, these emissaries first met with the Defence Attaché who, in turn, introduced the officers to members of the State Department.

The discussions had been warm and friendly, establishing a basis for further exchanges. To date, these trusted men had already met in secret with Malaysian and Singaporean officials. The common ground, upon which Soeharto wished to initiate a rapprochement with his President's declared enemies, had been established. At first they had been treated with extreme suspicion. The Federation of Malaysia had been at war with its giant neighbour for almost two years and there was considerable fence-mending required before the officers could make any real headway. Eventually, as the Malaysians genuinely desired restoration of former relationships across the Straits, they accepted the messages of hope, indicating that there would soon be moves to end Confrontation.

As the afternoon progressed, each of the officers had been taken quietly aside by the CIA Station Chief and given envelopes as a token of America's gratitude for their contribution in restoring dialogue with the West. The men were ecstatic with the reception, and the obvious support for their endeavours. The Ambassador repeated his Defence Attaché's commitment, undertaking to provide support to the Indonesians when the time arrived. The colonel heading the delegation was then given a sealed envelope to be delivered to his commander, and the officers were escorted back to the airport where they were flown to Singapore. Once there, still dressed in their civilian attire, the men caught the Cathay Pacific flight home to Djakarta.

That evening, Major General Soeharto sat quietly reading the letter he had been given by his emissaries. He was pleased. It had been his own initiative to establish contact secretly with the Malaysians and Singaporeans to allay their fears that there would be increased military activity in the future. He expected that his approach would be treated cynically, as he was, after all, the Deputy Commander of the Crush Malaysia campaign. Soeharto understood that their attempts to threaten their neighbours had been futile. Due to heavy losses in Sarawak, the Army had resisted sending paratroopers in support of Soekarno's request for massive airdrops over Malaysia. Instead, the Airforce were obliged to wear the brunt of the exercise, which failed miserably. Dissent had grown dramatically during the past months, resulting in his decision to establish contact with the opposing forces.

The general read through the contents one more time and,

satisfied with the support he had received from the Americans, destroyed the letter carefully. He closed his eyes and smiled. Time was running out for them all. And only he would be prepared when the moment finally arrived.

* * * * * *

Semarang

General Prajogo, the Diponegoro Commander, walked together with his old friend, listening, deeply disturbed by what the other man imparted. They had left the Command Headquarters and walked away from the other officers as his colleague had indicated that he wished to speak privately to his fellow general.

'We have always been able to share a confidence, Mas,' the visiting Brigadier General had stated, *'but what I'm about to disclose to you must remain only with you. It could mean my career, perhaps even my life. Do you understand?'*

'Sounds very intriguing indeed.' The Diponegoro Commander smiled. His friend had always enjoyed the melodramatic, ever since they had attended basic training together.

The general looked back sharply. *'No, Mas,'* he insisted, *'this is really the most serious discussion you and I might ever have. I must have your word that, whatever I say to you, under no circumstances will you repeat this information, for whatever reason. Do you agree?'* The commander looked closely at the other man and was surprised at the concern in his old friend's voice. He thought for a moment before answering.

'Only if what you tell me doesn't compromise me in any way, or commits me to something I may disagree with.' Then he smiled again, just to ease some of the tension between them. After all, they were practically brothers. Their careers had taken similar paths, both had achieved their first stars in the same year.

'I am taking you into my confidence, Mas, as I expect that you, of all people, should have been invited to participate in what is planned. I don't understand why you have not already been approached.' The commander listened, concerned with the direction their conversation was taking.

'Go on,' he urged, suddenly eager for the rest.

'As you know, Mas, I have been seconded to Pak Yani's staff in Djakarta.'

'*Yes, I had heard,*' the commander said, a little impatiently. General Yani's position as Chief of Army Staff was one of the most powerful in the country. The commander did not believe the position should be Yani's. In his opinion, there had been others more deserving.

'*Have you heard mention of the Dewan Djenderal, Mas?*' the other officer suddenly asked, almost in a whisper. The commander immediately stiffened at the mention of the Council of Generals. As far as he was concerned, these generals had grown fat at their country's expense and represented the very epitome of corruption at the top.

'*I have heard some rumours. Why?*' he asked, cautiously. They were treading on very dangerous ground, even for two men who had known each other so well.

The visiting general hesitated, then continued. '*Mas, once again I must remind you that you can not repeat anything of what I'm about to reveal to you.*' He then looked at the Diponegoro Commander enquiringly, who had stopped and turned to his companion, curiosity aroused.

'*Agreed. Now what about this so called Council of Generals, what are they up to?*' he asked, attempting a weak smile.

'*Over the past weeks the generals have solicited support from officers they believe they can trust. I have only just been approached. And by Pak Yani personally! It would appear that they have been successful in their recruitment as they are confident that the majority of all the Army's field officers will move with them.*'

'*Move? Move where?*' the commander asked.

'*No, no, Mas. Not move, mobilise. The Council is going to sack Bung Karno and move against the PKI!*' he answered, bubbling with excitement, unable to contain the information any longer. '*We're going to sack the President and abolish the Communist Party, Mas,* he repeated, grinning from ear to ear in satisfaction, as if it were his own idea, '*and then we're going to put this country back in order.*'

The commander froze where he stood, shocked by the revelation. Was this really possible? He stared at his visitor, almost disbelievingly. When he observed the other man's excitement, he realised it was true.

'*When?*' he asked with difficulty, his mouth dry. Why hadn't he been approached before this? Had he and his Command been deliberately overlooked, until now?

'Remember, Mas, only a select few are to know. I will advise the Council when I return that they can count on your Command for support. There will be much more information to follow. The most important point is that you are prepared to move on the day, with the rest of us. Will you be ready?' he asked, forgetting to reveal the target date in his excitement. The commander thought quickly. Of course he must commit as a matter of self-preservation. He did not hesitate.

'The 7th Division of the Diponegoro Command will be ready. When do we move?'

'The Fifth of October, Mas,' he laughed, pleased with the surprised look on the other man's face. 'That's right, Mas,' he repeated, in a conspiratorial voice, 'Armed Forces Day. It will be so simple. Our Military will summon only those Commands which support the Council, to attend the parades scheduled to be held throughout the capital. Even Soekarno has given his blessing to making this year's effort greater than previous celebrations. He thinks this will distract the rakjat from their empty bellies as our tanks rumble through the streets. There should be little or no bloodshed. Our troops will control the city from the moment they enter Djakarta. The entire concept is brilliant,' he boasted, proud to be part of the planned revolt.

The two generals discussed which Army units had already committed to the coup attempt. By late afternoon, the Diponegoro Commander had memorised most of the detail he had heard. Later, after his visitor had departed, convinced of his friend's loyalty, the commander returned to his home where he remained alone, brooding over the day's startling events. By morning, having not slept throughout the night, he had considered all of his options then made his decision. The only common ground he could identify with the conspirators was the fact that both he and the Council would eventually abolish the Indonesian Communist Party.

He considered how his Army superiors were slowly but surely delivering their country to the Americans. This, more than the knowledge that these men had grown fat at others' expense, raised the fire in his stomach. He could not understand how they could betray the Republik knowing that just a few short years before, the United States financed teams from Taiwan and South Korea which occupied Indonesian territory, joined rebel movements and endeavoured to destroy national unity. How could they have forgotten the aerial attacks flown from American bases in the Philippines and the thousands who died defending Indonesia against the American-sponsored uprisings? He believed he had no other choice, for failure to move quickly would ultimately result in the very men he despised taking control of the *Republik*. The decision to inform his other enemies, the communists, of the proposed move by the Council on the Fifth of October did not sit well on his mind.

General Prajogo still believed that his President's position of non-alignment was the only acceptable political position to take, ignoring the overtures of the Americans and Soviets. As for the communists, well, once he had moved to Djakarta and left the Diponegoro Conmmand in the hands of his trustworthy officers, he would use the Communists as they had used others. He would have their leaders removed and the PKI abolished. But first, it was imperative to his own strategy that the PKI make the first move and pre-empt the others. Prajogo had to find some means whereby the communist leadership could be alerted to what was happening in the Nasution camp.

Before the late-morning *lohor* prayers had commenced, the commander had put his own play in effect. He now realised that the task ahead was too great for him to carry out alone. He would go to Djakarta in search of the one man who still commanded his deepest respect. A man who had also once been the ranking officer commanding the Diponegoro Divisions, and a man he knew he could trust to support a fellow general's pursuit for a better Indonesia. He would seek this man's assistance. But first, there was another matter he must attend to.

The Commander called his aide and instructed the officer to summon Colonel Sutarmin. He had a mission for the veteran who had just recently returned from the jungles of Kalimantan. A mission which the combat-hardened colonel would most surely relish. One which would provide an opportunity to partly repay the Australians for the thousands of Indonesian soldiers who had perished, slaughtered by their SAS during their illegal raids over Indonesian soil.

* * * * * *

Beijing, 16th September

Indonesian Airforce General Omar Dhani listened in dismay as China's powerful Chou En Lai carefully laid the information before him. The second most powerful man in China after Chairman Mao Tse Tung, refrained from clucking at the man's ignorance. It was obvious that the Indonesian general before him had very little appreciation of what was really taking place in his own country. With the assistance of an interpreter, senior Minister Chou En Lai explained to Dhani, for the third time, how the information came to him.

The Indonesian Airforce Chief of Staff was confused. Why did these people always have to talk in riddles, he wondered? The information the Chinese had insisted was absolutely accurate alarmed him greatly. Dhani knew that the Army had been planning something because they had gone to incredible lengths to exclude him and the Navy from their secret meetings. Even so, the Airforce general had great difficulty in accepting Chou En Lai's startling information, which suggested that Nasution's Council of Generals would effect what amounted to a coup d'etat in less than three weeks. In his mind, the idea was preposterous, or it had been until the Minister then went on to substantiate the claim, with damning evidence.

'Should they succeed, General Dhani, the first to go will be our dear friend Soekarno. There is no doubt in our minds that the Council would then move to eradicate the Communist Party in your country, sparing none.' This had sent a shiver down Dhani's spine. He was painfully aware that should such a situation evolve, he would be one of the first to be incarcerated by the Army generals. Chou En Lai then went on. *'Here is proof of the Americans' involvement in the subversive attempt not just to destroy President Soekarno and Aidit's Party, but also to provide the means for the West to completely ensconce their own Military in the Indonesian Republic.'* The Chinese Minister paused for effect. *'The Americans are even more imperialistic in their foreign policy than the British,'* he said, uncertain that the man before him would understand, but he continued anyway in the hope that Dhani might learn at least something from the people who were currently providing the necessary support to his associates in the PKI.

'First, they attempted to take China and our great Chairman chased

their puppets' tails across the sea to Taiwan. Then they tried Korea, even sending tens of thousands of Chiang Kai Shek's so-called National Army into Burma to bark at our heels. This too failed, leaving their soldiers nothing but access to the white powder which destroys their brains. Now they are at war with Ho Chi Minh and it is inevitable that the Americans must lose. Make no mistake, General, this information is real and you would do well by your country to leave here immediately and return home, where you will then be in a position to prevent what is planned.'

Omar Dhani examined the information again. He did not wish to challenge the detail offered and could find no reason to do so. Suddenly he was pleased that these people were his friends. He admired their uncanny ability to survive, wherever they established their communities. And now, because one of his fellow officers had developed strong personal and commercial ties with a Chinese back in Djakarta, ties which had resulted in the flow of information at hand, Dhani believed that he had been given the opportunity to pre-empt the moves of others. Moves which would, undoubtedly, have resulted in his own death, had they been successful.

Dhani and most of his contemporaries had similar relationships to that described between the major general and the Chinese trader mentioned in the report. The expatriate Chinaman had been clever, following the Army officer's career through the years. They had remained loyal to each other and enjoyed the fruits of their relationship. Now, unwittingly, that very same relationship had provided the means whereby the Indonesian Communist Party could advance its own cause by pre-empting the Council of Generals move to topple the popular President and deliver their country to the Americans.

Dhani read through the information again and shook his head. Apparently the major general had held in-depth discussions with one of his own, which resulted in the disclosure that Nasution and his secret Council intended moving against the Government on Armed Forces Day, the Fifth of October. It appeared that the general had decided that there was little he could do to prevent the more powerful faction from effecting their move. Instead, understanding the ramifications of such a successful action, he had discussed the intended coup in depth with his close Chinese friend who participated in his *kongsi*, their business house, and suggested that he and his family ensure that they remove themselves from any possible harm which may result from the power struggle.

The report made it clear that the major general had been given an assurance that the information he had passed to his old Chinese friend would, in no way, be revealed to others. The Chinese trader had been grateful for the warning and moved quickly to protect not just his family and friends, but, in typical style, his business interests as well. The closely-guarded secret was passed from trader to trader within hours until finally, the Chinese Embassy in Djalan Hajam Wuruk was abuzz with the facts.

The Ambassador had apparently wasted little time in telexing this incredible information directly to the Minister in Beijing requesting advice as to what action should be taken by the Embassy and staff, knowing that when Nasution and his generals took control, the Chinese would, once again, be punished for whatever ills prevailed at that time. The Ambassador had pointed out that Nasution had arrested many Chinese merchants just a few years before, and seized their businesses on the pretext that they had been involved in supplying arms and providing support to the rebels.

Following Chou En Lai's advice, Omar Dhani departed immediately for Djakarta, flying directly in on of his own Airforce jets. He arrived early the following morning and went directly to Aidit and Soebandrio where he delivered the incredible news. The three spent the day closely locked in secret at Colonel Latief's house, as they formulated their own plan to circumvent Nasution's move to take control of the country.

'We have no choice but to advance our own plans,' Aidit insisted.

'But how?' Soebandrio complained, understanding the logistical nightmare in bringing their people together a month before the scheduled seizure of power from the Military.

'We will just have to move with what we have and trust that the element of surprise will still be to our advantage. Also, it is now more imperative than ever that, when our troops move into the city, they first must take every member of the Council and place them under immediate arrest.'

'But what about their personal security?' Dhani asked. All the generals would be well protected by their own trusted guards.

'We will use the Tjakrabirawa teams supported by the Gerwani. The original plan has not changed, it's only a matter of advancing the timing.'

344

It will still work, as planned,' Aidit insisted.

'And we should make this move when?' Soebandrio asked. He would not be involved in the actual attack. His role would be to muster provincial support as the movement gained momentum once they had established control over the capital.

Aidit thought for a while then smiled. *'We are most indebted to our Chinese friends. As we must make the move before the Fifth of October, why not agree to enter the city and arrest the Council on the anniversary of the People's Republic of China?'* Both Soebandrio and Dhani were supportive of the suggestion. It did not leave much time but, there again, there was little choice. If they failed to move quickly, then all would be lost. They agreed. The plan would be known as *'Gerakan 30 September'*, the 30th September Movement, even though the actual attack was planned for the early hours on the morning of the following day. Their commanders were all summoned and briefed.

The communists would make their move to take control over the capital and the Military, on the morning of the Anniversary of the Peoples' Republic of China. Each and every person involved in the operation clearly understood that they had very little time left in which to implement their strategies if they were to be ready to move on that momentous day, the First of October.

KERRY B.COLLISON

Chapter 18

Melbourne
Thursday 23 September

Susan stared at the walls and wondered why she had insisted that Harry give her the bungalow. Now she couldn't stand the place. Everywhere she looked, memories interrupted the tranquillity she needed so desperately. She couldn't even be sure that he wouldn't just reappear, and offer one of his casual explanations as he had so often in their past. She prayed desperately for some evidence that he was really dead. How long could she be expected to carry on like this, not quite a widow? The thought crossed her mind momentarily that he had done this just to punish her.

Susan read Zach's almost impersonal cable again and then crumpled it in her hands. At least she'd had the company of Murray for lunch when he was in town. Apart from Muriel Stephenson, there had been few visitors. Most did not offer condolences, she noticed, just support. Muriel had stayed over twice. She was a godsend, always there, assisting with the child without being asked. Susan rose and moved over to the cocktail cabinet and made another drink. She grimaced as she swallowed, the alcohol biting hard. It was her sixth for the day and it wasn't even five o'clock, she noticed. What the hell, she thought, angry with Steven's almost impersonal letter. Susan then wandered around the lounge area, moodily, lifting cushions and throwing them back onto the cane settee. As she passed the painting to the left of the bar one more time, Susan stopped and examined the lush island vegetation against a full tropical sunset. She stared at the picture for several minutes. It was the trigger she needed.

Without thinking further, she raced into her bedroom and checked inside the cupboard for cash and, satisfied there were sufficient funds, she dialled information and scribbled down the numbers. Then Susan phoned Muriel Stephenson and pleaded for her to keep her son for another week. Murray's mother was only too happy to do so. Two, three weeks, she laughed, suggesting that Susan should take a complete break away from the uncertainty which surrounded her life at present.

Muriel was surprised that she had grown fond of Susan Bradshaw. And it was not just because she suspected that the child was her grandson, but more because, considering the circumstances under which the lonely woman lived, Susan had consistently displayed a resilience Muriel had not thought possible. She thought her own son a fool, but had forgiven him his indiscretion. The matter had never been raised, not since the christening.

Susan made two more calls, then danced into the bedroom and packed. She had a flight to Singapore and it departed in less than four hours. There was so much to do. She remembered her passport and that there was no valid visa for Indonesia. Deciding that this could be arranged in Singapore upon arrival, Susan completed her packing, then bathed. Thirty minutes later, she phoned the overseas cable service and dictated a message, which the operator confirmed would arrive the following day at its destination. She listened as the woman read her cable back before advising of the charges. Susan smiled as she replaced the receiver, knowing that her impetuous behaviour would, no doubt, attract strong criticism from her circle of friends. She shrugged her shoulders at this thought and then locked the house and drove back up to Melbourne and Essendon Airport.

The Qantas 707 four engined jet deposited her in Singapore in the sleepy morning hours where, to her dismay, Susan discovered that her passport had to be sent to Djakarta for endorsement, due to confusion resulting from the *konfrontasi* conflict. Disappointed, she checked into the Raffles Hotel and waited, while the High Commission assisted with her travel documents.

When she received the call, Susan was ready to leave but unable to get a seat on the overcrowded flights. It seemed that suddenly everyone was heading into Indonesia. She had already spent four days by herself, wandering through Collyer Quay and its quaint Change Alley more times than she cared to count. She had visited Robinson's Department Store and marvelled at their displays, and sampled the extraordinary choices of Asian cuisine unique to the crossroads city, before returning exhausted to the colonial splendour of her magnificent Raffles suite.

The next day, Susan Bradshaw managed to catch a Cathay Pacific flight to the Indonesian capital. As the aircraft banked, then turned on its final approach into Kemayoran Airport, Susan smiled as she recognised the harbour below. She remembered her first visit and the violence she had witnessed and, for the first time since leaving Australia, Susan wondered if she had made the correct decision in returning to Indonesia.

The Boeing's undercarriage groaned as hydraulics completed the procedure locking the wheels into place, and Susan managed to complete the last of her complicated arrival forms as the tyres screamed, announcing their arrival. As the aircraft came to a halt outside the terminal, she checked the forms once again and sighed at the date. It was almost the end of another month. She looked out through the porthole at the dilapidated buildings and was suddenly overcome by a feeling of helplessness. An ominous hiss indicated that the passenger exit door had been opened. Susan took a deep breath, then stepped from the aircraft.

* * * * * *

Djakarta, Tuesday, 28th September

Murray received the call via the Embassy switchboard. Once he had replaced the receiver, he cursed loudly at the woman's stupidity then went directly in search of Steven Zach. Susan had said that she had already tried to speak to Steven, and had been advised that he was still on his round of morning appointments.

He discovered Zach in the Embassy foyer talking to one of the other Attachés.

'Steven,' Murray called, his voice urgent, 'sorry to butt in. It's important.' He smiled at the Air Attaché and led Zach away by the arm.

'Well, what's up?' Zach asked, concerned by Murray's sombre expression. He listened, his face growing dark with the news. 'Why the hell didn't she let us know?' he asked. They both knew that this was no time to be distracted from their responsibilities. Something was brewing out there on the streets and both men believed that trouble was imminent. There had been rolling demonstrations every day, clouds of dark smoke rising high into the city's sky, identifying the hot spots. Their latest estimates indicated that in the course of the past month alone, more than six hundred had been killed as a direct result of demonstrations and looting in the capital.

'Beats me, she's booked into the Hotel Indonesia. Guess she wants you to hold her hand,' Murray said. Zach looked at his friend sharply, then accepted that the comment was not meant unkindly.

'I'll ring her right away. Thanks, Murray,' Zach said, patting the Station Chief's arm. 'Did she say how long she was staying?'

'Sounded pretty much open-ended.' Murray hesitated before continuing, then decided to say it anyway. 'It's tricky, Steve. She shouldn't be here right now and you're probably the only one who can tell her that.' Zach nodded in agreement.

'I'll ring her first, then shoot down to the hotel. Catch you later,' he said, leaving Murray alone in the Chancery lobby. Then he frowned. Why hadn't his own people picked this up? Her name should have triggered all sorts of alarm bells when she had departed Australia. How did she manage a visa?

Returning to the security wing behind the Consulate section, he went into his Number Two's room and briefed the agent on the woman's presence. It was protocol. The Second Secretary merely nodded and offered to keep an eye on her should the Station Chief consider this necessary.

'No,' Murray had said, 'let's see how long she's staying first,' hoping silently that Susan would listen to common sense and leave the troubled city. He then telephoned the operator and advised her to take messages for the rest of the day as he would be out of his office. Murray left for his appointment with the lieutenant colonel from Semarang, his thoughts pre-occupied with the brief and enigmatic telephone conversation they'd had the day before. Murray could not recall the officer from his earlier visits to the Central Javanese city, although the suggestion that the man had information vital to Murray's personal safety was sufficient to interest him. He had asked for more detail on the telephone but the officer insisted that they meet in person. Intrigued, he had agreed to meet at the location nominated. But before doing so, Murray removed his P9S automatic with its double-action lock from the safe, checked the nine-round magazine, and placed the German weapon inside his briefcase. These were dangerous times in Indonesia, he knew, and to attend a meeting so shrouded in secrecy, unarmed, would be extreme folly.

* * * * * *

'No, I did not receive your cable. And, quite frankly Susan, if I had, then you would not be here,' Zach said sternly. Susan pouted.

'You aren't pleased to see me, Steven?' she asked, feeling foolish. Perhaps her visit may have been just a little too reckless.

'Of course I'm pleased to see you. He ran his fingers through his hair and looked at her in exasperation. 'It's just that you couldn't have picked a worse time. Susan, didn't you notice anything on your way in from the airport? Didn't you see what is happening out there?' he jabbed his finger emphatically in the direction of the hotel's window. Susan's eyes followed the movement. It all seemed normal enough outside. And she hadn't seen anything unusual on her way into town.

'Look, Steven,' she started, 'I wont be in your way. I needed to get out of Melbourne and I thought you might be pleased to see me.' She searched his eyes. 'It's been hell, Steven,' she said, struggling to contain the tears. 'You have no idea what I've been through. They don't even know if he's dead!' She began to look down at the floor like some scolded child. It was too much for Zach. He stepped forward and lifted her off the couch and into his arms, holding her close and whispering soothing words.

'I'll leave immediately, Steven, if that's what you wish,' she mumbled, hoarsely into his chest. Then she pushed away slowly and looked into his eyes. 'Is that what you want, Steven?'

'No. No, it's not what I want,' he replied, 'it's just that the city is no place for you to be right now, Susan.' He then thought for a moment before continuing. 'If you do stay, then you must agree to listen and abide by what I'm about to say. Okay?' Immediately, she moved back closer and placed her head on his shoulder. Zach couldn't see the almost childish smile.

'Okay,' Susan agreed. 'You lay the ground rules and I'll follow.' He had acquiesced. It had not been as difficult as she had anticipated. Susan stroked the rough beginnings of stubble on his cheek.

'Good, then here's rule one. Stay in the hotel until I return. I don't want you wandering around outside under any circumstances, especially alone.' He held her away and smiled. 'Now, I must return to the Embassy. I'll try to be back before six o'clock. Okay?'

'Fine by me, darling. I'll just sit around the pool and read or something.' She looked at him and smiled. 'Thank you, Steven,' she said, rising up onto her heels and kissing him softly. The warmth of her mouth made him want to linger but he pushed her gently away. He had to go. He squeezed her hand and left, hurrying back to the Embassy.

When he got there, his assistant greeted him with a number of priority signals which had been received during his brief absence. He went to work immediately, examining the information that had been forwarded from the Directorate of Army Intelligence in Australia. An hour later, Zach also left the Embassy to attend an urgent conference at the United States Embassy where he spent most of the remaining day deep in discussions. It was during this meeting that Zach decided to take at least one night off and spend it with Susan up in the Puncak Pass before sending her back to Australia. He believed that she would be more receptive to his suggestions to return home once they were together in the hill bungalows, where they had first become involved. He knew she should leave as soon as possible but decided that, as long as she boarded her flight before the forthcoming Military parades, she would be relatively safe.

Zach checked the bungalow roster upon his return to the Embassy, then telephoned around in an attempt to locate one of the other Embassy members who might be receptive to his request to exchange their rostered turns in the mountain resort area. It seemed that many of the wives had prearranged parties and guests right through until the following weekend. They too had decided to stay away from the city as troops continued to pour into the capital in preparation for the Fifth of October parades.

There was only one opportunity and it was late-midweek. Steven checked his schedule and found that he could afford the one night away. It was in just a few more days. He then checked the airline flights and booked Susan out for the afternoon following their return from the mountain retreat. He circled the calendar on his desk, and wrote 'Susan leaves' alongside the date. It was the coming

Friday. He then telephoned Susan to tell her of the arrangements. She was thrilled with the opportunity to return to the cool mountain lodge. As it was already Tuesday, she was pleased that they would be in the mountains alone together, in just two more days.

* * * * * *

Tandjung Priok Harbour

Murray directed the driver towards the row of long *godowns* which blocked the view into Djakarta's filthy harbour. He instructed the driver to stop alongside the perimeter fence and examined the faded notice, still hanging where it had been placed many years before. He checked his watch and observed that he was only a few minutes late. Murray knew that this would have little significance in a land which practised *djam karet*, or rubber time, as a matter of course.

'*Stay here,*' he ordered the driver, opening the rear door. He was assailed by a wave of heat as he climbed out of the airconditioned vehicle. The driver's pained expression immediately changed to relief as he realised that he would not be expected to accompany the *tuan* down the narrow gang between the old port warehouses. '*I'll be back in half an hour so you'd better kill the engine,*' Murray suggested, then left his driver alone. As soon as Murray disappeared down the narrow lane, the driver looked back over his shoulder, checked the rear-vision mirrors and wriggled uncomfortably in his seat. Remembering where he was, the driver then reached over behind and locked the rear doors first, before checking those in front. '*Tuan Murray must be a little crazy,*' he thought, but most of the drivers already knew this.

Murray continued down through the maze of dilapidated buildings, checking the oversized numbers painted on stained cream walls. The warehouses all appeared empty as he continued to move through the neglected site, searching for the *gudang* number which would lead him to his designated meeting place. There didn't seem to be any security around, and this surprised the Station Chief. Then he shrugged this off, assuming that the security would most likely be asleep, resting from the stifling midday heat.

He continued his search. There appeared to be no sequence to the numbering of buildings. Murray looked back and checked again to confirm the random figures painted on both sides of the huge open doorways and, quite by accident, noticed the number he had been searching for just a few metres back. He turned and walked over to the building; then stopped and opened his case. He placed the automatic inside his belt, then held the light case directly in front of his body as he entered the long silent warehouse.

'*Kolonel*,' he called out, remaining near to the entrance, scanning the huge empty expanse inside the old storage centre. There was no response. He called out again, '*Kolonel, it's Stephenson.*' Still there was no answer. Murray walked deep into the building, and came to a halt almost directly in the middle of the dust-covered concrete floor. He could see that little, if any, traffic had disturbed the dust at his feet. He peered down the length of the building. Murray estimated that the far wall was more than one hundred metres from where he stood. Pencils of light pierced the stillness as the midday sun penetrated the rusting galvanised roof overhead. He called out again, then waited. Suddenly he heard a slight noise in the distance. He checked his watch and turned. The colonel was only fifteen minutes late. Nothing, really, in this country, where even soldiers could not be relied upon to be punctual.

The ambient temperature in the old warehouse was most probably ten degrees hotter than outside, and the perspiration was drenching his body. He decided to move back to the entrance where it was slightly cooler. As he turned, he heard the unfamiliar sounds again and decided that this, at last, must be the colonel. He walked slowly towards the entrance and, when he was within fifty metres of the huge sliding doors, a figure appeared, framed by the open space.

'*Tuan Stephenson?*' the man called, his voice echoing through the empty building. Murray stopped, not forty metres from the figure and answered.

'*Yes, I'm Stephenson. Are you Kolonel ...*' he started to ask but stopped in mid-sentence as he identified the swift movement and the weapon's silhouette. He dropped his brief-case and rolled to his right as the world exploded all around. The first bullets punched through the short distance to where he had stood, their velocity so great Murray could feel the shock waves against his body. He came up to his feet still holding the P9S fully extended, fired the first three rounds without aiming, then threw himself hard to his left, ignoring the sharp jabbing pain which stabbed his knee as it hit the concrete. Murray fired again, then again, before taking more deliberate aim at his attacker. He heard the man scream. Murray fired again, recognising the dull thudding sound bullets make when they hit a man's body. He saw the killer's arm swing, bringing the deadly weapon to bear and so he rolled once more, this time again to the left.

The air was shattered with a screaming staccato of bullets as they hit the ground to ricochet around the *gudang*. In desperation, Murray fired his last three rounds, cursing himself for not bringing a spare magazine. His assailant, wounded at least once, turned to flee but buckled, staggered, and then collapsed into a heap, his weapon still clasped firmly as he fell. Murray waited, trying to determine whether the man could still return fire. Had his last shot found its mark? He ran across to his right, watching for movement. He approached the crumpled figure from the side, remaining half crouched, expecting the soldier to turn at any moment and recommence firing. But there was no further movement from the fallen man. Murray had hit twice. His first bullet had merely grazed the soldier's arm but the second had entered through the stomach and shattered the man's spine.

He knew it wasn't necessary to check for a pulse. Quickly and with expert hands, the Station Chief examined the dead man's pockets. He removed the contents. Apart from some identification there was little of significance to find. The soldier was wearing a non-issue tunic. Murray unzipped the thin jacket to reveal the soldier's uniform and immediately recognised the identifying flashes of the Diponegoro 7th Division based in Semarang. He checked the dead soldier's weapon. It was a Swedish 9mm M-45 Carl-Gustaf automatic machine gun. Murray pried it out of the dead man's hands and then realised just how close he had been to death. He knew that this weapon's rate of fire was controlled by finger action and not by fire control. Had it been otherwise, his killer might have succeeded. Almost half of the magazine's 36 rounds remained intact.

Murray left the body and peered outside. He couldn't be certain, but it appeared that the soldier had acted alone. He then retrieved his brief-case, and found the leather torn where one of the 9mm rounds had grazed the surface, searing a path from one end to the other. He placed his automatic back inside the case and, checking outside once again, walked quickly back along the narrow lane and across to where his driver waited.

They drove back in silence. Murray felt it best not to raise the question of gun-fire and he knew that, with any luck, the driver would not have necessarily associated the brief bursts with his *tuan's* presence in the harbour area. Gunfire was not unusual in Djakarta. Anyway, from the stuffy odour which greeted him inside the car, it was fairly obvious that the driver had kept all of the windows closed during his *tuan's* absence, further reducing the likelihood that his driver had heard anything. He instructed the driver to return to the Embassy. As he sat in the rear of the sedan, even he was surprised at how coolly he had reacted. He looked at his hands and smiled. They were not shaking. He felt absurdly like laughing out loud.

When Murray arrived, his Number Two handed him several incoming messages, which he knew could wait until the following day. He opened his safe and extracted the spare clip of 9mm rounds and slipped it into his pocket. He had already decided on his way back to the Embassy that he would never again venture outside without at least one spare clip for his P9S. He had been lucky and he knew it. Next time — and he now believed there would be a next time — he would be better prepared.

There had now been two attempts on his life, and both carried out, in all probability, by members of the 7th Diponegoro Division. As he was driven to his residence, Murray recalled his visits to Semarang and the discussions that had taken place with Harry Bradshaw and the general. Suddenly a thought crossed his mind. Surely the attempts on his life had to be related to the information the former ASIS Chief had given the general concerning his man Sulistio! They had accused the man of betraying the general. Now, he believed, he was being held to account for Sulistio's death. Murray considered this scenario and believed that he was on the right track. He had to be, he thought. What other possible explanation could there be for elements of the Diponegoro Command to want him dead?

* * * * * *

MERDEKA SQUARE

Halim Perdanakusama Airforce Base,
Djakarta

Yanti settled down with the other Gerwani women and tried to sleep. They had been gathering here, at the AURI Airforce Base, over the past two weeks. She had counted almost 2,000 volunteers for the permanent troops; all had joined under the newly-created communist Central Command. There was a strong feeling of pride as the young men and women gathered in their makeshift billets, preparing their weapons, ready for the imminent orders to move into the capital.

Yanti was particularly proud. She had been promoted and selected to head the Gerwani assault teams which would accompany other units, consisting of the Tjakrabirawa Palace Guards, the Pasopati troops, the KODAM V Djaya Infantry Brigade, the AURI Kavaleri and Pasukan Gerak Tjepat units, as well as two companies from the Bhimasakti which stood ready, under the command of Captain Soeradi. Yanti's Gerwani were ordered to accompany the Pasopati troops, because they had been assigned probably the most important task when the moment came. They were to arrest the Council of Generals and bring them, dead or alive, back to the Halim Airforce Base. They were to be part of the operation designated 'Takari'.

The strategic Airforce base had been chosen as the final staging point for the communist forces. The Airforce Chief of Staff, Omar Dhani, had approved the use of his facilities for this purpose well before he had departed for Mainland China to organise the armament shipments which had now all but been completed. When questioned by his peers as to why there were so many non-Airforce personnel occupying the base, Dhani had easily convinced his fellow officers that the additional ground forces had been brought in as part of the airfield defence exercises aimed at preparing for the possibility of a Malaysian air attack on the capital. On the 26th of September, the majority of the volunteers, spawned by the Pemuda Rakjat, the BTI, Gerwani and SOBSI moved into the Halim Airforce Base as part of the ground defence exercise named *Lubang Buaya*, or Crocodile Hole. Airforce officers carried out the training as instructed by their Chief of Staff and cleverly disguised the substantial build-up of communist forces within the military complex.

The mood was restless as they waited for the final command. Yanti knew that this was imminent, as she had heard that almost all of the senior Communist Party officials had already departed, as planned, for selected provincial centres where they would provide additional support to PKI followers in those distant locations. Comrade Aidit had decided that he should remain in Djakarta until power had been successfully seized. The others, including Dr. Soebandrio, had already left for their destinations where they would remain, until word of the successful coup d'etat signalled the planned move throughout the entire archipelago, to seize power from all the provincial authorities. There had been almost a mass exodus of senior Communist Party officials over the past two days. Yanti had seen many of them depart directly from the Halim Airforce base. She had not been surprised that the majority of the Airforce personnel had, in fact, joined the communist cause. Yanti believed that most of their Navy had done likewise. They had both borne the brunt of most of the fighting over the past two years and wished now to take revenge on the Army and its demanding generals.

Yanti was tired but had difficulty sleeping. She wished she had had more time with Murray the week before but he too had been extremely busy with his responsibilities at the Embassy and could not spend more than the one evening with her. She smiled. The memory of their last night together comforted her as she lay in the overcrowded quarters. Images of their love-making gradually soothed her tension and, as the rhythm of her breathing changed, Yanti finally drifted off to sleep.

* * * * * *

Presidential Palace

Soekarno stood silently, deep in thought. He felt tired, and knew that the accumulated effect of the medications he had been given by the doctors for his kidney ailment, only partly contributed to the general feeling of malaise he now experienced. As President, he felt saddened by the decision he had been obliged to take.

He loved his people dearly and had endeavoured to provide the leadership they so desperately needed. Now, it would seem, there was to be even more bloodshed as elements within his Government prepared to push their *Republik* even closer to the edge of chaos and disaster.

He had listened as Aidit and Soebandrio had provided details of the Council of Generals' treacherous plan to move, within days, on the Palace. Soekarno now understood that he had been deceived by his Military, aware that 20,000 soldiers had been camped around the Senajan Sports Complex in preparation for the Armed Forces Day parade, and that these additional units had added to the largest military gathering ever seen in the capital.

Soekarno was bitter as he recalled the many conversations he had held with the Military leadership, the last only days before when he had demanded that General Yani disclose the real purpose of the secret Dewan Djenderal. He remembered that Yani had been adamant, admitting that there was a group of his fellow senior officers which had been casually referred to as a Council of sorts. However, he had insisted, the membership consisted only of senior command officers who met to discuss military matters in private. Yani had sworn to him that he and his fellow officers had no secret agenda and now, the PKI Chairman and his Deputy First Prime Minister were telling him that Yani had been lying. Soekarno had cursed his Army Chief of Staff for his apparent disloyalty.

As President, he believed that it was imperative that he maintain a balance between the political parties and his country's military establishment. Now, as he listened, Soekarno realised that he had failed. There was no other choice. He approved the plan in principle, believing that the Council of Generals had, at all costs, to be prevented from succeeding with their plan to overthrow the Government and establish their own military dictatorship. Soekarno snorted at the thought of Nasution being welcomed at the White House by a grateful American President. No, he thought bitterly, he would never permit this to happen. He and his people had struggled far too long against the neo-colonialists and old guard imperialists to throw it all away now. Nasution and his crowd had to be stopped. Aidit's strategy seemed sound and Soekarno had given it his blessing.

Soekarno bade farewell to his two senior advisers and slumped in his chair. He loosened the top button of his tunic and wiped the sweat from his face. Although he had hidden it from the eyes of his subordinates he had been suffering increasing nausea and dizziness as the meeting progressed. He reached out for the bell to summon an attendant for some water and, seconds later, he reeled sideways from his chair and slid heavily to the floor. He was rushed to his Japanese wife's home in Selipi where the resident Chinese doctors quickly took charge.

Soekarno could not know that the plan to which he had so cordially given his blessing at his last meeting was in fact a plan to arrest the country's most senior generals. He would never have approved such drastic measures.

As Aidit well knew.

* * * * * *

Philippines
U.S. Airforce Base, Clarke Field

The barometer had been falling for over an hour as the Flight Control Officer made his way up the steep stairwell and into the Officer Commanding's presence. The Airforce general snatched the clipboard impatiently and quickly examined the list, then cursed.

'Goddamn mothers,' he snarled, chewing through the sloppy end of his Havana cigar. He pulled it away from his mouth and spat into the waste-paper receptacle. He passed the clipboard back to his major and snarled. 'How reliable is this intelligence?' The major was not offended by the suggestion that his report may be suspect. He could only provide interpretations and evaluations on the information given without wandering into the world of supposition. The major, like most experienced Intelligence officers, was painfully aware that those who collected intelligence information operated under the most difficult conditions, and often opted to provide what their masters wanted to hear, and not what was necessarily an accurate assessment of a true situation in the field.

'We couldn't get any photography, General, but subsequent overflys confirmed the situation.' The OC snarled at no-one in particular. The drops had been a disaster and he could only blame the incompetents in the meteorological station. Their weather forecasts had been disastrous. The unseasonal hurricane had presented his boys with one hell of a curly flight plan. Weather over the past week had all but cancelled most of his flights south into Indonesia and, as the weather seemed to break creating a window for his pilots, he had stacked the backlogged flights, and sent them all down within a twelve-hour time frame in order to meet the drop deadline. Weston, one of his most experienced pilots, had led the first mission and dropped his cargo along with signal beacons for the other flights to follow. Weston had missed his target by more than fifteen miles, and seven more loads were then dumped all over the rough terrain. They had dropped enough weapons and ammunition to equip a small army.

And over the wrong target.

* * * * * *

A village in Java

Throughout the following day, the villagers collected the weapons and boxes of ammunition that had curiously arrived during the night. They had heard the sounds of aircraft flying overhead and even sighted one of the twin-engined planes during the morning and wondered why they had been given so many rifles and bullets. The village *lurah*, as the *kampung's* elected head, had ordered that the parachutes be collected along with their cargo and delivered to the *balai kampung*, as this meeting hall was the only building which could house so many boxes.

This isolated *kampung* had remained almost untouched by outside influence for hundreds of years. Almost, that is, except by the encroaching influence introduced by the people from Kampung Kali Ketjil, the adjacent villagers who lived nearer the sea and followed the teachings of their Christian God. As in many other villages, there was but one radio around which these simple people would gather with their children, to listen whenever their President addressed his people. They adored Bung Karno, although they had never seen the Great Leader of the Revolution. He was one of them, and a true believer.

The village chief addressed his fellow villagers and explained that the weapons were a gift from *Allah, The One and Only True God*, and that they should all consider the delivery as a very special sign. He led them in prayer in accordance with the fundamental teachings of the Prophet Mohammed, as they prayed for guidance and direction. The *lurah* then ordered that the arsenal be guarded as he and the other devout Moslem villagers waited patiently for a sign which would enlighten them all.

It was Tuesday morning, the 29th of September.

* * * * * *

Lembah Njiur

They all laughed as Brigadier General Sujoto finished telling his story. Major General Parman leaned over and slapped his friend's leg playfully, enjoying the anecdote as related by the younger officer. The mood was almost festive as they had finished their meeting, confident that all was in place for the following Monday's momentous occasion. Harjono smiled at Pandjaitan, then winked at Suprapto. They were on the final countdown, with just six days to go.

The full Council had gathered. It was to be their last meeting before the Monday parades when they would lead their men down through the streets of the capital as teams of select men and officers occupied the Palace and placed Soekarno under arrest. They were not surprised at just how easy it had all been, to muster such incredible numbers around the city under the guise of preparing for the Armed Forces Day celebrations. As far as they were concerned, it was already a fait accompli. They believed that it was not even necessary to wait for the following week as they had already successfully occupied the nation's capital. Within the week, the country would be under their direct control and there would be a new President. The Communist Party would be banned and any Fifth Force resistance would be dealt with severely. Brigadier General Pandjaitan burst out laughing again as Sujoto repeated his story, feigning a serious face as he recounted his meeting with the *Tjakrabirawa* colonel.

The Palace Guard officer had insisted that his information was accurate and was furious with the general for not giving any credence to his report. He was adamant and almost on the verge of tears when Sujoto had suddenly burst into laughter at the suggestion. The brigadier was then obliged to reprimand his colonel for carrying such ridiculous stories out of the Palace. He had sent the officer away, suitably chagrined by the admonishment he had received from the general.

'Oh, I agree, said Soekarno. Let's attack the Military before they can do us any harm,' Sujoto repeated, bringing tears to the eyes of the others present as he mocked the colonel's story, suggesting that he had overheard a conversation which supposedly took place between Aidit, Soebandrio and their erstwhile President. 'And then Aidit said, aduh, Bung, I would be proud to lead the PKI against the treasonous Yani and his generals!' with which the room broke immediately into raucous laughter at the very suggestion that Aidit could muster enough support to even consider challenging the might of the Military leadership.

The meeting then broke up as it had commenced, in fine spirits. Soon the whole world would know all of their names.

Chapter 19

30th September 1965
0500 Hours

The first morning prayers had come and gone. Subuh stretched, preparing himself for the rituals he had followed for most of his sixty-four years. Then the holy man prayed. There were no intonations, no vocal prayers. Instead, there was silence as the *maha guru* transcended to a higher level. The Master remained still.

His physical being receded as he concentrated on his inner self, enjoying the floating sensation of separation as the *latihan* commenced. After many years of dedication, he no longer experienced the urgency which had accompanied the first transition as his consciousness distanced itself from his mortal presence.

The holy man's inner being settled peacefully into its own plane. He was only conscious of thought patterns established through years of dedicated compliance. Then suddenly, the ugly images reappeared, threatening the tranquillity of the moment and, as the *maha guru* summoned all of his powers, he feared, for the first time, that he would lose this struggle.

The world appeared before him, confused and in disarray. As his spirit passed through the many-dimensional barriers, he encountered the most terrifying scenes. Voices echoed through the darkness as images of familiar faces flashed across his mind like splinters of light. He had transcended into a world of terror and destruction. As his soul prepared itself against the onslaught of evil, he recognised a fierce, distant voice. In that moment, shadows twisted and changed as darkness gave way to light, and he immediately identified the face of the man who had been summoned to act against the powers of evil.

When he awoke, the spiritual leader was surrounded by a sea of concerned faces. He smiled, absorbing their warmth, and rose slowly. Upon discovering his unconscious body, his followers had carried him carefully to his protected chamber. He, however, refused to be pampered, insisting instead that he be driven into the city for a most important meeting. Reluctantly, the guru's most senior followers acquiesced, and drove their master to the destination in Menteng. Upon arrival, he once again refused their assistance as he climbed with obvious difficulty out of the car and entered the house alone. The armed guards recognised the man and bowed in deference as he shuffled through the barbed wire gate towards the main house. He knew that his presence required no formal announcement.

Subuh remained inside briefly, politely refusing the proffered refreshments as he spoke quietly to the solemn-faced Javanese general. An hour passed before the holy man emerged, smiling wearily at the armed sentries as he moved slowly down the pathway into the waiting sedan. The soldiers guarding the residence on Djalan Waringan watched his car disappear round the corner.

Inside, Major General Soeharto sat reviewing the vision seen by the *maha guru*. Suddenly, he too felt the heavy burden of responsibility. Being Javanese, he understood that his people had long developed psychic faculties and it was not uncommon for such visions to be seen. He sensed that to ignore the dream and its interpretations would most certainly invite disaster.

He sincerely believed that the holy man had been destined to shape his life. Was it not Subuh who had precipitated the changes which had influenced his early childhood years? Now the guru had returned to warn him of impending danger. The Javanese general believed that his world had been shaped not by mortal hands, but by the gods who had created the heavens and earth. He closed his eyes and offered his thanks to those powers which continued to steer him safely through life's maze. He remembered his wife and children, and asked that he and his family be protected from the approaching evil which, he could now sense, endangered them all.

The general's thoughts were interrupted as his wife, Tien, entered the room and reminded him that she wished to leave early to take their son to the hospital. The boy's condition had deteriorated during the night and, having already bathed and fed the youngest of her six children, she was ready to leave with him. The general watched as they were driven away, and then he too departed, arriving at his KOSTRAD offices well after the Thursday morning parade was over.

* * * * * *

1030 Hours

Murray thanked the Military Attaché's assistant for the coffee, then waited for the Warrant Officer to leave his colonel's office before continuing their conversation.

'I'm pleased she's agreed to return to Melbourne, Steve. This is no place for her right now, as you know,' he said, relieved. He knew how distracting having a woman around could be. Earlier, he had left Ade still dressing as he had dashed to the Embassy just in time for his first appointment. It always seemed to happen whenever Ade stayed over, although he was not complaining. She filled a void in his life and Murray had appreciated her company, particularly over the past two days. On Tuesday night, when Ade had arrived unannounced, she discovered him sitting alone in the bedroom, half-undressed, his whole body shaking. Quickly she had finished removing his clothes and forced Murray to lie down while she went in search of a sponge and water. She was very worried and wanted to call the Embassy doctor but he had insisted that it was nothing, citing a reccurring attack of malaria. By the time Ade had returned to the bedroom, he had ceased shaking. The delayed shock from events of a few hours before had finally surfaced, and, what is more, he knew that he was still not out of danger.

Murray had slept in late that morning, electing to arrive at the Embassy just in time for the weekly prayers meeting which was always scheduled for ten o'clock Wednesday morning. The session had dragged on for almost two hours as the Ambassador listened to the Attachés brief his Counsellor regarding the rapidly deteriorating military situation. The Station Chief had then spent a few hours in his own office, catching up on the sudden increase in communications traffic which threatened to bury his desk. By early afternoon, he'd had enough. He telephoned the hotel and spoke briefly with Susan, then left the Embassy compound, swinging by his house for a change of clothes. An hour later, as he completed his workout, Murray climbed out of the hotel pool and joined Susan as she sat sunning herself in the late afternoon sun. He remained only long enough to greet Zach when he arrived, then returned to his residence on Djalan Serang, where he knew Ade would be waiting.

The servants had prepared dinner and they remained indoors. He believed that whoever wanted him dead would wait for an opportunity when he strayed away from locations which were well frequented by other expatriates. In the meantime, Murray kept his P9S close at hand, although away from Ade's curious eye. As he had rushed out the door earlier, she had called out to remind him that she would not be staying over again that night, promising to come back before the weekend. He had blown her a kiss and hurried away, missing another breakfast as well.

His thoughts returned to Susan and Zach, as he sipped the strong Arabica coffee.

'When is she leaving?' he asked. Zach moved uncomfortably in his swivel chair then raised his own cup, sipping the aromatic brew.

'Hopefully, Friday afternoon,' he answered. Murray raised his eyebrows and placed his coffee down.

'What in the hell does that mean?' he asked, surprised at Zach's response.

'I'm taking Susan back up to the bungalows late this afternoon. We'll spend the night. I'll break the news to her then.' Steven looked directly at his friend, who merely shrugged.

'Better you than me,' Murray said, anticipating Susan's resistance. He had seen her stubborn streak before. 'When are you leaving for the hills?' he enquired. Come to thing of it, it wasn't such a bad idea taking her to the mountains, as she had been stuck in the hotel grounds for more than two days now.

'We'll get away about three and return first thing in the morning. I have her booked out on the last flight,' Zach advised.

'Best get away early, Steve. The military traffic could slow you down somewhat.' They went on to discuss the substantial build-up of troops around the Senajan Sports Complex and arrangements for the following Tuesday's celebrations.

All embassy officials were expected to attend the parades. Invitations had begun to flow in days before, requesting their presence at a number of official venues during the celebrations. It was considered mandatory that all Military Attachés attend. Murray left Zach and returned to his mountain of paperwork, striving to clear his desk as the other Embassy officers had begun to leave for the day. It was just after two in the afternoon.

* * * * * *

Halim Perdanakusumah Airforce Base, 1430 Hours

Yanti smiled sweetly at the driver as she climbed into the truck and slammed the door firmly. Her features did not betray her excitement as the heavy troop vehicle rumbled through the main security gates and headed towards the by-pass road. She held on to the cabin strap as the truck made its way through the broken macadam, lurching over the large pot-holes.

Yanti checked her watch again, impatiently. She knew there was very little time left. She also knew that all hell would break loose if the other team leaders became aware of her absence from the exclusive compound, which now housed all of the Gerwani units. Yanti and her command had been placed on full alert just hours before. The moment had come.

Yanti's team had received their orders and been secretly briefed. They were to accompany several of the Pasopati units on their mission to arrest the members of the Council of Generals, and take them back to their compound in the Halim Airforce Base. They would depart not long after midnight, when they would be briefed for the final time, then covering the 25 kilometres into the city in two columns before dispersing into five attack groups. They, in turn, would be followed by units of the Tjakrabirawa Palace Guards whose deadly purpose would be to secure the inner city areas of Menteng and Tjikini where most of the senior Military officers lived and certainly the majority of all foreigners.

Yanti had listened in disbelief when their leader, Colonel Untung had casually remarked that he had given explicit orders to the Palace Guard troops to shoot and kill any foreigners who might attempt to leave their houses for their Embassies.

It was imperative, he emphasised, that the foreigners not be permitted to alert their own missions once the attack had commenced. He warned that there were many foreign elements present in Djakarta whose sole aim was to support the Council of Generals Westernization of their *Republik*, and that any interference would not be tolerated. Hence his orders to shoot any foreigners they encountered, on sight. He had smiled, then suggesting that foreigners should not be out on the streets at all, considering the hour. Didn't they know that Djakarta's streets were considered dangerous at night? Many of those present at the briefing had laughed, some, including Yanti, nervously. Murray had to be warned. She knew what he was like, staying out with his friends to all hours of the morning. He would be in danger. She had to tell him to stay indoors.

As the truck bumped along then came to a halt at the by-pass intersection, Yanti looked sternly at the driver. What was he waiting for, she thought impatiently, urging the man to hurry. The soldier smiled at the attractive Sundanese girl, then slowly removed his foot from the clutch. The truck lurched forward and stalled, immediately blocking the southbound traffic. The driver cursed and shuffled the gears while leaning on the starter and, reluctantly, the old cylinders sprang to life, in a cloud of smoke. Ignoring the cacophonous sounds blasting from horns all around, he guided the truck across the main road and down onto Djalan Gatot Subroto. As they passed the Airforce Headquarters, Yanti checked her watch again and knew that Murray would already be home. She hoped feverently that this would be one of those rare occasions when he would not go visiting.

Yanti knew most of the places Murray frequented and shook her head at the thought that she might have to go searching for him without the benefit of transport. The soldier had only agreed to drop her near to the Senajan Complex where his own unit was billeted. Yanti knew she could jump on a bus along Djalan Djenderal Sudirman, then take a *betjak* the short distance through Menteng to Murray's house. Impatiently she looked at her watch yet again. She hardly had time to get to his house and back to Halim, before she was missed. They crossed the clover-leaf-shaped junction and Yanti asked the driver to stop and let her out. She jumped out of the high cabin and ran down to the divided road, searching the oncoming traffic for signs of a bus. Yanti started walking towards the city. It was only a few kilometres and she could easily identify the Intercontinental Hotel in the distance. She rubbed her watch nervously, refusing to look as valuable seconds ticked by. As she walked on, Yanti looked back over her shoulder and was relieved to see a yellow bus moving towards her, and she waved it down. Yanti jumped onto the step, unable to go any further as the bus was already jammed full. The bus then groaned and moved forward, painfully slowly, belching its poisonous fumes in the faces of pedestrians by the roadside. Yanti wanted to scream. It would have been faster to walk. She glanced at her watch. *Aduh!* She wasn't going to make it!

* * * * * *

The bus carrying Yanti rolled slowly towards the Welcome Roundabout and she could clearly see the Selamat Datang statues standing high in the air, their arms frozen in gestures of greeting. As Yanti stepped down, a blue and white Holden passed her heading in the other direction. The Embassy driver leaned on the car's horn to clear a path ahead as he sped south and away from the Hotel Indonesia.

'When do you expect we'll arrive, Steven?' Susan asked, in reply to Steven's explanation that the traffic was particularly heavy due to the Armed Forces celebrations, which were crowding the streets with endless convoys of soldiers.

'It will probably take most of three hours. Sorry,' he apologised, annoyed about losing valuable time in the mountains together. He had hoped they would have the opportunity to take a walk in the tea plantation, as they had once before. It was there that he hoped to encourage Susan to leave the following day. The driver expertly weaved through the heavy traffic, blowing the horn even more so than before.

Steven's estimate had been accurate and the couple arrived at the hill station bungalows just before six. As they gratefully climbed from the vehicle, the air was filled with the *Mahgrib*, the Moslem evening call to prayer, and they both hurried inside where they were greeted by the old woman who cleaned and cooked for the white *tuans*. 'How lovely!' Susan had exclaimed, rushing over to the fire which had been lit as the sun went down. They opened the small box containing supplies and gave the food to the cook, then settled down to sip their glasses of Mouton Cadet. They smiled at each other, and suddenly Steven didn't have the heart to broach the subject of her departure. He decided to leave it until later, or even the following morning.

Susan kicked her shoes away and made herself more comfortable on the large colourful floor cushions. She smiled as Steven joined her, placing his wine on the floor beside hers. He placed his arm around her shoulders and pulled her gently towards him. They embraced, then kissed. As Steven stroked her hair, Susan sighed softly in contentment. There was no other place in the whole world she would rather be than here, with Steven, in these tranquil mountains outside Djakarta.

* * * * * *

1730 Hours

Yanti had missed Murray by only a few minutes. His servants had no idea where he had gone and she decided that it would be futile to go searching for him. Yanti was almost beside herself. Common sense dictated that she should leave without wasting another moment. If she failed to return before the next scheduled check, her absence would most certainly trigger a search and then, she was certain, alarm. Reckless of her own peril, she elected to remain at the villa and wait for Murray to return. An hour passed, then two. Then the phone rang and Yanti sprang to grab the receiver.

'Allo,' she answered, expecting the voice to be that of Murray's. Instead, there was a brief pause before the other party spoke.

'Who is that?' the woman asked. Yanti knew immediately that it was Ade.

'It's Yanti,' she said, hoping that Ade would be annoyed with her being at Murray's house.

'Let me speak to Murray,' Ade demanded. She hated the Gerwani woman.

'Murray's not here, Ade,' Yanti replied, knowing that the other woman would not believe her. The line went dead as Ade banged her phone down. The momentary distraction did little to alleviate Yanti's fears that Murray would not come. By the time she heard the amplified prayer call from the Mosque, Yanti began to panic. She telephoned the Embassy but no one answered her call.

The minutes continued to tick by. Where in the hell is he! she thought wildly. It started to rain and she knew that this too would hinder her return to Halim. And then she heard the heavy iron gates as the *djaga* opened the way for someone to enter. *'Let it be Murray,'* she pleaded running out through the main door as he stepped out of the car.

'Quickly, Mahree,' Yanti called excitedly, *'we don't have much time.'* Murray laughed as he hurried out of the rain and stepped inside. He was surprised to see her and, at the same time, relieved that Ade had not remained for another night.

'What are you doing here?' he asked, picking her up and giving her a playful hug. *'I thought you might have run away with someone else,'* he teased. He knew of her involvement with training the new Gerwani recruits. Sometimes he just could not bring himself to believe that the beautiful young woman who was so loving and exciting in bed could actually be a member of the hardened communist women's brigade.

'Mahree, we must talk,' she whispered, leading him into the bedroom. *'I really don't have much time.'* As they closed the door behind them, she observed that he cleared the bedside table and placed his brief-case there. She had never seen him take work into the bedroom before.

'Okay, manis, let's talk,' Murray said, undressing quickly. Yanti frowned. She knew that she had to approach this situation carefully. *'If only there was more time,'* she thought, bitterly.

'Come on manis, are we going to talk or just play?' he laughed, reaching for her arm and pulling her down to the bed. Suddenly she decided that perhaps it was best to do this first. Quickly, Yanti removed her own clothes and rolled onto the bed beside him, and kissed him playfully on his hardened stomach, then stroked him as she had so many times before as they prepared each other for what was to follow. Yanti moved with a sense of urgency, surprising Murray with her impatient love-play. As they moved together, he sensed her mood and became excited by her demanding rhythm, losing control of the love-making as Yanti rolled, moving herself in the dominant position. Within moments it was all over. As they lay together, Murray looked down and was surprised to see her eyes filled with tears. Yanti had never cried. Ade, yes, but not Yanti, not that he could recall. He sat up and rolled her over to face him.

'*Mahree, I love you,*' she said, while pushing herself into a sitting position on the bed. '*I love you enough to care what happens to you.*' Murray had never seen her as serious as this before. Something was troubling her deeply.

'*Sure, Yanti, I know. But nothing's going to happen to me, okay?*' he said, wondering what Yanti would say if she knew of what had happened just two days before. A thought crossed his mind but he immediately dismissed it. There could not possibly be any connection between what had happened at the harbour and Yanti's strange behaviour now.

'*Mahree, if I tell you something which would get me into the most serious trouble should others know, would you promise not to mention it to anyone?*' Murray cocked his head and looked directly at her beautiful serious face.

'*Of course, Yanti,*' he replied, becoming concerned with her strange behaviour. She hesitated, then took both of his hands in hers.

'*Mahree, if I asked you to stay here all night tonight would you promise me you would, without asking why?*' He looked at her pleading expression and wanted to smile. Yanti was up to one of her little games she often played. He decided to go along with it.

'*Okay, sure,*' he promised, keeping a straight face, and wondering what she would do next. Yanti's face clouded over. She could see that he was not taking her seriously.

'*Mahree, listen. You must promise, okay?*' she asked, her voice almost breaking into sobs. '*I want you to promise me that after I leave here tonight, soon, you will remain inside until I phone you in the morning. Promise me Murray, okay?*' He looked at her face. This was no game.

'*And if I asked you why...?*'

'*You can't. You must not. I will not tell, even if you do.*'

'*If it means that much to you, of course I'll stay. I hadn't any plans to go out anyway.*'

'*Do you really promise?*' she insisted, squeezing his hands as one of her nails dug deeply. '*Please don't make a joke of this, Mahree. It is very important. Tomorrow I will explain. Okay?*'

'*Okay, manis,*' he sighed and threw the sheet back as he slid off the bed.

'*No, Mahree, I'm late. Let me go first, please,*' she said, jumping off the bed quickly and running into the ensuite. He heard the shower and got up to join her there. Murray enjoyed having his back scrubbed. He did not believe that she really had to leave in such a rush. Indonesians rarely hurried. Time was always flexible. As he moved to the end of the bed he reached down and retrieved Yanti's clothes, which had fallen to the floor during their brief tryst. Murray smiled at the camouflage-coloured uniform. He remembered this as the regular Gerwani dress which they often wore to parades. Getting ready for Monday's parades, he thought, throwing the clothes onto the rattan chair and, as he did so, the contents of her unbuttoned jacket pocket spilled onto the carpet runner. It was a note book.

He bent down again and was about to place this on top of her clothes, when he recognised something of what had been written on the exposed notebook page. He frowned, then flicked through the rest of the small pages. These were full of annotations relating to units with times and names scribbled inside. He couldn't make head nor tail of what she had written. Murray then flicked back to the first page and looked at what Yanti had written there and suddenly a chill passed through him. It was a list of names. He had seen it before, or at least one very much like it. Murray heard the shower door open, then close. He read through the list quickly, trying to memorize what he could before Yanti returned from the bathroom but she stepped back into the bedroom, still towelling her body, before he could return the pocketbook to her jacket.

Murray looked up in surprise then, as casually as he could, flicked the small book onto her clothes. Yanti remained still, staring at him as she dripped water onto the floor. He could see from her eyes that she knew he had seen was written in her secret notes. She lunged forward and snatched the book up and opened the pages as if there would be evidence of his invasion of her privacy. She turned sharply and glared.

'What did you read, Mahree?' she demanded, the softness all gone. 'Why did you read my personal letters?' she challenged.

'It fell out, Yanti. Your book just fell out when I picked your clothes off the floor. Why are you so upset?'

'Did you read it all, Mahree?' she asked again, knowing that he would have. There had been enough time.

'Some,' he replied, gauging her reaction to this admission. 'It *just caught my eye, that's all,'* he lied. *'What's the list for, Yanti?'* he asked, still watching her eyes as they narrowed slightly then looked away from his gaze.

'What list?' she answered, sharply.

'The list of generals. The list in the front of your notes. That list!'

'It's not a list,' she snapped back angrily. *'These are just notes for Monday's parades,'* she lied. *'The Gerwani will be participating in the parades, Mahree. These are just my notes concerning what I must do as one of the team leaders.'*

Murray walked over to her and said quietly, *'Tell me, manis, why have you listed those generals in your book. And why do you insist that I remain here tonight?'* he watched her as she commenced towelling herself again quickly. She ignored the questions and grabbed her clothes. Dressing quickly, she prepared to leave the room. Her eyes softened and she turned back to Murray and touched his arm with her hand.

'Remember what I said, please Mahree. Stay home tonight. If you don't, it could be dangerous. I can say no more,' with which she reached up and kissed him on the cheek. Murray tried to stop her from leaving but she pulled away angrily and opened the bedroom and turned. *'I came here tonight at great risk to myself because I love you, Mahree. Don't betray me. And please, please listen to my warning. Stay home tonight. The streets are going to be very dangerous!'*

'Yanti,' he called but she moved too quickly. He grabbed at the sheet and pulled this around his body, chasing after her, calling for her to wait. But she was gone even before he could make it to the front door. Murray stared out into the drizzle and cursed. He showered and dressed hurriedly, then telephoned the duty officer and requested that his car be sent immediately to take him to the Embassy. The rostered official responded to the urgency in the First Secretary's voice and sent the duty driver around immediately.

Twenty minutes later, Murray sat in his office examining a file to which only he had access. These were his Diponegoro notes and assumptions. The only other ASIS officer to have had access was now missing, perhaps even dead.

He flipped through the documents, searching for the one loose page he had placed there after he and Harry Bradshaw had visited Semarang together. Murray swore as he flipped through the pages, searching frantically. At last, with a triumphant cry he discovered that it was still there and, as he extracted the single sheet and placed it under the light, he stared at the names in disbelief. The list was almost identical to that of Yanti's. Murray stared at one of the names which had been crossed out. The name of the major general who led the Army Strategic Reserve Command, KOSTRAD.

He sat there stunned, staring at the damning evidence, confused by the information which had fallen into his hands. Then, as the cold realisation of what was planned swept across his mind, Murray raced into the Registry, unlocking doors as he went, and leaving these open behind. He entered the main safe and turned the telex machines on to warm them up then suddenly had another idea. The radio! He fumbled through the Embassy telephone directory until he located the Assistant Naval Attaché's number. Then he grabbed the nearest telephone and dialled out. A voice answered, but it was not the Chief Petty Officer. His *djongos* advised that the *tuan* was out and was not expected until late. Sometimes his tuan stayed over at his friends house. No, he did not know where his *tuan's* friend lived. Murray thanked the houseboy, then swore at the system which provided only one qualified radio operator for the clandestine transmitter. The communications aerial farm which hung all over the Embassy was so obvious, he had often wondered why the Indonesian Foreign Office had not already ordered the illegal facility to be taken down.

The Station Chief knew that even the highest priority message would be dependent on just how quickly the Indonesian postal services would respond and onforward the encrypted five-group-worded message. He knew from experience that this could range from three hours to three days. Murray was no longer sure just where the Americans or the Brits would sit when the communists made their move. And he had no real hard evidence to support his conclusions. He was not entirely sure that they would give him access to their own networks, as his country's allies could easily have their own agenda. Even so, protocol demanded that he first communicate directly with ASIS and Central Plans. The rest would be up to them. Frustrated by this knowledge, he had no other choice but to drag the only other man back who, due to his active operational experience in the jungles of Borneo, could operate the damn complicated apparatus. Even then Murray was not certain that he had sufficient time. He could feel it in his bones.

He knew the communists were going to make a move. And the information which he had gleaned from Yanti's notes, and her warning for him to remain inside, indicated in every way that this was the night. He had to get Zach back. Immediately.

* * * * * *

Senajan Sports Stadium, 1900 Hours

Aidit, the Communist Party Chairman, was pleased that Soekarno had recovered enough to attend the rally, as it was essential to his general plan. He stood alongside the President as Soekarno addressed the gathering of Indonesian technicians who were members of the communist-backed labour movement. Aidit smiled as his leader spoke. Soekarno was in his element, his charismatic style captivating all who listened. The Great Leader of the Revolution, and President for Life spoke without the assistance of a prepared speech. As the loyal followers listened and watched, they gasped in surprise when the President suddenly stopped halfway through his speech and clutched at his chest. In pain, he was assisted back to chair as the crowd surged forward only to be pushed back by the Tjakrabirawa Palace Guards. Many broke into tears as they watched their President grimace, in obvious pain as he clutched at his chest.

Aidit and the other committee members crowded around, loosening Soekarno's tie and rubbing his chest with ice. The crowd was hushed as those surrounding their President moved slowly away, exposing their leader as he rose weakly and raised his hands in salute. He had suffered from an extreme attack of heartburn and, once it had passed, Soekarno smiled at his audience and continued with his speech. When he finished, the crowd roared their approval for the sixty-four year-old hero. They chanted his name as he left the stadium, and touched the hands of all those closest as he passed among them along the exit route. He was loved. He was their President. And the morrow would see those who disagreed removed from the very institutions they led against him. He entered the Presidential limousine and returned to Sari Dewi's house in Selipi to spend the night in the arms of his Japanese wife.

* * * * * *

MERDEKA SQUARE

Gerwani Group Compound, Halim, 2000 Hours

Yanti had to stop and regain her breath. She had run across the airfield, then behind the enormous aircraft hangers until reaching the area across from where her strike teams were billeted. She knew that there would be perimeter security watching and she walked the remaining two hundred metres knowing that she would be observed.

'Halt!' the soldier called, advancing towards her with his rifle extended in her direction. She stopped, her heart beating furiously. As he approached and identified her clothing, the soldier demanded to know what she was doing outside the secured area. She had already prepared her response, knowing she would be challenged.

'Kolonel Untung had sent for me earlier,' she lied, knowing that this soldier would not know whether this was true or not. He advanced closer, suspicious.

'Why have you returned from this direction?' he challenged, looking past her to see if she had been with any others. Yanti moved towards the soldier and let him see the unbuttoned jacket. She was not wearing anything underneath. The soldier grinned as he could see most of one of her breasts from the side.

'The kolonel wanted to be discreet,' Yanti replied, moving slightly to the side so that he could have the benefit of the overhead perimeter lights. The soldier lowered his weapon and moved closer.

'And where is your kolonel now?' he asked, standing very close. He smiled at her and placed his hand on her shoulder. When she offered no resistance, he moved to place his hand inside her jacket. As he leaned forward, Yanti placed her right hand around his free wrist, leaned backwards as she turned and rolled the guard over onto his back. The movement was quick and very professional. The soldier lay stunned, and embarrassed, his weapon already in her hands as she stood over him.

'My kolonel is probably back in bed already. Where you should be. He would be furious that one of his soldiers had been so easily unarmed by a mere Gerwani,' she teased, before stepping back from the prostrate figure. At the mention of the colonel, he jumped back to his feet and brushed himself off quickly. Yanti returned his rifle and walked on towards her own barracks leaving the soldier wishing he had smashed her to the ground.

As she entered her compound, Yanti was relieved to see that the second briefing had not commenced as her companions were still milling around waiting to be summoned. She moved amongst her women and offered reassurances where needed. Yanti could see the excitement building as the AURI Cavalry mingled with the several companies of the Airforce's Rapid Deployment troops. She overheard grumblings of disapproval from a group of angry Tjakrabirawa soldiers when they were informed that the Bandung Cavalry contingent would not be coming. For some reason yet to be discovered, both companies' loyal communist officers were replaced on that very day.

A whistle sounded, calling all section commanders to their second briefing. They gathered inside the Central Command quarters and listened attentively as colonel Untung and his commanders briefed those present. As she listened to the colonel praising his officers for their dedication to the Party and cause, Yanti was pleased that she had been chosen to lead the two teams of Gerwani in what had been named Operation Takari. Their forces consisted of three commands, each broken down into four teams. Yanti's team were in the First Command, which had been given the responsibility of assisting with the kidnappings and transportation of the generals back to Halim. Each of these targets were given code names to be used during radio communication. They had all been expected to memorise the codes and, as Yanti prepared for the signal to move, she ran these through her mind so as not to forget. Nasution's code was 'Nurdin' she remembered, while General Pandjaitan's was 'Singer' and General Sutojo's was 'Toyota'. Yanti ran the others through her mind, recognising that one was missing. She searched her memory for the remaining code on her list which correlated to General Yani's name, and was relieved when she also remembered that the Army Chief of Staff had been designated 'Jonson'. It was then that Yanti, along with the other section commanders, was instructed by Colonel Untung that the generals were to be taken, dead or alive. This startled Yanti.

She had realised from the very beginning that she might be required to kill and could even be killed herself. She felt a sense of doubt. Faced with the reality of her own involvement, Yanti's mind wandered. She wondered what Murray might think of a woman who had blood on her hands. Immediately she struggled to refocus her attention on the important information being given at the briefing. Yanti forced herself to regain her composure and listen as the team leaders were instructed in communication procedures.

They then rehearsed identification codes and signals. Yanti's teams were to answer *'Takari'* whenever challenged by the call *'Ampera'*, and were instructed to blow their horns three times in response to any challenge of two blasts from any of their number. The Operation Takari Commander, First Lieutenant Dul Arief, insisted that they continue to rehearse this information in their minds knowing that it would be difficult, later in the dark, to distinguish friend from foe.

The excitement continued to build and Yanti suddenly discovered that she had her hands full overseeing preparations for the early morning attack. Preoccupied with her troops, Yanti had little time to reflect on Murray's earlier reaction to information in her notebook. She had wondered, briefly, whether or not the small pad had in fact accidentally fallen from her jacket, or whether he had gone through her pockets. His curiosity had been aroused and, the more she considered the incident, the more Yanti felt uneasy with the knowledge that he seen the list. She hoped that her lover would be unable to relate these to anything more sinister than the explanation she had given to him. Not, that is, until they had completed their mission. Only then, she was sure, would Murray associate the names mentioned in her book as belonging to those senior officers who would, by then, be in custody at the Halim Airforce Base. With a wry smile, she wondered how Murray would react, when he learned that his Yanti had been partly responsible for the operation which kidnapped the entire Council of Generals, and had carried them all away.

* * * * * *

2100 Hours

Murray checked his watch and resisted the temptation to push the driver any harder. As it was, the man had almost killed them twice already. The Station Chief moved around uncomfortably. He adjusted his automatic under his batik shirt.

There were no white lines, no warning signs or other aids on these roads to assist the drivers. Trucks, buses and even armoured vehicles tore through the night, often without headlights to warn oncoming traffic. As they had followed the dark road around one corner, Murray yelled, warning the driver in time to avoid the truck parked without lights, broken down in the middle of the main highway. They had swerved in time, barely missing the men who sat repairing the truck's differential. Once they reached Bogor, the road narrowed even more. As they commenced the climb through the foothills, Murray checked his watch again. They were losing more time than he could afford.

On they drove, passing other vehicles on dangerous curves, overtaking buses and trucks as they struggled up the steep incline. As they neared the turnoff halfway up the mountain, the driver pulled out and overtook a slower sedan, only to be run off the road by an oncoming Army truck. The Holden swerved and slipped as the driver's side wheels lost traction along the soft shoulder. The inept *supir* panicked and overcompensated, causing Murray to stifle a cry as they came perilously close to overturning and rolling down the steep incline. Enough was enough. Murray ordered the driver out of his seat and took charge. He gunned the engine, spinning the wheels on the soft damp soil, correcting the car's path, powering them forward onto the bitumen.

After several kilometres, Murray turned the wheel abruptly, leaving the main highway to Bandung and followed the gravel road up into the Embassy compound. He killed the engine, ran up the bungalow steps and knocked loudly. A frightened old woman appeared, who, on discovering Murray's familiar face, broke into a toothless smile.

'What's wrong *tuan* Murray?' she asked, unlocking the porch doors with an old key.

'It's okay, *'bu,'* he reassured her, moving quickly to the door he knew would lead to the master bedroom. He knocked loudly.

'Steve, it's Murray. Sorry, but it's really very urgent,' he called, continuing to knock. Steve opened the door abruptly, dressed only in a towel. He looked at Murray and scowled.

'For Chrissakes, what's the racket all about?' he demanded, squinting at the light. 'What are you doing here, Murray?'

'We don't have time to talk. Grab your clothes and you can dress in the car,' he said, moving into the room uninvited and switching the light on. Immediately Susan pulled the sheets even higher to hide her naked body. Shocked by the intrusion, she glared at their friend.

'What is it, Murray?' she also demanded, embarrassed and angry.

He thought quickly. They couldn't leave her there as it might be too dangerous. He decided to take her with them. At least he could put her back in the hotel where she would be safe.

'Get dressed,' he barked, startling his friends. 'I don't have time to explain. Just do as I say, please. Get dressed and, if you can't find something, leave it behind. Come on, let's go, quickly,' he ordered, leaving them to dress. Zach knew from Murray's tone that they should do as he said. His mind raced as they searched for clothes which had been thrown around the room at random.

The Station Chief had them dressed, packed and in the vehicle in less than five minutes. He glared at the driver, telling him to remain behind as Murray desperately needed to talk to the Military Attaché in secrecy. At first, the *supir* had ignored the *tuan* and started to argue until the *tuan* clenched his fists and took several steps towards him. At that, the driver had then shrugged his shoulders, reached back into the car to retrieve his cigarettes, then held the door open for Susan.

'Go back to the Embassy with the kolonel's driver tomorrow morning,' Murray called to his driver as he slipped behind the wheel and reversed savagely out of the driveway, then headed back down the narrow dirt track towards the mountain highway. Steven sat alongside Murray as they re-joined the sealed macadam and turned towards Djakarta. He finished lacing his shoes and looked across at the Station Chief.

'Well?' Zach asked, waiting for an explanation. Murray looked into his rear-vision mirror and observed Susan combing her untidy hair. She looked distressed. He was concerned that she would hear everything he had to say and, with that in mind, Murray cautioned Zach with a brief hand signal. He leaned back slightly and lifted his shirt with his free hand to remove the uncomfortable weapon which he placed on the seat. Zach's eyes narrowed. He had not known that the Station Chief was carrying the P9S.

'I have every reason to believe that the communists are planning to make a move on the Government, Steve,' he started, holding the steering wheel tightly as he was forced to swing wide to avoid something which had moved along the dark roadside. Steven said nothing, waiting for him to continue. 'I need your help. I don't know where the hell the radio operator is, and I couldn't think of anyone else who could punch the signals out in his place.'

'Shit! How soon?' Zach asked. Murray was the senior Intelligence officer and he respected his judgement. If Murray Stephenson said there was going to be a move on the Government, it was good enough for him. Murray would never speculate without sound fact to support his observations. The communists' move probably would not amount to much, he thought, having seen recent evaluations of their strengths and weaknesses. Zach knew that his Director of Military Intelligence in Melbourne thought that the PKI were lacking in experienced military leadership, in spite of the Navy and Airforce being predominantly communist at the top.

'As we speak, I'm afraid,' Murray answered, braking to avoid running into an oncoming vehicle which had pulled out to overtake yet another stalled truck. Susan cried out as she lost her balance and bumped her head on the side window.

'Do we have to go this fast?' she called out angrily, but was ignored by both men.

'So, what's happening?' the colonel asked, glancing at Susan through the corner of his eye as they spoke. She was busy with the buttons on her blouse.

'They have a list, Steve. A bloody hit list!' he said, dropping his voice a little. 'If I'm not wrong, they're going to take a crack at the members of Nasution's Council of Generals and, once they've succeeded, they'll most likely grab the Palace as well.' Zach was a man not normally given to surprise, but in this instance he frowned and stared back at Stephenson. Was it possible that the communists would have any chance of succeeding against Nasution and his powerful associates? Obviously Stephenson thought so.

'I won't ask you how you came by this information Murray but, for Chrissakes, are you absolutely certain?' Zach asked. 'If we're going to hit the air-waves, my friend, we'd bloody well better be confident that you are right. You're talking about a possible coup d'etat here Murray. And against the Indonesian Military! Jesus, Murray, I hope you've got something to back this up.'

'Sure,' was all Murray said. Zach did not have to know that Murray was acting primarily on a gut feeling, and a voice in the back of his head which kept telling him that, somehow, Harold Bradshaw's disappearance had something to do with all of this. The list was the common denominator. Murray looked across at his friend. He knew that once they had successfully signalled his Director in Melbourne, the contents would be disseminated within the hour to all friendly countries which, in turn, would communicate directly with their own embassies and consulates in Djakarta. He was simply taking a short-cut.

Murray knew that raising the alarm via Australia would carry more credence than if the news first broke via dubious Indonesian sources. Lives could be saved, as long as he could have Zach back in the radio room before the situation deteriorated further. There was no way of determining just how the communist move might affect the security of foreigners throughout the country, once the blood-letting commenced.

'I'll let you have a look at what I have when we get back,' he said to Zach, hitting the brake pedal again as they rounded a corner and were confronted with two oncoming trucks occupying both sides of the road. He managed to pull off the road in time to avoid a collision.

'All right?' Zach asked, reaching over to Susan and placing his hand on her knee. She grabbed his hand and held it tightly. She had been petrified from the moment they had left the bungalow. Zach squeezed her hand firmly, then released his grip and turned back to Stephenson, who had already brought the car's speed back to a dangerous level. He glanced at his friend's features, and was reminded of the grim, determined men with whom he had fought alongside against the Indonesian soldiers in Kalimantan.

Zach decided not to distract Stephenson any further. The road was dangerous and he was impressed by his friend's driving skills, glad that it was not he who sat behind the wheel. Zach looked at his watch and noted that it was well after midnight. He wondered what the new day would bring.

* * * * * *

Friday, 1st October, 1965, 0130 Hours

Yanti walked to the back of the truck second in line and checked that her teams were all settled. They had boarded the trucks almost half an hour before and had already become restless with the inactivity. She told them to quieten down, then moved on to the third vehicle, climbed into the driver's cabin and waited for the signal to roll. Moments ticked by and suddenly she saw officers from their Central Command walk by briskly. They were led by Brigadier General Supardjo. As she watched, the soldiers came to a halt and dispersed. Colonel Latief moved towards the other column while Major Gatot Sukresno continued to follow the other officers, Supeno and Suradi. There was a hushed excitement in the air as she looked across at the parallel convoy and knew that the soldiers there were ready.

Yanti was scared, but was careful not to show any outward sign. She hoped the uneasy sensation in her stomach would pass once they were under way. The Gerakan 30 September forces had drawn units from all sections of the Indonesian Armed Forces. Yanti had seen regimental flashes on soldiers shoulders identifying units from the Tjakribirawa, Brawidjaja and AURI Commands. She was particularly surprised to see soldiers strutting around from the 454th Company, which she knew was one of the Diponegoro Command's best units. It seemed that the Indonesian Communist Party had been successful in securing support from a major cross-section of the country's military, the *Tentara Nasional Indonesia*.

She returned a wave from one of the commanders as he walked past. Yanti remembered that this officer would take two units and occupy the telecommunications centre, then move on to secure the radio and television stations. They knew that their task had been made less difficult by commencing their attack when most of the city's inhabitants slept. Their Central Command had planned the strike to take place well before the capital stirred as first prayers were called in the early morning darkness. Nervous, Yanti was disappointed to see that the hands on her watch had hardly advanced since she had last checked. Suddenly, she saw two men run up to the lead truck and hit the driver's door firmly, before continuing onto the next truck loaded with armed Airforce troops, and repeating the signal. Her heart leaped into her mouth as the driver alongside her hit the starter and their engine roared into life. It had started and they were on their way into the city. Suddenly she opened her window and vomited violently. The driver leaned across and slapped her lightly across her back and, as their truck groaned slowly forward, she turned, and looked with embarrassment at the seasoned soldier.

'*Tidak apa-apa,*' the Malaysian campaign veteran offered, telling her it was all right. Yanti grinned gratefully and returned to concentrate on her Gerwani's role in the attack.

The trucks rolled slowly along the airfield's dirt roads, crossing the concrete hard-standing area past a selection of unserviceable American Hercules transports, and continued on past a row of empty aircraft hangers, then down to the western perimeter gates where they stopped. Security checked the convoy one last time. They were joined by a number of Toyota jeeps carrying mobile radio equipment ,and another jeep which had just returned from reconnaissance, where Sergeant Major Sulaiman was familiarized with General Suprapto's house in Djalan Besuki. The barbed-wire-covered gates were slowly drawn open and the lead vehicle lurched forward.

* * * * * *

Djakarta, 0200 Hours

They drove on in silence. Murray had managed to get them back to within twenty kilometres of the city well before two o'clock. He slowed at the junction to the west of the huge Halim Airforce Base and turned towards the city. He was pushing the engine to its limits along Djenderal Gatot Subroto, when he came up behind an Army convoy and was obliged to slow abruptly. He could not overtake. The soldiers standing in the rear truck indicated with a wave that he was to remain behind. Murray was tempted to blow the horn but resisted, knowing that this was an offence and could get him into trouble with the soldiers ahead. He fumed, angry that they had managed to make reasonable time on the return trip only to be delayed now.

When they reached the first roundabout, Murray decided to turn right and save time by cutting back behind the eastern suburbs and enter Menteng via Tjikini and the Senen roads. They followed the circle around and Murray caught a glimpse of the full convoy as it continued on towards Senajan. In those brief moments as a dark cloud passed across the sky, smothering the moon's rays, he could just make out that all the trucks were loaded with soldiers. The thought never occurred to him that the convoy might be part of the communist contingent, heading into the city, on their way to create a new chapter in Indonesia's history.

* * * * * *

0215 Hours

The air was still as the President moved outside and away from the air-conditioning. He had never really enjoyed the artificial cooling, preferring instead the soft breeze of an overhead fan. His lower back ached. He bent and rubbed the area surrounding his right side, knowing that it would make little difference. The kidney stones remained and reminded him of his failure to heed advice given many years before concerning his diet.

Soekarno moved slowly across the terrace and stood in the partial darkness observing the sky. On the far side of the courtyard he could see the glow of a clove *kretek* cigarette being smoked by one of his Tjakrabirawa Palace Guards. He raised his head, thinking he had heard the cry of a bird, then sadly remembered just how long it had been since he had heard the cry of anything wild, or free. A soft puff of wind fanned across his face and he looked to the heavens where thick dark clouds crossed the sky heralding further rain. The Wet Season was gaining momentum.

He had not been able to sleep. His mind was filled with the events which had overtaken his life, his Presidency, his people. He felt he had been betrayed by those closest to him. He had refused to entertain any discussion about what would happen to those who had plotted his overthrow. It was sufficient that they had been discovered in time and he, as President, had once again been given the opportunity to act, in the interests of his people. Soekarno loved his *rakjat*. In the twenty years of his Presidency, not once had he taken from the people. He had fought for them, then struggled for them and been imprisoned for them. The years of sacrifice had

388

thankfully ended in independence for the Indonesian people. In material terms he had nothing. His wives and children lived simply. They had never once taken advantage of his position nor his power, for these things had little value in his world. He had struggled to introduce the basic principles of Pantja Sila, so that the people of his great country would have a set of values to guide them through life, and remind them of who and what they were. Diversified they might be, he thought, but at least after this night they would remain united. The Council of Generals would be destroyed forever and, in their ashes, a new generation would grow. He and those who had supported the principles of *Merdeka*, of freedom, had done so to protect their generation and those which followed.

Soekarno turned and shuffled across the terrace into the magnificently-appointed bedroom where he edged towards his bed. He was still in considerable pain and so placed his arms behind, then carefully lowered himself down onto the pillows. Suddenly he felt a little better and looked across at the Japanese woman sleeping by his side. He smiled. Dewi remained asleep, and he was pleased that this was so. Sometimes, he admitted silently, the former hostess could be very demanding.

* * * * * *

Murray had dropped Susan at the Hotel Indonesia first, then he and Zach swung back round the quiet roundabout and down Djalan Iman Bondjol towards Tjikini and Djalan Pegangsaan Timur and the Australian Embassy. He was exhausted.

Zach remained deep in thought as they sped down the deserted road lined with an unkempt nature strip where itinerants huddled together in sleep.

'Doesn't exactly look like they've started beating the drums,' Zach said. But as an experienced field soldier he was more than aware that an enemy rarely saw the first strike.

'Don't wish for something we don't need,' Murray muttered, blinking. His eyes felt gritty with fatigue. They arrived at the Embassy, gave the *djaga* on duty a perfunctory wave and hurried into the Embassy, unlocking and relocking doors with Murray's keys as they went. They opened the restricted access door leading into the radio room and searched for the light switch. Zach cursed loudly as he cracked his head on a protruding shelf hidden in the dark. Murray located the lights and Zach set about warming up the radio while Murray returned to the Registry and encrypted the message. He rushed back to Zach who had established direct contact with the Australian spy-ship positioned in the South China Sea, and had requested its officers to stand by. He would send a confirmation copy to the secret signals listening base in Singapore as well. Murray returned and handed the encrypted message to Zach for despatch. It hadn't been too long since the colonel had used Morse code, and he managed to complete the transmission in less than twelve minutes, then closed the station having received acknowledgement from the receiving operator. Zach rubbed his right hand as it had begun to cramp, then turned to Murray.

'What's next?' he asked, flexing his fingers.

'I'm going to try to warn the generals,' Murray replied. Zach immediately shook his head.

'Don't do it. Don't get involved,' he warned. 'They are all well guarded, Murray. Who knows, perhaps they'll snuff this whole thing out even before it starts.'

'I have to at least give it a try,' the Station Chief replied, lifting the automatic and placing it back in his belt. Zach observed the movement and shook his head.

'I think you're being foolish,' Zach said. 'Just what do you think you can do at this late hour?' He then paused. 'You might already be too late.'

'Well, it would be useless trying to ring them, that's for sure. Even if someone did answer at this hour, do you think a servant would take it upon himself to wake his general on the advice of a telephone call from a foreigner? I don't think so. No, there's no other choice. They must be warned.'

Steven Zach looked at the Station Chief's determined face and knew there was no point in arguing any further.

'Okay, Murray,' he said, wearily, 'let's go.' Stephenson hesitated at the Military Attaché's offer to assist. Should their attempts to warn the men on the list fail and the Indonesians later discovered that an Australian Army officer had been involved, he knew that such ramifications would be most damaging to their country's relationship with its giant neighbour.

On the other hand, Zach was a most competent officer, and

Murray was pleased that he had offered.

'We'll start with General Harjono as he lives just a few doors down from my place. We've spoken once or twice. If we can get him to listen, maybe he'll believe us and contact the others.' Zach agreed and they left the building hurriedly.

It was just after three o'clock in the morning.

* * * * * *

The Australian spy-ship had been positioned in these waters throughout the duration of the Crush Malaysia campaign, and remained in the area specifically to accept all radio transmissions from South-East Asian stations. Once the ship had received the coded signal, the communication was then pumped into the atmosphere through a powerful transmitter, and received via the Australian Army secret intelligence listening post in Toowoomba, Queensland. This listening station, located in the most unlikely of places, was manned by a battery of highly qualified signals specialists whose life was dedicated to picking the air clean of all radio transmissions which emanated from Asia.

Army Warrant Officer Nicholas 'Nicko' Denison listened intently, writing the Morse code down faster than many clerks could type. He acknowledged the message and tore his headset off and ran to the command desk. The officer of the day took one look at the highly sensitive classification and telephoned Melbourne to alert the early morning watch that he was about to despatch a signal bearing 'eyes only' classification. He then moved to the bank of antiquated telex machines and instructed an operator to send the message as it appeared on the written receiving report.

The typist-cum-telex operator punched the keyboard sending the five letter coded message directly to a similar machine in Melbourne. She had to slow her typing movements as the machine could not accommodate her speed and started to choke. Five minutes passed before the duty officer was able to place the long thin tape punctured with thousands of tiny holes, alongside a matching tape which acted as the deciphering 'twin', As the deciphering mechanisms clattered away, the officer on duty in what they called The Factory, observed the initial notification which stated, 'Eyes Only OYSTER' followed by the signal's priority. In the young officer's short career he had never seen any communication which had been graded 'FLASH' before. Immediately he called his superior. This grading was only used by troops fighting on the front line when they first sighted the enemy. He knew there had to be something wrong.

The Melbourne-based Officer Commanding, Colonel Sharpe, was summoned from his quarters, near St. Kilda Road. A further fifteen minutes passed before he read the communication, then phoned Canberra. After this, the colonel telephoned ASIS Acting Director Anderson at his home in Melbourne, apologised for the hour, then requested the Intelligence Chief's immediate presence.

Less than twenty minutes later, Anderson climbed wearily from his ageing Ford Customline and made his way into the dark, well-disguised buildings. He joined the others where they sat, sipping instant coffee. He cursed Stephenson. Why hadn't he taken steps to remove the Djakarta Station Chief when the opportunity had first arisen? Anderson read the signals and snorted contemptuously. In his own opinion, there was no valid reason to suggest that the Indonesian communists could possibly effect a successful coup d'etat. The ASIS Director believed that the Djakarta Station Chief was grandstanding and his behaviour was most probably related in some way to the disappearance of Harold Bradshaw. This message only confirmed his suspicions. Murray Stephenson had been in Indonesia far too long.

As Acting ASIS Chief, he had discussed the Indonesian situation just the day before with Agency representatives in the American Embassy in Canberra. There had been no suggestion that the PKI was in any position to carry out such a grandiose scheme. In fact, he had been given access to sensitive information which totally contradicted what Stephenson was now suggesting. During the one-on-one meeting with the CIA Director, he had been informed that the United States had entered into an understanding with senior officers of the Indonesian Military to support their move to take control of the Government, and this was only a matter of days away. The generals had agreed to dismiss Soekarno and dismantle the complex political system which had enabled the communists to consolidate their position in Indonesia. The ASIS Chief undertook to protect the integrity of this information, agreeing not to disseminate any of the intelligence to other agencies until cleared by his counterpart. It was apparent to Anderson that whatever Stephenson had seen was merely one piece of the overall strategy being put into place by the American initiatives in Djakarta. He knew that Stephenson had misread the situation.

Anderson advised the other Intelligence officers who had also been called in urgently that he would personally take charge of the situation. He pocketed the communication and thanked the surprised group of analysts, then returned to his well-appointed accommodation. As his head touched the pillow, Anderson already knew what his first business of the day would be, when he arrived at his office in Central Plans the next morning. The Acting Director smiled, as he easily gave way to sleep, pleased that he would soon be rid of his predecessor's protege.

Chapter 20

0310 Hours

The Embassy guards waved as they drove through the gates and headed towards Murray's residence. He turned into Djalan Professor Moh Yamin and drove towards the Intercontinental Hotel for two blocks, then turned left into Djalan Tjik Ditiro as the engine spluttered, then died. Murray turned the starter as he peered at the dash instruments then swore, realising that they had run out of gas. Immediately, both men jumped out and jogged towards the villa on Djalan Serang. They had less than four hundred metres to cover now. They had just turned the corner together when Murray pulled Zach urgently to the side of the broken footpath.

'We're too late!' he hissed, bending low to the ground, watching the fury of activity less than a hundred metres away. Soldiers poured out of the three trucks and ran along the road while others forced their way past the alarmed sentries guarding Major General Harjono's house and family. Murray was within twenty metres of his own villa. He realised that there was little they could do for his important neighbour. He looked at Zach and signalled, pointing across at his residence.

'Let's get to a bloody phone, and quick. We must alert the Ambassador and the other Attachés now we have solid evidence of what's happening. Also anyone else we can contact. There's nothing we can do now, for them,' he nodded in the direction of where the soldiers had congregated. They could hear shouts and signs of resistance as the communist Takari teams easily overran Harjono's own security. They rose from their crouched positions and started across the street. Suddenly, a soldier shouted and they knew, instantly, they had been spotted.

'*Stop!*' the voice demanded. Zach and Murray both froze.

'*Stop!*' the soldier screamed and raised his weapon at them where they stood half-way across the road. Suddenly, Zach realised the soldier was going to shoot.

'Run!' he yelled, and Murray sprang into action and legged it across the road as fast as he could.

'Keep going!' Zach yelled, bending down to reduce the target. They had just about made it to the other side of the road when the soldier began shooting, sending a spray of automatic fire in their direction. The first bullets hit the footpath ahead and ricocheted into the night. They both turned away from the onslaught and ran furiously back across from where they came, bullets following their pounding footsteps. Suddenly the whole street seemed to come alive as the soldier was joined by his comrades, shooting wildly at the running figures.

'Shit,' Murray called loudly, 'the bastards are trying to kill us!'

'Then for Chrissakes man, run!' Zach ordered. Murray didn't know how they managed to make it back to the corner unscathed. They ran as fast as their legs would carry them, crossing Djalan Tjik Ditiro. The sounds of running soldiers signalled that they were not too far behind. Just then, Murray fell, and as he hit the ground bullets whipped dangerously close to where he lay. He screamed in pain and Zach thought the Station Chief had been hit. Instead, it was an old injury, come back to haunt him. Murray knew, as he struggled to his feet that the excruciating pain in his ankle would foil their attempts to escape. Zach saw the problem and pulled Murray to his feet, scooping his friend up effortlessly as the soldiers approached closer. Bullets broke the air around their heads and Zach was forced to throw them both to the ground, causing Murray to scream in pain.

'Give me the gun,' he hissed, groping for the automatic Murray carried.

'No, hell no!' Murray yelled, fighting against Zach as the colonel gripped the P9S and pulled the handgun free. 'They'll shoot you dead if they see you armed,' he shouted, not realising how ridiculous this sounded to the seasoned veteran.

'Shit, Murray, what the hell do you think the bastards have just tried to do,' Zach hissed, turning with the weapon and pointing it directly at the approaching soldiers. There were three of them, all dressed in battle fatigues and armed with what Zach guessed from the rapid fire would be either Soviet Sudarevs or Spaghins sub-machine guns. The weapons could even be Stens, he thought. It really didn't matter. He knew from his anti-guerrilla sweeps in the jungles of Sarawak that the Indonesians had both. The leading soldier fired from the hip as he crossed to their side of the road, sending a spray of bullets just off to their right, ripping chunks of cement from the adjacent wall. Zach believed he had no choice. He aimed the pistol and fired three shots in rapid succession. The soldiers behind threw themselves to the ground as one of Zach's bullets found its target. The Indonesian soldier's body jerked back, and then sideways, and he was dead before he even hit the ground. Zach then charged towards the other two startled soldiers, and fired two shots as he scrambled towards their fallen comrade.

Zach dropped down heavily beside the dead man, using the body for cover. He stuck the P9S into his belt. There were still four rounds left in the automatic's magazine. He ripped the sub-machine gun from the soldier's hands and pointed the Soviet PPS at the other two soldiers and squeezed the trigger. The SMG Sudarev pulled to the right as the remainder of the thirty-five 7.62 mm rounds tore from the barrel, sending flames out the side of the weapon's circular cooling holes. Both soldiers scrambled in a vain attempt to escape, their faces twisted as they fell in the fierce hail of bullets.

Zach ran across to where they lay, and crouched beside them. He removed one of the weapons, checked the curved box magazine and threw the empty Sudarev aside in disgust. Damned obsolete Soviet junk, he thought. He rolled over the other body and checked the second machine-gun. There were still rounds in the magazine so he grabbed the weapon and ran to the injured Murray.

Zach responded to Murray's enquiring look with a quick shake of his head, indicating that the men were all dead. Murray knew that the colonel had had little choice. They could not afford to leave any witnesses who could identify them as having exchanged fire with the Indonesian soldiers. Zach pulled Murray to his feet, then put his head under the injured man's arm and half-carried, half-dragged him away from the scene of carnage.

As they struggled along, Murray kept looking over his shoulder, expecting another attack from behind. But none came. Instead, the remaining soldiers concentrated on their task at hand, the immediate capture and arrest Major General Harjono. Zach checked the automatic. It was too obvious, he knew. He buried it inside his shirt, still held in place by his belt. They hobbled along, careful of the broken pavement, Zach acting as Murray's crutch. The men pushed on until reaching the junction of Prof. Mohamad Yamin and Tjik Ditiro. They rested, and Zach waved at a passing *betjak* which stopped and accepted the fare from what he believed were two drunken *tuans*. Murray Stephenson and Colonel Steven Zach were already well out of earshot when the staccato sounds of Sten fire pierced the air along the street known as Djalan Serang.

* * * * * *

0320 Hours

When their contingent had first arrived, Sergeant Major Bungkus, as team leader, had jumped down from his jeep and disposed of the sleeping security without effort. He had then run to the front door and banged loudly, calling out to those inside. Mrs. Harjono awoke with a start and left their bedroom, passing through the family room and across to the side entrance where she peered through the curtains. She was startled to see soldiers dressed in Tjakrabirawa Palace Guard uniforms. Others were gathering in her front yard and she immediately became concerned. She stepped out through the side door and confronted the men there.

'*I must speak to Bapak Djenderal Harjono,*' the sergeant demanded. Harjono's wife gasped at the NCO's insolent attitude.

'*The Djenderal is asleep,*' she replied defiantly, but Sergeant Major Bungkus knew this not to be so. He suspected that the general was awake and had sent the woman out to investigate. '*What are you doing here?*' she then demanded.

'*The Bapak Djenderal has been called urgently by the President,*' Sergeant Major Bungkus lied.

'*Stay where you are. I will inform the Djenderal,*' Ibu Harjono instructed the soldier. She returned inside, leaving the side door open, then hurried into her bedroom. '*Pak, Pak,*' she whispered urgently, '*there are Tjakra Palace Guards outside insisting that you go with them. They said that they are to take you to see the President!*' Djenderal Harjono was alarmed by his wife's wild-eyed expression.

398

'*Tell them to leave immediately,*' he asked his wife, then added, '*and tell them to come back in the morning. At 0800 Hours.*' They both listened to the distant gunfire and became even more alarmed. Ibu Harjono did as asked, returning downstairs to confront the soldiers who waited there.

'*You are to return tomorrow morning,*' she called to the men outside through a half-opened door.

'*The Bapak is to come with us now!*' the sergeant outside demanded once more. She was shocked by his insolence.

'*The Bapak Djenderal is not well,*' she lied. '*Come back in the morning as he has ordered.*' For a brief moment there was silence, and then Ibu Harjono thought she could hear the soldiers outside talking.

'*Go away,*' she called through the small opening, wishing that the general's own men had been present. She listened but there was no response. Ibu Harjono then proceeded to close and lock the front door. Suddenly she was startled by a loud banging noise as the door's timbers screamed under the soldier's onslaught.

'*Aduh, aduh,*' she cried in alarm, running back to her bedroom.

'*What is happening?*' the general asked, panic rising in his voice.

'*They refuse to go, Pak,*' replied the anguished Ibu Harjono. '*They tried to break into our house!*'

General Harjono suddenly realised that he was in grave danger, and that the men outside were there to take his life. '*Get the children. Quickly!*' he ordered. Ibu Harjono started to cry, lost in the sudden turmoil. She put her hands to her face.

'*What do they want?*' she cried, fearing that she already knew the answer.

'*Do as I say, now. Get the children and stay with them in the next room. Lock the door. I will go and talk to the men and then send them away.*' As he spoke, they both heard Sergeant Bungkus scream angrily.

'*Come out now, Djenderal, or we will kill your whole family!*' General Harjono knew then that he was to die. He turned to his wife and held her tightly.

'*Go. Now. Get the children as I asked. Take them into the next room and stay there. You will be safe. I promise you.*' He attempted a smile as he quickly touched his wife's face. She turned and hurried away to do as her husband had instructed. Ibu Harjono knew that it was now her responsibility to ensure the safety of their children. She didn't look back at her husband of thirty-one years as she hurried to the other room.

'Come down, Djenderal!' she heard the soldiers demand menacingly. Suddenly there was a burst of machine-gun fire. She grabbed the children, fled to the safety of the back room, and bolted the door behind, leaving her husband cut off from his family. Ibu Harjono could hear the general moving around. It seemed that he was moving their furniture in the bedroom.

Sergeant Arlian opened fire with his Sten while Private Subakir half-emptied his own Sten's magazine, shooting through the thick teak door. Bungkus then burst through the doorway and found the room in darkness.

'Get some light in here!' Bungkus yelled. Immediately, one of the soldiers set fire to some loose newspaper sheets and threw this inside the large room. They then entered as the flames flickered, casting an eerie light through the darkness. Something moved, catching the intruders off-guard. It was Djenderal Harjono.

'You bastards!' he screamed, lunging forward to attack with only his fists. He had been unable to find a weapon in the bedroom. He leapt forward and wrestled with one of the soldiers, throwing Private Subakir to the floor. He groped for the man's weapon unsuccessfully, and, as flames died out, returning the room to darkness, he moved to the farthest corner, crouching beside a built-in cupboard. Private Subakir was back on his feet within moments.

'Kill him!' a voice commanded from somewhere behind in the darkness. Immediately, Subakir unleashed a hail of bullets sending the heavy-set general crashing to the ground.

In the adjacent room his wife and children screamed loudly, crying for help as they heard the bullets rip through the walls.

'Shut up in there or we will kill all of you as well!' Bungkus threatened. The children huddled together, petrified. Suddenly they heard another burst of fire from one of the Stens and they whimpered, knowing that it was all over. General Harjono was dead.

The communists dragged the half-dressed body out into the family room. Harjono's singlet and short pants were smothered in blood and, as he was unceremoniously dragged outside, over the terrace and through the front garden, his body left an ugly trail of blood. Sergeant Major Bungkus, assisted by Subakir, Wagirem, and some of

Yanti's Gerwani, threw the general's corpse into the waiting truck. The Gerwani women shrieked with pleasure at their unit's success.

One of Harjono's children raced outside to be confronted by the grisly spectacle.

'*Bapak! Bapak!*' the child called out in anguish at the sight.

'*I said shut up!*' Private Wagirem screamed as he knocked the child unconscious with a vicious blow from the butt of his machine-gun. The soldiers then all boarded their truck and drove away. As soon as she realised that they had gone, Ibu Harjono fled into the darkness outside. She cried out loudly for assistance as she ran to the homes of General Parman and her husband's other close friend, General Suprapto. But she was too late.

* * * * * *

And so it went on. As the attack had commenced against General Harjono, the houses of the other generals had also come under siege. Major General Parman and his wife were awoken by sounds of movement outside and, suspecting that the neighbours on their right were being burgled, the general went outside to investigate and, if necessary, lend assistance to his friends next door.

'*Who's there?*' Parman challenged, but there was no reply. His wife had remained inside. '*Ada siapa?*' he called again, but still there was no response. Suddenly he recognized the sound of army boots hitting the ground somewhere nearby.

'*Who is there?*' he challenged once more, now wishing he had carried his revolver with him. Within seconds he was surrounded. Parman knew instantly what was happening. What a fool he had been! He had left his family unprotected.

The soldiers had been obliged to jump the small iron garden gate as this had been locked by the security guard earlier. At first General Parman was relieved, as he identified the uniform of the Tjakrabirawa Palace Guards. His fears were allayed. He had no way of seeing the Gerwani women soldiers who were hidden, out of sight, in the truck parked outside.

'*What are you men doing here?*' he demanded to know. The group's leader, Sergeant Major Satar came to attention and saluted convincingly.

'*Bapak Djenderal, we have been sent to escort you to the Palace. The*

President has asked that you come immediately, as it concerns national security. President Soekarno has instructed us to inform you, sir, that it is very important that you come.' Sergeant Major Satar lied very convincingly. As he peered over the sergeant's shoulder, General Parman briefly caught a glimpse of a man standing there, almost in the shadows. For a moment, Parman thought he recognised the face but then decided that it could not be the same man, as this one wore the 'Tjakra' uniform. He started to call out to him but then hesitated. The man he remembered was still serving in Semarang, with the Diponegoro Divisions. No, he thought, it couldn't be him.

General Parman's role as the most senior Intelligence general often demanded his presence at the oddest of times, and he was accustomed to being called to the Palace by the President. Parman was an exceptionally good officer. He loved his country and remained loyal to his President even though others in the Council did not.

'I will not be long,' he said to the sergeant, turning to re-enter his house while permitting the Tjakrabirawa guards to follow. He believed there was nothing amiss.Two soldiers also entered, their weapons bearing fixed bayonets. Ibu Parman, also awakened by the noise, was shocked by this presumptuous invasion.

'Where are your written orders?' the outspoken woman demanded. She was not accustomed to such behaviour in her home.

'The NCO outside has these, ibu,' they had lied in response.

'Then go and get it for me,' she ordered, but the soldiers did not budge. The soldiers started to follow her around the house. Suddenly her temper flared.

'Why are you following me? Stop this behaviour and leave my home immediately!' she demanded.

'Sudahlah,' the soldier responded, telling her that he would accept no more of her manner. She was shocked.

'What are you doing here,' she cried, alarmed as other soldiers entered the room. Her husband could not hear the exchange as he was in the bathroom washing his face and changing into his dress uniform to meet the President. When he reappeared he sensed that something was gravely wrong. General Parman saw the look of terror growing on his wife's face and he turned to re-enter their bedroom.

'Cigarettes,' he called, searching for an excuse, leaving the room only to be followed by one of the bayonet-wielding soldiers.

'*You must hurry,*' the soldier insisted. Parman became enraged at the man's insolence.

'*Get out of my room! Immediately!*' he demanded. When the corporal merely laughed, General Parman knew instantly that his situation was hopeless. He shook his head in dismay.

'*Wait outside,*' he ordered, but the soldier simply smiled and grabbed him roughly by the arm and escorted the general out of the house. When Parman reached the front door, he turned and looked back at his wife and then smiled.

'*Call General Yani and tell him that I have been summoned by the President,*' he asked. Immediately his wife moved towards the telephone to do as her husband had instructed. '*Stop!*' Corporal Chairuman cried, as he leapt across the room, smashed the telephone to the floor, then ripped the line from the wall.

'*Outside!*' the sergeant barked, enjoying the role reversal. Parman stood in the doorway refusing to move further. Corporal Chairuman took two quick steps and hit the general brutally with his rifle stock. As he doubled over, the other soldiers moved to his side and ushered their captive outside.

'*No! Please no!*' Ibu Parman cried in desperation. What was happening here? How could this be happening to them? Sergeant Major Satar turned and grinned sardonically. He was enjoying all of this.

'*We will take good care of the Bapak. Don't you worry, 'bu!*' he said, his voice full of sarcasm as he too then marched out into the courtyard to oversee his troops. Ibu Parman followed outside, too scared to cry. She witnessed her husband being thrown into the lead truck.

'*Parman! Parman!*' she called in desperation after her husband, then fled inside as one of the soldiers turned towards her, hate in his eyes. Before she aware of it, they were gone. The communist contingent sped through the quiet city, on their way back to the place they called Crocodile Hole, where they had planned to detain their captives inside the Halim Airforce Base.

Only minutes had passed when Ibu Harjono suddenly appeared at the Parman residence. Sobbing uncontrollably, she told the terrified Ibu Parman that General Harjono had just been shot and that his body had been taken away. Ibu Parman collapsed.

* * * * * *

0345 Hours

Zach provided support to Murray as they hopped up the Hotel Indonesia steps. They had decided to return there, as the hotel's phones would probably still be working. Zach had suggested that the communists had probably cut all Embassy and other foreign communications, but he doubted if they would have attempted to disrupt the Hotel Indonesia's lines, as this may have alerted others to their game. They went immediately to Susan's room and knocked loudly on her door. Susan looked tired and scared as she opened the door.

'My God!' she gasped, alarmed at their dishevelled appearance. 'What happened?'

'Later, Susan. Later. Just help me get him inside,' Zach said. She held Murray carefully and helped as he hobbled into the room. Murray sat on the bed by the telephone and started dialling. Susan clucked admonishingly, believing that he should at least rest for a while. Murray ignored her and continued with the task at hand. He could remember only a handful of the residential numbers and, in each case, no-one answered. It was just too damn early in the morning, he thought angrily, wishing they had gone to the Embassy where all the numbers were stored.

'Steve, this is no good. I'm not getting anywhere. We have to go to the Embassy and try from there. If the phones are out as you suggest, at least we can grab the staff directory then beat it back here. What do you say?' he asked, pulling himself to his feet, wincing with pain. Zach knew that Murray was in no shape to venture back outside. He would only slow him down.

'You stay here. There's no need for both of us to go. Give me your keys, Murray. Besides, you can't even walk, let alone run.' He looked at Susan and smiled, anticipating her objection. 'I wont be long. Why don't you rustle up some room service for, say, five o'clock, and we'll all have breakfast when I return?' Zach took Susan in his arms briefly and kissed her cheek. She stiffened, then stepped back and lifted his shirt, exposing the P9S automatic. There was a moment of silence in the room as she looked up into his eyes, then turned questioningly towards Murray. Knowing that an explanation would be too difficult, Zach then left, promising to return within the hour.

* * * * * *

0410 Hours

Yanti stood alongside the soldier as they prepared to enter General Suprapto's home. She had watched the general's arrival prior to the 'Tjakra' team's departure from Halim.

The procedure was much the same as when General Parman was successfully captured. The team was fortunate that Suprapto had suffered severe toothache through the night and had risen from his bed to paint, as a means of distraction. He was extremely tired.

The team had waited outside where through the windows, they could see Suprapto work until the early hours of the morning on a painting. Yanti knew Suprapto was an artist of some standing. She had seen his work on the walls of the Djakarta Art Gallery and was aware from newspaper reports that he had arranged to have his paintings displayed in the Djogyakarta Museum. At about four o'clock they saw him put down his brushes and retire to his bedroom. They waited, giving the general time to fall to sleep. Then it was time to move.

As the assault team crossed into Suprapto's front yard, the neighbour's dog heard their movements and started to bark. The general awoke with a start. Within moments he was joined by his wife. They peered outside and identified the Tjakrabirawa Palace Guards.

'What are you doing here at this time of the day,' he challenged, calling to the soldiers through the open window.

'The President has instructed us to escort you to the Palace, Pak Djenderal. The President has asked that you come immediately as the situation is urgent.' Suprapto shook his head and made his way down to the front of the house and unlocked the front door. Immediately, he was confronted by Sergeant Sulaiman, the team leader. General Suprapto looked across at the men assembled there and, for a moment, thought he had spotted a familiar face. When he looked again, it was gone.

'Djoko?' he called, but the face had disappeared. What was he doing in Djakarta? he wondered.

The general always obeyed his superiors. His President was the Commander-in-Chief, and had ordered him to the Palace. That was sufficient. He nodded to the sergeant, accepting that he would have to go.

'Wait here,' he ordered, *'I will first change into my uniform.'*

'No, there isn't time,' the sergeant insisted and, at that moment, they lowered their bayonets at his stomach.

'What ...' Suprapto called in surprise, but had no further chance to summon help as the soldiers pounced heavily and threw him down. As his head smashed against the marble floor, he uttered a muffled scream.

'Tie him up!' the team leader ordered.

Yanti motioned to the other Gerwani women and they ran forward. The general was hauled outside through his front garden and thrown into the waiting truck. The women climbed aboard, kicking and punching the terrified man until he lost consciousness. Then they drove through the sleeping city and out to the Crocodile Hole in Halim Airforce Base.

The general's wife, alarmed at the commotion, had ventured cautitously back into their living room. Immediately she was confronted by a dozen or more soldiers. Ibu Suprapto didn't hesitate, making a grab for the telephone.

' Kill her!' one of the soldiers shouted, but one of Yanti's troops stepped forward and struck the woman hard, across the face. She fell, then rose and scrambled away from her attackers.

'No! Don't kill me!' she cried, falling to her knees as she tried to escape. The soldier ripped the telephone from its wires and threw it across the room. He looked at his sergeant who shook his head, indicating that the woman was not to be harmed further.

Struggling to her feet, Ibu Suprapto fled back into her bedroom and opened the windows there. Bravely, she leaned out and could see the garden full of soldiers in red berets, wearing the uniform of the Palace Guard.

Ibu Suprapto could not believe the treacherous behaviour of President Soekarno's own personal guards. She watched and listened as the kidnappers departed. When she was certain that they had all left, Ibu Suprapto ran to the front of her house and slammed the doors firmly shut. Her heart was still pounding and she felt faint. Forcing herself to the study, she scribbled a note for General Parman, hoping that he would be able to help her husband who had just been kidnapped from his home. She sealed the envelope and went in search of one of her servants. They lived behind in separate quarters and, surprisingly, seemed to be unaware of what had just transpired. She was about to send one of her servants out into the night when there was a knock at her door.

'*Bu?*' the voice called, but she did not dare to open the door. Fearing for her life, she refused to answer. Finally, she checked from the upstairs window and was relieved to discover that her caller was alone.

'*Who's there?*' she asked, unable to see the woman clearly.

'*They have killed my husband, Djenderal Harjono!*' the woman cried out. Stunned by this news, she hurriedly let Ibu Harjono in and the terrified women clung to each other. Both described the horror which had occurred in their houses.

'*There is no use in sending your note to Pak Parman,*' Ibu Harjono told General Suprapto's wife. '*He too has been kidnapped.*' The women then locked the doors just in case the soldiers returned to kill them also. After all, they were witnesses.

* * * * * *

0425 Hours

Zach cursed as he sorted through the keys. He had taken a *betjak* from the hotel and arrived at the Embassy in less than ten minutes. As he passed through the front gate, he stopped and gave one of the guards a handful of rupiah and explained where the unguarded Embassy car could be found. Rostered drivers would start their day within the hour and he assumed they would have fuel in the workshop. He then went about unlocking the Embassy, wishing that he had asked Murray to identify which keys he would need, thereby saving precious time.

Zach wasted fifteen minutes making his way into the Consulate section where lists of all staff were pinned to the Consul's inside wall. He commenced dialling, first the Ambassador, then the Counsellor, making his way down the list according to seniority. When a telephone continued to ring unanswered for more than twenty seconds, he moved to the next number on the list. Within twenty minutes, he had managed to contact eleven of the fifteen permanent Embassy officers. Satisfied that there was little else he could achieve, Steven Zach returned to the hotel.

* * * * * *

While the Australian Military Attaché was in the process of alerting Embassy officers, one of the Takari kidnap teams arrived at the home of General Sutojo Siswomihardjo and knocked brazenly on the general's front door. Meanwhile, members of the communist team slipped quietly down the side of his home and seized his houseboy, threatening him with their bayonets. Petrified, the ageing *djongos* unlocked the rear doors which led directly into the main house. General Sutojo heard the noise and went directly to his front door.

'Who are you?' he demanded, annoyed that his security had not prevented whoever it was from disturbing him at such an ungodly hour.

'It's Gondo from Malang,' the soldier answered. His curiosity aroused, Sutojo foolishly opened the door. He stood there for a moment trying to identify the soldier. Suddenly, he was attacked.

'What the hell ...!' Sutojo yelled, as he was seized by two of the kidnappers.

'Gag him, quickly!' the team leader ordered, then delivered several punishing blows to the general's head. As they dragged the unconscious general away, Ibu Sutojo emerged from their bedroom, alarmed at the noise. She was terrified, believing that they had been invaded by robbers, a not-uncommon event around the city. At that moment, soldiers entered from the rear of her house. She stood, stunned, as they went about destroying everything in her home.

'No!' she cried, as the soldiers moved around the lounge room hurling loose furniture around, ignoring her presence.

'No!' Ibu Sutojo cried aloud in anguish,'not that!' as one of the men use his rifle butt to destory her prize Ming vase. She collapsed to the floor as the rampage continued. Glasses were smashed, plates thrown to the floor and family pictures destroyed. Ibu Sutojo pleaded with the men to stop, but they ignored her, continuing to smash everything in sight. She ran to the front door only to catch a glimpse of her husband being lifted into one of the two trucks which had brought the kidnappers to her home.

She tried to cry out, but choked in fear as one of their attackers suddenly appeared, menacingly, and pointed his bayonet at her. She listened in silence to the shrill cries of the Gerwani women as they kicked and punched her husband insensible.

Ibu Sutojo moved slowly away from the threatening soldier and turned, re-entering her home. Amidst the incredible scene of soldiers laughing and smashing her prized possessions, she had the presence of mind to slip back into her bedroom and lock the door. There was an extension in her room. She grabbed the phone and dialled. It seemed to ring and ring for ages, unanswered. She was about to place the telephone down when, suddenly, she heard a voice.

'*Siapa ini?*' someone asked. Immediately Ibu Sutojo held the telephone closer and whispered urgently.

'*This is Djenderal Sutojo's wife. Call Bapak Suthardio, quickly! Someone here is trying to kill us!*' She had connected to the home of the Minister for Justice, Brigadier General Suthardio, who also acted as the country's Attorney General.

'*The Bapak is still ...*' Suddenly, as she was speaking to Suthardio's servant, the line was broken. The kidnappers had ripped the wires from the wall in the living room. She sat there in the dark and held her breath, believing she could hear footsteps approaching. Then, after what seemed to be an immeasurable time, there was silence. She waited, listening to what was happening outside her room. Suddenly, she remembered. The children! Ibu Sutojo jumped to her feet and darted from the dark room, hitting furniture as she made her way towards the children's room. She heard a noise. Alarmed, she stopped and listened. Then, deciding that it was safe, she continued on, reaching her children's room safely. There, she was relieved to discover them unharmed. She gathered them together and ran down the road to the Attorney-General's house.

Upon arrival, Sutojo's wife explained to Suthardio what had happened, deposited her children, then hurried off to her other friend's home only to discover that General Parman had also been taken. Ibu Sutojo remained with Ibu Parman and prayed. Their world had been irrevocably destroyed.

* * * * * *

Less than one kilometre away, another Takari team entered General Pandjaitan's front yard and moved to the rear of the two-storey home. There they discovered a connecting pavilion, and attempted to break through the small building's door. Inside there were three young men sleeping. These were the general's nephews.

'What the ...' the oldest called, startled by the noise.

'Open the door!' a voice from outside demanded. The older boys were not impressed. Their uncle was a general. And they had their own guns.

'Who the hell is it?' they demanded, searching around in the darkened room for clothes. The youngest boy buried his head under the sheets of the top bunk where he had been sleeping, as the two older brothers jumped out of their beds. One of the nephews groped in the dark for the revolver he kept hidden in the closet.

'Open this door or we will shoot!' the menacing voice called.

'Go away!' the second eldest called, frightened. 'Don't you know that this is Bapak Djenderal Pandjaitan's house?' As this was followed by a few moments of silence the nephews felt that this had worked. Obviously the men outside were thieves. 'Wait 'til the general's security catches these arseholes!' they sniggered amongst themselves, envisaging their attackers fleeing at the discovery that they had mistakenly attacked such a place. The oldest boy still searched around in the dark for the revolver he had hidden. Where in the hell had he put the bloody thing!

Before he could arm himself, the door crashed open. Two NCO's stepped inside and opened fire at point-blank range, killing both the young men instantly. The third boy remained hidden, his fear almost giving him away as the soldiers then filed through the pavilion, gaining access to the main house. Meanwhile, several of the soldiers outside fired directly into the upstairs windows, breaking all the glass and smashing the light which had just been switched on. Sergeant Sukardjo led the first assault into the house. He ran to the bottom of the stairs and yelled loudly.

'Bapak Djenderal, you must come downstairs,' Sukardjo ordered. He then took several steps and looked further up into the second storey but couldn't see too much there as the upstairs hallway was in darkness.

'Who are you? What do you want?' General Pandjaitan shouted, his head protruding from the master-bedroom door. The shots had smashed through his room but fortunately only damaged the furnishings. He looked at his wife. She sat on the bed, her hands covering her face in shock. And then he thought of his children. They were in the adjacent bedrooms. His mind raced. His gun was downstairs locked inside his desk.

'General, we have been sent here by the President. You are to come with us immediately.' Sergeant Sukardjo was quickly losing patience and signalled to the others that he would move up the stairs, ordering them to remain below. *'General,'* he called again, *'General, we are from the Tjakrabirawa Regiment. The President has instructed us to escort you to the Palace. It is urgent.'* Seconds ticked by and there was no response. Sukardjo started moving up the stairs when Pandjaitan suddenly called out, telling them to wait while he changed. More minutes passed and, to their surprise, the general emerged, dressed in his parade uniform complete with medals and ribbons. He walked down the stairs and into the family room. The kidnap team circled the general with their bayonets and in that moment, he knew that he would die.

'Move,' Corporal Dikin ordered, shoving the high-ranking officer roughly towards the open front door. *'I said, move!'* the young Corporal screamed, and kicked the general in the knee savagely. Pandjaitan was led out into the front garden where Dikin, with several cruel blows to the back of the general's head, sent him crashing to the ground. Pandjaitan lay there groaning. Dazed, he looked up but instantly knew that these soldiers were there to kill him. As the man attempted to rise to his knees and pray, both the young corporals opened fire with their Thompsons and Stens, shooting at point-blank range. His head exploded, throwing hideous lumps of bone and tissue around the garden. The kidnappers then threw his body over the fence onto the footpath, where others loaded it into the waiting truck. They too then returned to the Halim Airforce Base. Another mission successfully accomplished.

* * * * * *

Over at Lieutenant General Yani's house in Djalan Lembang, soldiers from the Presidential Guard poured into the Chief of Army Staff's driveway, where the general's security guards greeted the kidnappers cordially, recognising the respected Tjakribirawa uniforms. The unsuspecting guards were easily overpowered and the communist team, led by Sergeant Major Raswad, moved directly into the general's house.

Yani's seven-year-old daughter had woken and was in the process of wandering around her home in search of her mother. She had forgotten that the following day would be her mother's birthday, and that Ibu Yani had spent the night in her husband's official residence over at Taman Surapati. The child was the first to encounter the soldiers who had stormed into her home.

'Where is your father?' Sergeant Raswad asked the child. He had a daughter of his own.

'He's still asleep,' the young girl replied, not in the least concerned. Her father was the Army Chief and she was used to soldiers being present in their house at all hours of the day.

'Would you go and wake your father, please,' he coaxed the girl, *'and tell him that Bapak President wishes to speak to him urgently.'* She smiled at the soldier and went to her father's room to do as she was asked. Meanwhile, Yani's second daughter had woken, startled by the noises outside. She woke her eleven-year-old brother and, frightened by the strange sounds, they also ran to their father's room.

When General Yani emerged, he was still dressed in his pyjamas. He was furious that someone had so easily compromised his security and entered his home.

'What are you doing in my home?' he yelled at the men as they moved towards him.

'President Soekarno has instructed us to take you to him,' came the rehearsed reply. General Yani was livid. He detected the insolence in the sergeant's manner. He continued to stare angrily at the intruders, then turned to re-enter his room.

'Wait outside. I will bathe first then change,' he ordered. Raswad stepped forward and raised the muzzle of his weapon.

'That won't be necessary,' he sneered, and turned to smile at his comrades just as General Yani stepped closer to the soldier and hit him with all of his strength. The Palace Guard fell heavily to the marble floor. Yani recognised his peril and turned to flee. He ran through the kitchen and managed to reach the rear door when he heard the shouts from behind.

'Gijadi, shoot!' Raswad screamed at his comrade who was blocking the other's line of fire. Immediately, Gijadi opened fire, spraying bullets along the corridor and through the glass doors as the Thompson jerked in his hands. General Yani died instantly, seven of the bullets reaching their target. The children had remained in their father's room, as ordered. Now, huddled together as the sound

of machine-gun fire ripped through their home, they trembled in fear and began to cry.

Their father's body was dragged through the house and out through the front door. His blood stained the entire length of the house as the killers carelessly rolled his corpse out into the front yard. Members of the Communist Youth Movement then took over and threw Yani's body into one of the waiting Toyota jeeps. A solitary figure moved out of the deep shadows and climbed into the truck to examine the body. Satisfied, he leaped from the back of the vehicle and vanished back into the night. The sergeant barked at the rest of his troops and they boarded the truck. Then they too returned to their headquarters at Halim.

* * * * * *

0435 Hours

The conspirators were aware that their plan to overthrow the Military could fail if they missed their most important target, Indonesia's most senior and respected general, Abdul Haris Nasution. The man was a legend throughout the country, and was greatly admired by the people of Indonesia. The communists knew that his capture would have to be executed with precision as Nasution was always surrounded by well-disciplined soldiers who would give their lives to protect their national hero. It was for this reason that a full company of soldiers was designated the responsibility of kidnapping this powerful officer, the nation's Minister for Defence.

Before moving on Nasution's home, the kidnappers disarmed soldiers and guards down the road at the Deputy Prime Minister's residence. There, the Tjakrabirawa soldiers encountered resistance, resulting in the death of a senior police officer, Brigadier Satsuit Tubun. The communist soldiers then moved quickly to complete their mission, disarming Nasution's own guards and forcing their way into his home. The intruders smashed their way through doors and windows in search of the general. Ibu Nasution urged her husband to flee immediately and, reluctantly, he hurried out through the rear of their home and into a neighbouring yard, where he hid behind the pump house. The residence was protected by diplomatic privilege, being the home of one of the Iranian Charge d'Affaires in Djakarta.

Moments later, the Tjakrabirawa soldiers opened fire, shattering the bedroom door behind which Nasution's wife hid in terror. A hail of bullets tore through the wooden louvered door but, incredibly, Ibu Nasution remained unharmed.

The nanny screamed in terror as the entire house exploded with the sounds of machine-gun fire. She grabbed the child and ran through the house, screaming as bullets punctured the walls and ceilings. Several finally found their mark as the woman fell, still holding the little girl tightly in her arms. Corporal Hargijono's orders had been to kill the general. Instead, three of his bullets ripped through the five-year-old girl's tiny frame, tearing through flesh and bone as they exited, breaking her spine. The nanny was wounded, two of the bullets passing through her hand before entering the child she had tried to protect. Irma Surjani Nasution died instantly, her young life snuffed out even before she had seen her sixth birthday.

In a small pavilion located at the rear of the house, two officers leaped from their beds, startled by the sounds of gunfire. Both men were Nasution's adjutants and were quartered there in the small building.

Lieutenant Tendean ran outside, armed with his revolver, while Hamdan, his police offsider, remained inside still searching for his weapon. The Army adjutant was immediately confronted by the Palace Guard troops and disarmed. Suddenly, an unfamiliar officer appeared and took charge. He looked at the adjutant's face and smiled. Tendean bore a remarkable resemblance to Nasution, and in the dark yard he was mistakenly taken for his superior. He was immediately arrested and dragged outside, where he was bound and placed on the floor of the team leader's jeep. Satisfied that they had captured General Nasution, the soldiers drove their prisoner directly to Halim, believing that Operation Takari had been successfully completed. The Council of Generals had been destroyed. Indonesia was now in the hands of the communists.

Concealed behind the overgrown structure built over his neighbour's well, Nasution thought he recognised the voice of the officer who had appeared and ordered the arrest of his adjutant. He shook his head, confused. It had sounded like Djoko! But he knew this could not be. The Diponegoro officer was supposed to be in Semarang, looking after things in Central Java. As he sat alone, the cold realisation of what was really happening suddenly occurred to him. He closed his eyes and prayed, shocked that he had been betrayed. Nasution then knew, that if he was to survive, he dare not reveal his whereabouts to anyone.

* * * * * *

Lubang Buaja -Halim Alirforce Base, 0530 Hours

The atmosphere surrounding the return of the last contingent was euphoric, as the team leaders gathered to see Nasution. The other captives, Generals Parman, Sutojo, Suprapto and Lieutenant Tendean had been tied together, and placed alongside the bodies of the other generals, Harjono, Pandjaitan and the Army Chief of Staff, General Yani, whose bloody corpse remained dressed in pyjamas.

Their success had driven the Gerwani women into a frenzy. Someone had produced a bottle of *arak*, a dangerously overproof extract derived from palm fruit, and toasted the success of the 30th September Movement and their comrades. Exaggerated tales of bravery and cunning were swapped around the fire as news of each successful kidnapping was announced. One by one, the units returned carrying bodies or prisoners. The bodies of the three dead generals had been laid out for all to see. Some of the Gerwani women, intoxicated by the deadly mixture of *arak* and the euphoria of bloody success, danced around the fire's flames laughing, singing, and mocking the once powerful men before them. Then, as the occasion deteriorated even further, the women began to chant, and shout obscenities at their prisoners.

Yanti walked proudly amongst her troops as they enjoyed their moment of triumph. The *arak* had helped. As she swallowed her first sip and felt the fire touch her insides, Yanti let out a yell of joy, and danced around with her friends as they shared the bottle of powerful spirits. Very few of their number had ever taken alcohol before. Someone added more fuel to the bonfire around which more than two hundred had gathered to celebrate the mission, the first step in achieving their Party's goals.

The prostrate forms of the three dead generals seemed to bother no-one. Some of the women, in unaccustomed alcoholic frenzy, tore their clothes away and danced, naked. An older woman spat on the corpse closest to where she stood and her friends laughed, teasing her that she was still frightened of the dead, whereapon she stepped forward quickly and kicked the body to prove that she was not afraid. The others laughed and so did she, warmed by the alcohol and the camaraderie. Another women, not to be outdone, took one of the soldiers bayonets from his scabbard and drove the steel blade into the dead man's chest. For a moment there was silence as they watched the woman extract the blade and hold the bayonet up for them to see.

Yanti did not like the way the mood was changing and held her breath in apprehension. Suddenly a loud cheer filled the early morning air as the women scrambled to see who could desecrate the other bodies first. Within moments there was pandemonium as they struggled with each other to see who could do the most damage. They kicked and pushed, tore at each others eyes, screamed obscenities and even drew blood as teeth sank deep into an adversary's limb. Yanti could see that they had lost control. There was only one thing that she could do. The violence was escalating dangerously quickly as some of the soldiers joined in the melee when Yanti's shot rang out, bringing the violence to an end.

'Why are you doing this to each other?' she screamed angrily, still holding the gun in her shaking hand. 'They're the ones who are your enemy,' Yanti yelled loudly pointing at the three men who had been tied and gagged then left to await their own fate. Lieutenant Tendean, the officer who had been mistaken for General Nasution, watched the young woman walk across to where he lay. The camp was suddenly silent. Tendean shuddered at the sound of the metallic click as the hammer of the revolver was slowly pulled back into place. He closed his eyes and whispered a prayer. Then he heard the whispering metallic sound of the action as Yanti pulled the Colt .38 trigger, sending the hammer roaring back into contact with the cartridge.

The bullet's impact brought an immediate roar of approval from her comrades. Yanti believed she had executed the country's most powerful solider, General Nasution. She threw the weapon to one of her team, who walked across and pointed the gun at the other prisoners. The young woman teased by pointing the gun first at one, then another, then shot General Parman through the eye. The communist soldiers and women roared again, and joined in the executions of the last two captives, Suprapto and Sutojo. The two remaining generals were trampled, beaten and gouged to death as the women fought over who would deliver the final blow to the former Military leaders.

The frenzy continued as the generals' bodies were further mutilated. Finally they were carried across the yard and thrown into the deep dry well behind the Gerwani billet. And then, as suddenly as they had started, the celebrations ceased.

* * * * * *

Lieutenant General Nasution was not aware that his six year old daughter had died in the attack. As the main body of communist soldiers departed, Nasution continued to hide in his neighbour's yard. He could still see Tjakrabirawa soldiers wandering around nearby. Reports of the attack on his home finally reached the Fifth Military Area Commander, General Umar Wirahadikusumah, who despatched a number of light tanks to the scene. It was not until well after six o'clock that Nasution was able to move to a safer location, assisted by Lieutenant Colonel Hidajat Wirasondjaja. Less than an hour later, he heard the radio broadcasts announcing the coup, and Nasution immediately contacted the Strategic Reserves Commander, Major General Soeharto, who had just arrived at his own headquarters along Merdeka Square. Immediately, Soeharto went in search of his President. But Soekarno was nowhere to be found.

Kerry B.Collison

Chapter 21

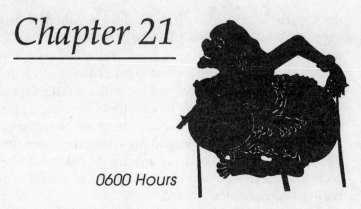

0600 Hours

One could not blame a casual observer for thinking that nothing had really changed in the capital. Clouds cleared and the sun rose over Djakarta while its inhabitants went about their chores, as they had for as long as they could remember. The communist forces had taken several strategic locations around the city, successfully occupying the radio, television and other communication stations even before first prayers had been called for the day. Captain Soeradi's communist soldiers had taken most of the strategic buildings around Merdeka Square, without any real resistance.

The two Australians had hired a pirate taxi from outside the hotel and instructed the driver to take them down town. At first, Murray could not see anything which would indicate that a military coup d'etat was well under way until Zach pointed at the two Armed Personnel Carriers of British origin positioned where they could control all traffic moving towards Radio Republik Indonesia, the national broadcast station.

'First time I've seen them bring out the Saracens, Zach whispered, indicating the two APC's. 'The Brits would be pleased to see their export drive making inroads at last,' he joked weakly. They were tired.

'Over there,' he said, pointing across Murray's side of the car. 'Soviet APCs,' he said. 'They're fully amphibious,' Zach added, making a face, then indicated to the driver that he should slow down. They drove past the Soviet BTR-50Ps and Murray could see at least half a dozen soldiers standing ready, inside the open top.

'They're new additions too,' Zach commented, nodding in the direction of the pile of sandbags which had been stacked around what appeared to be a heavy machine-gun battery. Murray squinted through the window, his vision slightly impaired by the early morning sun. 'You wouldn't want to be in their line of fire,' Zach continued. 'Those Czech guns spew out 12.7 mm bullets at a rate of eighty rounds per minute. And they have four barrels.' Zach then scratched his head. 'They're mainly used for anti-aircraft purposes,' he said, 'doesn't make much sense having them here unless it's mainly for show.' Murray knew that the Military Attaché was suggesting that the Indonesian Airforce would not attack the communist position. They then attempted to drive around the National Monument but were prevented from doing so. Soldiers had begun to blockade the western access to the Square.

'Communists?' Murray asked, unable to determine which faction was in control of the military there. Zach stared across at the men in uniform and shook his head.

'Impossible to tell.' Zach went on. 'They could be Government forces but I'm not sure. Let's drive down towards the Palace and see what's happening there.' Murray agreed, and ordered the driver to turn into Djalan Veteran then down Djalan Nusantara towards the Presidential Palace.

The driver followed their directions, taking the tuans past the Palace before turning into the main arterial road which led down Kota, Djakarta's Chinatown. The traffic had already become congested here as thousands of bicycles and *betjak* joined the vehicles thronging the narrow road.

Zach noticed that the foreign mainland Chinese community had wasted little time in commencing celebrations for their national day. Red Chinese flags, signalling the beginning of the October First Chinese anniversary activities, had already been raised along most of Djalan Hajam Wuruk and, as the morning sea breeze floated in from the north, the colourful flags danced. Satisfied that all appeared normal around the old city quarter, Murray then instructed the driver to take them out to the Senajan Sports Stadium. They were surprised to discover that the scene here too appeared normal. The tens of thousands of troops had already risen and were casually attending to their early morning ablutions as the Australians drove slowly by.

'It almost seems as if someone has forgotten to tell them what's going on,' Murray remarked. Everything just seemed too normal. He checked the time and suggested they go to the Embassy. Zach agreed, stopping off at his villa for a quick shower and change of clothes while Murray made his way to his own house to do likewise. The driver turned off Djalan Iman Bondjol and into Tjik Ditiro, then stopped. Murray could see that the road had been barricaded where it intersected with his street, Djalan Serang. There were soldiers running around everywhere, fully armed and looking very menacing. He told the driver to wait, climbed out of the taxi and started limping in the direction of the junction where he had almost been shot just hours before. As he approached the corner, two soldiers jumped forward and pointed their weapons directly at his chest. Murray sighed. His ankle hurt, his head ached, and the last thing he needed then was to be refused entry to his own home.

'*I live in that house over there,*' he told the soldiers, pointing at his villa.

'*What is your name? Which country are you from?*' was the terse demand. Murray could see that these men were agitated, armed, and ready to fire. So, tired as he was, Murray forced a smile.

'*I'm Australian. I work at the Embassy. That is my home over there. Please let me through.*' The soldiers were still not sure. One of them turned and went in search of an officer, returning with his Captain. Murray repeated what he'd just explained to the other soldier and, accompanied by the officer, was escorted down the street into his villa.

Exhausted, he dragged himself slowly into the house where his surprised servants fussed over him. They had been worried about their *tuan* when they too discovered what had occurred along their street just hours before. He stripped and bathed, standing uncomfortably on one leg, but enjoying the luxury of the luke-warm shower. Murray closed his eyes. He could still visualise the soldiers running after them, shooting wildly as both he and Zach ran for their lives. He wondered how the generals had all fared, and how many of those on the list he had seen had been able to defend themselves or avoid whatever the communists had planned for them. As the dull ache across his temples slowly disappeared, Murray felt the waves of fatigue take over. He limped from the shower and towelled himself dry in the airconditioned bedroom, then sat naked on the soft, cool double bed. Before he was aware of what was happening, he placed his head on the tempting feather pillows and closed his eyes for a moment's rest. Exhausted, he fell deeply asleep, unaware that Zach had been trying to contact him by telephone.

As he waited for Murray to return, Zach listened to Djakarta's central radio station and caught the broadcast announcing Untung's successful arrest of the entire Council of Generals. Unable to communicate this information due to the disrupted telephone system, Zach left a message with his own servants for when Murray returned, then left his residence and hailed a *betjak* to take him to the Embassy. Zach had little doubt that once foreign governments were alerted to the dangerous turn of events, many, including the Australian Forces, would go immediately onto full war alert. As Military Attaché, his presence in the Embassy would be crucial to the decision-making process which would undoubtedly follow. He would catch up with the Station Chief later.

* * * * * *

0700 Hours

Djakarta's inhabitants had no idea that there had been an attempted coup d'etat until Radio Republik Indonesia's early morning broadcasts announced that Lieutenant Colonel Untung had arrested several high-ranking Army officers. The surprise announcement went on to advise that Untung had initiated these steps to pre-empt similar action by the Council of Generals themselves. The capital was stunned to discover that those responsible, acting under the banner of the 30th September Movement, had already taken control of many strategic positions in and around the city. The station's listeners were then advised that there would be a Revolutionary Council established to take control of government. A decree was then issued, the first of several, abolishing the Dwikora Cabinet and demanding that all officers who previously held the rank of lieutenant colonel or higher, write immediately to the Revolutionary Council, pledging their loyalty to the new authority.

It became apparent that the communists had successfully executed their coup d'etat and were now in full control of the city, if not the whole country. As the capital's population became aware of the ramifications relating to the communist take-over, so did the rest of the world. Communication centres around the globe became alive with the news that the world's fifth largest population had suddenly fallen under the control of Chairman Aidit and his Communist Party.

The Naval Chief Petty Officer had arrived at the Embassy and immediately realized from the activity that he should have maintained contact. He was rushed into the radio room where he was greeted by a mountain of priority signals requiring immediate despatch. The Chief threw himself into the task and, within five minutes, no less than five listening stations had caught his signals. The first of these was an Army NCO who was about to go off shift from what had been another relatively boring night at his station in 7 Signals Regiment in Toowoomba. He was looking forward to the weekend and, when he picked up the tiny radio beeps, he looked around the section quickly, believing at first that someone was playing a prank. Then he wrote the code down quickly. The signal had been designated 'FLASH' in terms of priority. As the entire text became clear, the corporal tore the message from his pad and raced this quickly to the officer on duty who grabbed the red telephone, and within seconds was communicating directly with the Director of Military Intelligence in Melbourne.

Around the world, signals intelligence intensified as, station by station, codes were decyphered and verification was sought of the alarming news. In Singapore, all leave was cancelled as the British Forces went directly to full alert. The Vulcan bombers, having returned but a few hours before from a run over the archipelago, were refuelled and sent back into the air as the crews awaited further instructions. At Butterworth in Malaysia, the RAAF went to red alert status, as the squadron of Sabres was moved out of the hangars. RAAF Central Command in Canberra flashed signals around the country placing Australia's limited Airforce, too, on red alert. A squadron of Mirage jets left the ground from Williamstown and headed directly for Darwin.

The United States Airforce Commander at Clarke Field read his revised orders for the day and swore. They had already scheduled fifteen more flights into 'Nam for the day and now he had been asked to place one squadron on stand-by in the event that these B-52's may be required to strike at the Madiun Airforce Base where the Indonesian TU-16's sat threateningly, ready for flight. By 0900 hours, the West was ready. All that remained was to wait and see which way the communists would move.

* * * * * *

1000 Hours

Those few members of the Communist planning committee who understood something of military strategy had always suspected that their only weakness would be the lack of experienced military leadership within their ranks, once the coup had commenced. Their initial putsch had, indeed, been relatively successful, considering that many units committed earlier had failed to appear. As the morning progressed, the Communists were elated to discover that they had, in fact, achieved control. Radio broadcasts convinced the populace that the PKI had taken over the Government, and Military Commanders throughout the country waited for orders as confusion continued, due to the loss of their most senior officers. Communist elements within regional Military posts moved quickly to establish control, removing officers and disarming those who were not supportive of the 30th September Movement. And then, due to lack of direction, the Communists vacillated.

Chairman Aidit had always believed that, once his forces had established control over strategic targets within the capital and arrested or removed the members of Nasution's Council, the President would then throw his support behind their Movement and the battle would be won. When Soekarno left his wife Dewi's house in Selipi that morning, he drove directly to the Halim Airforce Base to meet with the coup leaders. He remained there throughout the morning and it was at this time that he was informed that Operation Takari had not been as successful as was first reported. Reluctantly, the communist officers revealed to Soekarno that they had mistakenly kidnapped one of Nasution's adjutants, believing that the officer was in fact the four-star general.

The President was livid. Immediately, he knew that the communists could not win, as Nasution could easily rally the Army behind him and, once this happened, he had no doubt that his old foe would initiate steps to remove him as President. Soekarno decided to cut his and the PKI's losses. He ordered General Soepardjo

424

to cease all military action in support of the coup to avoid further bloodshed. The general refused, knowing that once a military operation lost momentum, it would most certainly fail. Many within the PKI leadership elected to ignore the President's demands, although Colonel Untung feared that by doing so the Communists could not achieve the level of support they desperately needed to maintain control. The Revolutionary Council entered into heated debate and, incredibly, the leadership collapsed and the coup fell into limbo.

Untung believed that not having captured General Nasution was the major contributing factor behind his President's failure to continue support for their cause. In consequence, he despatched elements from the 530th Battalion to return to the city and search for the missing general. Soekarno then announced the appointment of a caretaker Chief of Army Staff, naming Major General Pranoto to replace Yani. The President believed that he could trust Pranoto as the man was known to have close relationships with the PKI leadership. Before six o'clock that afternoon, another decree was broadcast advising that the President was well, and had assumed leadership of the Armed Forces as well. A signed copy of this decree and that of General Pranoto's appointment was then sent by messenger to the Strategic Reserve Forces' Commander, Major General Soeharto.

Soeharto was advised that the President required the presence of Pranoto immediately, at Halim. Although Soeharto was junior to Pranoto, he was the KOSTRAD Commander and refused to permit the officer to leave, resulting in a stand-off. Thirty minutes later, still suffering from the shock of his daughter's death and his spirit near broken, Nasution arrived at the KOSTRAD headquarters. He had remained hidden in the home of his neighbour, the Iranian Charge de Affaires until he was satisfied that it was safe to venture outside these premises which were protected by diplomatic privelege. But before leaving this sanctuary, he held secret talks with members of the American Embassy whom he had alerted as to his predicament. It was the Americans who later informed him of his daughter's demise.

At KOSTRAD Headquarters, Nasution discussed the tense situation with Soeharto. They had both been informed that the President had summoned others to join him at Halim, in a show of solidarity. Helicopters had arrived carrying the Minister and Chief of Police, Inspector General Sutjipto Judodihardjo and the Minister and Chief of Naval Staff, Admiral Martadinata. There were others too, who had heeded their President's call, including the Deputy Prime Minister, Dr. Leimena. It was obvious to Nasution and Soeharto that these men were communist supporters, and that their presence was an attempt to consolidate the PKI's power.

An hour later, an ultimatum was delivered to the communist forces at Halim to either surrender, or prepare to be attacked by the full might of Soeharto's Strategic Reserve Forces Command. The message was ignored. Soeharto then sent one of the President's adjutants with a letter in which he advised that he, and not Pranoto, would assume leadership of the Army. Soeharto also advised Soekarno that he should deal only through him, and that it would be best if Soekarno left Halim immediately as KOSTRAD was preparing to attack the communist forces at the Airforce base.

Major General Soeharto then ordered the RPKAD, the Army's Paratroop Regiment, to retake and occupy all positions which had fallen to the communists. In less than an hour, Soeharto's soldiers had routed the enemy forces and retaken the radio, television and other communication centres. The coup was all but over. Soekarno reiterated his demands that the communists cease any further attempts to take control, and then left Halim before it came under attack. The Airforce Chief of Staff, Air Marshall Omar Dhani attempted to convince Soekarno to follow him to Central Java but the President refused, recognising that he should remain close to the capital. Just before midnight on the first day of the failed coup d'etat, President Soekarno left Halim Airforce Base by car and was driven directly to the Bogor Summer Palace. Upon arrival, his adjutant phoned General Soeharto who acknowledged the President's whereabouts. Soeharto then moved on the collapsing communist forces at Halim. He attacked at 0300 hours on the morning of the second day of October, less than twenty-four hours after the communists had made their first move on the Council of Generals.

Just one hour before the Government forces attacked, the Chairman of the Indonesian Communist Party, Comrade Aidit, climbed aboard an AURI aircraft and fled Halim Airforce Base, for Djogyakarta in Central Java, leaving behind remnants of his shattered dream for a communist state. Brigadier General Supardjo proposed that their forces remain and defend Halim, to the death, against Nasution and Soeharto. Air Marshall Omar Dhani suggested to Colonel Untung and his right hand man, Latief, that AURI and the 30th September Movement integrate their forces to protect Halim, but the Airforce Chief was left alone as Untung and Latief fled, also to Central Java. The dispirited soldiers watched in dismay as their officers deserted, many changing into civilian dress as they fled from the Halim camp known as Lubang Buaja, the Crocodile Hole, where Yanti and her Gerwani troops remained, ready to fight.

* * * * * *

1100 Hours

Murray woke with a start, his heart racing as he sat upright in the bed.

'Tuan Mahree, bangun! You must wake up!' the voice called, somewhere in the back of his brain. Suddenly he realised that it was the *djongos* calling from outside his bedroom door. He jumped out of bed quickly and tore the door open, not quite knowing what to expect. His ankle throbbed painfully.

'Tuan, there is a driver outside. You must go to the Embassy now, it is urgent,' his houseboy explained, concerned that he had woken the tuan when he so obviously needed rest. Murray thanked the man, threw water quickly over his face and changed. He looked at his watch and swore loudly. On his way through the house he checked the phone and found that the lines were still out of order. Murray hobbled out to the waiting car and climbed in as the driver gunned it recklessly. It wasn't until they'd reached the corner that Murray realised the barricades were gone. He turned quickly, and observed that the street which had been full of soldiers just hours before, was now deserted.

He ordered the driver to stop, then reverse the vehicle back down the street. The driver slowed, when they came up to his gates thinking the tuan may have forgotten something but Murray insisted that they continue backing down the narrow street past his own villa. When they came to where General Harjono lived, Murray ordered the driver to stop. From inside where he sat, he inspected the area surrounding Harjono's house. It was deserted.

'*Sudah pergi, tuan, semua,*' the driver said, explaining that the occupants had all vacated the villa. Murray thought about this for several moments then instructed the driver to return to the Embassy. During the short time he had slept, life in the city had moved on, and quickly, he observed. The general's family must have been moved. Murray then realized that this would explain why security had suddenly disappeared from his street. He looked at the driver and smiled dryly, remembering just how quickly information passed through the drivers' network. He took advantage of this to bring himself up to date on events as they made their way to the Embassy.

The Embassy was alive with activity as officers scurried around their sections, yelling at each other, frustrated by the congested communications system, and the absence of many of the local staff who had opted to remain home with their families. The Consul waddled around officiously calling out to all, reminding them of the standing orders governing behaviour during such crises. It was his responsibility to contact all registered members of the Australian community and warn them of the dangers of leaving their homes. The telephones were a disaster and, in the absence of sufficient drivers to convey messages by car, the Consul had no idea how he could carry out his duties effectively.

'Oh, Murray,' he called, spotting the First Secretary on his way through the lobby. 'You are wanted in the Ambassador's office. There is a prayer session under way,' he said, checking his watch as he spoke, 'and they've been at it for more than an hour already.'

'Damn!' Murray muttered under his breath, changed direction and went straight to where the other senior Attachés had gathered. The Ambassador's secretary spotted him approaching and rose from her desk to escort him into the meeting.

'You're very late,' she whispered as he smiled tiredly at her.

'Slept in again,' he said, grinning, knowing that she would not believe this possible at this time.

The secretary knocked softly, then opened the door permitting Murray to enter the inner sanctum. All heads turned as he limped in, acknowledging his presence with a nod or a mumbled greeting. The Ambassador peered over the top of his glasses at the man he disliked most in the entire Embassy.

'Where have you been? All departments were advised of this meeting more than two hours ago,' the Ambassador complained. Murray deliberately ignored the senior public servant and apologised instead to the others.

'Sorry gentlemen,' he said, 'have I missed much?' Zach jumped to his defence.

'I can fill you in later. Right now we are trying to assess where we're at, in terms of the communists' strengths and whether or not they will be able to hold onto the gains they've made. As Army Attaché, I have to say that I'd never have believed it possible for the communists to take the city as quickly as this.' The colonel pointed to the map of Djakarta on which some of the known communist positions had been marked. 'What is surprising,' he went on, 'is that there has been no apparent counter-attack from any of the TNI forces. It's almost as if there is no opposition.' He then looked at Murray and, recognising the signal, passed the floor to him.

'Gentlemen, the lack of opposition is probably a result of Government troops not having commanders.' He had their attention. Even the Ambassador frowned, confused by the statement. 'There is strong evidence to suggest that the communists have been very clever indeed. I believe that they first moved to remove most of the Military's senior officers even before occupying these positions in the city,' he nodded in the direction of the map. There was a brief silence as those present considered his opinion. Then the Consul spoke.

'What evidence would that be, Murray?' he asked. Murray cleared his throat before answering.

'Our intelligence suggests that the PKI made a move late last night to arrest members of Nasution's Council of Generals, and perhaps other high-ranking officers as well. We know there was an attempt on General Harjono's life during the early hours of this morning. There is sufficient evidence to suggest that others, including Nasution himself, could already be in communist hands.' Murray turned to the Military Attaché. 'Wouldn't this account for the fact that there has been no response from the Government troops? Why hasn't Nasution appeared to reassure the public, and where is their Army Chief, Yani?'

They considered what the Station Chief said. Was it possible? It sounded highly improbable that such senior officers could be taken as easily as Murray suggested. Some voiced doubts.

'The radio broadcasts confirm that the communists are in control of communications, radio, television and lord knows what else. If Yani and Nasution are still around, why don't they just take those positions back?' Murray repeated, feeling a sense of frustration at the inability of the others to understand what was happening. There was a knock at the door and the secretary interrupted.

'Group Captain,' she said, addressing the Air Attaché, 'I have been asked by your Assistant, Sergeant Cooke, to advise you that there has been a further broadcast from Radio Indonesia. He says that the general text of the message is another Revolutionary Council decree stating that the ...' she hesitated, checking her notes, 'ah, the Dwikora Cabinet has been declared officially disbanded, and that the Communist Party has President Soekarno at Halim. The President is reported to be safe and well, and continues to direct the affairs of the Government on behalf of the people.' She finished reading the message, then slipped quietly away.

'Seems that Soekarno has thrown his lot in with the Communists,' the Counsellor suggested, breaking the silence. The others in the room merely nodded, considering the enormous implications of this information. They all knew that the situation was bloody serious. Soekarno's open support for the Communists against his own Military could tear the country apart. In the light of this news they discussed, for some time, the final format of a communiqué to be sent to Canberra, the essence of which contained the respective opinions and recommendations of the joint military Attaché's, diplomatic and political sections. A final draft was circulated early in the afternoon and Zach and Murray, who had eaten nothing all day, sent one of the drivers out to buy *nasi goreng* with *sate*. They ate the roadside food straight from the banana leaf packets, understanding the risks, but too preoccupied to care. As the afternoon progressed, the mass of intelligence matter had grown. They remained huddled together, listening to communist radio broadcasts while they re-examined the data from reports flowing in from friendly stations around the globe. Hours passed without the men becoming conscious that night had fallen. Zach suddenly said something which caught Murray by surprise.

'They've blown it, Murray! The communists have lost the initiative. Look at this!' he said, showing Murray the British Embassy report compiled by their own Defence Attachés. It showed quite clearly that, having ensconced themselves in the major centres, the Communists had done nothing with their military gains and had, in fact, withdrawn from several strategic locations due to lack of logistic support. The coup was already crumbling. British listening stations in Singapore and Malaysia confirmed that the Indonesian Army signal traffic had been sent in clear language, and most indicated that the Strategic Forces along with the Army's para-commandoes were preparing a counter attack. It seemed to be an incredible turnaround in just a few hours. What would happen now? Another hour passed as they mulled over possible outcomes. Finally Murray leaned back in his chair and rubbed his face vigorously. He was tired. And annoyed.

There had been nothing back from Central Plans and he could not understand why. The city's postal communication services had all but collapsed but the Embassy still had its radio channel open. ASIS traffic would have been awarded first priority, Murray knew. There had been no response whatsoever from down south and he was annoyed with the breakdown in communications. He was surprised to see that it was already well into the evening. Murray gazed across at his companion. Zach looked like he had not slept for days.

'That's it,' Murray said, pushing his chair back from the desk and stretching. 'I'm away from here. Do you want a lift down to the hotel?' he asked, hoping Zach would refuse. There were no drivers available and he really did not want to be stuck entertaining Susan. Steven Zach smiled and said nothing. He too stood, stretched and then smothered a yawn. He placed his hand on Murray's shoulder, then left the building. It was almost midnight, too late to telephone Susan. Zach went home to catch up on some well-deserved sleep.

Murray followed not far behind the colonel as he too signalled a *betjak*. He listened as they moved slowly along the street where Zach had saved his life just the evening before, amazed that so much had happened in such a short time, and without leaving any signs of what had transpired. As the *betjak* driver turned into Djalan Serang, it seemed impossibly quiet. Murray climbed down from his ride and looked in amazement down the deadly silent street.

He had lived in Indonesia long enough to know that violence lay waiting, just below the fragile surface. The *betjak* peddled away with an occasional clang as the driver warned others of his presence. His gaze then returned to the scene where he had almost lost his life. Twice. Then he looked back down towards General Harjono's deserted home and wondered if, in the future, anyone would remember that this street had been the scene of the start of the Communists' attempt to seize control of the country.

* * * * * *

1600 Hours

The Gerwani women had slept well into late morning, by which time the euphoria of earlier events had passed away. Hungover and tired, Yanti and her colleagues moved around slowly, listlessly, almost without direction as the general mood throughout the camp changed to one of deep depression. The women experienced an emptiness as they waited for word from their leaders that it was time for them to leave their camp and return to their homes. But, as the day progressed, the word never came. Instead, they watched in disbelief as their President came, then left, and their leaders argued amongst themselves. Night came and, to their dismay, they were suddenly urged to flee. Until that moment, Yanti and the others had no idea that their coup had failed. By the time they were alerted to the fact that Government forces were on their way, it was already too late for many of their number. When the Red Berets attacked, dozens of the young Gerwani girls were simply bayoneted to death as the soldiers stormed through. The brutal attack lasted less than three hours and, as the first rays pierced the dull morning sky, it was all over.

When it was obvious that they were doomed, Yanti had escaped with a small group of her friends along the very same path that she had taken the day before. She led the three young women across the fields, away from the onslaught of Soeharto's forces. The women had discarded their uniform jackets and made their way along the airfield perimeter fence, to an area where Yanti knew it would be safe to hide. There the group remained all through the day, terrified that they would be discovered. Night fell. They had been without food and water since the bloody festivities of the night before. Under cover of darkness, they made their way towards a small group of huts occupied by itinerant workers, and begged for food, but were turned away. Yanti suggested that they separate and make their own way back to their villages as best they could. Two of the girls agreed but the third clung to Yanti, refusing to leave. She had no place to go and insisted on staying with her leader.

The two walked through the night. They had no money, no food, and were in danger of being arrested at any moment by any one of the many passing military vehicles. Their world had been turned upside down and they were lost, with nowhere to go and no-one to go to. And then Yanti made her decision. It would be a long walk, almost twenty more kilometres, but she knew there was little choice. The pair set out together and headed into the city. Yanti knew, that providing they walked through the night, it was possible to reach their destination before morning and, hopefully, before he went to the office. She took her companion by the arm and started to walk, hoping that Murray would not be too upset that she had brought a friend.

* * * * * *

1700 Hours

Susan was of two minds about having missed the flight. She wanted to go but did not wish to leave Steven behind. What had been annoying though, she felt, was being left alone at the hotel. There was little else to do except sit around the swimming pool and eat. When Steven finally managed to call, their conversation was abruptly disconnected by the operator. Susan had finally given up in frustration and left a message with both the operator and reception that she could be located at the pool. By late afternoon she was bored and a little put out that neither Steven nor Murray had made any further attempt to contact her again.

There had been little information available as to what the latest developments were, outside in the streets. Susan decided that she would wait and hear what it had all been about, first hand, once Steven arrived. She ordered another gin and tonic and settled back to enjoy the afternoon rays as the sun galloped on its way to the west. At six o'clock she showered, changed and returned to the lobby, then settled down in the Baris Lounge Bar to wait. By late evening, Susan was more than a little tipsy and decided to return to her room, bored and annoyed with her most monotonous day. All in all, Susan felt, she could not have been abandoned in a more unexciting place. She fell asleep, not knowing that at that precise moment, Major General Soeharto's troops had left the city, and were, at that very moment, on their way to place their stamp on Halim.

And history.

Chapter 22

Friday 2nd October.

Yanti told her friend to be quiet. She knew that soon the morning light would remove the advantage of darkness so they hurried through the city's outskirts, along the secondary roads, arriving at last at Tjikini. Yanti knew that their clothing would probably be enough to warrant closer inspection should they be spotted by the roving military police. She warned her friend, Erika, to be quiet as a foot patrol passed nearby.

When she considered it safe, Yanti grabbed her tired friend's wrist, dragging her across the railway crossing and down the street following the canal. If necessary, Yanti was prepared to throw herself over into the filthy *kali* to avoid arrest. They continued along the street, conscious of the aggressive looks from the many itinerants who lived along the canal's banks. Yanti had counted on their presence, prepared to move amongst their number to disguise their own presence if they should encounter passing patrols. She knew that if they were stopped and questioned, it would be all over for them. They had thrown all of their identification away, knowing that these would most certainly incriminate them if they were caught.

They arrived, exhausted, outside Murray's house just as the night *djaga* was leaving his security post to return home. Yanti held her friend's hand and waited for the servant to pedal off down the street. Then they slipped into the grounds, moving down the side of the building, using the servant's access to the kitchen and laundry area. Yanti knew that the servants did not like her, probably due to Ade's influence. It was still early and Yanti knew that the cook would not have arrived for work, and the other servant who slept behind the laundry would still be asleep.

She opened the side door which was always left unlocked to permit the servants access into the main house. Yanti held her finger to her mouth urging Erika to be silent. Then, opening the interconnecting door to the main guest room, she peered inside.

Satisfied that there were no others present, she then tugged her friend's hand, and went inside. She whispered to Erika to remain where she was, then carefully opened the door leading into Murray's room. As she slowly opened the door, and slipped through the narrow space she had created for herself, Yanti felt the rush of cold air from the air-conditioned room.

The force of the blow as Murray's fist smashed through the darkness almost ripped her head from the rest of her body. The impact threw Yanti back into the wall, knocking her unconscious. She collapsed to the floor. Seconds passed, and Murray had already jumped back waiting for what might follow. He heard someone running towards his bedroom and, as the footsteps approached, he flung the door open quickly, then slammed it shut, with the full force of his body. He felt the heavy door wobble, almost springing back on itself. He heard the muffled cry of pain, and pulled the door back open quickly, ready to kick at whoever was there.

The crumpled body of a girl lay unconscious where she had fallen. Murray, nonplussed at the sight, moved back behind the doorway, listening for any other attackers who might be following. He knelt down in the semi-darkness, moving his hands over the first intruder's body. Surprised, he rose and flicked the light switch.

'Yanti! What the...' Quickly, he scooped Yanti's unconscious body up and placed her on his bed. Then he reopened the bedroom door and examined the other young woman lying there. He lifted her too, and placed her alongside Yanti on the bed.

For a brief moment, Murray stood back and observed the two women. He could judge from their appearance that they had been in trouble. Then he stared closely at Yanti and wondered just what his young friend's contribution may have been towards the communists' attempt to take control over the country. He frowned at the two and shook his head as one would at errant children. He went in search of his servants to have them take care of his two intruders. Murray could have no knowledge that the young women who lay on his bed had played their part in the kidnapping, mutilation, and eventual death of the missing generals.

* * * * * *

Colonel Suhendra parked his jeep so as not to be conspicuous. He was tired and knew it would be extremely difficult to remain alert. The journey from Semarang had taken much longer than anticipated, due to the numerous road blocks already in place as a result of the communist uprising. He had dropped General Prajogo at Djalan Tjendana, not far from where he now rested. The Diponegoro colonel settled back and closed his eyes for a few minutes. He doubted if the people inside would emerge before he could snatch a few minutes rest. He looked across the dark intersection and noticed the movement from the corner of his eye. He sighed, and stretched. As he watched the two wretches cross the road and enter the foreigner's house he suddenly frowned. Then he smiled, wondering just what the two would steal from the Australian's house while he slept inside.

* * * * * *

Meanwhile, Soeharto's Strategic Reserves together with the RPKAD had met with little resistance as they swept across the Halim Airforce Base. When a number of PT-76 tanks trundled across the main runway, the 'Tjakra' battalions retreated without a fight. Then the rest of the communist forces collapsed and ran, terrified as Red Beret troops attacked, swarming all over their enemy's positions. Most of the heavy fighting was all over within hours and the Government troops swept through the area mopping up what was left of the communist resistance. By late afternoon on the following day, Halim had been re-taken and the communist forces completely routed.

President Soekarno remained in Bogor, directing the country's affairs from the safety of his Summer Palace. At no time did he divulge any information as to his knowledge of the whereabouts of the missing generals, although he was most curious as to why he had not been asked. He listened to the Radio Indonesia broadcasts, then back in its rightful hands, and not once had any of the announcers alluded to the fact that Yani and his fellow officers might be dead. The Army had retaken control of the capital, and it appeared that the memory of the communists' unsuccessful coup d'etat would quickly fade away.

* * * * * *

On the other side of the city, Ade sat and listened attentively to the radio broadcast announcing the re-taking of the communications station. She thought about what had taken place throughout the capital and wondered how her friends had fared. She was still annoyed that Murray had made no attempt to contact her. She assumed that his communist friend, Yanti, would have fled the city along with all of her comrades now that they had failed in their attempts to take power from the Government. In a way, Ade was pleased. At least she would not have to compete with her any longer and, with these thoughts in mind, the young Javanese woman continued on her way out to meet with some of her friends. They had all agreed to attend the *latihan* sessions at Subud together. At this terrible time they felt the need for spiritual support. There was another scheduled for the following day, Saturday, and Ade decided that once the group session had finished, she would catch a bus into the city and drop in on Murray. It had been more than a week and she just knew that he would be pleased to see her.

* * * * * *

Murray had left instructions with his servants to let the two girls sleep and, when they awoke, the *koki* was to feed them. The old woman accepted her *tuan's* instructions although she was not all that happy having Yanti in the house. Along with the other servants, she believed that Yanti's presence could only bring trouble. They all knew that it would only be a matter of time before the hunt would start for those who participated in the abortive coup. Servants had their own lines of communication and often they knew what was going on even before their *tuans*.

Murray once again spent most of his day at the Embassy with Zach and the others, discussing intelligence material which had been made available from friendly sources, and generally following through with his own reporting for the teams in Central Plans. He had been surprised, however, that there was only one brief message from Anderson. The tersely-worded text, once deciphered, left little doubt in Murray's mind that the new ASIS Director disliked him.

Murray thought about this as he sipped his cup of Robusta coffee back in his own office. He was growing tired of the whole damned business. Now that Harry was no longer the head of Central Plans, he was somehow unable to maintain the same level of interest and loyalty to the organisation. Ever since his old friend's unexplained disappearance, Murray had been toying with the possibility of moving on, and creating a new career for himself. It was an attractive idea. He had few ties left in Australia and the contacts he had developed over his years as a result of his time in Indonesia would stand him in good stead. Murray decided that, once the pressure was off and the excitement surrounding the communists' failed move on the Government paled with time, he would give the matter some serious thought.

Right now, though, he had to stay on top of what was happening. Or rather what was not happening. He could not understand why there had not been anything in the media concerning the generals who had been captured by the communists more than two days before. Murray suspected that they were most probably still being held as hostages to afford Chairman Aidit and his followers some negotiating power. None of the men had come forward since their disappearance, adding evidence to this supposition. He completed his report which highlighted this conclusion then took it over to Zach's office before he sent it to Melbourne. The communications centre in Australia worked a seven day schedule. Even though this was a Saturday, their messages would be treated as if it were any other work day. They went over the contents together.

Zach read the first part of the report and smiled. 'You're right! These guys have never missed an opportunity to have their pictures in the paper. Suddenly, their names aren't even being mentioned. Something's going on, Murray, and I'll bet your evaluation is spot on. The bastards still have Yani and his mates locked up somewhere and are using them to negotiate themselves out of the mess they have created for themselves.'

'It's interesting that Soeharto seems to have stepped in and is taking a strong position against the communists. Considering their relationship in the past, why do you think Nasution let Soeharto pick up the ball, virtually by himself and run with it?' Murray asked. This question had been on everyone's mind.

'Could be that he's just doing what a good Commander would

do when the other senior officers are missing. Soeharto reports to Yani. The Army Chief of Staff is being held, or so we believe, incommunicado somewhere. Nasution narrowly escapes death and discovers that his fellow members of the so-called Council of Generals have all disappeared as well. Who else could he turn to?' Zach asked rhetorically.

'I don't know, Steve,' Murray said, almost contemplatively. 'When we remember that Nasution is still the senior officer and has the support of the people, why wouldn't he have taken control of the Halim attack?'

'We shouldn't forget that he lost a very young daughter during the bungled kidnapping. Who knows just how much influence this may have had on his own judgement at the time. It is Soeharto's responsibility, as Commander of the Strategic Reserves, to move as Nasution directs. Perhaps we'll understand more as time goes by, Murray. It's bloody difficult to speculate about what is really going through their minds. Let's see what happens when Yani returns. It's my bet that nothing much will change because Nasution's fellow Council members have substantial support from within the Army.' Zach thought for a moment then added, 'I wouldn't say the same for the President, though. He's really screwed up in a big way, this time. Word is, even the junior officers in the Army are yelling for his guts. In my opinion, Soekarno committed a major political error in moving out to Halim with the communists. I was stunned when the news broke on radio, yesterday. It is obvious that he's somehow involved in the 30th September Movement or, at least, he was aware of what the communists had planned.'

'Seems he's set up camp in Bogor. That's more than a little ironic. Nasution once drove a tank up to the Palace steps there and demanded that Soekarno step down as President. Bung Karno talked him out of it!' Murray laughed lightly at the fact that circumstances had almost gone full circle. Nasution was in the capital cleaning up after another of the Great Leader's misadventures. As the ranking officer, it would seem that General Nasution would once again be obliged to confront his President as he had done before. On the steps of the Bogor Palace. Their conversation then turned briefly to Susan.

Zach said, 'I have her booked out tomorrow. You can imagine the trouble we've had trying to get a flight. The airport is jammed with locals with fistfuls of dollars ready to pay any amount to get out. Probably most of them have had some sort of relationship with the commies, and don't wish to stay around. Can't say I blame them. Anyway, the important thing is we'll have Susan out of here by tomorrow night.'

'Great. I'll try and drop in before she leaves.' Murray then left Zach alone and, as it was again already late, he called for a motor-pool driver to take him home. As they drove the short distance to his villa, Murray had little time to reflect on the day's events. The driver turned into Tjik Ditiro and headed for Djalan Serang. Murray observed that traffic was unusually light and, as they turned into his street and pulled up outside his house, he failed to notice the Toyota jeep still parked across the intersection. It had been there all day. He climbed out of the Embassy car and walked down through the servants' entrance, as he had done so many times be-fore. Yanti and her friend Erika were sitting with the cook, eating together. When she saw him, Yanti jumped up to greet Murray and squeezed him tightly as the old *koki* shook her head and walked out of the kitchen.

'*Mahree, you're so late,*' Yanti said, her strong arms encircling his body. He laughed and broke her grip, pushing her back to the seat and the unfinished meal. Although they had obviously washed the clothes they had worn to his house the evening before, Murray could see that they belonged in the rubbish bin. Apart from a slight swelling on the side of her jaw, Yanti seemed none the worse for wear. He looked closely at Erika and decided that she too had been extremely fortunate not to have suffered more serious injuries from his blows.

'*Mahree, do you want something to eat? Erika is a fantastic cook,*' she said, pointing at the other and younger girl with her spoon.

'*No thanks,*' he said, not wanting to cause trouble with his cook. Leaving the two alone to finish their meal, he showered. As the water washed away the day's accumulated tiredness, he thought about what he should do with Yanti and her friend. Murray knew they should leave. But it would make little difference if they stayed another day. It might even give him the opportunity to talk to them about what they had been up to and what they saw at Halim. He towelled himself dry and wrapped a batik sarong around his waist. Then he called the girls into his room to avoid having his servants

441

overhear their conversation.

The girls were relieved when Murray told them they could stay over for another night. This had been in their thoughts all day. They were still scared. He gave Yanti a handful of rupiah and told her to send one of the female servants out to the evening market to buy some clothes. He then spoke to the cook who burst into a toothless smile when he told her to prepare something for him. The two young women went off to inspect their temporary quarters.

When he had finished eating, Murray checked his telephone. The lines were still down somewhere. His telephone call to Susan could wait until tomorrow. Right then he was just too tired to go out again. Murray went to the refrigerator beside his small bamboo bar and grabbed one of the huge cans of Victorian Bitter. He then moved back into his bedroom, and lay on the wide double bed, falling asleep before he could finish the beer.

Some hours had passed when Murray was awakened by an unfamiliar sound. He pulled the bedside drawer open quickly and extracted the P9S. He slipped from the bed and moved through the dark room, then carefully, and slowly, turned the door handle and peered into the dimly lit guest room. Both Yanti and her friend sat cross-legged in the middle of the large room, and Murray could hear that the younger girl, Erika, was crying. He opened the door wider and approached the two sitting on the carpet square, directly under the overhead fan. Yanti turned and saw Murray and immediately jumped to her feet.

'Maaf, Mahree. I'm sorry. We woke you.' It was a simple statement but Murray identified her sincerity. *'We're scared, Mahree,'* she said, then bent down and placed her arm around her friend. Erika looked up then also climbed to her feet.

'I'm sorry too Mahree,' she cried, choking on the sobs as she spoke. Murray looked at them both and realised that the women were not just scared. They were traumatised by the events of the past days. He stepped closer to the two and wrapped his arms around them both, drawing them to his chest.

'Why are you still frightened?' he asked, although he suspected he already knew why.

'Mahree, the servants don't like us being here. We're worried that they will tell the police,' Yanti said. After Murray had retired, she said, the cook had snapped at them both and asked when they would

be leaving. Yanti then forced a sad smile and looked up at Murray. *'We are scared, Murray. You don't understand what has happened. If they inform the police it will be very bad for us. Very bad,'* she repeated.

Murray looked at their worried faces and attempted a reassuring smile. He took them by the hand and led them both back into his bedroom. He knew that this would be sufficient to silence the servants. They would be miffed by the girls' presence but would not even consider informing the police while there was any chance that their *tuan* still enjoyed their company. The two girls undressed and climbed into the huge bed, enjoying the feel of the cool sheets as they slipped between these quietly. He then climbed in alongside Yanti who lay in the middle of the bed. Murray reached for his unfinished beer. The contents were warm but he drank anyway, sipping slowly as his thoughts returned to the warning Yanti had given him, just days before. And then he understood just what Yanti had done for him. She had taken grave risks in order to warn him from venturing outside his villa that night. She had known that there would be troops in his street during the time the Communists planned to kidnap his neighbour, General Harjono. She had also known that he would most probably have been awakened by what was taking place outside and, as a matter of course, would have wandered outside and into the street. She had saved his life. Murray thought about this as he rolled onto his side and prepared for sleep. Soon his thoughts cleared and his breathing fell into a soft deep rhythm. The girls too slept, comforted by Murray's presence. The streets outside also became quiet as the city's inhabitants retired for the day, locking their doors and windows as they went about securing their homes in preparation for the night ahead.

* * * * * *

A hundred metres down the road from where the Australian slept soundly, a car engine broke through the stillness. Kolonel Suhendra then gunned the jeep's engine and drove away, disappointed that he had so little to report. He drove towards the barracks where he knew there would be a bed. He would stop along the roadside and buy something to eat. Then he would rest for a few hours before returning to his post to wait for the Australian to leave his villa alone. The colonel thought about this as he drove away in search of a roadside *martabak* stall. He hoped that this mission would not take too long, as his presence was required back in Semarang.

* * * * * *

Halim Airforce Base, Sunday 3rd October

Government troops were in the process of completing their final sweep through the remnants of the area known as the Crocodile Hole, when they discovered a dry well covered with leaves and branches. Suspecting this was used to hide weapons, the soldiers cleared the well. There, in the gloom, tumbled together like discarded sacks of refuse lay the bodies of their missing officers. News of the discovery swept the capital. And then the whole country. The corpses were removed and photographed, and these in turn were published in every newspaper throughout Indonesia. The people were shocked at the condition of the dead bodies. The suffering of the men before they died was unimaginable. Evidence of the mutilations, some showing testicles removed and eyes gouged from their sockets, proved to be too much for the Indonesian people. The country roared its disapproval, and the Communists were immediately held responsible for the atrocities carried out at Lubang Buaja. When interrogated, the captured Communist soldiers immediately blamed the excesses on the Gerwani women.

As the city awoke to the news of the slaughter of General Yani and his fellow officers, anti-Communist factions hit the streets demanding revenge for what had happened. Within hours, the city streets swelled with incredible numbers of students chanting for the removal of their President for permitting such atrocities to happen under his guardianship. The mood was violent. The people demanded revenge. Terrified by their sudden change in fortunes, the Communists and their supporters immediately went to ground. Known Communist sympathisers were dragged out of their houses and killed. Teachers identified as being sympathetic to the PKI were stoned as they arrived at their schools. Violence continued to erupt throughout the city and finally spilled over into the countryside.

In the first hours following the broadcasts, thousands upon thousands died. Few of these were true Communists.

* * * * * *

At first, when Ade had been shown the early morning newspaper, she refused to believe that Indonesians could do such things to each other. The photographs were most explicit and, as she stared at the mutilated corpses and read the names of the men who had been tortured before they died, Ade cried. Depressed by these atrocities, she felt she could not go to the *latihan* sessions and elected instead to go directly to Murray. She needed desperately to be with him. Ade caught the bus from the station at Blok M, and then a *betjak* from outside the Intercontinental Hotel. It was not until nine o'clock on Sunday morning that Ade walked into the front yard and peered down the small access used by Murray's servants. She hesitated, then decided to enter via the kitchen as she had so many times before.

'*Pagi, ibu,*' she said kindly, spotting the old cook pottering around in her kitchen. The toothless woman looked up, startled, and did not know what to say to the unexpected visitor. Ade sensed that there was something a little strange about her behaviour but just smiled as she continued through the house towards Murray's bedroom. The old cook shuffled outside and called the other servants and explained excitedly what was happening. They all gathered in the kitchen and listened, holding the servery door open just enough so they could hear.

Ade opened the bedroom door and closed it behind her, softly. It seemed that Murray had slept in. He often did on a Sunday. She tip-toed across the dark, windowless room and went into the bathroom. There were no public conveniences anywhere in the city and she had waited a little longer than expected for her bus to arrive. Hearing the noise, Murray awoke with a start, reached for the beside light and then remembered what had happened before falling asleep the night before. He looked across at the two women. They were still sound asleep. Yanti had pulled the sheets across the bed exposing Erika's naked body to the cold air. Murray slipped his feet out of bed and was about to go to the bathroom himself when he heard the toilet flush. He turned and looked at the two girls lying on his bed, and was confused. Then Ade opened the bathroom door and walked into his bedroom.

At first she faltered, then remained still, in shock. Yanti and

another young woman lay on Murray's bed, both obviously naked. She looked at Murray, her face reflecting the disbelief that he
could do such a thing, that he could have these type of women in
house, let alone his bed. Ade shouted at him as he stepped forward and raised both fists and pounded his naked chest, cursing
Murray in Javanese. Both the girls jumped up, startled by the
screams in the confined space. As soon as Yanti realised what had
happened, she grabbed Erika's arm and dragged her into the bathroom, past the screaming Ade, and locked the door behind them.

'*Mahree, how could you do this?*' Ade screamed, her hands now
held in Murray's firm grip to prevent further blows. He could not
believe what was happening. Why did she have to pick this, of all
times, to visit, he thought angrily. He hadn't even slept with the
women! Or, at least, not with Erika.

'*Take it easy, Ade. Just cool down. You know we have an agreement.
You shouldn't get angry. Okay?*' he asked, releasing his grip, hoping
she had settled down.

'*Mahree,*' she cried out loudly, '*you don't understand. Yanti and
her Gerwani friends are all murderers. They killed Bapak Yani and the
other generals!*' Suddenly Murray's stomach felt as if a cold hand
had gripped it. He grabbed Ade by the shoulders and shook her
roughly.

'*What do you mean? How do you know this, Ade?*' he asked quickly,
as she began to sob. Not now, Ade, he thought, not now, hoping
that she wouldn't lose it altogether. '*Tell me, Ade, what do you know
about Yanti and her friends?*' She grabbed his wrists. Murray was
hurting her as he continued to shake her shoulders.

'*Ask your servants to get you a newspaper. Better still, listen to the
radio. The reports are all over the news. They killed the generals, Mahree,*'
she yelled loudly, '*and they even murdered Bapak Nasution's five-year-
old daughter!*' she added, before losing control and breaking into
chest-heaving sobs. Behind the bathroom door, Yanti and Erika
looked at each other, their faces covered with fear.

'*Are all the generals dead?*' Murray asked stunned by Ade's revelation.

'*Yes, Mahree, yes. And you have let that filth stay here, hiding in your
house,*' she cried, accusingly. '*How could you have done such a thing?*'
She felt weak. Murray caught her as she fainted. He lifted her easily and placed her on the bed. Then he grabbed at the bathroom

door handle and pulled angrily.

'*Okay, get dressed. Quickly!*' he hissed as both women rushed past and hurriedly searched for their clothes.

'*Mahree, I'm sorry,*' Yanti started to say but stopped when she caught the look in his eyes. Suddenly she was even more frightened than before.

'*Get dressed,*' he snapped angrily, moving towards the bedroom door, '*then get out there and wait. Don't move from those chairs until I tell you, Yanti or so help me, I will call the police myself!*' Erika grabbed her shoes and fled from the room. Yanti followed as soon as she finished dressing. Murray called to his houseboy and told him to watch the girls. Yanti and her friend were not to leave, he told his excited servants. Then he returned to Ade who, by this time, had begun to recover. He helped her sit up, then rubbed the back of her neck.

'*Are they gone?*' she asked, looking around the room.

'*I told them to wait outside ...*'

'*Mahree, you can't let them stay. You just can't!*' she pleaded, gripping his arm tightly. He felt the nails biting into his flesh.

'*It's okay, Ade. It's okay. I will send them away just as soon as it's safe. You wouldn't want them being caught as they left here, would you?*' he suggested, knowing that what he said made sense. Murray wanted the opportunity to speak to the girls alone. He needed to find out more about what happened at Halim. He dressed quickly and told Ade to remain in the bedroom. Then he went outside and sat with the distressed pair who were, by now, also near to tears. He understood that they probably already knew what would be in store for them once they were caught and taken away to prison. If they were lucky, that is.

'*Okay, Yanti,*' he started, '*I want to hear the whole story. No lies, no embellishments, just what happened.*' She looked at him, fighting back the tears. She hadn't cried for such a long, long time. '*Yanti,*' he said, leaning across and placing his hand on her shoulder, '*I know you probably saved my life the other night. For that alone, I will help you both as much as I can. But you must tell me exactly everything that happened. Okay?*' He waited for her to respond and, catching his servants hanging around in the kitchen with the door slightly ajar, he called his *djongos* and told the houseboy to bring coffee and rice porridge for them all.

They sat together and talked. Murray listened, prompting only when he could see that they had left something out. The girls explained their role in the kidnappings and how the prisoners were taken to the Crocodile Hole at Halim. They lied, blaming others for the mutilations and executions knowing that to do otherwise would not serve their cause. They described how the bodies were thrown down the old dry well, and then covered with leaves and branches.

Erika cried as she told how the Red Berets had killed the Gerwani women. Then they explained how they had managed to escape and seek safety with Murray. When they had finished, Murray went back into the bedroom and spoke briefly to Ade. He told her to remain where she was until the others had left. Reluctantly, she agreed. He then called his servants and warned them not to say anything to anyone, and suggested that if they did and this resulted in the police coming to his home, then they too would most surely be suspected of hiding the girls. When the old cook heard this, she wanted to leave immediately, but Murray managed to convince her that it would be safe, in the long run, to remain. He then sent the *djongos* out to find a pirate taxi, and have the driver park his car inside the yard. Then they waited.

'Where will we go, Mahree?' the girl called Erika asked. Murray looked at her and attempted a smile. He had decided on a course of action which, he knew, depended on assistance from others whom he really had no right to ask. Almost an hour passed before they heard the car pull up outside and the creak of the front gates as the houseboy returned. Murray bundled them into the American sedan and told them to sit down low in the seat without creating the impression that they were hiding. He wanted anyone along the street who may have been watching to observe the vehicle departing with passengers. Murray only hoped that the servants' gossip had not been overly explicit. He had listened to the eleven o'clock broadcast and knew that it would not take too much for even the back streets of Djakarta to burst into violence.

He called Yanti and told her to take the letter he had written, and give it only to the man whose name appeared on the envelope. She had reached up and kissed him but Murray could not bring himself to respond. He knew her account of the deaths of the country's military leaders was essentially a lie. He then gave the driver an excessive amount of rupiah and sent the two former Gerwani women on their way.

* * * * * *

Colonel Suhendra watched with interest as an old Buick pulled up outside the Australian's house, then backed into the driveway. He assumed that the car would remain as the servants had then closed the iron gates. He had seen the attractive young Indonesian girl enter more than an hour before and assumed that she was involved somehow with the foreigner. Then he recalled the unkempt women who, some hours earlier, he had seen slip like thieves into the yard. When he had driven away late the night before, Suhendra had assumed that the two women, after getting what they could, had slipped out again and moved down the street out of his sight.

The scraping sound of metal on metal alerted him. The colonel watched as the gates were opened and the Buick pulled out of the driveway and turned in his direction. He could see that there were at least two passengers in the back seat. He started the jeep and waited for them to pass, then he followed the illegal taxi as it moved sluggishly down the street.

* * * * * *

Zach sat opposite Susan as they ate their way through lunch. He had already finished and she felt he had rushed his meal. Suddenly it seemed that everything was going wrong again, just as before. Her flight was scheduled to depart at five-thirty. Susan thought that he was overly preoccupied with whatever was happening outside.

'Is it really that serious?' she had asked in response to his comment that they should leave plenty of time to get to the airport due to the unrest.

'Worse,' he had replied, abruptly.

'Do you want to leave now?' Susan asked. There seemed little point in his staying. They still had most of the afternoon to kill and it was noisy around the pool. Sundays attracted a larger crowd than usual and Zach would have known most of the faces present. He ordered another drink as the waiter passed by and tilted his head politely in Susan's direction to see if she too wanted her drink topped up. She nodded, lifted her half-finished gin and tonic and finished the remains of her fifth drink for the day. Susan was not happy.

Actually, she thought that he should be punished. After all, Steven had shown her so little attention since her arrival, leaving her to spend so much time alone. All in all, she thought, the trip had not had the remedial effect that she had anticipated. She looked across at Zach and wished she could read his thoughts. She noticed other women casting admiring looks. He was handsome, intelligent and she cared for him. But she was annoyed. He seemed to be so distant. There had been little opportunity for them to have any real time together on this trip. Susan was not impressed with the excuses he had given. The streets had seemed relatively quiet. The stories of some coup and the country's upheaval were all lost on her. It seemed to her that there had been far more street violence the last time she had visited than what was evident now. Maybe he had already become bored with the relationship, and was too embarrassed to say. Susan knew she was becoming tipsy, but didn't care. She looked at him and suddenly realised that their romance had mainly been the result of her own loneliness. Then she thought of Harry and wondered if he was really dead, or had he just run away. Susan knew that it wouldn't have been another woman in Harry's case but felt bitter about the way she had been left in limbo. She smiled at Steven and wished that they had met elsewhere and under entirely different circumstances. Her own world was full of uncertainties. She wasn't even sure if she was still legally married or even had a husband. Somewhere.

Their drinks arrived and Susan finished hers before Zach was halfway though his. Then she stood and asked Steven to take her back to her room. Somehow the magic had vanished and she wanted to leave. The special moments they had enjoyed together would always be just that. An interlude. Steven Zach had merely filled a vacuum in her life, although looking across at the handsome man, Susan knew that it would be most unlikely she would be attracted to anyone as powerfully again. In that instant, she knew what she must do. Susan smiled and placed her hand on his. He looked at her and smiled back. Had he read her thoughts? Then they strolled slowly back to her suite and waited together through the afternoon until it was time to leave. There was no suggestion that they would make love. Later, when there was nothing left to say to each other, Zach escorted Susan to the airport.

* * * * * *

Murray had not told Ade where he had sent Yanti and her friend, and she didn't ask. Satisfied that they were gone forever, Ade had eventually left his bedroom and wandered around the house, letting the servants see that she was still there, and very much in control of the situation.

Almost 12 kilometres to the south, the ageing Buick coughed and hesitated as the poorly-maintained fuel lines restricted the flow of fuel to the engine. The passengers sat quietly in the back of the sedan while the driver worked on the problem. An hour later they continued on their way, and were pleased to discover that their destination was not all that far from where the car had broken down. The driver entered the compound and stopped directly inside the front gates. He had already been paid by Murray, but this was as far as he wanted to go. The two girls scrambled from the taxi and went in search of the man whose name was on the envelope Yanti carried.

Outside the entrance to the Subud complex, Suhendra stopped his jeep and left it alongside the road. He then entered the unguarded centre and followed the two women he had seen leave the Buick. It was obvious to him that they had never been there before. They appeared lost. After some minutes he observed that they were met and taken across a small parking area surrounded by Banyan trees. Then they were ushered inside a chapel-like building. He waited. The afternoon dragged on slowly and he became restless with the inactivity. It seemed to him that the two he had followed would not reappear. Then, when he was about to leave, suddenly, they both emerged. For a moment they stood talking to an old man dressed in white robes. They walked towards the compound's main entrance. He followed.

* * * * * *

Yanti and Erika had spent the time inside waiting for Murray's letter to be delivered, and read. As the afternoon slowly passed they had become increasingly worried, at the uncertainty of their situation. Finally, they were escorted through the building and across a garden to a small pavilion set in a pleasant landscape. They removed their shoes before entering, and were ushered into a small room, devoid of furnishings. Inside, they discovered an old man, sitting alone, as if in prayer. He looked up and smiled, then indicated that they too should sit on the *tikar* carpet. They did as instructed. Immediately, Yanti felt at ease in the presence of the guru. She sensed a warmth emanating from him and, without knowing why, knew that they would be safe in his care.

She had taken Erika's hand and sat, cross-legged, and watched as the old man had taken Murray's letter and read it slowly. After a time, he rose and smiled at them both, without speaking. It had felt as if they had only been in his presence for no more than a few minutes but, when he ushered them outside, Yanti looked at her watch and was startled to see that they had been sitting there, alone and at peace, for more than an hour. Neither of the two could remember speaking during their time in the small chamber, and yet both recognised that some exchange had taken place. As they bid farewell to the guru, they were given directions for where they should go next.

When they left, Yanti and Erika walked from the compound and looked for some form of transport. They had been instructed to stay with a family on the outskirts of the city and were also given a letter for the people who would take care of them until the situation changed, permitting their return to their own villages. As they waited, they were observed. Suhendra watched as they looked around for transport, and waited. Two hours later, he followed them to the small house on the road to Bogor, and concluded that this where they would remain. He then returned to Djakarta, and reported what had transpired.

During the early evening, a team of Red Beret soldiers raided the house and arrested all of those present. When the owner resisted, he was shot. Then his wife screamed at the soldiers and she too was silenced as they beat her to the ground with the stocks of their rifles. The two women who had been followed from the Australian's house were taken into custody and escorted to the Military detention centre, where they were interrogated. They were beaten with a rattan cane until their bodies were covered with blood.

The questions continued. Erika, nowhere near as resilient as Yanti, broke first. As she cried out in pain and finally admitted to their complicity in the kidnappings, Yanti knew it was all over. She was taken into the adjoining cell where the punishing interrogation continued. Each time she regained consciousness, Yanti would be thrashed again, the strokes ripping through her flesh.

She collapsed in agony, only to be revived by her interrogators. They wanted her to tell them about the Australian but she had nothing to tell. She sobbed, choking on her own blood in a valiant attempt to convince them that they were only lovers, and that he was not involved with the Communists. They refused to believe her, continuing with the brutal flogging until finally, unable to withstand any further punishment, Yanti bit through her own tongue then collapsed. The interrogator rushed outside, then returned before she could choke on her own blood and pierced Yanti's tongue with the piece of wire, then ran this through her cheek to prevent her from swallowing the muscle. Yanti never regained consciousness. When it became obvious that neither of the two Gerwani detainees could be of further use, their battered and bruised bodies were dragged from the interrogation centre and they were placed with a number of other prisoners.

As the first morning prayers were called, the ten-man squad took their positions and waited for the command to fire. They raised their automatic weapons and looked down through the sights at the seven women who lay on the ground not twenty metres away. In the distance a voice carried through the air, breaking the morning silence, calling the faithful to prayer. As the words *Allahu Akhbar* reached the ears of those who believed and followed the teachings of *The Merciful One*, the morning air exploded with sounds of rapid fire as the soldiers squeezed the triggers of their recently-acquired American rifles.

As the sun forced its way into the sky and the morning light touched the trees, then roof tops across the city, Ade murmured softly and moved her body closer to the warmth of the man she loved.

Chapter 23

Djakarta

It was appropriate that the murdered soldiers be buried on the very day normally reserved for parades and celebrations to mark Armed Forces Day. The city's inhabitants flocked to the main thoroughfare to observe the funeral procession as it passed on its way to the Heroes' Cemetery, Kalibata. There was an eerie silence as the six caskets were paraded slowly through the capital. But the city would have little time to mourn. The morning papers carried more photographs of the murdered generals, which further inflamed the people against the PKI and those associated with the 30th September Movement. Accusations were made suggesting that Indonesia's minority Chinese population had prior knowledge of the PKI's plans, and these were underlined by the fact that the attempted coup d'etat coincided with the anniversary of Mao Tse Tung's Peoples' Republic of China. A groundswell of anti-Chinese feeling grew quickly, fuelled further by leaked reports relating to the secret arms supply agreement put in place by the Air Force Chief, Omar Dhani. As demonstrations continued to sweep the country, the Chinese locked their shops, barricaded their homes, and prepared for the worst blood-letting the country had ever known.

Reports of the President's meeting in Bogor had already filtered back to the capital. Soekarno had summoned the nation's leaders in an attempt to restore solidarity amongst the warring factions, but he had failed. The President had then issued a statement condemning the 30th September Movement, and called for a day of national mourning for the slain officers who were the first victims of the failed coup. The six officers were then officially declared Heroes of the Revolution.

Two more days passed before Soekarno called an interim Cabinet meeting. A further statement was then issued further condemning the Communists and their Revolutionary Council, while appealing to the nation for calm and continued support for the real Revolution against Neo-colonialism. On the ninth day of October, just eight days after he had fled Halim, President Soekarno left the safety of the Bogor Palace and was flown by helicopter back to Djakarta. At all times, the responsibility for his safety remained with units of the tarnished Tjakrabirawa Guards. Soekarno then attempted to restore the country's leadership to what it had been prior to the failed communist movement, but discovered a formidable opponent who refused to permit the re-instatement of left-wing elements into the Government. A struggle for power commenced behind closed doors and, on the 14th day of October, two weeks from the day of General Yani's murder, Major General Soeharto took his place as Chief, and Minister of the Indonesian Army.

* * * * * *

A remote village in Java

The villagers all gathered to hear what their *lurah* had to say. As they assembled together in the *balai kampung*, the village meeting place was unable to accommodate everyone, compelling many to stand outside. This was the third such meeting called by their leader. Following both the first and second assemblies, there had been discussions as to what they should do and, unable to reach their traditional form of consensus, a further meeting was agreed upon to provide the entire village with the opportunity to have their say. Outside, stacked in rows for the gathering to see, was the arsenal of American weapons sent to them from the sky. The head man had ordered that the boxes be moved out of the village meeting hall and opened, for his villagers to see.

Mothers, delicately balancing baskets of cloves, garlic and peanuts on their heads, stood, holding their children. Most of the older women chewed betel-nut as they listened to the village elders have their say. The well-worn dirt yard which was the *kampung* square was dotted with blood-red lumps where the women had spat out the glutinous remains of the mixture of chalk, tobacco and *gambir* nuts. Produce was left unguarded across the square where their central market provided a communal outlet for all their needs. It would be a rare thing for someone to steal from another in this village. They lived together peacefully as had their parents before them. And, like their forebears, these people followed the strict teachings of the Prophet Mohammad and the Holy Koran.

There was a hush as the *lurah* called out to the villagers to listen. He was their unchallenged leader. He could read and write, and knew more about the outside world than any of their number. More importantly, he ensured that the people followed the dictates of their faith. He raised his right hand and indicated to the villagers that the meeting had commenced.

'We have heard from the elders and now you must have your say as well. Many of you sat with me and listened to Bung Karno as he spoke of the evils of those who would destroy our land. These people are called communists,' he said fiercely, then even louder, *'and we all know where they live.'* The *lurah's* statement was met with a roar of approval for they knew just who he was referring to. The people who lived over the mountain in the village they called Kampung Kali Ketjil were obviously all involved with what had happened. They prayed to a different god and had even attempted to bring that influence into this village.

'Last night we listened to the radio and heard how the evil these communists have introduced to our land has spread through the country. We heard our leaders tell us that we must help them prevent their influence from growing further. We also heard them say that the only way to ensure that we remain safe from the terrible influences of these godless people was to remove the evil from our soil, as one would tear a diseased plant from the ground.' The villagers murmured loudly in support.

'We have been warned. There will be no further harvests unless we act now to remove these weeds which threaten our families and children. And like the diseased plant that would spoil the others we must act and follow what has been said. We must tear these plants from the ground, right down to their diseased roots!' The villagers roared again.

He continued to speak, and the people became even more excited. Their anger grew, and the mood became violent. Several of the village men started shouting that it was time to act, and a loud cheer followed the suggestion that they take the weapons and chase the Communists and sympathisers away. The villagers' appetite whetted, and consensus finally reached, the *lurah* agreed to lead the men on an armed attack across the mountain, and into the nearest village.

The following morning, as women prepared for the day and children played in the dirt outside their modest dwellings, the people of Kampung Kali Ketjil were attacked by the neighbouring villagers. The small Catholic church was razed to the ground and the priest's decapitated head was placed on a pole outside his place of worship. Volley after volley of gunfire could be heard reverberating along the small river as men, women and children were slaughtered during the raid. The village was then burned to the ground and the river boats destroyed. The attack had lasted no more than two hours. The last survivors were dragged from their hiding places, dismembered and left in the village square as a warning. Then the *lurah* led his men back across the mountain. The following week they mounted yet another attack, venturing much farther afield, where they again destroyed an entire community simply because some of the villagers had converted to Christianity.

Across the nation the story was much the same. As the weeks progressed, reports of mass slaughter and terror reached the cities. The entire archipelago erupted into an horrific nightmare of blood feuds and genocide, fuelled also by the likes of Colonel Sarwo Edhi who moved his RPKAD troops through Central Java, destroying villages and whole communities suspected of being communist or sympathetic to their cause. And, as civil war continued, tens of thousands of young children fell victim to the policy of destroying communism down to its very roots. Most were murdered simply because one of the members of their family might have been seen in the company of a known communist. Villages attacked each other settling old scores, families attacked neighbours over the most minor of disputes, and brother killed brother out of sheer sibling rivalry.

In Bali, the people living on the Island of the Gods moved quickly, slaughtering a greater proportion of the population than in any other part of Indonesia. They killed many of their own, but also took advantage of the situation to remove all signs of Javanese presence from their island. The carnage was to continue unabated, finally dribbling to a close more than one year later, leaving in its trail more than half a million dead and many more maimed or scarred for the rest of their lives. Even Djakarta City was not spared the marauding gangs. They plundered the countryside, running amok as they broke into houses, killing the occupants and burning their homes to the ground. Not even houses under the umbrella of diplomatic status were safe. Several of the foreign legations lodged official complaints concerning attempts on their staff.

It was on the evening following the announcement of Soeharto's appointment as the new Army Chief that Murray learned just what it was like, to wake suddenly in the dark, and discover that one's house was on fire.

* * * * * *

It was the smoke which first alerted Murray. He coughed, waking immediately to the acrid smell that had crept under the door and slowly enveloped the room. He fumbled for the bedside light and squeezed the switch. Nothing happened. The air inside the room was sticky and then he realised that the airconditioner was also not working. He moved through the dark and unlocked his bedroom door. A cloud of smoke billowed through the doorway followed by flames. Shocked, he closed the door. Fighting down the rising panic, he stumbled through to the ensuite bathroom and turned the tap. Nothing. He cursed. The water pump would have ceased functioning the moment power had stopped flowing. His mind raced quickly.

Murray moved back into his bedroom and groped for the bedside table. He opened the drawer, located his wallet and passport and placed these on top of the table. Then he extracted the P9S from the back of the drawer. Valuable seconds were lost as he stumbled around in the dark, finding the wardrobe, where he quickly ran his fingers over the clothing. He pulled at the denims and put these on. Then he took one of his T-shirts and made his way back into the bathroom, removed the top of the water cistern, then dipped the shirt. He threw some of the water over his face and body, then slipped into the wet clothing. Making his way back into the bedroom, Murray shoved his documents inside his back pocket and the automatic inside the waistband of his jeans. Feeling around on the floor, he discovered the casuals he had worn the day before.

He slipped these on as well, then readied himself for what he knew was waiting outside.

As Murray opened the solid teak door he was hit with the full force of the fire. The heat was incredible and he held his hand up to cover his face as the searing blast of air sucked the oxygen from the room. He slammed the door shut again, and groped around for the towel he had thrown down after showering the night before. Murray grabbed it, then ran back into the bathroom and immersed it in the remaining cistern water. He wound the towel around his head and neck, then opened the door once more, and, without hesitating, ran blindly through the area of the house which he knew like the back of his hand. The heat sucked the air from his lungs but he continued through the smoke-filled room as the ceiling collapsed above the wall adjoining the kitchen. He grabbed at the door handle, screaming in pain when the metal burned deeply through flesh.

Fear gripped him, but he stepped back and then lunged forward, smashing the door with all the force he could muster. There was no air and Murray knew that he was about to pass out. He threw himself through the kitchen and kicked furiously at the external door, bursting thankfully out onto the small pathway alongside the house as the door timbers folded under his weight. He struggled to his feet and stumbled the few metres down to the servants quarters where he found his houseboy lying on the floor. He staggered around feeling for others who might have stayed over with his *djongos*. Satisfied that he had been alone, Murray lifted the small frame and threw him over his shoulder. Then he headed out along the narrow passage used mainly by his servants, until reaching the front garden. He stumbled, regained his footing, then fell again. Murray reached down and grabbed the houseboy by the arm and dragged him the rest of the short distance out onto the street where a large crowd had already gathered.

He dropped his houseboy on the far side of the street and then fell to the ground, sucking in deep breaths of air. He looked for his security guard amongst the onlookers but could not see him anywhere. Murray shook his head knowing that the man would have disappeared to avoid being blamed. He had probably fallen asleep, Murray guessed, and had panicked when the fire had broken out.

There was an explosion somewhere out the back of the villa

and the crowd ducked as flying debris landed near where they stood. Murray guessed that there would be more, knowing that there were at least three gas bottles stored behind the building. A servant from down the street who was friendly with Murray's *djongos*, tugged at his arm and drew his attention back to the unconscious servant. Murray asked the young man to take his injured friend down to his *tuan's* house and care for him there, away from the fire. The flames had reached well into the sky, lighting the whole area as Murray watched the roof cave in. The neighbours had already left their house waiting anxiously to see if the fire would spread. It didn't. By morning it had burned itself out, leaving only the brick walls standing as evidence.

Murray had remained around until the fire had burned itself out. He had no telephone, no car, and no servants. Or at least, not until his old cook had arrived and, even then, once *koki* discovered that her place of employment had been destroyed, she too had to be assisted, overcome by shock. He then went down the street to check on his *djongos*. Murray was worried that the houseboy had not reappeared that morning. They had been together for some years and Murray treated him, as he did the old cook, almost as if they were family. He approached the house and could see that a number of other servants from along the street had gathered to check on their friend. As Murray moved into the driveway, he sensed that something was wrong. He pushed passed the servants blocking the side entrance and entered the small room. His *djongos* lay on his back on the narrow bed. He was dead. Murray moved across to the body and bent down to examine his small friend. In the early morning light he could see the look of anguish on the man's face. One of the servants pointed to a minute puncture hole low on the houseboy's back.

Murray checked the small wound and concluded that the weapon used was probably a knitting needle. Murray had heard of similar killings before. He knew this style of killing was quite common amongst the cross-boy gangs which had suddenly emerged during the past weeks. One of their number would merely walk up behind their intended victim and drive a knitting needle deep into the lower back, leaving only the smallest of puncture holes as evidence of an attack. Often the victims would feel a sharp stabbing pain and continue walking without realising that they had been seriously wounded, until finally collapsing, as their insides filled with blood from the wound. Then, like Murray's houseboy, they would die. The Station Chief rose and placed his hand on the body, nodded silently at the still face of his servant, and friend. He clenched his fists and swore silently, knowing that the man before him had been murdered. Somehow, he had to put an end to his feud with the Diponegoro soldiers, even if it meant going back to Semarang to speak to the men there.

He stepped outside and spoke quietly to the owner of the house. Murray thanked his neighbour and assured them that he would bear the cost of funeral arrangements. Then he walked down the street watching for a passing *betjak*. As he stood on the intersection of his street and Tjik Ditiro, he noticed that something was out of place. Tired and distressed by what had happened, Murray shook his head and, out of habit, rubbed his face.

He heard the clanging bell of an approaching *betjak* and waved. He then climbed aboard. As his driver peddled slowly away, Murray turned back and looked across his shoulder, without knowing why. Suddenly he remembered what it was that didn't fit in the scene back at the intersection. It was the jeep. The jeep was missing. And then the thought struck him. Every day, as he had been driven to the Embassy over the past week, he had noticed the Army vehicle as the Embassy driver had slowed each time before turning into Tjik Ditiro. It had not really registered before. There had been too much else on his mind.

He tried to recall returning to his villa each night, and whether or not he had sighted the jeep as his driver turned into Djalan Serang. The more he thought about it, the more convinced he became that there had been something there, waiting. Waiting for him. Suddenly he experienced a familiar chill pass down his back. He leaned forward to see if anyone followed. Then he felt for the automatic, still tucked away inside his jeans.

* * * * * *

Murray was surprised when he detected the hesitation in Zach's response. He had telephoned and asked if it would be all right for him to bed down at his house until the Embassy could find somewhere suitable for him to stay. He had spent his first hours cleaning up at the Hotel Indonesia. Then he had gone directly to the Embassy and submitted his report to the Ambassador, through the Consul. Murray had reported that the fire was accidental, caused by a leaking LPG bottle. A more detailed copy was then despatched through his own channels directly to Central Plans in Melbourne. He still did not reveal that there had been another attempt on his life.

Before heading off to replace his sparse wardrobe, Murray dialled the colonel's extension. He had expected a warmer response to his suggestion and immediately regretted having asked. He really needed a friend right then and was disappointed with Zach's obvious reluctance to have him around.

'Anytime after tomorrow, Murray, okay?' Zach had said. 'I've got something on my plate right now. Anyway, a night in the hotel won't do you any harm.'

'That's fine, Steve,' Murray had replied, wondering why he couldn't move directly into one of the three empty bedrooms in the Military Attaché's residence. Then the thought struck him that Steve probably had a woman staying over and was embarrassed because of Susan. Murray smiled and shook his head. The following day, Murray moved into Zach's residence.

* * * * * *

The United States Embassy

The resident CIA Station Chief, Samuel Preston, was not at all happy. He read through the classified reports and shook his head at the incompetence of the so-called Military advisers on Embassy staff. These were the same so-called experts who had been unable to ascertain who was doing what to whom over at Halim when the commies had taken charge, and then told the Ambassador that General Yani and the others were most probably alive and only being held as hostages. And, before that, dropped weapons into unfriendly hands, delivered equipment mistakenly to the communists and, if all that wasn't enough, had five of their number arrested and thrown into jail for breaking the goddamn local curfew! He chewed angrily on his unlit Havana, reading through the remaining reports.

When he came to the blue-coded files, he pushed everything else aside and snapped the cover of the first document open. There was a recent photograph attached to the inside cover sheet. He examined the man's face, and then eyes. First he read the running observation report on Colonel Steven Zach. Then he read the recent communications on Stephenson. When he had finished, he took the files and personally returned the sensitive documents to CIA/Per/Only registry and lodged a security error breach against the officer who had left the highly-classified documents on his desk unattended. Then Preston bit through the soggy tip of the cigar and spat into the rubbish bin beside his desk. With a well-rehearsed movement, the Chief flicked his Zippo lighter and held the flame to his Havana. He drew on the cigar until the tip glowed, then inhaled deeply. Satisfied, he went on with business.

Over in the adjacent building, the United States Ambassador to Indonesia sat across from the major general and nodded to his interpreter. The young State Department officer, not quite equipped for the idiosyncrasies of the Indonesian language struggled, as he attempted to pass the gist of what his Ambassador had said to the Indonesian officer. They had picked him to act as interpreter only because of his security clearance. There was no-one in the entire Embassy capable of interpreting fluently at this level. His head ached. They had been at it for over an hour.

'General, the United States Government wishes to thank you for what you have said today.' He then checked his notes. 'Hmmm... We wish to say that we applaud your efforts in removing the communists who threaten your country. Hmm...We wish also to say that although we have heard conflicting reports concerning the.... the exaggerated numbers of dead, the United States Government have no... sympathy for those people and we... encourage your Government to continue with its valiant efforts to...' again, he checked his notes — 'continue to... eradicate the communists. We pledge our support to you, and send our President's personal congratulations to you on your recent appointment. We look forward to the future and a time when we are able to discuss more...hmmm... concrete proposals concerning Defence Co-operation. Thank you.'

Major General Soeharto merely smiled. These were the words he had expected to hear. There would be more accolades, he knew, but not at this time. He rose, shook hands with the Ambassador, and was escorted down through the private access used for moments such as these. The Ambassador then called his secretary and asked for a few minutes before his next appointment. He spent a few quite moments alone, thinking. He mumbled a short prayer while holding his father's Bible, which had been passed down to him when his father had retired from the ministry. He then spent a short time washing his face and hands before returning to his desk. Refreshed, he signalled his secretary that he was ready.

When his next guest shuffled into the private reception area, the Ambassador stood until the older man had settled comfortably in the matching deerskin-covered chairs. They talked for more than an hour together before the guru rose and smiled at the American, then shuffled back out of the magnificently appointed chamber.

The Ambassador leaned back in his thick leather chair and reflected on his two recent visitors. It was obvious that both were leaders with strong convictions. He was convinced that each would achieve a very strong following some time in the future.

As he recalled their responses and reactions during the private discussions, the Ambassador was amused to discover that his two visitors were actually very much alike. He stretched, then leaned forward and lifted the photograph on his desk. Then he looked across at the wall decorated with flags and a photograph of Lyndon B. Johnson watching from the wall, and smiled. The President was preoccupied with his escalating war in Vietnam. That left the team from the State Department to do practically whatever it wished in Soekarno's Indonesia.

Chapter 24

CIA Headquarters, Langley,
Virginia U.S.A.

The agent was burdened with the knowledge that his KGB masters would believe that he had revealed details of the Soviet network inside the CIA. Interrogation techniques could easily extract such information. The mole also knew that the KGB would use him as an example and punish his son who still lived in Moscow.

If it had not been for the ongoing background noise which always affected those working on this level, many more agents would have heard the shouts, moments before the loud shot. Instead of throwing themselves to the floor as they were trained, the few amongst their number who immediately recognised the sound for what it was, turned towards the gunshot and stared in disbelief. Senior Agent Richards along with several others had yelled as the officer jumped to his feet, placed the .38 Police Special to his mouth and pulled the trigger. Immediately, the senior administrators moved to damage control.

The dead agent had known the moment he had been confronted with the evidence. Intuition had told him that there was something wrong. He had sensed it for days. And then, out of the blue, he knew he had finally been discovered. He elected not to face the mandatory weeks of interrogation. Consequently, he took the only steps which he believed would convince his superiors back in the Kremlin that he had not betrayed his country. His son would be safe.

Senior Agent Richards had moved quickly to squash all speculation about the man's motives, citing a terminal disease and associated stress. The Director had called an urgent meeting of his departmental heads to review their options. The active operations which had been running at the time of the Soviet mole's suicide were discussed. As a result of the agent's suicide, the CIA had discovered that an operation, similar to their own, had already been initiated by the Soviets. Only the targets were different. Any such action by the Russians had the potential of jeopardising years of American planning. The United States Government's most valuable resource within the Indonesian Military had come under threat. Someone had given the order to kill Soeharto, a leader who had suddenly become one of the most powerful men in his country. And if he died, responsibility for his death might well be laid at the feet of the CIA.

* * * * * *

Semarang

The Siliwangi and Dipongoro Commands had worked together planning their operation to support the anti-Communist sweep through the island of Java. In the first few weeks following the failed coup, Colonel Sarwo Edhi had already cut and slashed his way through most of what he claimed were Communist communities. Reports of his RPKAD Para-commandoes cleansing operations had already accounted for tens of thousands of so-called 'enemies'.

Brigadier General Prajogo was pleased with the course of events. The communists had made their move first and failed. Now, under new leadership, the Army would see that the PKI would be removed from the country forever. He thought about the Council of Generals and the deaths of the six officers. Although saddened, he now believed that their demise had served their country well, creating the necessary groundswell required to move against the communists in the harshest way. He was particularly saddened by the news of the death of Nasution's daughter and was pleased that officers such as Sarwo Edhi had extracted their revenge on those who had supported the treacherous PKI.

His thoughts turned to the Australian who apparently led a most charmed life. The general firmly believed that the Communist threat was still very real, and as long as elements existed which continued to support Soekarno's soft stand against the Left, the Republic would remain in danger. He looked at the daily reports and re-examined the annotations made by his aides. There was a request to accept a courtesy call from a visiting foreign officer on tour through Java. The general knew what that really meant.

The foreigners were becoming restless with the reports that Sarwo Edhi's cleansing campaign had been excessive. He had read several of the foreign press clippings charging that the Indonesian Army had embarked on a campaign of genocide, spear-headed by the RPKAD colonel. The request to visit had been accompanied by the Deputy Chief of Army Staff's recommendation supporting the tour and, in consequence, the general had little choice but to agree, even though it conflicted with other arrangements, already in place. He signed his name approving the Military Attaché's visit, then read the BAKIN intelligence report on the officer, Colonel Steven Zach.

* * * * * *

Djakarta

Zach could tell that Murray was keeping something back. He looked across the table at his friend and waited, but the Station Chief remained silent. When Zach had advised those present at the Wednesday prayers meeting that he had received approval to tour Central Java, Murray's initial reaction had been very supportive, but later had turned to one of concern. They had just finished dinner. The Embassy still hadn't found suitable accommodation for Murray and he had remained at Zach's house while the search went on.

'Why don't you come with me?' Zach suggested. 'I'll only be gone for ten days or so.'

Murray looked at the other man and seemed to be considering the idea. He played with a toothpick.

'I could do with a first-hand assessment of what's really going on around Solo and Surakarta,' he said, then added, 'They got Aidit today. The info came in just after you left.' Zach hadn't heard. Without their Chairman, the PKI had no real leadership left.

'I'd like to be present when they interrogate him,' the colonel smiled, knowing just how impossible that would be.

'He's dead. They took him out as soon as they discovered who

469

he was,' Murray said.

'I'm not surprised. There were most probably standing orders from above to ensure his silence. Aidit would have had information on many of the boys still sitting close to the top. They'll be running scared until this business is over, once and for all.' Zach poured himself some more coffee.

'Soekarno is keeping the game alive, Steve,' Murray said, discarding the broken toothpick. 'Don't hold your breath waiting for the Communists to just give up and go away. They know that their very survival might depend on the President's goodwill. Or even on those who secretly supported their Movement but now find themselves between a rock and the proverbial.' Zach listened to Murray. The man's understanding of how the Indonesians thought was second to none in the Intelligence community.

'Will you think about coming with me? It'll give you the chance to show off some of those places you're always bragging about.' said Zach, urging Murray to agree. 'We could swing back through Bandung on the way back from Semarang instead of going along the coast.' At the suggestion of the port city, Murray looked up quickly. He thought he'd caught a flicker in his friend's eyes. He was tempted to accept.

Murray knew that he had to resolve the ongoing problem with the Diponegor officers in Semarang. If only he could sit down and talk with them, he just might be able to settle their differences. He was sick to death of peering over his shoulder the whole time. Since the fire, he had not noticed any further surveillance of his movements. Perhaps whoever was directing the feud had decided that enough was enough, although Murray knew that this was probably wishful thinking on his part. He sat thinking about Zach's offer. If they were together, Murray believed that he would be safe, although he was not entirely comfortable with the prospect of taking the chance just to find out.

'And you won't even have to interpret for me,' Zach was saying, as Murray half-listened to the other man's encouragement. It might be the solution to his problem. He had an idea.

'If we're going together, best put my name down as your official interpreter. If the Army approves my travel, I'll go.' Murray then looked up and smiled at the grin on Zach's face. They had become good friends. Murray trusted the man.

'Great,' the colonel responded, grinning broadly. 'I'll have the W.O. process the request first thing tomorrow morning.' He clapped his hands together, then went in search for one of the servants. They needed more wine. As Steven Zach wandered out of the dining room, Murray considered his decision and hoped he had not been too adventurous in electing to throw himself into the enemy's camp. Zach returned with another bottle of claret and they sat together talking, sipping the red wine, while the servants cleared the table. When they had finished, the men went to their respective rooms and threw themselves into bed. Having consumed his fair share of the wine, Murray had little difficulty sleeping. Within moments of closing his eyes, the gentle hum of the airconditioner lulled him to sleep, and he dreamed of his first trip to the magical islands surrounding Pulau Putri, and the special moments he had enjoyed while still a student at the university. Then his dream twisted, becoming convoluted, and the mood changed. Suddenly he could see Yanti running along the sand, calling to him as she was chased by soldiers, but he was unable to help. His feet were being held as he tried to swim the few metres back to the beach to help her, and each time he attempted to kick free, his body would sink a little further into the deep water. And then he was cold. Very cold. And the dream changed as he was chased down the street by a crowd of servants who had gathered and called out to him, accusing him of killing his houseboy and, as he ran to escape, his path was blocked by a row of soldiers wearing the insignia of the Diponegoro 7th Regiment. And then he began screaming ...

Murray awoke with a start. He was covered in sweat yet the cold air-conditioned air continued to blow across his body. He sat up and shivered, then the waves of nausea rose through his stomach and he knew that he was going to be ill.

The following morning he had recovered from the attack but still appeared grey around the face when Zach sat down to have coffee with him. They rarely ate a real breakfast, not that Murray was in any condition to do so this day. Zach shot an enquirng look across at the Station Chief but Murray recognising the look, just shook his head in disgust.

'I was going to suggest you shoot your cook,' Murray attempted to make light of his debilitating attack. Few expatriates successfully completed a tour of the country without at least one serious illness during their stay. Zach smiled knowingly and left Murray behind, offering to send the driver back later. At ten o'clock Zach telephoned to see how he was.

'Are you up to some good news?' he asked, pleased that his assistant had been able to wait for the approval and return with the travel warrant already signed. The Army protocol section had merely added Murray's name to the colonel's already approved tour, as he was listed as the Military Attaché's interpreter. No other formal clearance had been necessary. Zach promised to send the driver straight around to bring Murray to the Embassy.

He went back into his bedroom to change, while thinking about the tour with Zach which would take him back to Semarang, and the Diponegoro officers. He knew that his dream had been a result of the seafood they had eaten but couldn't help thinking that perhaps there was an omen there somewhere. 'Omen indeed! You've been here too long, my friend,' he said to his reflection as he dressed in front of the mirror.

* * * * * *

Murray knew that it would not be appropriate for him to have Ade stay while he remained in Zach's house. He had no doubt that the colonel would have agreed had he asked but, understanding how the Military functioned, Murray believed that having an Indonesian girl stay over at the Attaché's house would most definitely be frowned upon by the wives. He knew that gossip had ruined more than one officer's career over the years.

There had been little opportunity for Murray to take time to catch up with Ade since his house had been burned. She had discovered what happened only days after his narrow escape, and had telephoned him at the Embassy to see that he was unharmed. He had taken her to the Tjahaja Kota restaurant twice but they had not been able to spend the night together. Neither had mentioned Yanti's name although Murray wondered how she had fared. He thought it probable that she had managed to return to her village and remained in hiding, out of reach of those who continued to search for all who were involved in the Crocodile Hole massacre. Murray hoped that she was safe. He could not understand what had driven Yanti to be party to the mutilations at Halim. Ade, on the other hand, tried not to think about her. Secretly, she hoped that Yanti was dead.

As he would be departing for Semarang within a few days, Murray sent her a letter with one of the drivers, suggesting that they meet at the Hotel Duta for an early dinner. He would rent one of their rooms and then spend what he could of the evening with her. The driver returned within the hour with her reply. She would meet with him at the hotel.

That evening, as they lay awake together, Murray told Ade that he would be going away with Zach on a tour through Central Java.

'Why are you going, Mahree, isn't it still too dangerous?' she asked. There were reports of continued fighting between the Army and the communists.

'Well, Zach asked me to go, and I agreed. Besides, his Indonesian is not as good as he thinks,' Murray lied. He had to provide some reason for accompanying the Military Attaché. Ade appeared to accept this and he changed the direction of their conversation, knowing that it was difficult for him to justify venturing through Central Java when fighting had been reported as being so heavy. He needed to establish just how strong the Communist resistance really was, as Central Plans had expressed concern that the information being passed out by the Indonesian authorities had been drastically altered in their favour. Once Murray had alerted Melbourne that he would accompany the Military Attaché on a tour through the area, he was immediately given a list of target information requirements from his superiors.

They left the hotel together before midnight, promising to meet as soon as Murray returned from his tour with Zach. He was pleased that he had made the extra effort to spend the evening with Ade, deciding that all in all, he was very lucky to have her around.

* * * * * *

Embassy of the Union of the
Soviet Socialists Republic, Djakarta

Colonel Kololotov sat thinking about the last directive he had received from Moscow. The report had been hand-delivered by courier and included recommendations from the Head of KGB activities for S.E. Asia, General Konstantinov. The former Canberra-based Russian spy chief had become the first senior KGB officer to be promoted to that rank while still serving outside the USSR and, as Kololotov knew, this made the regional head one of the most influential members of the *Komissia Gosudarstvennoy Bezopasnosti*, the KGB.

The colonel was concerned about his career. Bring stuck in Dja-karta during the current problems was proving to be disastrous for him. Chairman Aidit's premature move against the American supported Council of Generals had not only resulted in the demise of the Indonesian Communist Party, but had greatly strengthened America's position in influencing Indonesian affairs. Senior Military officers on whom the Soviets had pinned their hopes to move their Government back into the Kremlin's fold had suddenly been removed or shuffled away from positions of any real power. Years of building relationships with the Indonesians had all but been lost. The PKI's failure to remove General Nasution and the death of the others had only precipitated a sudden rise in anti-Communist feeling throughout the country. To the Soviets' dismay, much of this was also directed at the USSR. When mobs of angry demonstrators crowded their Embassy, the Kremlin had been furious. At least they had not burned the building, Kololotov thought, remembering the damage done to the Chinese Embassy days before. Yes, his masters in Moscow were most unhappy with the current state of affairs in Indonesia. Alarmed by the sudden swing towards their enemy's camp, the Russians had demanded that swift action be taken to correct American initiatives to subvert Soviet influence in the Republic. Kololotov had been ordered to follow the directive now sitting in the folder on his desk.

He sighed, knowing that what they had asked would most probably cost him his career if he failed. And his life, if he was not careful. With this thought, he unlocked the top drawer of his desk and checked that the 7.63 Mauser was fully loaded. The German automatic lay there with its spare ten-round magazine. He lifted the heavy weapon as if gauging its suitability for what he had in mind, moved the safety with his right thumb, then laid it gently back in the drawer. Kololotov then re-locked the desk and leaned back in his chair, looking over his left shoulder into Djalan Iman Bondjol where he could see a convoy of military vehicles moving towards the roundabout.

The Embassy's double-glazed windows all but eliminated the siren's sounds as he observed two military police motorbikes clearing the way for the speeding vehicles behind. Kololotov snorted in disgust as he recognised the assortment of Soviet, American and Japanese equipment knowing that there had been a shift away from using his country's hardware only because the Indonesians could not pay the country's massive debt to their Soviet benefactors. He watched as the convoy entered the roundabout and then cut across the road directly into the Hotel Indonesia. Surprised, the KGB officer unlocked his desk again and reached for the binoculars there. He turned back quickly and adjusted the focus slightly, just as the well-guarded figure emerged from the second vehicle, and walked confidently up the Intercontinental's steps before disappearing from view. Kololotov leaned back in his chair again, unconsciously chewing the binoculars strap as he wondered about the man's sudden rise to the Army's most senior post. Then, he shrugged to himself and reached back into the desk to replace the glasses knowing, that in a few more days, it would no longer be an issue. Kololotov recalled the Kremlin's conclusions as to how this officer's name might have been overlooked on the night of the kidnappings. But he could not support their findings. Nobody, he believed, could really be that stupid. The colonel had lived in the dark world of subterfuge and lies long enough to realise that even in a land where people thrived on the mystique, the simple explanation of how that general managed to be overlooked on that fateful night just did not wash with him. He was convinced that there had to have been another agenda, and that it was most unlikely that he, or any other than those directly involved, would ever know the truth of what really transpired during that night.

Suddenly, he sighed. These thoughts were taking him nowhere. Kololotov pushed the subject aside and returned to the tasks before him. He had much to do before leaving on his trip. The KGB colonel telephoned downstairs and confirmed that he would be requiring one of the unmarked Embassy sedans. Then he picked the dossier and file up from his desk and went down the passageway to discuss his journey with the Political Counsellor. He would require his assistance in accessing the huge safe in the Ambassador's office where funds for all covert missions were kept under lock and key. Kololotov knew that the Counsellor would require time to arrange the cash and have it all checked, before surrendering such a large amount to him. As he made his way through the second storey of the Embassy, the KGB colonel wondered if things would really change once he had effected payment to the man. His superiors on Dzerdzhinsky Square obvious thought so, believing that they really had very few other options. They had proposed the plan and left the details for him to arrange. He had cursed them all when he had first been advised. The task they had given him was practically suicidal. Security around the capital had become virtually impenetrable since the kidnappings. The KGB colonel had instructed his source inside Army Headquarters to keep him informed, and finally the news he had hoped for, came. There would be a brief tour outside the city. He knew that they must take this opportunity, away from the watchful eyes of his bodyguards. The Americans would then be blamed.

Kololotov knocked, then entered as the voice inside answered. He then went together with the Counsellor to make arrangements for the US Dollars he had been instructed to deliver to the officer in Semarang, wondering as he did so whether their man in the Diponegoro really had what it took to see the assassination through.

* * * * * *

CIA Headquarters, Langley, Virginia

Senior Agent Richards left the meeting with the Director and immediately returned to his own office where he drafted messages to his Station Chiefs in Djakarta and Australia. When he had finished, he personally carried the signals over to the communications centre where he identified a familiar face and motioned for the cipher clerk to approach.

'I'll wait while you do these,' Richards advised, handing the messages to the woman. 'And Jean,' he added, before releasing the pages, 'there will be no copies and no logged despatch for these. Okay?' The request was unusual and she raised an eyebrow in surprise. Richards had anticipated her reaction. She was one of the centre's best operators and knew how to keep her mouth buttoned. 'Director's orders,' he said, releasing the pages into her hands. Jean then went to work and, less than fifteen minutes later, both signals had been despatched to their addressees. These were not recorded in her work log, and she returned the hand-written pages to the senior agent. Richards thanked the operator and returned to his own office where he shredded the two signals.

Across the globe, the messages were received and passed to their respective communications officers who, upon sighting the addressee's name, alerted the officer designated that there was an encrypted and urgent signal waiting for him in the Embassy. Within half an hour, the messages had been read then destroyed in both Djakarta, and Canberra. The United States CIA Station Chief in the Indonesian capital phoned BAKIN and made arrangements with his contact to meet later that day.

In Canberra, a similar conversation took place and a meeting was set up for the next morning. As soon as he had replaced the receiver, Anderson buzzed his secretary, Madge, and instructed her to book a flight for him to Canberra. Then he sat in deep thought trying to untangle the enigmatic message that had been passed to him, and wondered just what his Djakarta Station Chief had done that had ruffled their American cousins' feathers so.

Chapter 25

Java

Zach leaned forward and attempted to stretch. He was uncomfortable from the many hours of just sitting, with Murray, in the rear of the Holden. They had just finished their brief one-day stopover at Solo, during which time Zach paid a courtesy call on the local Army commander. They discovered there, too, that the story was the same as it had been wherever they had stopped. It was obvious that the local commanders had all been given an identical brief on how to respond during conversations with the visiting Military Attaché. They had learned very little from these officers. Instead, evidence of what was really taking place could be seen along the roadside as they passed through the densely populated centres.

Their tour had taken them up along the central highlands, through Bandung down to Tjilatjap and back up into Djogyakarta. They had spent almost five days on the road before reaching the special area still ruled by the Sultan. Zach had been invited to a small gathering hosted by Hamengkubuwono, the Ninth Sultan who, until recently, had served as a member of Soekarno's Cabinet. Zach had been keen to meet with the Sultan as he believed that they would glean more from any discussion with him than they might from the local garrison commanders.

It had been a frustrating week. They could see that Central Java had suffered badly from the ongoing civil war. When they had stopped at a roadside stall not far from the southern coastal port of Tjtjalap, the *nasi goreng* vendor had talked enthusiastically of the ongoing slaughter of Communists in the neighbouring villages. Zach had not been overly keen when Murray had pushed for a slight detour, one which would take them through the turbulent area.

Ten kilometres down the narrow provincial road, the driver had suddenly braked, refusing to continue. At first, neither of the passengers understood until Zach swore and yelled at the driver to go forward to the next side road, and turn around. Murray reached for his brief-case, reacting to the possibility of danger.

Alongside the red dirt road, stacked as if they were piles of logs, were rows upon rows of bodies. These had been placed, Zach thought, to assist with the count. In places, the piles were stacked more than four to five bodies high, and the rows continued along the village road, almost as far as they could see. Neither spoke. Murray silently photographed the terrifying scene. Zach later said that he had carried out a quick count as they had driven by, estimating that there were at least a thousand dead, stacked off to the side of the road, only partly hidden in the knee-length grass. And these weren't just the bodies of men. Murray's jaw tightened as he identified the bodies of children amongst those thrown onto the piles of dead. It was a grisly discovery.

The driver started to drive faster, as more and more bodies came into view. Neither of the two *tuans* prevented him from doing so. They had seen enough. More than enough, Murray felt, sick to the stomach fighting back waves of despair. It reminded him of images of a Hitler death camp. As they drove away, Murray wondered just how many more would die before the President called a halt to the genocide.

A few days later, they had met with Hamengkubuwono, briefly, in the royal court, and warmed to the Sultan immediately. He asked had they driven through the areas where fighting continued. When he discovered they had, Murray saw a look of concern cross the ageing Sultan's face as Zach described what they had seen. The Australians knew that there was little that the royal leader could do to rectify the situation. His authority as Sultan was severely restricted to the special area of Djogyakarta and its surrounds and, although greatly respected by the people of Indonesia, he was unable to exert any real influence over the Government. Hospitable and gracious, the Sultan had provided escorts while the men remained within his domain. The following day, they left for Semarang.

* * * * * *

Semarang

Pak Didi, the Hotel Istana manager, was excited with the sudden surge in the number of guests. The past month had been disastrous, since few were willing to travel through the country due to the ongoing political unrest. He went through the bookings and checked the names and nationalities against the rooms allocated. Satisfied that all was in order, he then completed the mandatory daily police report and instructed one of his staff to take this down to the station.

The authorities insisted on keeping tabs on all visitors, not just the occasional foreigner who might be passing through. Pak Didi sighed. He had wished that the town had more to offer than just being on the road to Borobudur and Djogya. It seemed that the port city had so little to offer the tourists. Rarely did his guests stay more than one night, using the Istana Hotel merely as a way-station. At least, he thought, collecting a copy of the guest list for his file, there were still some foreign guests willing to brave the countryside and visit.

He then went about arranging for fruit baskets to be placed in the rooms to welcome his foreign guests. It was a thoughtful touch, he knew. Deciding to check on the arrangements himself, the fastidious manager climbed the staircase. He checked the first two overlooking the garden, which he had allocated to the Australian group, and was satisfied that all was in order. Then he moved along the passageway and inspected the smaller room facing the street. He stepped inside and looked around. Pak Didi then turned and left, closing the door behind as he did so.

Then, with a slight display of arrogance, and knowing that he would not be seen, the manager made a face as he walked back down the passageway. Pak Didi resented the fact that he had a Russian booked into his hotel room. In his experience, they had never shown any gratitude for his gestures of hospitality, and besides, he thought they were generally uncouth. Pak Didi knew that, had it not been for the fact that the Istana Hotel was the only recognised accommodations where foreigners were permitted to stay, the Russian would most probably have been just as comfortable staying in one of the local *losmen*. With this thought, Pak Didi went down to the kitchen and cancelled the fruit basket for room 208.

* * * * * *

Diponegoro Headquarters

Colonel Suhendra's stomach growled as he sat nervously, considering how he would have to change his rostered duties with one of the others officers, to enable him to slip away in time to meet with Kololotov. He had been surprised when the Russian had contacted him by telephone. Suhendra lived in continuing fear that he would, some day, be compromised by his Soviet colleagues through their often amateurish ways. He had discovered, much to his dismay, that whenever the Russians had attempted to communicate with him, over the past four years, their clumsy methods had almost cost him his life. Suhendra recalled an earlier meeting with his Soviet Embassy contact some months before. The stupid fool had simply sent a letter to Suhendra's home instructing him to meet with the Russian in a popular beer garden. When the note had arrived, his wife had opened the envelope and, unable to understand the contents, accused her husband of having an affair. Later, he had still met with his contact. But not at the predetermined location. It was just too risky.

Suhendra had been responsible for revealing Colonel Sulistio's relationship with the Americans. Subsequently, when Lieutenant Colonel Sulistio did not return from one of his evening patrols, Suhendra knew immediately that the information he had passed to his Soviet controller had been effective. They had obviously wasted little time in orchestrating the colonel's demise and, at the time, he was relieved that the American sympathiser was no longer around to complicate his life. This had been difficult enough, what with the frequent visits his Commander made to Djakarta, often insisting that he drive with the general. At least he had been able to do something constructive during the last visit. Suddenly Suhendra smiled as he recalled the success he'd had in observing the Australian's activities during Prajogo's recent visit to the capital. It hadn't bothered him when, after their arrest, he had discovered that the two detainees were members of Gerwani. He had no time for this women's group, even though they were pro-Communist.

Suhendra had been recruited by Kololotov's over-zealous predecessor in 1958, when, along with many others, the Javanese officer had become disillusioned with his country's unsuccessful attempts to prevent the Americans' ongoing intrusions into Indonesian territory. It had not been difficult to influence the young Lieutenant, whose brother had been killed in Sumatra during a coastal patrol off Padang. Indonesian Intelligence had been informed by Soviet sources that the Americans had been offloading tons of ammunition from two submarines along the Sumatran coast. Sadly for Suhendra's brother and most members of his marine patrol, their craft came under fire and was sunk during one such US Navy mission.

Survivors had confirmed sighting the submarines, although the United States Government hotly denied the claims. Suhendra's father had been a communist. He had died in late 1948, during the fierce fighting in Madiun when the TNI brutally prevented a Communist uprising from succeeding. He and his brother had been orphaned. They had barely survived, living hand-to-mouth, along with millions of others. When the time came, they joined the Military. After their country gained formal recognition of its Independence, political infighting had started, throwing the country into disarray. They learned quickly, understanding that they had to be circumspect regarding their political affiliations. Promotions were overlooked by those who were anti-Communist. The young officers both maintained their father's political convictions. However, neither registered as members of the PKI.

At the time they were still young officers, the Americans moved to create a major split in the Republic. Rebellion broke out on several fronts, and Suhendra was soon dragged into the conflict, as was his brother, as members of the fledgling Armed Forces. It was then, as a junior Intelligence officer, that the young lieutenant discovered just how serious the Americans had become in their efforts not only to destabilise the Republic, but to create three separate and independent states under their influence. Then he lost his brother.

Suhendra had been bitterly disappointed with Soekarno's permissive attitude towards those who would drag his country into a pro-Peking communist alliance. He strongly believed that his country needed to remain ideologically identified with the Soviets. Suhendra was convinced that the Indonesian Communist Party would deliver his people into the hands of the Chinese. When news first broke of the Halim massacres, he too wanted to rush out to join in the search for those who had kidnapped and mutilated their own people. But later, he realised that the PKI had, in fact, assisted his own ally's cause by removing those who had steered Indonesia towards American control. And now even the PKI had failed.

Suhendra understood that the events surrounding the 30th September Movement had driven his country's leadership further away from Communism, and that those who now influenced the Government had made it quite clear that Indonesia would never tolerate any re-emergence of the Left in any form. Suhendra fiercely believed that those who had taken charge since the abortive coup d'etat, should be prevented from delivering the country back into the hands of the neo-colonialists. Also, there were the financial considerations. Even a good Communist needed money. He had agreed to participate in the plot which would follow through from where the PKI had failed. Only, this time, he was determined that no-one from their list would survive.

* * * * * *

Army Chief of Staff Offices, Djakarta

Arrangements had been confirmed for Soeharto's flight. At first, he had been reluctant to ask AURI for the use of one of their aircraft, knowing that many of the Indonesian Airforce officers were still loyal to Air Marshall Omar Dhani and the PKI. It was only after he was assured that the crew had been hand-selected by Army Intelligence that the Chief of Staff agreed to fly. His schedule would first take him down to Djogyakarta from where he would then proceed by staff car to Solo and Surakarta. The general wished to see what was happening for himself. In view of this, he would return to Djogyakarta and fly the short distance across the fertile plains, before dropping down to visit old friends. He was looking forward to seeing his former Command, and the officers of the Diponegoro Divisions based in Semarang.

* * * * * *

Melbourne

Director Anderson sat stunned, his face grave as his visitor revealed the startling evidence with its damning implications. He glared at the document holder stamped 'Most Secret - C.I.A. Director Only' across the face.

'I'm sorry,' the American said, sincerely. He had flown down from Canberra then gone directly to the address in St. Kilda Road. The CIA Station Chief looked at the grey-headed Australian and genuinely felt sorry for him. The flurry of activity generated by the contents of the report he carried was nothing when compared with the accusations and soul-searching that had taken place back in Langley, after the suicide. The experienced Chief also knew that if the Australians refused to rectify the problem immediately, then his own people would not hesitate to remove the danger themselves.

'I can't accept this as irrefutable proof that Stephenson is one of theirs,' Anderson said a little too sharply. The American knew that this was going to be tough. No one wanted to hear that they had been betrayed. 'Shit,' he thought, 'if only this man knew the whole goddamn story!' He sat quietly, waiting for the Australian Intelligence Head to get it all out, as he knew he would.

'Granted, Stephenson's been known to be a little unorthodox from time to time in the way he handles his duties,' Anderson went on, 'but we've never been given any reason whatsoever to suspect that he has, in any way, compromised this agency.' The American waited. He knew there would be more before the recriminations started. 'It should be clear to your people that his relationship with elements of the Indonesian Communist Party were a result of directives from this office.'

'Our sources in Indonesia are beyond reproach. There is more than sufficient evidence to support Langley's conclusions. Otherwise, why would we be having this conversation?' he suggested.

'Murray Stephenson is our Station Chief. Langley knows that. Situations are rarely as clear-cut as they appear to be. Aside from his instructions to associate with the communist students and elements of the PKI as an integral part of his cover, Murray Stephenson has never been associated with anyone who could even be considered 'pro-Soviet.' He paused, collecting his thoughts.

'The suggestion that Stephenson might be a threat to Soeharto is, quite frankly, absurd.' He was angry not only at the suggestion that one of his agents may be involved in some plot to remove one of Indonesia's brightest stars, but also because his anger was evident. He had meant to keep his temper.

'I'm sorry, but the evidence does point to his involvement. Even if you're not convinced, our agency is. We should accept their findings,' the American said, not offhandedly. He found it difficult dealing with people who failed to understand that the United States was working in their interests, too. Seemed to him that half of the goddamn world failed to appreciate this. He had been instructed by his Director not to reveal the additional information he carried unless it became apparent that the Australians were reluctant to accept the American findings.

'Your predecessor, Bradshaw, recruited Stephenson, I believe?' he asked, already knowing that this was true. Anderson frowned and nodded, anxious as he watched his visitor push yet another folder across the table. It had the same security warnings blazened across the cover as the other. Suddenly Anderson didn't want to know what was contained in this second folder. He looked at the other man. His eyes narrowed as his stomach tightened. There was silence. Then the ASIS Director snapped the binding away from the document and opened the report.

The inside covering sheet contained a full head and shoulders photograph of his predecessor, smiling as if he'd posed for the shot. For a brief moment, Anderson was taken aback, having already forgotten just how charming Harry Bradshaw could be. He flipped through the preamble and commenced reading the CIA profile report on the man who had been Australia's most experienced field agent and, later, Head of its clandestine Intelligence forces. As he read through the file, even he was surprised at the depth of the information contained in the document. Harry's early life and associates were all well-documented, including extracts of Soviet reports relating to his activities when employed by the British MI6. Anderson paused, removed his glasses and rubbed an itchy eye before returning to the fascinating reading. Then he paled. As he turned the following page, there was another photograph. And another. These showed a considerably younger Harry in Berlin. Anderson was embarrassed by what these photographs obviously inferred. Then he was angry. Why hadn't their allies produced these damning reports before? Why wait until the man was missing, probably dead, before they revealed what they had? Had Harry been compromised by the Americans? Had they been using him as well? These and other questions raced through the Director's mind as he turned the pages, one by one, following the damaging evidence of Harry's dark secrets. He stopped and rose slowly from the long mahogany table and shuffled like an old man over to where coffee and biscuits had been left by his secretary. He poured the coffee and turned back to his visitor. The American nodded. Anderson then returned to the table and placed one of the cups in front of his visitor.

'How long has the Agency had this file on Bradshaw?' he asked, almost casually. The American sipped the dark liquid. He thought it tasted like crap.

'You know how it goes. Everyone keeps tabs on everyone else. In Bradshaw's case, we had him on file ever since he was working with the Brits. You probably don't know this but our boys are paranoid about giving anything to the limeys, and that goes back even before the shit hit the fan with Philby, Burgess and Maclean, just to mention a few. Their MI6 is like a ship full of leaks. Hell, no one wants to deal with them anymore. Bradshaw came to our attention when he worked for MI6. They had him over in Berlin. But you know all about that. To be honest, we didn't know about his little idiosyncrasies until we caught him in Bangkok. Then, due to the sensitivity of our relationships with Australia, we decided to keep him in check just in case your own people weren't doing their job.'

'What happened to him?' Anderson asked, knowing that the Americans had the answer. The CIA officer was taken aback at the bluntness and waited for a time before replying. There was still a great deal more on file which wasn't revealed here in the documents he'd shown Anderson. He crossed his arms and looked down at the table.

'We believe that Boris got him,' was all he said. It was Anderson's turn to be surprised. He had believed his department's conclusion that Harry had fallen victim to one of the groups of thieves which thrived in Thailand by robbing tourists. His body had obviously been dumped somewhere discreet. 'Perhaps even in the crocodile farms on the outskirts of the city,' he suddenly thought.

'The Russians?' he asked, disbelievingly. The American nodded slowly and leaned across to check the second file Anderson had been reading. He found what he'd been looking for and showed the report to the ASIS Chief. Again, there were photographs attached. Anderson read through the pages and then leaned back in his chair.

'We know all about those visits. They were all well-documented at his request. It was, he said, his way of maintaining civilised communications with the Kremlin. I could show you these if you feel they're important. Personally, I believed at the time that Harry should have left the ongoing contact well enough alone, but he was the Director and dictated most of the policy around here while he was in the chair. No, I don't accept that there was anything sinister in these visits.' Then looked across the table. 'Why does the CIA believe otherwise?' he asked, watching the American's face to see if there was anything there which might indicate just how much more they knew. That they weren't telling. Anderson understood how the game worked. His visitor unlocked his arms and placed his hands on the table. Anderson was then certain that there was, indeed, a great deal more that hadn't been disclosed.

'You'll have to leave that with us for the time being. We have something in play, as we speak. When it's finished, I'm sure my Director would be happy to discuss this with you further. In the meantime, he's looking for a reassurance that your man Stephenson will be removed from the area, at least until we can clarify the situation.' Anderson understood quite clearly that this was not a request. He was furious that he would be obliged to agree to their demands. He did not accept their suppositions based on Stephenson's known relationship with the former Director. What they were suggesting was absurd. Ludicrous! But he would have to comply, knowing that to refuse could jeopardise their close working relationship with the American Intelligence Services. Not to mention the danger Stephenson would then be in. Anderson knew that it wouldn't be the first time the Americans had taken out one of their own friendlies whose presence interfered with one of their own operations.

'Stephenson will be told,' Anderson said, unhappy with his own response. His visitor immediately smiled, then rose. He retrieved both the document holders and extended his hand.

'The Director will be very pleased. I will inform him of your co-operation.' They shook hands. Nothing further was said. Anderson walked with the American as far as the first security level and passed him on to his secretary, then returned to his office and thought through his meeting with the Agency representative. Then he waited for his secretary to return to take his instructions. Within the hour, two messages had been encrypted and sent across to com-munications for despatch. These were passed through the encipher-ing machines and coded, then directed through the central des-patch unit located in Canberra.

At the post office in Djakarta, the messages were placed inside small envelopes, and placed in the Australian Embassy box. An hour passed before one of the drivers arrived and cleared the mes-sages, taking these directly to the rostered duty-officer. He, in turn, went immediately to the Embassy and passed the signals through the first stage of decipher, which indicated that the signals were for the political section. The officer telephoned around to locate those concerned, and found the Second Secretary at home. Murray Stephenson, he said, would not be at the colonel's house as they had both left that afternoon by car for Central Java.

The officer went directly into the Embassy and went through the complicated process of deciphering one of the messages as it was, in fact, addressed to him anyway. He placed the other on the First Secretary's desk for when he returned. Only Murray would be able to decipher that particular message as each had their own codes locked in individual safes. Half an hour later, having read his own message, Murray's Number Two went in search for the Chief Petty Officer to see if he could send a most urgent despatch by radio back to Central Plans in Melbourne. He had to inform the Director that Stephenson had left on his trip, and that it would be most unlikely that either he or the Military Attaché would be contactable due to the current crisis. Even at the best of times, tel-ephones rarely worked in the countryside.

At ten o'clock that evening, Anderson sat behind his desk glar-ing at the incoming signal. There was no way he could now pre-vent the Americans from taking remedial action, which is precisely what they would do once they discovered Murray was already on his way to Central Java and could not be recalled. Anderson summoned one of the night-duty secretaries and dictated a message to Langley. He informed the CIA that Murray had been contacted and would be returning to Djakarta.

That night, before he closed his eyes and wished for sleep, the Director considered his decision to mislead the Americans. He'd really had no choice. Stephenson was far from being Anderson's first choice as Station Chief in Djakarta, and he had often held his own reservations as to the man's integrity. Nevertheless, he found the accusation that Murray Stephenson had embarked on a mission to assist with the assassination of the new Indonesian Chief of Army Staff, Major General Soeharto, absolutely incomprehensible.

Chapter 26

Semarang

Zach stepped out of the car and smiled at the porters who hurried out to assist with the luggage. He was pleased to be in Semarang, as it was the last military post he was to visit on the tour. There would be a number of courtesy calls to be made and then, with a little luck, he expected to be back in Djakarta before the end of the week.

'*Pagi, tuan,*' the porters called, almost in unison as they waited for the driver to open the rear of the sedan. The porters were all dressed in white trousers and jackets, with the familiar black *pitji* sitting on their heads. Zach and Murray left them to take care of their luggage and strolled into the large open foyer where they were met by the ebullient manager, Pak Didi.

'*Welcome, gentlemen,*' he said, smiling profusely, waiting to see whether or not he should shake their hands. Many foreigners, he knew from experience, didn't care to do so. Murray stepped forward and extended his hand. Pak Didi was pleased. He had always liked Australians. '*I have arranged two suites as requested by your Embassy. These are adjacent, on the second floor.*' They thanked the manager and then moved to the reception desk where they were required to show not only their passports but also the travel pass issued by Army Head-quarters in Djakarta. They registered, then went to their rooms to clean up before lunch. Zach had meetings arranged for the afternoon and asked Murray if he wished to accompany him.

Murray had thought long and hard about his position, and the danger he would be in once his presence in the coastal town was known. He realised that this would be only a matter of hours, as a copy of the colonel's travel warrant would soon pass from the hotel registry desk to the local police station. From there, they would telephone and inform the local Army garrison of the Military

KERRY B. COLLISON

Attaché's arrival. Chances were, his name might not be mentioned as the accompanying interpreter, and he hoped that this would be so. Murray was anxious to meet with the Commander and establish some dialogue with the man.

He had to convince the brigadier somehow, that he should not be held responsible for the circumstances which led to Colonel Sulistio's demise. He knew that this was imperative for his own safety. The problem was how, as Murray really didn't wish to float in with Zach, unannounced, and place his friend in a difficult position. He had also thought about Steven Zach as they had driven through Java together. He admired the man and respected their friendship. A strong bond had developed between them and, apart from the early discomfort he'd felt concerning Zach's affair with Susan, Murray believed that their relationship had strengthened considerably over the past months. Zach had explained what had happened the day Susan departed. He explained that, afterwards, he'd felt a little guilty at being relieved that she had gone.

It was then that Murray understood Zach's earlier reluctance to have him stay at his house. An embarrassed Zach admitted that he had invited the Ambassador's secretary around to his villa twice, although nothing had come out of the discreet encounters. Later, he had even suggested that he might give their relationship another try, once things had settled down in Indonesia and he could take some real time away and visit Susan in Melbourne. Murray was pleased with this. He understood just how difficult it would be for them both, considering Harry Bradshaw's disappearance. Murray believed that if he was to secure his friend's total support, he would have no choice but to disclose how he had nearly been killed in the harbour warehouse, and circumstances relating to the other attacks. He thought about this throughout their long drive together and finally decided, as they neared Semarang, that he would explain what had happened, and leave it up to Zach to decide whether or not Murray should accompany him to meet the general.

Murray knew that it would be most unlikely for the Diponegoro Commander to agree to meet with the man his troops had attempted to kill. Murray wished he could resolve his problem alone but realised that he really had no choice but to seek Zach's assistance.

* * * * * *

492

Moscow

It was obvious that they had lost one of their most valuable assets. Fortunately, he was not alone in his service to the USSR for, over the years, there had been many within the American Government who were receptive to payments in exchange for information. When their senior agent failed to communicate later that day, the alarms went off, causing officers in the Soviet Embassy in Washington to work through the night.

By mid-morning, their worst fears were founded. Their deep-cover operative had been uncovered. When the news was announced during an urgently-called Intelligence briefing, not one of the officers present even thought to commend their patriot's actions in taking his own life. Instead, they were angry. Coded messages passed back and forth until it was decided that the mission previously ordered to be implemented by General Konstantinov, should be temporarily put on hold. The Soviets suspected that their plans had been compromised. Their mole had been unable to protect the integrity of the mission. They assumed that the Americans had been alerted. The assassination attempt was not to proceed as they then believed that discovery of their involvement would be inevitable. The KGB immediately communicated this decision to their agent at the Soviet Embassy in Djakarta. Colonel Kololotov was already preparing to leave Semarang and return to Djakarta when he received his new instructions. He cursed them all, knowing that he might not be able to contact Major Suhendra again, or in time.

* * * * * *

Diponegoro Headquarters

The Commander smiled cordially as they shook hands. Zach was then introduced to the other senior officers present, including Colonel Suhendra. The courtesy call went well, Zach deciding to avoid any further attempts to pry information from the Central Java commands as to what the status really was in respect to the Communist clean-up. He knew that they would deliberately mislead him and believed that he had already acquired sufficient information for his final report. During the course of their conversations Zach heard the distant sounds of sirens approaching. When it became obvious that his host had another guest, he suggested that he return when it was more convenient for the officer.

'No, please stay, Kolonel,' the Commander had insisted. He was impressed with the Australian who spoke their language, acknowledging the effort it would have taken. *'But you will excuse me while I greet my other guest.'* Zach was then entertained by the other officers for almost half an hour as he sat wondering who was with their Commanding Officer in the adjacent building. He was about to leave when the door opened and the Commander returned. He entered the room smiling, obviously pleased with himself.

'Kolonel, have you met my guest before?' he asked, stepping aside as all the officers present jumped to their feet. Momentarily surprised, Zach had done likewise, standing at attention as a sign of respect to the Chief of Army Staff who had entered.

'Pak General,' he said, waiting for the distinguished officer to make the first move. Major General Soeharto smiled and stepped forward, offering his hand to Zach. They exchanged greetings, then the general turned to the other officers and merely nodded for them to sit.

'So, Kolonel Zach,' the Chief of Staff said, still smiling at the Australian, *'you have been touring through Java. What do you think?'* Zach was surprised by the question and wasn't quite sure how to respond. He smiled back.

'I think your country is very beautiful. I would like to see more,' he replied diplomatically. His answer was well-received. The Major General then turned and spoke to his fellow officer in his own dialect. Zach at first thought this rude, then he remembered that all of the officers present were Javanese.

'Kolonel, you have been invited to join us tonight. We are having a small reception for Djenderal Soeharto.' Zach accepted immediately, acknowledging the honour of being invited to join these men during their private dinner. The function would be held at the hotel where he was staying. Zach was later to discover from Murray that this was the only real venue in town, and that any function held by the Army would most probably be paid for by the local merchants.

They talked for a while longer then, knowing when to leave,

Zach apologised to the officers and departed, returning to the hotel to catch up with Murray. He was escorted to his car by Colonel Suhendra. Zach's driver saw him coming and started the engine to cool the vehicle's interior. The officers saluted each other.

'Thank you for your hospitality, Kolonel,' Zach said, sincerely. 'If you come to Djakarta please contact me at the Embassy. I would be delighted to see you again.'

'Oh, you'll see me before then,' Suhendra suggested, smiling at the confused look on the other man's face. 'I will also be attending the function tonight at your hotel. It is a command performance. All of the senior Diponegoro officers must attend.' Zach laughed, knowing from his own experience what they meant in military terms. They then shook hands and parted, agreeing to speak again later that evening.

Zach's car left the compound and the Indonesian soldier's smile vanished. As he stared after the departing vehicle he wondered how the Australian's presence that evening might interfere with his plans. Suhendra returned to his own office to consider how best to ensure that the foreign Military Attaché's presence later that day would not jeopardise his preparations in any way. It was not in his plans that a foreigner should die. But if he had no other choice, then the visiting colonel would become one of the unfortunate casualties.

* * * * * *

Hotel Istana, Semarang

Murray sat sipping his second beer, enjoying the lobby setting. Overhead fans turned slowly, moving the air gently around the old colonial structure. Rattan chairs, with high and intricately woven backs, were positioned in pairs, facing oval-shaped tables. Orchids sprinkled with deep violet colours decorated the tall columns, while arrangements of hibiscus were carefully placed at each end of the bar. Had it not been for the threatening cloud of depression hanging around as he waited for Zach to return, Murray would almost have been happy.

They had discussed his predicament at lunch that day. Zach had expressed surprise that he'd waited so long to reveal the situation, reminding that the violence could have followed when Murray moved in with him. At first, Steven Zach had been quite annoyed that he hadn't been told. Then, as Murray explained the complicated relationship he'd had with Bradshaw and Central Plans, Zach began to understand why Murray had concealed what had happened from his new Director in Melbourne. They had ordered lunch but neither had eaten. Murray knew that Zach's trust was imperative, and even though Zach had not responded warmly at first, for the first time he felt comfortable with the knowledge that someone else was also aware of the threats on his life.

Steven Zach had been adamant. He could see no advantage to either of them should Murray accompany him during his courtesy call on the local military authorities. They had discussed this at length until both reached the same conclusion. Any approach by Murray would be treated with contempt, as long as the Diponegoro officers still believed that he was involved with the Communists, and may have been responsible for the demise of their Lieutenant Colonel, Sulistio. Finally, Murray accepted, albeit unwillingly, his friend's advice not to attend Zach's meetings with the Army. He remained behind, settled down with a bottle of Bir Bintang and waited for the Military Attaché to return.

Towards two o'clock, he heard a Russian voice echoing through the empty, high-ceilinged lobby. Murray had turned around and spotted Kololotov immediately. Kololotov had been trying to telephone his Embassy in Djakarta and had been disconnected several times while attempting to do so. He had stormed down to the reception and accused the operator of eavesdropping. Murray attempted to look away quickly. But not before Kololotov had caught the look in the Australian agent's eye which told him instantly that he had been observed by the enemy.

The Djakarta-based KGB operative was obliged to leave the hotel and place his call directly from the local P.T.T. When he returned, he passed back through the hotel lobby and observed that the other foreigner was still sitting alone, drinking. Recalling the annoying conversation he'd had with the Counsellor, Kololotov approached reception and informed the staff he might be staying yet another day. Then he went to his room to consider just how he could contact Colonel Suhendra again, knowing that the officer would have left the compound along with the others at three o'clock. He checked his watch and swore to himself. Had communications been what they should, he would have been able to telephone the colonel in time and arrange a meeting during the afternoon. Now he had no other choice. Kololotov knew that Suhendra would arrive at the Hotel Istana around six o'clock for the function. He would wait and speak to him then.

Murray watched the Russian from the corner of his eye and wondered what the Station KGB Chief would be doing in such a place. Certainly there was little for the Soviets here, he thought, remembering the deep anti-Communist feelings which ran through the local community. He considered asking the reception how long Kololotov had been there when he spotted Zach walking up the steps into the lobby.

* * * * * *

'How did it go?' he asked, noticing his friend's discomfort with the heat. There were damp spots under Zach's armpits.

'Better than expected,' he replied, nodding to the waiter who had suddenly appeared. He pointed to Murray's bottle of beer. 'Met Soeharto,' he said, resisting the temptation to smile as he watched his friend's reaction.

'Sure you did,' Murray responded, sceptically. Then he saw from Steven's expression that he was indeed serious. 'No bullshit?' His friend played with him for a moment, almost ignoring the response. He accepted the glass of beer, sipped the thin layer of froth, then placed his glass back onto the round rattan table before replying. He knew Murray would find this annoying.

'No bullshit,' he said, smiling, as he wiped his mouth with the paper serviette. Then he continued to play the game. 'What have you been doing with yourself while I was away?' Murray leaned over and shook his fist playfully.

'Come on, Steve, give. What happened. Did you have a chance to talk to the Commander privately?' Suddenly Zach remembered the seriousness of Murray's situation and dropped the game.

'No, Murray, I'm sorry. Soeharto arrived just as I was building up to asking for some private time. But don't be too alarmed. I have been invited to attend their cosy little gathering here, tonight. Right here, Murray, in the Istana Hotel.' Murray listened intently. He wasn't overly distressed by this news. Perhaps an opportunity would present itself to manipulate a meeting with the general, somehow. He considered that possibility.

'Can you get me an invite?' he asked, knowing that this was most unlikely. Zach looked at his friend, knowing what might be going through his mind. He had to do whatever he could to help clear the dangerous problem. Zach understood the stakes that were involved.

'How about you just turn up,' he said, then waved his hand knowing that this would not be acceptable. 'What if I phone and ask if I may bring my interpreter,' he suggested, thinking quickly, before shaking his head as he realised that this also wouldn't work. 'No, that's no good either. They already know I speak their language.'

'How about we wait for me to pass through the lobby at an opportune time, and you can step forward and pretend we've just bumped into each other?' Murray asked, knowing that there was always the possibility that he had already been spotted. Or the receptionist's report would have reached the Army Intelligence desk officer of the day and someone there might have remembered Murray's name. It was possible, Murray thought, he had been there before. And now he was well-known to the Diponegoro officers. At least, to some of them. Suddenly the idea lost its appeal. Murray began to think that perhaps the only solution would be to approach the problem through Djakarta contacts. The trip had been an error in judgement. Or at least the visit to Semarang was, he now believed.

'Maybe I'd best give it a miss. It wasn't one of my best ideas,' he said, rather despondently. He raised the beer to his mouth and took a long swallow. 'Let's cut our losses. Why don't you attend alone, then we'll head back early tomorrow?' Zach considered what he'd said.

'Okay. But we'll still have to work on your problem.' He looked at Murray with a sympathetic smile.

'By the way,' Murray said, nodding over his shoulder without looking, 'there's a Boris running around the hotel yelling at the staff.' Zach lifted his head but couldn't see anyone resembling a foreigner.

'There's thousands of them. Probably an agent for one of their ships.'

'No, this one is on our lists. It's Kololotov.' Suddenly Zach was interested. He was familiar with the name and what he represented. The KGB had never been overly clever, nor discreet, when it came to disguising their agents.

'Are you sure?' he challenged.

'Sure? Of course I'm sure. He virtually threw a tantrum right over there within earshot. Seems his phone wasn't working in his room and he'd missed reporting in to Big Boris, or something like that.' Murray had been drinking a little longer than he normally would at this time of the day. He was becoming a little aggressive. Zach finished his beer and rose. Murray didn't move. He had no reason to. Zach looked up at the lobby clock which informed the hotel guests helpfully what the time might have been in Moscow and Tokyo. It was apparent no-one liked the Americans. Not that it would have mattered as all three clocks had stopped. He checked his wrist-watch. There was still an hour or more to go before he would have to dress for dinner. He told Murray to take it easy and left him alone, hoping that his friend knew it was time to take a quick afternoon nap. As one would do in Djakarta, under the same circumstances. Then Zach went for a stroll outside.

* * * * * *

Semarang Harbour

Kololotov sat alone listening to the filthy harbour water slapping against the wooden poles which supported the small seafood restaurant. The thick, foul-smelling combination of rotting seaweed, discharge from ships' tanks and whatever waste fifty-thousand port-dwellers had hurled into the dark waters did not bother the Russian. The KGB colonel waited in the small shanty-styled structure, irritated that he was there and not already on his way back to Djakarta.

He had been unable to telephone Suhendra, and now he was really concerned. He had sent a rather ambiguous note to the officer by hotel taxi, hoping that someone over at the Army base would have enough initiative to take the two dollars affixed to the envelope and pass it on to the colonel, wherever he was now billeted. Kololotov then caught a *betjak* down to the harbour and waited, on the assumption that the letter would be delivered, and understood. He had argued with the driver over the fare. He despised these people, they were always wanting more. Finally, and to avoid becoming overly conspicuous, Kololotov had paid the additional two-and-a-half rupiah, throwing the note to the ground in anger. He had then entered the shanty-styled structure to wait.

The two hours dragged by slowly. Finally, the Russian accepted that his man had not received his note. He left the small restaurant and looked for a ride. Outside, he noticed the man who had peddled him down to the harbour earlier, waiting with some others. The group of *betjak* drivers sat atop their machines and ignored the Soviet. Even they had their pride. He then started the long walk back to the Istana Hotel.

* * * * * *

Diponegoro Army Married Quarters
Barracks, Semarang

Suhendra's wife received the note and sent the driver away. Her husband was not there. She opened the envelope and frowned at the writing, wondering if the note could be from another woman. She had never studied foreign languages and certainly could not understand whatever was written there. Anyway, she wasn't overly fussed. Her husband had already left, missing his customary afternoon nap. She made a face, remembering how he had returned to their quarters briefly, undressed and taken a quick *mandi*, then changed into his dress uniform before disappearing again, while muttering something about looking after visiting dignitaries.

She really didn't feel too annoyed. These days one was fortunate to be still considered one of the 'active' wives. Her husband had been married twice already and, somehow, with the number of nights when he stayed away until late becoming ever more frequent, she assumed the worst. He was probably going to take a third wife. She sighed and looked out the window at their three children, all still in primary school. Then she cleared her head of these negative thoughts and went about preparing the evening meal, knowing that no good could possibly come from worrying about what her husband may be doing.

* * * * * *

Diponegoro Ordnance Depot

Suhendra took the key and opened the third door to his left. As the senior officer, he had not been questioned when he walked past the drowsy guards and entered the storage facility which was located as far away from the other buildings as could be managed. He walked down the musty corridors covered on both sides with chicken wire to permit ventilation through the dangerous stores. He looked up. The plastic skylights were dirty, restricting the necessary natural light into the explosive goods area. He made a mental note to have the roof cleaned and proceeded along the four-metre-high racks of explosive devices and weapons. Suhendra was happy here. He understood the complicated weapons and explosives which were laid out here in the central store, under his control. His responsibility.

He knew the neatly-arranged items almost as if he had created them. Suhendra knew that he could come and go, remove almost anything he wished without the other officers questioning his access. And Suhendra was pleased that this was so, for it was here that he had hidden his money, knowing that the bundle of cash would be safe, buried under the explosives.

He stopped to examine the new storage bins he'd introduced to accommodate the various mortars his Government had purchased. The colonel nodded confidently as he sighted the boxes containing the Danish Madsen 51mm mortars, and then, alongside, the British hand-held two inch weapons. He snorted, looking beyond to the Soviet M1938s sitting beside the smaller American version, knowing that most of the Soviet equipment would soon be replaced if he was unsuccessful in his mission.

Suhendra was immediately reminded of his purpose in entering the huge weapons facility. He quickened his pace, knowing exactly where to go. He turned to his left past a number of unopened cases of Italian 7.62 BM59 Berettas which were awaiting despatch, and moved across to 'G' section. There he found what he wanted. He placed the detonator and timer inside his trouser pocket and continued on his search.

Suhendra smiled, stopped, then picked up the block of TM-200 explosive. It originated from Czechoslovakia, he knew. He had selected the area under where the explosives were stored to hide the money the Russians always gave him, knowing that even the most inquisitive of his fellow officers would not dare venture this far into the dangerous storage area. Let alone check under the supply of TM-200!

He placed the explosives inside his case casually, before running his hands across the adjacent boxes. These contained grenades. Again, the colonel knew that he had an ample choice here. There had been no shortage of suppliers eager to fill his country's warehouses with their expensive tools of war. The boxes had all been opened and the covers discarded. The first contained the British 36-M anti-personnel grenades. He passed over these quickly, not because they were not efficient, but because they did not fit his plan. Then he stopped and picked up one of his old favourites, the Soviet RDG-33. A soldier could throw that a long way, he thought, holding the torch-like shape as if it were just a toy. Finally, he hesitated alongside the box which contained the American MK2 fragmentation grenade.

Suhendra took one of the half-kilo olive-drab weights and threw it casually into the air before catching it again. He thought that it would only be fitting for the assassination to be carried out with at least some American components, as he knew that most of these had been given, not only covertly to his superiors, but also without cost, even though eventually many had benefited financially along the way. He ran his hands across the raised criss-crossed bumps on the grenade's surface, and the thought crossed his mind that these may even be remnants of the shipments his brother had died for, when he had been ordered to search for the American submarines along the Sumatran coast just a few years before. His face clouded with the memory and he turned to leave.

He stopped suddenly, as if unsure of what he'd taken from the case. He rubbed his hand across the plastic cover, checking that the explosive was there. Suhendra knew that these this would do the job. Then his mind turned to the grenade still gripped tightly in his hand. The compact explosives were wrapped in a deeply grooved cast iron body, criss-crossed for maximum effect. After detonation, anyone within ten metres of the explosion would suffer severe injuries. He knew this from experience. Some of his men had used these on the range against PKI detainees. He returned the grenade to its case. Satisfied that he had all he needed, Colonel Suhendra then left the munitions warehouse as easily as he had entered. He headed towards the reception for the Chief of Staff at the Istana Hotel. At that time, he still had not received Colonel Kololotov's message.

* * * * * *

Hotel Istana

Zach walked back in the direction of his hotel, deep in thought. He was concerned for Murray, convinced that the local Army garrison had to be approached by a third party to convince them that their position regarding the Station Chief was all wrong. He turned the corner and waited for the oncoming group of *betjak* to pass before attempting to cross the wide street. Then he noticed the tall foreigner, dressed in light-coloured trousers and short sleeves, walking quickly towards the Istana Hotel. Zach remained where he was on the side of the road, watching. When he observed the man swing determinedly into the hotel drive, Zach decided that this would have to be the Russian, Kololotov. He followed, also entering via the hotel's main driveway.

When he entered the lobby, the Australian was surprised at the transformation that had taken place in his brief absence. The columns had already been decorated with palm leaves, tied across at the top presenting an appearance similar to a bridal path formed by green and yellow tinted branches. The lounge chairs had been moved closer to the reception area while at the other end, staff were furiously running around throwing white tablecloths over the long collapsible tables, now standing in one line.

Flower arrangements had started to arrive. Zach looked at several of these tall, almost wreath-like displays of lilies and smiled, observing that the local merchants had not been backward in demonstrating that it was they who were funding the evening's festivities. He was surprised also at the number of guests expected. Zach had envisaged that there would be only a few tables, mainly to accommodate the senior officers, but he could see that there would be many more. To Zach, it appeared almost as if the function was still growing in numbers as the hotel manager fussed around checking the arrangements, obviously not really prepared for the additional catering he would be obliged to provide. Zach estimated that there would be no less than a hundred guests expected: many more than even he had anticipated. He wandered over to the reception and asked for his key. It was then that the electricity died. Zach sighed, walked slowly up to his room and entered. He went directly to the windows and opened them, knowing that it would probably be some time before the power was restored. He looked at the silent airconditioner and shook his head. The country had some very serious infrastructure problems, he knew, and electricity supply definitely headed the list.

Zach sat on his bed waiting for power to return before showering. Without the airconditioner it would merely be a waste of time. He undid his shirt and strolled back to the window overlooking the secluded beer garden and stood, willing whatever breeze was out there to cool his sweaty chest. He looked down to the courtyard covered with moss-coloured bricks and near the corner he noticed figures, partly covered by the thick-leaved frangipani tree. Then one of the figures moved and he could see that it was the Russian, Kololotov. He leaned out of the window then tilted his head to the side. Zach could then see that the other man was an Indonesian Army officer, and obviously one of the evening's guests as the soldier was wearing the white officer's formal attire. Zach moved back slightly, to avoid being observed. Then he listened, catching only a few words of the sharp exchange. They spoke in Russian. Zach was surprised, as he caught some of their conversation.

'You will do as I say, if you...' the speaker's voice was muffled and Zach was unable to hear all they said. '... then you will compromise us all!' he heard, barely catching the hissed words. He could tell that this had been the Russian speaking. He strained for more.

'... talk to me in this manner. I am... and this is still my country!' the other man had replied, with a similar amount of venom. The exchange was heated, he could tell. Suddenly, Kololotov swore at the other man, which resulted in a slight scuffle. The Indonesian cursed back and threatened him. The Russian swore again, followed by silence and what he thought were footsteps. Then he could not hear either of the men at all. Zach leaned out of the window again and was surprised to see that the Russian had gone. The other man had remained, and was standing alone, straightening his uniform.

Zach could then clearly see the face of the soldier. It was Colonel Suhendra, and he was obviously very, very angry. As quietly as he could, Zach leaned back into his room and snatched his shirt from the back of the chair. He hurried down the hallway as he buttoned his clothing, and followed the steps down into the lobby, ignoring Kololotov as they passed on the stairs. He walked directly out into the rear garden area to find the Indonesian, but he had already slipped away. Surprised and disappointed, he turned and re-entered the lobby, only to find that Murray, who had been having a sleep, had reappeared. Zach told the Station Chief what he'd seen.

'What do you read into it?' Murray asked.

'Obviously Suhendra is their man here. Or at least one of them. Boris would normally have more but I'd be surprised if there are others of the colonel's rank down here. The Diponegoro boys may not be overly fond of the Americans themselves, but having said that, we shouldn't forget that it's here, in this province, that the communists are taking their worst hiding.'

'What do you think they're up to?'

Zach remained deep in thought. The exchange he'd overheard had most definitely been vitriolic. There were possibly even blows exchanged, or at least some serious shoving.

'Got to admit, I really have no idea what it's all about,' he answered.

'Let's talk to the reception and see how long Kololotov intends staying. Maybe we could stay over another day ourselves. I'm still of two minds about leaving here without first settling my problems with the Army.' Zach considered this and nodded. Murray then wandered over to the reception and started talking casually to the staff. Zach could see them talking and smiling. He knew that the staff would tell him what he wanted to know, seeing them warm to Murray's friendly face. Murray strolled back to the bar where Zach was sipping a whisky.

'Seems that our friend has already booked out once today. Curious, he hasn't checked back in yet, but the staff seem to think that he might stay another night. He's still upstairs in his room,' Murray reported. Suddenly, lights blinked in the fading sunlight. Assorted mechanical whirring noises indicated that the power had been restored. They both moved upstairs to shower and, in Zach's case, to prepare for the function which would soon commence. He entered his room and went immediately to the windows, closing them before undressing then showering in the antiquated bathroom.

* * * * * *

Kololotov was livid. He remained in his room trying to decide what course of action to take next. It had never been his plan to remain another night, but he now believed that it was imperative that he do so. He thought back over the altercation. Colonel Suhendra had become unreasonable. No, more than that, he decided. The colonel had become irrational. When he'd been informed that the operation was cancelled, Kololotov had been shocked with the response ...

'It's too late to change your minds now,' Suhendra said, anger evident in his voice.

'You must also return the money,' Kololotov insisted. His masters would never believe that he had been unable to recover the funds once the mission had been aborted. He had to take the money back to the Counsellor.

'No!' Suhendra hissed, his voice rising, 'The money is mine to keep. I will have expenses,' he demanded. Kololotov's own anger flared.

'You will do as I say. If you continue with the original plan it will most certainly fail. Then you will compromise us all!' the Russian hissed back at the stubborn Indonesian.

'You have no right to talk to me in this manner. I am an officer of the Army and you are nothing.' He dropped his voice even further, 'We must continue with the plan. It is for the good of my people. You don't understand. We must proceed. I am making this decision myself now, and this is still my country.'

'You are a fool!' Kololotov accused harshly, knowing then that it was unlikely that he was going to recover the funds. He would have great difficulty convincing his superiors that the money had, in fact, been paid. 'I will abandon you now and inform my people that you are no longer to be trusted,' he hissed again, moving closer, Suhendra recoiling from the bad breath.

'You are a pig,' the Indonesian spat angrily at the Russian.

Kololotov grabbed the front of his uniform and jerked his arm upwards, lifting the smaller man almost off the ground. They scuffled briefly then froze, as one of the staff passed by almost within view. The Russian whispered threateningly into the colonel's ear, then stomped away in anger, returning to his room to think things through. His hands were tied. Somehow he must take steps to prevent the assassination attempt from continuing as planned.

* * * * * *

Suhendra remained behind, shaking in rage. He hated the man who had so easily intimidated him. Had he been in possession of his dangerous package right then, he would have willingly selected a new target and forgone the other, just to repay the Russian for this confrontation. Looking down he saw that his uniform had been rumpled and, straightening the jacket, he walked quickly away. How he wished he had not informed Kololotov about the function that would take place in the hotel later. He had to think. And he knew that he also had to regain his composure. Suhendra moved through the rear of the garden and sought out his jeep. His hands were still shaking when he leaned behind the seat and checked that the metal box he'd placed there earlier that afternoon had not been disturbed. He sat alone for some minutes, considering his options now that the Soviets had aborted the original plan. It took but a few moments before Suhendra decided that it would still be in his interests to proceed. Only now he would modify his plan to accommodate his target's revised itinerary.

When Suhendra's Commander had informed his staff that the new Chief of Staff would visit, the Army's own guest house, maintained only for VIP visits, was immediately prepared. Suhendra had planned to place the explosive in the major general's quarters before he retired. When the explosion took place, he would be back in his own quarters, asleep. Now, as the general had decided not to remain overnight, Suhendra's options had been severely restricted. He had thought about the limited time left, and even considered placing the explosives close to where his target would sit during the function. Suhendra knew that his own Commander was not one of the American supporters. Suhendra admired the man and decided that he would not be responsible for his death as well. The function as a possible venue for Soeharto's assassination was therefore discounted completely. There would be no other opportunity, he felt, apart from the general's transport. Suhendra knew that it would be almost impossible for him to place the explosives in the correct vehicle, and at the right time. There were just too many unknown factors involved for him to take that risk. Finally he had decided to place the device on board the departing aircraft, which would transport Indonesia's most powerful soldier back to the capital. Once the man was dead, others who waited in the wings would not hesitate. Even Nasution would not be missed this time.

He thought about what he must do, when the time arrived. As a member of the Commander's personal staff, he would have little difficulty in boarding the airplane prior to its departure. Then he would set the timer and place the package on the aircraft. The explosion would do the rest. Satisfied that the changes to his plan would not be difficult to incorporate, he waited inside his jeep for other invitees to arrive.

Chapter 27

Semarang

Kololotov remained in his room until well after the loud music had started downstairs. Then he remembered that he had not confirmed with reception that he would be staying for another night. He had to remain, there was no other choice. When the situation presented itself, he would go downstairs and confront Suhendra again, if possible, and convince him to reconsider. He must find some way of attracting the colonel's attention during the function without being overly obvious to the other guests. Only then could he consider leaving the city and driving back to Djakarta. Kololotov bathed and changed into a long-sleeve white shirt and dark trousers, so as not to appear too conspicuous once he had moved down amongst the many guests. He knew that his presence would not be challenged. The Indonesians were too polite for that. Instead, those present would assume that either he was an invited guest or as a resident in-house, had wandered into the function believing that it was open to all the hotel guests.

* * * * * *

Murray was unhappy with the commitment he had given Zach to remain out of sight in his room. But both understood that he would be recognised once a few of the Diponegoro officers remembered his face from earlier visits. So, reluctantly, he had agreed. Zach had undertaken to make a concerted effort to deal with Murray's problem the next day.

Murray had ordered a half of Scotch and settled back with a generous serving of local dishes to keep himself occupied. Within the hour, he had become restless and bored. The music teased as he listened to the orchestra play, and he was fascinated by the number of string instruments supporting the traditional, almost calypso-style music which filled the tropical night. Murray turned his airconditioner off, then opened his windows to allow the sounds to filter through. He ignored the mosquitoes which flowed through the large opening. Even with almost a quarter of the bottle already under his belt he was not relaxed. Murray moved to his bed and lay back in the darkened room, listening.

* * * * * *

The lobby filled quickly as guests flowed into the large high-ceilinged space, their voices carrying through the building. The manager, Pak Didi, ran around nervously, watching as the mixture of local merchants and military crowded into the reception area. He looked across at the receiving line and was pleased that he had managed to arrange everything in time considering the incredibly short notice he had been given. The men who stood waiting together, as hosts, were amongst the most powerful in his country. Suddenly he felt his chest swell with pride as he danced quickly towards the kitchen.

Zach entered the lobby and accepted a warm beer poured over ice. When the next waiter passed, he exchanged this quickly for what appeared to be whisky, then stood observing the other guests as they formed small groups and conversed. The noise level rose quickly and, as he mingled with some of the Indonesian officers and their wives, he spotted Colonel Suhendra standing alone. He moved towards the man immediately.

'Hello, and selamat malam, Kolonel,' he said, wishing the officer a good evening. They didn't shake hands. Both men had already spoken during the course of his meeting earlier in the day. 'This is quite a function,' he stated, hoping to engage the colonel in conversation.

'Yes, it is,' replied the colonel, matter-of-factly, as if such occasions were common in his city.

'There are not many foreigners present,' Zach suggested, directing the conversation.

'There not too many who would be welcome at such a gathering,' Suhendra replied. Zach detected an air of hostility. 'It is difficult

510

these days for my Government to know who to trust.'

'*I hope you don't include the Australians in that observation,'* Zach parried. Now that Suhendra was apart from his peers his prickly attitude was more apparent. Zach pushed ahead.

'*I believe I saw you here earlier,'* he said, watching for a reaction, '*out in that magnificent rear garden setting.'* He observed Suhendra's reaction. The colonel's face froze as his eyes moved to stare aggressively into Zach's. This, Zach knew, was considered confrontationalist in this country. He knew he had hit a nerve.

'*I think you must be mistaken,'* the colonel responded, emphatically. He then waved at someone across the room and forced a smile. '*Excuse me, I am called,'* with which he quickly walked away and through the crowded lobby.

The Australian Military Attaché lifted himself unobtrusively onto tiptoe and glanced in the direction the man had taken to see if he had, in fact, been summoned. Suhendra had already disappeared from sight. Zach then strolled across to another group and introduced himself, hoping to speak again with the colonel later. As he was speaking to the wife of one of the other guests, a loud gong sounded the buffet's commencement. Zach stepped back, knowing that there would be a rush.

The buffet came under attack as the guests filled their plates with the fine assortment of food which had been prepared for them at the local traders' expense. He waited before taking a small plate of *sate*, then stepped back to watch the other guests enjoy themselves. As he pulled the charcoal-cooked chicken meat off the skewer with his teeth, careful not to drip the soya sauce, he spotted Kololotov standing at the bar section, looking like some imported foreign bartender who had lost his way. Zach moved slightly, standing almost out of view behind a group of younger officers. He observed the KGB officer staring across the room. Zach followed the Russian's line of sight and discovered that Suhendra had returned. He continued to watch the two, as Kololotov's efforts to attract the other man's attention were obviously being ignored by the Indonesian officer. Then he watched with interest as the poorly-dressed Soviet attempted to move through the throng of guests, heading directly towards the man who refused to recognise what Zach had thought were obvious signals to talk, or meet outside. He continued to observe the move, and was not surprised when he saw the Indonesian turn suddenly and walk away from what might have been a confrontation, towards the far end of the lobby. Then he noticed Kololotov pause before following the other man who had exited in the direction of the toilets.

Zach made his way to the far end of the lobby and stood so that his view of the reception area was unhindered. Minutes passed, then, as he anticipated, first one of the men re-appeared, followed by the other at a respectable interval. Zach was caught off-guard when the Russian returned to the lobby, but instead of rejoining the gathering, he turned to his left and climbed the staircase, obviously heading for his room. Zack moved back and stood alongside a small group of smiling local businessmen who had finished eating, but remained standing around talking not far from the other guests. Zach smiled, introduced himself, and started to talk to one of the merchants when he observed Suhenra trying to look inconspicuous. Zach understood the movements. He apologised, mentioning he had forgotten something and moved away, just as Suhendra turned from where he was standing close to the stairwell, and climbed the carpeted stairs. Zach noted his exit then returned to the guests at hand. He remained close to this station waiting for the Indonesian colonel to re-appear. Some minutes later, he felt a hand on his arm and turned to see the commander smiling at him.

'You are enjoying our reception for the Chief of Staff?' he asked, not insincerely.

'I am. Very much. Thank you for the honour of the invitation,' Zach replied. He wanted to move slightly so as to keep his peripheral vision open to the staircase leading upstairs.

'You are driving back tomorrow?' the Commander asked, knowing that this was fact.

'Yes, unfortunately,' Zach responded again. Then he remembered Murray. 'I might stay over another day, if there was an opportunity to meet with you, Bapak,' he said, using the term of respect which was not lost on the senior officer. The Indonesian smiled at him.

'I will not be here. Pak Soeharto has asked me to join him tonight on his flight back to Djakarta.' The Commander seemed pleased that he would be leaving with his old friend. He had yet to announce his departure to those other than his aides and senior officers. He would do this shortly.

'*Ah,*' Zach said, making small talk, '*then you will arrive back in the capital even before I leave the province.*' The general smiled again and nodded in affirmation. Then he suddenly became serious.

'*Wait here,*' he ordered, leaving Zach standing alone. Only moments had passed when a captain walked over and took him by his elbow.

'*Pak Kolonel,*' he said to the surprised Attaché, '*the Bapak wishes to speak to you.*' Zach followed, conscious of the stares as he did so. The young officer took him through the congested hall, holding his hand in front as he made way for them both until they reached the hosts who were seated off to one side. The general indicated that he should sit.

'*I hear that you don't enjoy driving so much?*' Soeharto asked. The others in his group smiled knowingly. One of the ladies even giggled. Zach felt slightly embarrassed.

'*It isn't that I don't enjoy the beautiful countryside,*' he said, searching for the more difficult words, '*it is that sometimes I become impatient to be at my next destination.*' The group were flattered with his reply. They had all, at some time or another, travelled the long journey across the broken roads to their villages. Here was a foreigner who really understood how to behave. They were impressed.

'*You are invited to join us tonight, if you wish,*' the general offered. Zach was caught off-guard again and, for once, wasn't quite sure how to respond. If the invitation was sincere, he would have to go. There would be the added advantage that he may be given the opportunity to speak to the other officer, alone. On the other hand, had the general's invitation merely been a polite gesture, he should find an acceptable way to refuse.

'*You are very kind, General.*' Zach replied, knowing that they were all watching to see how he would response. '*I would be pleased to join you on your flight. Terima kasih,*' he said, hoping that he had made the correct decision. The wives clapped their hands as one would expect young school girls to react. The two generals smiled.

'*Well, that's it then,*' the Commander said, '*Captain Suhardjo there will take care of the arrangements.*' Zach decided that this was his signal to leave. He excused himself, thanked the generals again, and walked away followed by envious eyes. He mingled with the officers who seemed suddenly eager to be seen talking to the foreigner who had found the ear of their commander. And the new

Chief of Army Staff. Zach laughed and talked, enjoying the moment. He didn't even notice when Colonel Suhendra surreptitiously rejoined the party.

* * * * * *

Murray felt drowsy. Although the windows were open and the music continued to drift into his room, he could still hear the sounds of staff as they walked along the corridor. There had been a lull in the noise when the band had taken a short break. He felt his eyes closing as the soft breath of the evening sea-breeze wafted gently through the open windows. He had finished almost half of the whisky and, when he at first heard the sounds, thought nothing of them. Then he heard the noises again, and sat up immediately, alert. Surely the noise had been a cry of pain?

He moved through the semi-darkness and placed his hand inside the case, removing the automatic and checking the magazine as a matter of habit. He stood by the door and listened. There! He was sure he'd heard it again. There was little to be heard but the sounds downstairs, as the guests went about jostling each other over the buffet. Minutes passed, and Murray waited. But he could hear nothing more. Slowly he lowered himself back onto the bed and closed his eyes, listening. Then he drifted back to sleep.

* * * * * *

Suhendra had followed Kololotov upstairs to his room. They had quarrelled.

'You must not execute the plan. If you do, it will be the end of both of us,' the Russian had warned. Why wouldn't this man listen? 'I will wait here until tomorrow, Kolonel. The money I gave you must be returned.'

'This is no longer your plan,' Suhendra spat at the KGB officer. 'The major general isn't even staying here. Your plan would have failed. Tell me, would you still have demanded the money be returned had I destroyed an empty guest house?' he asked sarcastically.

'It was your information we had acted on. You cannot blame anyone but yourself. You have no choice, return the money!' Kololotov demanded, once again.

'*I will keep the money. I will also complete the mission. For me, nothing has changed.*' Suhendra said, with a menacing smile. '*If you threaten me with exposure, then you only threaten yourself. You cannot accuse me without involving your own Government.*' The Russian's face muscles tightened as his eyes narrowed.

'*You are a fool, Kolonel,*' he growled. '*I am covered by diplomatic privilege. You, on the other hand, are not.*' Suhendra thought quickly about this. What the Russian had said was true. Would the Russian go that far to ensure that the mission was cancelled? Suddenly the possibility seemed real. Suhendra attempted another approach.

'*Listen. I have already made the arrangements. It will be merely a simple matter of the general's aircraft disappearing on its return flight to the capital. No one will suspect. There will be no danger for you or your Government.*' Kololotov understood immediately. The colonel was going to place explosives on board the aircraft before it departed. He had to find out more. The Russian attempted a knowing smile. One of a fellow conspirator.

'*When will you do this?*' he asked, as if receptive to the plan. He observed the Indonesian officer closely, watching his eyes as he replied.

'*He intends returning once the function downstairs is finished. I will accompany the other officers as they escort the Chief of Staff out to the airfield. I will board the aircraft and place the explosives to the rear of the cabin. I will set the timer as soon as he leaves the hotel. It will not be difficult to accomplish.*' Suhendra appeared calm. He apparently cared nothing for the crew and other passengers on that return flight to Djakarta. But Kololotov understood clearly how these men would die. Those who survived the blast would probably live long enough to experience the terror of falling from the sky, knowing as they screamed that nothing could save them from certain death. How they died was not of any great import to him. Who was killed in the accident was his only consideration at this time.

'*I order you not to proceed with this plan,*' he snapped, surprising the colonel. There was a moment when silence engulfed the room, before Suhendra realised that he had been tricked. He glared at the Russian and turned to leave. Kololotov lunged across the narrow space, losing his footing on the loose bedside carpet. He crashed face-down onto the wooden floor, stunned. Suhendra recognised his opportunity but stopped as he was about to flee. The burly

Russian had already begun to rise groggily to his knees.

Suhendra's mind raced. He reached across and lifted the thick, solid glass ashtray and smashed it with all of his force against the side of the Russian's head. Kololotov collapsed to the floor again, screaming in pain, blood pouring from the wound. Suhendra stepped back. He was shaking all over. The ashtray slipped from his hands. The screams became indistinct, died away, but had they been overheard?

He bent down cautiously and inspected the body and, as he did so, Kololotov moved and groaned. Alarmed, Suhendra sprang back, watching, horrified as the injured man moved slightly, then lifted his head. Colonel Suhendra panicked, retrieved the glass weapon then wielded it savagely, again and again, smashing the man's head. Suddenly he stopped, out of breath, glaring down at the prostrate body. Kololotov appeared to be dead.

Suhendra raised his head and listened to the sounds from below. The band had begun playing again. Startled, he checked his watch. He had been away from the function for almost half an hour. Standing up quickly, he checked his uniform for blood and, satisfied there was none, straightened his clothes and left quietly down the long corridor which led to the stairs. Minutes later, he stood amongst the other guests and officers, holding a small plate of food in his hands. He looked down at his hands. They had nearly stopped shaking. Everything was going to be all right.

* * * * * *

Captain Suhardjo found the Australian Military Attaché engrossed in conversation with several of his fellow officers and wives. He waited for the officer to finish speaking before he moved forward and interrupted.

'Kolonel Zach, I am to inform you that the general's party will leave in fifteen minutes. If you have luggage you wish to take, I will wait for you just outside, over there,' he indicated a tall tree behind which Zach could see the white painted lines on the helmets of the military police. He thanked the officer and excused himself from the group, and went directly upstairs. There wasn't much to pack. Then he knocked rather loudly on Murray's door and waited. Moments later, a tired Station Chief opened the door, still rubbing his eyes.

'Well, how was the bash?' Murray asked, relocking the door behind Zach and indicating that he should sit. He yawned, looked at his wrist watch and clicked his tongue in annoyance at having fallen asleep so early.

'I'm off, Murray,' Zach said, and explained what had taken place downstairs. Murray seemed annoyed at first, until Zach said it would be an excellent opportunity to talk directly to the Commander about Murray during the flight. Murray thought about this and nodded his head in agreement.

'There's not much point in trying for an appointment tomorrow now that he's going to be leaving on that flight. You may as well go with him, Steve. At least, that way something might just come out of it.'

'When will you head back, yourself?' Zach asked. Murray thought for only a few moments before replying.

'First light. I really don't want to stay around here any longer than I have to. There's no reason to hang around.' Then he remembered. 'Will you let the reception and our driver know?' he asked, wishing to avoid going back down to the lobby while the Army personnel were still there. Zach agreed. He then left Murray, checking first to see if there was anything he could do before leaving.

'No, Steve, thanks. Think I'll give food a miss and just crash again. It's a hell of drive back tomorrow.' Zach nodded, then went down to the reception to inform them that he was leaving and ask that the account be presented to his friend in room 201. He asked for his luggage to be brought down while he went in search of their driver. Zach stepped out into the musty evening air and peered through the carpark. It was packed full of vehicles, most of which belonged to the Army. There were soldiers and drivers milling around everywhere. He could see four jeeps lined up together, and recognised the gold stars attached to the rear number-plates indicating that these were the general's transport. Zach walked over to a group of men squatting under one of the palms and asked if they had seen his driver. They called out in the partially-lighted area and, within a few minutes, the man appeared. Zach gave him Murray's message and, as he turned to leave, he spotted one of the mobile roadside vendors cooking inside the hotel grounds, serving food to the soldiers and drivers. Zach smiled, knowing that the *martabak* was one of Murray's favourites.

'Get one of those for yourself, and one for tuan Murray. Okay?' he instructed the driver, while digging into his wallet for small notes. He pulled out a one hundred rupiah note, 'Give tuan Murray the change,' he insisted, then gave a wave as he then went in search of Captain Suhardjo. When he caught up with the aide, the officer was busy organising the general's departure. Zach's one piece of luggage arrived, and this was stored in the rear of one of the jeeps while he remained there, in the carpark, wondering how much longer he would have to wait. He saw the driver collect the large Indian omelette filled with chillies, and walk towards the hotel. Zach smiled knowing that Murray would probably curse the intrusion as first, then thank him once he discovered the food. Then the two generals appeared, smiling and shaking hands as they bid farewell to the officers and wives who would not accompany them to the airport. Zach joined the senior officers and, twenty minutes later, the military motorcade entered the Semarang airport and crossed the field to the AURI hangers where the C-47 transport waited.

Zach stood by the aircraft, and to the side, as the Indonesian officers talked amongst themselves on the tarmac. He observed some of the crew moving around the twin-engined plane and saw Colonel Suhendra board, then leave some minutes later. He waved to the colonel as the Indonesian climbed down from the aircraft and waited beside the steps as the commander continued talking to the major general and others, just out of earshot. Then they were given the signal to depart. Zach waited until the Commander and General Soeharto boarded, and then he followed. As he stepped into the aircraft, he turned and waived once again to the colonel standing outside, smiling as he did so. Suhendra returned the smile and stepped away as the starboard engine started, blasting a tunnel of smoke in his direction. Then Zach heard the cabin door locked. They were ready to depart.

* * * * * *

The driver was prevented from entering the hotel lobby through the main entrance because of the presence of VIP's. Instead, he was redirected around the main building and told to use the side access which took him through the rear garden. He passed through a short walkway and into the reception. He knew that he should not be there and attempted to attract the attention of one of the waiters to take the food up to the *tuan*. The manager passed close by but did not notice the Embassy driver for, at that moment, he heard the whistles outside, alerting the police and military escorts to the general's imminent departure. Finally the driver caught the eye of one of the waiters.

'What do you want in here?' the waiter demanded, officiously, looking over his shoulder in case he was seen by Pak Didi. It was against the rules for a driver to be in this part of the hotel.

'I have a martabak for tuan Murray, upstairs. Would you take this up to him for me?' he asked. The waiter looked concerned. He was not permitted upstairs. That responsibility rested with the kitchen waiters. He belonged to the lobby bar service area where Pak Didi had first placed him, almost two years before. He shook his head.

'No, I can't. Ask one of the kitchen waiters,' he suggested, wishing that he could have helped as he knew that the foreign *tuans* tipped exceptionally well.

'Look, why don't you just do it. The kitchen staff will only tell me to ask the manager, you know that,' he argued, knowing that the man was only looking for a few rupiah for himself. The waiter could see no value in offering to assist the driver who, as he could see, wasn't even Javanese.

'Give me five rupiah and I'll do it,' he said, glancing around again to ensure that Pak Didi was still preoccupied with the guests outside. The driver was furious. The request was exorbitant. Besides, he had no right to give *tuan* Zach's money away to this man. He refused.

'Then do it yourself,' the waiter retorted, turning away, ignoring remarks which followed him. The driver looked at the omelette wrapped in newspaper and banana leaves. Then he looked up at the stairs. He turned his head and saw quite clearly that almost everyone present had moved away from the reception area and towards the main entrance to farewell the visiting general. He didn't hesitate. Moving up the stairs two steps at a time, he soon covered the short distance arriving at the corridor which led down to the suite rooms. Then he frowned, knowing that he should have first checked to see in which room *tuan* Murray stayed. He walked along the carpeted hallway looking at the bottom of each door to see

which still had lights burning. The driver moved along slowly, checking as he passed room 201, then 203 which had been allotted to the Australians. There were no lights and so he continued down to the end of the corridor where he discovered that the lights to 208 were still burning. He knocked and waited. He knocked loudly, again. Then he heard the loud moan from inside.

* * * * * *

Murray had just drifted into sleep when he thought he heard knocking. He opened his eyes and listened. The sounds were coming from further down the passageway, so Murray closed his eyes again. He felt hungry. Why hadn't he asked Zach to send a platter of food up with one of the waiters?

He heard the loud knocking again. Curious, Murray listened. Suddenly he heard someone call out, *'Tuan, tuan!'* and he threw himself out of bed, unlocked his door and peered cautiously through the narrow gap, preparing himself for danger. He couldn't see anything at all. The shouts came again, calling from somewhere down the hallway. Murray considered grabbing his weapon, but decided to wait until he learned more about what was happening. Then he saw his driver appear from the far room and run in his direction. Murray swung his door open and grabbed the man as he passed, pulling him savagely into the darkened room. He slammed the door shut and flicked the lights on as he held his forearm across the driver's throat.

'What have you been up to?' Murray demanded, relieving some of the pressure against the man's neck. The driver's eyes remained opened wide, filled with terror. He thought he had been attacked by whoever had hurt the other *tuan* down the hall. *'I said, what have you been doing down there?'* Murray hissed at his driver, between clenched teeth. He then shook the man roughly and released his grip. The driver slid to the floor, then raised his hands over his head for protection.

'Nothing, tuan, nothing!' he wailed, horrified with the sudden turn in events. Why had he gone upstairs with the food? Now look at the trouble he was in!

'What happened?' Murray snapped, raising his hands threateningly.

'Nothing, tuan, nothing. I didn't do anything, I swear!' he sobbed, curling his feet up underneath his body. 'Tuan Zach told me to buy some martabak for you and I thought you were in the other room,' he choked, forcing the words out. Then he remembered. 'Tuan! There's a man down there who's hurt badly. It's another tuan,' he gushed, excitedly. Murray knew immediately who it would be. There had only been three foreigners staying in the hotel and Zach had already departed. He dragged his trousers and shirt off the chair and pulled these on quickly. He shoved his P9S inside his belt. Then he slipped into his shoes and killed the light.

'Wait here,' he ordered the driver, before opening the door and moving out into the hallway. He walked slowly towards the far room. Arriving at 208 he found the door ajar. Inside, Kololotov, who was bleeding profusely, had dragged himself up into a half-sitting position. He saw Murray and attempted to crawl towards the bedside table. Murray guessed that the Russian would have a weapon there somewhere. He closed the door with one hand and moved to block the man's path. The Russian slid back to the floor and moaned loudly.

'You, ... who are you?' he asked, his voice barely audible as he dragged himself into a sitting position. His vision seemed impaired. Murray looked at the bloodied mess around the man's face and head. He couldn't understand how he was still conscious having taken such punishment.

'I'm a guest,' he answered slowly. What in the hell had happened here? Murray wondered, glancing around. Then he noticed the ashtray and sucked in air through his teeth. This had been the weapon. 'What happened?' he asked.

Kololotov gasped with pain as he finally managed an upright sitting position, leaning against the bed end. He looked as if he would pass out again at any moment. Murray looked around and spotted the thermos flask filled with boiled drinking water. There was no refrigerator. He moved over and poured a glass of the tepid water and placed this in the Russian's hands, careful not to position himself to his disadvantage. Kololotov took the glass and raised it to his lips, spilling more than he drank. He coughed, and as he did, his face contorted in pain. Murray removed the glass.

'Want to tell me what happened? Should I ask reception to get the police?' he asked, knowing that this would most probably be the last thing the Russian would want. Kololotov appeared to ignore the suggestion. He seemed to be having difficulty maintaining consciousness. 'Has this something to do with your friend, the Diponegoro colonel you were seen with earlier?' Murray went on. Kololotov seemed to understood this, his hands tensed, forming a fist.

Murray moved away as if intending to leave. 'I'll go downstairs and see if someone can find him if you want,' he suggested, realising that the Russian's mind was still confused from the savage bashing he taken.

'Are they ... still downstairs?' he asked, groaning.

'Who?' Murray asked, his curiosity more than aroused by now. 'Who should be downstairs?' he asked, hoping that the man wouldn't pass out.

'The ... the ... general. Has he ... has he already ... left for ...' He stopped, the pain preventing him from continuing. Murray bent down and placed his hand on the Russian's shoulder. He knew that there would be no danger from this man now. Odds were, from the look of him, he might not make it.

'Left for where?' Murray asked, gripping the man to let him know that he was there to help. 'Where was the general going?' he asked, knowing the answer himself, but curious that this was of interest to a man who might be dying. He wanted to shake the man but knew this would probably kill him. Suddenly there was a loud groan.

'Has ... the ... general gone to ... the airport?' the Russian managed, almost fainting with the exertion. Murray could see where part of the man's head had been opened wide. The sight of the gash made him feel ill.

'What about the general?' Murray tried again, suddenly very concerned. A familiar feeling of dread started down his back. How did the Russian know so much about the general's movements? 'Listen, what about the general?' he asked again, slowly and clearly. He could see that the man was almost gone, his eyes had begun to glaze over.

'Suhendra ...' Kololotov suddenly said, spitting the name out with a groan of agony. He seemed to be trying to form the words but they just wouldn't come. 'Suhendra ... he must not continue ...' again the words fell off. Murray could not quite make out what he was saying. It sounded like someone's name. Who in the hell was he referring to?

'What must he do?' Murray asked almost irritably. Kololotov tried again, and he opened his eyes and blinked. Suddenly it appeared as if he could recognise what was happening in the room and could see the other man clearly.

'Suhendra ... Suhendra ... must cancel ... the mission.' The words were almost indistinguishable now, as his voice slurred. 'Not ...Soeharto,' he said, fighting to stay conscious 'Not ...not ...now.' And then Kololotov died, his body sliding to one side and onto the floor. Murray knelt, then felt his pulse. He knew the man was dead even before he checked, surprised that Kololotov had survived this long. He rose, and stood staring down at the dead KGB officer. Murray frowned, trying to make sense of what the dying man had said. Was he saying Sunda? No, he thought, it sounded more like... and suddenly he realised what the Russian was trying to say. The words raced through his mind and he swore loudly, recognising the name of the colonel that Zach had spotted in the hotel garden.

He turned and raced down the corridor as fast as he could, repeating the words which had so suddenly alarmed him. Airport, Suhendra, mission, Soeharto! He couldn't believe that what he was thinking might be true. The Soviets were involved somehow in a plan which concerned the major general and his aircraft. His mind continued to race with the possibilities. Was there going to be an attempt on the Chief of Staff's life?

He banged his bedroom door open violently and grabbed his driver, half-dragging the frightened man along the corridor with him as he ran down the staircase and through the lobby. There were still a number of guests who had remained behind to enjoy what was left of the buffet and each other's company. They heard the shouts and turned, surprised, as the foreigner rushed through the reception dragging his driver behind. The hotel manager stood with his mouth open when the two almost collided with him as they blundered through the lobby and down the steps into the carpark.

Murray took one look and did not need to be told that Zach's party had already departed. He cursed loudly, then yelled at the driver to run faster as they headed for the Embassy car parked across the enclosure. Suddenly there was a shout from behind, as one of the Army officers ran into the carpark yelling to the others waiting there. He had seen the Australian run through the lobby and couldn't believe his eyes. He was certain that it was the same man from Djakarta. What was he doing there?

Murray and his terrified driver made it to their vehicle first. The Embassy driver didn't need to be told to drive quickly: he did, not knowing which direction to take and spinning the car wheels on the loose gravel surface. The engine screamed as the driver pushed the six-cylinder motor past its limits, missing the gear change in panic, expecting the car lights behind to belong to the military police. He thought that he would be accused of harming the injured guest in 208, and that *tuan* Murray was trying to save his life.

'Go straight to the airport,' Murray ordered. The driver looked at him in disbelief.

'But tuan, it would be better if we drove the other way,' he complained, knowing that they would surely be caught if he took that road. 'We are faster. They won't be able to catch us if we just drive to Tjirebon,' he implored, indicating that they were already being pursued by the other vehicle.

'Just drive as fast as you can to the airport or I'll throw you out here and drive myself, okay, mas?' Murray snapped, cursing for not having taken the wheel himself. He turned in his seat and caught a glimpse of the car behind. 'Go faster!' he urged, just as the hapless driver hit a large pothole and almost lost control. Murray swore loudly as his head hit the roof. Glancing back he could see that the car following had also plunged one of its wheels into the hole as headlight beams flashed wildly in all directions. Their driver had overcorrected and spun off the road.

'For Chrissakes, go faster can't you!' he screamed at the driver, knowing that this would be their opportunity to lose the others. They accelerated away and within minutes the town lights started to disappear behind. 'Go down there!' he snapped, pointing to a side road. The driver obeyed, losing a little speed as he threw the sedan into the corner, fishtailing wildly on the dirt track.

'Stop over there, quickly,' Murray ordered. They came to an abrupt halt and a cloud of dust engulfed their vehicle. 'Now get out, mas,' he said, sliding across and forcing the driver to move away as he leaned over and opened the door. It happened all too quickly for the surprised driver. He fell out as Murray moved into the driving position and wound the window down.

'*Stay here,*' he shouted at the stunned man. '*I'll send someone back for you.*'

'*No, tuan, no! Please don't leave me here,*' he screamed, but his words were drowned as Murray gunned the engine and turned the wheel, throwing gravel everywhere. He headed back in the direction of the airport, hoping that those who had been following would, by now, assume that he had gone on through the city and was still well ahead of them. Murray looked down at the speedometer then back at the narrow road, willing the car to go faster.

He knew that the airport would only be a fifteen minute run at this time of night. The road was quiet due to the curfew. Only a few more minutes had passed when he spotted outlines of the airport buildings in the distance. As he sped along the perimeter fence road, he couldn't see an aircraft anywhere. He ground his teeth and muttered, hoping that he was not too late. When he reached the turn-off to the airport main entrance, he swung the car into it and drove towards the main guard gate to the joint civilian and military field. The boom was still open but, in the distance, he could see that there were soldiers standing around nearby. He stared down the driveway as he accelerated towards the open gate, willing the men not to stand in front of his speeding vehicle, nor to lower the boom. Suddenly, Murray caught the flash of headlights in his rear-vision mirror again. He knew it would be them. He drove the gas-pedal all the way to the floor.

The main-gate guards had been standing around waiting for the vehicles which had entered some time before, to return, so that they could go back to sleep again. The airport had no more than two flights each day, and rarely any at night. There were no night-landing facilities available there, although this never bothered the military flights. Once the general's entourage had departed, they would be able to get back to sleeping until morning, when they would be relieved for the day.

The soldiers looked at the car speeding towards them and wondered what had been forgotten by the previous group. They could see that this driver was in one hell of a hurry and stood back as the car swept by, throwing a cloud of dust and small pebbles through the air as it did so. The guard officer could see that there were two vehicles, and waited for the second to scream past before stepping back onto the road. He shook his head at the reckless drivers, wondering what would have happened had he insisted that they stop. Then he turned back to talk to one of his men as the two vehicles sped on through the field.

Murray swung the car first to the left and then the right as he looked for a way around the aircraft hangars. He was driving blindly, guessing at where to turn next. As he slowed, the car behind caught up and now he could see that there was not a great deal of distance between the two. He knocked the rear-vision mirror away with his hand to prevent the other car's high-beams from blinding him. Then he began to panic that he had missed the flight. Murray turned once more, and rounded the remaining hangar spotting the line of jeeps waiting on the hardstand surface. These were surrounded by soldiers. He was within a hundred metres and he could see that these soldiers were surprised at the appearance of the two vehicles, one obviously in pursuit of the other. Murray searched for the aircraft and felt his heart sink. He was too late! Then, as he passed another building, he caught a glimpse of the freighter moving towards the main runway, taxi-ing slowly. He didn't hesitate. Aiming his vehicle directly at the runway, he drove across the grass strips and over deep gutters which carried excess rainwater away. He could hear the heavy tearing noises underneath, as exhaust assembly and other parts of the vehicle were ripped away. The soldiers behind remained locked on his tail, their headlights bouncing all over the airfield as they drove across the slight undulations and gutters in full chase. Murray could see the C-47 turn, then face down the main runway, hazard lights blinking. He drove directly at the stationary plane, flashing his lights. There was less than a thousand metres to go.

Inside the cockpit the AURI colonel looked quizzically at his co-pilot.

'What the hell are those two vehicles doing?' the pilot snapped. He watched the two pairs of lights dance across the perimeter until finally turning into his flight path. The co-pilot shook his head, raising his eyebrows to indicate that he too didn't understand. The thought flashed through his mind that these were the jeeps which had brought the generals out to the airfield and might have decided to line the strip providing additional light. He shook his head again, knowing that this was precisely the sort of dangerous cowboy behaviour he had seen so many time before, when flying in and out of the Army-controlled airfields. He moved the stick forward as his CO nodded. The engine pitch immediately changed, sending their screaming messages to those all around that the plane had commenced take-off. Committed, the aircraft started to accelerate forward.

The officer riding in the chase vehicle yelled at the others inside his car when he suddenly realised what the mad Australian was going to do. They had gained on the smaller car and were now alongside. He could see the determined look on the foreigner's face. The crazy fool intended to ram the aircraft with his own car! He screamed at his driver to go faster and force the foreigner off the airstrip. The driver kicked the gas-pedal hard and pulled the heavy eight-cylinder American Plymouth across the gap which separated the two vehicles.

Murray flinched as the sound of screaming metal on metal accompanied the collision, forcing his own car to swerve violently to his left, then right, before losing control as the Plymouth collided again. Suddenly Murray knew that it was all over. The Holden rose on its side and was plunged wildly off the runway as the much heavier vehicle ploughed on through. He felt the wheels leave the ground and, for a brief moment, caught a glimpse of the oncoming aircraft as it too had been forced to swerve from the path of the duelling sedans. In those seconds, as his car rolled and thumped then rolled again, Murray cried out in pain and his body was flung violently around inside. Suddenly, the screams of twisting metal ceased, and his head smashed forward into the steering wheel, bursting the cartilage in his nose and knocking him unconscious.

By now the shocked soldiers who had been standing around waiting for their senior officers to depart had recognised what was happening and driven their jeeps recklessly towards where the aircraft had ground to a halt. They had their weapons ready to shoot. Uncertain as to which of the two vehicles had intended attacking the aircraft they encircled the wrecked cars and pointed their weapons threateningly at those inside. The senior officer jumped down from his jeep and ran across to the aircraft which, by now, had come to a complete standstill askew from the runway. The pilot had kept the engines running waiting to see what developed next.

He cursed the stupidity of the two drivers, thankful that he had braked and kicked the rudder as hard as he had, to move out of the path of the hurtling mass of metal. He had no doubt the oncoming cars would have struck his undercarriage. As he stared back and across at the confused scene, as arriving jeeps focused their lights on the wrecks, he felt a hand touch his shoulder. Turning to the Army officer, he acknowledged the signal and instructed his co-pilot to close the engines down. Then he levered himself out of the captain's seat and went back into the cabin to check on his VIPs.

Zach had already moved amongst the other passengers, confirming that none had been injured when their aircraft had bounced around, then suddenly come to an abrupt halt slightly off the main runway. He peered through the porthole at the wrecked cars.

Suddenly, as one of the approaching jeeps swung towards the damaged vehicles on his left, Zach was stunned. The jeep's headlights picked out the Australian Corps Diplomatique number plate hanging off the back of the car. Without hesitation, he leapt over, snapped the cabin door open, then jumped to the ground. He ran to the wreck and, when he saw the driver, called out for assistance.

'Get over here, quickly,' he screamed at the soldiers in the jeeps. 'Give me a hand here!' he called again, leaning inside to see how best to pull Murray from the wreck. 'Murray, Murray,' he yelled, running his hands over the unconscious body. 'Murray, can you hear me?' He felt around for a pulse. There. He found one. He was still alive. He called again, 'Murray, Murray, can you hear me?' Just then one of the soldiers approached with a torch and shone the light onto the injured foreigner's face. It was covered with blood. The Indonesian soldier called out to the others.

'Put a guard around this car, quickly,' he ordered. Zach heard the man's commands but these didn't register. He was too concerned with Murray's condition. Slowly he managed to free the body from inside the wreck and, unaided, drag the unconscious man onto the grass. He ran his hands expertly over his friend's body, relieved to discover that there were no severe injuries. He checked inside his mouth and ears. Then he called for water. There was none on the jeeps.

'Kolonel,' he called, addressing one of the guard officers, 'would you please help here. This man needs water. There would be some on the aircraft,' he suggested, and waited for his assistance. Instead, the officer stepped forward and withdrew his pistol. He didn't wish to go anywhere near the aircraft.

'*No water. This man is under arrest,*' Suhendra shouted angrily. Zach was dumbfounded.

'*Arrest?*' he shouted back, rising to his feet, '*What for?*'

He stepped between Murray and the Indonesian colonel.

'*He tried to kill the general!*' the colonel screamed angrily, then grabbed a pistol from one of the security guards. He waved this threateningly. Steven Zach knew that they were in grave danger. The situation was extremely volatile and he knew whatever he did next might just determine their fate. He looked over and noticed that the VIP passengers had remained close to the waiting aircraft. He raised his hand to wave but there was no response. The Commander was in deep discussion with some of the men who had been pulled from the wrecked Plymouth and Zach could see them pointing in his direction. He turned back to the colonel and Zach's mind flashed back to other images, other times, when he had seen similar looks on men's faces during the heat of battle. There was a loud groan from behind and Zach turned quickly, in time to see Murray open his eyes and cough, as blood had trickled down into his breathing passage.

'Murray, wait,' he said, bending down to help him into a sitting position. If there was any more bleeding this would be more comfortable. 'Take it easy, Murray, it's okay,' Zach said, considering what to do next. He had to remain close to Murray. He could see that Suhendra intended to kill him, given the chance. Murray coughed again and wiped his face with the back of his bloodied hands. These had been cut as he'd been flung around during the crash. His vision was still blurred, but he knew that Zach was there. He gripped Zach's arm and dragged him closer.

'Get away from the plane!' he whispered hoarsely, the urgency in his voice startling Zach. Until then, he hadn't even wondered what the hell Murray was doing there. There hadn't been time for that. He leaned closer and placed his ear near Murray's mouth. 'Get them away from the plane!' Murray repeated, whispering just as hoarsely as before. 'It's going to blow!' he warned, then broke into a heavy cough throwing more blood onto the tarmac. Zach was stunned.

'Jesus, Murray, are you sure?' he whispered back. The injured man coughed, then sucked in as much air as he could, wincing from his bruised ribs.

'Suhendra ...' he gasped, 'it's Suhendra. I think he's interfered with the aircraft somehow.' He coughed again, grimacing with pain.

'How, Murray, for Chrissakes how?' Zach pressed, cradling the injured man.

'I'm not sure ...' Murray replied, taking as small a breath as possible as the sharp jabbing sensation continued around his ribs. 'Kololotov is dead ... Suhendra killed him. Of that ... I'm sure. He said Suhendra's name ... just before he died.' Murray stopped for a moment, to take another small breath. Zach waited impatiently. 'He also mentioned the flight ... and Soeharto.'

'Get away from that man. He is under arrest,' they heard the colonel yell at them. He then screamed at the other soldiers standing with their weapons at the ready. *'Take that man over to my jeep, now!'* Zach was about to stand when Murray gripped his arm and pulled him back.

'Get ... them ... away ... from the bloody aircraft,' he hissed, dragging himself upright.

Zach placed his arm around Murray's back to assist him to his feet. Murray looked at the officer standing directly in front of him and squinted. The jeep headlights presented the colonel merely as a silhouette. Zach suddenly understood why he couldn't permit Suhendra to take charge. He would most certainly kill Murray Stephenson. He looked across to the generals still standing at a distance. Then he called out loudly.

'Commander, this man has just saved your life!' He could see the men break into animated conversation. The officer who had pursued the Australian had raised his voice and was waving his hands around wildly. Zach looked sideways at Suhendra.

'General,' he called out to the Chief of Army Staff who had been surrounded by security just in case his life was further threatened. *'General, this man has saved your life as well. Please, bapak, listen to what he has to say.'* Suhendra started to move forward and raise his gun, pointing it at the two Australians.

'Stop!' a voice commanded, and Suhendra turned slightly to see who had issued the order. He kept his gun pointed directly at the foreigners. Zach could see the finger tightening.

'I said stop!' the deep voice barked again, closer this time as the

men approached. Suhendra turned and saw the group of VIP's moving away from the aircraft. In that moment he knew that he had failed. He tensed, then squeezed the pistol's trigger.

Zach saw the hammer pull back as the weapon cocked to fire and, in that millisecond, he knew Murray was dead. The hammer snapped forward sending the high tensile steel smashing towards the chamber and, even before either of them could scream, the deathly silence exploded with a sharp click. The chamber was empty. Shock and surprise flashed across Suhendra's face as what happened registered in his brain, and he squeezed the pistol again. Zach had already moved, anticipating the colonel's reaction, kicking high and hard as he threw himself into the air, his right shoe heel striking the arm in which the officer held the weapon.

'*Stop this! Immediately!,*' the Commander yelled, and two of his aides moved quickly to recover the revolver which had spun through the air and landed some metres from where Suhendra stood, holding his wrist in pain. Suhendra knew that this would be the end. He glared at the two Australians. How did they know? The question flashed through his mind. Then he cursed himself for not checking the other soldier's weapon. He stood there, head lowered, knowing that soon he would most certainly die. Suhendra looked back at the aircraft. If only it had taken off just seconds sooner, he thought bitterly.

General Prajogo eyes were filled with hate. After focussing on Suhendra he turned to Murray. '*You have committed a grave act against the Indonesian people,*' the Commander snarled, staring at the face of the man he'd tried to have killed. He could see that his aide had correctly identified the Australian who moved with the Communists. He looked sternly at Zach.

'*I know this man, Kolonel Zach. He has been here before. He ...*'

'For Chrissakes Steve,' Murray interrupted, his voice still hoarse. 'Tell him about Kololotov. And Suhendra,' he added, still wincing in pain. The general glared at him.

'*General,*' Zach started, watching Suhendra as he spoke, '*Murray Stephenson did this to stop our plane from departing. What he did might have saved our lives. Will you at least give us the chance to explain. He deserves at least that.*' The Commander started to shake his head when his superior interceded.

'*Let him speak. I wish to hear what he has to say,*' Soeharto ordered.

Suddenly everyone became quiet. Murray cleared his voice.

'There may be a bomb on your aircraft, bapak. It could detonate at any minute. I believe that this officer knows what I'm talking about,' he said, indicating Suhendra. The Commander stepped closer to his Chief of Staff and whispered something.

'I am told that you are not like Kolonel Zach. The Commander says that you are our enemy. Why should we believe you?' he asked. Murray looked at the serious Javanese and rolled his eyes in exasperation.

'Why then would I do this?' he asked, moving his head from side to side slowly indicating the wrecks.

'It's true, general,' Zach interrupted. *'Why would he have risked his life? What did he have to gain?'* The officers stood waiting. They were still not convinced.

'Ask Suhendra what he did to the plane,' Murray insisted with difficulty, as blood continued to flow from his broken nose. He was angry that they refused to believe him. *'Why not have the plane checked?'* Suhendra was silent, rubbing his injured wrist.

'Suhendra?' the Commander asked, looking at his colonel.

'I don't understand what this foreigner is talking about, Bapak. There could be nothing wrong with the aircraft as the crews themselves had it thoroughly checked. Why am I being accused? Surely it's these foreigners that should be questioned, not me. He's the one who tried to drive his car into your aircraft. Why am I being treated in this way?' he asked. The Diponegoro Commander thought for a moment. Suhendra was one of his finest officers. He trusted him implicitly, and besides, he sounded so convincing.

'Take the Australian, Stephenson, away for questioning. Take him back to the barracks,' he ordered, then he spoke privately to the other general. He nodded. They seemed to be in agreement over whatever he'd said.

'General, you can't do this!' Zach pleaded. He realised immediately what would happen once Murray was out of his sight. *'If you take him, then you must also take me,'* he challenged. The Commander flashed him an angry glare as he turned and took the arm of his friend, and senior officer, then started back towards the aircraft. They would depart as planned. He called out for the crew to remove Zach's luggage. The crew obediently entered the aircraft.

'General,' Zach called as he watched them both move towards the plane. *'Please don't do this,'* he implored, and went to move after

them but stopped when several of the security guards raised their machine pistols at him. He stood there in dismay as one of the other guards motioned with his weapon that they were both to follow him. As they walked over to the jeeps, suddenly he heard shouts coming from the direction of the aircraft. Soldiers ran towards the plane and ushered their senior officers away, providing a protective shield as they did so. The crew, dressed in their orange flying suits, jumped out of the aircraft and started to run. The guards hurried their VIPs towards the waiting jeeps and moved around behind these as a shield. Zach knew instantly that they had discovered something to cause all this panic while searching for his luggage to offload.

'Get down over there,' he yelled, warning Murray. The soldiers guarding them turned and watched the confusion. Zach then yelled at them also. There was another shout and Zach looked up just in time to see Colonel Suhendra running towards the aircraft.

'Stop him,' the Commander roared, and two of his aides jumped to their feet and fired. But they were too late. Suhendra leaped into the open cabin and pulled the door shut behind him, locking it in position. He stood there gripping the handle, then he turned and saw the container lying on the floor. The container which would have changed the course of Indonesia's history had it not been discovered. Suhendra moved slowly towards the metal box and knelt down beside it.

The Indonesians and Australians all remained hidden behind the row of vehicles not one hundred metres from the C-47, waiting. As the minutes dragged by, the tension on the silent airfield grew intense. Zach sat against one of the jeep's wheels wondering what in the hell Suhendra was doing inside. If he was going to blow the plane, why hadn't he already done so? He looked across at Murray and observed that he too was safely positioned behind a wheel waiting for the explosion. Zach looked across at the group of soldiers sitting, half-crouched around their leaders and wondered what was going through their minds right at that moment.

Inside the aircraft, Suhendra had sat down alongside the metal container and placed his hands on his knees and sobbed. From the moment he'd discovered that his Commander would accompany Soeharto on the flight, everything had seemed to go wrong. He cursed Kololotov. When Suhendra had returned to the function and discovered that the generals would be travelling together, his immediate reaction was to cancel his plans. But then he realized that the Russians would discover what had happened in Semarang and would move to take their revenge. Suhendra understood that this would be his one and only opportunity and, although he wished it could be otherwise, his own Commander would die too.

Suhendra looked again at the bomb he had prepared and suddenly his father's image flashed across his mind. The hardship which followed his death. Then he remembered his brother and the resolution he had made when he had been killed by the Americans. The tears stopped and he wiped his eyes with the back of his wrist. He reached down and smiled at the open container, remembering the large amount of money he had hidden away in the ordnance depot. And how he had booby-trapped the box covering his hoard. Then he laughed at his own joke and advanced the timing mechanism manually.

Those surrounding the aircraft had come to suspect that either the bomb was faulty, or Suhendra had changed his mind. When the explosion came, the blast lifted the vehicles some inches off the ground, blasting everyone away from behind their protective wall as the air compressed then expanded under the violent detonation. The aircraft's fuel tanks ignited and contributed to the deafening explosion, throwing huge pieces of the plane across the field in a continuous fiery blaze. The scorched air seared flesh, causing all the men to shield their faces from the heat. Within seconds it was all over.

The men lifted themselves slowly to their feet. They were shocked to see how little was left of the plane. Small fires were evident around the field as parts of the aircraft continued to burn, flames dancing like ghosts wherever the soldiers looked.

* * * * * *

'Murray?' Zach asked, looking in his direction. He was still sitting down, facing away from the blast.

'I'm okay. You?'

'I'm a lot better than I would have been had you not been such a lousy driver,' he answered, forcing a smile. Murray could barely detect the grin in the semi-darkness.

'What about that lot?' he asked, still pissed that they had to go through all of this. Zach looked over and watched the men climbing into their Jeeps.

'They're okay. Look's like they're leaving. Do we want a ride?' he asked, still grinning. It was good to be alive. As he spoke, the soldiers called to them and Zach helped Murray to his feet.

'*Come, we will take you back to the hotel,*' the Commander said. '*And then we can talk.*' Zach looked at Murray who sighed in relief. It was all over. Now he would be able to walk the streets of Djakarta again without having to look over his shoulder all the time. He couldn't smile but he did the next best thing. He placed his hand on Zach's shoulder, then limped towards one of the waiting jeeps. He started to climb into the Army vehicle.

'*No,*' he heard the officer say, causing him to look up. '*You will ride with us here,*' the major general said. The soldiers all looked at the Australian, then at the two generals. Murray stepped back and moved around to the staff car. He looked up into the faces of two of the most powerful men in the country, and they both smiled. Then he knew that everything was really going to be all right. Suddenly the soldiers all cheered as the Commander offered his hand and assisted Murray into the rear of his jeep.

The four vehicles drove away from the scene of devastation weaving their way through pieces of wreckage and across the airfield. Zach looked back and observed Murray sitting in the rear, disguising his pain as he talked. Throughout his military career, Zach had seen many men risk their lives for others, but Murray's endeavour had indeed been exceptional. He was a true hero. A clandestine warrior of the highest calibre. Zach looked up at the brilliance of the starry sky and smiled.

Chapter 28

Djakarta

Murray looked at the letter delivered by diplomatic courier from Australia. He used the short-bladed letter-opener shaped in the design of a silver *keris* to slice carefully through the end of the envelope. It was stamped on both sides with the appropriate warnings and security classifications. He read the brief enclosure then let it fall back onto the desk. He hadn't expected the official notification of his transfer back to Melbourne for at least another six months. Following his return from Semarang, he had submitted to Central Plans an in-depth report of the political atmosphere and what he had witnessed during his tour through Central Java. Zach had agreed with him that it would not be in their best interests, nor in those of the Indonesians, to disclose the events surrounding the assassination attempt. They understood all too clearly that the current political uncertainty which prevailed could all too easily be manipulated to the disadvantage of the West, and that disclosure of yet another attempt on the country's generals might further inflame the people.

He told curious members of the Embassy that he'd broken his nose in a *betjak* collision, and they'd accepted his explanation without question, although there was the odd knowing wink from some of them. Murray's reputation had long been the subject of embellishment and rumour. He had been invited to Army Headquarters unofficially, where he met again with not only the Chief of Staff, but also his former enemy, the Diponegoro Commander. The three enjoyed an informal discussion and, it appeared, the Semarang Commander was satisfied with the Australian's political position in relation to the Communists. He was not directly asked about his relationship with the PKI students, nor was he questioned in relation to his earlier visits to the Diponegoro Divisional Head-quarters with Harry Bradshaw. Instead, the meeting was conducted in typical Javanese style, with questions presented politely, but obliquely. Murray understood that it would be most unlikely that they would become close friends, even though he had saved the general's life, for there would always be that unanswered question in their minds about Murray's role in those earlier machinations which cost Colonel Sulistio his life. But no further mention was made of the incident, nor the near-fatal attempt on their own lives. And then there was Ade.

Murray had visited the Indonesian Intelligence Agency, BAKIN, within days upon his return to his office. It was a courtesy call, and one which was expected of all foreign Embassy officials who had journeyed through the country in any official status. He had ar-rived almost an hour early for his appointment, hoping that he could clear the mandatory interview earlier than scheduled. Murray's face was known to the desk security officer who, unable to contact the appropriate extension upstairs, escorted the Aus-tralian up to the third level where he was instructed to wait. Murray was aware from previous visits, that this was the section which attempted to maintain surveillance over members of the foreign community, a daunting enough task, he knew, considering BAKIN's limited resources. He heard voices inside, and laughter. Then the door opened and the pair came out together, still smiling at their private joke.

Ade's face froze as Murray looked at her, completely caught by surprise. She tried to speak but the words wouldn't come. Instead, she dropped her eyes and continued past without so much as a sound. The Indonesian Intelligence officer, obviously flustered by the embarrassing encounter, stammered an invitation for Murray to enter his office. He did so, staring back over his shoulder at the woman who had shared his bed all those years. Later, when she telephoned asking if they could meet, Ade explained that she had been down to the Intelligence Agency arranging a security clear-ance for her cousin in Java. But to Murray, the story had no sub-stance. He knew that the office she'd visited was in no way con-cerned with such matters. Instead, he had files in his safe which described quite clearly how the Intelligence Agency had developed a special corps of young women, who were employed to keep tabs on specific foreign targets. It was clear to Murray that Ade had been their conduit for some time.

They did meet, but only for dinner. Murray said it was to say goodbye, as he was returning to Australia. She cried through the meal. Murray felt saddened that even this relationship had been tainted by the devious world in which he had chosen to live. They had parted that evening, not even as friends. Later he would recall the coincidence of her journey to Australia when he returned to Melbourne. Murray's disappointment grew even greater as he came to believe that her placement by his side was far too sophisticated for the Indonesians. Ade had to have been working in conjunction with an outside agency. And he thought he knew which one that would be.

* * * * * *

Melbourne

He walked through the long corridors and observed that nothing had really changed since he was first escorted through these bleak offices by Harold Bradshaw. Anderson's secretary had smiled warmly when he arrived, taking him straight through into the Director's well-appointed chamber. She left, closing the door behind her.

'Well, that's about it then,' Murray said, placing the file on Anderson's desk. It was his final clearance document which had required that he meet and be interviewed by no fewer than twenty other Intelligence offices from various agencies within the Australian Government. Then, as he had completed these sessions, each of the agents had signed him off, but very few bothered to shake his hand and wish him well. Murray had no idea whatsoever how he had become a pariah within his own organisation. He put this down to his allegiance over the years to the former Director who, having been missing for more than a few months, was now considered to be a potential defector. He had heard the rumours. And the whispers when the others had thought he was out of earshot. Now, as of this moment, he was his own man again.

'What are your plans?' Anderson asked. Murray knew they would maintain a file on him and keep it current.

'I have decided to return to Djakarta,' he said, knowing that this would be of concern to all within the ASIS community. Central Plans' personnel would all, no doubt, be briefed as to what they should do in the future if they were to come into contact with the former senior agent. Anderson looked unhappy with this news.

'Do you think that wise?' he enquired.

'Why not? I have sound contacts there and thought I might try my hand at something else for a change.' He knew they would find out eventually. They always did. Anderson shook his head as if in the company of some errant schoolchild. He stood.

'I'll see you out, as it's your last visit,' he said, almost with a tone of regret. Murray turned as Madge entered and raised her eyebrows at her Director. He wondered where Anderson kept the button which had signalled her to come.

'Bye, Madge,' he said, bending down quickly and kissing the surprised woman on the forehead. She clucked her tongue and turned away as the two men left the Director's office and walked slowly down the linoleum-covered passageway. They continued down through the maze of smaller offices, neither speaking as they went. Murray looked directly ahead, ignoring the rows of smaller offices, the nerve centre of the Secret Service. As he walked along the corridor he knew, without looking, that each of the agents there would be aware of his departure and wondered how many of their number had bothered to look up and smile.

They stopped in the central clearance foyer and Anderson extended his hand for the last time. As he did so, a young man entered via the security doors and walked directly towards the two men.

'Good morning,' the newcomer offered with a youthful smile. Murray returned the smile and wondered if he had been that young when he'd first been recruited. Anderson hesitated, then decided that they should be introduced.

'Murray, even though you're returning to Djakarta in your own capacity, I have no doubt that you will wish to keep your finger on the pulse of things. I don't have to remind you that you are, and will continue to be, covered by the Official Secrets Act.' Anderson turned to the young smiling officer who Murray thought could be no more than twenty years old, and placed a paternal hand on the young agent's shoulder. 'This young man is one of our bright new stars. You will see him in Djakarta within the next few months, if you're there. He'll be taking up a position you yourself once held in the Embassy, Second Secretary Political.'

Murray smiled, reminded of his own youthful experiences in Indonesia. He spoke warmly to the younger man.

'Well, when you arrive and get settled, look me up. I'm Murray Stephenson,' he said, extending his hand which the younger man took, then shook cordially as he introduced himself.

'Yes, I've heard a great deal about you,' he said admiringly. 'And thanks, I'll certainly do that.' The young man turned to the Director and said, 'I'll wait in your office,' and smiling, walked away.

Murray watched the agent as he climbed the stairs on the far side of the room. Then he turned, nodded at the Director and passed through the security doors for the very last time.

Anderson watched Stephenson depart. He hadn't liked the former agent, but he had to admit he had been one of the best. He almost grinned in pleasure as he turned away and moved back towards the steps which led up to his office. He would dedicate some hours to briefing the young agent, a man he was convinced would develop into one of ASIS's finest agents. Only an exceptional recruit would have the same instincts and level of commitment as Stephenson, but he was confident the young man waiting for him would be equally willing to commit himself to the demands of the Service.

Satisfied that the day had worked out precisely as he had planned, Director Anderson returned to his office.

The young man's name was Stephen Coleman.

KERRY B.COLLISON

542

Epilogue

Merdeka Square

There was a moment when the crowd fell silent. For hours they had jostled, pushed, yelled and even laughed, waiting together until their charismatic leader appeared.

A soft breeze touched the faces of the spectators as they waited patiently. Now only a few spoke. They could feel that the moment was near. As the crowd of almost one hundred thousand waited, they observed the evening sky become brighter as the pale moonlight slowly spread across the heavens.

Suddenly there was a cry, followed quickly by others calling loudly as the moon's light struck the figure standing alone on the dais. Within moments the multitude reacted, overwhelmed by the presence of the great man. They called out to their leader, their voices falling into a rhythmic chorus while they chanted his name. Then they commenced swaying together as they chanted, *'Hiduplah Bung Karno, Long Live Bung Karno, Long Live President Soekarno...'*

Their voices reverberated across Merdeka Square and through the buildings surrounding the huge gold-leafed obelisk. Voices rang through the side streets and into the restaurants, even down the main thoroughfare leading into Chinatown until finally, in the distance, their chanting became but a whisper, barely audible at all. And at that moment it was as if the gods had sent a signal to correct the destinies of the two great men, born together to become leaders of the Indonesian Nation.

* * * * * *

As Soekarno's power diminished, the spiritual leadership of Subuh grew in intensity until his star could be seen as brightly as

543

any other in the heavens. It had been ordained. The SUBUD following would grow to be even greater than that of their master's namesake, Soekarno.

Soon the sounds became mere whispers as the Great Leader moved away, his evening shadow all that was left for them to remember him by. As the faithful shuffled across the open field and looked up to where he had once stood, only a few shed tears for what had been, and their glorious past. As the moon crossed the heavens and gave way to the thickening clouds, the bright light quickly faded, moving away out of sight until it disappeared altogether, only to be replaced by another.

Within a few short months, Great Leader of the Revolution, President for Life, Bapak President Soekarno, moved from his Palace of dreams in Djakarta, into his house of exile in Bogor, where he was destined to spend the remaining days of his life. There, he acted out the remaining chapter, playing it through as if it were some intricate part of the shadow plays which had captivated his soul and dominated his thinking since he could first remember. And, in compliance with the prophecies long mooted by those who claimed to hold the keys to understanding the mysterious powers which govern the Javanese culture and mind, the people of Indonesia transferred their love and loyalty to another.

On that violent stormy day in the small town of Bogor, the inhabitants were surprised when the skies cleared overhead, and the wind dropped. They had all looked up in awe as a magnificent rainbow suddenly appeared, displaying a brilliance of colours none of their number had ever witnessed before. The people stood transfixed and their eyes followed the colourful shapes which gently touched the lines of the Summer Palace where their former President remained. A prisoner. They knew it was a sign. An omen. And at that moment, as the rainbow suddenly disappeared and the sky turned ominously dark, a soul moved from earth and took its place in the heavens to wait for the moment when it could return. Inside the Palace, the man who had founded the Indonesian Republic and first enunciated the philosophy of *Pantja Sila* which would continue to guide his people through their lives passed away quietly in his sleep, alone.

Author's Note

Merdeka Square is a work of fiction, written while I lived in Vietnam. It is based on my imagination, on research into historical facts, and my personal recollections from my period of service in Djakarta. As the reader might imagine, there are obvious reasons why I found it necessary to tell the story of this fascinating period in this fictional form.

No doubt many readers , and in particular my critics, will have difficulty in differentiating between what appears to be fiction in the story, and what is undeniable fact. Obviously most of the characters are fictitious, but it is a fact that the Head of the Soviet KGB Station in Indonesia during the time I served in the Australian Embassy was General Konstantinov and, as mentioned in this novel, he was the first KGB officer to be promoted to the rank of general while serving outside the USSR. I met with the man, a leading Soviet spymaster, several times during the course of my service. He was later replaced by Kololotov, with whom I spent many wonderful Sunday afternoons sipping Georgian Brandy up in the Coolibah Estate in the mountains of Puntjak Pass.

Perhaps the most controversial aspect of this account is the murder of the Indonesian generals on that fateful morning of the 1st October 1965. There has been considerable debate as to whether the captured generals had been tortured, and to what extent the Gerwani played a role in these officers' deaths.

The surrounding events have been poorly documented in the West over the years, but I have seen sufficient intelligence material to convince me that the Gerwani did, in fact, play a significant role in what happened to the prisoners once they had been escorted to the Crocodile Hole at Halim. The descriptive passages relating to the kidnapping, murder and frenzied mutilation of the generals and other officers are taken directly from interrogation reports which I have read. I have attempted to maintain the integrity of those real details in the story line.

There are those who maintain that these women were innocent of many of the accusations made about them. I have been present at interviews with those who would refute such claims. Of one thing we can be certain. The Gerwani were present during the last hours of those generals who were dragged from their homes and families in front of their children, only to be brutally murdered at the Halim Air Force Base. Autopsy reports 'discovered' by academics later indicated that the generals had not been tortured.

It would seem most fortuitous that such revealing documents had 'accidentally' been discovered by a foreign academic while sifting through medical records in Indonesia. Such a controversial discovery would obviously benefit the anti-New Order lobby and I have great difficulty in accepting the validity of the documents, although I certainly do not question the integrity of those foreigners who were involved in their discovery or those who differ from my view.

The role of Western powers in these events is also controversial. There is substantial information in the public domain made available by authors such as Brian Toohey in his exposé of the Australian Secret Intelligence Service (ASIS), *Oyster*, in which Toohey tells us how senior Australian agents not only established networks in Indonesia, but also infiltrated the secret religious cult known to many as Subud.

This book is in no way intended to offend the followers of Subuh, nor the association known as SUBUD. The heritage left by Subuh is obviously of great spiritual wealth. The SUBUD following throughout the world is large and influential and is well supported by Western intellectuals. In Australia this little-known sect has a dozen or more chapters and many followers. There is little hard information in the public domain about SUBUD.

It is a fact that the founder of this organisation, the late Bapak Subuh, was born at approximately the same time as Indonesia's charismatic President, Soekarno. The Javanese believe that a man's name is all-important, being directly related to his destiny. It is therefore interesting to note that the spiritualist was born with the name Soekarno, and later changed it to Subuh. Likewise, the man who became Indonesia's first President was born with the name Subuh, and changed this to Soekarno. It seemed that their destinies were to follow a parallel path and only when his namesake fell from power did the spiritual leader's star move to the ascent. Also, we should note that Indonesia's second President was not born with the name Soeharto.

Under the Rules of Disclosure, it is not yet possible to obtain accurate details of the American and Australian Government's involvement in the era known to many as The Years of Living Dangerously. Fortunately, institutions such as Cornell University in the USA have successfully identified substantial pieces of evidence. Their information suggests that the CIA had established dialogue with senior officers of the Central Java Army Division known as the Diponegoro Command in 1965. Their aim was to support a coup d'etat against what they considered to be an anti-American President and his communist friends.

There are still many questions left unanswered as to what role the Western powers actually played in President Soekarno's downfall, and how Australia's spies contributed to the outcome of the complicated power struggle which resulted, subsequently, in the massacre of half a million Indonesian people, most of whom were guilty of nothing more than simple ignorance. There is strong evidence that foreign powers had developed a sophisticated network of Indonesians who were loyal to the concept of destroying their President. Estimates place this number in the thousands, financed mainly by the CIA.

Records tell us that this was once President Soeharto's own Command, from which he was unceremoniously removed by (then) General Nasution. We also now know that at least three of the six assassination attempts made against Soekarno were financed by the CIA. Although there have been strong rumours of attempts made against President Soeharto, none of these have ever been given any credence by the Palace, often the very source of such innuendo.

During post coup trials held in camera, evidence was given by Dr. Soebandrio, Soekarno's Foreign Minister and Deputy Prime Minister, that elements within the powerful Indonesian Military had, at that time, formed a secret group known amongst themselves at the Council of Generals, whose aim was to overthrow Soekarno's Government and destroy the Communists. Soebandrio claimed to be present when the then Army Chief, General Yani, confirmed the covert Council's existence to the President.

Documentary evidence also supports the fact that China's Chou En Lai had commenced sending arms to the Indonesian communists to assist with the creation of a militant Fifth Force within the Republic. We can safely assume that at the time of September 1965, there were at least three plots afoot to overthrow the Government of Indonesia. A great deal more could be said but, due to restrictions placed on the writer, readers will have to wait for more details to be released.

As to events following those described in this book, the people of Indonesia quickly tired of the brutal conflict which cost their country more than half a million lives. Three quarters of a million had been arrested, many never to be seen again. The Indonesian Communist Party, the PKI, had virtually disappeared. Its leaders had either been murdered or jailed. But their ghosts remain with us. Massive demonstrations against the Chinese for their past support of the PKI-Peking Axis seriously affected the nation's security and economy. Emerging student groups, KAMI, and later KAPPI, quickly realised that they had the power to influence national policy and, not unlike the PKI, demonstrated en masse, day after day, until their voices were finally heard.

When President Soekarno moved to have the student groups banned, the country moved back into chaos. During a Cabinet meeting on 11th March 1966, the President's Palace Guard Commander warned his leader that Sarwo Edhi had sent his RPKAD troops against the Palace. Soekarno fled, once again, to Bogor by helicopter. Later that day, confronted by Generals Basuki Rahmat, Amir Machmud and Mohammed Yusuf, the man who had been appointed President for Life surrendered his power to Major General Soeharto.

One year later, Soeharto was appointed Acting President by his supporters. Another year passed and, on 27th March, General Soeharto was officially installed as the second President of Indonesia. A new era for the people of the archipelago had begun.

Finally, for reasons of historical accuracy I have presented all Indonesian words, names and place names in the spelling which was used in those times.

Yes, this book is a work of fiction, but it is very definitely based on historical fact. As to the rest, I will leave you, the reader, to judge.

Kerry B. Collison, Yangon, Myanmar

Glossary of Terms

Although many readers would have visited Indonesia, this simple glossary of the *Bahasa Indonesia* and other words used throughout the novel may assist others who have not yet been fortunate enough to visit the beautiful archipelago and become familiar with its multi-faceted culture and language.

ABRI	Indonesian armed forces
adjal	destiny
aduh	exclamation of complaint
akan	will do
ALRI	Indonesian navy
Antara	Indonesian News Service
Apa kabar?	How are you?
ari-ari	placenta
ASEAN	Association of Southeast Asian Nations
ASIO	Australian Security Intelligence Organisation — the Australian domestic spy service
ASIS	Australian Security Intelligence Service — the Australian overseas spy service
AURI	Indonesian Air Force
awas!	be careful!
babu	old term used to refer to a female servant
bagus	good
Bahasa	language
BAKIN	Badan Koordinasi Intelidjen Indonesia — the Indonesian equivalent of the CIA
balai	hall, meeting place
bangsat	arsehole
Bapak/Pak	a term of respect to an older or more senior person
baru	new
betapa	how
beliau	His Honor, Sir

berita	news
betapa	how
betjak	tricycle taxi
bingung	confused
bioskop	cinema
bisa	can
bohong	liar, lie
brengsek	something/somebody incompatible
bule	derogatory slang for foreigner — 'whitey'
bulu-babi	sea urchin
Bung	older brother
bunuh	kill/murder
CIA	Central Intelligence Agency — US foreign spy service
cinta abadi	eternal love
cyclo	tricycle taxi
desa	small village
dia	he/she
djaga	guard
djahanam	curse/hell
djalan	road
djelaskan	explain
Dji Sam Soe	cigarette brand
djongos	servant (male)
djuga	also
DMI	Directory of Military Intelligence
dukun	witch doctor
dulu	before
enggak/tidak	no
fadjar	dawn/daybreak
gamelan	Indonesian orchestra
ganja	cannabis
ganyang	to chew savagely
GERWANI	Indonesian Women's Movement — Communist-affiliated group
golok	large field knife
gotong-royong	working together
gudang	storage room
gunung	mountain

halaman	garden/court
HANKAM	Department of Defence
hidup	live
hormati	to respect
ibu ('bu)	mother, Mrs, older woman
Idulfitri	end of fasting period feast
itu	that, it
jangan	don't
journos	journalists
kali	stream
KAMI	Student Action Front
KAPPI	Student Action Group
kampung	village
Kapten	Captain
kawin	marry
kenapa	why
kepulauan	island group
kita	we
koki	cook
Konfrontasi	War against Malaysian Federation
kongsi	union/company/society
KOPASGAT	Indonesian SAS
Korp Komando	Indonesian Marines
KOSTRAD	Strategic Reserve Command
krait	deadly poisonous snake
kretek	clove cigarette
ladang	arable land
Laksamana Laut	Vice Admiral
Laksamana Madya	Admiral
langganan	dealer/client
Langley	CIA headquarters, USA
Lebaran	a religious feast
Letnan Satu	First Lieutenant
losmen	housing — barracks
lubang maut	death hole
lurah	village head
maaf	apology
mandi	bath, bathe
manis	term of endearment/sweet

Mas	address to a man
"masuk kandang kambing mengembik"	when in Rome, ...
mati	dead
mengerti	understand
Merdeka	independent, free
mereka	they
MI5	British Secret service, domestic
MI6	British equivalent of CIA and ASIS
mudah	young
nama	name
NASAKOM	Nationalism, Religion and Communism
nasi putih	steamed rice
nenek	grandmother
nenek mojang	ancestors
njonja	address to an older woman, or married woman
obrol-obrol	chatting/gossiping
OPM	Free Papua Movement
OPSUS	Government Special Operations Unit
orang asing	foreigner
pagi	morning
Pantja Sila	the Five Principles of Indonesian National Philosophy
panggil	call
parang	sword
Parlimen	Parliament
pasar	market
pasti	certain, sure
pemerintah	Government
perahu	fishing boat, outrigger canoe
perwira	officer
pitji	black cap worn by men
PKI	Indonesian Communist Party
PLN	Electric Company
Presiden	President
pribumi	indigenous people — 'sons of the soil'
protokol	protocol

MERDEKA SQUARE

PTT	Post, Telegraph and Telephone
pulau	island
rakjat	people, of the country
Ramadhan	the ninth month of the Moslem year
Ramayana	Indonesian epic originally from India
rambutan	red fruit with hairy rind
randjau	landmine
rezeki	good fortune
rendang	spicy meat dish
ringgit	Malaysian currency (dollar)
rotan	rattan, cane
RPKAD	Indonesian Para-Commando Army Regiment
rupiah	Indonesian currency
sabar	patience
sampai	until
sawah	rice fields
saya	I
sedih	sad
sekolah	school
selamat datang	welcome
selamat djalan	goodbye
selamat pagi	good morning
semua	all
serta	with
sialan	damn
siapa namanja?	what's his/her name?
silahkan	please
simpati	sympathy
sisihkan	to put to one side
sop buntut	ox-tail soup
SUBUD	religious cult — Susili Budi Dharma
subuh	dawn, first light
sudah	already
sumpah	swear
tamu	guests
Tandjung Priok	Djakarta harbour
tas	handbag
tenangkan	calmed

tentu sadja	of course
terima kasih	thank you
terpaksa(lah)	forced to
terserah	do as you please
tinggi	high
Tjakrabirawa	Presidential Guard
tjap	stamp
tjengkeh	cloves
tjepat	fast
tjewek	girl
TNI	Indonesian National Forces — military
toko	shop
tua	old
tuan	sir
Tuhan/Allah	God
tukang	labourer/worker
VOC	Dutch East Indies Company
wajang kulit	shadow puppets
walaupun	although
waris	legal heir
warisan	inheritance
yang	which, who

Kerry B. Collison, the author, followed a distinguished period of service as a member of the Australian Embassy Air Attaché Corps in Indonesia with a successful business career in Southeast Asia.

As a former member of the prestigious Young Presidents' Organisation and the only Australian ever to be personally granted citizenship by President Suharto, he brings unique qualifications to writing *Merdeka Square*.

His best-selling first novel, *The Tim-Tim Man*, takes up the turbulent events which shook the archipelago after the fall of Soekarno, and the third volume in this trilogy, *Jakarta*, will be published in 1998.

Photo of the author by Samantha Studdert, published
by courtesy of the *Daily Advertiser*, Wagga Wagga.

*To order more copies of Merdeka Square
or The Tim-Tim Man,*

photocopy this page and mail or fax it to:
Sid Harta Publishers P.O. Box 1102, Hartwell Victoria 3125 Australia
Fax: (03) 9803 4414 or (03) 9889 1132
Email: sidharta.com.au

Please supply.................copy/copies of **The Tim-Tim Man**

Please supply.................copy/copies of **Merdeka Square**

Price per copy including post and packing:

Within Australia — Aus $19.95, overseas orders — US $19.95

Enclosed is Cheque /Money Order for $............................

Name ‾‾‾

Address ‾‾‾‾‾‾‾‾‾‾‾‾‾‾‾‾‾‾‾‾‾‾‾‾‾‾‾‾‾‾‾‾‾‾‾‾‾‾‾

‾‾

‾‾

Country...Post/zip code...........................

PAYMENT BY CREDIT CARD

Amex ☐   Mastercard ☐   Visa ☐   Diners Club ☐

Expiry date: ☐☐ ☐☐   Payment in: Aus $ ☐   Us $ ☐
           month   year

....
Cardholder's name

....
Cardholder's signature

Card number:

☐☐☐☐ ☐☐☐☐ ☐☐☐☐ ☐☐☐☐   Total: ☐

May be charged in equivalent New Zealand dollars

Enquiries from booksellers or distributors are welcome.